doing it

By the same author

An Angel for May
Bloodtide
Burning Issy
Junk
Kite
Lady
Loving April
The Baby and Fly Pie
The Cry of the Wolf
The Earth Giant
The Ghost Behind the Wall
Tiger Tiger

MELVIN BURGESS

doing it

Andersen Press

First published in 2003 by
Andersen Press Limited,
20 Vauxhall Bridge Road, London SW1V 2SA
www.andersenpress.co.uk

Reprinted 2003 (twice)

British Library Cataloguing in Publication Data available
ISBN 0 86264 788 6

Typeset in 12/14.5pt Bembo by FiSH Books, London WC1
Cover design by Rebecca Garrill
Printed and bound in Great Britain by
Mackays of Chatham Ltd., Chatham, Kent

With thanks to Mr Knobby Knobster

1
Either Or

'OK,' said Jonathon. 'The choice is this. You either have to shag Jenny Gibson – or else that homeless woman who begs spare change outside Cramner's bakers.'

Dino and Ben recoiled in disgust. Jenny was known as the ugliest girl in the school but the beggar woman was filthy. Her teeth!

'You are so gross,' said Ben disgustedly.

Jonathon acknowledged the compliment smugly and nodded. He was the King of this.

'At least they're both female,' said Dino.

'I'd take the homeless,' said Ben, after a moment's thought. 'She wouldn't be so bad once you'd cleaned her up.'

Jonathon shook his head. 'You have to take her as is.'

'Agh! You're the one who thinks of this stuff,' Dino pointed out. But that was the delicious horror of it. You had to make a decision. You had to consider it yourself.

Ben squirmed as he tried to focus his mind on the actuality. It was beyond a matter of taste. Disease came into it.

'Can I shag her from behind?'

'No, from the front. With the lights on. Snogging and everything. And you have to do oral sex on her, too.'

'*Jonathon!*' hissed Dino.

'You never said anything about oral sex,' said Ben.

'Oral sex until she comes.'

Ben winced as his mind shrank back like a slug on salt. 'You are *disgusting*. Well, if I could have her cleaned up, I'd do the tramp, but if she has to be filthy, I'd do Jenny. *But* . . . if you had to leave Jenny out on the street for a few months until she was as dirty as the tramp, I'd do the tramp. What about you?'

'I'd take Jenny,' said Jonathon promptly.

'That's just because it's the only way you could get a shag.'

'She's ugly, but I bet her body isn't too bad. It'd be all right once you got going. And the tramp would have rotten teeth and smelly breath, bits of old kebab rotting in her teeth. Cold sores, probably. Ulcers, that sort of thing.'

'Yuk.'

'OK, Ben,' said Dino. 'What about . . . Jenny or Mrs Woods.'

They hissed with laughter. It was a clever one. Mrs Woods was at least sixty, obviously hated anyone under the age of twenty and her breath smelt of tinned cabbage – but at some time in the distant past, she might well have been a bit of a looker.

Ben paused. 'Are they both clean?'

'More or less.'

'Mrs Woods,' said Ben boldly.

'Mrs Woods?' said Dino, acting appalled. 'I mean, Jenny is ugly, but Mrs Woods is *old*.'

'Old is better than ugly,' said Ben definitively. The

other two looked at him curiously. That was Ben; he always knew exactly what he wanted. 'You're really quite weird, aren't you?' said Jonathon. 'Nothing is worse than old. What about personality? Jenny's quite a nice sort of a person, but Mrs Woods is a monster.'

'Yeah, but she wouldn't be a monster if I was shagging her, would she? She'd be...'

'Friendly?' suggested Jon.

'Yeah.'

'So old is better than ugly and personality doesn't come into it?' asked Jonathon.

'We're talking shags here, not marriage. No one mentioned having to talk to them,' pointed out Ben.

The boys laughed.

'I'd do Jenny,' said Dino.

'And me,' said Jon.

Ben shrugged and smiled. 'Ah, but at least I got to shag a teacher,' he teased. 'And she'd be experienced.'

'A woman as horrible as her would probably be prepared to do anything,' Jonathon agreed.

'Let's not go there. OK,' said Ben. 'My turn. Mrs Woods or... Mrs Thatcher.'

Dino sighed. He hated this. It was, in his opinion, one of the few things he wasn't any good at.

'OK,' he said. 'Mrs Thatcher. She's uglier and older...'

'And she's had a bit of a stroke,' pointed out Jon.

'... but you'd have to see Mrs Woods at school every day, whereas with Thatcher, you'd never have to see her ever again. Definitely Thatcher.'

'Coffin snatcher.'

Dino grinned sheepishly.

'I'd do Mrs Woods. Thatcher's practically dead,' pointed out Jon.

'I know one,' said Dino happily. 'The Queen... or Deborah Sanderson?'

'Not Deborah again!' protested Jonathon. The Queen was hideous, no one in their right mind would sleep with her even if they were eighty years old and called the Duke of Edinburgh, whereas Deborah's only crime was that she was a bit on the plump side. She and Jon were good friends. The theory was that Jonathon fancied her to bits and was too embarrassed to admit it.

'You have to answer,' insisted Ben.

'Deborah, then.'

'Ah ha!'

'But only because *anything's* better than the Queen.'

'Bollocks,' said Ben. 'It's because you fancy her. The Queen is obviously far more attractive. I'd rather sleep with the Queen, any day. What about you, Dino?'

'The Queen, definitely.'

'You lying bastards! You're only saying that to wind me up!'

'No way. I mean, Deborah! Fat!'

'Plump!' hissed Jonathon.

'Still, you know what they say. Fat Girls Are Grateful For It,' said Ben.

'Yeah,' said Dino. 'She's probably the only woman living who'd be prepared to sink to your level. I knew you fancied her all the time.'

'Right.' Jonathon pointed a finger at Dino. He had one

4

that would see them off all right

'Either you can sleep with any w
woman, at any time. They can't say no. T
beautiful and gorgeous, all you have to do is as
disposal. And they have to do whatever you want t
to. *Anything*. But. You ALSO have to be buggered. Once
a year for twenty minutes. On the radio.'

'On the radio? Why not on telly?' demanded Ben.

'Because on the radio you'd try and keep really quiet
so that no one would know it was you, but you wouldn't
be able to. Little noises would escape. Oh. Oh. Oo. Ow.
You know. Mmm. Ah. Mmm. Woo. Ah. Na–ha. And if you
don't, then you get no sex ever. Never. No one. For life.'

Dino tried to think about it, but he couldn't. No sex
was impossible. So was being buggered.

'I'm not answering that.'

'You have to.'

'No way. I'm out. Anyway, you asked it, you have to
answer it.'

'Easy. I'd take the endless women and the buggery. It'd
be worth it.'

'Me too,' said Ben. 'Think of the rewards! Anyone. S
Club 7. Kylie. Jackie Atkins . . . ?'

'Poofs,' said Dino weakly, but he'd already lost.

'OK, you,' Jonathon pointing his finger at Ben.

But Ben spread his hands and smiled. 'No thanks. You
win. Again.'

'You can't just back out!'

'Yes I can. I know what you're going to say. The same as
last time. My dad or my mum. I'm not doing either of them.'

insisted Dino.

say *anything*,' said

both of you took it

you never know till you try.'

ing on a Saturday night,'

'It p...u're a suppressed homosexual, they're alway... that hate it the most.'

Dino pulled a f... 'I might as well be.'

'Still no punanni,' said Ben sympathetically

'You should get a girlfriend. Punanni is usually found in the same vicinity. Unless you get one of those plastic ones,' Jonathon pointed out.

'Shut up,' said Dino; and Jonathon did.

'Give it up, Dino,' advised Ben. 'She isn't interested.'

'I'm not thinking of her,' insisted Dino. 'There just isn't anyone else I fancy at the moment.'

'What a stupid waste,' said Jonathon. 'Half the girls in the school are wetting themselves for him, and there he is, mission impossible, Jackie Atkins or nothing. Only the most gorgeous will do for our Deen.'

Dino shuffled his feet and smiled.

'You'll probably get it before I do,' he said. He left Jonathon smiling fondly at this thought and headed off home.

As he left the cloak room, Dino paused to look at himself in the mirror. He liked what he saw. Jackie was the most gorgeous creature in the school – with one possible exception: himself. Dino was It. He had dark hair speckled with honey blond, even features with just a hint of rough, a wide mouth, full lips and deep golden-brown eyes. Girls fell into them and disappeared without ever being seen again.

But Jackie was more than gorgeous; she was sensible. She already had a boyfriend years older than her and she thought that Dino was a prat. Dino knew better. As the two officially most gorgeous people in the school, he and she belonged together. He deserved her. His crush on her had gone on for so long he never said anything anymore, but he didn't believe she didn't want him, he never had. It was just a question of how long he was prepared to wait.

2
The Incredible Journey

Three nights later, Dino strolled across the room of the Strawberry Hill Youth Club with just the slightest backward glance to check that Jon and Ben were following. He leaned on the wall next to the Coke machine and began a lively conversation with two girls who came up to use it. One of them bought him a Coke. Dino smiled with pleasure, like a lamp slowly lighting up, and the girl shone straight back.

Jon leaned across to Ben.

'The rustling of nipples stiffening against the poly-cotton pads of a thousand Wonderbras. The gentle hiss of a roomful of drenching gussets,' he said.

'Shut up,' said Ben.

'Sorry.'

The Youth Club wasn't the sort of the place where the boys usually hung out. Dino had persuaded his friends to come along because Jackie was there. Jackie came to fence. She'd been there the whole time, getting togged up, and now she came into view in the big hall at the other end of the room. Dino knew her at once, even covered as she was with protective clothing and the wire mask. She began making passes with the rapier, her hand poised in the air behind her head. He was hoping for a snog later on. No chance. Jackie was right: Dino was a prat. He was even too big a prat to understand he had no chance, despite any number of very clear messages about it.

Dino was unfazed. Jackie obviously didn't understand something. He had right on his side – his good looks, a sudden smile that could charm the knickers off a supermodel and a disarming openness that took you by surprise over and over again. And the voice. Dino had a voice like a lecherous teddy bear. It was magic.

And he was It. That's what really counted.

'Tonight's the night,' he said.

'No chance,' said Ben. 'I told you. She thinks you're a prat.'

'And you *are* a prat, too,' observed Jonathon.

Dino laughed, then sighed. 'I'm scared,' he confessed, and swigged his Coke. The girl who had bought it for him, who had been waiting by his side uncomfortably being ignored for five minutes, walked off in a huff. Dino watched her go, his mind on other things.

'Perhaps you ought to give it a miss,' suggested Jonathon. Dino scowled. 'You're supposed to be helping here, not letting me down,' he said. 'Thanks, friend.'

Jon was immediately mortified. 'I didn't mean it like that . . .'

Dino rolled his eyes and snorted, but he let it drop. Jon and Ben exchanged a wry glance. Dino walked through life like a blind man on the edge of a cliff, but angels guided his steps and he never fell or tripped. It was just a matter of time. Surely, that time was now.

★

One reason why Jackie despised Dino so very much was because she was It, too. She'd been It since she was little, just like Dino. Unlike Dino, she'd put such childishness behind her. She knew that she thought far too much of herself, and didn't like herself for it, but she couldn't avoid the conclusions that she was far more mature than most of her fellow students – certainly far more than any of the boys, who were mere children. That didn't stop them from wanting her, of course. They knew she would, they knew she had, they knew she *did* – but not with the likes of them. To get anywhere with Jackie, you had to be so grown up you were almost old. Her boyfriend, Simon, was eight years older than she was. He occasionally picked her up after school in his car. He had his own flat where she often stayed over, with her parents' consent. They trusted him. By his side, Dino was a foolish boy-child. There was no reason on earth for her to swap.

She only snogged him that night out of curiosity. The club held its monthly disco that evening. People let their hair down a bit, had a few slow dances, got into a clinch or two, a bit of a grope. Jackie had been going out with Simon for two years, she was very faithful but she was starting to feel that she was missing out on this kind of thing. Perhaps that was why, when Dino came up and asked her to dance, instead of rolling her eyes and telling him NO! again, she shrugged and let him hold her close and waltz around the room with her. She allowed him to manoeuvre his thigh between hers, felt him swell against her stomach and felt – tickled. Tickled enough to allow him to kiss her as the track was ending. Just out of curiosity.

The kiss went further than she intended. She ground herself against him. Her legs went. When he pulled back, she still hadn't finished and hung around his neck, eyes half closed, dazed. She felt like a leech prematurely pulled away from its host. Dino looked into her eyes and exclaimed, 'God!' passionately, before he pressed her to him again and murmured over her head, 'That makes me so happy!'

Jackie started to think, What a crap line! But even as she did she knew it wasn't a line. It was *true*. He meant it. She'd made him happy. She tried to stand up and her legs twitched. Her pelvic floor clenched involuntarily. She panted three times. Dino was a Popsicle; she could lick him all up. He pulled back to look at her again as if he couldn't believe what she was doing to him. His face was shining. It was as if he had just handed her the glowing ball of his happiness, and could she let it drop?

He rested one hand against the side of her face in a way that made her feel both slightly threatened and vulnerable. 'Come out with me. For a walk or something. Tomorrow afternoon?' he begged. 'Please?'

'Oh. OK.'

'Thanks.' Dino squeezed her tight again and his heart beat against her like a bird. He didn't hang around. Some instinct made him leave her and go home before she changed her mind. Suddenly abandoned, Jackie staggered back to her little group of friends.

'Enjoy?' someone asked.

'Don't get it myself,' she replied coolly, but her heart had already begun the incredible, traitorous journey

11

down to you-know-where. And once her heart had lodged in you-know-what, she was doomed. There is no fate more humiliating than falling in love with a lust object as arrogant and as charming as Dino the Lozenge.

'See?' said Dino, as they walked home.

'But how?' wondered Jonathon. He was amazed. He had been positively scared of the damage to Dino's fragile but massive ego when Jackie inevitably spurned him. Instead, here he was, beaming like a lighthouse, still licking the taste of her off his lips.

'She let me feel her tits as well,' he confided.

'Really? What are they like?' asked Jonathon.

'She has nice tits,' Dino replied.

'How does he do it?' demanded Jonathon. 'Do you think she forgot who he was? Do you think she suffered a temporary hallucination and thought he was Brad Pitt?'

'I think she wants his body,' said Ben.

'Wow.' Jonathon could only wonder at the luck of having a girl want you for your body, let alone someone like Jackie.

'Well, he has the personality of a doof, what else can it be?' asked Ben.

'Don't be stupid,' said Dino. He felt like a lion. If he'd been on his own, he would have roared.

By the time she got home, Jackie still hadn't realised what was happening to her, but she was concerned enough to ring up her best friend Sue.

'You snogged Dino?' repeated Sue incredulously. 'You have a date with *Dino*?'

'It's not a date,' insisted Jackie.

'You snog a boy and then arrange to meet him and it's not a date?'

'Don't be such an old hen, nothing's going to happen.'

'So why go?'

'So why not?'

Sue began to feel anxious on her friend's behalf. 'You don't like him, remember? What's the point of going out with a boy you don't like?'

'Just because. Why not?'

'Stop saying why not! WHY?'

'What's up with you?' asked Jackie, and Sue replied,

'I. Smell. Trouble.'

Jackie just laughed. She felt mildly giddy. Look at Sue going all mumsy just because she let herself do something crazy for once! Sue giving *her* advice. It was always her who advised Sue. Sue had the lousiest taste in boys in the world – hopeless. She just couldn't help herself.

'I'm curious,' insisted Jackie, and to her annoyance, Sue laughed at her.

'Listen to me, dolly,' said Sue. 'Blokes like Dino, they're like some sort of horrible addiction. You always think you can handle it, that you're the one who can try them out just to see what they're like. Then you're hooked, and your whole life becomes ridiculous.'

'*You're* being ridiculous,' snapped Jackie. She refused the advice on principle, and went to the park to spite her friend as much as anything.

They walked along. He tried to hold her hand and she didn't let him, but he didn't seem put out. In fact, he was smiling his head off — at her, at the grass, at the dogs, at the people, at himself.

'You look happy,' she said.

Dino glanced around as if they were being spied on, then leaned across and whispered huskily close to her ear.

'You're beautiful, I expect people tell you that all the time. You could be in one of those magazines. I just think... I just feel... I don't know what to say! It's you. You make me so *happy*!'

It was part ridiculous — like a girl in one of those magazines! — and part nonsense, and part pathetic; but it was all gorgeous. The words sent a shiver all the way up and down her insides. Dino adored her. He couldn't believe his luck. Where was his caution? Here he was, handing her his heart on a plate, just like that, before her very eyes, even though she had spent the past ten years telling him to get lost. He meant every word he said. He was as open as the sky.

Then he sort of tugged her off into the shrubbery for another snog and she let him.

Afterwards, Jackie thought, In the *shrubbery*? She had a boyfriend, he had a flat they could go to. What for? But at the time she didn't even think about it. Maybe she didn't even want to do it, but suddenly there she was leaning up against a tree with Dino's hand down her knickers, just like she'd been planning on it all week long. It was just the most intoxicating thing she'd ever done. She was hanging round his neck moaning, 'Dino... oh.

14

Oh. Oh. Dino!' in a little surprised voice. Saying his name like that turned her on even more. They were at it for ages. In the end he had to stop because his wrist was getting cramp. They were very tight jeans. They staggered out into the day, blinking at the light, and she was in such a dazed, hormone-sodden state that she agreed to a date at the cinema mid-week.

Jackie couldn't work out if she spent the next few days in a dream or a nightmare. Dino was still a prat, only now, she realised, he was a mind-meltingly delicious prat. She kept picking up the phone to cancel the date and then putting it down without ringing. She was thinking, I could just go along for the ride... and then she'd think – What ride? She couldn't get him out of her mind. Like Sue said...

'Good-looking, horny and arrogant. Irresistible, huh?'

'It's awful. Am I in love?'

'This is lust, babe. Enjoy!'

'But you can't fancy someone you don't even like!' insisted Jackie.

Sue shrugged. 'I think they're supposed to happen at the same time but I'm not sure it always works like that,' she said.

'What am I going to do?' begged Jackie, feeling suddenly tearful.

'What about Simon? You're supposed to be in love with *him*.'

'I *am* in love with him,' she told her.

'Then forget Dino.'

'I don't need you to give me advice,' she snapped.

'You've got it bad,' said Sue.

'No I haven't. I'll just do the date and then tell him I don't want to see him again.'

'Why not tell him now? Why didn't you do it yesterday before it was too late?'

'It isn't too late, that's silly.'

'How often do you think about him?'

'All the time,' she confessed. 'The things we did in the park. And he's such a wanker. It's just gross.'

Sue laughed. 'He sounds just like my sort of boy. Tell you what, leave Dino to me. I've had loads of them. He'll make me unhappy and I'll shag his brains out. When you see what's left you won't want it.'

It was true, Sue ate Dinos for breakfast, even though they gave her severe indigestion. But there was no way.

'Don't you dare!' snapped Jackie, and they both wet themselves laughing, although it wasn't in the least bit funny.

So she went to the film and it was the most fantastic experience of her life. They never watched a second of it. When she undressed that night, she had little bits of sticky popcorn all over her, which must have worked their way under her clothes while he kept feeling her all over. She felt like a drawer that had been thoroughly rummaged through. Dino was over the moon, he couldn't leave her alone. When he kissed her, she could feel his heart not beating in his chest but literally fluttering. After the film they walked the streets and he talked. He confessed all his secrets to her and she felt as if she was being showered with jewels. He made her feel as

16

if she was the only person in the world that mattered to him, that he was giving her everything he had. He made her walk with him for hours, because he couldn't bear this to stop and he was so anxious that in the morning the magic would be gone and never come back. She got home at half one the next morning, to be roared at by her dad for being so late without ringing. Only as she stood in the shower rinsing away the popcorn, did she realise that in five hours she had barely said a word to him about herself, and he hadn't even asked.

'Oh, shit,' she murmured, but she didn't care. It was too late. Her heart had burrowed its way down and made a cosy little nest for itself just below her womb, where it snuggled in and pulsed and glowed and purred happily. It wasn't coming out of there for love nor money. She was going to have to tear it to little pieces and chuck them away one by one to shift it. She'd fallen in lust.

3
The Secret History

As he caught the bus away from school that Tuesday afternoon, Ben felt like a man with a chest full of treasure. Hot wet jewels. Palpitating doubloons. Warm golden breath and silver shivers going up and down, up and down. Riches beyond all measure.

That didn't stop him feeling anxious as he rode on the top deck and watched the houses and gardens flick past. Treasure can be lost or stolen. What if it isn't yours? What if it's so seductive and dangerous that you shouldn't be playing with it in the first place? What if it was cursed?

It was just great; if you didn't have it you were worried about getting it and if you did have it you were worried about losing it. Whatever, it was perfectly certain that if he was ever caught running his fingers, his face, his tongue or anything else through the contents of this particular box, all hell would blow up around him. It was bound to happen. He felt as if he was muttering a dark enchantment under his breath, which one day was suddenly going to work and release every demon God could dream up, scorching up out of hell towards him. And where would his soul – or his education – be after that?

But you know what? It was worth every hot, wet, little second of it. It was an education in itself, and while he was fairly certain he could get another crack at his A-levels, he wasn't sure how often this sort of chance came along.

The bus took him right to the outskirts of town until it was running past hedgerows and pasture. He got off and walked up the road a little way, then back the way he'd just gone. If a car went past he speeded up, as if he had somewhere to go. It was April, a wet, clean day. The nettles were out in soft clumps, there were little white flowers in the hedge, the hawthorns were covered in little green sprouts. Someone had told him they called it bread and cheese. He broke one off and nibbled it. What sort of bread, what sort of cheese? It tasted nothing like.

After about ten minutes, a yellow Renault came driving out of town and pulled up next to him.

'Hi.'

The young woman inside leaned over and opened the door for him. Ben climbed in and they drove off.

She was chatty today. Asking about the day at school and what he'd done at the weekend. Ali was a gossip. She told him a great story about Mr Haide (Maths) whose wife was having a nervous breakdown. Apparently she'd started pruning the privet hedge outside their house at two in the morning because she was scared that the wind would whip the long branches against the windows and break them. As always, Ben was amazed. He couldn't even begin to relate to the home life of teachers. It's like something you might get on a natural history programme.

Food gathering and mating and what territories they have, that sort of thing. Mr Haide! Poor old sod. Haide was a miserable old wombat. Ben didn't want to feel sorry for him.

At her place she made coffee and they sat on the sofa drinking it in silence. Then she got up and pulled all the curtains, made him stand in the middle of the floor and undressed him.

She did that one most times. He often thought that one day he'd like to do it to her. She took everything off, one after another, as if she was unwrapping him, until there he was, stark bollock naked in the middle of the room with an erection on the front of him like a concrete pillar. In some ways, it was uncomfortable standing there like that with your teacher stalking round you, but what came next was so indescribably delicious, he could put up with just about anything for it. She took his erection in one warm hand and gave a long, deep kiss. He could have harpooned a walrus with it. He pulled up her blouse and slid his hands round to unhook her bra, and then she crouched down and took it in her mouth.

He was one lucky boy.

Ben's affair with Ali Young had been sown over three years ago when he was in Year 9, involved in the school production for that year, *West Side Story*. Ben was helping with the lighting and sound engineering. She was very familiar right from the start, always trying to tease bits and pieces of information about the other students from him in exchange for titbits about the teachers while they were backstage sorting out gels and fixing the lights. Ben was flattered and enthralled, even though he felt a little uncomfortable with some of the information she gave him.

The headmaster had a hernia operation last May, and by all accounts was walking around for weeks beforehand with half his digestive system in his scrotum. Mr Collins (History) had a cat who shat in the house, and he left the turds there for three days before cleaning it up, on the grounds that it was easier to deal with when it was dry. Mr Collins' wife had died of cancer of the bowel the year before, did Ben think there was a connection? Mr Wells in History had had an affair with Mrs Stanton in Geography. And so on.

'That's just between us, Ben, OK?'

How could he disagree? It wasn't often that you got a truly adult peep into the world of school, especially from an attractive young woman. Ben fancied her something chronic. They all did. She was just out of college, this was her first job and she dressed like the girls he knew dressed when they were out of school. Over the weeks they got very relaxed together. There was a lot of talk and fooling around together. His friends teased him about it. He even had pleasant little fantasies in which the teasings were true.

Then came an incident which changed everything. She was up on a chair backstage fiddling with one of the lamps, when she tripped, fell over and rolled on her back with her legs in the air. Ben went rushing over to help, all excited and embarrassed because he'd seen her knickers. He embarrassed himself further by actually trying to brush her down. It seemed like a good excuse at the time. He knew what he was doing. He couldn't keep his hands off her.

'I can do that, thanks, Ben,' she said. He smiled self-consciously at her, going red at the same time, because he'd overstepped the mark by quite a bit. But she just smiled at him. 'Did you enjoy that?' she asked him.

'Sorry, Miss. I did, Miss, yes.'

'Then how about this...' And she did a silly little dance for him, lifting up her skirt and waggling her bum. It only lasted for a second, but Ben almost died. Her knickers were tiny. He was such a kid at the time. She flushed red with embarrassment as she realised what she'd done.

'...Oh God, I shouldn't have done that. Let's pretend I never did that,' she said waving her hands in front of her face as if she could chase the previous seconds away.

'I won't tell, Miss.'

He kept his word: he never told a soul. Not Dino, not Jonathon, not no one. He was determined to be loyal, but the incident dented their relationship. The long conversations about lighting and sound, as well as the gossip, came to an abrupt halt. Ben understood. She was a teacher and she'd showed him her underwear. It was magic, but it was also an amazingly stupid thing to do. Imagine if she'd done it to Dino or Jonathon – it would have been all over the school in hours. She could have lost her job. She'd put herself in his power, and from then on, the relationship waned. She'd overstepped the mark and now she put a distance between them to get things back on track.

Ben was sad but he admired her enormously for being so spontaneous. She wasn't like the others – she regarded the students as people, not as a bunch of sausages to process. For years afterwards, the image of her bum waggling at him in those tiny low-line knickers drove him mad with lust. It kept him supplied with fantasies for years.

Ben knew all about fantasies – he kept a stack of them heaped up in a wicker basket in his bedroom – and they all had one thing in common. Whether it was the just-possible ones, like falling on top of her by accident into a costume basket in the wings off stage and her closing the lid, or meeting her in a pub and having a few drinks and then ho-ho; or the middling ones, like her inviting him to peel the knickers off that pert bottom she was sticking out to him, or the wholly unlikely ones, like him blackmailing her, or her deciding to become a nun but wanting to have a really filthy sex orgy with him before she said goodbye to the pleasures of the flesh forever – the one thing you could say about them all was this: they weren't gonna happen. They were fantasies. That was the whole point.

Gradually the fantasies faded and new ones replaced them. He had little to do with her. The following year he didn't take part in the school production and she never asked why. But Ben kept faith. No one knew, no one was going to know; it was as simple as that. There were plenty of occasions when he might have told the story of how she lifted her skirt and wiggled her bum at him, but he never did. He would have loved to tell her that he was doing this for her, to reassure her that he had kept quiet, that he understood why she had withdrawn. He knew she was worried about it still, because he noticed her looking at him from time to time. She wasn't assessing his performance for a mark at drama, that was for sure. It was a lingering, appraising look. He had no way of knowing that it was nothing to do with anxiety; it was lust. Miss Young was having fantasies of her own.

Another year went by. Even the odd looks stopped. As the new school year began, he had offered his services again for the Christmas show. The bum dance was three years ago, a thing of childhood. He attended the first technical rehearsals, helping set things up backstage. Once again, those odd, lingering looks began and once again, he thought she was worrying about him.

Things changed forever one afternoon when she had to go to the theatrical suppliers for gels. Ben went with her into town to help.

She made small talk for the first ten minutes or so, then fell silent. Ben reached down inside himself and picked up the courage to speak.

'I never told anyone, you know,' he told her.

She twitched in her seat.

'What? What did you say?'

'I never told anyone. None of my friends, no one. About that day you fell off the steps. I never told anyone.'

There was a pause while she just carried on driving. Ben ploughed on.

'I just wanted you to know because I thought you might be worried about it. So you don't have to be, because I never told anyone. OK?'

They drove on a bit further in silence. Ben was scared. Maybe he should have kept his mouth shut.

'I appreciate that, Ben. I appreciate you telling me that. I thought you must have told at least a few people.'

'Well, I didn't.'

'No one at all?'

'No one, not one.'

'Well, I believe you. Do you know why I believe you?'

'No,' said Ben.

'Because you brought it up. You told me without me asking. If I'd asked you if you'd told anyone, of course you'd have said no. You'd have to. So I know it's true. Do you see?'

'Yes, yes, I see,' said Ben nervously, although he wasn't really sure at all.

'You were worried about me worrying,' she said.

'I could tell you were worried by the way you were looking at me, that's why I said,' said Ben.

She laughed, he had no idea why. 'You're a very grown-up boy, you know that? Very grown-up. Very mature.'

'Thank you,' said Ben. He knew that. He was more mature than Dino or Jonathon, both of whom were just kids in one way or another. But it was nice to have someone say it for him.

'More mature than me in some ways,' she added.

'I don't know about that,' he said.

'Well, you never showed me your bum, did you?' she said, and then added, 'More's the pity.' She looked sideways at him and smiled. Ben smiled back and his

25

heart started beating, beating, beating in his chest like some kind of alarm machine.

Miss Young was in a hurry at Straelers, the theatrical suppliers. She rushed through the choice of gels that they'd spent so long talking about earlier, and on the way back she suggested that since they were early, they could stop off at her place to have a cup of coffee.

Ben sat awkwardly on her sofa drinking the coffee she'd hastily made, while she continued to be impressed by his honesty and faithfulness.

'It's a question of trust,' she told him. 'You kept our little secret.'

Afterwards, Ben spent many, many hours trying to work out how many clues there had been to what was going to happen next. He decided that there were about six hundred thousand at least, but he was still surprised every single time it happened. She started talking about boys and girls, and then Ben and girls. Having discovered that he had no girlfriends, she wanted to know what sort of sexual experiences he'd had. Ben, by now hopelessly out of his depth, told her that surely this was private stuff, wasn't it? She nodded approvingly. Then she stood up, brushed down her little skirt and smiled at him.

'Sorry, but I've been wanting to do this for a long time. Ever since I showed you my knickers,' she added. Then she leaned down to him and gave him a dirty big snog. Ben responded with his tongue and she almost fell on top of him, running her hands over his face and up under his sweatshirt. Blinded by a sudden rush of hormones he put his hand on her hip, then let it slide down to the side of her bum. She pulled up her blouse, and Ben slid his hand up and cupped a breast. He thought he was going to faint with lust and had to sit up.

Miss Young – 'Call me Miss' – pulled him back onto the cushions and kissed him even more deeply, making little moaning noises deep in her throat as though she was eating something surprisingly delicious. Her hand caressed his thigh and stroked the bulge in his school trousers. Ben heard himself muttering, 'Jesus,' three times, one after the other. They carried on kissing. She unzipped him. Mad with lust but terrified by authority, Ben suddenly froze up and couldn't think what to do next, but that didn't seem to bother her.

'I guess I'm going to have to take the lead, aren't I?' she said. She reached behind and undid her bra, pulled her jumper up so that only the thin material of her blouse was covering her breasts. He could see the deeper colour of her nipples showing through. She took his hand and placed it on her breast.

'Go on,' she told him.

As he did as he was told, Ben found himself thinking that this was how young girls must feel when they are seduced by an older man. He was so bewildered and sexed up he could hardly think. There was no question of him having any choice about what was happening.

When she began to peel his trousers over his feet, he panicked.

'I've never done this before,' he told her. 'I don't think this is a good idea,' he said. 'Are you sure?' he asked. Or was it, 'Please, Miss?' He could never remember.

'Ben,' she said. 'I'm your teacher. Do as you're told.'

Ben did as he was told.

An hour later he found himself deposited back at school, fixing the new gels to the lamps while Ali, who had transformed herself back into Miss Young like some sort of dark fairy, sorted out a group of Year Sevens who needed to learn how to walk in step. He thought to himself, 'I just lost my virginity during school hours. To a teacher.' He felt immensely proud and privileged. 'I sucked Miss's tits,' he thought. 'I know what colour pubes she has.' He wanted so bad to boast about it to someone, but he knew he never could, not for years and years, maybe even never. But who cared? Even though he'd just come three times in the previous hour he was still more horny than he had ever been before. OK, the whole thing had been awkward and embarrassing as well – but it was easily the nicest half an hour he'd ever had in his life. Fleshy, filthy and holy. It had everything.

'You lucky bastard,' he thought to himself. 'You lucky, lucky bastard.'

4
Dino

Going out with Jackie is the best thing that ever
happened to me. The best. I knew it was going to
happen. It felt right. By the time she said yes I felt like I'd
been waiting forever.

'It might be right for you but it certainly isn't right for
me,' she said once before she realised, and there were her
and her mates laughing away. But it can't be like that, can
it? With those sorts of feelings, it can't be right for one
person and not for the other. That would be wrong.

The main thing about Jackie is, she's gorgeous. People
look at her all the time. When I'm walking along and
she's holding onto my arm, she makes me feel like I'm on
a red carpet in front of the world. As long as I can
remember, she was always out there, growing up ahead of
me. She was always the one everyone fancied, even at
Primary School. And now here I am, watching her long
fingers pop open the top button on her jeans for me
while I stroke her tits in the rhododendron bushes down
Crab Lane on the way home, and it makes me feel so
fucking good.

'Not here, don't be daft,' she says in a little while, but
both of us are panting like steam engines by then. Wow!

I mean! I stood back and watched as she did up her zip and pushed the button back into place.

'You should wear a skirt,' I said. It felt like my blood had turned into boiling hot soup. That's what she does to me. I felt like a cow in the slaughter house with a bolt going through its head.

'More accessible,' she said.

I can be a bit of an arse sometimes. I admit it. I'm my own worst enemy. I couldn't help it. I stood there watching her zipping up, I was almost mad with lust and I was thinking how she never wore a skirt or a dress for me. I was thinking, This is how it's gonna go. We'll go home to my place, I'll strip her to the waist, we'll get our hands down each other's pants and spend about an hour writhing around like a pair of earthworms . . . and that's it. That's as far as it was going to go. Her jeans would not go below her hips.

You know? It's been a month now, a whole month and I'm still a virgin. I mean, it's practically like I was saving myself for her, because there's loads of other girls I could have had. You ask anyone, there's loads of girls would love to go out with me, they'd shag me tomorrow if I just went up and asked. It's like that. You get my point? And she won't. So what's that all about?

You don't know Jackie. She's as stubborn as a brick in a wall. She smiled at me and walked out of the bushes and onto the road, and I knew I should have kept my mouth shut but I just started before I even had time to think about it.

'I've got some contraceptives,' I said.

30

'No,' said Jackie. Then she added under her breath, 'Not this again.'

'But you want to, why not?' I asked. I slid my hand down her arse and tickled her crack.

'Get off me! Not here.' She wriggled away. 'I'm not a bloody dog or something.'

'What's up with you? You didn't mind a minute ago.'

'That was in there.'

'You'd sleep with me if you loved me.'

'Dino, stop it!'

'It's true.'

'What's love got to do with it? You don't love me.'

'I *do* love you,' I said.

'Dino!'

'I do!'

'You don't know what love is.'

That's how she goes on at me. Like I'm some sort of kid. As if I'm ten years old and she's about twenty-something.

'But don't you love me, then?' I said.

She looked at me closely. 'I like you very much.'

'Is that all? Like? Just *like*?'

'Anyway, even if I did love you, I wouldn't sleep with you.'

'What?'

'I don't want to talk about it.'

'I want to know. I'm interested,' I whined. I could hear myself whining, but I still couldn't stop myself. 'I just want to know. I mean, is it me? Is there something about me you don't like? Is there something wrong with me?'

'It just doesn't feel right.'

'It felt pretty good with Simon.'

'Leave it!'

'So what was so great about Simon? Why aren't you going out with him? What's the difference between him and me?'

'Well, he was eight years older than you for a start.'

'Oh, right. I'm too young, am I? Not mature enough for you?' I was really pissed off but I knew I shouldn't be going on like that, I was really blowing my chances. I just can't help it sometimes. 'I get it. I'm stupid. I'm just a kid. You're all so grown up and I'm not!'

'You're behaving like a kid,' said Jackie coldly.

'I don't behave like a kid – you do!' I yelled.

And that was it. She was off, pulling her coat around her and storming off down the road. I thought, Shit! Why do I do this? I mean, I don't mind having a row. I don't mind throwing tantrums and sulking – it was pretty bloody unreasonable of her not to sleep with me, after all. But why did I have to do it *then*?

I ran after her, shouting, 'Sorry – please don't go, don't go!' But it was too late. She pulled her arm away from me and shouted,

'Just fuck off!'

I froze. I was furious. Shouting at me like that. Right in the middle of the street! I could see people looking.

Listen – no one tells me to fuck off.

'Fuck you too!' I yelled. I stood on the pavement watching her, furious with her and furious with myself, too. I mean, all right, she won't shag but she'll do almost anything else. Almost anything else isn't shagging, but it isn't bad and now I wasn't even getting that. I'm such a dick! I just can't help it. She drives me mad. I just want — you know. I just want to do it with her so much.

★ ★ ★

As he walked sadly back home alone, Dino distracted himself by imagining that a mighty power-beam grew out of each of his temples, destroying everything they touched. All that lay behind his step was crushed by his passing. Trees, houses, lampposts, even small hills were all reduced to trash or broken neatly off where the beam struck them. If he stood on tiptoe, he could peer over the devastation. The world below his nose was a tangled mass of rubble and destruction.

He'd been doing this as he walked along ever since he was about six. It was very childish, but it passed the time and since no one in the world knew about it, who cared?

Slowly, he turned in a circle and cut a kilometre-wide circle in the surrounding houses. Rising up on tiptoes, he peered over the allotment fence tangled with ivy, over the cabbages and beans and the brown earth on this blue afternoon to where his own house stood, miraculously preserved amid the devastation. The house stared back out of the window on the second floor and said, 'You think it's gonna be fun? Do ya? Do ya?'

As he approached the front door Dino failed to notice the strange car, which had in any case been parked up the road as a precaution. He walked straight up to the door and just as he was about to put the key in the lock, he looked sideways and caught a beautiful view of his mum in a clinch with a man through the bay window. They were kissing passionately. Her blouse was open. She was wearing a red bra which hung loosely off her breasts. The man was slowly hitching her skirt up from behind.

'More accessible,' whispered Dino to himself.

He watched in slow motion as the skirt hitched up right above her bum and the man's hand began to ease its way down the back of her tights. Then, before they turned their heads and saw him he fell on the spot to his knees, bruising them painfully on the hard plastic shoe scraper. He suppressed a howl of agony into a choked grunt. He glanced behind him to make sure no one was watching from the street. Right in front of the window! How could they? The neighbours! But in fact they were behind the wall; it was only from his position by the front door that they could be seen. As he crouched, Dino realised that he hadn't looked at the man's face at all. All he had noticed was his mum's mouth moving hungrily on the strange lips. There had been a moustache, he felt. Somehow, the fact that his mum had been getting another man's facial hair in her mouth made it even worse.

Dino scuttled rapidly backwards so he could get out of sight, stood back up and walked boldly up to the door again, this time staring straight ahead as he noisily put his key in the hole and opened it up. He ignored the alarmed scurrying sounds from the front room and walked through to the kitchen to get a drink. He flung his bag on the floor with a thud.

'Who's that?' called his mother in a surprised voice

34

from the front room.

'Mum?' said Dino, also in a surprised voice. 'It's me.'

'What are you doing home?' she asked. Her voice sounded heavy. Dino had a vision of her standing there doing her bra up.

'History was cancelled. What are you doing home?'

'English was cancelled,' said his mum, and laughed. Her laugh sounded like china dropping to the floor. Dino walked through and opened the front room door. His mum was standing there on one side of the coffee table and on the other was Dave Short, a teacher at his mum's college. He was smoothing down – or perhaps wiping – his moustache. Dave taught technology, Dino remembered.

'Was technology cancelled too?' he asked. To his surprise, Dave Short blushed as pink as a boy. Dino blushed back.

Dino spent a lot of time that evening in his room trying to think of nice things like Jackie or football or a good film, but all his mind would show him was his mum sucking Dave Short's moustache, in vivid, spitty close-up. The image was ghastly beyond belief. What was going to happen? Was his family going to break up? Did his little brother Mat have any idea what was going on? His mother was old, how could anyone want to kiss her? Did he have to tell his father? Did his mother know that he knew, did she suspect – or had he fooled them both completely?

As for Dave Short – I could blackmail the bastard, thought Dino, and at once, he realised that he was on to a good thing. Dave Short was a balding man with a dense, badger-coloured moustache and a fair amount of badly placed fat on his stocky little frame; utterly repulsive, the last sort of man you'd want as a stepfather. So repulsive, in fact, that Dino couldn't believe that his mum actually wanted to be doing sex things with him at all. Probably *he* was blackmailing *her*! So that was it! Blackmail! The bastard!

His mother needed rescuing.

Then he thought about the way she'd kissed him. Perhaps she did want to be doing sex things with him after all.

That just meant he could get both of them. Why not? The bitch was trying to ruin his life. Just because she was his mother...

But first that bastard Short. He sat down at his desk and began to compose a blackmail note. He got through a couple of drafts before he was called down to tea.

Knives and forks rattled on the plates, but Dino was miles away, thinking about money. Soon he'd be rich. He'd be able to get a car, at least. Maybe life would be *better* because his mum was having an affair, not worse.

As the word 'affair' rebounded in his head he looked guiltily up. No one seemed to notice he was thinking the unthinkable. For a moment, he became acutely aware of his ability to think things with no one knowing what he was doing. Deliberately, he began to conjure up the filthiest thoughts he could manage about Jackie – and they really were pretty filthy. No one seemed to notice. It was bizarre that you could sit there innocently eating mash next to your little bruv while your head was immersed in the most depraved filth man could dream up. It was disturbing but fun, until his mind began, quite against his will, to imagine the same filthy thoughts about his mother.

Bad mistake. He felt ill with anxiety and disgust. At that very moment, Dave Short might be eating his dinner with his family and thinking the exact same kinds of things about his mum — and he'd be *enjoying* it! Even worse, maybe his mother was thinking filthy thoughts about Dave Short. Sitting there, all alone in the middle of his family, Dino blushed a bright, bright red.

'What's up with you, wet your pants?' asked Mat. Mat was only nine. Dino sneered at him and looked away.

He began thinking about all the money he was going to earn again, when his dad's voice interrupted him.

'. . . going away for the weekend.'

'What?'

'Me and your mum are going away for the weekend.'

'Where?'

'We don't know yet.'

'What for?' asked Dino.

His dad laughed. 'What do you mean, what for? To go away for the weekend, that's what for.'

'You're so dumb, Dodo,' sneered Mat.

'Mat,' said his mother mildly. 'We haven't been away together on our own for ages,' she explained. Dino stared at her. She smiled fondly at his dad. She looked like a woman with no secrets at all.

'Mat's going to stay with Gran...'

'No!' wailed Mat.

'You haven't been for ages. It'll be OK, she'll get some vids out.'

'It's boring!'

'So you'll be on your own, Dino. Do you reckon you can manage it? You *must* be old enough to be responsible now.'

'I'll be fine,' said Dino. 'Do I look like a baby? You go. Have a nice time.' He didn't mean it but it came out all sarcastic.

'What's that for?' his dad asked him.

'Nothing. Everything's fine, isn't it?' Dino glanced at his mum who smiled and − was it his imagination? − avoided his eye. Then, as if to prove him wrong, she turned and looked at him so directly that Dino almost started to blush again. But he didn't, he just smiled straight back. He thought, I can be as innocent as you can. It went on for too long, though, and they both looked away suddenly in confusion.

I could blackmail you, he thought, you bitch.

After dinner, as he was wiping the pots, Dino found himself staring down at his mother's back as she bent to the dishes in the dishwasher. He could see her bra strap through her blouse. It wasn't red anymore, it was her usual off-white job. Built for comfort, she used to say. She was quite well stacked upfront.

As he looked down at her, a number of thoughts flashed through Dino's mind. One was the memory of a story she often told about him, how when he was about five or six he was curious about breast feeding and had apparently asked her if she had any milk in them now.

'No, not now,' she said.

'Perhaps we should have a try just to see,' he'd told her. She told the story now to make him blush. Another thought was that seeing your mum with nothing on would be like seeing someone stripped of their skin, some sort of carcass. The third, was that he wished he'd stayed and lingered at the bay window for just a bit longer, to see if Mr Short was going to lift her bra up, so he could have caught a better look at her breasts. The fourth was, how nice if she'd talk to him about what he'd seen that afternoon. This was one secret he definitely didn't want.

Without thinking, he bent down and playfully snapped her bra strap.

'Twang!' he said.

His mother jumped upright, blazing at him. 'How dare you do that to me!' she demanded, glaring inches from his face. 'How dare you!' she repeated, brushing the hair out of her face.

'Sorry,' muttered Dino. He was amazed. He couldn't work out what the fuss was about.

'Don't you ever do that again!' she ordered. She turned and marched out of the room, but at the door she turned and looked back at him curiously.

'Sorry,' said Dino again, shrugging. 'It was just a joke.' His mum didn't say anything but stood there watching him carefully, examining his face, and he knew exactly what she was thinking. She was thinking, Did he see or didn't he? Does he know?

'What?' he asked. 'What?' And he pulled a grim, mirthless little smile. His mother turned and left the room. A little later, Dino went back upstairs. He was half expecting her to come up and talk to him, but she never did.

'Ah-ha! And you know what that means, don't you?' said Ben.

'Party!' said Jonathon. Yes. Dino had to have a party. He'd made Jonathon have a party when his parents went away, partly by insisting that's what he'd do. It'd be awful. Ray and Alan Wicks would turn up late and chuck bottles up and down the road. The stereo would get broken.

'It's not so bad,' said Jonathon. 'People help you clear up. Those girls can clear up like magic. My parents never even knew.'

'Until your mum tried on those shoes and found out they were full of puke.'

'I said that was me.'

'Did you tell them it was you pissed on the sofa in the conservatory, too?'

'I did mention I had a few friends round in the end. OK, I got caught, but listen. It was a great party. It was worth it.'

And that was the truth.

'Anyway,' said Dino. 'There's another possibility. Like, Jackie.'

'Ah, right,' said Ben. 'Two days all alone in the house.

Better than a party.'

'Parents out, Dino in. Yum yum,' said Jon.

'Except she doesn't, does she?'

'An empty house,' said Dino.

'Will it make any difference?' asked Ben. 'If she says it doesn't feel right, why should an empty house make any difference?'

'She's been stringing me along for weeks, it's not fair.' He appealed to them. 'It could be the perfect chance. Do you want me to stay a virgin forever?'

He convinced Jon and Ben, but Jackie was another matter. When she heard about the empty house, she favoured the party. Dino stared sulkily at her.

'What?' she said.

'It's just, you know. An empty house. You and me.'

Jackie chewed her lips and looked at him. 'You stand more chance of getting a girl into bed if she's had a few drinks first,' she told him, and smiled.

'Party's on,' said Dino.

5
Knickers On

Dino was discovering that despite living with them for over sixteen years, his parents were strangers to him. What did they think, what did they feel? Long ago they used to read stories to him and wipe away his tears and he'd tell them his secrets – but what were *their* secrets? They might have been secret balloonists or Welsh people putting on an English accent for all he knew. He had assumed that the whole of their emotional selves was tied up in him, his brother and each other, but that brief glimpse through the window of his mother snogging like a schoolgirl had blown that vision right out of the water. They weren't just parents. They were friends and lovers, betrayers and cheaters and fallers-in-love. There was a whole crowd of them in there.

Did they have a love life? What did they get up to? It could be anything. Did they get kinky? Did they watch in the mirror? Did they do oral? Of course, he'd wondered about such things before in a kind of shuddery, jokey sort of way. Now, to his disgust, he found himself actually turned on by the thought. Just because he had seen her getting felt up by another man, his mother had turned into a sexual object. It was horrible but he couldn't stop it. It made him feel like some sort of a machine.

Whenever he'd thought of parents and sex before, the term 'making love' came into his mind – a comforting, elderly kind of union. But it hadn't looked as if that was what his mum had wanted with Dave Short. It looked more like she wanted a bloody good shag.

One afternoon that week, he crept into their bedroom to see if he could find any evidence. He went in the drawers and under the bed, looking for stockings and suspenders, vibrators, pornography, membership cards to swing clubs, nipple clamps, peek-a-boo bras, massage oil, anything. He found nothing, not even any contraception. His heart sank. It'd be separate beds next. He crept out feeling like a skunk.

On the other hand, so what if his mum was having an affair? It's what people did. Read the papers, watch the telly. They were all at it, banging away at each other like it was keeping the world turning. Who cared anymore? On the third hand, though – how did he know for certain that anything had really happened in the first place? What if there had been some kind of misunderstanding? Maybe he had mis-seen what was going on in the front room, like they do in films. His mum could have been doing any number of innocent things with Dave Short. Showing him a piece of jewellery. Looking at a cut on his nose. Having him adjust her blouse. He'd been so horned up over Jacks that he'd hallucinated the snog, the breasts, the urgent hands. It was all a mistake. That would explain why his mum hadn't come to have a word with him about it.

The trouble with this theory was the images crowding round his brain. It was almost a form of sexual harassment, by his own mother. He considered asking her about it, but that was impossible. He could talk to Jackie, perhaps, but he had no idea how to talk about it. She was coming round on Friday after his parents had left to help him sort the place out for the party. Maybe he'd have a word with her then – sort of drop it in accidentally. She'd know what was going on. He could imagine what she'd say...

'Well, obviously it was a rehearsal for the school play/she was showing him her brooch/blouse...her button fell off and he was helping her with it...And you actually thought they were kissing! You twat, Dino!'

Something like that.

But maybe she wouldn't.

His parents left after the rush hour on Friday. He helped his dad carry out the bags to the car.

'You expect me to help you pack for your dirty weekend?' asked Dino. His dad decided it was a joke and laughed.

'I should be so lucky,' he said.

'Is it just you two, or are you having someone else along? You know what they say – two's company, but three's fun,' he said.

'I should be so lucky,' said his dad. Too lazy to think of another reply. He opened the back of the car and put the bags inside.

'It might be a good idea,' advised Dino. 'Help perk up

44

your sex life. Married for all those years. Maybe you need a bit of a booster pack.' His dad smiled wanly as his mum hurried out with her walking boots in her hand.

'All ready?' she said.

'Are you having an affair?' said Dino.

He said it so plainly. As soon as it was out of his mouth he nearly fainted. What on earth induced him to say that, of all things? He grinned maniacally, he would have started to laugh but he knew he'd sound like Doctor Strange.

His parents stopped in mid-movement to stare at him. His father looked just on the edge of getting cross for this over-familiarity; his mum looked horrified.

'I should be so...' began his dad.

'What?' said his mum.

'Ahhhh... are you having an affair? It's like the two of you are off for a dirty weekend. Ha ha!'

His mother laughed too loudly, and chucked him under the chin. 'If only you knew, boy,' she growled. Laughing anxiously, she and he climbed into the car and drove off. As his dad wound the steering wheel round, Dino watched once again as his mum watched him watching them with that curious expression on her face, like someone watching the arrest of the man who had gunned down her family. An incomprehensible look. Dino waved as they got to the end of the road, then rang Jacks.

When she got ready to go out that night, Jackie was only planning on jeans and a t-shirt, but she got carried away. It started with brushing her hair. She had long hair

45

which shone like copper when she brushed it, and as she watched it come to life in the mirror, she was inspired to spend a bit more time on her make-up. It was fun, but it was too much for the clothes she'd put on. She was going to take it off, but she had some spare time so she went to try on a few dresses and skirts. As she turned and twisted in front of the long mirror on her wall, she found she was getting excited. How much Dino loved it when she dressed up. The transformation from plain schoolgirl to the full vision with lippy and scent and tight t-shirt and a flash of tummy and leg made him go weak at the knees. So she kept it all on, just for fun — why take it off when she'd gone to so much trouble, and it would tickle Dino so much?

Self-consciously, she hid herself under her coat before she said goodbye to her mum and dad, but even so they spotted it at once.

'Wow — party time!' said her dad brightly, but her mum scowled.

'I thought you were staying in at Dino's tonight?' she asked suspiciously.

'We changed our minds, all right?' demanded Jackie. Then she had to invent a bar they were going to before she closed the door and stamped bad-naturedly out of the house.

'Get a taxi back if you're late. Ring us!' called her dad after her.

As she walked the half-mile to Dino's place, Jackie felt unaccountably furious. Her mum had probably seen right through her even before she had. She was ludicrously overdressed for a night in. She was on the pull. Why had she worn a dress? 'More accessible,' she thought. Maybe, tonight was the night that she was going to make Dino's dreams come true. For a long time she'd tried, and managed, to enjoy the intoxicating effects of going so far and then stopping, but she had to admit, these days it gave her a severe headache.

Jackie wasn't entirely sure why she was so reluctant to go all the way with Dino. The official line was that she didn't feel sure of his feelings for her and that she was waiting for their relationship to grow, but her hormones had another, simpler plan, which involved getting carried away one night. Unbeknown to Dino, she'd had a pack of condoms sitting accusingly in her handbag for weeks in case the night was now.

'This is a nightmare,' said a knowing voice in the back of her head.

'Shut up,' said Jackie. She speeded up to try and drown out the dissenting voice, but it was no use. She looked like a million dollars and she was certain Dino was going to try and have her for a fiver.

But when the door opened, Dino beamed, he just beamed at her, she looked so beautiful. He took her in his arms, kissed her and leaned back on his heels, lifting her up into the air pressed tight against him. He rocked her from side to side on his pelvis.

'You're so beautiful!' he crooned. A warm, tickly glow spread out from her stomach into her arms and legs. And bless him, poor old Dino was so embarrassed at showing his enthusiasm that he blushed bright red behind his smile. Jackie rested her hands on his broad shoulders, looked into his big smiling face and felt she was going to melt away on the spot.

The poor sap had no idea why she was so touched. Dino was one of those people who thought the world of his bad points and was ashamed of all his good ones. He was perfectly unaware of how attractive his openness and his eagerness to please were, which just made Jackie love him all the more. Already he was beginning to scowl at his own embarrassment. She leaned forward from her perch on his pelvis and kissed him deeply until he melted back down.

Inside, Jackie took a bottle of Ice Head out of the fridge and started gabbling away. She felt like ripping his clothes to rags and riding him round the room but instead she ran to the CD player to pick out her favourite tracks, talking some nonsense about her mum while he stood there bemused, wondering what to do with his seething blood. As soon as she turned to fiddle with the CD Dino came up and held her from behind. He pulled her dress right up her back, nuzzling her neck and pushing himself into her.

'You're so amazing. I'd like to take your knickers off tonight,' he murmured. Jackie spun round and seized hold of his hands as if he was about to do it that moment.

'No, no, naughty boy, naughty,' she shrieked, sounding like some kind of maiden aunt even to her own ears. She leaned forward and pushed her mouth into his ear and breathed a tickly whisper right inside him. But why not?

Why not let him take them off and every other scrap as well? Why not tonight?

She pushed him off. 'Come on, let's make a tart, I mean a start,' she said. She gestured at the plates Dino's mother had displayed on the wall. The house had to be made safe for the party, which was why she was supposed to be here. She put down her Ice Head. Dino grabbed her bum again as soon as she turned round and she had to waddle to the wall with him still stuck to her back, where she began removing the plates. Dino felt like something she'd sat in.

'We can do all that tomorrow,' he complained. But Jackie just smiled at him over her shoulder.

'Go and get the newspaper,' she told him. After a brief pause, Dino went to do as he was told.

Dino's mother was always collecting things. She'd build up a good number of whatever it was, sell them all off and start again. It had been these plates, a 1940s series painted with characters from Dickens, for about a year now. Before that it had been hatpins, and before that, egg cups. The plates were worth quite a bit of money. Dino had never thought about them on the wall, but now, holding them in his hands, he realised how horribly fragile they were.

'Maybe this party isn't such a good idea,' he said anxiously, after they'd taken down and wrapped up the first few.

'It'll be OK. I know how to pack them up.' Jackie enjoyed the preparation. Soon all twenty-five plates, some as small as dinner plates, some great round chargers you could serve a swan on, were all wrapped up and coffined away in cardboard boxes ready to be taken upstairs and stowed away in the spare room.

That done, they pushed the furniture back to get an idea of what the place would look like empty. The room was knocked through; emptied, the space looked enormous.

'Wow, look at it . . . space,' said Jackie. Dino pressed the CD to get 'They Always Do', Jackie started to rock her hips and they jived about the living room. Dino was a poor dancer, and he felt better when a slow one came on. They cuddled up on the dance floor, big long slow kisses, and in a minute they were in a clinch on the sofa.

She kissed him deeply as he unbuttoned her dress and exposed her breasts. She could see him peeping down at them secretly, which just slayed her. She wriggled as he eased her dress right up above her tummy and ran his palm over her knickers, tiny low ones that barely covered her pubes. Dino ran his fingers inside the edges, and then began to roll them down, first this side, then the other. Jackie sighed and lifted her bum for him. It was going to happen, they were coming off – but then just as they were about to pass the point of no return, she suddenly sat up, entirely against her will, and lifted her finger.

'Knickers ON,' she snapped, and she leaned over to pick up her drink.

'Why not now?' he mewed. He couldn't understand it. They were alone. They were in lust. He didn't know that Jackie couldn't understand it either.

'I – don't feel right . . .' she began.

'It's never going to be right, is it? Is it?' said Dino between clenched teeth.

'Yes, it will,' shrilled Jackie, but she could have howled with frustration, because he was quite right. In some ways that was the most humiliating thing about it – that a dope like Dino, who knew nothing, was in a position to tell her, who was actually quite sorted, what was going on. She could have killed him for that. She got up and started rearranging her clothes.

'Tomorrow,' she said. 'After the party.'

'What about tonight?'

'I can't, Mum and Dad are expecting me back, but they think I'm staying over with Sue tomorrow. We'll have all night long. All night.' Jackie had no idea why she was making such a rash promise. Maybe she was just fed up with being put in the wrong all the time, maybe somewhere deep inside her, she'd decided that she'd waited long enough for things to work out right – she just had to do what she had to do.

'Me and you in the place on our own, after everyone's gone home,' she promised. 'We'll do it then. OK?' She felt as if she was withholding sweets from a child.

'I can easily find someone who will, you know. You're not the only fish in the sea.' Dino scowled slightly to himself. Had he really said that? The lovely, unexpected things he came out with now and then that Jackie loved so much were matched only by these astounding pieces of oafishness. He had no idea himself where they came from. He peered at her to see how out of order it was. She was staring at him with a thin little smile.

'Tomorrow's another day,' she said.

'Don't forget you promised.'

Dino looked suspiciously at her, then beamed. He was in love again. He was happy. He came to hold her in his arms, and pressed her tightly up against him.

'You don't know how happy that makes me,' he murmured in a thick voice. Jackie could feel herself melting away like a jelly. With her chin on his shoulder, she grimaced resentfully.

'I know. I know, Dino. Honestly.' She'd made him happy and she loved him for it – but only for a bit.

I'm going to get hurt, she thought. But she already was.

6
Jackie

Can you believe him? 'You're not the only fish in the sea.' Who does he think he *is*? And me! Letting him. Well, that's it. If he thinks I'm going to go to bed with him at his ridiculous party, he's living on another planet. It's not just what he says — it's the way he wraps me round his little finger afterwards. You know? Gives me a big hug and a smile and thinks that makes everything all right. And the worst thing is, it *does* make everything all right, for a bit anyway, just for long enough to watch a bit of telly and walk back to my place, and I'm getting angrier and angrier so that by the time we get to my door I can hardly speak I'm so furious, and you know what he says? 'What's the matter with you?' What's the matter with *me*? Can you believe it?

I've got no excuse, I've known what he's like for years. There was a time at Primary School, I remember, he brought in this enormous cowboy hat — very appropriate — and he walked around the playground with a crowd of other little boys all begging him to let them have a go wearing it. It was huge, a great big black thing with silver tassels all the way around the edge. It was about three sizes too big even for his head, it looked ridiculous. If it had been any other kid, they'd have all teased him about it, but some-how Dino managed to make that stupid hat into something they were all just desperate to have on their heads.

I should have listened to Sue right at the start.

'Just use him,' she told me. 'Use his body and then fling it back. Why not? Simon will never know.' But did I do it? Did I hell! And do you know why? Because I'm not that sort of girl! How stupid is that? That's how I see myself. I would never shag someone just for sex and betray my boyfriend. Other girls might do that but not me, oh no – I have to have a decent relationship with them before you get down to that sort of thing. I have to like them and respect them and have them respect me – even if it's a total arse like Dino! He doesn't even know what respect is. All the time I thought I was safe because I was sensible, and sensible people only fall for other sensible people. Only idiots fall for idiots. But when a sensible person falls for an idiot, that's the person who really suffers, because a person who isn't sensible just does mad things and likes it, but a sensible one spends her whole time trying to make an impossible situation sensible. I am so useless!

I keep thinking he's going to get it. I keep kidding myself he's going to grow up. But why should he? He gets everything he wants by just being a wanker. Except me. He just waved goodbye to that.

The first time I chucked him was after we went to see a film together – I forget which one it was, we go to films quite a bit. We sit and snog all the way through. It's great. Anyway. I was still seeing Simon as well at the time. After the film we went for a walk in the car park and I gave him – well – I don't want to say. Oh, God, I'm blushing. You know. A blow job. It was the first time I did that for him. It sounds horrible but it was really lovely, actually. I enjoyed doing it. It felt right somehow. Not sordid at all. I was floating on this lovely cushion of sex. And then on the way home, he started. He had a stiffie again immediately and he wanted to do a knee trembler in the car park but I wasn't into that, that would have felt horrible. He went on and on and on, and by the time I got home I wasn't feeling wonderful anymore, I was feeling horrible and crabby and frustrated and pissed off. Trust him to spoil it. I was thinking I'd go to bed and have a diddle down there and think about all the things we did, but instead I had a shower and went to bed feeling ridiculous, as if crouching down and sucking him in the bloody car park was some sort of compromise that wasn't really good enough.

I thought, That's it. This bloke's just awful. I gave him a ring the next day and told him. I was furious. And he was devastated – everyone said so. He begged me to go back out with him and what did I do? I said yes! Why? For a couple of weeks, I juggled Dino and Simon, trying to decide what to do but in the end there was no way round it. I had to tell Simon I needed a break. He was really upset. He kept sending me letters. Every other morning for a fortnight I'd open them at breakfast and weep into my cornflakes. I rang him up a few times and told him it was just for a bit. I really thought I'd end up going back to him in a few weeks.

'I see,' said Sue. 'You shag Dino's brains out for a few weeks, give him the elbow and go back to Simon for a mature, lasting relationship. Wouldn't it be easier to just have an affair with Dino?'

'I'm not shagging him,' I told her.

'What do you mean, you're not shagging him?'

'Not until I'm sure it's the right thing.'

'Shagging him is the single possible reason for going out with Dino. If you don't shag him, why bother?'

'I'll give him a reasonable chance. If it's no go, I'll put him back on the shelf.'

Sue looked at me wearily. 'This is wrong,' she said. 'Prepare to get hurt.'

'I'm not like you, Sue,' I said. 'Either it's serious, or it's off.'

Sue looked at me like I was mad, but Dino has got his nice sides. He's a sweetheart. I know that doesn't sound like him, but he is. He blushes like a baby. And he's so open – really. You can see what's going on in there like a goldfish in a bowl, he just can't help himself. When he's not thinking about how cool he is, he's actually very charming.

It's not just that he's desperate to sleep with me. *I'm* desperate to sleep with *him*. Really. He makes me feel like – ooooh. Sometimes I feel like weeping with frustration. When we ... well, I don't want to talk about that but you would not believe how horny I get. And I'm not going to do it unless I feel right, and how can you feel right when your boyfriend's so selfish? Isn't that stupid?

But ... the thing is ... you can't blame him. Maybe we

deserve each other. I've been leading him on for ages. I'm either chucking him or preparing to sleep with him practically every week, and every time I chuck him we get back together and every time I try to sleep with him I back out at the last minute. I guess I'm frightened of getting hurt. Which is totally stupid, because I'm getting hurt, anyway. And so's Dino.

Maybe if I did it... I mean, what if that's the problem? Poor boy, he must get so confused, he isn't really all that selfish inside, he's just not very good with feelings. That's the problem, really. If I did shag him, maybe it would make everything all right? If I made him feel secure like that? And I do want to.

Tomorrow. After the party. I'm going to do it. Even if it makes me feel like shit afterwards, I'll never be able to live with myself if I don't. I'll have a word with Sue about it in the morning. Yes! Oh, God. What am I like?

7
Pressure

While Jackie and Dino were jumping on each other in the sitting room, Ben was outside the little row of shops just down the road from his place, on his mobile to Ali Young. They were having an almost argument.

'It's my birthday,' she was saying.

'It's your birthday *today*,' he told her.

'You know I've got to see my friends tonight.'

'Ah ha, well, I have to see mine tomorrow.'

There was a pause. Miss was not happy.

'You could make the effort.'

'What would I tell Dino? It's his party, he's my best friend. I can't tell him I can't come to his party because it's your birthday, can I?'

'Make an excuse.'

'I can't.'

'Of course you can. If you wanted.'

'I can't! Look, I'll see you Sunday...'

'Don't tell me when you'll see me,' said Ali sharply. Ben took the phone from his ear and stared at it suspiciously. He felt completely fazed every time, when she veered from lover Miss to school Miss in mid-sentence.

'All right,' he said. 'I'd like to see you on Sunday.'

Another pause.

'It's as if you're ashamed of me,' she complained.

Ben didn't know what to say. This was getting complicated.

'Well?' she said.

'Well what?'

'Are you? Ashamed of me?'

'It's not that! We can't exactly go public, can we? I mean, it's not like...'

'Like what?'

'Well. It's not quite the same as if you were my girlfriend, is it?'

There was another pause, so long this time that he got alarmed. He was just saying, 'Hello,' when she replied,

'I've got to go now, Ben, that's someone on the mobile, I'll see you on Sunday, then. And don't you dare go with anyone else – I'll find out, you know. Goodbye.' And she was gone.

Ben tucked his mobile back into his pocket and went into the newsagent to buy a chocolate bar. He was surprised at how pissed off the conversation had left him.

What did she want? He'd thought it was sex but now he wasn't sure. He was seventeen years old, and he wasn't sure he wanted anyone to want him for anything. Not yet. Not for a long time.

Shagging Miss had always been scary, but lately there were other worries beginning to creep in. It wasn't just the question of where it was all going. It seemed ungrateful, but he was missing girls of his own age. He sometimes actually felt jealous of Dino's problems with

Jackie; it all seemed so sweet and innocent and sexy. Miss not only knew it all, she'd done it all and if there was anything she'd accidentally missed she was keen to try it out. Measured against such monumental stark bollock naked, spread open, rampant rudeness, having a snog and a grope in the shrubbery seemed like a childhood game, a lost pleasure like toy cars and pogo sticks.

Then again, what if his sex drive got worn out? What if some sweet, shy girl came along and offered herself to him and he had to get her to swing from the light fittings with a telescope up her fanny and pegs on her tits before he could get it up?

Stupid. He was getting greedy. He was the man with more treasure than he could count, and here he was jealous of their little coins. As if he had any need to feel bad about himself.

8
The Party

The idea was to have the Hand Dogs banging it out as people came through the door.

Look at you with your thigh-boots on,
Oh yeaaaah.
Won't you let me dance with you?
Oh yeaaaah.
Stand up with you,
Lie down with you,
All over yoou-hooooo-hoooo.
Kirry-kirry oooooooo.

The trouble was, when *were* they going to arrive? Everything was set by five o'clock in the afternoon. Jackie had come round again in the morning to help get things ready, then disappeared for the afternoon to get her homework done and get ready. Ben turned up about lunchtime, Jonathon at about three. They drank Coke and watched Dino check on his mobile to make sure everyone knew exactly what to do that evening: be there. Jonathon started nagging to open the beers and get stuck in.

'There's not enough as it is,' said Dino. 'We don't want to get too pissed before the party's even begun.'

'Don't we?' said Jonathon, who seemed genuinely surprised. Ben wagged his finger at him.

'What about the girlies, Jon? We don't want to be out of action for them.'

Jonathon, uncomfortable with a subject he felt unequal to, nodded and shrugged and tried to look cool.

Fasil turned up at six to drop off his famous party tapes, and then incurred Dino's ire by clearing off to get on with his training and homework.

'You can't, I'm having a party,' explained Dino, but Fasil was unmoved.

'There's no such thing as a party at six o'clock in the evening,' he said. The door closed behind him, and the long wait began again.

'I'm scared,' admitted Dino an hour or so later, just after Jackie arrived. 'In fact,' he added about an hour after that, 'I'm terrified.'

'Calm down,' advised Ben. 'It's going to be a great party.'

'I'm having a good time already,' said Jonathon.

The rest of the gang from school arrived shortly afterwards, but Dino cheered up only briefly. The main bulk were surely going to turn up any second now; the party needed to get hot. He kept running in and out of the front room putting the Hand Dogs on in case the first guests turned up, but by the time it'd played about ten times everyone was begging him to take it off.

Dino was laughing and loafing about, but inside he felt sick. What if no one came? He'd have emptied the house for a handful of mates and they'd all feel sorry for him. At nine Fasil turned up and began DJ-ing. The party had been started so many times that Dino was getting attacks of *déjà vu* and had to go into the garden to calm down with Jacks.

They wandered up past the lawn towards the patch of garden where his father grew vegetables. The music sounded tinny at this distance, nothing to do with him, almost. They had a snog. Jackie stopped him mussing her hair and made promises for later on. After the music. After the dancing. After the drink and the smoke and the sweat. After the noise, there would be love. Dino began to feel better.

'Perhaps it'd be better to just wait out here until it gets going,' suggested Jackie, but Dino was anxious to watch the agony of his party's birth pangs.

By ten, he was in despair. He was in the kitchen talking to Jackie and Sue and pretending to be cool when two things happened. The music went off. There was a long, loud silence in which the doorbell rang.

Dino ran excitedly down the hall, looked out of the window and saw about six thousand people clutching bottles, standing there like snowmen outside an eerily silent door.

'Wait! Wait!' he hissed. 'Don't let them in . . .' He burst into the front room. The hardcore were all in there dancing like maniacs to no music.

'What's this, you freaks?' he screamed. 'What are you *on*?'

'Are you deaf?' sneered Snoops. Everyone started to make out that the CD player was on full blast and that Dino was the only one who couldn't hear it, yelling things at one another and pretending they could hardly make it out. And – this shows what a state Dino was in – for a second or two he was ready to believe them.

'Huh?' he said. 'Huh?' and he was staring at the player trying to work out how come he could hear them and not it. They all hooted at him like baboons and began pogoing to no noise again. Dino blushed his deepest, most crimson red. Behind him, someone opened the door and a long queue of people came in. Two or three of them stood and stared in amazement at the collection of freaks head-banging to the silence. Outside in the corridor, Dino could hear the others, their voices booming and squeaking in an embarrassed way in the silent house.

One look at the happy little faces of his friends proved anything he wanted to know. They were already off their heads. Useless! He'd issued instructions not to Not to NOT TO before the thing was going, but here they were, peaking like Linford Christie already.

'Can't anyone here even think?' he groaned. Then Fasil walked in, strutting about like he was the only one with a clue in the world and pressed the button. A deafening soup of thick, chunky noise hollered out. At last! Dino poked his head out down the corridor. Everyone was standing still, heads turned to the opened door that was suddenly bellowing music at them.

'Drink, drink, drink!' he instructed them. If he got them drunk or stoned or something no one would even know whether they were having a good time or not. He herded them along to the kitchen and as soon as he was wedged into the corridor, someone turned the music up.

It was so loud he couldn't talk to his guests even a hallway and a room away. The bastards! His own mates! They'd reached two o'clock in the morning while everyone else was still at 5pm. Dino was furious. The crowd was so thick in the hallway he couldn't even get back to the dance room without a fight. It was awful. Hang your coats there, no, put them in the boxroom, drinks, smoke in the garden please. He was turning into someone's mother, for God's sake! People were milling about in little groups not knowing what to do, it was pathetic. He felt like screaming at them, What's wrong with you, don't you know how to have a good time? Do you need *lessons*?

Suddenly he'd had enough. He fled the kitchen – leave the bastards to it – and made a dive for his friends in the dance room. He hid in the thick wall of music, drank a bottle of Ice Head quick, had a toke on a spliff and tried to relax. It didn't work, so he rushed across the room, seized hold of Jackie and gave her a good snogging in a corner for ten minutes.

It was perfect. It silenced conversation utterly. No one likes to interrupt a good, hard snog. By the time he'd done, someone tapped him on the shoulder, he was feeling cool already. Jackie hung in his arms, her face turned up, ready for more – ready for anything by the looks of her. Dino answered the question about coats, and gave it to her again.

'Oh, *Dino!*' She pushed herself right up against him and stroked his face and whispered right in his ear, 'That was some kiss. Oo-oo-oo...' she panted, which made Dino feel very good indeed. The next time they came up for air again Dino was ready for a look around. It was getting there. The music was down so you could hear people if you screamed, the dance floor was moving, people were talking.

He'd done it. He'd survived by snogging with a good-looking girl in the corner of the dance floor. Cool or what? And now it was safe to go and mingle. Jackie had other ideas. She was thinking, Right, right. She could see Sue scowling and trying not to look at her over people's heads, but she'd made up her mind. Tonight was the night. She just had to shag Dino. She was going to do it right now. She'd take him upstairs and ride him like a . . .

'Come on,' she said, pulling him into her. But Dino was already turning away.

'Just a bit . . .'

'Dino! Where are you going?'

'Got to go see, Jacks. Won't be long.'

'Dino!'

But it was too late. Dino was out of the door and off to socialise. He had no idea how close he'd just got. Furious, Jackie looked over at Sue, who was talking loudly in a corner and refused to meet her eye.

Dino did the rounds, shaking hands, five high, five low, great do! How are you? Things were looking good.

'Welcome to the Guesthouse Dinoroso,' he whispered to himself, and imagined that he was walking on air and that everyone was looking at him shyly, out of the corners of their eyes. He elevated his power beams to a foot above everyone's head so they had nothing to worry about. Fasil was doing great with the music – he didn't have to worry about that. He didn't have to worry about anything.

What did you expect? Yeah – Dino did a great party. He walked up the hall and around the kitchen. He snogged Grace by the back door – it was a party, it was what people did – and coolly resisted her suggestion to go for a walk. Back inside, as he passed down the hall, he met with Ben in the hall, staring at something on the stairway. As Dino came up to him he saw what it was, an amazing sight – Jonathon enjoying a feeding frenzy with Deborah Sanderson on the stairs.

Jonathon had no idea how it had happened. They'd been talking at the bottom of the stairs and it was bit embarrassing because every time someone went up or down they had to squeeze past and Deborah had to push right up against him. That was a bit obvious, Deborah being a bit of a plumper. Jonathon was embarrassed – partly for her, but mainly because he didn't want to be seen squashed up against her like that. He got teased enough about his friendship with her without that.

The kiss had come out of nowhere – he couldn't even remember how it started. He had wondered so often how you actually knew when it was right to kiss a girl, that even as he was doing it, he was trying to work out what had happened so he could use it next time with someone he really fancied. Then, once it had started, it just went on. Deborah sighed, closed her eyes, pulled him almost on top of her and let him sink into her. Immediately, he was overtaken with a rage of hormones. Deborah felt his erection against her stomach and smiled up at him. She grabbed hold of his bum and moved him gently from side to side so that it rocked against her, twitching like Frankenstein's monster in an electric storm. He let his hands creep round her to cuddle a breast. They half fell, half walked a couple of steps up the stairs and collapsed. Jonathon slid his hand under her top and stroked her bra.

Not having known how it started, he had no idea how to stop it, either, even though he was embarrassed to be snogging a fat girl on the stairs where everyone could not only see but had to squeeze past in order to get up and down. Under her loose clothes he felt her all over – every bit that he could get to, anyway. Only when he began to ferret under her knickers did she open her eyes and whisper, 'Not here.' She smiled a languid, warm smile at him and her eyes drifted up to the landing. Terrified, Jonathon closed his eyes and kissed her again, more deeply than ever. He didn't want to be doing this. Or did he? Traitorously, his penis had turned to super hard concrete in his jeans. Deborah was surreptitiously rubbing it with the back of her hand and he felt so good, he thought he could happily die.

'But I don't fancy her!' Jonathon tried unconsciously to explain, but Mr Knobby Knobster grinned his woozy little hard man's smile and said, 'Yeah? But I do.'

It seemed to go on for hours. He was curled up almost on top of her and they were taking big, long, syrupy slurps of each other's face. A steady stream of people were squeezing past on their way up and down the stairs. In the course of half an hour or so, everyone there would have seen what he was up to, and who it was with. He was feeling more and more uncomfortable, but he had no idea how to extricate himself.

'Jonathon. I see you're having a good party.'

He opened his eyes and saw Dino and Ben standing at the bottom of the stairs watching him. Dino was smiling like a flint. Ben was staring at Deborah, fascinated by this sudden glimpse of the woman sunk in a sexual trance. Deborah's face hung beneath him, her eyes closed, her lips wet, half open, relaxed, hungry. She opened her eyes and looked sideways at Ben. Ben smiled, made a 'Hi,' face, but she just smiled slightly at him before closing her eyes and held her face back under Jonathon's to be kissed. Lowering his, he began to feed. When he peeked out again a moment later, they were gone.

Jonathon came to a sudden decision.

'I need a wee,' he said, and immediately panicked at the thought that she might want to come with him up the stairs. 'Out in the garden, the queue's too long,' he finished quickly. He leapt off her; the image came into his mind of a small raptor leaping off the carcass of a dead sauropod. Wincing, he jumped down the stairs and ran out into the kitchen.

Behind him, Deborah got up and rearranged her clothes. She fancied Jonathon something rotten but never thought she stood a chance. They had so much in common. She and Jon spent ages happily chatting together at school but they'd never seen each other out of it. She'd dreamt that something might happen at the party, but never thought it would. The way he'd leaped on her! She'd actually gasped with surprise. It might have been just a party snog, but he'd been so enthusiastic – it had to mean something. No one had ever told her that a stiff knob means a stiff knob and no more.

'It was just a snog,' Jonathon told Dino in the kitchen a little later.

Dino pulled a face. 'I don't know how you could do it, that's just gross,' he said.

'What?'

'Gross.'

'What's gross about it?'

'She's fat.'

'She's not that fat,' he said, and Dino replied,

'Fat enough.'

Jonathon tried to be dismissive. 'A snog's a snog, so what?' he said. He thought of suggesting she had nice tits – something he'd heard people say dismissively about a girl they'd been with they didn't fancy – but he just couldn't do that to her.

'She still has feelings you know,' said Ben severely. 'Just because she's overweight...'

'Fat,' said Dino. 'She's fat.'

'She's plump,' said Ben. 'Some people find that very attractive.'

'People like Jonathon,' said Dino, and Ben snorted in amusement.

'Better than Jackie the beanpole,' said Jonathon.

Dino rolled his eyes. Who did he think he was kidding?

'She's a nice person and she's very fond of you, just don't hurt her, that's all,' said Ben.

'Fat's fat. That's all there is to it,' pointed out Dino.

'She has feelings.'

'Just fat feelings, though,' said Jonathon, who was utterly unable to resist a joke; and then felt awful the way both of them looked at him. His head was whirling. At that moment Jackie and Sue emerged meaningfully out of the crowd and cornered him.

'Are you serious about Debs?' asked Sue.

'What?'

'Are you serious about her?'

'What?'

'Don't keep saying What!'

'Do you really fancy her?' asked Jackie severely.

Jonathon was horrified. Part of him refused to give Dino the pleasure of thinking that he didn't fancy Debs merely because she was fat; part of him was scared of Ben and the girls thinking he was just using her; and part of him genuinely liked Deborah and didn't want to hurt her. He just didn't fancy her, but he wasn't sure he had any right not to.

'Well? Do you?'

'You're being a bit quick, aren't you?' said Ben.

'She's really fond of you, do you know that? She really likes you,' said Sue. 'You don't know how lucky you are, she's such a nice person. You're not just stringing her along, are you?'

'No, of course I'm not...'

'Do you fancy her then?'

Jonathon writhed, caught between Dino, Ben and these fearsome young women. 'Well, yes of course I fancy her, I was kissing her, wasn't I?' On the tip of his tongue were the words, 'But that doesn't mean ...' But somehow they couldn't emerge.

'Good.'

'You've done it now,' said Dino after they'd left. 'They've probably gone to tell her that you want to go out with her.'

'I didn't know you felt like that,' said Ben.

'Neither did I,' said Jon. He pushed his way through the crowd to escape. He was definitely not in control of the situation.

'So you like fat girls too, then,' Dino told Ben, leering at him. Ben smiled blandly and slipped away to the back door.

The fact was, Ben was jealous. Not of Deborah herself, although he liked her. He was jealous of the sort of relationship she and Jon could have together. They got on well together. He thought how comfortable they'd looked on the stairs. He wished them well.

Bollocks, he thought to himself, as he stuck his head out into the garden and gulped down the cool air. All these lovely girls. All those lucky boys getting off with them, snogging with them, sleeping with them, feeling them up – and he couldn't do it. As she'd said, Ali would find out somehow and give him hell. Ben was a popular and good-looking boy, there were any number of attractive girls who would have got into a clinch with him, but he didn't dare. There wasn't anyone he could talk to. Stupid though it was, for someone who was getting quality sex from an expert, he was feeling left out.

Oh well, he thought. One thing anyway, at least the old harpy can't come here. The thought made him shudder.

Apart from having to watch one of his friends kiss a fat girl, Dino had ordeals yet to come: he spotted Jackie snogging Fasil in the kitchen. Suddenly, all the feel-good drained away out of the hole in his bottom. Out of order, or what?

Dino didn't mess about; he interrupted.

Fasil did the right thing. He grinned meekly, abandoned all hopes of single number status for the rest of his life and scuttled off. But Jackie turned round and eyed him aggressively.

'My girlfriend. My party,' said Dino. 'You snog me.'

'I snog anyone I want.'

The thing that really pissed Dino off wasn't just that they'd snogged. It was that they'd snogged in public. There was his girlfriend snogging one of his friends in full view of everyone. It was all cut and dried. Except...

'You were snogging Grace, you two-faced bastard,' Jackie snarled. It was true. Dino blushed. He'd been a twat, but that just made him angrier than ever. The one thing he really couldn't bear was to feel like a twat.

He bent down and hissed in her ear, 'Shut up, will you? Everyone's going to think I'm a right twat.'

'Is that all you're worried about? *Looking* like a twat? You *are* a twat! Twat!' she bellowed, and off she shoved, leaving Dino standing there feeling more twat-like than he had ever done before.

Dino was furious. 'Slut,' he called after her. 'Slapper,' loud enough for everyone to hear. She turned round all little girlie and squeaked in a stupid voice,

'Oh, Dino, I was only practising so I could kiss you better later on. Everyone knows you kiss sooooooooooo gooooooooood.' And she said this in such a way that indicated – can you believe this? – that Dino was a crap kisser. Then she flounced off.

He stood there like a bare arse. He could feel his cheeks flushing redder and redder. Everyone had heard the whole exchange. He began, 'Don't give me that bollocks, everyone knows I kiss like a...' And then he had to stop because now he was putting his foot in it very badly indeed. Boasting about how well you kiss! God, that was so childish.

Having no idea what else to do, he just turned round and walked out. Right out. Out of the room, out of the hall, out of the house. He was blind with rage and humiliation. Let them have fun! Let them enjoy themselves, the whole lot of them. He didn't want anything to do with any of them.

Dino got halfway home before he remembered that he'd been at home in the first place. There was nowhere else to go. For a moment he thought about going back to the party and throwing everyone out, but even as he thought it, he realised it was impossible. That would not be a very cool thing to do.

He walked back. From outside it sounded as if the

party was going like a bomb. He lurked, wondering what to do. It was a while before he realised the way out. Thank God! He'd been in the wrong! All he had to do was admit it. Admitting you were in the wrong was a cool thing to do. It made you more human, somehow. He'd been snogging people, so had Jacks. So what was the problem? Of course, he'd much rather not have stormed out, or lost his cool; and he'd *very* much rather Jackie had never snogged with Fas. But what was done was done.

He hung around a bit longer, plucking up courage. He practised laughing at himself. Then he took the plunge and went to ring the doorbell. It really was pretty funny, after all.

'I went home,' Dino told Stu, and started laughing and laughing. 'Outta my head!' he howled. Stu grinned back, and Dino knew he was going to get away with it. Once he'd recovered laughing at how out of his head he'd been, he went to look for Jackie and apologised. She forgave him at once.

'OK?' he said and she said,

'OK.'

Dino leaned in and whispered, 'Sorry.'

'Yeah, so am I.'

'No more snogging other people, eh?'

'No more snogging other people.'

Dino thought, I'm still in. 'I'm still in? Later?' he said.

'Mmmmm . . . OK. If you're good.'

But it had been a close thing. He found Fasil and – this was really cool – had a chat with him about nothing much, just to show no hard feelings. But warned him off as well.

'I reckon I'm in with Jackie after,' he said.

'Mmm,' said Fasil.

Dino leaned up right close to his face and breathed, 'Virgin hole,' right in his face. Fasil moved his head back and stared at Dino with a horrified expression. Dino winked and leered.

The party went from quiet to friendly, to busy, to loud, to frantic. Dino had a few smokes and a couple more Ice Head beers and gradually a holy, rosy glow started to hover around him. It was a good party. He was a saint, really. All these people having such a good time, just because of him. His Holiness Pope Dino the First, he felt like, as he went from group to group, bestowing his benedictions upon them. The hardcore were like a bunch of apes by comparison, they were all jiggering about and shouting. They had indulged in something a bit stronger than a few spliffs. Dino himself declined. He didn't want to do anything that might interfere with his session with Jackie later on. That, after all, was the main event of the evening. He didn't want his vital parts shrivelled up like a frightened slug. He wanted big, stiff parts for that night's action.

People were rushing up and down the stairs shrieking. People were yelling in the kitchen and having fights over the limited quantities of alcohol. Couples had moved into the bedrooms, or, if the bedrooms were full, into the garden and under blankets in the downstairs room. A row of them were snogging up the stairs.

76

'What's this, the queue for the bedrooms?' bellowed Jonathon up at them. Standing in a group three metres and about fifty people away, Deborah looked at him and laughed far too loud. Jonathon pretended he hadn't noticed. A crowd in the sitting room discovered that if they all danced up and down hard enough they could make the piano next to the door advance on them. It looked threatening and stupid at the same time, and someone christened it Dino's Dad, because it looked like it was coming to chuck them all out.

A girl called Sam made love in Dino's parents' bed with a boy called Robby, who was sick on the sheets next to her as soon as he'd finished. They covered it up with the duvet and went home. Next door in the boxroom a kid called Simon Tiptree pretended to pass out on top of a pile of coats. When he was left alone, he began systematically to go through all the pockets and bags, looking for money and valuables. At about the same time downstairs in the kitchen, a thin girl in a tiny pink dress was opening the fridge door. She stared rapturously inside. Treasure! Cheese, pork pie, cold cooked sausages! Paradise. Cream cake! What comes next on the ladder up after cold sausage paradise? Cream cake paradise, of course. Without even pausing to moan in pleasure, she reached in and seized an oozing triangle of pleasure, and bit in.

At that moment Jonathon entered the kitchen, trying to duck out of sight of Deborah. It was getting severe. So what if he'd snogged her? Sod it, why couldn't he have a snog just because she was a tubber? Now she was following him. It

77

was awful. And so public! Whenever he lifted his head, there she was, looking at him, walking towards him, eyeing him sideways, craning her neck in between people to try and spot him. Jonathon was being hunted. By good fortune he turned up as the slight girl was opening the fridge door, just in time to duck behind it out of Deborah's sight. The thought, 'Never hide from a fat girl in the fridge', crossed his mind, but there was nowhere else to go. He lowered his head as if to peer inside.

'Yum,' he said to the girl standing next to him. She waved a wedge of cream cake at him.

'No' bad,' said the girl thickly. The little pink dress was so short she showed her knickers every time she bent over or lifted her arms; a pussy pelmet, as his dad would have called it. It occurred to Jonathon that it would be a good thing if Deborah saw him in close-up with a pretty girl like this. She might get the message.

'I'm Jonathon,' he told her, moving in, something he'd never have dared to do unless he had another reason other than to get close.

'Zoë,' she said thickly. She waved her cake into the fridge, generously inviting Jonathon to help himself. Jonathon reached in and took out one of the cold cooked sausages lying on a plate inside. He held it between his fingers, and on a sudden impulse – 'May I?' – reached across and dipped the tip of the sausage into the cream of the girl's cake, wiping it along so it had a big dollop on the end. As he did it he had a nasty feeling he might regret it. He held the sausage up in his fingers and waited.

'You disgusting thing,' said Zoë, but even as she spoke

she burst into laughter, snorting around her cake. Jonathon bobbed the sausage up and down like a little finger puppet.

'Mr Porky is wearing a white hat today,' he began. He was about to launch into a puppet show, but the girl laughed in surprise right through her mouthful of cream cake and sprayed all over the inside of the fridge. Everything was covered.

'Jesus, sick in the fridge,' said Jonathon. The girl was delighted with him, it was great. But at that inopportune moment, Fasil turned up.

'What is this? What are you doing?' he asked them. He looked in amazement at the sausage and then angrily at the girl's handful of cake. Then he saw what looked like sick sprayed all over the inside of the fridge. Despite being caught snogging Dino's girlfriend, Fasil was a man of principles.

'That's his fridge! That's his food. You can't do that!'

'Who's this?' asked the girl. 'Someone's dad?'

'What are you doing?' Fasil asked Jonathon. Jonathon smiled weakly. 'It's just a sausage . . .'

'Look at that, she's got half his cream cake there,' complained Fasil. 'She's spat it all over the fridge and you're encouraging her.'

'Is this how you *party*?' the girl asked. 'Is this how you have *fun*?' Fasil was pulling the fridge door shut on them. Revealed to the kitchen, Jonathon looked round. Sure enough, Deborah was there, right there. Two steps and she was on him.

'Oooh,' she said. 'Sausage and cream. My favourite.' She

reached forward, took the sausage off Jon and licked the cream off the end of it.

'I see,' said Jonathon.

Taking advantage of the distraction, the girl in the pink dress dodged out of sight, past Fasil, who was staring at Deborah and her sausage as if he'd just seen a cat lay an egg, and out into the hall, where she leaned against a wall and finished off the cream cake greedily.

Zoë had started out the night before in a bar called Kas the Wanderer, drinking Red Bull and vodka with a group of friends. She'd done a load of e at another party, stayed up all day watching TV at a friend's house before going to Dino's. One of her friends was going out with one of Jackie's, which was how they'd found out about it. The others had had enough fairly early on and gone home, but Zoë had nowhere better to go. She hung around in the hope of doing a bit of looting. She'd had nothing to eat all day and she was starving hungry and exhausted.

That guy with the sausage had been nice. She liked funny boys.

When she'd finished she picked up a drink someone had left on a windowsill and took a swig. Snake bite — cider and lager. She whacked down the glassful, pulled a face. She put a hand behind her to steady herself against the sill. Her head was swimming. She decided to have a look upstairs, see if she couldn't find a place to get her head down right now. The stairway was solid. The first room she found was the boxroom, where Simon Tiptree had to quickly pretend he'd passed out on his back on a pile of coats. Zoë watched him closely, staring at him for a full minute, listening to his breath, until she was sure he was asleep. She went up and prodded him with her foot. He didn't stir.

Satisfied that he really was out cold, Zoë began to go through the pockets of the coats heaped on the bed beside him. In his false sleep, Simon was outraged — a thief, standing there stealing while he was asleep! The awful thing was, there was nothing he could do about it. If he woke up and nabbed her, she might make a fuss, and then someone might come in and find his own bag full of their valuables. He just had to lie there and take it.

The girl was disappointed to find so little money. She went through the coats — nothing. Then the bags, but it wasn't until she opened an unpromising looking nylon rucksack that she suddenly struck it rich. It rattled like a collection box with handfuls of loose change. Inside were watches, bits of jewellery, paper money. There must have been fifty or sixty pounds in cash there.

'Oh yeah,' she whispered. She stared intently at Simon, who lay on his back in fury, still trying to appear fast asleep. His face twitched slightly.

'Thanks, sweetheart,' she told him, and slipped out.

She knew she should leave right then. But she was truly exhausted. The slice of cream cake was about all she'd eaten for twelve hours or more, she was full of vodka and cider and needed to lie down. She poked her head next door into one of the bedrooms. There was a couple lying side by side on the double bed on top of the duvet. She couldn't tell if they were post coital or just past it, but there was a small sofa under the window with a candlewick cover lying on it. She got onto the sofa, pulled the cover on top of her, and went to sleep.

Next door, Simon was furious. After all the trouble he'd been to! He'd had plans for that money, it was important to him. But what could he do? As soon as she left the room, he sat up, groaned and held his head in his hands. The vile little bitch was so tiny! It was infuriating – a small person getting one over on him like that! The funny thing about it was, he felt so violated – he the thief – because he'd been robbed of his thievings. Frustrated and sullen, he jumped up and stamped downstairs with the idea of finding the girl, following her home and mugging her to get his money back. But he didn't see her again. He went home with a headache, empty handed. But there was one lesson to be learned, he realised: if you're going to steal, steal from a thief. They are the least likely to report it.

At two, Ray and Alan Wicks started throwing bottles on the street outside the house – a sure sign that the party was over. There was nothing left to drink, the strangers had left; acquaintances and semi-friends were already pulling on their coats. There was a flurry of fury when people discovered that their bags had been raided. A few of them had nothing to get home with and had to borrow from those who had been more careful with their things. Taxis turned up and ferried people away. There was a final clump of dedicated smokers getting happily stoned on the landing, who made Dino feel very uncool as he booted them out. The semi-hardcore hung about searching through the bottles for dregs, then left in a lump, leaving Jacks, Ben, Fas, Sue and her boyfriend Dave. And Jonathon. And Deborah.

There had been a weak attempt to begin the clearing up, but Jackie evidently had other things on her mind. People were drinking coffee, but she was sitting next to Dino on the sofa sighing and leaning her head on his shoulder. Whenever he turned to look at her, she kissed him.

'I guess it's time to go,' said Sue. She stood up and smiled at Jackie. 'Come on, let's go and get the coats for the dregs. Speed things up.' Jackie got up and they went upstairs together.

Jonathon leered. 'You don't have to boot us out, Dino,' he said. 'You don't need the whole house for that.' He smiled awkwardly at Deborah, who was sitting next to him clutching his hand.

'Yeah, yeah, yeah,' said Dino.

'Do you need the downstairs for some sort of overflow system?' said Jonathon. 'Is it your organ size? Do you need the extra room to manoeuvre it? Perhaps some of us could help with the positioning?'

'Shut yer trap,' said Dino. But he loved all this.

Upstairs, Sue and Jackie were in Dino's parents' bedroom.

'So this is the holy of holies.' Sue tested the bed by pressing down on it and bouncing it up and down. 'Plenty of give, should give a good return service...'

'Shut up!'

'Did you change the sheets?'

'Shut *up*!'

'There's nothing worse than waking up to the smell of his dad.'

'Yeah, I know, I made him do them yesterday.'

'Did you? Make *him* do it?'

'Yeah,' said Jackie. Which was a lie. She just thought she needed a bit more cred.

Sue sighed. 'So you're finally going to go through with it?'

'Yes.' Jackie's voice came out all high and funny, but she was determined this time. The thought of it made her squeak with excitement.

'Well. I'll be thinking of you. I'll get the coats. You get into bed, eh?' Jackie burst out into a fit of nervous giggles, but she kicked off her shoes and started to unbutton her top. She paused when she noticed that Sue was still standing on the other side of the bed, smiling and watching her.

'Go away!' she scolded, turning her back.

'I hope he appreciates what he's getting,' said Sue, and she left to get the coats. Jackie walked excitedly round the room a couple of times, anxious about getting in naked. She ran to the door to listen and make sure no one else was coming up, then she took all her clothes off. Naked, she looked at herself in the mirror. Her eyes weaved their way across to the bits she didn't like. Her hips, which seemed to stick out sideways like a set of lard shelves. Her buttocks quivered as she walked – disgusting! Her breasts looked fine when she was standing, but headed south for her armpits as soon as she lay on her back, and when she

84

stood up with her legs together, instead of her thighs touching each other on the way up to a neat triangle at the top, she had a slight bow in between her thighs which ended abruptly. These were secret faults, of course, only for lovers ever to see — which was of course precisely what she didn't want.

She scowled and tried to concentrate on her good points. She turned sideways, looked at her breasts and her tummy and her skin. Nothing's perfect but ...

'Pretty good,' she told herself uncertainly.

She paused, unsure whether or not to wait up and give him a flash as he came in — she looked at her best standing, when gravity worked for her — or to get into bed and risk him finding he had to feel under armpits to find her boobs. She went to hover by the bed. She turned off the main light and put one of the bedside ones on. She decided to wait. She pulled on a gown she found on the back of the door. She'd slip it off as she heard him on the stairs and give him a second or two of full frontal as he came in, then she'd slip in between the sheets. She went to stand by the bed and pulled back the crumpled cover so she could jump in quick.

9
Dino

Sue came back down with the coats. 'Time to go home,' she said.

'Mighta known, prefers his hole to his mates, typical,' groaned Jonathon, and I thought, Man! I am the One. I mean. They were going home and me — what was I gonna do? Me and Jacks. If you saw her, you'd know what you're missing.

I saw them out. They were all as jealous as a cat in a fish shop — or, put it another way — jealous as cats watching another cat in a fish shop, and that cat was me. I closed the door. I caught a glimpse of Jonathon turning to face Debs with a funny look on his face. Poor sod, I thought to myself, and Jacks is upstairs, all ready, in bed, probably with nothing on, waiting for me.

Up I went, up the stairs with a couple of bottles of Ice Head all ready to make it and what was waiting in the bed for me? You know what was there? A big heap of sick.

I think I nearly went mad for a moment. It was just lying there where she should be, and there was a definite second when I thought she'd actually been turned into a pile of squashed puke. Then I realised — she'd been ill! Just my luck – she's bloody drunk so much she's been sick and now the whole thing's off again!

I ran out to the landing and into the bathroom, but she wasn't there. I called, 'Jacks!' down the stairs, but there was no reply. Right then, I knew. In fact, I reckon I knew even before, as soon as I saw the puke. I started to think that maybe she was hiding from me, or maybe she'd passed out and was lying on the floor out of sight. I ran around the house checking behind all the chairs and things like that, but I knew she wasn't there.

The thing is, it was squashed sick. It was well slept on, that puke. I ran back up to check and tested the temperature of the vomit with the tip of my elbow – I know, it's mad, you have to remember what I was going through. I didn't want to touch it with my fingers. I had no idea of the cool rate of vomit, but this was stone cold.

'This is not my fault,' I hissed to myself. I'd even got her clean sheets to put on the bed! How could she do this to me! I stood there steaming, then I thought to look for her coat in the boxroom, ran through . . . It wasn't there. That was the final proof. The bitch had sneaked out without even telling me. I ran to the front door to shout after her, but I didn't dare to shout very loud; it was too humiliating. There was no answer.

Can you believe that? Why me? Just a few minutes before, I was about the happiest bloke on earth. It was so perfect, showing your friends out of the front door, while your beautiful girlfriend is sliding all naked and gorgeous and ready and waiting into the sheets upstairs. And now look! It's all just . . . a pile of puke.

I walked back along the hallway and I suddenly realised what a horrible fucking mess everything was. There were crumpled plastic cups everywhere. Some of them had spilt, some of them were full of dog ends and other crap. I couldn't bear to go back into the living room, I just went straight up the stairs, but I could feel the presence of the mess in every corner of the house, like a haunting. Stinking beer and dog ends, ash, mud and puke on the carpets and in the beds. I remembered now that someone had been sick actually *in the fridge*. Even along the landing it was filthy. There were dark puddles on the carpet. Someone had rubbed the black rubber of their shoes along the skirting boards. There was broken glass on the top few stairs. There was a row of dog ends standing like a little fence on the little table by my bedroom door. Some of them had fallen down and charred the wood.

And I was still a virgin.

I went back into my parents' bedroom to have another look at the sick, like it might not be there this time, or it'd turned back into Jackie. It was really well ground in. I stared at it for a minute. I thought to myself, If I shag the sick instead of Jackie will I still be a virgin? . . . because just then I'd have done anything on the planet not to be a virgin. I'd destroyed my parents' house and it hadn't worked. What did I have to do? I took a deep breath into the depths of my lungs and I screamed,

'AHHHHHHHHHHHHHHHHHHHHHHHHHHHHHH HHHHHHHHHHHHHHHHHH!' as loud as I could, and someone right next to me screamed back so loud I think I died briefly as I jumped about ten metres into the air.

10
Jonathon

Dino closed the door and Sue and her bloke shot off home. It was Ben, Fas and Meandeborah. All I wanted was for it to be Ben and Fas and me and Deborah. Or even better Fas and Deborah and Ben and me. Or better still, Deborah, Ben, Fas and me on the other side of the whole fucking sentence, but there I was – Meandeborah. Help.

Ben was being very nice. He can be very...courteous, I suppose. Fasil was quiet, I knew he disapproved. Well, Ben disapproved too, but he disapproved because he thought I was going to hurt Debs. He was probably right. Fasil disapproved because he thought that going with a fat girl was morally reprehensible.

I was coming down. I felt like my nervous system had been wired up to some sort of fairground attraction. Have you ever had that feeling where everyone looks like machines? You know? Only pretending to be human beings? What do they want? What are they *up* to?

So this was hilarious, really. We'd just got to the t-junction on the main road when there was this low, moaning call. It sounded like mating wombats lost in the drains or something.

'Was that *Dino*?' someone asked.

We all stopped and the call came again.

'Yaaaackeeee . . .' As if Dino, if indeed Dino it was, was scared of shouting too loud in case it punctured his status.

'Could be,' said Ben. We waited for a while, but there was no more noise, so we carried on a little way. Then, feet, clip-clopping down the road. It was like a movie. Like the camera crew and the lighting guys were going to come running backwards round the corner at any moment filming something coming towards us.

'I think it's coming towards us,' I hissed, and Deborah laughed too loudly. It was so late there were no cars about, everything was dead quiet. We all turned at once to watch the t–junction behind us, just as if we'd been told to.

Clop clop clop clop clop, they went. I turned to look at Ben to see if he was aware that we were in some sort of production; he just smiled at me sideways and raised his eyebrows.

Clop clop clop clop clop clop. It was like, will it be, won't it be, will it be . . . ?

It was. Jackie.

As soon as she saw us she stopped dead in her tracks and stared at us, before turning and heading fast up the road in the opposite direction.

'Jackie, where you going? Are you all right?' called Deborah. Jackie turned and looked at her, nodded, then shook her head and leaned her arm against the wall and rested her forehead on it. Deborah told me to wait for her and went clopping off herself to see to her, with Fasil, who fancies Jackie chronically, trailing behind her.

Ben looked at me and I looked at Ben – and we both just

cracked up. Poor old Dino! After all that. We had to turn our backs so we couldn't be seen. He was so sure he was on to it tonight. And here she was running away! Poor old Jackie was obviously in a right state and we couldn't show her how hysterical we were. We didn't say a word, we just stood there with our backs to them, trying not to shake too hard.

Finally we got ourselves under control. Debs and Jacks were having a heart to heart with Fasil hanging around the edge, like he was looking for a spare bone. As if he didn't have enough bone already.

I was starting to move over towards them, but Ben hung back. He put his hands in his pockets and sort of rocked on his feet and said, 'Well, looks like there's enough gooseberries about. I think I'll go home.' And he smiled grimly at me.

'You bastard,' I hissed.

We looked across. Deborah was trying to listen sympathetically to Jackie and keep an eye on me at the same time.

'Make a run for it now?' suggested Ben.

There was a pause. He always scares me by lunging straight into things.

'It was just a snog,' I insisted.

'Not for her. She's smitten, I think,' he said. Then he looked at me and said, 'But it's nice to have someone who's smitten with you, isn't it?' I didn't say anything, so he asked me right out, 'Do you fancy her or not?'

'Yes,' I lied. 'Of course I do. But . . .'

'But?'

'I just don't want to go out with anyone at the moment.'

Ben smiled wryly. 'You'll just have to tell her then,' he

said. He wagged a finger at me, and I could have strangled the bastard. I suppose he was only offering me a piece of advice but it felt like torture. He knew very well I couldn't bring myself to do that. Didn't he?

'See you,' said Ben, and he left, giving me a friendly little wave over his shoulder as he slid off.

So I sauntered over to see what was going on, like a puppet in a puppet show. Free will? Don't make me laugh.

Deborah looked as if she was having a good time. She has this gift, Deborah, she always manages to look as if she's having a good time. Maybe she is, who knows? – but on the other hand, maybe she was doing it for Jackie, who kept giggling and bursting into tears. Fasil was standing there staring at her like a weasel. He kept offering to walk her home every minute or so, until Debs snapped at him to shut up going on, couldn't he see she was upset?

So, of course Deborah had to offer to walk home with her. Which should have been great because I could have said, OK, see you later... What a pity! Just as we were getting to grips with each other, you have to rescue a friend! Oh well, I'll try not to be disappointed. Maybe another time (which will never come). But Deborah said, 'You can keep us company,' so I had to go along.

That bit was quite funny actually. Fas came along too, and we ended up walking behind, like a pair of shotgun riders or something. I tried to make conversation with him, but Fas, he gets so stoned, he could hardly say a word. He just kept staring at me with these big dopey eyes every time I said anything, so I shut up and we walked along in silence. Meanwhile, ahead of us, Deborah was being magnificent as usual. She was sorting Jackie out, no problem. They were laughing and talking, and Debs kept patting her and comforting her. She's just great like that.

Finally we got Jackie home. Goodbye goodbye goodbye. Fasil off in one direction, Jackie flung her arms round Debs and went indoors and there it was, Meandeborah all on our own. She linked her arm through mine and smiled.

'I've been waiting to get you on your own all night,' she told me, and lifted her eyebrows up and gave me one of those big lovely smiles, so I knew what was in store. And of course Mr Knobby, the traitorous little fletch, stood up at the mere thought.

We walked along a bit, and then Deborah started cracking up, and had to tell me the story. See, Jackie had got herself all ready, all powdered and washed and lovely and naked and plumped up and ready in the bedroom, pulled back the covers to the bed to get in so she'd be like a nice tender, juicy little filling when Dino came up . . . and there under the sheets was this huge pile of cold puke lying there, all squidged up into the covers. And she was so offended, she put her clothes straight back on and left. Deborah just cracked up — it was pretty bloody funny. I mean, it wasn't even Dino's fault. She stormed out — very quietly by all accounts — and was halfway home before she realised she'd sabotaged her own shag.

'So why didn't she just go back?' I asked, and Deborah said,

'Because she didn't want to!' She thought this was priceless, Debs, she just kept bending over and roaring with laughter.

It was a real gas, that walk home, actually. We started pretending to be Jackie and Dino, with her dying to shag him and then panicking every time he took his knob out. I really lost it, actually. I started pretending I was Dino's knob in *disguise*, trying to look all friendly. I found some roses and sprinkled some petals on my head and ran around Deb with this crazy, knobby walk, wagging at her and promising all sorts of things if she'd just let me get in her. Deborah was killing herself. I was off my head – pretending to be Dino's knob! God, if he ever found out he'd never speak to me again. It was great. Then we got near to her place and I felt myself lose it again and got all quiet and anxious. We stood there holding hands. She moved up very close to me and said, 'Aren't you going to see if I run away screaming from yours?'

I said something, I don't know what it was. She came right up to me and kissed me and put her hand on it so it went up like a rocket inside my jeans.

'Yum,' she whispered.

So we stood hidden round the corner to where she lived, and we had this huge, magic, mammoth snog. It was just fantastic. And I felt her all over. It was like . . . well, how can you describe that? It was like drinking Fine Old Wine. I mean, not really – I've never drunk Fine Old Wine, only once, you know, and I didn't like it all that much. But it was like you'd imagine it might be. Or swimming in Fine Old Wine or something like that. Just rich and filling up all your senses and well – gorgeous and thick and loads of it.

I'd felt up other girls before, but Deborah was *womanly*. Tits and belly and bum. She smelt like a piece of fruit cake.

I was really getting into it, and there was this little bit of my mind that was watching the whole thing, and another bit that was imagining someone else was watching us, which really turned me on. I got her jumper hoisted up and her tits out of her bra and right out into the air, and I kept turning her so that the street light was shining on her, and imagining that someone could see what was going on. She was breathing these deep, heavy breaths and staring up at me like she was stunned or something. She kept glancing up the road but I don't think she minded. I kept bending to kiss them and they got all wet. I kept trying to pull her knickers down too. I had this vision of her standing there with her tits out and her knickers round her knees that was making me go mad, but she wouldn't have it. And all the time she had Mr Knobby out in her hand, working away with him. She was having little looks at what she was doing. And finally – this was just so great – finally, she pulled away slightly to get a really big look, like it was a big treat for her, and stroked and pulled until I came all over her hand and on her skirt.

'Sorry,' I groaned, hanging onto the wall to stop falling down. It was all over her clothes. She roared with laughter.

'I enjoyed it,' she insisted.

'What about you?' I whispered, when I'd got my breath back. I'd spent the past ten minutes labouring away down there, with no success.

'I'll be all right,' she said. She paused and then added, 'I'll show you how another time.'

I stared down at her. She was looking up at me, her white teeth smiling in the dull light. I was thinking, Does that mean I don't know how? Yes, it does. And does it mean that she's expecting to see me again? Yes, it does.

And do I want to?

'You know what?' a little voice in my head said. 'I haven't got a clue.'

'I'd better go in now,' Deborah said.

'OK. Thanks.'

She laughed at me. 'You don't need to say thanks!' she gurgled.

'Did you really like it?'

'Yes!' she roared, as if that was a great joke, too. It was beyond me what she got from it, but she seemed to be telling the truth.

'Are you helping clear up at Dino's tomorrow?' she asked.

'I said I would.'

'See you there then. About midday?' She reached up and kissed me. When she pulled back she put her hand on the side of my face for a moment, a very tender touch, then she turned and went inside. And I thought, That was so gorgeous.

Help!

11
Party Fairy

'AHHHHHHHHHHHHHHHHHHHHHHHHHHHHHH!'

What was it? A murderer? Jackie? The sick? Please, please not the sick shouting at him! He spun in a circle and landed facing the opposite way. The candlewick cover on the little settee under the window had opened up and inside it was a pale, grubby girl. Her bare arms made her look like a child. Her eyes were as big as saucers popping out from under her curly brown hair. She looked as terrified as he was. She was pretty. In the first fraction of a second, Dino had another mental illusion. As soon as he realised she wasn't the sick he wondered if she might be a fairy.

'Who are you? Jesus! What are you doing there?' Dino asked.

'I was asleep, sorry, sorry.'

'Jesus,' he said again. 'You look like a bloody fairy. What are doing there?'

'I fell asleep.' She looked around the room anxiously and tried to smile. 'A party fairy, that's me. Do you want three wishes?' As soon as she said it, she regretted it and blushed. Then she tried to smile as if she was being funny.

Dino thought, What? And then his heart went bang

bang bang because there they were, alone in the bedroom, strangers – and she was offering three wishes. A shag, a blow job and a ... He'd think of the other one later. He was so terrified by the thought that he hardly dared to look at her for a few seconds and walked round in a circle instead. Of course it was ridiculous – she was just saying it for a joke. But you never knew. When he looked back at her she was scowling.

'Do I really look like a fairy?' she asked suspiciously.

'Everyone's gone home,' he told her.

The girl stood up. She was wearing a tiny pink dress, which she tugged down over her thighs. She looked so bare standing there in her party dress that Dino thought again that she might be offering. Maybe she was waiting for him to ask. He remembered what someone had once said to him about girls: if you don't ask you don't get.

'What?' he said anxiously.

'Got a fag?' she asked.

'I don't smoke,' he told her. 'I expect there's some somewhere, though.'

'Hang on ...' She walked to the side of the bed and bent down to pick up a packet of Marlborough Lights and a lighter lying on the floor by the bed. She shook it; the pack rattled. She took one out and lit it. She stood there smoking and looking sideways at Dino.

'Someone must've left 'em behind,' she said, shaking the packet at him.

'Yeah.' Then for some reason Dino looked at the bed. Her eyes followed his. Then they both looked at each other.

'I better go,' said the girl.

'Someone was sick,' said Dino. 'Look.' The girl looked at the bed again.

'Oh, yeah,' she said.

Dino began, 'My girl ... I mean, this girl did that and walked out,' he said. 'Just now. Did you see her?'

'I was asleep.' said the girl, and she took a big hard drag on her fag. She looked pissed off, but she wasn't leaving, not so far. She was just standing there, looking all bare with her arms wrapped round herself, holding tight to her fag. Her legs were grubby, too, he noticed. Actually, she looked like a bit of a tart. Make-up smudged all over the place, grubby legs — what did she have grubby legs for? She saw him staring and tugged at her dress again.

'Been a long party,' she said, and laughed.

'All night,' said Dino.

'Two bloody days I've been at it!'

'Oh ... Well. Wow. You've had a good time, then.'

'Huh, yeah!'

She took another big drag on her fag and then she said, 'What's the time?'

'I dunno, maybe three.'

The girl sighed and said, 'Look, it's late, I don't like to ask, but can you put me up here?'

'My parents are back tomorrow evening.'

'I'll be gone by then, I won't be any trouble, I can sleep here.'

And Dino thought, Oh ho! But he was scared to ask her if she'd sleep with him, so he said, 'Will you help me clean up in the morning?' instead.

'Yeah!' She looked pleased about it. It was a deal. 'Yeah! All right. Thanks.'

'All right!'

'OK, then.' She nodded. 'Thanks.' Then she sat down on the settee and said, 'See you then.'

'No, you better...' Dino was about to be the host and say that she could sleep in a bed, but the word bed froze on his lips. Then he thought, Sod this – she knows what I want. What sort of Wally would find a situation like this on their hands and then not try it on? What would he say to his mates? 'Nah, we just had a chat and then she went to bed...'

He said, 'Do you want a cup of tea.'

'Nah. I'll just sleep.'

He frowned. She knew what he wanted all right! There she was with her party dress up round her knickers... So he did it. He said,

'You can stay the night... So long as you stay with me.'

She didn't look at him at once. Her mouth opened slightly. Then she glanced up. Dino half smiled and took a step towards her. She didn't move when he sat there awkwardly next to her on the little settee. Dino knew, suddenly, without knowing why, that he could do anything he liked to this girl and she'd let him; he just knew.

He put an arm round her. Her shoulders were cold. He kissed her, she tasted sour and faggy. She shook her head and said, 'Don't.'

'Go on,' he told her. It was so obvious she wasn't going to stop him, it was as clear as day. He pulled her

100

backwards and sideways onto her back and looked down. Her little dress had ridden up and there was a little white triangle of knickers. He kissed her again and stuck his hand down there straight away, no messing. She wriggled slightly and turned her head away. He kissed her neck instead, nudged her legs apart and rubbed into her. He lifted his head to see her face and he was put out to see that her eyes were open as well. She was on her back looking away from him, staring at something on the other side of the room. Dino looked over in alarm. There was nothing there, just the wardrobe. But it put him off, her staring like that.

She said, 'I'm cold,' in a whiny little voice.

'We can use my bed,' he told her. He stood up and gave her his hand, which she took, and led her by the hand through to his room. Her expression looked so odd that he actually said to her,

'You don't mind.'

She shrugged, and he thought to himself it would be truer to say she didn't care. It was awkward, standing by the bed. He kissed her again to stop her mouth in case she complained. Then he pulled the pink dress over her head and there she was, with her knickers hardly covering her bush and her little titties out. Dino said, 'Oh, oh, oh.'

He pushed her gently to the bed, and she got in. He took his trousers off and got in after her. She asked him to turn the light off, but he took no notice. He peeled her knickers off and she lifted her legs to help him. And then . . . and then . . .

Dino began to lose it.

She was lying there, she felt all chilly under his hands as if she'd just come out of the fridge and he was trying to spread her on his bread. He kissed her again, hard, to try and stop his erection collapsing. Quickly, before it went altogether, he rolled on top of her and pushed her knees apart with his knees, giving himself a bit of a rub with one hand and holding himself up with the other. But by now the thing was almost hanging. He rubbed it between her legs and even gave an optimistic push, but it just bent. He kissed her again. He reached down and stroked her down there again, and began to nibble her breasts, but it did no good. He thought about getting cross with her because she just lay there like she didn't care, but it was too embarrassing. He rubbed his pubis on hers, but as his fear of failure grew, so his knob got softer and softer and now at last it was nothing but a felty slug hanging off him.

And that was it. It was over. It had just melted away. It was terrifying how easy it was for it to just melt away. The girl lay under him looking up with a half smile on her face, and Dino had never felt so alone as he did then, in bed with a girl and no erection.

'It's ... I must be tired or something, I dunno. It's been ages.' Desperate for an excuse, Dino blurted, 'I've forgotten how, it's been a while since.' Then he stared at her in yet more horror. Had he really said that? Was she going to notice how ridiculous that was? The girl slipped sideways from under him and put her arms around him with her little white face pressed hard against his.

'Don't mind.' She giggled. It was a very pretty giggle,

even Dino had to appreciate that. 'After all that,' she said, because he'd been so big and hard making her sleep with him and now he was all soft and pathetic and . . .

'Sweet,' she said. Then, bless her, she tickled him under the ribs, so of course he tickled her back. They had a little struggle in which the covers came off her and Dino got hard again. Quick as he could, before it disappeared again, he kissed her, very hard, suddenly. She said, 'Ouch!' because he banged her lips.

'Sorry, sorry,' he muttered. She watched his face curiously this time as he rubbed his hands over her everywhere, like a pirate running his hands through treasure. And it might have worked – Dino was sure it could have, although he was scared of the moment of penetration. But the girl suddenly lifted her hands, took his head between them and said, 'Don't. Please don't.'

'Sorry,' he said again.

'Don't worry,' she said. 'This is nice enough, isn't it?'

'Yeah,' said Dino miserably. She smiled.

'Are you gonna stay here with me?' she asked.

'Oh, yeah,' he said, thinking he might do it later on. The girl smiled again and cuddled up close to him. She looked really happy, lying there snuggled up with him. She put her face on his elbow and sighed.

'I've never done this before,' she said in muffled voice.

'What?'

'No, I mean, just cuddle up to someone all night, you know?'

'Oh, yeah,' said Dino.

'Like there's nothing to worry about. All cuddled up,

here in your arms,' she murmured. Dino lay there listening to his own heartbeat and to her breathing. Here in his arms. Nothing to worry about. It seemed to him such a curious thing to say, perfectly amazing, that she was so relaxed with him even though he'd almost . . . even though he'd been such an arse. He was flattered. She was safe in his arms. In about half a minute she was asleep. Dino thought, Poor little thing, she must be worn out. He stroked her hair. He felt bad now that he'd tried to blackmail her into staying with him. It was nice to let her have her wish and spend all night in his arms with nothing to worry about, and then he fell asleep as well.

He awoke in an eerie dawn light. He lay peacefully on his side for a moment wondering what had woken him up before he felt the warm body next to his and the memory hit him, and there he was, wide awake, wishing only that he was alone in his catastrophe. The girl lay sleeping peacefully up against his back, her breath on his shoulder. He didn't dare move for fear of waking her. Her skin was warm and heavy, her face relaxed and so peaceful that Dino, in his electrified state, thought she looked like an angel. First a fairy, then an angel. She smelt like nothing he had ever smelt, like nothing on earth. She was just an inconvenience to his misery.

I have a failure rate of One Hundred per cent, thought Dino to himself, even though he knew he was being unfair. What was really scary about it was he had no control over it at all. You can wink your eye, you can stretch your toes, you can waggle your tongue. Some people can even waggle their ears. But not your knob. You can flex any muscle but that one. It has to do it for you.

Dino knew he'd never be at peace with himself until he had managed a successful shag. Who knows how long that could be? Jackie had run away. He'd sworn anyway to chuck her if she didn't come up with the goods tonight, and she hadn't in a big way. This girl lying so peacefully by his side had been his final destruction. He watched her little pointy face half out of the duvet and he thought, She must be a right little slut to come to bed with me just like that. Dino wasn't all that familiar with sluts. The girls he hung around with were quite picky. There were some, particularly in the year below him, who let just about anyone feel them up but he doubted if even they'd go to a party and end up shagging someone they'd only known for five minutes just to get a place to sleep. What a slapper! He wondered if maybe it was her fault that he hadn't got it up. Maybe he needed a decent girl to turn him on. If she didn't care who stuck it up her, that was pretty off-putting.

But it was no good. Dino didn't want to get it up just for decent girls. He wanted to do it with slappers, slags and sluts as well. So long as they were good looking, who cared? The more the merrier.

None of these abusive thoughts about the girl felt true inside him. For one thing she was so lovely in her sleep. She'd been so pleased to just cuddle up. She'd stroked him and comforted him even though he'd bullied her. How could you say that someone was a slut if they were kind to you and happy to be with you?

Even so . . . There she was, lying stark bollock naked in bed next to him. He couldn't afford to let this night end without shagging her or he would suffer for weeks, months, maybe even years. He had to have her. He was thinking, all he had to do was wake her up and he could shag her. In fact, he probably didn't even have to do that – she wouldn't mind. She'd probably let him do anything to her he liked. And he bloody couldn't do it!

The girl rolled over. She was flat on her back, with her head tipped to one side and her mouth open. Slag or not, she really was very pretty. Very softly and quietly, Dino lifted the duvet up so that he could see down her body. He looked at the shadows on her body, her small breasts, the deep shadows around her stomach in the dull light. He could make out the dark rings of her nipples.

Ever so, ever so softly, Dino reached out with one arm and fumbled at the small bedside lamp on his table. At last it clicked on. The girl just lay there. Now he could see a lot more. Her nipples were pretty and pink, and there was the furry place down below. He could see his own body too, and his limp traitorous penis lying just inches away from this naked pleasure house; not a twitch. He looked from himself to her, but nothing stirred. Carefully, very softly, very gently so as not to wake her, Dino began to stroke himself under the covers, glancing from his own hand to her body in an attempt to get himself going. At first there was nothing, but then he started thinking dirty and gradually it began to move. It was so tatty, peeping Tom on a girl in bed with you – but, oh, yes, things were stirring! Dino speeded up his tempo, beat, beat, beat. The

106

mattress moved slightly under him and her breasts moved gently with the rhythm; that was good. He thought, if he could get it nice and stiff he'd have another go, although in fact he was already nice and stiff. It was hard to stop though . . . just another little bit more . . .

'Mmm?'

Oh, God, no.

'What are you doing?'

'Eh?'

'What you doing?'

'Ah . . . Do you wanna cup of tea?' he said.

'What's the time?' The girl – whose name he didn't even know, he realised – sat up and pulled the covers up to her chin. She must think he was some sort of nutter, perving away at her like that. She was right.

Dino glanced at the clock. 'Five o'cock,' he replied, as his erection slipped into oblivion.

'Eh?'

'Do you wanna cup a tea?' he begged again.

She pulled a thoughtful face. 'I'm hungry,' she said.

'Cereal? Sandwich? I do a great egg sandwich.'

'Yeah!'

'What'll you have?'

'Both.'

12
Dino

I went downstairs and put the gas on. It was endless! First Jackie disappears just when she's ready to open her legs, then there's sick in the bed, then my willy doesn't do it and now I've been caught wanking. From shagger to wanker to waiter in the space of about two hours. Being caught wanking is the worst thing that can happen to you. The only important thing now was to keep her away from my mates in case she told anyone.

It shows you what a state I was in, I was actually hoping she'd have done a runner by the time I got back. But there she was, sitting up in bed with her little pink party dress back on, waiting for me.

'S'great. Great!' she said when she saw the food. I put the tray on the bed in front of her and sat on the side of the bed feeling like her dad, and watched her eat it up. I was still trying to make my willy work. I was thinking, She's not got any knickers on under there, and trying to remember what her body looked like. But it wasn't working.

'Still here, then?' I asked her.

'What?'

'I thought you might be gone,' I said, and she said, 'Why?'

'I was a bit of a...' I was about to say tosser, but that might be giving the game away. I mean, maybe she hadn't seen what I was doing.

'Tosser?' she said.

I blushed. I hate blushing. It's my worst thing. 'I don't mean that,' I said. 'I mean, about last night. Making you stay like that. Making you sleep with me. I don't normally behave like that. I'm sorry.'

She shrugged her skinny little shoulders. 'I just wanted a bed for the night. Look, I just do anything, mate, I just do it. So don't come on all moral at me. At least I don't use other people. I just do what I want, right?'

'You didn't look all that happy when I told you you had to...'

'Yeah, well, no one likes being ordered around. I just wanted a bed for the night,' she said again, and she sank her teeth deep into her egg sandwich and dribbled ketchup on her chin.

There was a pause. 'I'm Dino,' I told her.

'I know, I heard people call you that last night.'

'And you?' I asked.

'Siobhan,' she said. 'Siobhan Carey.' She finished the sandwich and started on the cornflakes. 'Anyway, I know what you're really sorry about. You're sorry you couldn't get it up.'

'No!'

'Yeah.'

'Well, maybe,' I confessed. 'But that doesn't mean I'm not sorry about the other thing as well.'

'Don't worry about it. It'll come back. Dragging its tail...' she laughed.

I was blushing again. I felt so awful. She must have seen me blushing because she said, 'No, don't feel bad about it.'

All I could do was pull a face.

The girl looked curiously at me. 'I liked you for that, you know. I did – I liked you better for not getting it up than I did when you told me I had to shag you or get out.'

'I never said that!'

'That's what it meant, though, didn't it?'

'No,' I said, but she was right.

The girl was thinking about it. 'It made me feel safe,' she said. And when she said that, this weird thing happened. Her eyes filled with tears. I never realised that . . . I don't know what, I just never realised. I didn't know what it meant. I reached out and touched her shoulder. I'd have liked to hug her, but I didn't want her to think I was coming on.

'I wouldn't really have booted you out, you know,' I told her.

'You'd have gone on at me all night. Blokes do.' She finished her cornflakes and dusted her palms together. 'C'mere . . .' She leaned over her tray and put her arms around me. It was nice. After a couple of seconds she broke off, put the tray on the floor, and moved over so I could sit closer to her. We put our arms round each other and she pressed tight – making herself feel safe, I thought.

We sat on the bed hugging awkwardly until she said she was getting cold, then we got back together under the covers. She stroked the back of my head. By that time, I was feeling pretty safe myself, if you know what I mean, and I was thinking, Ho ho!

I kissed her and she kissed me back. She'd got her

knickers back on, so they came off and up went the little pink dress. I pulled my stuff off. It was great, both of us naked. I had a raging erection. I put my hand . . . well, work it out for yourself. It was gorgeous. I pushed her legs apart really wide and she let me. And then I got on her . . . and down it went again. I could just feel the blood draining away like something had been turned off.

'Don't worry, you'll be able to do it in the morning, I expect,' she said, and that 'I expect' – the bottom just fell out of the whole world. That was it. Once it'd learned to go down, it was staying down, I was certain of it. I had a lifetime of impotence ahead.

We were lying half in the bed and half out. In one way, I was slightly relieved. Is that really weird? See, it meant I didn't have to try anymore. I mean, it was such a bloody bother, it was just hard work really. You're better off wanking. Now I didn't have to bother. But I knew I wasn't going to be feeling like that for long.

But I did have another idea. OK, it was no sex life, no shagging. I was doomed to descend to about Number One Billion. Even Jonathon was better off than I was and he was with a fat girl. But, you know – it was still a pity to waste the chance.

'Can I have a look?' I said.

'What?'

'You know.' I nodded down the bed. Jackie used to let me touch but she was always scared to let me take her knickers off in case things went too far. I once tried to have a peek by pulling her knickers to one side, but she had her jeans on and couldn't open her legs. I wanted to see a proper spread.

'Have a look?' she repeated.

'Yeah. You know. I'd like to . . . see it.'

She giggled and grabbed hold of the bedclothes. 'I'm shy!' she screeched.

'Oh, right.' I backed off, but Siobhan seemed to be pleased for some reason. She was slapping out at me and screeching as if I was tickling her.

'No! Don't, don't!' she giggled, pushing me away, even though I wasn't doing anything, so of course I grabbed hold of the covers and tried to pull them down. 'Stop now!' she said, so I did. She held the covers tightly round her neck and thought about it. 'It's not very pretty,' she said.

'I don't mind.'

'What do you mean, you don't mind?' she scolded.

'I mean – I dunno.' I made as if to lift the covers at the bottom and she grabbed hold of my ears and screeched again.

'NO! I tell you what. Stop it. You can get – no, stop it. Stop! Under the bedclothes and have a look if you like,' she said.

'Can I?'

'Yeah. If you like.'

'I won't be able to see anything . . .' I began, but even as I spoke I found my eyes drifting across to the little bedside lamp.

'NO!' she howled, reaching out to grab my arm, but I fended her off.

'There's no point if I can't see!'

'No!'

'Yes!'

112

'But I'll be in the dark,' she complained.

'I won't.'

She let go of my ears and lay back in the bed. Down I went, under the covers. She didn't stop me when I pushed her legs apart and bent up her knees.

'All right?' she asked, shyly. But I couldn't say anything. It was just... I mean, I'd seen pictures but they give you no idea, really. The real thing! It was bigger than I thought, and redder and hairier and it was just stunning. It had this amazing spicy, pee-y smell. It was pure sex. I pulled it open and my knob began pulsing like some sort of atomic weapon.

'Wow,' I said. It was awesome. The pictures don't tell you anything, really. Still staring, I wormed my hand out towards the bedroom table.

'What you doing?'

'Looking for a condom.'

She laughed at me, but I didn't care. It must have been really weird for her, with the light on her fanny and me under there examining her. But you know what? I think it turned her on. She found one and handed it down to me. I struggled under the covers to hold the lamp, put the condom on my vast, iron hard stiffie, and keep looking at it all at the same time.

I tented the covers and came up for air. 'I never saw anything like that before,' I told her. I held her and kissed her, hooking her leg up with one arm. She smiled up at me and reached down to guide me to the right place with her hand, and I just slid in.

13
Ben

It was nearly eleven by the time I got out of bed, so I was late for starters. Had a shower. Couldn't face breakfast. Got my footie gear together. Her birthday present, a CD, 'The Handsome Cult'. I was planning on bringing something else for her – my old school uniform.

I'd got it all together. The blazer was at the back of my wardrobe – Mum had kept it in case my brother Neil ever needed it spare but he kicked up such a fuss about getting it second-hand, he never used it. The polo and sweatshirt were in Neil's cupboard – spares again, glad I'm not a younger brother – and so was a pair of trousers. I found the shoes right at the back of the cupboard in the end, all dried up. I'd cleaned them up a couple of nights before and they still fitted. I'd been kidding myself that I'd grown over the past year, but evidently not in the foot department anyhow.

But in the end I left it behind. I felt too ill. Just the thought – yuk. I just stuck my footie gear in my bag and cleared off.

'See you!'

'Where are you going?' yelled my dad.

'Footie.'

'Have you had breakfast, you need breakfast if you're playing sports,' yelled my mum.

'Yes,' I lied, and left the house. I felt sick, my head hurt. I just wanted to go back to bed.

That school uniform thing. She's always on at me about that. She put on a maid's uniform once. Sat me down in an armchair with a beer and waltzed around the flat doing the dusting, leaning over me so I could see down her top and bending over the table so this tiny little skirt rode up. No knickers. You know? Then I had to tell her off for missing bits. I was supposed to order her to do all sorts of jobs so I could get an eyeful but I wasn't very good at it. Too self-conscious. She didn't seem to care. She flitted around a bit, took all my clothes off, just the same as usual, except she called me 'Sir' as she did it. God knows what she'll get up to once she gets me dressed up like a schoolboy.

Kinky. I don't mind the uniform stuff and games and all that, but some of it really gives me the twitches. She does stuff at school – does that count as kinky as well? It wasn't too bad at first. She used to take me out to the store cupboard and give me a big snog and I'd feel her tits. That was pretty good actually, but it was still scary. There was this time she got me backstage, pulled up my top and her top, popped herself out of her bra and gave me this big, wet snog, skin to skin backstage with half the cast of *Toad of Toad Hall* just the other side of the curtains. I thought I was going to die. It was still pretty amazing though.

But it's getting out of hand. I think the thing is, she likes the risk. She always used to do things like grab my packet when I was standing behind her and there were other people in the room – you know, shielding me with her body so no one could see. Then she started giving me detentions so I had to stay behind after school. It was outrageous – right in front of the whole class. She said I was doing something stupid – I wasn't doing a thing. It was all so obvious. I thought she was going to make me shag her, but it was worse than that. She got me back-stage behind the curtains, took my jeans down and gave me a blow job. The sick thing was, she made me face the curtains so I could peer through the curtains and see people in the hall coming and going.

'You'll have to keep an eye out in case people come,' she said. I tried to stop her but – I don't know, I just don't seem to be able to say no. She always gets it her own way. It's not fair.

14
Mother Love

At first he thought she hadn't heard the bell, but just as his finger was lifting towards the buzzer again he heard someone shuffling towards the door in such a way that set his heart beating fearfully, even though he knew that it wasn't, say, a wounded water buffalo or a starving tiger that was coming towards him, but Miss. She opened the door to reveal herself, hair in a rumpled mess on the back of her head, face a crumpled mess on the front. The air stank of stale drink, tobacco smoke and polish.

'Ben,' she groaned. She held her hand to her head and turned away. He followed her into the flat.

It was all wrong. For a moment he thought that he'd come by some impossible chance to the wrong flat and she happened to be in it – with a new lover...? But it wasn't that. It was the flat itself that had gone crazy.

Miss's flat was always messy. She kept her clean clothes and her dirty clothes in separate heaps on the floor and didn't touch the washing up until there was enough to bother with. Dusting wasn't her thing, she was waiting to find a window cleaner, wiped the surfaces only when something sticky refused to dry out, and only did the kitchen floor when it stuck to the soles of her slippers.

Every now and then she had a blitz, but what had happened here was something else. The place was spotless. More than spotless; it was sterile.

'What happened?' asked Ben, as she waved a despairing hand around, but he already knew the answer.

'My mother gate-crashed my birthday party. Put the kettle on,' she replied and shuffled back to the bedroom.

There are many different sorts of mothers depending on what they make you do or feel. There are love-mothers and hate-mothers, guilt-mothers and sad-mothers, rage-mothers, glad-mothers, sleep-mothers, mania-mothers, laughter-mothers, fear-mothers, hit-mothers, tear-mothers, bore-mothers, sick-mothers, work-mothers and safe-mothers, to name just a few. It works for dads, too. Alison Young had a lobotomy-mother. Whenever her mother visited her she spent the rest of the day walking around like a narcoleptic zombie.

Ben had seen it before. He'd come round one Sunday a couple of months ago and found her like this, in bed with what seemed like a huge hangover because of her mother visiting. It looked at first as though she had a drunk-mother, but it wasn't that. Her mother made her feel like a great lump of shit.

He made his way into the kitchen to make coffee and found, just like last time, that the place had been totally rearranged.

'Where have the cups gone?' he asked.

'Wherever that fat bitch put them,' said Ali. So it was. The cups were where the tins had been, the tins were

118

where the bowls had been, the bowls – who knew where the bowls were?

'She pretends she does it by accident,' murmured Ali, sipping her coffee a little later. 'She empties everything out so she can clean in the cupboards and then puts them back somewhere else *better*.' She leaked tears and leaned across for a tissue.

Ben already knew a whole host of stories about Mrs Young. How she'd convinced Ali to have a fourteenth birthday party, swore she'd keep out of the way and then stayed anyway and forced everyone to play party games.

'Blind Man's Bluff. Postman's Knock! Imagine being forced to play Postman's Knock when you're fourteen by your mother. Being locked in the cupboard like that...' raged Ali.

How, when Ali had her first period, her mother had taken her up to the bathroom to sort her out and then come back down and announced it to the whole family at tea. And for the week after, to anyone who happened to come into the house.

'"She's having her first period!" she'd say, and she'd point at my crotch. I swear it. And, of course, people would look down there for a second, just following her finger. I felt like they could see it!' wailed Ali.

This time, Mrs Young had travelled down to surprise her daughter on her birthday. Ali had had a few friends round. They'd gone out for drinks and then come back for more of the same.

Mrs Young marched in unannounced – Ali had no idea she'd got keys cut for herself. She didn't look too happy, according to Ali, to find other people there, but she made the best of it by serving drinks and snacks. She didn't do small talk. She left the 'young people' to it and went into the kitchen to begin her ritualistic clean. After she'd emptied all the cupboards onto the floor and made the kitchen impassable, she changed her mind and came out to begin on the living room, starting quietly by vacuuming in the corners but gradually moving into the middle until she'd achieved her objective, and people made their excuses and left.

Ali had asked her if that was what she wanted and they'd had a huge, blazing row that she could bear for about five minutes before bursting into tears and rushing hysterically to her bedroom in tears while her mother mercilessly cleaned and shouted at her over the vacuum. It was so humiliating. Why couldn't she *stop* her? Why did it *get* to her so much? Wasn't she pathetic? Why did it have to happen to her?

Ben listened in sympathetic amazement. Part of him was appalled, part of him was amused. Ali seemed a pretty effective sort of person – why so helpless with her own mother? It seemed all wrong. After she'd drunk her coffee, she flung herself sideways in the bed, pulled the blankets up and buried her face on the pillow. Ben stood by the edge of the bed feeling awkward.

'Are you all right?'

'I'll be OK.' But she didn't look OK.

'Are you going back to sleep?' he asked hopefully.

She glanced up at him. 'You can give me a cuddle if you like.'

Ben hesitated a moment. He wanted to say he had things to do, but she knew he hadn't, so he slipped off his shoes and made to get into the bed.

'Not like that, I want some skin,' she complained. He pulled off his jeans and shirt and slid in next to her. She pushed her back up against him, and he put his arms round her and squeezed.

'Hmm,' she said. He wondered if he was supposed to make love to her. Although he'd felt exhausted on the way round and had wanted to get back to bed, he felt wide awake now. He felt like getting up and rushing busily around. In a minute she turned round and nestled her head on his shoulder. 'Mmm,' she said again, and closed her eyes with a sigh. As he lay watching her he noticed for the first time two very straight, white scars running neatly from one side of each of her wrists to the other. Then he fell asleep.

15
Nemesis Rising

The girl Dino knew as Siobhan was really called Zoë by doting parents whom she despised. When she woke up the night after the party in bed with Dino, she smiled with pleasure at the thought that she'd spent the night with a boy who thought she was someone else. Over breakfast, without thinking or caring why, she'd started to tell him more lies just to amuse herself.

Her dad was a vet who specialised in reptiles. She was seventeen years old, the youngest of five. An accident, her parents didn't want her. They hated and controlled her in equal measures. If they knew she was having sex they'd go mad. They'd probably kill the boy. It would be better for Dino never to call her at home.

Dino believed everything.

In fact, Zoë was only fourteen but she had for many years had an irresistible appetite for trouble. She loved it, lived it, was it. The imaginary father she conjured up for Dino wrestled with alligators with toothache and giant pythons with sore backs, trying to get them to take their medication. The real one supervised a production line in a yoghurt factory. He kept his hands so clean, the skin cracked through over-washing. He'd have run a mile at the sight of anything in scales. She thought of reptiles, partly because her father was one, but also because he'd gone ballistic only that weekend when she'd tried to sneak out of the house dressed only in a tank top and pair of skin-tight snakeskin pants.

'It looks like something's swallowed you,' he snarled, barring her way out of the front door.

Zoë had run back upstairs shouting, 'Is that rage or lust making your eyeballs bulge?' She changed into her pink party dress, came down and threw the hot pants onto the gas fire.

'I'll never wear them again,' she screamed. The hot pants shrivelled and stank and melted down the coals and Zoë zipped out of the door. Out on the street she ran down the road listening to her father's bellows retreat as she turned the corner. She was furious with herself for letting her dad catch her dressed to kill and for throwing her pants away like that. She was so full of red hot life and danger it surprised her she didn't just sizzle her way through the pavement all the way down to hell.

She'd liked Dino that morning. Once he'd stopped trying to throw his weight around he was undeniably sweet. And rather gorgeous. Dino was a looker all right, every bit of him was lovely, but she hadn't forgotten either that he *had* tried to throw his weight around, or that she had unaccountably let him. The whole time they spent in bed, she was wondering whether or not to bite it hard or kick him suddenly in the goolies. She was quite capable of doing either. One thing she did know: Dino was going to suffer, no matter how much she liked him.

Telling him a huge pack of lies was an amusing form of revenge, but it wasn't enough. The poor boy thought he was using her. Sooner or later, he was going to find out differently.

In the meantime, she was enjoying herself. They spent the morning romping about in bed like a pair of kids on a bouncy castle. She would have been happy to stay all day – she had nowhere better to go, certainly not home – but as soon as she found out that Dino's friends were coming round to help him clean up, she remembered that she was going bowling. She jumped out of bed and was dressed before he really knew she was going. He just had time to make a date at the weekend with her before she was out of the door and gone.

Zoë caught a bus into town and dialled a number from a phone kiosk.

'Hi, Sam.'

'So how was the party?'

'I stayed all night.'

'Zoë!'

Zoë laughed at her friend's scandalised tone. 'I stayed with the guy whose house it was.'

'What's he like?'

'Gorgeous, very. You remember that one with the dark hair with little goldy bits in it?'

'Him? Ohhh, nice.'

'But stupid. I'm seeing him again. Or at least, he thinks I am!' She roared with laughter.

Sam roared too, uncertainly. 'You're a bad girl, Zoë Trent.'

'No, listen. I told him the most monstrous pack of lies. You wouldn't believe it. Wrong name, wrong age, wrong everything.'

'What did you do that for?'

'I don't know why, I don't know why, I just did it!' roared Zoë, who was certainly not going to admit that she'd been gate-crashed into sleeping with someone. 'He thinks my dad's a reptile doctor – no, really! He thinks my name is Siobhan. He thinks we have an indoor swimming pool and that my parents trust me so much, they let me have the house at weekends when they're away.' That wasn't all true – she hadn't actually told Dino the last two things, but the fact was, Zoë was an inventive and helpless liar. She just did it as she went along. 'Not only that,' she went on. 'Listen; I got a bag full of money.'

'Zoë!'

'About sixty pounds.'

'Where from?'

'Where'd you think?'

But Sam wasn't having it. 'Zoë, that's really tight, those people were at that party in good faith.'

'Oh, don't be such a whingebag. They're all fat soft kids, they've got families and homes, they won't miss it.'

'Fat soft kids. You're a fat soft kid!'

'Not fat, not soft, not a kid, either. D'you wanna help me spend it?'

'No.'

'Come on! Sixty quid!'

'I can't today. What do you want to do that for, Zoë? Anyway, I've got loads of homework.'

'Homework!'

'Yeah, well, some of us want to have a life, you know.'

'Sixty quid, Sam.'

Sam paused. 'Sixty quid, that's a lot of money.'

'Come on. We can spend it all. Every penny. Today. All in one go.'

'OK. Right!'

'Good girl! Down town. See you in Stred's in an hour?'

'I'm going to have to finish my homework first. I'll be a couple of hours at least.'

'Come on, Sam, I'm paying.'

'Two hours. OK?'

'OK,' agreed Zoë grudgingly. It wasn't fair. She was paying, wasn't she? She wasn't sure Sam had the right to say no, but that was Sam. She was prepared to be as mad as anyone, but only after she'd finished being sensible and only if she was certain she wasn't going to get found out. She was a master of disguise, was Sam.

Zoë put down the phone and stood looking up the streets. Two hours to kill. Boring. Boring boring boring! Why was life so boring?

It was gone eight o'clock on Sunday evening by the time Zoë got back home. They'd had a great time. There wasn't a penny left. They'd seen a film, gone bowling, eaten a mountain of crisps and sweets and bought a CD each. Zoë had to leave hers round at Sam's because her parents searched her room regularly. She hadn't been there since Friday evening.

Her parents popped out of the front room like a pair of armed badgers before she even had time to close the front door.

'You just don't care, do you?' yelled her dad. 'We've been worried sick and you don't even care.'

'I'll bet.'

'It's not fair!' he yelped.

'Darling, what makes you behave like this?' cried her mother, the waterworks already coming on. Her eyes glistened, but her father put out his hand to silence her.

'You have absolutely no regard for anyone else. You don't think about anyone else, you don't have any feelings for anyone else. It's just you you you all the time. Well?'

Well, what could she say? It was true, every word. The thing was – she didn't care. She really truly did not care. She felt like the princess in the fairy story who had been brought up by strangers. She just didn't fit. Her parents weren't so bad to her. They had their faults, sure. Her father was high handed and obviously didn't like kids; her mother couldn't understand her and rather pathetically never gave up trying to. Even when Zoë was a little girl, her mum used to hide outside the door for hours listening to her playing dolls with her friends to try and work her strange, elfin daughter out. She'd tried, you had to give her that. No, it was quite clear, it was Zoë who was the problem and no one else. She made herself feel like shit, the way she went on. She just couldn't stop.

Her mother stood staring at her, flaunting her tears like the Crown Jewels, but Zoë refused guilt of any kind. Was

127

it her fault she had caring parents? No. She stamped upstairs.

'I ought to have had a couple of thugs, you two are bloody wasted on me,' she shouted downstairs. She went into her bedroom, then came out again. 'Stop making me feel guilty!' she yelled.

'Zoë, all we ask is that you let us know where you are. You're only fourteen, we need to know you're all right. We're responsible . . .' said her mother.

'Yes, responsible, responsible, remember about being responsible?' bawled her dad. 'But I don't suppose that word means very much to you, does it?'

Zoë slammed the door. 'Weaklings,' she growled. It was true. Her father blustered and her mother wept, but neither of them had the slightest clue how to keep their daughter in check. Inside, she prowled around her room. Why did she have nowhere else to go? Why was she so abandoned and alone in her own home? Why didn't her father come up and knock her about the place, when she treated them like shit?

'Pants! Shit! Cunts!' she yelled downstairs at them, but answer came there none. She crept downstairs. Her parents were watching a quiz show on TV and eating nuts as if they didn't have a care in the world. Zoë wanted to murder them, but all she did was run upstairs and weep on her bed instead. She couldn't kill them, but someone was going to have to die, and soon. It was just a question of who.

16
Happiness is a Full Binbag

Sex? No prob, bruv! He was a natural.

I'm good at that, thought Dino. That girl . . . he'd almost driven her mad with pleasure. Jackie didn't know what she was missing. He felt so pleased about it, he was almost willing to forgive her. In fact, he probably would have if it wasn't for the fact that he didn't have to. He had a new girlfriend now.

About half an hour after Siobhan left, Jackie rang him, full of apologies. She was horrified at herself. She couldn't understand how, or why she'd run off. That sick had just offended her so much, she was out of the house before she knew what she was doing.

'We need to talk,' she said.

'I don't think there's anything to say.'

'I do want to sleep with you.'

'Well, someone else did last night, too, so just . . . don't bother,' he'd said, and he put down the phone.

Jackie was history.

Dino was so relieved at having successfully lost his virginity that he had no idea how unhappy this new situation made him for all sorts of reasons. For starters, he didn't trust Siobhan as far as he could throw her. His behaviour at blackmailing her into having sex with him had left a very nasty taste in his own mouth and badly dented his self-esteem. Jackie had rejected him yet again, which hurt very much indeed. Finally, even while he was busy congratulating himself on having chucked her, he was terrified at the thought of losing her.

He was in love with her and he didn't even know it.

After dismissing her, Dino went downstairs to eat some cereal. That had showed her. He tried to imagine doing the things he'd done with Siobhan with Jackie, but it made him feel queasy and odd. A little later he looked at the clock and saw with a shock that it had somehow become one o'clock. People were supposed to come round at midday! His parents . . . ! The house looked as if someone had thrown a party in it.

Dino's anxiety levels began to rise alarmingly. He rushed back to the phone and rang his friends one after the other, but every one of them was too busy lying in bed to speak to him. He began running around from room to room throwing rubbish into a binbag, but in half an hour nothing seemed to have changed. Already, he was very seriously regretting having told Jackie about Siobhan, richly though she deserved it. It wasn't until gone two that the doorbell rang. He rushed to open it; it was Deborah. She smiled beatifically at him.

'Is Jon here yet?' she asked.

'Quick,' he yelped. 'We have to clean up!'

To his amazement, Debs didn't seem to get the message. The first thing she did was try to ring Jon, but there was no answer from his phone and his mobile was switched off.

Then she wanted to go round to wake him up, and Dino had to keep watching the front door in case she sneaked out. And the rest of them? Not one of the lying, cheating bastards had showed up. The house was a death pit of household destruction. Fag ends in the carpet, plastic cups ground underfoot in puddles of sour, stinking beer. There were all the breakables to unwrap and puddles of sick lurking in places that no one had as yet even discovered. His parents were due home in just a few hours and there was a week's work for twenty strong men still left to do.

By the time Ben came round at three, Dino didn't know whether to cuddle him or punch him for being so late.

'Where the fuck were you?' he whimpered.

'Hangover,' said Ben. 'Don't worry, we'll get it done. Where's Jackie?'

Half an hour later, there was another knock at the door. Both Deborah and Dino ran to open it. There stood Jackie and Sue.

'Deborah!' gasped Jackie. Was this who Dino had spent the night with? 'You!'

'Have you seen Jonathon?' demanded Deborah. 'What? What have I done?' she added, seeing Jackie's horrified face.

It took a while to sort it out. Deborah, who had just spent an hour on her own with Dino, had had enough, and left. Jackie, realising that she'd made a mistake, apologised to her and started trying to make it up with Dino, but he was too agitated about getting the house clean to realise that she was offering to sleep with him again. Shouting started. Sue was furious with herself for coming at all. Jackie had rung her at an hour of Sunday morning she didn't previously know existed. She had a bad hangover and this was not her problem. It was all cobblers, anyway. She hadn't believed Dino's story about sleeping with someone else for a second.

'There wasn't anyone else there, what did he do, ring an escort agency?' she'd asked when Jackie rang her on her mobile. How obvious was it that as soon as they got there, Jackie and Dino would stand and shout at each other while she'd be expected to run around and actually help with the housework?

It was a point of principle. Sue never helped with the housework.

'OK,' she snarled. 'I'll do *one* bedroom and then I'm going. I have homework to do.'

'You came to the party too,' yelled Dino. 'You enjoyed it!'

'It was a crap party,' she snapped, and stamped upstairs to the big bedroom only to find that she'd forgotten about the offending vomit.

Jackie thought she was going to go hysterical. 'We have to talk,' she blubbed as Sue thumped upstairs.

'We have to *clean*,' insisted Dino.

'How can I do housework when you spent the night with someone else?' she screamed.

One brief glimpse at Jackie's face was enough to tell Dino that if he stuck to his story, he was unlikely to get so much as a light dusting out of her. Even guilt at running out on him wasn't going to help her to see reason. His parents were due back in a few hours. Deborah had gone, Sue was unreliable, Ben was male. What could he do?

'I was lying,' he lied.

'You were *lying*?'

'Yeah.'

'You just wanted to hurt me!'

'Jacks, you ran out on me. You promised. And you promised to help get the place together and here it is, it's half past three and look at it, it's a shit hole. I'm sorry I told a fib but can we please, *please* get this place put together. Please?'

Jackie blinked through her tears at the chaos all around them. It was after all, her who was in the wrong. He was a lying bastard, but at least he was lying about *not* having slept with someone rather than the other way round.

'OK,' she said. 'But after this, we have to talk. OK?'

'I love you!' cried Dino. He grabbed her, hugged her and kissed her. He was happy again, and the poor deluded girl smiled with pleasure. It was one of Dino's greatest gifts; he was infectious. He broadcast his feelings. If he felt bad, so did anyone near him. If he smiled, the world smiled with him. It was all so perfect. He'd lost his virginity! He wasn't going to chuck Jackie! She was going to help him clean! He put his arms round her and squeezed her and radiated pleasure. Jackie was swamped by it. She held her face up to him and felt his joy sparkle in her eyes and fizz and tingle in her spine and in her belly. Ben, standing at the back of the room with a binbag full of beer cans, laughed to see them. Upstairs, Sue scowled as pleasure fizzed up through her feet. She thought, Why? And Deborah, plodding on her way home trying not to cry, thought of Jonathon waking up in bed and getting anxious and confused about her, and she forgave him suddenly for no reason at all.

17
Dino

It was like magic once Jacks got there. The whole place just cleaned itself. Man! Just like that. She even got Sue into it, they liked it. Sue was humming to herself as she vacuumed the landing. That's girls for you. I can't even work out how to keep my room clean.

As we worked, I started thinking about my position and you know... I started to think that maybe, it was a pretty good position. I mean, it could actually work out pretty well for everyone, but for me in particular. Siobhan's all very well, but I don't know if I fancy her as a girlfriend. You know what I mean? She's a bit of a slapper. Not like Jackie. On the other hand, Siobhan shags and Jackie doesn't and that shagging business – that's something I want to do a great deal more of.

What I'm saying is – why not both of them? I could go out with Jackie and shag Siobhan. Siobhan and me, that's not going to last, but what's to stop me seeing her a few more times without Jackie knowing anything about it? It's perfect. It'd take the pressure off Jacks to give out, and then when she does...

'Wow, Dino, if only I'd known! I'd have done it months ago...'

I'll have had loads of practice! Cool or what?

Seriously, though, it's true I won't be nagging her so much for sex because I'll be getting it elsewhere... and she'll think I'm being all sensitive and understanding! Nice, eh? Anyhow, what does she expect? She's been mucking me around for weeks, I'm bound to go looking for it somewhere else sooner or later.

I saw everyone out of the house by half four. Sue has a car, she went to drop off all the extra binbags at the dump – that was her idea. She's done this before. What would happen if Mum and Dad looked in the wheelie bin and found all those cups and fag ends and cans and so on, you know?

And I was on my own in a nice clean house waiting for Mum and Dad to come back.

★ ★ ★

But as soon as he was on his own, Dino's anxiety levels began to rise again. He started to get worried that they'd done the place too much. What had Ben been thinking of, polishing the table so well? That table never got polished, and now look – it shone like an advertisement. Jackie had sponged down the curtains where someone had spilled some beer on them and made a big clean patch right down one side. Sue had gone out and bought some shake 'n' vac and other smellies to cover up the old beer and fag end smell lingering around the place. Since when did the house smell like that? They'd know! He rang Jacks on her mobile for advice but she'd turned it off, the selfish cow. Gone back to bed probably, just when he needed her. He began to deconstruct the cleaning job. He sponged down the half of the curtain that was still dirty, then he got to work on the table, trying to take off that sharp shine and get it back to its natural dullness. He rubbed his sweaty hands on it, but that just made it look like a polished table that someone had wiped their hands on, so he got a little sausage grease out of the grill pan, put it on a J-cloth and rubbed it vigorously onto the shine. That made it look duller, but greasy.

Then there was the key in the door and his mum's voice cheerily calling out, 'We're home!'

In that very second Dino remembered in a blinding flash of darkness what he hadn't thought about for two whole days. He ran halfway up the stairs before they came in, trying to escape; but where to? His mum was having an affair with some wanky bloke from her school. He'd just lost his virginity, it should have been one of the best days of his life. He had not one but two girlfriends, things ought to be just brilliant, but did he feel great? No. And why? Because of his stupid fucking mother.

His parents came chattering up the hall like a pair of children. If only his dad knew what Dino knew — that'd wipe the smile off his face. They came to a stop at the bottom of the stairs looking up at him. Dino glared back down.

'Well, that's a fine greeting,' said his dad. Behind him, Dino's mum had stopped smiling. Dino was obviously a bit of a downer as far as she was concerned.

'Welcome home?' she said in a little voice. Dino sneered and went upstairs. What shit! He was furious. What right had they to spoil this moment for him? Sick to death about his *parents'* sex life on the very day his had just begun! It couldn't be more awful. How selfish they were. How self-obsessed. This was HIS day, HIS moment, and instead of swaggering about feeling great he was sweating with anxiety.

He went to lie down on the bed and tried to remember what sex had been like – his hands on Siobhan's breasts, the hot feel of her moving underneath him – but all he could think about was Dave Short doing the same things to his mum.

He heard her coming up the stairs and his heart began to beat violently in his chest. She was going to talk about it! She knew he knew! She knocked, popped her head round the door and asked, how come the table smelt of sausages?

Dino was amazed. Was that it? Was that all she could say after a whole week of unacknowledged knowing? He waved her imperiously away from his door with a hand, and – can you believe this? The bitch got cross with him for being rude. She got cross with *him*! Suddenly, Dino was screaming at her and then his dad came up to have a go at him for speaking to his mother like that. Get that! Both of them at the end of the bed telling him how many different kinds of shit he was and all the time he was thinking, You people have no idea. If they had the slightest inkling of what he could do just by opening his mouth and uttering the secret words. He was a time bomb. He was a fucking Cruise Missile. He could not believe he was having to put up with this shit.

★

While his dad was out picking up Mat and his mum was getting tea, Dino decided that the only explanation had to be that it didn't matter. They'd obviously had a nice time away. They seemed to like one another. Why should he worry? All sorts of things could be going on. Maybe they had an open marriage. Or they'd decided that the marriage was over but they ought to stay together for the sake of the children. It could be that. They could be swingers! Well — it happened. Someone's mum and dad had to be swingers. Maybe it just happened to be his.

'Did you have a good time, then?' he asked them at dinner that evening. He gave his mum a little wink. She stared blankly at him.

'Great. Thanks for asking,' said his dad sarcastically.

'Just the two of you, was it?'

'It'd be rather difficult to have a romantic weekend with more than two, wouldn't it?' asked Dad.

'Dirty weekend, you mean,' corrected Mat, but everyone ignored him. Dino smirked. He wanted to let them know that he knew what was going on. He stared at his mum until he caught her eye and gave a leering kind of look.

'You look flushed,' his dad said to her.

'Yes! Must be the menopause or something, I expect!' said his mum, fanning herself with her hand frantically. Everyone stared at her.

'What's that?' asked Mat suspiciously.

'I can't say I'd noticed anything menopausal,' observed his dad.

Dino lost patience. It was like some stupid game they

were all playing. Ridiculous. So he just said it straight out.

'So, did Dave Short go with you, then?' he asked, and even as he said it he knew he shouldn't have. His own jaw fell open with horror as the words fell out of his mouth.

His mother was still flushed from her blush; now the blood drained out of her face.

'Dave Short? Dave Short? Dave Short?' said his dad nervously. 'Dave Short?'

In desperation, Dino started to laugh as if he'd made a great joke. 'Ha, ha, ha!' he said. He sounded like a dog coughing. 'Oh – so you're not swingers then,' he said. Suddenly he desperately, desperately wanted to rescue his mum. He was trying so hard to laugh he began to choke. Then his mum started laughing as well, a hollow, amateur dramatics kind of thing... 'He he he he he he,' she said. Then Mat joined in, properly. Even though he had no idea what was going on he always found other people laughing funny. Perhaps it was hysteria, perhaps it was the sound of a true laugh against their own hollow impressions, but Mat started Dino and his mum laughing properly, too, and that made if even funnier. Pretty soon they were all howling and wiping the tears off their faces. Only his dad sat there holding his knife and fork in his hands, staring at them all as if he was on his own in a crowd of strangers.

Later that evening, when Dino was in bed, the shouting started.

18
Jonathon

'So, let's get this straight,' I said. 'Jackie threw up in your bed and then cleared off. Maybe it was some sort of hideous perversion. What do you called vomit perverts? Sickophilia? Is she a pukeophage?'

'Yeah, yeah, yeah,' said Dino, rolling his eyes.

'Not exactly what you were expecting,' said Ben.

'I thought it was party on, knickers off. Are you sure it wasn't a failed attempt at oral sex you don't want to tell us about?'

'I was upset about it,' said Dino grimly.

'Because if it was I don't blame her for throwing up. The mere thought...'

'Bloody shut up,' hissed Dino. And there it was: the look. It's not fair. I ought to be able to talk the pants off him but all he has to do is look at me and I just shrivel up.

'Sorry, Deen,' I snivelled, but it was too late: I had ceased to exist.

Ben wagged his finger at Dino and smiled fondly at him. 'You said this was her last chance.'

Dino pulled a face.

'You can't force someone to do sex with you,' I pointed out, but he ignored me.

'So?' Ben asked him.

'I don't know how much she really likes me,' Dino complained.

'I don't think there's much doubt that she's very much smitten,' I said. He half smiled at me. Flattery will get you everywhere with the Lozenge.

That's what I call him. Dino the Lozenge. I can't remember why. He must remind me of a cough sweet in some indefinable way.

'Jon's right,' said Ben; and Dino looked so pleased about it, Ben and I exchanged a fond glance. Funny, isn't it? Why on earth should we feel so happy because Dino is pleased about something?

He scowled lightly. 'Do you think I'd be a bit of wanker to go back out with her? After all that?'

'It all depends,' said Ben. 'How much do you like her?' There was a pause, in which Dino looked at him as if he'd just asked what unicorn he was wearing today.

'What do you *feel* for her?' I asked. Dino looked all confused, and then he blushed. Ah! Bless.

'I've never thought about it,' he said coyly.

Was it possible? After all the dozens of times he'd talked to us about Jackie, and he'd never actually thought about what he *felt*?

'Not even once?' I asked.

'Well, of course I have,' snapped Dino, through his blush. 'But . . .'

'Ah, now,' said Ben. 'I think old Dino likes her more than he cares to admit.'

Dino smiled shyly. He nodded. 'It's true,' he said,

colouring up again. 'She's lovely.'

Nice, isn't he nice? As well as being a bastard, of course.

'So you might as well keep on with her, unless you've got someone better to do,' I said. Which was just a joke to cover up his embarrassment, actually, but he looked at me as if I'd said some horrible blasphemy.

'No, of course not,' he snarled. So there I was back in the depths of the shit heap again, without really knowing why this time. And it was at that moment, just at the height of my confusion, that I looked up and saw her standing by the lockers.

DeborAGHHHHHHHHHHH!

She was talking to Sue and Lesley. As I watched, she turned round, saw me, smiled and gave me a big wave. I looked away and pretended I hadn't seen her – much too late. Ouch – that must have hurt! Poor Debs. Out of the corner of my eye, I saw her turn away back to her friends.

'Do you want to talk about it?' said Ben. I looked at him. He was nodding over to Debs.

'No, no no no,' I said. Then, realising I was being far too emphatic, I shrugged casually. 'What's there to talk about? It was just a snog, that's all.'

'I bet they don't think so,' said Ben, nodding at the little huddle of girls by the lockers.

Dino leaned over to me. 'Your woman's nipples are shaking with anxiety,' he told me. I grinned weakly, but he terrified me. That was one of mine! I live in constant fear that someone is going to be as horrible to me as I am to them.

The thing is, poor old Debs is the butt of an awful lot

of jokes and most of them are mine. She never gets to hear them, of course. No one — especially me — would ever dream of hurting her feelings. She's too well liked. It's just that, well, jokes are funny. You know? And I like a joke more than anyone.

For example. Deborah has wrap-round tits. Her nipples have ended up behind her head. She has more skin than a elephant. She had so many folds and flaps on her, it's difficult finding the right one without a map. If you melted Deborah down and poured her into a fat-powered vehicle, you could drive to London and back without a refill. Some said it wasn't her fault, she had a problem with her glands.

'Sure,' I liked to point out. 'Too many gland sandwiches.'

See? I really am vile. I'd be mortified if she ever got to hear any of these witticisms, of course — but behind her back, yes, I'm ruthless!

'So, what was it liked to be entombed between her mighty thighs, then?' asked Ben. See? That's one of mine, too.

'Leave it out.'

'Have you wiped the grease marks off, yet?' said Dino, raising his voice so that although she never could hear, it *felt* as though she might. The bastard. That was one of mine, too. If she ever got to hear any of it I'd die of shame.

And so it went on all morning. It was all over school. I was amazed — really amazed at some of the attitudes that came out. I mean, all right: I am unbearably cruel, I know that — but it's all for the sake of a laugh. I'm callous. I go too far. I'm insensitive. But it's horribility by *accident*. Some of these guys really go for it. I'd always thought that the whole thing about fat girls was something you went on about because it was funny. It never occurred to me that some people actually seem to think that there's something morally wrong with it.

'Like sheep shagging or something,' said Snoops.

'Don't be ridiculous,' I snarled.

Snoops is a bastard, but even some of the nice guys like Fasil were all over the place on this one.

'Sorry, Jon, but I can't understand it...that sort of thing,' he said. That sort of thing? What does he mean by that? Even Ben, who's just about the nicest of us all.

'Not my personal cup of tea,' he said. 'But each to their own, eh, Jon?'

'Yeah, you stick by her,' said Dino.

'I shouldn't think it's all that easy to escape,' I said. Joke. Stick, fat, get stuck, see? Bastards! Even I was joining in. Oh, we were all having a great time at my expense.

I'm just as bad as they are. I've always taken the attitude that it doesn't actually matter what size and shape a girl is. It's the personality that counts. So how come I don't want Deborah? I like her. My glands obviously think she's great. Whenever I think about those twenty minutes outside the garage with the wind blowing around Mr Knobby Knobster and her tits out, I almost pull my trousers off from the inside. So what's my problem? Could it be that I've been kidding myself all the time, and that actually it's just that I'm *ashamed to be seen with her*?

Because let's face it, the humiliation would be endless. People would go on and on and on and on. It's so stupid. She isn't even that fat. She's chubby. It's just her bad luck that somewhere down the line she got appointed the school fat girl, and that's it.

But then, I always get like this. I mean – I like girls. I get on well with them. And I like sex. Not that I've had all that much experience of it – not with another person being in the room at the same time, anyway. I just can't somehow put the two together. I can be getting on really well with a girl but as soon as I get an inkling that there might be a chance of anything happening, I just freeze up. It's scary. Sex is . . . well it's so rude, isn't it? You wouldn't think girls would like sex. You'd think it's too rude for them. Doing sex with a girl, it's a bit like putting a frog down their backs or scaring them with dead mice or throwing worms at them. They're such sensible, grown-up sorts of people. And yet apparently even the nice ones like you sticking the rudest thing you have on your whole body up the exact, rudest part of their body that they have! It doesn't make a lot of sense to me.

The fact is, I can't put together the sort of feelings that I get when I'm having a dirty big wank together with the kind of feelings I get when I'm having a nice friendly chat with someone. It just doesn't work. But here's Deborah, who I get on very well with and she actually appears to want me to do those things. It sounds too good to be true, right? Even better, she wants to do them back to *me*. I mean. Saying no – it just seems so stupid.

Maybe I'm just scared. Maybe I need to bite the bullet and give her one and I'll feel better.

Nemesis came the next day. It was about the most embarrassing thing that ever happened to me.

I was talking about it to Ben and Dino, and a couple of others, the bastards. Ben was telling me off.

'You shouldn't have raised her hopes,' he said.

'She can't help being fat,' pointed out Fasil. 'Do you think she likes it? You've encouraged her to think that it doesn't matter.'

'But it *doesn't* matter,' I snarled. 'Some people *like* fat girls.'

'Ugh, there, I knew it,' said Snoops. 'That means you do fancy her. Gross.'

'I don't! I'm talking about other people. Christ!'

'You looked like you were having a good time to me,' said Dino.

I suppose I should have noticed that they'd started looking over my shoulder. Later, Ben said he tried to indicate what was going on with his chin. I'm not sure I believe him. He could have said, 'Oh, hi, Sue, Jenna and Jackie, how's it going?' instead of just doing odd things with his chin. So these three harpies emerged over my shoulder just in time to hear me come out with this prime piece of bullshit...

'I was doing her a favour,' I said.

I didn't even mean it. It was a joke. Try explaining that to them.

'You bastard!' shrieked Jenna in my ear.

146

I leapt round. I think I might have briefly fainted in mid-air.

'You're disgusting,' hissed Sue. 'She was doing you a favour, if only you knew.'

'I didn't mean I was doing her a favour, that sounded all wrong. I meant – Jesus! It was just a snog! It wouldn't matter if it was anyone else I'd snogged.'

'Yuk. All that flesh,' said Snoops.

'Shut up,' I said.

'Don't tell him to shut up, you're as bad as he is,' said Sue.

'You lot are the prejudiced ones,' I told them, wildly going onto the attack. 'If it was a thin person I'd snogged, no one could care less.'

'You made her think she was in with a chance, that's what's wrong with it,' said Fas piously.

'You *all* make me sick,' barked Sue. 'She's "in with a chance" with lots of people. She had a boyfriend, just recently. And *she* finished with *him*, what's more!'

'See?' I said.

'She's upset,' said Jackie seriously. She nodded across the common room. I looked sideways across. Debs was sitting at a table, half turned away. She must know they were talking about her. How could she bear it? Did she know all we were talking about was her weight?

'I was only joking about doing her a favour,' I repeated pathetically.

'You have to speak to her. You owe her that much.'

'All right. OK. I'll have a word with her, OK?' I begged. And all three girls answered as one:

147

'When?'

★ ★ ★

I am blessed among mortals. I know it's hard to believe just looking at me, I expect I seem just your average geek to you. Don't laugh. It's embarrassing. See, I have a small flock of invisible magical helpers to do my every bidding.

I know it's ludicrous. I'm obviously mad. But – just imagine. Suppose it's true. You don't know. You can't prove anything really. It's a question of faith. It's just the same with bloody old God, isn't it? He's no different, you can't see him either. You don't know if he's there or not. God, magic helpers – they all basically have a big credibility problem. Something to do with moving in mysterious ways, or being invisible as I like to call it.

There's all these stupid rules these beings have. They're so *moral*, which cuts out most of the stuff I want for starters. And they're so touchy about it. If for instance, you asked them to bring you the Taj Mahal, or give you a twelve-inch knob or turn you into a millionaire or something like that, something really desirable and useful, they wouldn't do it, even though they easily could if they wanted to. It'd be too obvious for them. It'd be like you were asking them to prove their existence to you, which would mean that you didn't really believe in them properly... and if they get the slightest sense that you don't believe in them properly, they go all stroppy and start sulking. What you have to do is ask them to do things that are within the realms of possibility. Things that mean *you never know for sure* if they've been brought about by chance, or by magic. Things like, for instance: *Please make Deborah stop fancying me.*

It's just exactly the sort of thing my magic helpers could help me with. All I have to do is work out what exactly they want me to ask them.

But please stop Deborah fancying me won't work because that would mean asking them to interfere in another human being's feelings, and they'd never do that. That's immoral. So how about this? *Please please please make Deborah **thin** . . .* but with big tits, so that I'd still have those wonderful bazookas to play with, but no one would sneer at me for going out with a fat girl.

Nice thought, but that wouldn't work either, because you can't just make someone change shape to suit you. Making their body change is just as bad as making their minds change. That would make my magic helpers all huffy and disappointed for sure. Even if she wanted to be thin with big tits – and there's a fair chance she does – it would still be immoral because it would be cheating. My magic helpers would expect her to go on a diet like everyone else.

So how about – *Make **me** fancy her!* What do you think? Maybe they already have. Mr Knobby certainly thinks so. But in that case, why does doing sex things with her make me feel so panicky? It's nice at the time – it's brilliant at the time – but thinking about it makes me feel awful. What's going on there? And anyhow, that's immoral too. Most things are, I find, when you start thinking about it. It's as wrong to change yourself to suit somebody else as it is to change someone else to suit you. Almost.

So what about this?

Please give me the courage to tell her that I like her very very much, but I just don't fancy her.

But they won't touch that one either because, of course, I could do it perfectly well myself. Magic is only for things you can't do yourself. And I'm certainly not going to do it as I am, and you know why? Because I'm a coward, that's why. So I'm shafted.

It makes you wonder. What use are they? They won't do anything to make it easier for me, and the difficult things they insist I do for myself.

I couldn't bear to hurt her feelings. Really, simply, couldn't bear it.

The easiest thing to do would be just to go out with her. Why not? For one thing, I am actually very fond of her. That's a start, isn't it? She's female for another. That counts for a lot. It means she has tits and a minge. Yes, I know, that's amazingly superficial of me, but there you go. Tits and minge are actually very important things to me in a girlfriend. In fact, they're just about the most important things I want in a girl. I dream about them. I think about them. I spend a lot of my spare time looking at them on my computer screen – tits and arses and minge till it comes out of my ears. And Deborah has them all. In fact, she has just about the best tits you can imagine. Big lovely womanly breasts with lovely big dark nipples and and . . . oooh, la, yum yum yum.

Maybe I should just be prepared to accept what comes my way. Beggars can't be choosers would be a bit harsh, but if I narrow my field down to the good-looking ones, I'm likely to stay a virgin forever. It's something I've noticed. The good-looking ones don't tend to fancy me all that much. I'm just not one of the beautiful people. And she likes me. We're mates. She could be my best friend, and having a best friend who lets you do sex with them – having a best friend who *wants* you to do sex with them – is something really worth having, I reckon. Me and Debs. Why not? She's clever and funny. We like the same things. We share a sense of humour. We spend ages chatting about all sorts of stuff. She's talented. I ought to be flattered, really. She does these amazing cartoons of people. It takes her about a minute, she just sits down, looks at you, draws a few lines and there it is, a really funny caricature. It's like magic watching her. She laughs at my jokes and listens to my opinions. You know what? I think I make her happy. Isn't that something? She was smiling and smiling and smiling at me at the end of the party when we were on the sofa next to each other holding hands. Isn't that worth having?

And then there's the tits and minge.

It wouldn't last, though. Once she got to know me she'd go off me dead quick. I mean, I'm pretty weird, really. I'm only ever nice to people because I want them to be nice to me. Pretty superficial, huh? I think much too much of myself. I'm quite good with words but that's about it, there's nothing else. School work – very patchy. People – I'm shy. Chatting girls up – hopeless. Knowing when to stop – can't do it. And that's not all. My head – you wouldn't believe the things that go through my head. My head is unbelievable, it's a quagmire in here. How could I have a relationship with someone when I have so many secrets? My wank life, for instance. All the time! I'm like a monkey. And my magic helpers. Childish or what? And other things. The thoughts that fill my head! Sometimes I lie in bed and I spend hours thinking the most deliberately horrible things I can. The worst curses. The most violent acts, the most uncharitable thoughts, the most disgusting perversions. You just would not believe.

But – the fact is, she seems to like me. She's clever and sweet and thoughtful, and she likes me.

But *Deborah*! As a friend she's great but as a girlfriend she's a joke. Is that what makes my hair stands on end? Because she's overweight? I know I'm crap but that really would be too petty even for me. But why else? My knob likes her, I like her – but something just shrivels up and dies of embarrassment at the thought of doing it with her.

★ ★ ★

By seven o'clock that evening when he arrived at the War Memorial in Scofield Park, Jonathon still hadn't got a clue what to do.

She wasn't there yet. He kicked around the monument waiting and wishing and hoping, and dreading that she wouldn't come. The truth about wishes is, they can come true – but only if you wish for the right thing. The wish that can come true fits in like a piece of a jigsaw puzzle and everything falls into place. What was the right wish here?

He was walking around a bench muttering to himself when she suddenly appeared. He jumped. She smiled anxiously.

'I was scared you wouldn't come,' she said.

'I said I would.'

They stood looking at each other and smiling.

'Walk?' she said.

'OK.'

They headed across the grass and around by the rosebeds. She took his hand. They walked right round the little park talking about school, about Dino, about why on earth Ben didn't get off with anyone when they were literally queuing up for him. Neither of them said a word about . . . things. When they got back to the monument, she leaned back against it and said, 'Kiss me.'

Jonathon put his arms around her and kissed her. She tasted of spices and winegums, which made him briefly want to giggle. Fat girl = winegums. He pressed his full weight right up against her, right down the length of her body and kissed her on the lips. She held him tight, her big bosoms pushed up against him. Mr Knobby rose up between them. Deborah pushed her tummy against it, and he pushed gently back.

'We get on so well together.'

'Yes.'

'So what's the problem?'

What could he say? Yes, I like you and I evidently do fancy you, but I can't bear the social humiliation of being seen out regularly with a fat girl? He shook his head and said, 'I don't know. I don't know. I'm . . . I need to think about it.'

Deborah looked away, then back at him. 'Is it my weight?' she asked.

153

'Good God, no! I don't care about that!'

She frowned. 'Then what?'

'I don't *know*,' insisted Jonathon.

'Look,' she said. 'I understand, you know.'

'What?' he asked, all panicky.

'You don't have to fancy me. I know I'm fat.'

'You're not fat!' insisted Jonathon furiously. 'Don't let them make you think that.'

Deborah laughed at his anger.

'You're not, you know you're not. Fat is — well, it's a lot bigger than you are.'

'Well, I'm chubby, then.'

'Plump, perhaps.'

'Plump,' she smiled.

'Don't you like being plump?'

She shrugged. 'No. But all the other girls' — She waved her hand over the park, the town, the world — 'they're all worried about being thin and the right shape and having the right boobs and the right everything. So I just think I'm not going to care about that. I'd like to be thin, I can't help that, but it's so stupid. Just fashion, isn't it? I don't go for fashion. It's like . . . being bullied, you know. I've decided to settle for being plump.'

'That's just so amazing. I think that's an amazing thing to do,' he told her fervently. Who else would think like that? Wasn't she something special? And she wanted to be his.

She smiled and wriggled her tum up against a grateful Mr Knobby.

'So don't you care what people think?' he asked her.

'Of course I do. I hate it. Of course I hate it. What did

154

you think, that I was a fat jolly person?'

'No, no, not that. You always seemed so – I dunno. Well adjusted.'

'The way people look at me. All those jokes.'

He blushed. Did she know?

'The way no one wants to dance with me at school dances.'

'I danced with you.'

'You're different.'

'Ben danced with you.'

'He's nice.'

'Everyone likes you,' he reminded her.

'Who wants to be nice?' asked Deborah. 'Everyone likes me, but no one fancies me. Well,' she amended, 'that's not actually true. Outside school loads of people do. It's just you lot.' She looked Jonathon in the eye. 'And I don't care about any of them, actually. It's just you. I like you a lot.'

Jonathon smiled grimly. 'I like you,' he said. He was relieved to be able to say something true.

'So,' she said. 'What do you say?'

He just stood there. He had no idea what to say and no idea what he felt, except for this: he felt confused and scared.

'You don't have to make up your mind now,' she said. She took his hand again and looked sadly at him.

'Is that all right?' he asked.

'It's OK. It's just that it would have been nice if you wanted to straight away. But you can have a few days,' she said. 'Come on . . . I'll buy you an ice-cream.'

She led the way across the park to where the ice-cream van waited underneath the poplar trees on the road outside. Jonathon tried to pay but she wouldn't let him. She smiled at him as they waited to be served. The ice-cream came down in swirls onto their cones.

'Looks like a dog shitting,' he said.

Deborah howled. 'What are you like!' she screamed. It was great. She even liked his awful shit jokes.

They walked back into the park and sat on a bench, side by side, licking their ices. After the cones had gone, she stood up and brushed down her jeans. 'You'll have to let me know by the weekend,' she told him.

'Yes'm.'

'Kiss me again,' she commanded.

Obediently, Jonathon walked forward to kiss and be kissed. He felt so helpless. Once again, up came Mr Red Cap. Deborah reached down and held him in her hand. She drew back and looked closely up into his face. He was so horned up he could hardly focus. He heard her speak in a kind of dream.

'You make me so horny,' she was saying.

'What?'

'I want to be your lover. I want to do it with you – I want to do everything,' she said again. Then she let him go. She walked away, glancing over her shoulder at him without smiling.

Jonathon's penis had reached an ebony-like degree of hardness that was positively uncomfortable. It felt as if someone had injected a litre of testosterone directly into it. He staggered around the bench, concussed by desire.

'You traitorous bastard,' he told Mr Knobby, but he wanted to shake hands so much that he had to walk swiftly home to relieve himself of the pressure. How could someone he didn't fancy turn him on so much? Was it possible? He was ravaged by hormones. He seemed to be bobbing upside down in them, just one more ingredient in a thick soup of lust. At home, he had to see to Mr Knobby three times, one after the other. Afterwards, he lay back and gazed at the fatal organ.

'You don't know when to start and you don't know when to stop,' he said severely.

Mr Knobby grinned back. 'Who cares about all that?' he said. 'You heard what she said.'

'She said, Everything. She wants to do everything.'

'And you know what they say.'

'Fat Girls Are Grateful For It,' said Jonathon dutifully. 'Fat Girls Will Do *Anything*.'

'It's the chance of a lifetime,' said Mr Knobby Knobster.

19
Sue

That's Jackie's big problem: she has to be right. If you disagree with her it's like some big insult. She goes on about it for hours and hours and in the end I just say, OK, OK. You're right, I'm wrong, but I don't care, I'm gonna do it/wear it/try it anyhow. What's wrong with being wrong? You get more done.

You'd have thought she had it all going for her. That's how it's supposed to be, isn't it? Be sensible, work hard, plan ahead and there it all is – good grades, good job, good kids, good husband. And then – Dino! What's that all about? All those years of getting it right, and then what? I mean, be irresponsible if you have to. But *Dino*?!

After the party, I thought even she'd be able to see what was going on. If she wanted any more proof that deep down inside she really did NOT want to sleep with him, then running away from his bed at two o'clock in the morning had to be it. I got her round to my place, sat her down in the lounge, told my mum we needed some space, and had another go.

I did it very carefully, very simply. Emotions by numbers. I pointed out all the things that mattered to her which her relationship with Dino was screwing up. Her work was suffering. She hates that. Jackie is the original topgirl. She was making a fool of herself. Horrible! She was losing her self-confidence. That made her wince. She always used to be in charge; now she was like a puppet on a string. And finally — and this was the so-so clever bit, see — I told her she was *using* Dino.

She looked like I'd just slapped her round the face. See, Jackie's not only sensible — she's nice.

'Dino's a boy,' I explained to her. She seemed to have forgotten this vital fact. Some people do. They think boys are like girls with knobs on. They're not.

'So what?' she asked belligerently.

'He wants a shag, right? But it's more than that. His feelings are all contained in the end of his knob. Try and imagine that that's where his heart is. Well, Dino wants to *give you his heart.*'

She scowled suspiciously, but I ploughed on.

'All this leading him on, Jackie — it's not fair. You're not just stopping him having a shag, you're rejecting him. How do you think that makes him feel?'

She didn't like that. 'Why all this concern for Dino suddenly?' she snapped.

'I don't give a shit about Dino, but since you can't do anything for yourself, maybe you can do it for him.'

'You want me to chuck Dino for *his* sake?'

'No, listen. The thing is, we've been talking about Dino as if he's just a selfish lump of meat who wants a shag. But it's more than that. He cares for you. You can't just treat him like he can turn it on and off like some sort of switch.'

'You've changed your tune,' she told me. 'According to

you, Dino's never given a shit about any living thing except himself.'

I shrugged. 'Maybe he's human after all.'

For a second I thought I'd gone too far, but she seemed to be prepared to believe anything. She began to nod slowly.

'So what you have to do, right? – is just deal with him straight. You have to try being honest with him.' I could see her bristle at that, but it was true. 'It's obvious you're not ready to sleep with him. Right? So, put it to him. Be truthful. Tell him, you want to go out with him – but no sex.'

'But that's what I've been doing!'

'No, you haven't. You've been *going* to have sex. That's different. It's been sex tomorrow, sex next week. You've been holding out jam for him. It's time to put the jam away.'

Jackie thought about it.

'He'll chuck me,' she said.

'You owe it to yourself, and you owe it to him,' I said. 'I mean, say yes or no, Jackie, but not like this, it's not fair.'

Just for a second I thought she was going to tell me to piss off, but suddenly she started to weep instead. It was amazing, actually. You know how plans like that, they never work? And here was this one all falling into place – it was like magic. For once in my life I must have got it right. Or maybe Jackie was just desperate for a way out.

I went over to give her a hug and she sniffed onto my shoulder. 'You're right,' she said in a muffled voice. 'I have to be straight with him. I have to tell him. No sex.'

And I thought, Yes! Got her! That was it. No way was Dino going to go along with that.

20
Ben

You know what heaven is? I'll tell you. You're lying across a big soft, king-size bed, so big you can stretch out in any direction without going over the edge. Everything's warm – the air's warm, your skin's warm, the sheets are warm and all rumpled up. There's an ice cold beer on the bedside table and a packet of chocolate-covered raisins on the sheet next to you. There's a good film on the telly. Then the door opens and Ali Young comes in with a bowl of Frosties, stark naked except for a pair of white socks. You watch her tits jiggle as she comes across the room.

'Are you looking at my tits?' she says, and you say,

'Yes, Miss.'

She puts the Frosties on the bed next to you, puts the backs of her hands underneath them and jiggles up and down. 'Jiggly-jiggly-jig-jig-jig,' she says, and then she bends over so they hang in your face like ... well. Like a beautiful pair of tits.

'Mmmmnuh,' I say. And that's what heaven is.

'What?' she says.

'Just *gorgeous*,' I reply.

It was the week after Dino's party. She'd just about

recovered from her mother and things were back to normal. Sometimes on a Tuesday evening she wants to grind her way around the sitting room – on the floor, on the table, you name it. Which is great, of course. But the thing I really like is just rolling about in her big bed, me on top, her on top, me behind. And then afterwards all shagged out with nothing on, titbits being carried to and fro, ready to start again any time you feel like it. It's the best thing.

Ali got into bed next to me and looked at the TV. It was a good movie – *Doubles* – but there were plenty more interesting things to do than watch a movie. I smiled fondly at her tits again and waited for her to look across and spot me doing it.

'One, two, one two,' she said, wiggling her chest.

'Yum yum yum,' I said. I leaned over and kissed them, and sighed happily.

'Stay over,' she said.

'God, isn't it?' I said, holding my head in my hand. In another hour or so I'd have to go back to parentland and sleep in my own narrow little bed, in my narrow little room, in a house full of people who felt like strangers just at that moment.

'Don't then.'

'I've got to.'

'Why?'

'They expect me. You know?'

'Ring 'em up. Tell them you want to stay over with a friend.'

'They know all my friends. They'll want the number.

They might ring back. Anyway, I never stay over on schooldays.'

'Ah, poor thing!' She smiled at me, a bit grimly I thought. 'Has iddle oodams got to be home on time, den? Come on, Ben, you're seventeen, they don't have to know where you are every second of the day.'

'Get off...' I muttered. I hate it when she comes on like that. It's bad enough as it is.

'Just ring them up and say. Tell them it's a new boy at school. Tell them it's a new girl!' She smiled at me. 'Are you allowed to have sex? Perhaps I should send a parental consent form home for you.'

'Don't be daft. Let's watch the movie.'

I could feel her looking at me, deciding whether or not to carry on with it. Just a moment ago it was drop-dead certain that I was going back in an hour or so, and now suddenly everything was all slippery. I felt like I was being dishonest in some way. She does that. She whips the ground from under your feet and you don't even know why.

And – well, let's be honest about it. I *wanted* to go home afterwards. I didn't want to spend the night in her bed. It made me feel uncomfortable.

'We should do this more often,' she said, snuggling down and holding onto my arm.

'Mmm.' I draped my arm over her shoulders.

'What about Thursdays?'

'Thursdays?'

'Why not? If you can't stay over?'

Maybe but... I didn't want to do that either. I suppose

163

it sounds stupid. One minute it's heaven and the next I want to go back home to Mum and Dad. Maybe you think I was being a bastard, but it's an edgy business, having it off with Miss. I suppose I just wanted to keep it at arm's length. I lay there for a bit trying to think of a good reason not to come on Thursdays. I have footie practice, there's a good programme on TV, I have to stay in and do homework. No no no no.

'Can't really get away.'

'Why not?'

'They're always on at me. I'm always out. I'm out tonight, I'm out seeing me mates tomorrow, I'm out with you on Sundays. You know.'

There was a silence.

'I feel as though I'm having to beg,' she said at last.

It was new, all this. So far she'd been very keen about keeping it down to a couple of times a week, not seeing too much of one another. She could lose her job – in fact, she could lose her whole career if anyone ever found out about it. No one'd ever give her a job in teaching again if they knew she shagged the students.

Shagging the students. I used to say that to her but it always made her cross.

'I shag you,' she said. 'Just one, Ben, in case you thought I was having it off with the rest of the year. I'm not, for your information.'

'Sorry, Miss.'

But. So why the change?

'What's this about?' I asked her.

'What's what about?'

'You wanting to start seeing more of me?'

'I'm just trying to find a way of doing this more often,' she said, all huffy.

'Really?'

'You're so paranoid!'

'You just sound . . . I mean I thought we'd agreed it was the right thing to be careful and not see too much of each other.'

'Just because I like the idea of another evening?'

'Sorry,' I said.

'You're so paranoid.'

I looked at her. 'Well, you know, I'd love to do it more often, but it's really awkward.'

'Why?'

'It just is. At home. Getting out. You know? It's not that they don't let me, but it's just difficult. I have to talk to them and tell them what I'm up to. It's just awkward. Like having an affair, I suppose,' I said.

That seemed to make sense to her. She nodded and pulled a face. 'I suppose. We'll have to try and think of something.'

I didn't say anything. I sat up and picked up the Frosties and tried to watch the film. I was scared she was going to go all hurt, but it was OK. I drank the beer, watched the movie and we had a lovely big snog on the doorstep before I went home. Delicious. Going home afterwards was fairly delicious, too.

21
Six Inches Away From Home

'Are you sure you're prepared to go through with this?' asked Sue.

'Go through it again.'

'You're very fond of him.'

'Right.'

'But for some reason' – Sue sighed impatiently – 'you can't bring yourself to sleep with him.'

'But I still want to go *out* with him.'

'Yes, but with no sex.'

'For now.'

'No, not for now! That sounds like maybe next week, same as usual. You don't want to even consider sex for the foreseeable future.'

'He'll chuck me!' wailed Jackie.

That's the plan, isn't it? hissed her friend silently to herself, but what she actually said was, 'Well, maybe, maybe not, who knows? Maybe it's like you say, he's more decent than you think. But if he loses interest just because of that, you don't want him. Right?'

Jackie pulled a face but she knew it was right. She couldn't keep on making promises about a sex life which, when it came down to it, she was unable to participate in.

'Either he's prepared to put up with it or he isn't. If he wants you for yourself, he'll say yes. And if he doesn't, that's that. And then perhaps we can stop having this conversation, and talk about something interesting. Like me, for instance,' she added hopefully.

Jackie rehearsed her lines, did her make-up, wept and did her make-up again. Sue soothed her and patted her and plied her with tissues and told her to be strong. She was fairly certain Dino would chuck her. It wouldn't last, of course, they'd be an item again within the week, but at least Jackie would gain a few Dino-free days. In the event, she didn't even manage that. At the time it was a complete surprise to Jackie the way things turned out and it was only in retrospect that she realised what a typically Dinoesque situation it was, the way he side-stepped her plans so effortlessly and manipulated her so blatantly, like a man working a complicated marionette puppet with one hand, while his real attention was taken up flicking through the TV channels with the other.

It started out so well. Her parents were out late that evening. Dino came round as arranged and they had a couple of hours ahead if necessary, although she wasn't expecting it to take anything like that long. She made him a cup of coffee and got straight on with it. She was very very fond of him but she didn't somehow feel confident enough of their relationship to sleep with him. Sleeping with someone, she explained, was a very special thing, a very close thing, a very intimate thing.

Of course, she fancied him something chronic, she couldn't keep her hands off him; but something was holding her back. She wasn't sure what it was, but she had decided that she had to respect it and she wanted Dino to respect it, too.

'Yeah. I think you're right,' said Dino.

'Pardon?'

'Right, I agree with you.'

'You agree?'

'Yeah. Let's give it a bit of time. There's no hurry. Maybe you have a problem in that department. Maybe there's some sort of experience you had once.'

'I don't think so, Dino,' she replied carefully.

'You must have covered it up. I dunno. But yes, you're right. Let's leave the sex for now. Is that what you wanted?' he added anxiously.

'Yes, yes, that's right,' exclaimed Jackie. Her hand was shaking so much she had to put her coffee carefully down on the table to avoid spilling it.

'God!' Dino clutched his chest. 'You gave me a fright. I thought you were chucking me there for a moment.'

'No no no.'

Dino shook his head. She really had scared him. He looked closely at her. 'You don't look very pleased,' he complained.

'Oh, I am. I really am.'

But the truth was, her first reaction was one of disappointment. She'd been thinking, that was it. No more worry and anxiety and fighting her better judgement. No more bullshit. Dino was going to behave

168

like an arse and that was that. Instead, he was just terrified that she was going to chuck him.

'You're sure about this?' she asked.

'You *are* chucking me, aren't you!'

'No. But . . .'

'What?'

'It's just that, you know . . . I really thought you wouldn't want to know.'

'What do you think I am? Some sort of arse? No, if that's how you feel, sure. I mean, of course.'

'Oh, Dino!' The disappointment passed. She was so pleased she jumped up and wrapped herself round him. She'd underestimated him! He loved her after all! See? Suddenly they were in a clinch on the settee loosening one another's jeans.

'Ooooo, that's nice,' said Jackie. She was just so grateful, so happy that Sue had been wrong. She sort of let go. After a bit, someone knocked the coffee table and one of the cups slopped over. Jackie got up to clean things up and Dino came up behind her and seized her from behind. He pushed her forward until she jammed up against the back of the settee. Jackie bent over it and he began banging himself against her bum. He was looking down, trying to imagine that the thin layers of jeans and knickers were gone, but he was still a good six inches from where he wanted to be. Jackie lay there and soaked into her jeans. At the back of her mouth the words formed,

'Go on then – take them off.' She could feel the sentence moving inside her. She whispered it soundlessly

169

just to see what it felt like and it felt just so gorgeous, so salty and sexy and true, that she wondered if, despite everything, she might actually say them.

'Go on then – take them off,' she heard herself saying.

Dino paused in his bangings. 'Are you sure?'

'Yes. Go on.'

She raised herself slightly off the settee while he felt underneath her for the zip. The zipper slid down with a growl. He tugged. Jeans and knickers came suddenly down and she felt the cool air on her bum.

'No!' she shrieked. She jumped up, spun round and tugged the jeans back up. 'Don't do that!' she snapped.

'But you said,' complained Dino.

For a second they both stood staring at one another.

'See?' she told him. 'I'm mad. I need looking after. Next time I tell you to do that – just don't, OK?'

'God,' said Dino. She put her hand to her mouth and started to shake with the giggles, while Dino stood watching her, lust vying with frustration vying with wanting to be sweet. Every time she looked at his face she laughed more. She kept expecting him to join in, but Dino just stood and stared at her with a wry smile on his face while she shook with hysterics. It went on for ages, until he got fed up with it and stalked out into the kitchen. Alone, she came suddenly to her senses, walked three times round the room and ran out to him to apologise. Amazingly, he was OK about it. More proof! She really had misjudged him.

They sat back down with their coffees. Jackie was delighted. He was sweet! He really was sweet! He hadn't

170

a clue what she was going through, but he was respecting it because she'd asked him to. And here she was still being an arse! That was pretty bloody good, wasn't it? Her initial instinct had been right after all – there was more to him than met the eye. Under the bullshit was a kind, sweet boy.

Dino leaned back on the sofa, basking in her approval. On the spur of the moment, he told her all about his mum and Dave Short. He hadn't planned on it. He had no idea why. He just found himself saying it.

'I was just remembering,' he said. 'My mum's having an affair with someone from her school. I caught them at it the other day in the front room.'

'*What*?'

'You know...' He looked sideways at her. 'She's having an affair.' Dino smiled at her. He meant it to be amused, but his smile was a terrible grimace. Suddenly it sounded awful – exactly what he didn't want it to be. He stopped smiling and scowled at Jackie, daring her to be appalled.

Jackie scowled back. 'When did this happen?'

'Just before the party,' admitted Dino, closely watching her face.

'Why didn't you tell me?'

'I don't know. The party and everything. Anyway, it doesn't matter.'

'Doesn't matter?' Jackie was desperately trying to work it out. Had his unexpected compliance got anything to do with this? She stood up and pulled her jeans up, as if they were still on the way down. She sat down again. 'OK. Go on.'

'There's nothing to tell, really,' said Dino. And then he told her everything – everything, that is, except for the fact that he had been alternating between total amnesia and utter turmoil about it ever since.

'I don't think she even knows I saw them,' he lied.

'If she didn't, she does now. After what you said to your dad about Dave Short going away with them for the weekend.'

'That didn't mean anything,' insisted Dino irritably. It was so typical! He'd been so understanding and grown-up and now look. Far from reassuring him, she was trying to make out it was some sort of disaster.

Jackie decided to take it at face value and be outraged. 'Well, how could she do that to your dad? And to you! In your own house! And she hasn't even come to speak to you about it. Oh, Dino, you must feel awful.'

'Not really,' he told her coolly. 'It's their business, isn't it?'

'It's your business too! Well, if she won't talk to you about it, you'll have to talk to her about it.'

'Don't be stupid.'

'Can't you? How awful.'

'No. It isn't that bad.'

'Isn't it?' Jackie looked carefully at him. It was happening: he was getting upset *with her*. He was looking to one side, pulling a face, sneering at her concern. She could watch it happening. Dino was rushing into denial.

'Dino?'

'Bollocks,' he told her, and turned away.

Jackie grabbed him by the arm and swung him round

to face her. This was important. He needed her, and here he was vanishing in front of her eyes.

'I care for you,' she hissed. 'How dare you just vanish on me. Dino! Look at me!'

Dino looked at her and began to sneer but before he finished it his eyes filled with tears. He was amazed. Tears? Where had they come from? What had he got to be upset about?

'Oh, Dino.' She put her hand gently on the side of his face. His whole face wobbled with sorrow and amazement. Then he took her in his arms, buried his face in her hair and sobbed.

An hour or so later, after she closed the door behind him, Jackie went to look at herself in the mirror in the front room. Her hair was still damp on one side where he had wept on it. Somewhere in the back of her mind a little voice – Sue's probably – was muttering away that there, see, he's done it again. Just as she thought he was being understanding and thoughtful it turned out he had an agenda of his own. Well, maybe – but Jackie didn't care. He'd clung tight like a big baby sobbing his heart out. He'd given her his bleeding heart. He needed her.

'I've never cried like that before,' he said to her afterwards. 'I don't think I could with anyone else.' And so he had wrapped her into his heart more tightly than ever.

Shortly after, the phone rang. It was Sue wanting to know how she got on.

'It was amazing,' said Jackie. 'He took it!'

173

'He what?' demanded Sue.

'He took it! He accepted the deal!'

'Are you sure?'

'Yes, of course I'm sure. He said he understood.'

'Understood?' asked Sue incredulously. Since when had Dino understood anything? 'What exactly did you say to him?'

'What we said. I told him. I said I needed more time to be sure of what we felt for each other, and he said that he agreed with me.'

'He *agreed*?'

'Yes,' insisted Jackie. 'He said he thought that we should just forget about sex for a while.'

'Dino said that?'

'Dino,' said Jackie.

'He's up to something.'

'Why do you have to be so suspicious?'

'Aren't you suspicious?'

'No,' said Jackie, in an offended voice. 'I mean, he's making all the right noises, isn't he? That was the deal, wasn't it?'

'I suppose the least you can say is, he knows the right noises to make. I wouldn't have even given him credit for that before.' Could it be that Dino was actually being clever? Surely not? But even that unlikely possibility was more believable than that he was being genuinely caring.

'He's up to something.'

'Don't be cynical. He was sweet.'

'It's better than his usual grunting, I suppose,' agreed Sue. 'But it's not like him, is it? Or are you going to give me some crap about this being the real Dino, the Dino beneath who has been waiting to emerge?'

'Oh, don't be patronising,' snapped Jackie. But although she would never admit to anything so foolish, really she did hope that it might be so. She had no idea of the depths of deceit that Dino was prepared to stoop to.

Before she put the phone down, Jackie hesitated. There was more to tell, but she knew exactly what Sue would say if she ever found out that Dino's mum was having an affair and that Dino had more or less grassed her up at the dinner table the week before. She put the phone down, Dino's secret kept, but she could hear Sue's voice ringing in her ears even as she put the phone down.

'Sucker! Why are you doing this to yourself?'

He needs me, thought Jackie in reply. He was like a six-foot teddy bear, right down to the sexy little growl when he whispered in her ear. He needed her. But did she need him?

22
Dino the Destroyer

Back home, Dino went straight up to his room. He felt calm inside, but his whole body was vibrating as if a perfectly balanced mechanism was spinning rapidly inside him. One jolt and he'd blow to pieces. He was furious with Jackie for making such a fuss. Look at the state he was in!

Below, he heard his mother's step on the stairs. He'd been dying for her to talk to him about it, but what good did talking do? He'd just talked about it to Jackie and look at him now. Talking just made it worse.

Her foot sounded on the creaky steps. The creaking paused, then restarted. Then paused. Then with a firm tread, she came upstairs. A knock. Dino flung himself sideways on the bed and closed his eyes. The door opened.

'Dino?'

Pause.

'Dino? Are you awake?'

'Uh. What? Mum?'

'Did you have a good day?'

'Yeah. All right, why?'

'You look . . .'

176

'I'm tired.' He glanced over to her through screwed-up eyes as if he was unused to the light and saw her watching him as if he was something you could open up, a box, a purse, and she could just pick out and throw away the bits she didn't want in there.

'Do you...? Is there anything...?'

'No.'

'Anything bothering...? Anything...'

'No.'

'...you want to talk about?' Dino suddenly couldn't work his mouth. He lay there and stared at her hopelessly until she gave in.

'Would you like a sandwich?' she asked.

'Yes!' That was more like it. Mother.

She smiled back at him, and for a second the two of them were complicitous in pretence, mother and son doing their mother and son stuff.

'Fried egg?'

'And ketchup.'

'Right.'

'Thanks, Mum!' he called after her. He meant it. He was so relieved, so pleased with her. All the business she had with him was a fried egg sandwich. He lay back down, exhausted.

'Things aren't as straightforward as they seem,' muttered Dino to himself. You ain't kidding. He closed his eyes and tried to blank everything out.

Ten minutes later, Kath Howther came upstairs, knocked gently on the door and went in with the fried egg sandwich on a small plate. Dino lay on his bed, fast asleep.

'Dino?' No answer. She went up close, put the plate down on the little table next to his bed and looked down into her son's pale face.

'Dino.' She said his name like a statement, as if she was testing to see if it still fitted this handsome, long man, who had been her baby son of just a few years ago. What was it like to be mother to a grown-up? How good would she be at it? She had thought it was going to be so much easier now, but look, she'd let go and thought of herself and here she was suddenly and hopelessly out of her depth. She had so much wanted the whole thing to work for them all – family, childhood, Mum and Dad. She loved him so much and here he was, already passing beyond her and her own feelings were suddenly too big, too soon.

'I'm sorry,' she whispered. She tiptoed out. She waited outside his door listening to see if he was awake really, but there was no sound.

One of the worst things about the whole mess was not knowing how long it would go on for, but she found out the answer to that very soon, when Dino destroyed his family the next morning accidentally, like a man with a shotgun pointing it at someone's head and pulling the trigger whilst suffering from a temporary illusion that he was really holding a feather duster. It started with an outrageous argument with his mother. Afterwards, he couldn't remember what it was about until she told him, much later on. It was socks. He had no clean socks. He called down asking where they were, and she yelled back up, 'Just a moment, Dino, I'm dealing with the cat.' Next thing, he was storming downstairs.

'Oh, the cat, the cat, the cat's all right, then. Always the bloody cat before anything else. You're mad about that bloody cat, I don't know why you don't marry it.' He burst into the kitchen, bleary-eyed and furious.

'Don't speak to your mother like that,' yelled his dad. First thing in the morning – not the time to start up. Before he could stop it, Dino's mouth opened and out it came.

'She might as well marry the cat, she's just a tart anyway. Come and get it, here it is. Pussy pussy pussy pussy pussy.'

In the silence that followed he watched his father's face change shape. He wasn't even conscious of being outrageous. It was true, wasn't it? His mother stood there with a tin of Katkins in her hand and her mouth open. Mat stared at him as if he was made of horror, a piece of toast halfway to his mouth.

'Just a tart,' Dino insisted in a squeaky voice. 'Pussy pussy,' he repeated. He couldn't understand what they were being so appalled about. His mother knew, his father knew – didn't he? They'd been arguing ever since he said that thing about Dave Short. The only person who was being kept in the dark was him. What did they expect?

His dad was rising to his feet and pushing the table out of the way. Dino was going to get hit. His mouth filled with wet, salty liquid. He smacked his lips, expecting to taste blood already. Now his father's mouth was opening and a stream of rage poured out of it.

'Fed on shit!' yelled Dino. He prepared to run for it, but then he remembered how small his father looked these days. He'd often had fantasies about beating the shit out of him. Well, maybe now was the time. He was fit and young; his father was a sad old bastard who couldn't even stop his wife shagging creeps like Dave Short in his own living room, probably in his own bed if Jackie was right and she usually was. Dino bent at the legs and moved his hands forward. His father was pushing the chairs out of the way. One went over. The milk spilled on the table. Mat jumped back.

It was all happening in slow motion but suddenly something broke out of the frame. His mother. It felt afterwards as if she'd jumped right over the table to get at him. She leapt on Dino, grabbed him tight, wrapped her arms round his neck and hugged him so hard it hurt.

Dino caught sight of his dad changing direction in mid-murder, face popping, swinging his arms to keep his balance and stop himself from colliding with them. His mother kept her face deep into his neck, just like Jackie sometimes did. His dad ricocheted off the edge of the work surface and banged his fist violently into the breadbin. His mother lifted her face to Dino's ear and whispered right in there, in words that sent a shiver and a tickle down his side until he squirmed, 'Don't do this to me.'

'Ah, oh, all right,' he yelled, wriggling and jumping because of the tickle.

'I'll speak to you about Dave. OK?'

'Right,' he said in a quieter voice.

She let go of him.

The room had escaped by the skin of its teeth. Mat suddenly ran out of it and up the stairs. Chairs down, milk spilled, tea slopped out of the cups, toast and crumbs everywhere. The air was ashes. It was amazing how much damage you could do in just a few seconds if you stopped bothering not to knock things over. His mum was already straightening things on the table, but his dad just stood there. He looked older, more wrinkled, smaller and more useless than ever. He seemed to have shrunk and his mother seemed to have grown.

She brushed herself down and said, 'But first I'd better tell your dad, don't you think?'

'I thought he knew,' said Dino.

'Tell me what?' said his dad.

'You were right,' she told him. 'I'm sorry.'

He shook his head and added even as she spoke, 'Don't tell me, I can guess.' He sat down at the table, and to everyone's pity and shame, began to weep bleakly, his head in his hands, his elbows crunching up the toast crusts. 'I knew it, I knew it, and you just kept denying it. Why did you have to keep denying it?' he wept.

'I'm sorry,' she said. 'Can we get the children off to school first?'

'She's been shouting at me about my suspicious mind,' he explained to Dino, his eyes glistening, his voice wobbling. He stopped, wiping his eyes, and looked up at the clock. 'But I have to go. I have that meeting.' He stood up. 'An important meeting, God help me, I was looking forward to it. Now look. What timing!' He glared at his wife and then at Dino, trying to swallow the things he wanted to say.

He moved around the kitchen picking things up and getting his jacket on as he wept. Dino, watching from the table, thought he looked like a man in a movie.

'Do you have to go now?' asked Kath.

'You've had how long to tell me – how long? Weeks? Months? How long?'

'We'll talk later,' she said, looking away.

His dad looked at Dino. 'Dino. None of this is your fault. OK?'

'Why should it?' asked Dino, but it sounded rude so he added, 'OK, Dad.'

'OK like hell, eh? I've got to go. Christ, what timing!'

'Let's take the day off, Mike. We can talk now,' said Kath.

He stood in the kitchen considering. 'No,' he said. 'No. Not like that. Not because you say so right now after so many ... so many lies. I'll take this afternoon off. See you here, OK?'

'The meeting too important for you, is it?'

'Don't be spiteful.'

'Sorry.' She looked away and bit her lip. 'Sorry.'

'See you later.' He clapped a hand on Dino's shoulder and walked out of the door.

Dino stood up. 'I'd better get going, too,' he said.

'No. We need to talk.'

'School ...'

'We'll take the morning off, both of us.'

'Sausages,' sneered Dino. He meant, she was treating

182

him and his dad like sausages – him in the morning and his dad in the afternoon. But she knew what he meant.

'No, important people I've neglected too long,' she said. 'I won't be a minute, I'll just get Mat away. We have to talk.'

She went upstairs after Mat. Dino ignored her instructions. Why should he go through this shit? Everything was going to stop for her? Nothing was going to stop for her! He went upstairs to get his things ready and slipped out while she was in the kitchen packing Mat's bag. He walked halfway down the road before he realised that if he went, he'd have to wait all day before finding out what was going on. He felt sick with anticipation already. He turned round and went home to listen to his mother's music.

Kath came back from taking Mat to school, stood in the hall and called his name.

'I'm in the kitchen,' he told her.

'Be with you, I just need to pee.' She ran upstairs to her bedroom and stood in front of the mirror doing her face, as if her son was an interviewer, or a lover or someone she had to look good for. What was she going to say? Poor Dino didn't even know how to think about this sort of thing. It was going to be a question of what mood he was in.

Not fair to him, she thought.

How much had he seen? Ouch – she couldn't even think of that. What a mess. She hadn't got a clue how to go about it.

She patted her hair and went down.

'It's all wrong, I should be speaking to your dad first, not you,' she said.

'I'll go to school, shall I?' said Dino.

'No, no, please. Oh, God, Dino. I'm not very good at this, am I?'

'You looked pretty good at it in the living room the other day.'

'How much did you see?' she asked, before she had time to think about it.

'Enough,' he muttered, and turned his face away to avoid having to watch her blush.

She walked two or three times up and down the room, turned, and put the kettle on.

'Tea.'

'Thanks.' Suddenly impatient, he squirmed in his chair and said, 'What do you want to say to me? I should be at school.'

His mother rubbed her eyes. 'I should have spoken to you ages ago. I didn't know...I mean, I wasn't sure if you'd seen us.'

Dino shrugged.

'Although I suppose I knew you'd seen us by the way you were behaving. You made it pretty clear, actually, considering it's almost impossible to get you to talk about anything.'

Dino laughed.

'Thanks for waiting for me, anyway,' she said.

'OK.'

184

He watched her as she turned to make the tea. This was a woman, he hardly knew her. She was like a tiny box he had held in his hand all his life, and he had pressed a catch and she'd opened up and here she was, big as the sky. She was like the bloody Tardis. He felt a wave of resentment that she had so much life.

She turned round to face him. 'Sorry. That's what I want to say. Sorry for bringing Dave home here. Sorry for you catching us. Sorry I never spoke to you about it until it was too late. You know what, when it comes to affairs of the heart we're all just about sixteen years old. But really, really sorry.'

Dino cleared his throat, and to his own amazement asked the only relevant question left between them.

'And sorry about Mr Short as well?'

She looked away and then back. 'I'm sorry for practically everything, aren't I? But I don't think I am sorry about that.'

'Are you going to live with him?'

'God, no! No, I don't love him, Dino.'

'You don't love him and you're not even sorry?'

'Dino. God. Talking to you like this! But . . . No I don't love him. The trouble is, I don't love your dad either. He drives me mad. I don't hate him, but he's like . . . he's like . . .' She took a deep breath. 'He's like someone I can't live with anymore.'

'Are you sure about that?'

'I'm sure.'

And having said it to her son, she was sure. She'd had enough. Kath Howther was out of there.

'I've known it for a long time,' she lied.

'Why didn't you go ages ago?'

'I was hoping things would change, I suppose.'

Dino shrugged. 'So leave,' he told her.

She gulped. *She* leave? *She* had to go?

'If that happens I don't know who would go, but there's one big problem at the moment.'

'What's that?'

'Money.' She shrugged. 'You know we don't have much at the moment.'

'You don't have much ever.'

'We can't afford two homes. Simple mathematics. The only trouble is, now it's out in the open, it might just become utterly unbearable.'

'So we all stay together, anyway.'

'I guess so.'

'So you'll just have to work it out?'

'I suppose . . .'

Dino felt a cloud lift off him. Everything was going to be all right. It wasn't his responsibility anymore. He had no more power. Great! He smiled, then paused, wondering vaguely why his mother was glaring at him. 'Can I go to school now?' he asked.

'I guess so,' she said, and he had his bag on his shoulder and was off down the road before she could say another word.

23
This is Me

The week after the party there was a youth club on at the school for Year Eleven and the sixth form. Dino, Ben, Jonathon and the other lads didn't very often go to these dos, but this time they were all meeting up.

Wood End School lay between two roads, one of them the main road leading into Wood End, and the other a busy A-road leading on to the motorway connections and nearby towns. Crab Lane connected the school with these two roads. It was a quiet road, blocked off at one end to stop it being used as a shortcut. The cracked tarmac was lined with old rhododendron trees, behind which stood a handful of big detached houses set back. Under cover of the rhododendrons were a number of nooks and crannies where generations of Wood End students had smoked their cigarettes and spliffs, drunk their beer, cider and alcopops and kissed and fondled their boyfriends and girlfriends. It was here that Dino had had his first serious kiss, and that he and Ben had seen their first fanny. It belonged to Julie Samuels in the year below theirs. It was a dark night, and Dino had lit up with a Zippo lighter, which he held so close Ben thought for a second he was going to set fire to it.

One of these hideaways, near the far end of the lane, had been formed from the space left by a couple of cypress trees, felled years before. One of the rhododendrons had snaked a long, low branch from one side of the space to the other, which made a bouncy seat, and the old stumps from the cypresses made another two. Dino, Ben and Jonathon went there to smoke some weed with Fasil before the dance. Dino and Fasil sat themselves down on the bouncing branch, while Ben and Jonathon crouched low on the sawn off-stumps on the dusty dry ground. It was early summer, still light, but the rhododendrons filtered most of it out and the boys sat in dusky silence as Fasil rolled up. His lighter flared and the red tip glowed like a coal.

'Nice stuff,' whispered Ben, wheezing on a lungful.

'It's skunk,' said Fasil.

Ben handed it on to Dino, who had his and handed it on to Jonathon.

'Skunk,' hissed Jonathon.

'It's skunk,' whispered Ben.

'Skunk,' said Dino.

'Skunk,' said Fasil.

All four of them laughed quietly down their noses, and then laughed again at the noise they were making. Jonathon handed the spliff back over to Fasil. The stump he was sitting on had speeded up. It was travelling at about seventy thousand miles an hour.

'Seeing Deborah tonight?' whispered Dino.

'Yeah.'

'How's it going?'

'Dunno.'

'Good luck with it, mate.'

'Thanks.' The spliff end flared up in the hushed darkness. They could just about see each other in outline. 'You seeing Jackie?'

'Yeah.'

'How's it going?'

'Great.'

'Great.'

'Hey,' whispered Jonathon a moment later. 'Look at these two. They're the two non-shaggers.'

'That's right, Fas and Ben the non-shaggers.'

'I'm shagging someone,' said Ben.

'Who?'

'Miss Young.'

Snorts of amusement went round the dark space.

'And me, I'm shagging someone too, I'm shagging everyone,' said Fasil, and he suddenly jumped up and started dancing around, swivelling on the dry dirt floor, hand jiving in front of his trousers. The other three cracked up laughing, holding their sides and wheezing helplessly into the darkness. Not being able to make a noise made it all the funnier. 'Me, yeah, I've 'ad 'em all. Look! This is me shagging everyone! This is me shagging the Queen, you know, man, I've done the Queen and I've done the Prime Minister's wife, me, I have. Cheree, baby!'

'Urrrgh,' they all wailed.

'Yeah, I've had anything, I have. I've had Carol Vorderman, Geri and Posh, Zoë Ball. I've had all your sisters and your mums, everyone, man!' Fasil whirled round on his heels, poking and pushing in all directions like a demon, shagging half the kingdom. It was hilarious. Dino, Jonathon and Ben rolled off their seats and tried not to hoot out loud.

'Here...here, what's this!' Jonathon jumped up, stretched himself in a cup shape as if he was spread over the back of an elephant and began humping.

'What's this? What's this?' he hissed.

'What?'

'This is me shagging Deborah.'

They were in fits. Dino developed a stitch from too much laughing.

'Shut up!'

'Ssssh! Someone'll hear!'

'Shit, that's so funny!'

'Here – what's this?' Dino jumped up, put one hand behind his head and did more pelvic thrusts. 'This is me doing Jackie standing up!'

Howls of laughter. Dino collapsed onto his haunches and hands.

'What's this? What's this?' Ben jumped up and lay flat on the ground, hands rigid by his sides in the dark. 'This is me lying down staring up Miss Young's minge while she gives me a blow job.'

'You filthy bastard! That's sooooo filthy, you bastard!'

'What's this?' Dino got back up and did Jonathon staggering about with his head stuck up Deborah's fanny, but Jonathon objected.

'You're only allowed to do your own!' So Dino did himself, trying to kneel without getting his trousers

190

dirty, thrusting and walking forward at the same time.

'This is me shagging Jackie from behind while she tries to crawl away! Come back here! Come back here! Come back here!' he hissed. Then Jonathon did doing Deborah first from the front, then behind, walking in a vast circle to do it; then Ben did being tied spread-eagled to the bed while Miss Young jumped about on top of him. Then Dino did shagging Jackie while he leaned on a tree eating a Twix bar. It was just so bad and so funny.

'You lot are sick. You're misogynists, that's what you are,' said Fasil.

'You started it!' objected Jonathon.

'Not with my own girlfriend! You ought to have more respect for your girlfriends. Look! This is me shagging all three of your girlfriends at the same time!' He jagged about to three points of the compass.

'You gotta do your own!' said Dino.

'No, that's not fair, he hasn't got one!'

'Ben hasn't got one either…'

'I'm only *imagining* shagging Miss Young,' said Fasil. 'It's the other two I'm really doing it to.'

'You leave Jackie out of it,' Dino told him, and they all stared at him to see if he was serious. He stared back at them, impassive in the half light.

'And you know what?' said Fasil. 'I'm gonna tell them, too. I'm gonna say to them that you guys *watched* me shagging them and you didn't care!'

'But we wouldn't do it if they were here. Christ! Imagine if they were here!'

At the thought of them being here, all four cracked up

191

and fell over again. They were convulsed.

'Anyway,' said Ben. 'You guys are disgusting. I agree with Fasil. You should show more respect.'

'Bastard,' said Dino.

'Let's go,' said someone, and then they were outside blinking at the light, saying hi to some friends on the road before they knew what was what.

Jonathon walked slowly around the dance floor. Deborah wasn't there yet. He sipped lager out of a Coke can and breathed slowly. His stomach had slowed down from 70,000 to a steady 300 or 400 mph.

'And . . . relax,' he said to himself.

The dance floor looked like a shadowy coral reef with brightly coloured fish swimming in and out of the sunlight. The teachers stalked about the edges like barracudas. The school was in fancy dress. Too many images! thought Jonathon, but he couldn't stop himself. Look at the girls! They were like a hundred species of exotic butterflies who had just emerged from the grub of their school-day selves. No more jumpers and jeans – it was low cut tops and short skirts, make-up, glitter, everything beautiful and exotic. All that skin – he could see so much skin! He never knew that the girls in his class had so much skin! Whole parts of them were practically stark naked.

He hadn't realised it before but almost every single one of the girls he went to school with was utterly desirable. When had they become so gorgeous? Why? Was it just their idea of fun? Was it a trap? Could it be that they actually wanted some spotty boy – maybe even some spotty boy like him – to come up and dance with them? Or kiss them? Or touch them and run his hands over them and under them and . . .

Jonathon lurched across the floor and suddenly came face to face with Susan Mallary. She had broad shoulders and a deep bosom. Jonathon was just stopped dead in his tracks by her cleavage.

'Wow,' he breathed. 'Susan! I never knew. I mean – you look amazing. You don't normally look gorgeous. What have you done to yourself?'

Susan laughed and spread her arms and shook her chest to show herself off. Before she knew what was going on, Jonathon had stepped into her arms and pushed up against them. He froze, realising he might have been too forward.

'Dance?' he croaked.

'OK,' she replied. Fortunately it was a slow one. They began to waltz clumsily around each other. Jonathon was amazed that he had got himself so close to those big, beautiful breasts.

Christ, I've asked someone to dance, he thought. He'd never had the courage to do it before. He clung onto her and stepped cautiously around her feet.

Two tracks later, Jonathon still hadn't thought of anything to say. She extricated herself by saying, 'Can we dance further apart?' They jiggled about in front of each other for a while, but the attraction had disappeared. Jonathon excused himself and scurried away to try and remember what he had said, in case he was ever brave enough to ask someone to dance again. He went over to stand by a pillar and sighed deeply. That had been so nice, but he felt embarrassed that he'd had nothing to say.

Deborah appeared in front of him with a little smile.

'Oh, hi,' he said.

'I hear you've been unfaithful to me,' she told him.

'It was just a dance.'

He looked closely at her, but couldn't work out if she was displeased or just didn't mind. She stood and watched the dance floor with him for a minute or two and then said, too seriously, 'Come for a walk with me?'

'All right.'

'I'll just get my coat. See you in the foyer?'

Jonathon tried to sneak out without being spotted. He nearly made it too, but Ben was lurking by the doors.

'What are you doing here?' asked Jon.

'Just taking a rest. What about you?'

Jonathon paused, but Deborah materialised by his side.

'Oh, you're off?' Ben asked.

'Yeah.'

'OK, have a nice time.'

Deborah led the way out and Jonathon cast his friend such an anxious glance that Ben gestured with his hands...Go on, get on with it, go on, it's all right. Jonathon paused a moment longer to look back inside. It was hot and dark and bright. He could have gone staggering from girl to girl in a fever if only...

'Would you rather stay?'

'No, no, of course not.'

They stepped out together and disappeared into the darkness. Ben turned back into the building and cautiously picked his way towards the dance floor. He'd have liked to get a few dances in, but there was no chance of that. Miss was hanging about the edges with her radar turned up full, keeping an eye on him.

Deborah and Jonathon walked out of the school towards the rhododendron drive, with nothing to say. It was awful. Jonathon tried to rattle on about school, or friends, but it all fell dead between them. At last she turned round and asked him if he'd made up his mind yet.

'Nearly,' he said.

Deborah looked sadly at him. 'You're taking too long,' she said.

'I know, I know, I know.'

'I'd rather be just friends than this. If you don't want to just say so.'

'Yes, I know.'

'So what's the problem?'

In order to stop her talking as much as anything else, Jonathon kissed her. Deborah kissed him back, pushing herself into him. Mr Knobby rose up at once.

'He seems to like me,' she said.

'Oh, Mr Knobby says yes, all right.'

They walked on a bit further, until they came to another little nest hidden away amongst the bushes. Jonathon guided her into it, pushed her gently up against a tree trunk and kissed her again, leaning into her. Once again, a flood of hormones rushed through him. It was like being hit on the back of the head with a frying pan. He stood back and looked at the ground.

'It's damp,' he said regretfully.

Deborah took off her little jacket and laid it down.

'We should use mine,' began Jonathon.

'I don't mind.' She took his hands and together they sat down on the coat and began to kiss again. Jonathon untucked her clothes. He fumbled with one hand at her bra strap, and she sat up and did it for him. Then, with a sigh, the two lovers lay down, half curled up on Deborah's jacket and kissed deeply.

'You're beautiful,' he whispered.

'In the dark.'

'My hands think you're beautiful,' he told her.

'That's a lovely thing to say,' she said. A little later she took his hand and pushed it down her tights.

'See if I'm beautiful down there, too,' she whispered.

She was.

'Do you?' asked Jonathon.

'With you I do – but not here.'

'No, not here.'

'Somewhere comfortable... You still haven't told me your answer.'

'I think it must be yes, mustn't it?' Jonathon said. They kissed, slowly and luxuriously and there in the darkness, Jonathon felt himself relax.

'You sure?' she whispered.

'Yeah.'

'Sure sure?'

'Sure sure sure.'

'It took you a long time to make up your mind.'

'I just...I don't know if I want a girlfriend. Except now I've got one, I'm glad it's you.'

They kissed again. He tried to rush with his tongue, but she held his face and brushed her lips against his very slowly. 'When, then?' he croaked.

'Slow down, tiger,' she laughed. 'Somewhere soon. We'll see.'

'Kiss me again like that,' he begged.

'Like what?'

'Like this. Slow...'

It was so lovely, Jonathon would have liked that moment to last forever, but they heard voices approaching and they froze, clinging together in the darkness.

'Oh, come on,' said a boy.

'I said no,' said a girl.

Inside their leafy cover, Debs and Jon looked at each other and smiled conspiratorially. It was Dino and Jackie.

'Why not?'

'Dino! I thought we'd put a stop to this.'

'That was shagging, I'm not talking about shagging. I want to...'

'We're not going to do that tonight.'

Dino laughed. Jackie was being crisp, but it wasn't clear whether he was teasing her or pushing her. Both probably.

'Come on, don't you want it?'

'I said no.'

'What about a bit of finger?'

'Don't be crude.'

'You like it normally.'

'I didn't say I didn't like it, I said I don't want to do it tonight.'

'Go on. Come here . . .'

There was a pause while Dino presumably kissed her. Then a bit more noise.

'I said, No.'

'Go on. Feel yer tits.'

'No.'

'Bit of finger.'

'No!'

'Just one.'

'No!' Jackie laughed at him. 'You dope.'

'Feel that,' said Dino. They could only guess in the dark. Jackie giggled at him.

'That's enough of that. Walk me up the lane and back. Just be together.'

The couple walked on. Jon and Deborah listened to the voices and footsteps disappearing and then began to kiss again. But Deborah was getting uncomfortable. They'd found a boggy bit.

'I'm getting damp,' she said. They got up. She dusted down her skirt and pulled on her jacket while Jonathon watched sadly.

'That was so nice. Can we do it again?' he asked.

'I'm a bit damp.'

'We can use my top this time.'

Deborah smiled. 'All right. Since we're going out together.' He took off his top, laid it down for her in an exaggerated gesture. She lay down and he snuggled in beside her and eased himself half on her.

'Is that all right?'
'You're crushing me,' she giggled.
He moved a bit. 'Like that?'
'That's lovely.'
'Undo your bra like you did last time,' he begged.
'Like this.'
'Like that. And that other button . . .'
'That one?'
'Lovely. Lovely. Lovely.'

24
Cool or What?

That weekend, Dino had his first date with Zoë. He was apprehensive about it – he hadn't said a word about her to anyone and he was worried about being seen. This two-timing business took a lot of nervous energy. He was looking forward to shagging her, of course, but in the end it didn't happen. Oddly, he wasn't sorry at all.

Zoë took what she wanted without a care what anyone else thought of it, but she had her pride. Dino had a few things to prove before she'd condescend to use him again. They met in town and Dino suggested a walk down the river. They walked hand in hand and kissed under Caversham Bridge. Dino's blood fizzed like champagne.

'Let's go somewhere. Let's do it,' he said.

'I don't think so,' she told him. 'Things went a bit too fast last time.' Dino grinned at her. She let him put his hand briefly up her top, but not down her jeans. At one point she almost gave in and let him fumble open the button, but then she took his hand away and got a little cross. Dino smiled happily. He was enjoying himself. He could wait – a bit.

'You're too much,' he growled in her ear. 'You don't know what you do to me!' Zoë hung around his neck and looked up at him blankly. Without even meaning to, he'd made her melt. She wasn't used to melting. If he'd put his hand down her jeans now, she wouldn't have stopped him.

They walked along the river and then back into town, where he bought her coffee and a pastry. He was sweating in his big coat. She teased him about his dress sense, without realising he'd only worn it so she had something to lie down on. All in all they had a really nice afternoon. He left her at the bus station with a kiss and went back for a date with Jackie after tea.

Two girlfriends. Was that cool or what? The way things turned out for him! It was like magic. He didn't have to think about it. He didn't even have to do anything. He just sort of hung out and it all fell into place. Which was, he supposed, the very essence of cool.

'I ought to trust myself more,' realised Dino.

Not only had he someone to shag, but he had taken the pressure off Jackie. She was going through a difficult patch for some reason and this gave him the opportunity to be understanding, to stand back a bit until she got herself together and at the same time give Zoë a taste of better things.

That last bit made him blush a little, but face it – it was true. You had to have the courage of your convictions. He was It. If there was a higher number than One, it'd be called Dino. Zoë was OK but normally, he'd be out of her class.

Even when he ballsed it up he got it right. Look for example at that business with his mum. At the time, blabbing in front of his dad had felt like a bad mistake, but now look. Result! The affair was out in the open. They were going to work it out. His mother had said so. The marriage was saved – thanks to him.

Even as Dino lay in bed that Sunday evening, congratulating himself on how he had saved his parents' marriage, they were downstairs doing a few sums. Things weren't as bad as Kath at first thought. There wasn't a lot of money but with some careful budgeting, renting a small flat was not impossible.

Kath smiled at the thought; Mike watched her coldly.

'Or we could work it out,' he said.

'Things have gone too far for that,' she said emphatically. 'It won't be so bad.'

'Don't tell me how bad it's not going to be,' snapped Mike. 'Bad for who? The one who stays here or the one who has to go and get the poky little flat and access every other weekend?'

'You agreed, Mat is too small, I have to stay with him.

Mike looked away. 'It'll take a few months to sort out,' he said.

'A few months? We could do this in weeks.'

Mike paused. 'I haven't agreed yet.'

'Yes, you bloody have, don't back out now!'

He glared at her. 'It's all right for you. What are you giving up? Your home? No. And don't say your marriage because you haven't wanted that for years.'

'And you have.'

'Yes, actually, I have.'

Kath looked at him. He'd had affairs in the past, one that she knew of, anyway. 'I wouldn't have guessed,' she said.

He pulled a face. 'What do you think love is, anyway, some sort of joint bank account? We all do stupid and selfish things over the years, me as well as you. People get through it.'

But she was determined. 'Well, we haven't.'

'It's not the only way. We could try to work it out.'

'No, Mike.'

'And there's the kids.'

'We can make it OK for them. It's better than the alternative.'

'Which is?'

'Living with parents who don't love one another,' said Kath, staring firmly into his eyes and uttering the magic mantra that all separating parents depend on.

'But I still love you.'

'But I don't love you. Sorry.'

He looked away, hurting. 'They've done pretty well out of it so far, despite the fact that you apparently haven't loved me for years, so please don't fool yourself into thinking this is for them. It's for you – just for you, Kath, and no one else.'

They both looked up to where, like bombs in their parents' hearts, Dino and Mat lay upstairs.

Dino was equally wrong with his assessment of how things were going with Jackie. Taking the pressure off? He was going on about it all the time. Of course, he didn't see it like that. He was just teasing her. Making light of it, really. He was barely able to let half an hour go by without some reference to how good he was being. There were endless little jokes about did she want a bit of dicky, or a few fingers, or how frigid she was, what a treat she had in store and so on. It was driving Jackie mad.

As for Zoë/Siobhan, Dino had no idea. Zoë was a beast with a very short attention span and he was safe only for as long as he could keep her amused, which was unlikely to be much longer than a few weeks. If he could hang on, she might just lose interest and simply allow him to drop off the edge of her attention. But one step wrong, and she'd pounce.

That weekend, Zoë had seen Dino at his best. For a few hours she'd been the centre of his universe. Whether it was because he wanted to shag her or hold her hand or make her laugh or stop her being cross with him, he hadn't thought about anyone or anything else all afternoon. He made her feel that he needed her. After the party he was some bloke who'd screwed her; that afternoon, she felt that she meant something to him. She was hooked. She was thinking, I was right. He really is a nice guy – and he adores me. Maybe I could actually go out with this one, who knows?

Zoë played it cool. She didn't rush things. She'd have liked to have rung him during the week but she didn't want to seem too eager, so she waited until the weekend as they'd agreed. It was a warm day in May. Dino didn't want to go into town so she suggested a picnic up the river. It was a very un-Zoë like activity, but she looked forward to it. She even cut some sandwiches and bought some Scotch eggs – he'd said he liked Scotch eggs – and a bottle of stolen wine to drink. They had a brilliant time. He didn't take his eyes off her all day. They walked along the river holding hands in the sunshine and found a quiet spot to go swimming in. They stripped to their underwear. It was freezing. The sun went in as soon as they got out and they had to run around to warm up and dry off. After, they hid themselves down in the grass, their underwear still damp. The sun came back out and he pulled her damp bra up around her neck and her damp knickers halfway down her thighs, and she had him in her hand until he spurted all over her hip. They giggled and wiped her clean with dock leaves, and Dino looked so sad when it was time to go home.

There was another date during the week, at the cinema. They hardly saw any of the film. By the weekend, Zoë had forgotten completely about the blackmail anymore. She was proud of herself. She'd held him at bay for three weeks even though she'd been practically barking for it. She'd also kept to a policy of two years' standing and not given him her address and telephone number and real name; but that weekend, if things went according to plan, she was going to bring him back to her place while her parents were out and make love to him on the settee in the sitting room.

And so it might have been if her friend Sam hadn't got her claws in. Zoë hadn't said a word to her or anyone else about the blackmail – that just wasn't the sort of thing that happened to her – but of course, her friend knew all about Dino. It had been one of Sam's other friends who had taken them to Dino's party in the first place. This friend knew about Jackie. It had to come.

'The bastard's two-timing you,' said Sam at school one morning.

'What do you mean?'

'She was at the party. He's been going out with her for ages. They keep getting together and splitting up.'

'Are you sure? Are they together now?'

'Yes. And they were together at the party. Apparently they almost split up after it, and you know why? Because she won't sleep with him. She keeps holding it out and holding it out, but never will do it.'

'How do you know all this?'

Sam explained her information route. It was impeccable.

'You can find out if you don't believe me. Give this Jackie a ring. I have her number right here.'

Zoë shook her head. Sam was certainly right, but she might have been a little gentler had she realised that Zoë was smitten.

'See what's going on? He's got a girlfriend, she won't sleep with him but you will. He's using you.'

Zoë turned pale around the throat.

'Are you going to chuck him?'

'Chuck him?' said Zoë. 'I'm going to fucking destroy him.'

25
Ben

It's all getting a bit much. A lot much, actually. In fact, it was a bit much right from the start when I think about it, although that was half the fun of it, I suppose. But the final thing, where I thought, This is getting out of hand, came last Tuesday morning when I came down to breakfast and Dad was sitting at the table with a letter in his hand.

'What's all this?' he said waving the letter at me. 'Maths,' he said.

'What about maths?'

He handed the letter over. It was from my maths teacher, Mr McGrath. Apparently I'd been falling behind. He was concerned. He suggested that I should stay in after school on Thursday to do extra maths and catch up in the areas I seemed to be having trouble with.

Since when have I been behind in maths? No one had said anything to me about it. But it was right. School notepaper, everything.

'But he got an A for his GCSE,' pointed out my mother. 'How come you got so far behind?'

'Mr McGrath didn't say anything about this to me.'

And then it clicked.

'This is...' I began; and then I stopped. What could I say? That it was a forgery?

'Ah... It's probably a mistake. Actually, I know what it is, it's a circular. The class in general has been falling behind, he wants us all to stay back. You know how they get...' I shrugged. 'League tables.'

'Wood End is very good on maths,' said Dad.

'Yeah, and they want to stay there. I'll talk to him about it. He may not mean me.' It was so stupid. Why pick maths, she knows I'm strong on maths. That's why I'm doing A-level, for God's sake.

I collared her in the corridor at lunch time.

'Maths tuition,' I said.

'Clever, eh?' she chortled. 'I'd love to have seen your face!'

'What if they checked up?'

'I'm sure you're equal to that, Ben, you're a born liar.' She raised her eyebrows and smiled. 'See you then, sweetie.' And she was off before I could say another word.

She's the liar. All this secrecy and plotting – I hate it. I think that's what she gets out of it. Maybe she actually wants to get caught, the risks she takes. Perhaps it turns her on, or something. She picked maths exactly because it's my strongest subject. More risk.

What about that business behind the curtains? Risky or what? She's always trying to get me into dodgy situations like that. She doesn't care, she likes it, but it does my head in. She made me shag her in the props cupboard last week. Sounds great? Don't you believe it. It felt like the whole school was listening outside the door.

And then she gets really pissy when I try to stop her.

'What's up with you?' she hisses.

'I don't want to.'

'Yes you do, you're as stiff as a rolling pin. Here...'

'No!'

'Why?'

'Someone might come in.'

'There's no reason for anyone to come in.'

'They might not need a reason.'

She put a broom under the door handle.

'There.' And so she got what she wanted, as usual. I ought to just say no, but somehow... I mean, she's Miss, you know what I mean?

'I'd get expelled,' I told her.

'It's worse for me. No one would ever give me another job in teaching. That'd be it. Career, income, gone. I'd be practically a paedophile. I don't know what you're making a fuss about.'

Another thing. I've had four detentions in the past two weeks. Everyone sees how odd it is, they're always on about it, teasing me about shagging her. If only they knew! In one of them she even made me sit down and write lines. Lines! So what's that about then?

This. Has got. To stop.

Apart from it getting a lot too much, there's another reason. I mean, girls my own age. You know? Someone I can talk to. Someone I could really fall for. I mean, the sex with Ali is great but it's not like the real thing, is it? It's just porn with a pulse. I want to... you know. Well. I want to fall in love.

Does that sound stupid? Maybe that's asking a bit much. It's just that I can't be myself with Ali. It's like a big game. It's not real.

OK, to be honest, there is this one girl I really fancy, which is a bit stupid because I've not even spoken to her that much. She's called Marianne and I do actually think I fell in love with her, or I started to anyway. I can remember the exact moment. She was going out with this lad from our year, Toby. He was there, too. He's a big tall lad – I'm quite short, and I thought they looked a bit mis-matched because she's quite short too, and he looked all over-sized and awkward standing next to her.

Anyway, we were all standing around talking, me and a few of the other lads and a couple of girls, and she was there with Toby, standing next to him and talking to someone opposite her. There was something about the way she stood there, close to Toby but listening to this other person. It was something about the way she was listening. She was holding some books up against her chest and she had her head to one side. I must have been staring at her because I saw her glance at me, and I smiled, and she gave me a little smile back.

Funny. She wasn't doing anything at all. I might even be making up all that stuff about her listening and standing protectively next to Toby to explain it, but I was really attracted to her. She's nice, that's all. And good-looking. Not in the usual way, like Jackie, but really pretty and neat.

I got embarrassed after that and I couldn't speak to her, but I watched her whenever I saw her. She can be quite chatty and lively, but I think she does listen well. You quite often see her listening to people. I know how to listen, too. A lot of people don't do that, you know?

She's pretty ordinary really – maybe that's what I want after Ali. Actually, thinking about it, I noticed her even before that during a gymnastics competition. That's pretty cheesy, isn't it? She was doing the dance on a mat – you know that thing they do. I think she came second or third, so she's fairly good at it. I thought she should have come first. She looked really good. She was flipping herself all over the place and running about, but she managed to look really serene and calm, as if it was no effort at all. It was only afterwards that she went red and sweaty, like she could hold it off until she wanted to, and I thought that was so great. I mean, that she was such a nice person and had such a great body as well.

That was last year. I mentioned it to Dino and Jon in the end.

'Ask her to go out with you,' said Dino.

'What if she says no?'

'Better than living in fear,' said Jonathon, as if you could miss out on something and ruin your life. It was a bit of cheek him saying that, because Jonathon would never dare ask a girl anything, but it made me think. So after a bit, I went and asked her. I got Jon and Dino to go along with me to her classroom for moral support, went in and asked her. She was very good about it. She said I was very nice and she was very flattered but she was going out with Toby at the time, and so she couldn't. I couldn't work out if it was an excuse or not. And you know what? I was broken hearted. But only for a bit, so it probably wasn't falling in love at all really.

I haven't had much to do with her since then, although we're at the same school. I was a bit shy of her, I suppose. Toby left and went to a sixth form college, but as far as I knew she was still seeing him. But the other day I came up behind her in the corridor. She was talking to some friends, and as I went past she gave me this big smile. It caught me unaware and I smiled back and went on. But I think it meant something, you know. Anyway, I asked around and apparently she and Toby stopped seeing each other a while ago. So maybe, I mean, under other circumstances, I could ask her again.

The lads are always on at me to get a girlfriend, they can't understand why I don't go out with someone. Dino was on about it the other day – did I still fancy Marianne? – and I had to say I didn't fancy her all that much anymore.

I don't dare do anything about it. For one thing, I bet Ali would make Marianne's life a misery. I bet she would. She's doing drama for GCSE. Which shows that I don't think all that much of Miss, you know, because that would be a really shit thing to do. You know what I think? I think she'll do anything she can to get what she wants. I was thinking that the other day. About a year ago, I'd have given almost anything to have done all the things I've done with Miss Young. And I have to say, it was great, but it was only great because I wanted to do all those things so much. It didn't really have anything to do with who I was doing them with. And some of it, I don't think I actually wanted to do with anyone. All that risky places stuff — that's not my thing. I'm more straightforward, I think.

If I ever manage to get rid of her and go out with Marianne, I'll go ever so slowly. I wouldn't try to sleep with her on the first dates. I'll try to kiss her and I may try to slip my hands under her top, but if she didn't want it, that'd be OK. And I'd keep it dead quiet, but not in the same way I keep it quiet about Ali. That's a secret because it's dirty and dangerous; this'd be a secret because it would be private. Some of my mates are really horrible, the way they go on about their girlfriends. Dino's the worst. He's always going on about Jackie — well, he used to anyway. I reckon I know as much about Jackie's body as he does. I know what size and shape her tits are, I know what colour her nipples are, how she plucks out the hairs around them with a pair of tweezers and goes yip! when she tugs them out. I know she hisses and whimpers when she comes. I even know that Dino can fit three fingers up her fanny but she doesn't like it much. That's personal stuff, man! You shouldn't say that stuff to anyone, not even your best friend! I bet poor Jackie would be pretty pissed off, I don't suppose she imagines that's going round the school. But then maybe she does, she's not an idiot.

Jonathon's different again. He's filthy, he's always been filthy, but it's just a show. I mean, he never says a word about him and Debs. Not a word. He's very discreet really. They're very different people, but I envy both of them because, at the end of it, I'd rather be kissing a girl and having her tell me to keep out of her pants, than spending hours and hours rolling around the floor with Miss, watching her trying to imagine new ways of doing the same thing over and over again. In school uniform. On the table. Over the sofa. It's like being trapped in a porn movie. I ought to grow a moustache. I ought to get rid of her. But I don't know how.

26
Jonathon

So – onwards and upwards. And inwards. Deborah has Found an Opportunity. Her parents are going away the weekend after next. This is it. I get to lose my cherry.

Only it's not a cherry – it's a big, fat, juicy plum. I have it right here in my hand.

'Ho ho ho!' says Mr Knobby Knobster.

'This is what you've been after the whole time, isn't it, you filthy little stalk of gristle and engorged flesh?'

'Yep.'

So Mr Knobby is happy. He thinks, right up to me ankles in hot meat. He thinks he's gonna have a good time. Well, don't say a word but there are things that Mr Knobby doesn't know. Secrets a knob would do better without. Hush! I'd hate him to get *worried*, you see. You understand me? Exactly. A worried knob is a limp knob.

Mr Knobby Knobster says: 'You fuck this up for me and I'll never forgive you.'

I have reason to believe that Mr Knobby is going to be very good at sex. You see, he *likes* it so much. Whenever there's a spare minute, there he is, asking for a hand. And since he's my best friend I'm always only too happy to oblige. In the bath, in bed. In front of the computer screen. I live in terror of the computer going wrong and someone sending it in to be fixed.

'Mr Green? Your computer. Upon delving into the hard drive we found a collection of filth which, quite apart from reflecting seriously on your morals also happens to be illegal. I realise that a great many of those women were doing those things to themselves – we expect to prosecute them as well. Your son, you say? You hardly ever use the computer? It's news to you? Ah. Now you understand why he kicked up such a fuss when you insisted on taking it in to get it fixed? Right, let's make that public knowledge as soon as possible...'

It will happen. I know it.

I'd like to put it on the record that a great deal of the porn I look at is only looked at for the sake of curiosity. The sight of someone chained up with a set of nipple clamps and a pregnant dog is not sexy to me. It just amazes me that it's out there and can be seen by perverts like me while they're looking for wholesome babes to drool over.

Oh, my God.

Hush! Mr Knobby Knobster is fast asleep. Lean closer. I can reveal that...

No. Not yet.

Secrets! I have thousands of them milling about in the black hole of my psyche, although nothing as awful as the one Mr Knobby must never know. For instance, this is an interesting one, I bet loads of people have this one but never dare admit it. When I was fourteen and going out with my first girlfriend, I couldn't find her fanny. How about that? I know, I know – how is it possible to miss something like that? I mean, it's about two-foot long, when you get up close. Impossible to miss, you'd think. But I did. Her name was Lucy Small, in the same year as me, and she picked me up – the only thing I ever pick is my nose – on a school Geology trip to Wales. Your first girlfriend and you met her in Wales – that's humiliating enough, surely? We went for a walk to post some letters, and then went to hide ourselves among the trees by the roadside for some Heavy Petting. She'd been after me for a while, but I was too shy. She'd been out with Alan Noble the night before, and he came back into the cabin and made us all sniff his finger to show that he'd been there. She only did it to make me jealous. So. I felt her tits – see, I'm not a complete goof, I knew where they were – and then she undid the button to her jeans, and I put my hand down and . . . it wasn't there. Nothing. I was amazed! What was going on? Was she deformed? Had I been unlucky enough to get a girlfriend with *no fanny*? Should I say something sympathetic – oh dear, no fanny, that's a stroke of bad luck. Or was I making some sort of mistake? That seemed the most likely, so I scratched about her bush, up down, all around, but there was no doubt about it: no fanny. Amazing.

That was obviously cobblers, even I could see that. What about Alan Noble's finger? Perhaps I'd found it already but it was completely different from what I had thought. Perhaps there was some secret way of opening it up. Open sesame! You know. Or a button or a flap or

217

something. Whatever. There *had* to be some explanation.

I went back and let everyone sniff my finger in the vague hope that I'd somehow got it in there without actually realising it, but they all agreed. No way.

I wasn't all that worried, to be honest. It had to be something totally obvious that I just hadn't thought about. You know what I mean? Those patches of ignorance? You get them all the time. You just have to hang on and see what happens next. And then, of course, when the answer comes, it's so simple you can't believe you missed it, even though it was impossible to work out just the night before. This had to be one of those.

So, the next night, me and Lucy took another walk and went into the bushes, and ... exactly the same. No fanny. I scratched around for ages. I couldn't ask her, could I? Excuse me, where's your fanny? I know you have one, Alan Noble made that very clear, but I need to know where it is. Not possible.

That's when I got dirty and started feeling around in a more adventurous fashion, further down. She didn't mind, somewhat to my surprise. I mean, that was bum territory, as far as I was concerned. I knew that girls were supposed to enjoy having their fannies felt, but even that seemed a bit doubtful – although I suppose if she didn't have a fanny then her bum might be the next best thing. So, anyway – I pushed further down and found – bits. Fleshy bits. I probed, I felt – and then suddenly, right down there, I mean right down there practically up her arse – there it was. She let out a little gasp as I found my way in. Bingo! I thought ... Aaah, so that's where she

218

keeps it! Amazing! And how embarrassing for those poor girls, having your private parts about half an inch away from your dirt box. Planning! I mean, who thought of that? It isn't even hygienic.

All those lessons in biology and no one ever told me that women keep their fannies practically halfway up their backs. I thought it was on the front. I mean, that's where your willy is, isn't it? Not right down between your legs. It sticks out in front. When blokes shag a girl, their bums go up and down, not to and fro. It was a logical assumption that fannies were in the same place.

Of course, looking back, it's obvious. I mean, those diagrams you get in biology – it's all down underneath her. But that's just diagrams – you can't take them seriously. I mean, if it was down to diagrams you wouldn't have a clue what a fanny actually looks like. All that red. And those bits. And it goes right from the back all the way up to their navels, practically. You don't get a real sense of the thing out of a diagram.

But it explained a lot. Like, for instance, why my willy stuck up in the air. Think about it; if fannies really were on the front, your knob ought to stick straight out. I used to worry about that, too. I used to try bending it down so it stuck straight out, but of course it always just sprang back up again. That day with Lucy Small, I discovered the basic physiology of minge, and I've never looked back.

So now I know what it is, and I know where it is. All I have to do now is put Mr Knobby in it.

It's tragic really, but it's also unbelievably stupid. Only

someone like me could ever get into such a mess about something so duh. So. Here it is. Ready? Well...

Hush now! It's a secret. Mr Knobby must never know. If he does – disaster. Total utter disaster. No Sex Forever. It's because... Oh, my God, it's so stupid and embarrassing and awful at the same time.

Here goes. OK. Mr Knobby has... *I* have... cancer.

There you go. Look. Well, you can't see it now, while Mr Knobby is fast asleep, but when I get an erection, there it is, halfway up the shaft. A big, squashy lump. Cancer. It's obvious... What?... No, don't laugh, not so loud, he's waking up – don't mention the word, if he hears it'll destroy him. Whatever you do don't mention the word **CANCER**!

'What?'

'Nothing!'

'What!'

'Nothing!'

'Really nothing?'

'No nothing!'

'What was that about cancer?'

'Yes! Yes! It's true! I can't hide it from you anymore. There, that lump. That's it!'

'**Ahhhhh!**'

'Yes!'

'I thought it was a vein. Take me to a doctor, quick!'

'No!'

'No? What do you mean, no?'

'Because if we go to a doctor and it *is* cancer...'

'Oh, my God!'

'Yes!'

'You mean...'

'They'll have to *chop you off*!'

That's it. I have cancer of the knob. Luckily it's been dormant up till now, but if I do anything silly like repeatedly sticking it in and out of Deborah for instance, the friction'll almost certainly set it off. And then... Well, then I'll have to make the worst choice any man has ever made. Death – or no knob.

I expect you think I'm joking. I'm not. It's stupid, you say? Oh, yes, I know that. The truth is obvious. It isn't cancer at all; it's a vein. Knobs are veiny kinds of things. That's why the lump gets bigger when I get wood. It swells up, same as the rest of it. Cancer wouldn't do that – *would it*? Ah, but who says? Who knows? You? Really? You know that? You're a knob expert? How sure are you? I mean, OK – *maybe* it would, but maybe it wouldn't. We don't know.

The obvious thing, of course, is to take Mr Knobby along to the doctor. And we all know what the doctor would say. He'd say, No, don't worry, this is just a vein, Jonathon, nothing to worry about, everything's fine. But. *But*. Although he almost certainly *would* say that, he might not. He might, even just a thousand to one chance might, take a long cool look at it and say,

'Hmm. Yes. A tumour of some sort, nothing to worry about, it's probably not malignant but just to be sure we'd better do a few tests...'

And then.

221

'I'm sorry, Mr Green, but I'm afraid you have a nasty case of knob cancer. Amputation is the only answer.'

So, OK, it's stupid, but it's got me. And the other thing is, it's so *embarrassing*. I mean, could you do it? Show another man your knob and ask him to examine it? Worse, I've been seeing that doctor for years. I could go in on an emergency appointment and get anyone who happens to be there to look at it. But that would be worse. It could be a woman.

That's where girls are so lucky. Doctors are always examining fannies. It's the first thing you do when you get a fanny, you take it down to the doctor and get it looked at. If you're a girl and you go down to the doctor with even a sore foot or something, the doctor looks at your foot and says, Fine, OK, ointment, bandages, whatever – Oh, and while you're here would you like me to look at your fanny? And the girl, says, Yeah, sure, might as well, and off they go. It happens all the time. Girls are used to it. But willies are different. No one *ever* shows the doctor their willy. Name me one person. I bet you know loads of people who've had their fannies examined. You know, smear tests and things, they happen almost once a week. But name one single person who's shown their knob to the doctor. You can't, can you? There's even a profession dedicated entirely to looking at fannies, gynaecologists. Have you ever even heard of a single doctor who specialises in knobs? A knobologist? Doesn't exist. Now, see, if a man goes down the doctor's and says, I want you to check my knob out, you'd get thrown out of the surgery just like that. What do you mean, you pervert, you want to show me your knob? Right, nurse, ring the police. What's more, I'm going to put this down on your medical records... There. Tried to show me his knob. So that it'll go down in history for ever and ever for any doctor and his mates to see ever after. Tries to show people his knob. Not to work with women and children. And if it was a female doctor, it'd be even worse. You'd get done for indecent exposure. She'd start screaming, Put it away, help, help. And that'd be it. You spend the next ten years in prison, dying of knob cancer.

And anyhow. I'm shy.

It's a horrible trap, sprung on me by my own mind. The thing that truly amazes me about myself is that I'm actually more scared of being embarrassed than anything else. I'd rather die than get a doctor to look at my knob. Isn't that unbelievable? But can you imagine what life would be like with no knob? I'd have to have no friends, ever. They'd all be looking at me. See that lad over there? He's the one with no knob. Yes, I know. I saw it in the changing rooms. It was *horrible*. Even my family would be unbearable. My mother would be sickeningly sympathetic, my father wouldn't know what to say. I'd be a hideous freak.

I've been worried about it on and off for years now. I've developed a hand technique that avoids the cancerous area, avoided thinking about it, told myself it's nothing. For long periods I've managed to forget all about it. Then, every now and again it comes back, and I worry a bit, and then I forget again. But this time, now that it's actually time to shag, I can't think of anything else.

Please, please, *please* let me not have cancer of the knob. Nah, won't work — too much like a miracle. How about, Let me stop worrying about my stupid vein. Or: Please let the cancer, if such it be, go away. Or: Let my vein get small again. Or finally, and I know this is the wish I need to wish, because it's the only possible one: Please, let me be brave enough to go down to the doctor's and get some decent medical opinion on the subject.

I'd rather die first.

27
Dino

And then, of course, when everything is absolutely perfect it all falls to pieces around you. One minute, One and One makes Dino. The next, it makes the biggest heap of shit you ever saw in your life.

First thing was my mum and dad. The weird thing was, it all looked as if they were getting on with it. Everything was just like normal. Socks in the drawer, breakfast on the table. No, that sounds bad, but you know what I mean. Like, if you were rude to her he'd tell you off, that sort of thing. Normal. They went out for drinks, they kissed goodbye, they smiled and made jokes and teased each other, you know?

Except, looking back, there were these few things that happened – kind of isolated things that'd rear up their heads and then disappear again. There was the time I woke up in the middle of the night, in total darkness and there was this hysterical sobbing coming from the landing. It was horrible. I thought, Poor old Mum. I lay there and listened and then went back to sleep. But the worst thing about it was, when I got up in the morning, Mat whispered to me, 'Did you hear Dad crying last night?'

All the hairs on my back stood up on end. Really. I

didn't even know I had hairs down the middle of my back, but they went all bristly then.

'What do you mean, Dad? It was Mum,' I said.

'Was it?' he asked, all hopeful.

'Yes,' I replied. But the thing was, I knew he was right. It had been Dad.

'Oh, I thought it was Dad,' he said, and he looked loads more cheerful, the little prick. Because, you know, it's bad enough to have your mum sobbing hysterically outside your door – but your dad? Sounding like your mum? Arghhh! And Mat had felt more miserable than me because he knew it was Dad, but now I knew it was Dad and he thought it was Mum, which meant he'd given all the extra misery to me. I was so cross, I kicked him, and he wailed and Mum came over.

'What was that for?' she hissed.

'For being a crud,' I told her, and stalked out of the kitchen with both of them yelling at me.

See what I mean? And then Dad comes down for breakfast all suited up and friendly and dadding about the kitchen, slurping his tea and teasing everyone and then dadding off out of the door as if nothing had happened. Just like normal. And they were normal that evening and normal the next day and normal the day after – it made me feel normal, too.

Of course, they had to pick that particular Saturday morning just when everything else was about to fall to pieces. That's what really gets me – the way it all happened at once. They got me just after breakfast. Mat had gone to play footie down at Beadles and they came into the room like a pair of coppers and sat me down in the living room around the coffee table.

'You know things have been difficult between me and your dad,' Mum began. Oh yeah? I thought. So whose fault's that, then?

'So?'

She glanced at Dad and he said, 'So we've decided, the best thing is for me to make a bit of space and . . . and move out. Just for a while.'

'How long for?' I asked. My heart was going away like mad.

'For as long as it takes to sort things out,' she said.

'Not too long, I hope,' said Dad, and he gave me this stupid little smile, and I thought, You idiot. Why should *he* go? I mean. Who was it shagging other people in the front room?

I just came straight out with it. 'Why should you go?' I said. 'She's the one who was being unfaithful.' I saw her scowl at me. Well, it was true, wasn't it? 'Why should you stay here and he gets booted out?' I asked her, and I saw him look at her and she nudged him with her elbow. You know? Like, go on, give him the line, ACT TOGETHER.

'It's our decision. A bit of space . . . time to think things through, clear the air . . .' he mumbled.

'What, do you want to go?'

'Of course not.'

'I don't see why he should go,' I told her. I was so pissed off! It was unfair.

'That's what we've decided,' she said crisply.

'That's what *you've* decided,' I told her. 'Why should he

go? She's the one who was doing it with Dave Short...'

'Dino!'

'Don't speak about your mother like that!' he said.

'It's true, she did. That's what this is all about, isn't it? She fancies someone else, so Dad moves out? It's not fair. If you want some space, you should move out, not make him move out when he doesn't want to.'

'Dino, I have to go.'

'Then I'm going with you,' I said.

'You can't,' snapped my mum.

'You can't stop me,' I said.

'Tell him,' she told my dad, and he said,

'Well, we haven't talked about this yet, have we?'

'We didn't need to, we knew the children were staying here.'

'Why should he go? Why don't you go, you're the one who...mucked it up,' I told her.

'Dino, your father works full time...'

'Why should you get the house and both of us and everything?'

'Because your mother is the main carer,' said Dad. 'She does all the mum things.'

'You do all the dad things.'

'Yes but...' And the poor twat looked at her to help him explain why he was being a twat.

'Dino, this isn't a discussion,' she went. 'We're telling you. We've talked it over and decided that this is the best thing. You're old enough to understand. These things happen, however difficult it may be. Our relationship... needs a break...'

'What about my relationship with Dad? What about Mat's? So why's your relationship with him so much more important than ours?'

'It's what we've *decided*. We're telling you before Mat because you're older and we thought you'd be able to understand better...'

'So,' I said, 'if it's just a break, how long for?'

'Not long,' said Dad.

'We don't know,' said Mum.

'Well, let's put a time limit on it, then,' I said.

'You can't put a time limit on these things...' began Mum, but I said,

'At least then we know it won't go on for ever. Put a time limit on it. So we know what's going on. So we can plan,' I said, which was a good one, because that's what my mum always says. You have to plan things. Yeah, sure. Unless it doesn't suit her.

She looked across at Dad.

'Why not?' he said. 'We could say, three months? That'd be long enough for you to...have some space. That's what you said.'

Mum glared. I'd got her.

'Six months,' she said crisply.

'Four,' I said, and Dad said, 'Four,' at the same time. So Mum pinched her lips together and nodded and I thought, Oh, yeah? See? I knew it was her all the time. She goes off shagging someone else and then tries to bully him into leaving home. And he's stupid enough to go along with it, too.

I was furious with Dad, too, though. Letting her push

229

him about like that. I mean, it's a bit pathetic having to have your son stand up to your wife, isn't it? But I was really pleased that I'd got a limit on it. If it was up to him he'd just go and do whatever she told him to do.

'OK, if that's the way it's going to be, but I don't like it,' I told them. I could see Mum glare at me as if to say, you know – like, what's it got to do with anything whether I like it or not? 'But I still want to go with my dad. OK?'

And my dad looked really pleased, and my mum looked so totally pissed off.

'Well,' he said. 'We'll talk about it.'

'We don't have enough money,' said Mum. 'You'd have to get enough room for him. Somewhere with two bed-rooms and so on...'

'Oh? What exactly did you have in mind for me, then? A bedsit, was it?' he asked. And she didn't say anything, and he said, 'My God, it's right, isn't it? You want me out and in the cheapest little hole possible. What am I going to be eating in this hovel of mine? White bread and marge?'

'I didn't mean it like that.'

'Well, how did you mean it, then?'

'Well, there's not much point in...' She paused. '...in spending too much,' she finished, and she winced.

'Oh! Not much point in spending too much? So that you don't have to go without, is that it? So that the kids don't have to suffer getting a cheaper pair of trainers? So that...'

'Stop it, Mike!'

'Oh, stop it now, is it?' he ranted, and she began ranting back and . . .

I got up and left them to it.

So that was a shit start to the day. What a pair of dorks. It was only another year or so before I left home to go to Uni., they could have waited that long. It was for Mat, see. If it was just me she'd have bloody gone, but of course Mat had to have his bloody mummy. So she took her wishes into account and Mat's wishes into account, and me and Dad just had to trail along with it, and why? Because he's too weak to stand up to her.

I couldn't get out of there fast enough. It was shit, but I still had a life to get on with. I had a date with Siobhan.

28
Set-Up

They met in the Arndale Centre – the Aardvark Venture,
Siobhan and Violet called it. Dino was feeling nervous.
He'd heard a great deal about Siobhan's friend Violet.
Siobhan evidently adored her.

They mooched about at the bottom of the escalator,
something which Dino felt uncomfortable with, partly
because he was worried about being seen with Siobhan,
and partly because he was worried about being seen
hanging around at the bottom of the escalator. That was
for poor people. Siobhan was carrying an old plastic bag
with some books and a couple of items of clothing in.
Her parents, it seemed, gave her a clothing allowance, and
she'd spent some of it before Dino turned up.

'What about the books?' he asked.

'Oh, they always like me reading books. If I spend the
clothing allowance on books, they give the money back
to me.'

Dino looked at the books. They were heavy, thick
things. '*Picasso – A Visual Biography*,' he read. 'I didn't
know you were interested in art.'

'I'm not. It's just, like, it's for free, innit?'

'Right.' He flipped to the back cover. '£32,' he read.

'Christ, they're generous, your parents, aren't they?'

'Vets earn quite a lot, especially when they do dangerous work for zoos and things,' said Siobhan. 'Dad did a job for Woburn the other day – taking the tonsils out of a hippo. It's tricky, you have to put your whole head inside and if the hippo yawns you can lose your life.'

'Don't they use anaesthetic?'

'Just local. Hippos react badly to going under.'

Dino picked out another of the books. '*Stalingrad*,' he read. 'Wow. Do you actually read this sort of thing?'

'I'm fascinated by war material. Hitler and all that. You know?'

'Wow.' Dino goggled. He hadn't realised how clever she was.

Siobhan and Violet burst out laughing. 'You dope – it's a present for my dad. It's his birthday next week.'

'Right.' Dino did his best to laugh at himself, but it came out rather hollow. He poked back in the bag and took out a CD.

'It's a present.'

'For who?'

'For you.'

'Really?' It was 'Spangles the Movie'. He'd been after that one. 'Wow, thanks, that's really generous.' Dino felt mean, because he was, after all, only in it for the shag. He put his arm round her and she pressed herself into him and wriggled in a way not really suited to a shopping mall.

'What are we doing today?' he whispered to her.

'Later.' She pulled away. 'We have some more shopping to do first.'

They rode up the escalator to the floor above and made their way to Debenhams. Dino was dismayed. He'd expected to have a good time. Instead he was going to get bored.

'Do we have to do this now? Can't you do it later? I thought we were going somewhere,' he complained, but Violet glared back at him so ferociously he sighed and shut up.

'She just wants to shop,' she hissed.

'It won't take long,' said Siobhan.

The girls went to the Miss Selfridge area and started racking their way through the clothes, while Dino lurked on the edges, feeling like a spare part. It went on for hours. Violet and Siobhan conferred, tried on a few things, conferred some more, asked Dino for his opinion, went back into the changing rooms, conferred some more. Dino thought he was going to go mad with boredom. At last they'd done – that's what he thought, anyway. They walked off together through the store, but in the perfumery, they told him what was going on.

'There's a great little top, I've got to have it, but I can't afford it.'

'How much is it?'

'Eighty quid.'

'Whoh!' said Dino. 'Sorry,' he added, getting the impression from the way they were looking at him that something was required of him. Eighty quid was not something he could do anything about.

'We're not going to buy it. You're going to nick it.'

'What? No way!' Dino started to laugh, but they

weren't laughing back. 'Really? No way!' He began to back off. The girls followed him, scowling and pressing in.

'Come on – what's wrong with you?'

'Don't be a wimp,' hissed Violet.

'I'm not nicking anything.'

'Why not? Not scared, are you?'

'No. Yes. It's stupid. What if I get caught?'

'You won't get caught. Just do as we say.'

'If you're so good at shoplifting, you do it.'

'Oh . . . all right then. But I think it's mean of you,' said Siobhan.

'Are you really going to nick it?'

'Yeah, 'course we are. You can watch – see how it's done.'

'Er . . .'

'Perhaps it'd be better if he waits outside,' suggested Violet. 'I don't think he's much good at this sort of thing.'

'OK, then,' agreed Siobhan. 'Here.' She handed him her plastic bag. 'Take this for me and wait outside. We'll see you outside Marks, OK?'

'Right.' Gratefully, Dino took the plastic bag and moved quickly off. Those girls were crazy, man! Shoplifting! You always got caught sooner or later. Imagine the humiliation, the fuss, getting nabbed outside the store, the police, the court case, his parents finding out! Unbearable.

He hurried through the scattering of shoppers – it wasn't lunch time yet, there weren't many people about. The perfumery was quite close to the entrance. Dino moved fast. He didn't want to be anywhere near that store when Siobhan and Violet came through the doors with the alarms ringing and the plain clothes men moving in.

He pushed through the doors and the alarms started ringing. He froze in his tracks – had they already worked out that he was an accomplice? – and someone took him by the arm.

'Excuse me, sir.'

?

'If I could just have a look in your bag, sir.'

Security guard. Big bloke. He took the bag from Dino's unresisting fingers. Another guard had appeared at Dino's other side and was standing close up. The first guard peered into the bag. Dino looked round. A number of other security guards had materialised around him.

'We'll have to ask you to step into the shop, please, sir. If you don't mind.'

No one was touching him at the moment, but Dino was surrounded. The guard stepped to one side and Dino walked back into the shop. As he went through the door he heard a voice – he wasn't sure whose it was, Siobhan or Violet or both – shouting out in the distance,

'Oh, Dino, you're so *sexy*!'

I've been set up, he realised.

'I've been set up,' he told the guards.

'That's what they all say, son,' said the guard.

After that, the endless humiliation. The humiliation of being walked through the store. Look! There he is! A shoplifter. The alarms went off and they got him. So that's what they look like. The humiliation of being walked

236

into the security manager's office and being searched. The items taken out of the bag one by one.

'My, you're a little sophisticate, aren't you?' The man held up a bra, black, frilly, edged with lace. Suspenders. 'Like a big of leg, do you?' The knickers, God help us, had a split crotch. 'Well, well.'

The CD. Then the books, one by one. '*Picasso. Stalingrad.* Educated, too. Or are these for your dad?'

'They're not stolen, they're . . .' But he didn't even bother to finish the sentence, because they were stolen, weren't they? Bound to be.

'I guess we'd better give Waterstones and HMV a ring.'

The humiliation of the endless wait for the police. The underwear lay like a set of exposed genitals (his) on the desk, for everyone to see. Then, the police themselves. Their amused disbelief when he told them his absurd story. More poring over the underwear, the policeman looking at him curiously, as if he was making Dino a reference point for future perverts before he dropped them briskly back in the bag.

'This sort of thing is for old men, son.'

The humiliation of his parents being called in to see their erring son. The long, boring, frightened wait. Their faces as they came into the room where he was being kept, pale and scared as if it was them who had committed a crime. The shocked drive back home and the inevitable, awful interview at the end of it.

'Dino, is this about your father and me? Is that what it is?'

'I told you, I didn't do it.'

237

'Dino . . .'

'I didn't!'

'I know it's been very stressful. I know. But this sort of thing . . . It isn't going to help.'

'I didn't *do* it!'

'Denying it isn't going to make it go away.'

'Fucking hell.'

'Dino!'

'How dare you!'

'Oh, God. I'm sorry, but I didn't do it! I'm not upset about you and Dad. I mean, of course I was upset but I didn't do it. OK?'

A long pause. 'OK,' said his mother.

'What?' said his dad.

'No, if Dino is insisting, we have to go along with it. He's our son. He's old enough to know right from wrong.'

'No, he's not, he's a shoplifter, they just caught him in the act. He's upset. He's stressed. He's *disturbed.*'

'I'm not disturbed!'

'Well, you've never behaved like this before.'

'We have to trust him. We have to show him we can trust him.'

'Trust?'

'Yes, trust. Not something you're very good at,' snipped Kath.

'What?' Dino's dad looked as if he'd stung. 'Is that what this is about? Are you sure you're not talking about yourself here?'

'Don't be ridiculous!'

'Am I?'

'Yes!'

'Then what's all this about me not being good at trusting?'

Dino listened in disbelief. He'd just been through the most awful ordeal of his life and his parents had changed the subject already.

'You always have to give me ulterior motives for everything I do. This isn't about me. It's about Dino.'

'You get caught in the act and you want to be trusted and now he's been caught in the act and you want him to be trusted? I think a little honesty's the way forward here.'

'For God's sake, not everything I do has to do with me and Dave Short!'

'All right!' Dino leapt to his feet. 'I did do it! I admit it! OK? All right? Happy now? I've been doing it for months. Now just . . . leave me alone!'

Bursting to his horror into tears, Dino fled upstairs, his mother in pursuit. She stood outside the locked door banging it and asking to be let in, to no avail. She went back downstairs, where, shortly, recriminations and rage began to float up the stairs in suppressed whispers.

Siobhan wasn't finished with him yet.

After the shock had worn off a bit he thought about ringing Jackie for sympathy and realised in the same split-second that it was impossible. There was another landslide hovering above him. Jackie! What was he going to say to her? Look, Jacks, I've been two-timing you with this girl, and she framed me for shoplifting. No way. But – what if she never knew? His only hope was that it all remained a secret. Why not? It was possible. His mum and dad weren't going to blab. What if someone who knew him had seen him being marched into the shop with the security guards? Then he was dead – but if they hadn't? If it never got into the papers. If he never said a word about it to anyone. If his mum and dad kept quiet . . . then it was just possible that no one who mattered would ever know. Maybe it was even likely. He just had to bite his lip and hope for the best.

He had to see Jackie that evening round at her house. It must have been obvious something was wrong, because she kept asking him, 'What's up with you? Are you all right?' It was an ordeal, but somehow he got through it without anything dire happening. But when he got up on Sunday morning, there was a little note waiting for him on the doormat.

'That'll teach you to two-time me, you shit. And don't think Miss Jackie Atkins of 17, Canton Road is going to stay ignorant for long either. Fuck you. Siobhan. (Not my real name.)'

Dino stood there for a moment feeling it sink in. Jackie, he thought. Jackie, Jackie, Jackie. Please not Jackie.

He dashed up to his room and rang her on her mobile.

'Hi, oh, Dino.'

'How are you?' he asked.

'Fine. You sound a bit weird.'

'Have you checked your mail today?'

'What, on the PC, no, why?'

'No, snail mail. Letters.'

240

'Well, it's Sunday, isn't it?'

'Oh, right!' Just for a second he thought, Great! But then he realised – he'd had mail. No stamps. Hand delivered. She'd put the note through the door by hand. A similar note could be lying there on Jackie's doormat that very minute.

'Dino? Are you OK?'

'Yeah.'

There was a pause in which he tried to think of something to say. Just as he began asking her what homework she had to do that day, she began the investigation.

'Why should I check my post? Have you sent me something?'

'No! No, look...'

'Just a minute...'

'Don't go, don't go, no – listen, listen, I've got something important to say!'

'Dino, what's going on?'

It was there all right. It was there, lying on her doormat like a nasty little piece of life-threatening dog shit. He had to deal with it.

'I ... got done for shoplifting yesterday.'

'Shoplifting? You?'

'I was set up.'

'Who by?'

'This girl.'

'What girl?'

'Just a girl. I met her down the Arndale.'

'What, just like that?'

'Well, no, not quite...'

'Well, how then? Why didn't you tell me yesterday?'

'I've been done for shoplifting and I didn't do it. What am I going to do?'

'But who's the girl?'

'It doesn't matter,' he begged. He tried to laugh, but it sounded evil.

There was a pause. 'Tell me what's going on, Dino.'

She wasn't even a little bit interested in the stuff about the shoplifting and Dino having a criminal record. All she wanted to know about was the girl. Who was she, why was he with her, did he know her from before? And then...

'Just a minute.'

'NOOO!' he bawled. But it was too late. He could hear her feet galloping down the stairs. There was a long pause. 'Please, please, please, please,' chanted Dino in a whisper. He didn't hear her come back up, but he did hear the crackle of paper as she picked up the phone.

'Jackie, listen to me, it isn't the way it seems, this girl is poisonous, she really is. She...'

'You two-timing bastard,' she hissed. 'All the time! No wonder you were being so understanding! Well, fuck. Fuck. Fuck fuck fuck fuck! Fuck you!'

'Jackie...!'

'Shit!'

'Why do you believe this crap, Jackie? Why do you believe her and not me?'

'Fuck you!'

'Please just trust me!'

'Fuck you!'

'And fuck you!' he yelled back at her, suddenly cracking up. He was so furious – everything was against him. 'And fuck everyone! And fuck everything!' he yelled, but she'd already gone.

Dino hung up and stood staring at the phone, daring himself to ring her back. But what could he say? The truth about Siobhan was as absurd and unlikely as any lie. It ought to be impossible to believe, but somehow it was stamped with the mark of truth. It just slotted into place so perfectly. There was no way he could explain this one away.

He sat down in the chair by the telephone and waited for something to happen. He was there for ages hardly moving at all, except to cross his legs and shift position slightly. He was there so long that everyone forgot where he was in the house, and his mum came into the room without knowing he was there. She stood in the doorway, completely unaware that she was being watched, and he got a good, long look at her face. She was thinking. She stuck her finger in her mouth and chewed the flesh on the edges around her nail, staring into space. It isn't often you see someone standing there thinking. He hardly thought of her as his mother at all. What was going on in there? What was she going to do? What was she going to change next?

Then she saw him and she jumped into the air.

'Christ! Dino! What are you doing there?'

'Just sitting.'

'Are you all right?'

'Fine,' he said. 'Just fine.' And he left her to it.

29
Ben

'He's a shit,' said Sue.

'Yes, but he's a mate, as well,' I said.

'You should pick your friends better,' said Sue. Well. I've known Dino for years. I didn't pick him. It's just given. Jonathon started going on about how there was no point in cutting him off, how was he ever going to change if he was just left on his own and so on.

'He's not going to change,' sneered Sue. 'Why should he? He doesn't need to, he gets it all just the way he is.'

A couple of days ago, I'd have agreed with her. That's Dino. He's the original Teflon man. No matter how stupid he is, he never looks stupid. No one ever manages to tease him. Jon's a past master at teasing and he can't do it. He just makes himself look stupid. It's weird. But this time, something's changed. Dino looks pathetic. All the other times, he's behaved pathetically and looked cool, but now, suddenly, he's just an arse.

Not that anyone really knows what's going on. There are so many rumours going around, especially about this girl, Siobhan or Violet or Zoë or whatever her name is. Dino says she's seventeen, everyone else says she's fourteen. Who knows? Dino isn't exactly trustworthy. Shagging her at the party? You're not trying to tell me he didn't make that up — but then there's the letter Jackie's supposed to have got. And shoplifting? Dino? You can't imagine Dino doing something like that. And his parents splitting up. And it's all public knowledge. Everyone knows everything.

Half the girls won't speak to him. Jackie won't even look at him. You can't blame her, although I don't see why the rest of them should be so down on him. He won't be the first one to two-time someone. It's his friends that really get me. It's like they say, you can really tell who your mates are at a time like this. Suddenly, he's a wanker. Suddenly, he was a wanker the whole time and everyone knew it.

Well, OK, it's true. Dino always was a wanker. You have to be a bit of a tosser to be that cool. How important is it to be admired? All that effort. And overnight he's turned into just some idiot with more problems than he can cope with, trying to look good and failing. You'd have thought he was the most popular guy in school last week and now all he's got is Jon and me. Bang! Gone, the lot of them.

'He's had it coming for a long time,' said Stu. 'Thinks he's It, doesn't he?'

'Poser,' said Snoops.

Fasil took the opportunity to give him a good old lecture. 'You don't know how to behave,' he kept saying.

Even Jonathon had a go, but not to his face of course.

'Those who the gods most wish to destroy, they first give an ego as big as a small town,' he said. I had a word with him about that.

'Well, he wasn't there, he couldn't hear me,' he said.

'What if someone tells him?' I asked, and he looked horrified.

'Do you think they would?'

'Do you?' I asked.

You could see the light dawning. 'The bastards.'

'I think old Dino needs a bit of looking after,' I said. So me and Jonathon decided to do a bit of taking care. We go round to his place a few times a week, walk home with him, hang around with him at school when he looks as if he needs company, stay away when he doesn't. Go running over when one of the girls or the other blokes look as if they're about to start on him. We're a regular little emotional bodyguard, we are. Poor old Dino! Not that it changes anything, I guess, but it's nice to have your mates around you. And he's so grateful for it. You can read Dino like a book, he's so open. It makes you feel that . . . well, he appreciates you. And you know what? There he is up to his neck in shit but I still envy him in a funny way. I'm nowhere near as good on that front. Let's face it, I've got myself into a bit of a mess. I could do with a bit of problem sharing, too.

Let's talk about secrets, shall we? Let's talk about talking. That's what Dino's got, even now when he's lost everything else. He can sit and tell you about what he did and what she did and what that makes him feel and how he thinks she feels till the cows come home. All right, a lot of it is self-centred crap. He tells loads of lies, I'm sure he does. And he gets embarrassed, he's blushing all the time when he's talking about it. But he does it anyway. I

246

can't do that, neither can Jonathon. Look at all that stuff with Deborah. I mean, OK, I don't know, maybe he's having a good time and that's all there is to it. But what do you bet? Why does he look like he'd got a hot spike up his bum whenever her name comes up? I mean, what's going on there? Try asking him. He practically runs away from you.

There was this really touching thing with Dino the other day. He was in a right state. The rumours were at their height, everyone was treating him like a leper. This girl was thirteen, he'd date-raped her at the party by refusing to let her stay if she didn't sleep with him, she was on the run from some home, you name it. It was about the third day after Jackie chucked him and she was refusing to talk to him. He'd obviously decided that they had to talk, so he really tried to pin her down. She walked away like she usually does but this time he followed her, and she suddenly turned round and shouted at him to fuck off, right there in front of everyone. It was awful. Everyone turned round to look. I really thought he was going to cry. He made the best of it, you know, shrugged as if he didn't care and walked off, but his face had gone the colour of ash. I tried to have a word with him, but he couldn't even talk, he just ran off and hid in the bogs.

He really was looking awful, so after lunch me and Jon collared him and told him we were taking him out. He nearly jumped up and punched us.

'What the fuck are you on about?'

'Take it easy. We're your friends,' I told him.

'Some friends. Leave me alone.'

247

'Come on, Dino,' said Jon. 'You need a drink. Come on, we'll buy you a pint or something. We're your mates, remember?'

Dino stared at him wildly.

'You need it, mate,' said Jonathon, and he just gave in and came along with us.

He didn't fancy the pub, so we wandered down Crab Lane and ended up at my place. I cracked open some beers, we sat down at the kitchen table...and out it all came. The lot. His parents. There'd been rumours going around about that one, started by Jackie I suppose, but it was the first time he'd talked to us about it. That explained a lot. Siobhan, him, Jackie, everything, from beginning to end. It was awesome. Boy, he really was going through it. And halfway through it, he began to cry – really properly cry, big sobs. You don't see that very often. We just sat on either side of him with our arms around him. He'd have broken your heart.

'Is it Mr Blubberhead paying us a visit?' said Jon, and I could have kicked him because it's just the sort of thing Dino might get pissy about, but he just giggled and blew snot down his nose, so it was all right. It went on for ages, him telling us another bit and then cracking up and crying some more and then blushing because he was being so wet and then crying some more.

Afterwards, he walked back to his place on his own. We wanted to go with him but he said he wanted to be alone. It was just me and Jon. I looked at him and he looked at me.

'What about that, then?' I said.

'Well, it was a privilege,' said Jon, which was about right. We both loved him for that, for losing it so completely with us there. He tries so hard to be Mr Cool, Numero Uno, but underneath he's just a really nice guy. Somewhere. If only he knew it. I can't tell you how much I'd like to be able to do that — just to sit down and tell them everything that's happened, and then break down and let it all out, the whole filthy mess. Instead of having this bloody secret.

Secrets. What's the point? This one's doing my head in. If I did talk about it — that'd be telling, wouldn't it? She's always going on about it. 'Oh, you never told anyone, Ben, you never boasted, never said a word. That's so mature of you.' What's so grown-up about cutting yourself off from everyone else? It's not like it's illegal, I am over sixteen. I just want some advice. Jon or Dino or someone. A friend. The way she goes on, that'd be like high treason.

It's what people do with little kids, isn't it? This is our secret, just you and me, you must never tell or awful things will happen. So what's that all about?

Secrets are dangerous. They turn on you. You think it's all nice and snug, just you-and-me, our private place — and then suddenly you can't get out.

Do you want to hear the latest? She loves me. What about that? Lucky old me.

We'd just had this lovely big long session and we were dozing away, and she said, 'I love making love to you, Ben.'

That was a bit odd to start with, because it wasn't

249

what I thought of as making love. It was shagging. There's a difference, isn't there? Now I come to think of it, we'd been doing less of the raunchy shaggy stuff and more of the slow sessions in bed sort of thing lately. Which was fine by me, I preferred it like that. In fact, it might have been all my fault because I think I might have suggested it. Anyhow, so then there's this pause and then she says,

'I love you. Do you know that?'

Everything went very still. Actually, perhaps it was me going very still. I suppose I didn't want her to know how shocked I was. I was scared. But at the same time I had this stupid urge to tell her that I loved her, too. I almost did say it, which would have been a disaster because it's completely untrue. It was just like it was the polite thing to say. Do you think that happens in real life? Do you think people spend their whole lives pretending to be in love with someone just because it's good manners?

I waited a bit more, and then she said, 'Did you hear me? I said I love you.'

I said, 'Since when did love come into it?'

She sat up and looked at me with a crooked little smile. 'That's not the reaction I was hoping for.'

'What was?'

'I was hoping you might be flattered. Or even pleased,' she said. Then she folded her arms and looked cross.

'You never said you loved me before,' I said.

'Well, I'm saying it now. Just because I'm a teacher and you're a student doesn't change how I feel about you.'

'It's not that, it's...' And then I bit the bullet. 'It's... well. It's that I don't think I love you.'

I turned to look at her and she was staring at me as if I'd slapped her. For a moment I thought she was going to flatten me, but she just looked away and slid back down into the bed.

'That's hard for me, then, isn't it?' she said.

There was a nasty silence. You know, when you hurt someone? It's horrible. I didn't want to hurt her.

I leaned forward in bed. 'It shouldn't have gone this far,' I said. I thought about it a bit and then I said, 'I think I better go.' I pulled back the sheet and got out of bed. She lay there with her back to me.

'You don't pick who you fall in love with, Ben. It just happens to you. I was just hoping it might have happened to you at the same time.'

'I'm really sorry, I'm really, really sorry,' I said. I got dressed, thinking to myself, Well, that's that. I mean, things had gone too far. We were going to have to call a halt to it, that much was obvious even to me. And you know what? I was pleased about it. My heart was going away like the clappers, but I was pleased. It was over. I was out of there.

She turned round to look at me. 'You don't have to go, you know,' she said.

'I think I should,' I replied.

She turned over to face the wall. Just as I was going to the door she said, 'See you on Tuesday, then.' I paused. My heart sank. I didn't want to see her on Tuesday! But I didn't say. I'd just hurt her once – how was I going to do it again right away? I just couldn't.

251

'OK,' I said. I waited a bit, then I let myself out. I felt awful. I didn't see her the next day at school, and I didn't see much of her on Tuesday either, but she did get in a wink in the corridor as I was going to a lesson. 'See you later,' she mouthed. She looked quite cheerful, which I thought was weird. Wasn't she supposed to have a broken heart or something... or maybe that's just me being romantic. It made me feel better, seeing her all cheerful. I hated hurting her. So I went round there and – it was OK. We had a bit of a heart to heart. She said she understood. She wouldn't put any pressure on me, I was still very young, all that sort of thing. She still wanted to see me. The annoying thing is, I went round there determined to say, Right, that's it, but when it came to it I couldn't. I don't know why, I always thought of myself as quite a straightforward sort of person. I think I was just so pleased she wasn't angry with me.

'I still want to see you,' she said.

'Even though I don't love you?' I asked.

'It'll happen,' she said. 'One day the penny will drop.' As if it was some kind of lesson I was being thick about.

She brushed her skirt down over her legs. 'Don't tell anyone about this, will you?' she said.

'Do I ever?' I said.

'I'm relying on you,' she said. Then she leaned over and kissed me.

I did get some advice the other day. Not from where you might think. In fact, it's embarrassing, it's such cobblers. Really cheesy. It's the sort of sad thing that happens if you don't have any real people to talk to. You remember that remark she made, about how falling in love was something that just happened to you, as if it was like a stone falling off a cliff, or a car accident, or being struck with lightning, you know? Shit happens. She was always saying those kinds of things. Like she'd had an abortion once, and that had just happened. I mean, how's that? She didn't want it, her boyfriend didn't want it, so it went, like she had no choice.

'You could have had it if you'd wanted it enough,' I said at the time.

'No one wanted it, you can't keep a baby no one wants, that's horrible,' she said. Which is true but it's not the point. I mean, she could have, couldn't she? If she'd wanted it. If she'd wanted to want it – you know what I mean? There is a choice. And doing drama was because she got on well with her drama teacher at school, and going out with me had been this spur of the moment thing. It was like her whole life was something that just happened to her, which didn't add up at all to me, because as far as I could see, she just does pretty well exactly what she likes. You try stopping her. So what's she got to feel so helpless about?

Right, so this is the embarrassing bit. I really hate this, but it's true, so there you go. It was my brother's birthday and I was in a shop getting a card for him. It was one of those big card shops, with gimmicks and mugs and loads of cards. There was a section with those signs you put on your wall. You know the sort of thing. 'You don't have to be mad to work here, but it helps.' Or, 'Just because you're paranoid it doesn't mean they're not out to get you.' Crap really, but sometimes there's a good one. Well, why not? I guess it doesn't cost any more to print something true than it does to print crap, except the market's probably smaller. Anyway, it went like this:

'Love isn't something that happens to you. It's a decision you make.'

What about that? It just caught me right between the eyes. I stood there staring at it. It felt so — well, I don't know if it was true or not but it fitted in so perfectly with what I was feeling about Miss at the time.

'It just happens,' she says — and there it was in black and white. No it doesn't. You *do* it. And — this is the thing — there was no way I was going to fall in love with her. No way. I'd have to be off my head to fall in love with her. But she'd *decided* to fall in love with me. You see? It didn't just happen. *She* was doing it. Not necessarily on purpose, I don't mean that. But she was doing it; and she hadn't done it *with* me. She'd done it to me.

Maybe that's fairly obvious, but it was like a revelation to me. It just shows what a state I was in. I hadn't realised I could say no.

See? I told you it was crap. No one to talk to, you start taking advice from greetings cards. That really is the pits.

'No,' I said to myself. It felt good. It felt great. I walked home saying it over to myself. 'Love is a decision that you make.' No, Miss Young. No, Alison. Oh, no. Thank you very much, but no.' It sounded so good.

She never asked me about anything, right from the start. I couldn't think of one single occasion when she'd been doing sex with me in those weird places, you know, the stockroom, backstage, in empty classrooms – not a single one of them where she asked me what I wanted.

'No,' I said again. Then I started to imagine saying it to her, and you know what? It already sounded a bit weak.

30
Jonathon

It's the night before the big day. Mr Knobby's in fine form, polishing his head until it shines, arranging his shirt around his neck at a jaunty angle.

'You lucky, lucky boy,' he croons, looking at himself at various angles in the mirror. As Mr Knobby's personal trainer and physiotherapist, I'm giving him plenty of massage and exercise – not so much as to wear him out, of course – just enough to keep him on form, so to speak.

That's how it should be anyway.

It's begun to hurt. That should be the final proof, but of course it's no proof at all. The pain might be psychosomatic. I spend hours every day focusing on the afflicted area, trying to work out if the pain is real or not, which is actually the worst possible thing to do. Did you know that cancer is the final, terminal stage of neurosis? I read that somewhere. The mind and the body are one. If you feel good about yourself you get healthy. If you're depressed you get spots and colds and 'flu and things. And if you worry too much, that gives you problems too – heart attacks, ulcers – and cancer.

You see? The sheer neurotic force of concentrated

256

anxiety for hour after hour on my willy will make it go cancerous in the end even if it wasn't in the first place! Yet another vicious twist to the trap. Every minute that I spend worrying about it is a step closer to malignancy.

I hardly dare even think about it anymore. When I do, I try to concentrate on being positive but it's not easy. I've tried those visualisation things that people do – you know, you imagine that the stricken part of the body is being attacked by arrows and Cruise Missiles and things, or rays of calming, healing energy. But it doesn't work. It can't work because I'm neurotic, and as a neurotic my attention is about as healing as a bucketful of plutonium.

See? I worry about it even when I'm trying not to. I reckon all this worry these past few weeks has already made it go bad. Pretty soon it'll be so swollen with tumours I won't be able to get it out of my flies. And then – off with the whole dirty job, knobectomy, chemo, the lot. And they'll all be running around saying, 'Why didn't you *say*? Knob cancer is one of the most easily treatable cancers so long as you get an early diagnosis. If you'd only said a few weeks ago we could have saved your knob, your dignity and your life.'

It's at the point really where nothing else seems to matter. I just go through the motions. Deborah keeps asking me what's wrong and I can't tell her. I actually envy Dino – imagine that, envying the Lozenge! That shows how low I've sunk. All the time I'm trying to cheer Dino up I'm thinking, Caught shoplifting? Easy. Try having your knob cut off, mate – that's suffering. Parents split up? Piece of piss. Lost your girlfriend?

257

Tough. Try losing your knob, see how that feels.

He's lucky. At least his problems are real. His girlfriend really has left him, his parents are actually splitting up. He has been done for shoplifting. Whereas with me, it's all in my imagination. Not only that, but I know exactly how to sort it out, and I can't do it. I'm literally dying of embarrassment. But it's just a vein! Can't you see that? Just the biggest little vein in the world.

And what about poor Debs? I'm going to have to dump her, it's no good. It's not fair to her. I could tell her I was gay or something – anything to avoid having to stick it in and make it go really malignant. Either that or she's going to chuck me. I really am pissing her off at the moment and you can't blame her. Just as I was getting to like having her as my girlfriend! Actually, I probably ought to chuck her for her own good. What if cancer is catching? When she gets some spunk on her skin, she might catch it. My spunk is bound to be terribly carcinogenic. Or in her mouth. She might get mouth cancer and it'll be all my fault. If I actually do manage to get it up, I could give her cancer of the minge. You see what a shit I am? I pretend to be supportive to Dino when really I don't care. I don't tell Debbie that she might already have the early stages of cancer – she's had enough of it on her in the past few weeks, that's for sure. And I don't even feel sorry for her. I feel sorry for me!

★ ★ ★

On the big day there was to be no forgetting. It was there when he woke and stayed all day until Deborah

258

rang him at twelve to give him the all-clear.

He kept hoping. It was embarrassing going up the stairs and embarrassing again getting undressed and sitting side by side on the double bed, shivering slightly in the cool air. He wanted to look at her naked, but he was too scared. Mr Knobby vanished up inside him. Under the covers, he kissed her and pressed her up against him, and tried to remember how he wanted it to be like. He wanted to spread her and stroke her and bang her and roll her over and gobble her all up like the lovely big banquet she was. But there was no movement. Mr Knobby had gone into a coma, hanging down there like a piece of scrap meat discarded by a low-class butcher as being unworthy even of the cheapest sausages. All he could do was cling helplessly to her breasts like a shipwrecked sailor. After a little bit she fetched a blow heater to warm things up and gave him a massage to help him relax. After she'd done his back she did his stomach. Jonathon was horribly conscious of his microscopic member. He kept trying to get little glimpses of her body, but whenever she met his eyes he looked away in embarrassment.

'It's all right, you can look,' she told him, but all he wanted to do was hide his face in his hands.

At last they gave up. Deborah went downstairs and came up in her gown, with tea and toast, which felt like cardboard in his mouth. Afterwards he made an excuse and left, even though they had planned on spending the night together.

'It's all right, it's not the end of the world, it happens

259

to loads of boys, it'll come back,' she told him. Jonathon smiled a tight little smile. She showed him out, sympathetic but disappointed, and very hurt that he wasn't staying; and he couldn't even tell her what was wrong.

31
Thaw

Dino had spent the weeks following the disaster in a fog of misery and incomprehension. He was the golden boy, things like this didn't happen to him in the first place, and if they did, it didn't matter. Somehow he always came up smelling of roses. He'd lost his girlfriend, his parents and his self respect all in one day. He was heartbroken about Jackie – he truly loved her in his own way – felt helpless and confused with what was happening at home, and just plain used by Siobhan. If he forgot one misery, another came flying up to sting him. One of the most unbearable things was the way it had made him feel like a nerd – one of those insecure, uncertain speccy kids who wander round on the edges of things never fitting in. It was just awful.

It took a while for it to sink in that it really was over between him and Jackie. She'd come back to him, she always did. He sulked for a couple of days – it was a bit much just chucking him after what he'd been through, after all. When she showed no signs of contrition, he tried to speak to her and was rebuffed like a pair of dirty underpants.

Ben and Jon were both being fantastic – that was the only good thing that came out of the whole episode; he

261

hadn't realised what good friends they were. He asked their advice about what to do about it, and was pissed off that they both thought he should leave it. After further pressing, they suggested begging forgiveness and declarations of love, so he tried bombarding her with emails, but after the first one, when she replied she was going to delete any others, he got no replies. He tried ringing her. She never answered her mobile and after a couple of poisonously hissing replies from her outraged mother, he gave that up too. He had no stomach for further humiliation.

It began to sink in. She didn't want him anymore. And it wasn't just her. The whole school had turned against him. Suddenly the magic was gone. It was like going blind. Even complete strangers seemed to know that he'd become a tosser. Girls in shops showed no interest in him whatsoever. He'd become so used to them smiling and laughing and fluttering and chatting up to him, he'd just accepted it as something that happened. Now, they served him without a smile and moved on to the next customer as if, he, Dino, was just anyone.

It was shit; but there's more than one sort of heartache, and out of all his troubles the thing that was causing him the most pain wasn't Jackie. It was what was happening with his parents. Their relationship was like some vast giant asleep under the land. What he had thought of as hills and valleys, slopes and plains turned out to be the muscle and bones of the sleeping giant. Now it was stirring and all the little buildings and roads he'd built over the years were crumbling like ash. He'd had no idea how much he relied on them. Like his skeleton, he'd taken them for granted.

Despite what his mum had said about trust, it was obvious that neither of them believed his story about being set up. He gave it up after a few days and started to pretend that he had done it. It was so much easier. Anyway, if it was a choice between being a shoplifter or a mug, he'd rather be a shoplifter. He had hoped that after his arrest, his parents would postpone or even call off his dad moving out, but he came home from school just a few days later to find his mum poring over the local paper for flats. She even had the gall to ask Dino to help her. He stormed out of the room in a rage. After that, he was barely able to even stay in the same room as either of them. He was enraged with his mum for pulling his world to pieces, with his dad for letting her and with himself for being affected by it.

Things couldn't go on as they were. Dino was going out of the room almost as soon as they came into it. His mum tried to have a word with him, but he just sat there in stony silence. Eventually she lost her temper with him spectacularly, screaming and throwing mugs at the wall and pounding the table with her fists. Dino was amazed – he'd had virtually no insights into his mother's state of mind apart from that sordid glimpse through the window all those weeks ago. Afterwards, she was desperate with apologies – she had no idea she had that in her herself, let alone that she could show it to Dino. He coolly listened to her apology and left her to it. The incident convinced him that she was rotten to the core.

The following Wednesday afternoon, when Dino had a couple of free periods at the end of the day, he came back to find his dad had come home early. He made his son a cup of tea and a sandwich, put them on the table in front of him and said, 'Let's talk.'

His dad used to make him sandwiches quite often a few years before, when his mum was re-training. He loaded the ham in and covered it with mustard, mayo and lettuce – Dino had forgotten how much he liked them.

'Yum,' he said.

'If I'd made more sandwiches and done less work, maybe it wouldn't be me who's moving out,' said his dad. He smiled wryly and folded his arms on the table.

'So what are we talking about?' asked Dino through a full mouth.

'Things. Me and you. Me and your mum. You and your mum. All that.'

'She's put you up to this,' accused Dino.

'We still decide things together. I took the afternoon off.'

Even though this was exactly what he wanted, Dino was embarrassed. 'Is it going to take long, I've got homework?' he asked.

'I don't know.'

'Go on then.' Dino busied himself with his sandwich.

'OK. Well, for starts, I don't want us to split up, as you know...'

'Then why are you going along with it?' demanded Dino, quick as a spike.

'Listen...'

'You don't have to.'

'Listen! She's stopped loving me...'

'Do you love her?'

'You're not listening.'

'But do you love her?'

'Yes.'

'Well, that's not fair, is it?'

'Dino, will you listen?'

Dino took a breath and picked up his sandwich. 'All right, then.'

'Right. Where was I? The marriage is over, it's as simple as that. She doesn't love me, I can't make her love me. She has the right to put an end to it. But I do think, I do think...' He raised his voice over Dino who was about to interrupt. '...I do think it's the wrong time — wrong for all of us...'

'But me in particular.'

'You included,' said Mike carefully. 'I think she should wait, give it another chance. But, she...' He was about to say, won't wait, but that was too easy. '...she, she feels she can't do it. The thing is, Dino, when I said that stuff about making sandwiches, it was a sort of joke, but not entirely. Your mum has done most of the childcare, the mothering. I did my bit, loads of it, actually. But she's been Mum, and she still is Mum and if things fall to bits, Mum stays and Dad goes. If I'd done the childcare it would be the other way round, but I didn't...'

'I'll bet,' sneered Dino.

'It's the kids come first. She's been the main carer.' He shrugged.

'So you get the shitty end of the stick.'

'I get the shitty end of the stick,' agreed his dad. 'She gets the house and kids and a great lump of my income, and I move away into some little flat, yes.'

'It's not fair. It's . . . pathetic. It's weak, isn't it?'

'Maybe. Or maybe it's being strong. It's certainly unfair, but I do know that kids come first.' His dad shrugged and smiled sourly. 'I don't say I like it. I don't say I agree with the way your mum's doing it. But since she is, this is what I'm stuck with.'

Dino couldn't believe it. 'But that's just crap! She has no right.'

Mike shrugged. 'You'll have to ask her about that.'

Dino waited. His dad sighed.

'She thinks it'll be better all round to get it out of the way and sorted, since this is what's going to happen anyway,' he said.

'So you're just going along with it.'

'There's not much choice.'

'You could refuse to go.'

'Dino, this has been going on a long time now. Years.' Mike paused again, not sure what to say. Secretly, he didn't just think his wife was wrong; he thought she was being a cow. She could have waited one more year. Mat was only nine, he had years to go at home, but he was a robust kid and Mike thought he'd be OK. But he knew his oldest boy; Dino was a lot more vulnerable than he realised. Kath said she'd been dying for years in this marriage, but another one wouldn't do that much damage.

'Men!' she'd exclaimed. 'You always want more!'

266

'We'll have to see what happens,' he told Dino. 'Maybe when she's on her own in here with you guys she'll realise it's not what she wants, I don't know. But the way things are at the moment, someone has to go and it ain't going to be her.' Mike glanced at his son. 'You can come with me if you like.'

'Can I?'

'You're seventeen. You can make up your own mind. I'd love to have you. I don't know if it's the best thing for you, though.'

'Why not?'

'Staying here would mean the least change. It's your choice. I'd like you to come – I'd feel better. But for your own sake I'd stay here if I were you.'

Dino swore he'd think about it, but he knew the answer already. This was a nice big house, it was comfy. He wasn't going anywhere.

At the end of it, Dino still wasn't sure whether his dad was being strong, weak or merely simple, but at least he seemed to know what he was doing. Like his dad, he'd have to put up with it, but he didn't have to like it. He was going to stay, but he'd do his best to make his mum's life a misery for forcing this on him in the meantime. He felt clearer about things, anyway.

About a week later, something else happened that cheered him up. There she was smiling her head off at the bottom of the stairs as he came down in the morning. She waved a letter at him.

'Come in and read this,' she said excitedly.

It seemed they'd been on to Miss Selfridge. His mum had

gone down there armed with school reports and an account of what had happened at home in the months leading up to his arrest. The manager had been sympathetic, but cool. It was out of his hands, he'd said – leniency was up to the police. Kath ploughed on. What was the point of prosecuting her son for a stupid prank, which he maybe didn't even commit, when there were so many other people who almost made a living shoplifting? Didn't the circumstances seem rather odd to him – just walking out like that? She could promise him it would never happen again, Dino had had the scare of his life, he was a changed boy.

The manager had listened politely and distantly, and said he'd think about it. She'd held out no hope – but here it was. He was prepared to drop charges, so long as Dino would do some charity work. It was a deal.

Dino leapt out of his chair and threw his arms around his mother. Sorted! It was going to be all right. No court, no prosecution, no having to watch those awful knickers brought out in public and waved before the courthouse. Bliss!

'I thought they had a policy of prosecution,' he said breathlessly when he'd calmed down.

'They do. But you see, you're a good boy, it does pay off. One slip like that – he must have seen the sense in what I said.'

That was one ordeal less, at least. On his way to school, Dino felt good for the first time in weeks. Life was picking up. No court case, the talk with his dad that night. He was feeling a bit more like himself.

32
Beauty and the Beast

The place to tell her was definitely at school. It was cowardly, but common sense. Ben was confident that she could him eat for breakfast any time, any place, but the opportunity to cram him down her gullet surrounded by one and a half thousand kids would be severely curtailed.

It wasn't going to be easy. Goodbyes hurt, and Ben was a soft heart. All he needed was ten minutes on his own with her – surely that would be long enough to get the word 'no' out of his mouth? For months now they had managed – *she* had managed – to get them on their own for at least that most days in the week, but Ali had such an instinct for getting things on her own terms, it was like a form of telepathy. Somehow, on this particular Monday morning, she was permanently busy.

'Sorry, Ben. I have a crisis in Year Eight.'

'When then?'

'Don't be greedy. I don't know. Not now.'

Monday swept by. Next day, Tuesday, he had a date at her place in the evening. Ben quailed: it'd be like asking a hyena for a bone in its own den. He had to get her in school.

Tuesday morning he never saw her. Tuesday afternoon

came and went. It was getting scarier and scarier. Words like hyena, dragon, hydra, beast, monster kept coming up into his mind as the evening drew near. It was unfair, he knew that. She had loads of nice qualities. There'd been months of loveliness, but now it was over. He made one last-ditch attempt to see her – a suggested meeting in a deserted classroom after school, something she always jumped at. It would be dangerous – after school, no one about; and, of course, her plans would be different from his. But it was better than doing it in her flat.

He collared her in between maths and a free lesson. Somehow he wasn't surprised when, with an unfailing instinct she managed to be busy then, too.

'Crisis in Year Nine.'

'You're working up, it was Year Eight yesterday.'

'I have a parent to see. See you at my place. Here's the key, I may be a bit late.'

She thrust a key into his hand and rushed off. Ben stared at the little piece of metal in his palm.

'No,' he said. 'No.' The word seemed to have emptied itself of all meaning.

After school, he went for a walk in the pastures near her place to try and clear his head. Was it better to be there before her, or after her? Should he cut and run and tell her later by telephone? Leave a letter? Tempting! But impossible. It was just too cowardly. So what was wrong with cowardice? He who fights and runs away...

'No,' said Ben, and tried to imagine the word conjuring elementals, demons and dragons out of the fields, from behind the houses, like the hero in a computer game. The no-dragon against the yes-beast. Maybe it would even work.

'Give me strength,' muttered Ben to himself as a tessellated, green and red-winged serpent loosened its coils over the housing. The dragon benevolently spread its great wings. Ben set off for the flat.

She was already in.

'Where have you been?' she demanded as she opened the door to the sound of his key rattling in the lock.

'... went for a walk...'

'Christ. What a day! I thought you might have had the kettle on or something. Kids with their teeth falling out. Kids suddenly going to see their families in Pakistan for three months halfway through rehearsals. Great! Kids torturing one another with sparklers. I hate kids!'

Ben stared at her sadly.

'Go on then, put the kettle on, I need a cup of tea. Do you want a drink? There's beer in the fridge. Christ! What an awful day. I hope you're all right, the last thing I need is more bloody trouble.' She eyed him sideways and went to fling herself on the sofa like a huge, carnivorous beetle. Ben staggered into the kitchen to make tea.

'Placatory offerings,' he muttered to himself. Tea seemed hardly enough. Fresh meat would be better. Or a virgin. Give her something to gnaw on while he ran for it.

'What about you, how are you, you seem a bit off colour this week?' she taunted him from her lair on the sofa.

'OK,' lied Ben, and winced at how quickly he was being carried away from his purpose.

The kettle boiled. He dropped tea bags into mugs.

'No,' he whimpered. 'I have a choice. No.'

From next door came a terrible strangulated, groaning roar. It seemed to express agony, rage and lust all at the same time. He'd never heard anything like it. There was something chitinous about it, as if a giant insect had suddenly discovered its mouth had air, and was giving voice to the accumulated desires and appetites of its kind for the past three hundred million years. With a cry he dropped the tea bags and ran next door. Alison was stretching out her legs.

'What?' she said, looking surprised at his terror-struck face peering out at her.

'That noise...'

'What noise?'

'That... noise. Didn't you hear it?'

'It was just me stretching.' She leered at him. 'You're jumpy today.'

Ben stared in amazement at her and went back into the kitchen. What was going on? Jumpy? What had jumpy to do with such terrifying, primal agony? As he picked up the mugs, he noticed how the tea was shaking in the cups as if a dinosaur was approaching. The dinosaur was his own heart. He put the mugs down and walked three times round the room. Then he picked them up again and walked into the den. He put the mugs down. Put his hands in his pockets and said,

'Listen...'

'Go and get me a piece of cake, will you?'

'A piece of cake?'

'Yes, there's some almond slices in the tin. God! I feel like I've spent the day in hell. The day in hell. The day in hell,' she repeated, watching dispassionately as he struggled to speak over her and failed. Ben went back to the kitchen. He was feeling weaker by the second. He took out two almond slices, one for her and one for him, and took them back to the prostrate monster next door.

'Mmm. Hungry. God. Sit down, you're making me nervous.'

Ben was standing above her looking down at her, munching on his almond slice. With his mouth full he couldn't speak, what choice did he have? Eating: another mistake. He sat down and waited while he finished his piece of cake.

'Don't gobble your food.' She burst out laughing – it was a permanent joke to her to treat him like a little kid. Ben swallowed and stood up.

'Listen. I've been thinking about, you know, you and me, and . . .'

She began speaking a second after he did and just carried on. 'Christ, what a day, those kids need a tamer, not a teacher, what am I doing here, I should have gone professional, a dog deserves better than this, I feel AWFUL!'

She had to almost bellow the last word because Ben was not giving up this time, he just carried on speaking, his voice rising to compete with hers.

'I want to stop. This. Us. I don't think we should see each other ANYMORE.'

She carried on as if she hadn't heard, made no reference to the fact that he had spoken at all.

'Nice cake, I like almond slices. Boy, what I'm going to do to you when I've fed, this is just for starters, the main course is gonna come all over...'

He waited until she stopped. Had her eyes twisted like little stones in her head as he spoke? Had she gone deaf? Was she ignoring him? She drew a breath, and in the uninterrupted silence, Ben spoke again.

'I said, I don't want to see you anymore.'

There was a terrible pause. No mistake this time. She sat there and stared at him, looking shocked and scared. Ben took a step back.

'You what?' she asked.

'I said...'

'I heard you!' she breathed. She took a long breath and began, fairly quietly at first. 'You choose now to tell me, now, now to tell me, now, after the day I've had? You fucking want to tell me about it now? Is that it?' Suddenly, she flung the remaining piece of cake on her plate at his head. It was soft, but Ben headed for the door anyway. There was no doubt; he'd done it at last.

'Don't run out on me, don't run out on me, Ben!' she begged, but he was off. She rose to her feet, scattering the plate and its crumbs around her feet, and ran after him. She grabbed his clothes as he fumbled with the door and he slapped her hand away with all his strength.

'Ow! Don't hit me...'

He was scared she was going to hurt him. He wrenched himself away and burst out of the flat and onto the

274

landing. He just had time to see the shocked face of an old woman struggling outside her door with four bulging plastic bags full of shopping. The bags fell over. Leeks and a carton of milk spilled out onto the floor. Ben leapt into space over the stairs and bounded down them three at a time. On the landing above him, Alison screamed.

'We have to talk!' she commanded, but Ben was gone, down three flights and out of the door like a rat down a hole.

'You could at least have helped this lady with her bags. Aaaahggh!' he heard her scream as he opened the front door and exited the building. Ben ran on. The houses and people and cars flashed by. It had been the hardest thing he had ever done.

Afterwards at home, he was sorry about how he'd done it. He'd only been thinking about how to make it easy on himself, when it was her he should have worried about. She'd been upset. Now he thought about it, hadn't there been tears on her face as she ran after him? He'd thought at the time she was after his blood, but maybe she just wanted to talk it through. Just blurting it out and running – it wasn't very clever.

He felt too jangled to give her a ring that day. He'd get her at school the next day, and say he was sorry he'd handled it so badly.

But he didn't see her the next day, which was odd; he nearly always managed to bump into her in the corridor. Thursday lunch time there was a rehearsal for the school play, in which he was as usual helping with the lighting.

275

He was feeling awful for still not ringing her, and dreaded having to see her, but she wasn't in that day. It was announced at break that she was ill.

Ben knew at once; it was him. He'd done her in. But how? Headache, heartache or death, he had no way of knowing. Fantasies spiralled in his mind; the beast slaughtered in her lair. But she wasn't a beast. She was a person, someone who loved him and whom he had once adored; and he had hurt her.

He was still too scared to ring her that evening and she wasn't at school again the next day. By then he felt utterly craven, weak with failure to do the right thing. He swore he'd do it the next night, but when he got home that Friday there was a call for him.

She wasn't angry anymore, he could hear that. Her voice was flat, wounded. She was sorry. She'd had a bad day, it came at the wrong time. Of course if that's the way he felt then he was doing the right thing. Could she just see him one more time? She didn't want to end like that, in a fight on the landing. Just this one thing for me. Don't let it end like this for me.

There were no signs of tears or bullying but his heart was going like a dinosaur again. He stared at the phone in his hand suspiciously, but he couldn't say no. It wasn't too much to ask, not much at all, but he couldn't get the thought out of his head that it was some sort of trap.

33
Ben

The door was ajar. I knocked and she said, 'Come in,' in a little voice. I went in and she was sitting on an armchair with her hands resting on the arms looking very pale.

'Hi,' I said, and she said, 'Hi,' back and looked at me with a funny crooked smile. She seemed embarrassed. Something was wrong with her but I couldn't work it out just yet. She looked down very briefly as if she couldn't help herself and then looked away to one side. My eyes went down. The armchair had a brown cover on. I took a few steps towards her but she jerked her head back as if I was going to hurt her even if I tried to be gentle. Then I noticed that the chair arms were all red.

'Are you all right?' I asked, and she pulled a funny face as if she wasn't bothered. I walked over and poked the material. It was damp. It took another moment to sink in. Where was the colour coming from? Then I saw. It was coming from her wrists.

She'd slit her wrists.

I think I said, 'Jesus!' and I ran for the phone to dial 999. She called after me but all I was bothered about was getting some help before she bled to death, just bled to death sitting there waiting for me. There were splashes of blood on the floor next to me and the phone was smeared with it. I got up to nine nine when she came up behind and pressed the button down to cut me off.

'What are you doing?' I begged.

'I don't need an ambulance. You can drive me.'

'Drive you?'

'It'll be quicker.'

'Will it?'

'Yes.' She shook her head and almost laughed. 'Don't worry, Ben. I'm not going to die.'

'How do you know?' I asked but even as the words came out of my mouth, I realised why. 'You've done it before,' I accused her. She'd never told me, but I'd seen the thin white scars on her wrists. I stood there with the phone in my hand wondering what to do, because I'd've very much preferred to call an ambulance and let them take her away from me.

'I can't drive,' I reminded her.

'You've got your provisional, I'll be sitting next to you.' She walked to the door. 'Come on. It won't take long.' She waved her hand at me and winced, and I could see the blood trickling out.

I was so scared I hardly knew what I was doing. I was scared of her, scared of the hospital, scared of the police, because...because you know why this had happened, don't you? I'd done it to her.

We got down to the car and set off. I was trembling, I could see my hands shaking on the wheel. 'Why did you do that?' I asked her.

'Because I'm stupid.' She sat very still, holding her

278

wrists on her lap, looking demurely down at them. She'd wrapped them in some blue-checked tea towels and the blood was slowly seeping through. After a little while she turned her head away from me and stared out of the side window. I kept having to brake hard and I was stalling and accelerating too quickly, and every time I did it, she stiffened up and pulled a face. She never said another word all the way there.

They made us wait for ages. A nurse came to have a quick look but there didn't seem to be any rush. I tried to speak to Ali but she just shook her head and said, 'No.' They left us waiting there for ages before they took her in and left me sitting there on my own.

'I'm not going to die,' she'd said. So what's the point of cutting your wrists if you're not going to die? I thought, I hope someone knows what's going on because I haven't got a fucking clue.

I sat there watching people come and go. There was this whole series of weird accidents coming in and out and I kept getting fits of the giggles. At one point the door burst open and this fat old Sikh man came in, clutching his bollocks and yelling, 'Nurse! Nurse! Oh, my God, oh, my God!' and these three younger blokes, his sons maybe, came banging in behind him and started prowling about. Poor bloke must have been in terrible pain, but I couldn't help it, I just started laughing. I had to run outside to hide it. It took me ages to calm down. Then this kid came in with his mum, and he had both hands bandaged. She was tiny, he was about eight and he was only a little smaller than she was, and they both had this funny waddling walk and they looked just like a pair of penguins coming into the waiting room. I felt like I was on some sort of drug. But then things got boring and I just sat there, waiting for ages until they asked me in to see her.

She was lying on a bed with her wrists bandaged up, smiling weakly at me.

'Hi,' she said.

'Are you going to be all right?'

She nodded. 'Stupid thing to do.' She shrugged.

'I didn't mean to hurt you . . .'

'It's not your fault. You weren't to know what a stupid cow I am, were you?'

'What did the doctors say?' I asked her.

She laughed. 'They said, next time I should use sleeping pills if I want to kill myself. They said I'd stand a better chance of being successful.'

'They said that? They said that to you?'

'It's too hard to kill yourself by slitting your wrists, the arteries are too deep.'

I was outraged. How could they say things like that? They were supposed to be sympathetic. 'We should complain,' I began, but she shook her head.

'They were just angry because they had some real accidents to deal with.' She smiled weakly. 'Not a little pretend case like mine.'

They brought us both a cup of tea and then I drove her home.

★

280

Back at the flat she asked him to stay with her. He rang his parents and told them he was staying over with a friend. They were surprised but didn't try to stop him. He opened tins of spaghetti and heated it up for supper and they went to bed early. She lay next to him, neither of them sleeping for a long time, then she wanted him to make love to her... one last time, gently.

He lay on top of her and moved slowly and softly. She buried her face in his neck and made soft little noises. He was distracted by the sight of her bandaged wrists. After a bit he grew desperate and started banging at her hard while she spread her knees and gasped.

'Is that too hard?' he asked her.

'No, it's all right, don't stop.'

He banged away until the bed rumbled under them and he silently came. He got off and she rolled over to hold him so gently he felt awful after his roughness. She began to weep silently.

'I'm back, aren't I?' whispered Ben. He stroked her head and let her cry.

34
Boy Siren

Jackie didn't notice it at first. Support for her in the school had been rock solid for weeks. Dino was a two-timing piece of toad shit; she was a used innocent. It was obvious. But behind her back the wind had already begun to change.

Of course Dino had behaved badly — but Jackie really had led him right up the garden path, hadn't she? All those promises. Dumping him on the night of his own party because someone had been sick in the bed! What was that about? He should have chucked her for that! You had to feel sorry for him. And the shoplifting. And his parents splitting up. Now Jackie dumping him on top of every-thing. It was a bit hard. Look at him! He was so *upset*.

No one said anything about this to Jackie but she began to notice that her exclamations of his guilt and general nastiness weren't getting quite the applause she expected.

'Stay angry,' Sue hissed in her ear, when she caught sight of Dino smiling hopefully across at Jackie one morning about a month after she'd chucked him. Jackie flashed him a glare that would have withered brickwork and promptly turned her back. Thus it was Sue who saw

Dino's reaction. What she saw in his face wasn't the usual anger, or contempt, or arrogance, or confusion. Something had happened. He wasn't disgusting anymore. His eyes turned red, his lips pursed. She saw a sore heart. Dino was in pain. Sue felt a pang.

'Pity?' she thought, amazed at herself. Instinctively she threw herself in between Dino's face and her friend, as if to protect Jackie from the siren song, the broadcast beams of Dino's pain.

She hadn't realised. He was so *vulnerable*.

So's Jackie, and I *like* her, thought Sue to herself as she followed her friend away from the disgraced boy. Dino had been in pain for weeks and he'd just looked pathetic. What was so different? She couldn't help glancing over her shoulder to where he stood with his face an open door to his distress. It was so touching – he couldn't hide it! His eyes were wet, he was wiping them with the back of his hand. It was all so unconscious. Staring over her shoulder to check how fast his tears were flowing, Sue collided with Jackie who had stopped to watch her.

'What are you doing?' hissed Jackie.

'Making sure the bastard doesn't follow us,' said Sue quickly. Jackie stared suspiciously over her shoulder. Sue ushered her away, but it was already too late.

'What was that about?' demanded Jackie when they were clear.

'Nothing!'

'He was crying, wasn't he?'

'Did you see?'

'I thought so. Really crying?'

'Meaningless tears,' insisted Sue.

'They made you stop.'

'I was just surprised, that's all.'

'He was crying. For me,' said Jackie, casting a longing glance away in Dino's direction.

'Stop it. Remember! He isn't worth it.'

But Jackie was immediately and suddenly certain that those tears were wept for her. Every instinct in her body longed to take him in her arms and comfort him and tell him she understood and would make it all better. He was stricken; she had struck him.

The annoying thing about it was, for the past few weeks she'd been enjoying her life for the first time in months. All the things that couples tend to let go of – going out with her friends, dances, just hanging about gassing. She'd taken up fencing again. She'd hardly missed him at all, but now somehow his pain was back in her heart, the siren song was in her ears: I need you, I need you, only you will do. It was irresistible.

She didn't immediately start wanting him; he just began to populate her brain. During the day she found herself endlessly explaining to him in her mind why they had to split up. At night she dreamt about him talking to her, making love to her, walking or dancing or just being there for her. In one dream she was sitting having tea and cake with friends in one room, while Dino was being dismembered with a razor-sharp kitchen knife in another just down the hall. No one said anything, but they all knew it was going on. She could see people exchanging glances. Dino was in silent agony, dying. Only she could save him. All she had to do was put down her cup and walk through, but she was unable to get up out of her chair.

Sue was exasperated but unsurprised. It all seemed so pointless. It wasn't even as though Jackie had a broken heart. Sue herself was in more pain several times a year when she dumped one of her string of blokes for no apparent reason, unless it was boredom. It pulled her to pieces every time — it was even worse when one of them dumped her, as they occasionally did. But this obsessive interest in someone who was no good for you — for someone who, as far as she could work out, Jackie didn't even like, was beyond her. The point was to have fun, wasn't it? And one day maybe to fall in love. This was neither.

For a few more days she did her best for her friend, but she was rapidly losing interest. Dino had already moved from pariah, to someone to be pitied, to someone really rather fanciable in just a few days. OK, maybe he was a tosser but — no one said it yet — so was Jackie.

'She's changed,' pointed out Deborah.

In other words, they deserved one another.

Sue was never very good with boredom. Enough was enough. Dino was obviously something Jackie had to go through. She was clearly beyond the help of medical science, and the kindest thing to do was put her out of her misery. If she had to obsess about Dino, she could do it with him, not her. Sue had had enough.

'I think you should talk to him,' she told her one day, suddenly no longer able to bear another word on the subject.

'Talk to him? Really? Do you really think that?'

'Definitely.'

'That's new. What's made you change your mind?'

'Boredom!' screamed Sue silently. But what she said was, 'I just think you have unfinished business with him.'

'Unfinished business?' Jackie's face flushed excitedly. She even let out a soft gasp of pleasure. 'Do you think so?'

'I really do. You need to talk to him, he needs to talk to you.' Sue nodded her head firmly. 'You need to talk to each other.'

'Really? You know, I think you might be right,' said Jackie. Her eyes sparkled excitedly. Sue was amazed that she didn't see any irony in this advice. It was like pressing the on button on a piece of kitchen equipment; off it went.

'Absolutely,' she said.

'Will you have a word with him for me?'

'Oh no, not me! Get someone else in on it.'

'OK.' Jackie nodded; she didn't seem to mind. 'Deborah will do it, I expect.' She smiled. 'He'll think I want to go back out with him. He's in for a surprise if he thinks that, isn't he?'

'Isn't he,' said Sue.

35
Two's Company

Every evening, Ben went to visit. Ali sat in her chair with her head up staring at the wall as if she'd lost her sight. He felt so stitched up. He kept thinking, She's done this on purpose, but it made no difference. On purpose, by accident, under your heels, over your head, because God wanted it or for no reason at all, whatever. She had him just where she wanted him. There was no way out. Just thinking about leaving her made him break out in prickles of guilt.

She'd cast a spell and frozen him solid. He wasn't going anywhere.

About halfway through the week, rumours began to spread through the school. Miss Young was depressed, she'd had an unhappy love affair, she'd tried to kill herself, an overdose, slit wrists. Gossip gossip gossip. Ben tried to see if anyone was watching him. Surely it was only a matter of time before he got caught.

'I didn't know,' he'd say to the head. 'I didn't realise, how could I?'

'It's a very serious matter. You took advantage of her. You more or less assaulted her, you couldn't have been

287

closer to Attempted Murder if you wielded the knife yourself. This was a vulnerable young woman, deeply in love with you. You have trifled with her feelings, sir!'

At the flat, Ali clutched his arm and made him sit next to her and kiss her still face. He made her cups of tea, cooked her snacks, read to her, fed her tissues. Every time she wanted him to make love to her. When he left she clung to him and buried her face in his collar bone. There was no more talk of splitting up.

She'd told the school that she was depressed and her friends that it was the break up of a love affair that had sent her over the edge. She had in fact spun a long tale about her boyfriend over the past few months to them, painting a complicated affair with a man from out of town who travelled great distances to see her, a married man who she could never visit but only visited her. It gave her an air of sorry glamour, but everyone was surprised at how badly it affected her; she'd never mentioned love. They all trooped round to visit the heartbroken woman. Ben lived in fear that sooner or later someone was going to catch him.

People would often phone up while he was there, and sometimes there would be a ring at the door. Ali had an intercom to the door of the block; she always answered it but so far she hadn't let anyone in while he was with her. Who knows how long that would last? She was mad, wasn't she? Ben begged her not to answer at all, but it caused more problems than it was worth. Was he ashamed of her, she wanted to know? (Yes.) Had he got something to hide? (Yes.) Was he so selfish as to be more worried about himself than her, even though she was in such a mess? (Yes.) And anyway, what harm would it do if someone did find him round there? She seemed to rather like the idea. So he kept his mouth shut and suffered terrors every time the phone or doorbell rang.

During the second half of the week, she began to pick up. She started talking and laughing, cracking little jokes, cooking bits and pieces for him, little treats. By the end of the second week she wanted to take him out somewhere at the weekend, to the pub or for a meal or something. Have a date.

'We've never had a proper date, not a proper going-out date,' she said. Ben smiled and quailed inside. Terror! They'd be seen! He was fairly sure now she was more or less angling for that. What did it mean? Boyfriend and girlfriend, that's what. She wanted to go public.

They went out on Friday night to an out of town pub, had a meal, a few drinks, then back to hers. He felt like her pet. It was an ordeal, but at least they didn't get spotted. He mentioned his relief later in the evening and she got irritated about it.

'What's your problem, Ben?'

'Well, if we got found out, you'd lose your job, wouldn't you?' he asked disingenuously.

Ali shrugged. 'I'm fed up with that job. Teaching isn't for me. I've been thinking of packing it in anyway. I might go down and get some careers advice when I'm feeling up to it.'

'When?'

'No hurry. I'm on the sick, aren't I? Next week, maybe.'

Careers advice? *Next week?* Ben said nothing but his brain went into overdrive. What possible reason would he have not to see her then — apart from his murderous dislike of her which he could never admit? She was clearing the way for them, a couple in love; except that he wasn't. Did it matter that he no longer liked her? It certainly made no difference to her. He wasn't sure she knew what being in love was in the first place.

Ben knew when he was beaten. He was out of his depth. He hadn't a clue what to do or who to turn to. All he knew was, he was in hell and no way out. It was one of the situations you just have to make the best of, like nursing a child sick with leprosy, or your partner of twenty years who's broken their neck and can't move.

No. The magic word. What an ineffectual little spell it was against this witch. The word had gone from his mind as anything of significance, but over the weekend it began to be slowly replaced by another idea — not something necessarily useful, perhaps, but something that might lead towards something useful.

A problem shared.

Dino had impressed him no end, suddenly laying out his whole life to him and Jon that day. Ben didn't know if it had made any real difference to Dino's life, telling them everything so shamelessly. After all, they had no power over the shoplifting or his parents or Jackie or Siobhan/Zoë...but even so, Ben felt that just by listening carefully, he and Jon had helped. One or other or both of them were round there at least three nights a week. They went out together at weekends. As usual, even in the midst of great shite, it was lucky old Dino. He had friends, he had sympathy, he had people with an eye out for him. So why shouldn't it be lucky old Ben? He was so completely alone here – no help, no advice, no sympathy, no nothing. His being true to her was encouraged by her in the first place and now she'd buried him with it. Maybe it was time to be true to himself.

But who to talk to? Mum, Dad? No way! School? *No* way. Some official thing – the doctor? The Citizens Advice Bureau? It wasn't that sort of talk he wanted, not yet, anyway. It was a friendly ear he wanted, and that meant Jonathon and Dino. What a pair! Dino was in a mess at the moment: Jon was in a mess more or less all the time, but he did have his good sides. He had some useful insights into things, even though he didn't always seem to know the difference between an insight and a one-liner. He was a known loud-mouth – but he could keep secrets when he really had to, and he *really* had to this time. He often got hopelessly carried away, especially when he was teasing, which he did far too much. He could be amazingly insensitive, but he could also be more sensitive than almost anyone else Ben knew.

As for Dino, he seemed to be improving, but he had enough on his plate without having to deal with this. After a little thought, Ben decided to leave Dino out. He was off his head just now. One at a time – he could always tell him afterwards if he wanted to. He felt bad about it; not so long ago he had been closer to Dino than he had to Jon, but things had changed lately. He told Jon after school that same day that he wanted to have a word with him. Jon looked horrified.

'What have I done?'

'Nothing.'

'Oh. Right. I thought I must have said something stupid to Dino.'

'No.'

'What is it then?'

'I just want to have a word.'

'Why?'

'Never mind why!'

'How can you have a word with me if you won't tell me what it's about?'

'Jonathon, this is serious.'

'Is it? Oh – I see. Sorry. What is it – *advice*?'

'No! Well, I don't know. I just... oh, fuck.'

'No, sorry. I'll be OK. I just don't know why you picked me, I'm not very good at this. Right, right now?'

'No, never mind.'

'No, really, I'll be OK. Come on, really, don't sulk, I wouldn't miss it for the world.'

Not a good start. But they went back to Ben's place and there he spilled the beans. He went through the whole thing – well, quite a lot of it anyway – from beginning to end. Halfway through Jonathon leapt to his feet.

'So – that night at the disco, it was all true? You really did lie down and get a blow job while you looked up her minge?'

Ben blushed. 'Never mind that.'

'But you did, didn't you? You lucky, lucky bastard! God!'

Despite himself, Ben smiled. 'Well, I'm paying for it now.'

'I should think anything would be worth it for that. Christ!'

For a moment it seemed to Ben that this might even be so. Jon was pacing excitedly around the room. 'Bloody hell,' he kept saying. 'Wow! I mean, what was it like? Miss Young! Christ! You jammy bastard. Is that really true?'

'It's true,' said Ben. And despite himself, he savoured his moment of glory.

Jonathon stopped and looked suspiciously at him.

'Why are you telling me this?' he wanted to know.

Ben rolled his eyes. 'Listen – you haven't heard half of it yet.'

By the time he got up to date, Jon was horrified.

'How awful! What an old bitch! What a cow!'

'Well, not a cow, not that bad, not really...'

'No, no, she really is!' Jon was pacing about again, this time in outrage. 'Christ. I mean, listen, Ben – she didn't do that to herself. She did it to *you*.'

'What?'

'Cutting her wrists, man!'

'She was trying to kill herself...' began Ben, but Jonathon shook his head.

'Bollocks, that's outrageous. That's just... abuse. She didn't try to kill herself. No, that's a cry for help. Or something. A cry for attention, in her case.'

Ben leaned forward. He knew this. As soon as Jon said it he knew he'd known it all along. He'd even said it to himself a hundred times, but then it had sounded like a shallow excuse. When Jon said it, it was real. In fact, it was obvious.

'Something like that. Fuck!' Jon was trying to calm himself, he was so excited. 'I mean, damaging herself isn't what she's after, is it? That's just a means to an end. She did that to *you*. Wow, who'd have thought it? She always looked so cool.' Jon shook his head. 'Christ. I can't believe this. It makes me feel dizzy just thinking it. Jesus! Mind you, I'd have thought it's worth any amount of shit to do the things you did with her – but that's big shit. That's the biggest shit I ever heard of. She's mad! Slicing her wrists just to put a lock on the door. She wants you. At any cost. No, scrub that – she wants *anyone* at any cost. Wow! Man! Incredible!'

Jonathon babbled away, trapped between amazement, envy and outrage. Ben tried to tease out some sort of advice about it.

'She's got you good and proper.'

'Yep.'

'She's had you good and proper the whole time,' realised Jonathon.

'The whole time,' remembered Ben; and through the mists of confusion he recalled his previous thoughts, which had been almost wiped out by the trauma. He'd never even once been able to say no when she wanted sex. He'd never once been asked about anything they did.

'I managed to avoid going on Thursdays for extra maths,' said Ben.

'Christ. She looks so normal. She must be stark raving bonkers. She's like some sort of carnivore. She really goes for it, doesn't she? That's awful. You poor bastard. How are you going to get out of that?'

Poor Ben shook his head and tried not to cry. Jonathon didn't know whether to put his arms around him or what. He sat next to him and put his hand on his back.

'She's a monster,' he said.

'I can't do anything, can I?' said Ben.

'Well, it's not as bad as all that. She wasn't really trying to kill herself, it's just a trick. A pretty severe trick though. That's the thing; how far will she go to stop you chucking her? Cutting her wrists, it's pretty dramatic, isn't it? But you have to leave her. Tell her she's better now, you haven't changed your mind, that's it.'

'But what'll she do next? That's the thing,' Ben muttered, his eyes filling up.

'That's her problem, not yours,' said Jon. 'It could be anything, but I bet it wouldn't be so bad — maybe she's done her worst. You've got to try. You can do it, can't you?'

Ben thought about it. It was unimaginable. 'No,' he said at last.

'Then tell someone, one of the authorities. You'd be doing her a favour, actually — she needs help. So do you.'

'Who do I tell?'

'The school?'

Ben shook his head. 'I can't do that.'

'Your parents.'

'Do me a favour.'

'Christ. Well, all I can say is, you need help. This is out of your depth. There must be *someone* who can do something. Unless you just want to stick it out until she gets fed up with you.'

'Thanks.'

'She will in the end, I bet you. The trouble is, I should think anything real that's horrible enough to see her off has been extinct for at least eighty million years,' said Jon, trying to jolly him along. 'Perhaps a geological event of some sort would help. A volcano. An earthquake. Ball lightning.'

'A pile up on the M1,' suggested Ben, wiping his eyes. 'Nuclear fission.'

'Something out of mythology. The gorgon Medusa. Something even more terrifying than she is. The Incredible Hulk. Superman. A giant anaconda. Another dragon even bigger and more terrible than she is. But where does such a creature exist?'

★ ★ ★

It was a good move, talking to Jon. It really helped. At first I didn't actually think he'd said anything I didn't already know, but at least he reminded me of what was real and what was me being paranoid. There were a lot of things that I'd forgotten about, I was so mixed up. Just having someone else say it for me made it real.

But I was still stuck. What he'd said about sticking it out until she got fed up with me sounded like the most likely scenario, but I didn't like it. It could go on for years. That's shit, isn't it? I mean, you got to *do* something, don't you? You don't just sit there and let it happen. But maybe that's just wishful thinking. Maybe that's life – just letting stuff happen, and keeping your eye out for a chance to dodge the next batch of shit coming your way.

She'd really done me in. I hadn't realised how much until I started crying that day, talking with Jonathon. I just sat there leaking tears while he cracked jokes to try and cheer me up. Everyone else had noticed already. My mum and dad kept asking me if I was ill, the teachers were the same – one of them even asked me if I wanted to see the school nurse the other day, I was so white. Even Dino noticed, which shows you just how bad it was.

'You are a bit pale, now I come to think about it,' he said. Which was quite perceptive for him – my skin looked like a pissy sheet, as Jonathon kindly pointed out.

So I'm buggered and she's loving it. She's being really nice – all tender and gentle, now she's got what she wants. It scares the hell out of me. She's all sorry for the way she was, sorry about cutting her wrists, sorry about being a bully. She's started using this little girlie voice, it drives me mad.

'Would oo like Ali to make oo a cuppa tea, nice Bennie?' she goes. I mean – she's in her twenties! It gives me the creeps.

Then, just when I'd more or less made up my mind that I'd just have to stick it out till she'd finished with me, I got an idea. It came from something Jon said, actually, a joke. You never know how what people say will come in handy. It was a really crazy idea. It was playing with fire – but that was the point, you see. What Jonathon said about a dragon even bigger than she was. I found one.

Poor old Ali! You've got to feel sorry for her. Jonathon went on about her being a monster, which she was, but she was the victim, too. Somewhere down the line she was *really* done in – worse than me – and I had a good idea who had done it, too. But I was out of my depth. I had to get out of there and I was willing to do it any way I could. Maybe it was too late for her – maybe not. But it sure wasn't too late for me and I wasn't going to wait until it was.

It was a great idea. And it was cruel and it was selfish and it was cowardly, and completely terrifying, but I was going to do it anyway. I was round at her place when I thought of it. Midweek. She'd popped out to get something, left me alone in the flat with orders not to let anyone in. The phone rang. Of course I didn't answer it, so then the answer phone comes on.

'Ali? Are you there, pick up the phone if you're there? Ali? I'm coming to visit you. It's been too long, you never ring, you could be dead as far as I'm concerned. My train gets in at five tomorrow afternoon. If you're not there to pick me up I'll catch a taxi. I know it's very short notice. You must ring me up more often if you want to avoid this sort of thing.'

The phone went down.

Her mother. I thought at once – monster. Not extinct, not mythological. She exists. And she was the only thing I ever saw that Ali was scared of.

I erased the message.

36
Jonathon

Someone was telling me this stuff the other day. It's a secret, I can't tell you. I guess I've got a reputation as a big mouth — in fact I know I have because this person was reluctant to tell me this stuff for that very reason. So I promised, and I won't even write it down, but it was just about the biggest secret you can imagine. And it was from someone who I'd never have guessed was under such a strain. Just like me, except that for this guy, there's no way out. We sat down and tried to sort it out for ages, but there's just no way. The — this woman — she's got him right by the knackers and you just know she'll never let go until she finds another pair to hold on to. God! Poor, lucky bastard.

It makes you realise. Everyone's got their troubles. This secret — I mean! That's real trouble. And Dino, too. I've been so crushed by this thing, I'd really started to believe I was going to have to die or spend the rest of my life in a state of misery, but it's not really true. I mean, Jackie's definitely not ever going to go out with him again. His parents really are going to separate. He can't change any of that. And this friend of mine is totally stuffed too, but I can do something for myself, however embarrassing it is. I can go to the doctor. The doctor will say, Fine, nope, nothing wrong – and I'll be OK. I have to do it. I just have to be prepared to get embarrassed.

This friend of mine. This problem he's got! Wow! You should hear about that. I could not believe my ears. I thought I had problems. I tell you, compared to what he has going on, imaginary cancer of the knob is nothing. I mean *nothing*. And it proves one thing. Sex is trouble. My mum always says, Sex rears its ugly head. Which I always supposed meant that she thought knobs are ugly, but perhaps she just means trouble.

I can't tell you. Really, it's impossible. It's not just being discreet, it's really serious stuff. Honestly, I can't say a word. It was so awful I got over excited and started jumping around the place and Ben had to make me sit down and think about it. All I wanted to ask him was about what she – this woman he's got himself around with – how it started and what they did, you know? And how on earth he can do anything about that, I do not know. All he can do is ride it out. But I was really flattered, you know – that he'd spoken to me. He must have thought I was worth telling. He could have told any number of people. He's a popular guy with the girls and the boys. I'm just a gob, really, but he chose to tell me. It made me think, maybe I'm not so useless after all. Maybe I even helped.

The funny thing about it was, all the stuff I was saying to him, all the advice, could have been applied to me. Like, 'You need help.' I said that to him. 'You have to tell someone who can do something about it.' See? If I'd had the courage to tell him what I was suffering from, he'd have said just the same back.

But I didn't. He can, I can't. Apart from anything else, I suppose, he's got a real problem while mine's just a joke.

I dunno. Maybe I shouldn't go to the doctor. Maybe I should tell this friend. But – it really is too embarrassing. I mean, his problem, it's awful but it's cool. Mine's just crap.

Who else could I tell? My mother?

'I'm worried about my penis, Mother. It's all lumpy.'

'Ah, poor dear. Let Mummy have a look at it. There, we'll just put a plaster on that. There! Good as new. Now, go out and stick it in a nice girl like a good boy.'

No way! My dad? We'd both sit there in a silent rictus of embarrassment until I got up and left and the matter would never be referred to again as long as we both shall live.

Maybe I should tell Debs... but I know what she'd tell me to do, so I might as well do it anyway.

Doctor.

Fuck it. I just wish so much I didn't have to do this. It's so horrible – but the alternatives are so much worse. It'll be utterly unbearable, utterly horrible, utterly unpleasant but – but at the end when it's all over, I'll still be here, won't I? Oh, OK, the doctor might say it is knob cancer – only he won't, will he? I know he won't. This is juju to make the fear go away. But it's going to work, because – well. Because I believe in doctors, I suppose.

What's actually going to happen is this. I'm going to get a new knob and be very, very, very happy.

I'm going to tell you this as quickly as possible because it was the most painful experience of my life. I can't bear to think about it, hardly. The suffering was so intense, I'm not sure that I survived intact psychologically. I may be scarred for life.

I didn't get an appointment for starters. The earliest proper appointment was the next week – too late. So I went down for the emergency appointments at five o'clock. I got there early to get it over with and sat there for hours and hours and hours waiting for my name to come up, scared silly that the doctor would throw me out for wasting emergency time with a neurotic knob. Well, listen – it was an emergency for me, OK? For all I knew, in the next hour or so I might be facing life with no knob, or certain death or years of chemo and surgery and radio and...

Or a new knob. If it was just a vein and I was – please God – just mad and not cancerous. But that was the last thing on my mind at the time. I just kept praying that the doctor would be the kind of person who'd not mind you showing them your knob, without actually *liking* it.

They called my name. I walked in and there was the worst of all possible worlds. A young female doctor. Very attractive. Short skirt. Legs. It was so awful. As soon as I went in I froze. I couldn't say a word. I could see it all. She'd think I was a pervert. Even if she did agree to look at it, it'd probably get stiff while she was examining it.

They'd be ringing around to see how many other surgeries I'd gone into to have my knob checked out. Prison, untreated cancer, amputation, death. Or possibly even just death there and then, because I was gasping for breath, my heart was cramping. I was going to choke to death on my own embarrassment.

'Hello, Jonathon. Sit down. What seems to be the problem?'

I stood there shivering. 'I have a problem,' I gurgled.

'That's why most people come to see us,' she smiled. 'What's yours?'

I stared at her in terror. Was she taking the piss? Did she know? What the fuck did she mean by that 'What's yours?' It was so...so informal. What's your poison? What do you fancy? How would you like me − over the desk, on the carpet? Please, please, don't let her try to seduce me!

'I...I have this lump. Well, this bump.'

'Whereabouts?'

'On. On. In,' I said. I just couldn't utter a word. I half stood up and looked at the door.

'Jonathon?' I made a little movement to go, but I'd frozen to the spot. She cocked her head sympathetically to one side. 'People come in here with all sorts of problems. I bet I've come across yours before. You'd be surprised.' She smiled at me and opened her palm towards the chair. 'Sit down. I'd tell you some of them, but what's said in this room is completely confidential. You should remember that. Nothing that gets said in here goes outside these four walls.'

I made a noise like a rat being grated alive.

'Please,' she said.

I followed her hand and sat down. She smiled.

'Something embarrassing?'

'Ah,' I croaked. I was trying to think of some other ailment I could lay claim to. The pox? Testicular gangrene? Anything but this!

'It's very brave of you to come to talk to me about it. Some people go through years of agony just because of embarrassment. But embarrassment can't hurt you: untreated problems can.'

'Ah,' I gasped. So! I did have cancer!

'Is it in a private place?'

'Um,' I agreed.

'Testicles?'

'Nun.'

'Good.' She waited a bit but I couldn't speak. 'Well,' she went on. 'That leaves only two other areas, doesn't it? But down below?'

I nodded but my mind was going bonkers. *Two* other places? I couldn't work it out for a minute, but then it occurred to me; she thought I might have cancer of the arse as well! Did that mean she'd want to get up there too? My God! That would be even more embarrassing! Just seconds before I'd been unable to imagine anything more embarrassing than showing her my willy and now she'd found one within minutes of my coming in to see her. What next?

'At your age I'd say it's most likely to be your penis. Correct?'

'Ah. Ahes,' I said.

She nodded. 'Where is this lump, on the shaft of your penis, or the head?'

'Jjj. Shi.'

'The shaft. OK, if you'd just go to the couch over there and take your pants down, I'll have a look for you.'

This was it. Pants down! Mortified! I went to the couch. She was over by the work surface putting on the plastic gloves. Plastic gloves? I'd washed it. My knob is spotless. Or was this for the arse examination?

I got my jeans down but I couldn't do the final thing. She came and stood by me. 'Come on then, I don't want to take them down myself.'

Like a little boy I jerked to attention and pulled them down. Out came the meat and two veg. Poor Mr Knobby!

'Right,' I said. 'Here's the lump just on this side I know it isn't very big now but it gets a lot bigger and and and and and harder when I've got annnnurrrection.'

'Yes, I see.' She prodded it with a finger and stood up. 'That's a vein,' she said. 'Perfectly normal. Penises are very veiny things. This particular vein happens to be close to the surface, that's all. It means you've got a good blood supply.'

'So it's all right then?' I said.

'Perfectly normal.' She'd pulled the gloves off and went to the sink to wash her hands. What did she think she was handling? She needed to wash after the plastic gloves? Were knob germs that deadly?

'So it's all right then?' I asked again. I wanted to make

absolutely sure, no mistake. I didn't want to have to go through this again.

'Perfectly fine. The thing about these sorts of things,' she said, washing her hands and looking over to me, 'is not to worry about them.'

'Yes. Yes. Right. I see, exactly, sometimes they just get a bit on top of you, I just wanted to get it cleared up. Exactly,' I said. 'Thank you very much. Goodbye.'

I ran out of the door. Just before I closed it behind me she said,

'Enjoy,' in a soft voice. As if she'd just given me something to eat.

On the way home I was dying, just dying. How had I ever managed to do that? It was awful, awful, awful. The hardest thing I'd ever done in my whole life. It wasn't until I was about halfway back, that I started thinking, Yes, that was very hard, very very very hard. And stupid and horrible. But now, my boy, you have a brand new knob. Thing is, to go and try it out.

37
Deborah

Scared? I was terrified. No, really, it was dreadful. I mean, boys and their willies. And girls are supposed to be the delicate ones. Talk about a prima donna – just because he couldn't get it up. He hardly said a word to me for a week. I mean – I try to be sympathetic but the least he could do was talk about it. You know, I like sex too. I didn't like to say, look you're my boyfriend, I expect to have sex with you, what's going on? It was making *me* neurotic. I was thinking it must be because I'm overweight. Really, he was being a real idiot about it. Not a word, hardly.

Then, finally, out it came. He was scared he was impotent, he said. Well, I mean, how stupid. The first time he's ever done it he can't get it up and he's impotent! Loads of people can't get it up the first time. I didn't say of course, but actually I was really cross. I'm his girlfriend, he can talk to me, can't he? If he can't tell me then who can he tell? His mates – do me a favour. That lot. So I had to pretend to be all sympathetic about the ridiculous little thing, even though he'd kept me hanging around for so long I thought I disgusted him.

Boys.

I must admit, I don't really understand it, why they get so worked up about it. He tried to explain to me. He said it was because willies are such temperamental things. What, more temperamental than girls? I asked him.

'Look,' he said. 'If I was with you, and you didn't get turned on, I'd hardly know, would I?'

Well, yes you would, I told him, because I'd be dry.

'Yes, but, it wouldn't be so obvious. And if I tried to stick it in anyway, I probably could, couldn't I?'

'I hope you wouldn't!'

'No! But all you have to do is lie there – you don't have to make something all stiff, do you? If it doesn't work for you it just means you're not in the mood.'

So maybe you weren't in the mood, I said, and he said, 'I would be if I could, though.'

What am I supposed to make of that?

That's boys for you. You know, I do really wonder if it's maybe something to do with me – no don't laugh – because this isn't the first time this has happened to me. Yes, really. This other one wasn't as bad as Jonathon though. At least he told me what was going on, how he felt. You'd have thought he was being sentenced to death. He was so depressed, I felt so sorry for him, but there was nothing I could do. We tried everything – no you mind your own business what. Well, use your imagination. But nothing worked. It would be sticking up straight as a poker and then as soon as he got anywhere near you-know-where, down it would go. He got so desperate. You know, he wanted to look at some porn pictures while he was putting it in! Yes! No way, I told him. Imagine it –

him turning the pages over my shoulder. I said, If I'm not good enough for you in the flesh, what do you think them paper girls are going to do for you? Well, I tell you how he justified it. Oh God, this is so embarrassing. He said, he said that if he could be looking at someone's fanny at the same time he reckoned it would stay up, and since it couldn't be my fanny, it had to be a paper one.

Oh God! Imagine! No, of course I wasn't angry. He was desperate, poor boy. He was dying. He did it from behind in the end, that seemed to work. Once he got back into his stride it was all right. It was all in the mind, you see. So when it happened to Jonathon, I thought, Oh no, not again! Jon was only my second, you see – that's a 100% per cent can't get it up rate! It doesn't exactly do a lot for your confidence. I have a problem too. Well, I'm not exactly six foot two and size 6, am I? I don't care enough to actually do anything about it, but I do like my food too much. Whenever I have problems with my boyfriends, I start to think straight away it's because of that. I do! I know it's stupid. Lots of boys like a bit extra, you know? 'I like to see a bit of movement,' my old boyfriend said! A bit of movement, oh dear, what am I saying? So I do worry about it, but it's just the same for everyone else, we all worry about our bodies. It's true. Even the thin gorgeous ones, they all think they're overweight. That's girls for you. With boys, it's their willies – with us it's our whole bodies. As soon as anything goes a bit wonky, I think it must be because I'm disgusting. It's a wonder people ever get to have babies at all!

So by the time we had another chance I was as scared as he was. I mean, if it went wrong again, what then? Maybe he'd never speak to me again! Maybe he'd have a nervous breakdown. He can talk the hind leg off a donkey, that boy, but hardly a word out of him for weeks. Oh, I love that boy. He makes me laugh, I'll go anywhere for a laugh. I'll do anything – within reason. No, don't look at me like that, I'm only joking.

There was another chance – my parents going out again – but I didn't dare say anything because he was so worried. I was just thinking, O-oh. I mean, it took him long enough to make up his mind if he wanted to go out with me in the first place. What if he didn't really want to? Maybe I was moving too quick for him. Because he comes on all talk and he's very clever and funny and all that, but deep down, I don't think he's got much confidence. And he thinks too much of himself. Does that sound strange? Maybe it is strange, but it's what I think. He's got a big ego and no confidence, exactly.

And then – it all changed overnight. Yes – just like that. Bang! One minute he could hardly move he was so worried, the next he was trying to push me out of my seat with his stiffie. He wanted to do it right there and then. I said, No way! Here on the floor with my mum in the kitchen? He just grinned, he was absolutely ready for anything. Something must have happened, but I don't know what. He never said. Never said a word. When I asked him, he just said he woke up one day and everything was all right. I said, Just like that? Well, I don't believe it. I wonder if there wasn't maybe something medical, but what? Maybe he thought he had a dose of something – no really, well, there has to be something behind it, doesn't there? But he wouldn't say.

So, the big day came. My parents were out. Oh, they do car boot sales. Yes! *Very* handy! I told Jon to come round at eleven. No need to hurry, is there – it wasn't a job – not like being a postman or something! I wanted to make myself ready. I had a shower. I made my room up. Changed the sheets. That made me smile, because of what my mum always says.

'I'm a woman and when I change the sheets on the bed, it means something.' That's what she says, so if I ever see her changing the sheets in her room, I just give her a wink and she gets all flustered.

I put a little vase with some plastic flowers on the bedside table and tidied up. Actually, I think Jon'd have felt more at home if I'd heaped smelly socks under the bed and spilt tea and milk on the sheets – or worse – and kept the windows closed for a week. That's boys – the ones I get to go out with anyway. And I got some little bits in from the supermarket, some hummus and stuff and some rice and a bit of curry I'd made for the family at the end of the week. I always cook once a week, sometimes twice, when my mum's at work. And I made the room a bit dim – but not too much. I was worried that once I took my clothes off, he'd see all my lumps and bumps and that'd put him off, even though he says he likes my lumps and bumps. He says they're womanly. But I didn't want to make it too dim, you know why, because a lot of people, a lot of boys, they like to see what they're getting. It was

311

a bit of a dilemma. Oh, God, this is embarrassing. Jon always likes to a have good old look, you know?

What am I like? Why am I telling you this?

So of course, I thought he'd be scared stiff again — I mean, scared not-stiff! But when he turned up, he was just great. He was in such a good mood. I was so surprised. He was jumping about and laughing and joking and teasing me. It was him who put me at ease! Normally he's so insecure. Sometimes you can see it in his face, he says the wrong thing or someone snaps at him and he looks confused and upset as if he doesn't know what's going on. He gets like that a lot. But this time, he'd been so weird for days and now suddenly everything was all right. I took him through to the kitchen and asked him if he wanted a drink, tea or coffee, and he said, No, why didn't we go straight through to the main course.

'I want to prod you with me stiffie,' he said, which made me laugh. He grabbed hold of me and kissed me and cuddled me and nuzzled my neck and tickled me. Such a good mood! So we went straight upstairs...and it was great. No problems. He made me feel good about how I looked, and how nice the room was. Well, he came almost at once, which was OK. He was a bit worried about that, so I told him I was flattered! That's how much I turned him on! And then we did it again almost at once and it was really lovely. Really lovely. He was so happy. I don't think I've ever seen him so happy with me before. Usually he's a bit cagey, you know? A bit anxious or withdrawn, ever since we've been going out together, but that day he was Mr Happy. Why? I just wish I knew. If he had some problem he got it sorted out, I can tell you! There was no stopping him after that! Every chance we got, he was all over me. It just goes to tell. Boys! What's going on in there? I think they're all mad. I know Jonathon is – oh well, so am I. You know what? I just fancy that boy so much, I think maybe I'm in love with him.

38
Ben

I wasn't sure if I'd recognise her. The station wasn't exactly heaving but there were still a fair few people about and a lot of them were getting on a bit. I'd found photos of her – I'd stolen one, actually. Ali's flat was full of them, she'd never miss one.

'Still keeping her beady little eyes on me, even in the bedroom. Even in the bloody toilet,' she used to say. It was true – I never thought about it until she pointed it out, but there was a picture of her mum in every room of the flat. Sometimes two. Her mum had given her them and hung them up or put them out. Once you looked there were thousands of them, it was scary. They all seemed to stand out and stare at you and follow you round the room. I asked her why she didn't take them down, but she said her mum knew them all by heart and kicked up such a stink if they were moved, it wasn't worth it.

I pinched a piccie from a drawer, but I didn't know how recent it was. She might have changed her hair or her make-up or her whole face for all I knew, but I spotted her all right. She was smaller than I expected, in a purple tweed coat and her hair up. She had one of those suitcases on wheels which was half as big as she was, but she was rattling along like some sort of rodent. I was a head higher than her but I had to hurry to catch up with her.

'Mrs Young?'

She looked over her shoulder at me.

'I'm a friend of your daughter. Alison. Can I have a word?'

She'd not stopped when I first spoke, but now she turned to look at me.

'You're very young for a friend,' she said. 'Do you go to her school?'

She had me sorted, first glance.

'Can I have a word?' I said again.

She looked up at the station clock hanging over the platform. 'I came to see my daughter.' She raised her eyebrows slightly, as if she was daring me to produce a reason worth her time.

'It's Ali I wanted to speak to you about.' She looked back up at the clock. You'd have thought just me turning up unexpectedly and asking would make her curious enough, but she really looked on the verge of walking off and leaving me. 'You really ought to know,' I said.

'Know what?' she asked at once.

'I can't tell you here,' I said. She pulled a face, but I had her now. 'There's a Costa Coffee over there,' I said. She pursed her lips and led the way there.

So where do you start? 'Well, I've been sleeping with your daughter but I want to chuck her now and I can't, so will you do it for me?'

315

I began with all the stuff about her being depressed and doing her wrists. That was the angle, you see. She was in trouble, I was worried about her, didn't know what to do. All that. Which was the truth – just not the whole truth. I mean, she was in a mess, and I was worried about her, but I was more worried about me. I wasn't the knight on a white charger. I was there for me. What a bastard. Well, OK. Being a bastard was all I had left.

Then she started asking questions and out it all came – Ali and me, teacher and pupil, having an affair. I wasn't happy about it, I said, but I couldn't see how to stop it since she was so... Well, what word do you use to someone about their daughter? Unstable, I said, and she almost hissed at me. I felt like a bigger and bigger shit every word I said. Because I was.

At last I ran out of things to say. She had pretty well the whole picture, or enough for her to fill in the gaps anyway. She sat there with her coffee cup in front of her – she'd bought for us both – and looked at me. I was waiting to see which way it was going to go. I was still hoping she'd understand me, I suppose.

'Young man,' she said, 'you have a lot to answer for.'

And I was surprised. I really was. I should have known, but I just wasn't expecting it.

'Me? What have I done?' I said, and I sounded like a whiny little schoolboy even to my own ears.

'Alison is a very vulnerable young woman and you've taken advantage of her.'

'Me?' I said again. I couldn't believe it. 'But I'm her pupil. She's my teacher.'

'Yes, every schoolboy's dream, I expect. Having an affair with an attractive young teacher. I suppose you had a great time boasting to all your mates about it.' She said 'mates' as if it was in inverted commas.

She began to get up. I was steaming. It was so unfair!

'But she was *in charge*,' I told her.

'Alison was never in charge of anything in her life,' she scoffed. And you know what – that pissed me off. All right, I know I was being dishonest in a lot of ways, and I know I should have just chucked her on my own, and I know... I know there's loads of things I should have done that I didn't do. And I know I was there for myself and not her, even though she was the one in trouble. But still. This was her bloody mother, and to her, Ali was just as big a piece of shit as I was. I was shit for taking advantage of her precious daughter, and Ali was shit for not being able to look after herself. I began to get a glimpse of why Ali hated her so much. I really wanted to tell her what I thought of her, but I couldn't get the words out so I just grinned.

'I'm glad you find it funny,' she sniffed.

'Mrs Young,' I said. 'Your daughter...' Suddenly I was so furious I just wanted to, you know, really hurt her. Or force her to understand. I wanted to say, Well, if she's fucked up, who fucked her up in the first place? But – what was the point? I just shut my mouth. Anything I had to say was just going to make it worse. The old bitch was going to go round and turn Ali into a lobotomy case all over again. I'd already given her the ammunition to do it, I wasn't going to make it worse than I had to.

I got up to leave. 'I didn't have to tell you,' I told her. 'I could have told the school.'

Mrs Young looked at me like I was an earthworm. 'Yes, and ruined her career for her. Well, you needn't worry about that. She won't be going back there.' And she said it with such confidence, I was sure she was right. She turned to go, and then glanced back.

'You are going to make some young woman very, very unhappy one day. I'm just glad I came to get my daughter in time.' And then she left, leaving me standing there with my mouth open, feeling like I'd just been discovered eating shit in public.

So – how big a bastard am I? Not in the way her mum was making out, though. I don't give a toss what she thinks of me. I suppose Ali is her little girl and I'm just another bloke who came along, shagged her and then dumped her when she was in trouble. What I did was about the worst thing I could have done to Ali. Her lobotomy-mother. There she is feeling hurt and vulnerable and suicidal, and I set the beast loose. Her worst nightmare. I suppose, really, the right thing to do was what Jonathon said – just wait and sit it out. Maybe I'd have been a better person if I'd done that. But – you've got to look after yourself, haven't you? Jon would have sat and waited, but not because he's a better person – because he'd be too scared to do anything else. Ali would have come out of it better, but he'd have suffered more. I suppose I could say, Well, maybe this'll teach her a lesson, maybe she won't do the same thing next time

318

and all that. But I don't believe all that. It was her or me, and no way was it going to be me, that's all. I don't mind taking my share, but no way was I going to just sit there and wait until she was ready to throw me away, thanks a lot.

So I don't feel proud about what I did, but you know what? I'd do it again. If that means I'm a bastard, then that's what I am. You can't always be Mr Nice. She had it her way the whole time – but not then. Not at the end. I had it my way. Maybe I'm even a little proud of it, because if it's a choice between being shat on and pissed on and used and being a bastard, I'll choose being a bastard any time.

And guess what – it worked. It worked like rocket fuel. That was it. She didn't come back to work, she was out of her flat by the end of the weekend and gone. Totalled. She didn't stand a chance. A couple of days later there was a supply teacher at school, the play was cancelled and then next half term there was a new drama teacher. Bang. Amazing!

So that was it. I was free. For ages I kept expecting her to pop up and murder me, but she never did. At long last I started to think maybe things were picking up. Summer was coming. Dino had started going on about this uncle of his who worked on a pleasure cruiser up in the Lakes, on Windermere, and that maybe he could get us jobs up there over the summer. You know? That sounded cool. Booze, girls. People on holiday having fun. A bit of money in your pocket. Even the hard work sounded OK.

I started chatting to Marianne again the other day and

I got the feeling that she was still interested. But it's too soon. Out of the frying pan – not that she's a fire in any way, but I just don't need another girl to go out with. Maybe after the holidays. I expect she'll be with someone else by then, girls like that just get snapped up. Well, that's the way it goes. I just want to get away for a while. Somewhere. 'Cause, you know what? I'm free, that's what. Free as a bird.

39
Dino

I was standing by the lockers with Jon and Ben watching Deborah go back to report to Jackie.

'She wants to go back out with me,' I said. Jonathon laughed. 'Do you know something I don't know?' I asked.

'Apparently.'

'What's so funny, then?'

'She's going to go out with you again, is she? After all that?'

'She's been telling everyone what a complete shit you were. And she was right, wasn't she?' said Ben.

'Bet you, that's what it is.'

They looked at each other, it made me giggle. They thought I was just being smug, but it was true. Because, you know what? I don't know what it was I lost for a while there, but I've got it back now. I could feel it. I could see it in the way people looked at me.

'Why else does she want to talk to me? Check up on my homework, I don't think so.'

Pause.

'He has a point,' said Ben.

'Well, if it is true then that's all my faith in girls gone forever. That would be pathetic.'

I shook my head. 'It's nothing to do with that,' I told him. 'She just fancies me something chronic, that's that.'

Ben laughed. 'And if she does, will you?' he asked.

I pulled a face. 'Dunno.'

'Another chance to enter her golden doors,' pointed out Jon.

'Another chance to get mucked around,' I said. 'She's not very reliable, is she? She wasn't exactly there for me, was she?'

'Not reliable?' said Jon, and they both fell around laughing, which pissed me off. So what's so funny about that?

'Yes, not reliable, what do you think?' I told him. And I was certain I was back on form then, because I had poor old Jon blushing away like he'd forgotten to zip up.

'I was just saying, you know.'

'Dino,' said Ben in his patient voice. 'You two-timed her. She was upset.'

Ben and Jon, they can go on a bit sometimes, but they're good mates. One thing I've learnt from all this shit, all that stuff about who's It and who's not and all that, that's for kids. Look at Jonathon – he's got about as much cred as a pair of y-fronts but he's been a much better mate than Stu and Snoops and the rest of them. And Ben – he still hasn't got a girlfriend, he hardly seems to be interested anymore. I wonder if maybe he's even gay. See? None of that stuff matters when it comes down to who your friends are. They're my mates – they showed that. And the rest of 'em are just so much crud.

But I was right about Jackie. I knew from the way she was looking at me. You don't smile at someone like that if you think they're a shit. She must have realised the sort of pressure I was under.

And I do know what I'm going to say to her, despite what I was saying to Ben and Jon. She's still the best-looking girl in the school, and I still fancy her something rotten. And we never – you know. It'd be a shame not to, wouldn't it?

We met outside the school gates and walked down the lane. She was all happy and smiley. It was great. It was, How are you, how you doing, how's your mum and dad, good news about the shoplifting, all that sort of thing. I didn't say anything much, just answered her questions. We were both smiling away at each other. After we were about halfway down she linked arms with me.

'Don't think this means anything, because it doesn't,' she said. 'We're just being friendly, OK?' But she said it in this little-girl sort of voice, kind of teasing, you know, so you couldn't really take what she said seriously.

'You made me very cross,' she scolded.

'Sorry about that,' I said, and she slapped at my arm lightly.

'You're not sorry at all, I can tell. Don't you ever dare do that again,' she said. There was a pause. 'I was really hurt,' she added.

'I really am sorry,' I said, smiling away, and she smiled back, kind of rueful this time, and then she held tighter onto my arm and sort of wriggled into me.

We got to the end of Crab Lane without anything happening. Jackie was sighing and standing there like she was waiting for something, so I carefully put my arms round her and she smiled up at me. She looked so happy, her eyes were all bright and shiny, it made me feel really horny. I kissed her. We had a good long snog, it was great. Then she sighed and leaned her head against my chest.

'Does this mean we're going out again?' she asked.

'I suppose so,' I said.

'You're a bad boy, Dino, I ought to...never mind. Kiss me again.'

So I kissed her again and...that was that.

'We better make a date,' she said. So we made a date for the next night. Sue was standing over by the bus stop; she looked really pissed off, she actually rolled her eyes at us. Jackie was still doing this little-girlie thing, all wriggly and silly and making a bit of a fool of herself, really. But it was a lovely horny snog, and what do I care about Sue, anyway?

So, that could have been that but...you know what? I went home, and I thought, Do I really want this all over again? It was just going to be the same kind of thing, really. Her all over me one moment and then all cold the next. And...well. There were other girls. Actually, to tell you the truth, I had already asked this other girl out at the weekend. Everyone fancies her, she's really nice. Now I was going to have to tell her it was off. I was thinking, maybe I preferred this other girl to Jackie. I used to think Jackie was all steady and straight, but she isn't really, she's all over the place. This other girl, she's pretty straightforward, which is probably more like what I need right now.

I didn't do anything just then. Next day it was all over the school about me and Jackie getting together again. No one could believe it, which was cool. I managed to avoid her most of the time, but by the end of the day I was pretty sure it was a mistake. So that night I gave her a ring and I told her it was off. I did it as nicely as possible. I still fancied her, but I didn't think it was going to work. She took it quite well. She was all pleased to hear from me and then all quiet and shocked when I told her. I felt bad about it, but it was better to do it that way than let it drag on. I guess we'd just mucked one another around for too long.

40
Sue

Rage. Tears. Hacking of air with the hands. Make-up all over her face. Ashes. Despair.

'How could he? After I *humiliated* myself for him!' she wailed.

It lasted about a week and then she was over it.

41
Finale

The idea was for them all to go to the cinema, or bowling or swimming or something – Jon and Deborah, Ben, Dino and Jackie. Except that Dino had given Jackie the push and was being very secretive about maybe someone else coming along.

'So I'll be the gooseberry again,' said Ben. But he came along anyway. He was thinking, if they went bowling he'd go too, if they went to the cinema he'd leave them to it. He did think about asking Marianne to go along with him – but it was too soon. Relationships. All that closeness. It was too much.

They met in a café by the leisure complex and sat at a table drinking soft drinks and eating crisps. About ten minutes later, Dino turned up with the new girl on his elbow.

'Hi,' he said self-consciously.

'Hello,' said Jonathon.

'Um,' said Ben.

'Hi, Marianne,' said Deborah.

Dino smiled happily. Marianne said hello and gave Ben a cool smile and a tilt of the head.

'So what are you two up to, then?' asked Jonathon,

to try and break the silence.

'We're going to walk about a bit, don't know really, see what happens,' said Dino. He was just so pleased with himself. Isn't she lovely? Isn't she gorgeous? Aren't you all pleased for me? Don't you all wish you were me?

Deborah started a brief conversation with Marianne about what there was to do in town. Dino stood and smiled anxiously at his two friends, who seemed to be a bit put out, he couldn't think why. After that, he and his new girl said goodbye and headed off for the door.

'See you later,' he called.

'Later,' said Jon. He waited until they were out of the door.

'The fucker,' he said.

Ben smiled and bobbed his head, blushing pinkly.

'What's up, you two were really off with him?' said Deborah.

'That's the one Ben fancies,' said Jonathon. Ben shook his head.

'That was ages ago,' he said, but his blush turned from pink to bright red.

'Oh, really, but, oh, that's so mean,' said Deborah. She pulled a face. 'Isn't that just so typical Dino?'

'He didn't know I still fancied her, did he?' insisted Ben.

'He knew,' said Jonathon, outraged on Ben's behalf. After all that running around looking after him! And after all that Ben had been through – he'd only just shaken free and now Dino had waltzed off with the one girl he really fancied!

'But he didn't *know*, did he?' said Ben. 'I mean, he was telling me I should ask her out only a couple of weeks ago and I wouldn't. Remember? I told him I didn't want to.'

'But...' began Jonathon. But it was true. Dino knew nothing about Alison Young. He had no idea why Ben hadn't asked Marianne out.

Neither did Deborah. 'But why didn't you ask her, I bet she'd have said yes,' said Deborah. 'You've got to ask, Ben, what's she supposed to do, wait for you or something?'

'No, no, it's right.'

'I don't care if he knew or not, he's still a shit. It can't be an accident,' insisted Jonathon. 'How can he be so accurate except on purpose?'

Ben grimaced.

'It's typical Dino,' said Deborah.

'It's just amazing. Bang on the nose. How does he do it?'

'It doesn't matter,' said Ben. He really didn't want to talk anymore about it.

He stayed and chatted a little longer. Jon and Debs tried to convince him to stay, but that was it, his heart was jolted out of place, the last thing he wanted was to hang around with a couple. He finished his drink and went off, leaving Jon and Debs to do their stuff on their own. He turned back to look at them through the window and saw that they'd leaned close together already, noses almost touching across the little wooden table. Sweet. He'd never seen Jon look so happy. He wandered off into HMV and looked at a few CDs he wanted but couldn't afford to buy, then caught the bus home. His parents were out shopping, his brother was at a friend's, he had the place to himself. Ben walked into the front room and stood there, gazing at the wall.

'Fuck,' he said. 'Fuck fuck fuck. Shit wank bollocks! ARRRRGGGHHH!' He ran over to the door and kicked it as hard as he could. It split. He was going to have to answer for that but he didn't care. He ran around the house yelling and throwing cushions and kicking walls and trying not to break anything valuable. Finally he flung himself down on the sofa. He felt like weeping or screaming or laughing or all three. He put his teeth into a hideous grimace and grinned like the devil at the ceiling.

In a minute he put his hands behind his head, sighed, and closed his eyes. Not that he'd had any intention of asking Marianne out, and it was totally unreasonable to expect her to wait around for him; but it just had to be Dino who got her, didn't it, and it had to be then, just days after he'd broken free. Like Jon said, it was too accurate to be an accident, but he was willing to bet Dino had no idea what he was doing.

Ben got up and looked at himself in the mirror. He had a good face, small even features, tight curly black hair. His eyes were bright and red with anger – he'd been close to tears – but he looked OK. The world was full of good-looking girls. Someone else would be there. Dino and Marianne wouldn't last for ever and he'd still be there. What was the hurry? He could wait if he wanted to, or not.

FORGOTTEN SACRIFICE

Dedicated to

Absent Friends

FORGOTTEN SACRIFICE

THE ARCTIC CONVOYS OF WORLD WAR II

MICHAEL G. WALLING

OSPREY
PUBLISHING

First published in Great Britain in 2012 by Osprey Publishing, Midland House, West Way, Botley, Oxford, OX2 0PH, UK
44-02 23rd Street, Suite 219, Long Island City, NY 11101, USA

E-mail: info@ospreypublishing.com

A CIP catalogue record for this book is available from the British Library.

Unless otherwise indicated, all images are in the public domain.

ISBN: 978 1 84908 718 6
Cover design by Gino Cieslik
Index by Sandra Shotter
Typeset in Minion Pro, American Typewriter and Palatino
Originated by PDQ Media, Bungay, UK
Printed in China through Worldprint Ltd

Cover photo © Topham/AP
Back cover image © IWM (A 27518)

12 13 14 15 16 10 9 8 7 6 5 4 3 2 1

Osprey Publishing is supporting the Woodland Trust, the UK's leading woodland conservation charity, by funding the dedication of trees. To celebrate the Queen's Diamond Jubilee we are proud to support the Woodland Trust's Jubilee Woods Project.

JUBILEEWOODS.ORG.UK

www.ospreypublishing.com

Acknowledgements

I am indebted to many people from many countries who gave their unstinting support for this most unusual project. First among these is my friend and mentor, Anatoly G. Uvarov in St. Petersburg, Russia. He arranged an exceptional itinerary for my research trip to that wonderful city, access to the Russian Naval Archives and State Library, and arranged for the excellent services of Maxim D. Melnikov as guide and interpreter. Maxim, a student at Herzen State Pedagogical University of Russia, effectively acted as my aide-de-camp, ensuring all went smoothly with interviews and getting around his city. A. Uvarov also arranged interviews with two remarkable veterans, Konstantin Sergeev and Israel Levinson.

Yelena V. Smirnova and Eric Johnson at the U.S. Consulate were very helpful and supportive during my visit. I am grateful for their support and assistance.

While in St. Petersburg, the members of the Polar Convoy Club, Juri Alexandrov, Anatoly L. Lifshits, Valentine V. Dremlyuga, V. V. Shehedrolosev, and Igor Kozyr graciously provided access to their remarkable collection of material and personal memories. Lifshits and Dremlyuga presented me with copies of their autobiographies, which have been a great help. Ludmilla V. Poljakova provided copies of the material as needed and also presented me with a signed copy of the Polar Convoy Club book *Polar Convoys in Photos and Statistics*.

My three-week Russia trip also included four days in Murmansk. There, Natalya K. Galeeva and Ekaterina V. "Kate" Yermolina of Gymnasium 9 were my hosts. Kate was my guide and interpreter, taking time off from her teaching duties to do so. These two remarkable women arranged for me to meet with Valentina I. Karepova, director of the Murmansk Shipping Company Museum. Karepova told me of Murmansk Shipping Company's history during the Great Patriotic War. While at the museum, I had the opportunity to interview three veterans: Alexander N. Kurganov, Vilen I. Astashin, and Yevgraf Y. Yakovlev. Each one served as a Ship's Boy during the Great Patriot War when they were in their early teens.

Also from Russia is Michael Suprun, who helped me with Russian sources about Lend-Lease and contacts with Russian authors.

Tony Cooper in the United Kingdom sent copies of thousands of documents from the British Naval Archives and, in many long conversations, helped me identify the most valuable ones for my research. Alan Blyth shared the letters from British veterans he corresponded with over the years regarding their experiences in the convoys. Nick Hewitt was kind enough to allow me to use material from his terrific paper *"Guns in the Night" HMS Belfast and the Battle of North Cape, 26 December 1943*.

From New Zealand, Chris King, president of the Russian Convoy Club of New Zealand, sent me his personal recollections of the convoys and granted permission to use articles from the club's newsletter.

Closer to home, George H. Evans in Canada sent me an autographed copy of his book *Through the Corridors of Hell* along with permission to use material from it. My good friend Dave Campbell in Nova Scotia spent hours with me on Skype evaluating my approach to the project, which helped me to avoid losing my focus. He also provided reassurance that I would get through this.

In the United States, John L. Haynes, a U.S. Naval Armed Guard veteran, autographed and sent me a copy of his book *Frozen Fury, the Murmansk Run of Convoy PQ-13* with his permission to use his memories as part of my work. Charles A. Lloyd, chairman and secretary treasurer of the U.S. Naval Armed Guard Association, assisted in locating information about U.S. Naval Armed Guard veterans and allowed me to use information and stories from the Association's magazine *The Pointer*.

The project would never have been conceived or written without my terrific Osprey editor Kelli Christiansen. It was her interest, great editing skills, and insights that helped make the project great fun.

I owe the most to my wife Mary, who has been my major supporter and cheerleader for yet another book. I don't have the words to express how deeply I love her.

Contents

CHAPTER 1

BRIEFING

The words "Murmansk Run" conjure visions of ice-laden ships and thoughts of freezing to death in minutes. Formally this was the Arctic Convoy run, fought primarily between three countries: Britain, the Soviet Union, and Germany. Numerous other forces also joined the convoys, including those from the United States, Canada, France, Holland, and Norway, and even as far away as Panama and India.

For five years, thousands of men and women from these countries and their allies battled ferociously in the coldest corner of hell on earth. Some fought for survival and some to help others survive, while many fought to crush their enemies. It was war without mercy. If manmade death didn't get you, the Arctic's weapons of ice and cold would. These natural weapons killed regardless of whose side you were on or how just was your cause. No one escaped unscathed the conflict's bitter essence—an essence distilled from fear, anger, killing lust, courage, self-sacrifice, and agonizing death, mixed with blood-stained, oil-tainted water.

Before we start this voyage into the heart of terror, death, and heroism, we'll first take a look at convoys, convoy escorts, the threats to the convoys, intelligence, the geopolitical landscape, and other related information.

CONVOYS

A "convoy" is two or more naval auxiliary vessels, merchant vessels, or both, assembled and organized for an operation or passage together; or a single naval auxiliary vessel or merchant vessel under escort of one or more warships.

Ships are the only way to move large amounts of material across an ocean. In peacetime, they sail alone and follow well-established routes between ports. The best way to protect merchant ships during war is to travel in a convoy with a screen of escorting warships for protection.

Going to sea any time is dangerous. Storms, ice, and fog, along with the risks of fire, mechanical breakdown, or collision await a ship. Crippling or fatal injuries are the penalties for a moment's inattention. War brings the added dangers of being torpedoed, bombed, or attacked by gunfire, or destroyed by a mine.

The best way to protect merchant ships is to gather them into a convoy. This way, fewer escorts can protect more ships at one time. However, convoys draw submarines, predatory aircraft, and enemy warships, increasing the danger. An analogy is a herd of sheep protected by sheep dogs. Trouble comes when there are too many predators and not enough sheep dogs—unless you're one of the predators.

History

The concept of convoying merchant ships in wartime dates back to the First Punic War between Carthage and Rome during the third century B.C. In England, convoys under the command of a naval officer were first employed by Edward III in the mid-1340s. During the following centuries, merchant convoys were employed during war or to protect against attacks by pirates in the Mediterranean Sea. When the threat was gone, the convoy system was abandoned. This was the case for England from the end of the Napoleonic Wars until well into World War I.

From August 1914 to November 1918, the first generation of German U-boats (*Unterseebooten*) sank 5,798 merchant ships. The losses threatened to starve Britain into submission. It wasn't until 1918, almost at the war's end, that the British Admiralty established convoys. That bitter lesson wasn't forgotten when World War II began in September 1939 and the Royal Navy immediately instituted a wide-ranging system of convoys.

Each convoy route was designated by a two- or three-letter code followed by the sequential convoy number. Initially, the Arctic convoys were assigned the letters "PQ" for the eastward voyage and "QP" for the return voyage to the west. The code PQ was chosen from the initials of Commander Phillip Quellyn Roberts, an operations officer in the British Admiralty. Later, the designations were randomly changed to "JW" for the eastbound and "RA" for the westbound convoys.

Convoy speed was governed by the slowest ship. In general, the Arctic convoys traveled at 8 knots. The distance from Reykjavik, Iceland, to Murmansk, Russia, is approximately 1,500 nautical miles (nm) and an additional 374 nm to Arkhangelsk. Thus, under ideal conditions, the voyage took roughly eight days to Murmansk and ten days to Arkhangelsk. Conditions were never ideal, however. Ice, storms, and German attacks forced diversions that often added days to each trip.

Organization

Convoys varied in size from as few as three to more than a hundred ships. The ships were positioned in columns 1,000 yards apart (one half of a nautical mile), and each ship in the column was positioned 500 yards astern of the ship in front of it. Each ship was identified not by name, but by a pennant flag number. The first was the column it was in, followed by the position in that column. For example, pennant number 64 was the fourth ship in the sixth column.

A medium-sized, 48-ship convoy arranged in 8 columns of 6 ships each covered an area almost 4 miles wide and 3.5 miles deep. Add the escort screen, and the convoy encompassed nearly 36 square miles of ocean.

Convoys were organized into two groups: the merchant ships under the direction of a civilian convoy commodore, in charge of the civilian ships when at sea, and the military escort commander, in charge of the accompanying warships.

The convoy commodore and a small staff of assistants rode on one of the merchant ships designated as the convoy's flagship. The military escort commander did not have authority over the commodore.

He could ask for, but not order, changes in the convoy operations or arrangement. The escort commander had the final say if there were any disagreements, however, and this command structure worked very well throughout World War II.

A major part of the commodore's responsibility was to retransmit any messages from the escort commander to the convoy at large directing evasive maneuvers. Because radio signals were easily picked up by the enemy, all messages were transmitted either by signal flags during clear weather or in Morse code by signal light when visibility was poor or at night. Traditionally, the only time a ship's captain was permitted to use his radio was to send a distress call if his ship had been torpedoed, attacked by a surface ship or aircraft, or if severely damaged by storms and in danger of sinking.

Before a convoy left port, a Navy officer held a briefing for all merchant ship captains. During the meeting, each master, as most merchant ship captains are called, was given copies of the convoy organization, the defensive zigzag patterns to be used, emergency communication instructions, and myriad other details needed to operate successfully in company with a city-sized flotilla of ships.

Rescue Ships

Before the addition of one or more rescue ships to a convoy in October 1941, the rear ship of each column was to serve as a rescue ship in the event of the sinking of one of the ships ahead of her. Although the rescue of survivors is an automatic reaction of any seaman, the task imposed considerable danger to the rescuer. In addition, the freeboard of a freighter or tanker in ballast and the unwieldy nature of merchant ships' boats made recovery of men in the water difficult.

With the increased sinkings of ships after mid-1940, the Admiralty sought to requisition certain small vessels for the specific duty of rescue ships. Principally small freighters with passenger accommodation, a good deal of work was required to fit them for their new role. To this end, they were equipped with special rescue boats (eventually one on either beam to guarantee a lee away from the wind), recovery equipment, cargo nets, and a properly equipped sickbay and operating theater staffed by a registered nurse surgeon officer and a sick berth attendant.

Within the ship, small, two-berth cabin accommodations were provided for officer survivors, while bunk-fitted messdecks were created in the tween decks for ratings. Additional, properly fitted washing and toilet facilities were provided for both sets of accommodations, and the original catering facilities of the ships were expanded. Staffing was increased to cope with the added numbers. Eventually, most rescue ships could accommodate some thirty officer survivors in cabins and in excess of 150 ratings in individual bunks.

Given that all survivors had only what they wore when rescued and all clothing was frequently fouled by oil fuel, replacement kits in rescue ships were essential. Every survivor received a set of underwear, socks, shoes, trousers, a jersey or cardigan, a raincoat or oilskin, a cap, and gloves. A toilet kit included razor, blades, soap, and toothpaste.

The completed vessels were allocated to convoys as specific rescue ships and usually were stationed at the rear of the center column of the convoy.

Unlike hospital ships, rescue ships were neither painted white nor identified with a Red Cross emblem on their sides or decks. Instead, painted gray and featuring the blue ensign of naval auxiliaries, they were targets like any other Allied ship. Another significant difference was that the rescue ships were heavily armed, including a 12-pounder, 40-mm Bofors, and 20-mm Oerlikons.

An additional benefit of the rescue ships was that almost all were eventually fitted with High Frequency Direction Finding equipment (see below), and three radio officers specially trained in its use were embarked in addition to the normal complement. These officers were able to take bearings on enemy radio transmissions and pass them to the senior officer escort (SOE) in order to provide a cross bearing in conjunction with his set. This facility added materially to the defense of the convoy and was of great value to the escort.

Arctic Convoy Bases

The primary Allied bases for the Arctic convoys were in Iceland at Faxaflói (Faxa Bay) off Reykjavik and at Hvalfjödur (Whale Bay) just north of Reykjavik, as well as secondary assembly and refueling bases at Seydhisfjordhurd on the east coast and Akureyri on the north coast; Loch Ewe and the River Clyde in Scotland; Scapa Flow in the Orkney Islands; and Murmansk and Arkhangelsk in the Soviet Union.

In the west, Reykjavik and Hvalfjödur were the primary assembly and destination bases from August 1941 through June 1942. After June 1942, operations were initially shifted to Loch Ewe and, later, south to the River Clyde.

At the eastern end of the route, convoys sailed to and from Arkhangelsk only in the short summer months since the Dvina River and the White Sea freeze during the winter. The Soviets strove to keep both Arkhangelsk and the neighboring unloading berths at Molotovsk, Ekonomiya, and Bakaritza open during the winter by the use of icebreakers, but during the first winters of the convoys, they couldn't accomplish the mission. Also, Arkhangelsk lies almost 400 miles further east from Reykjavik than Murmansk, which added several days to each voyage.

Murmansk is the only western Russian port to remain free of ice all year. The city is situated on the eastern side at the head of the Kola Inlet, 200 miles southeast of the North Cape of Norway. The facilities there were primitive. For example, there was no crane with a lift of more than 11 tons, which was needed for unloading tanks, so a crane ship had to be sent from Britain to do the job. The city itself was built largely of wood and, in consequence, suffered severely from the incendiary bombing raids by the Luftwaffe; only a few concrete buildings survived the bombing.

A few miles below Murmansk on the eastern shore of the inlet lies Vaenga Bay, where the oiler from which the British ships refueled was moored. It afforded a poor anchorage, the water being deep and the holding ground bad. At the time, the Soviets were unwilling to allow Allied warships other than submarines the use of their naval base at Polyarnoe, so the convoy escorts were obliged to anchor there. At the head of the bay was a pier, alongside which two destroyers could berth. Survivors from torpedoed ships were accommodated inside a hutted camp that had been constructed on shore.

The Soviet Northern Fleet naval base at Polyarnoe was a narrow, deep inlet off the Kola Inlet north of Murmansk. It afforded excellent shelter to the ships berthed at its wooden jetties. However, its facilities were not offered to the Allies for two years.

Convoy Routes

Three routes were available for getting supplies to the Soviet Union. The shortest but most dangerous was north around German-held Norway to Murmansk and Arkhangelsk. The second went south around Africa to the Persian Gulf, which seemed preferable, but there weren't the necessary rail lines or roads to move material quickly into Russia from the Persian ports. The third was into Vladivostok in Siberia. This was the longest and involved transiting Japanese-controlled waters. Also, from Vladivostok material had to be moved across thousands of miles by means of the Siberian Railway.

Almost all military deliveries went to the Soviet Union exclusively through Great Britain through the Barents Sea to Arkhangelsk and Murmansk. It took between ten and twelve days for each voyage.

The Arctic Convoy Route

Between the coasts of Greenland and Norway lies one of the most turbulent stretches of water in the world. Across it a never-ending succession of gales sweep northeastward, lashing the sea with their fury and pushing up waves to a tremendous height, which hurl themselves against the gnarled and rocky coast of Norway. Speeding round the North Cape, these storms enter the Barents Sea where, their destructive mission accomplished, the high barometric pressure over the polar icecap forces them into the upper atmosphere.

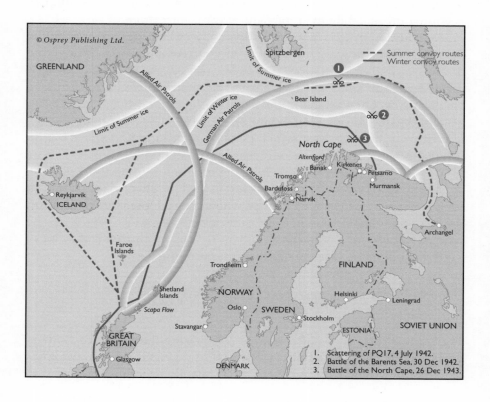

The warm waters of the Gulf Stream flow past the east coast of Iceland and on up the coast of Norway, where they divide: one stream turning north past Bear Island and along the west coast of Spitzbergen, the other flowing along the Murman coast and into the Barents Sea. The mingling of these comparatively warm waters with the colder and less saline waters of the polar region not only covers the region in frequent fog, but also provokes unusual variations in the thermal layers and the density of the sea, both of which are a great handicap to the operators of underwater sound detection apparatus searching for submarines that lie hidden in the depths. Furthermore, the temperature of the sea in these latitudes rarely exceeds 40 degrees Fahrenheit: A man unfortunate enough to find himself immersed in these icy waters has little chance of survival unless rescued within minutes.

The drift ice that forms the northern boundary of this tempestuous area advances and recedes with the seasons. During winter, the southern edge sometimes approaches to within 80 miles of Norway's North Cape, whereas in summer, clear water may be found around the shores of Spitzbergen, especially on the west coast, which, as already mentioned, is washed by an offshoot of the Gulf Stream.

An additional hazard of navigation in these latitudes arises from the freezing of the spray as it falls on a ship buffeting her way through the angry sea. If allowed to accumulate unchecked, the weight of ice thus formed can add so much weight to the superstructure and masts that a small ship becomes unstable and capsizes.

Finally, in time of war, when ships navigate without lights, the almost perpetual darkness which persists in latitude 77 degrees North, for instance, for 115 days in each year makes station-keeping in convoy or formation at these times one long nightmare throughout the voyage. And although concealing darkness for all its difficulties makes it harder for enemy aircraft to locate the ships which they are searching to destroy, the long summer days when the sun never sinks out of sight for the whole twenty-four hours enables them to attack "all round the clock" until defenders are worn out and ammunition runs low.

ESCORT OF CONVOY

The number and types of warships comprising the Escort of Convoy varied with the availability of warships as well as the convoy's destination. Arctic convoys were more heavily escorted compared to those sailing the North Atlantic routes or to those from England to the Mediterranean.

By February 1942, organization of the ocean escorts had been formalized into American, British, and Canadian groups, with each national group designated alpha-numerically. The British Royal Navy primarily covered the western approaches to England; the U.S. Navy protected the mid-Atlantic from its bases in Newfoundland and Iceland; and the Royal Canadian Navy protected the convoys as they departed or arrived off Newfoundland and Nova Scotia. Thus, the British Royal Navy was tasked to continue its role as the primary Arctic Convoy protector.

The Arctic convoy escort typically was divided into two forces. One was the close escort, initially composed of a cruiser accompanied by destroyers, corvettes, armed trawlers, and minesweepers. Later an escort carrier (see below for more information) was added to provide air support and extended antisubmarine warfare (ASW) coverage. The second was the covering force, positioned away from the convoy to counter attacks by German battleships, cruisers, and their accompanying destroyers. This second force was made up of battleships, heavy cruisers, and an accompanying screen of destroyers.

Providing ocean escort for the convoys fell to the Royal Navy. The Soviet Northern Fleet and Air Force were to provide local escort through the White Sea, and later when operations shifted to Murmansk, also along the Murman coast. The reason for this seemingly uneven distribution of responsibility was simple: the Soviet Northern Fleet did not have the resources or experience for long-range escort work.

At the beginning of the Great Patriotic War on June 22, 1941, the Northern Fleet, commanded by Rear Admiral Arseni G. Golovko, was a relatively small force. It consisted of eight destroyers, seven frigates, fifteen submarines, fifteen patrol boats, and several torpedo boats and minesweepers. There were 116 Northern Fleet Air Force aircraft, mostly older types.

The Northern Fleet's primary missions were to protect local Soviet convoys, interdict German convoys along the northern Norwegian and Finnish coasts, and provide support for the Soviet Army fighting on the Kola Peninsula. These missions were accomplished with great valor and sacrifice. As the war progressed, the fleet grew with the addition of aircraft, patrol boats, minesweepers, submarines, destroyers, a cruiser, and a battleship. Some of these were provided by the Allies or produced by the Soviets themselves.

CONVOY THREATS
U-boats

U-boats were the primary threat to convoys during World War II. A U-boat on the surface at night was virtually invisible. By keeping only its conning tower above water, it could get close to the flanks of a convoy or slip in between the columns without being detected. Because sonar and ASDIC (the British sound-detection system) only worked if a U-boat was submerged and until the escorts had radar, the night surface torpedo attack was perfect. To make the attacks more deadly, several U-boats would hit the convoy from different points in a coordinated action. This was the wolf pack.

The wolf pack concept (*die Rudeltakic*) was developed by Kapitän zur See (later Grossadmiral) Karl Dönitz in the late 1930s. Through radio communications, operations officers coordinated the attacks of multiple U-boats against a convoy. When information about a convoy's location, course, and speed was received from reconnaissance aircraft or by decoding radio signals at the shore-based operations center, messages were sent to selected boats directing them to locate the convoy precisely. The first U-boat to locate the convoy would transmit a homing signal for the others and then continue to shadow the convoy until the pack gathered. When the pack was gathered, the attack began.

The wolf pack's favored position was on the dark side of the convoy with a moon illuminating the ships, leaving the U-boat in the shadows. After attacking, the boats would pull away to regroup, rest, and report to headquarters. If contact with the convoy were maintained, they would surface out of visual range and trail behind or attempt to get ahead of the lumbering ships in order to gain a favorable position for the next night's work.

Aircraft

Arctic convoys faced the threat of two types of attacks not often encountered by their brethren in the Atlantic. The first was bomb- and torpedo-carrying aircraft. Luftwaffe bases in Norway enabled twin-engine Junkers Ju-88, Heinkel He-111, and Heinkel He-115 aircraft to reach the convoys throughout most of the voyage. In addition, Blohm & Voss BV-138 flying boats and four-engine Focke-Wulf FW-200 Condor long-range reconnaissance aircraft shadowed the convoys, providing the attackers with accurate location information. Both BV-138s and

Condors often carried bombs and were direct threats to ships. These aircraft would be joined by single-engine Ju-87 Stuka dive bombers when the convoys approached land.

He-111, He-115, and Ju-88 aircraft often teamed up for simultaneous high-altitude bombing and low-level torpedo attacks. While the bombers made their runs, the torpedo planes attacked from several different directions. This forced the convoy to split its anti-aircraft defensive fire power, which increased the chances of one or more ships being damaged or sunk.

Surface Ships

German *Kriegsmarine* (war navy) surface ships, including the battleship *Tirpitz* and battlecruisers *Scharnhorst* and *Gneisenau*, *Lützow*, and *Admiral Scheer* also operating from Norwegian bases, posed a significant threat to the convoys. German destroyers were more heavily armed than British destroyers, which gave them a significant advantage in ship-to-ship engagements. Although attacks by surface ships were rare, the threat was real for almost every convoy that sailed.

Surface ship tactics were fairly simple: Get past the escorting warships and destroy merchant ships with gunfire and torpedoes. Executing these tactics was more complex, however. First, the ships had to sortie from their Norwegian bases without being spotted either by reconnaissance aircraft or submarines. Often, word of these sorties was obtained by radio interception of coded signals (see "Intelligence" below).

After getting to open water, the ships needed accurate information as to the convoy's course and speed. This information had to be updated regularly in case of any significant change in the convoy's course or speed. Even then, though, interception wasn't guaranteed.

CONVOY DEFENSE

In addition to the escorting force of warships, merchant ships were fitted with guns of various quantities and sizes. When war broke out, the British Admiralty began arming merchantmen (Defensively Equipped Merchant Ships [DEMS]).

The Admiralty had laid aside surplus weapons and equipment that had survived the disarmament process at the end of World War I. The initial supply of weapons being very limited, many small ships in coastal waters received only machine guns, even then frequently on a loan basis, the guns withdrawn when the ships moved to less dangerous areas.

On British and Allied ships, these guns were manned either by merchant seamen or by crews from the Royal Navy or Regiment of Royal Artillery.

At first Soviet ships' gunnery crews were made up of soldiers from elite Red Army Guards units because they were the most reliable in the political sense and because Soviet authorities feared that ordinary seamen would desert as soon as they got to England. However, the Guards' lack of preparedness for sea service was quickly revealed, and they had to be replaced by ordinary sailors. Gun crew training was conducted by the Commissariat of the Navy.

When the United States entered the war in December 1941 after the attack on Pearl Harbor, her merchant ships were armed with a variety of weapons manned by teams of U.S. Navy Armed Guard. The teams, comprised of gunners, signalmen, and radiomen, served on both U.S. and Allied merchant ships.

No matter if they were British, American, or Soviet, the gunnery teams suffered higher percentages of casualties than their comrades assigned to warships since they were in combat situations during convoys more frequently.

Antisubmarine Warfare (ASW)

Depending on the size of the escort force and the convoy, two or more escorts typically swept across the front of the convoy, one or more on each side and at least one astern. If weather permitted, one or more escorts would be detached from the screen to range far ahead or to the sides during the day as much as 20 miles from the convoy, looking for ships that had either pulled ahead of the convoy (rompers) or lagged behind (stragglers). Additional sweeps would be made in hopes of surprising a surfaced U-boat. The key was to find the U-boat and at least prevent it from attacking the convoy, and the tactics to accomplish this varied with the number and experience of the escorts assigned to the convoy.

If the U-boat was on the surface, gunfire and ramming were used to destroy her. Ramming almost always disabled the escort, but the trade-off was deemed worth it. It was a different story, however, if a submarine was submerged.

ASDIC and sonar were the only means of detecting a submerged U-boat. Once contact was made, the escort went to full speed for the attack. Sonar could determine the range but not the depth, and, as the escort approached, contact would be lost as the vessel passed over the object. To counter the lack of depth information, a pattern of depth charges would be dropped, set to explode at different depths. Until the introduction of the forward-firing mouse-trap and, later, the Hedge-hog, whose charges only exploded if they hit a submarine, nothing could be done by a single escort to avoid losing the contact as it passed over the target. If there was the luxury of two escorts working a contact, one could feed range and bearing information to the second as the other swept in for the attack. No matter which approach was used, the exploding charges created a wall of bubbles that was impenetrable by sonar. This complicated follow-up attacks.

Sometimes when an escort got a doubtful contact, she would drop what were called "embarrassing" charges on the chance it was a U-boat and that the charges would either cause damage or at least keep it away from the convoy. A depth charge was lethal for a radius of less than 100 feet. Usually it was the accumulated pressure of several charges that cracked the U-boat's pressure hull.

The British began equipping their escorts with radar in 1941, but the sets weren't reliable and had a limited range. Even in moderate seas, a U-boat's conning tower was too small a target to be detected. Until a reliable surface search radar set was developed, there was no way to detect a surfaced U-boat at night except by eye. The best hope was to keep them far enough away during daylight so an attack could not be mounted at night.

During night attacks, specially designed ammunition-carrying magnesium flares attached to parachutes, known as "Star Shells" or "Snowflakes," were fired to illuminate the area and, with luck, a surfaced U-boat. Often, however, the only result was to give the U-boat better visibility for its attack.

Anti-aircraft, Antiship, and Countermine Measures

Massive firepower is the only effective means of defeating an air attack. As the threat from aircraft escalated, so did the number of anti-aircraft guns mounted on both navy and merchant ships.

Also, as air attacks increased, the British outfitted anti-aircraft ships equipped with the latest air search radars and guns designed to fire at high angles. In addition, these ships had more than the normal number of 20-mm Oerlikon and 40-mm Bofors anti-aircraft weapons. Two anti-aircraft cruisers, the HMS *Scylla* and HMS *Charybdis*, were outfitted in 1942 to counter the increasing number of air attacks on the convoys.

Early in the war, strictly defensive items supplied were kite balloons and kites, designed to be flown as a barrage to deter low-flying aircraft; "wiping" and "degaussing," the former a temporary and the latter a permanent defense against magnetic mines; and the Admiralty Net Defence fitted to certain vessels as a partial protection against torpedoes. Paravane gear, which streamed out on both sides of a ship, was fitted to many merchant ships as a defense against moored contact mines also.

In the early days of the convoys, several devices were provided, whose principal purpose was the maintenance of morale; however, danger from the devices was more likely to strike the user than the intended recipient. These included the Holman Projector, with which a primed hand grenade would be ejected by steam pressure from a metal tube aimed at an aircraft; PAC (parachute and cable), a rocket-propelled device that ejected a small parachute with a dependent wire into the track of an approaching aircraft; and "Pigtrough," which, both trainable and with variable elevation, launched a series of small rockets at a target.

Ship-borne fighter aircraft also were used. Initially these were carried on modified merchant ships known as Catapult Aircraft Merchant (CAM) ships. CAM ships were equipped with a rocket-propelled catapult launching a single Hawker Mark 1 Hurricane mounted on the forecastle (fo'c'sle) and carried their normal cargoes after conversion. The catapult could be moved from ship to ship as needed. The Royal Air Force pilot who flew the Hurricane could not land back on board, so he had to either bail out or ditch his plane when his mission was accomplished. In both cases he had to survive in the Arctic water, buoyed by his parachute and lifejacket, until rescued by the nearest escort vessel. CAM ships carried one Hurricane mounted and ready to launch as well as a second crated one stowed in the hold to be mounted when the ship reached its destination. As escort carriers became available, CAM ships were phased out.

In mid-1943, an escort carrier was usually assigned to each Arctic convoy. The escort aircraft carrier or escort carrier, also called a "jeep carrier" or "baby flattop" in the U.S. Navy or "Woolworth Carrier" (referring to the then-famous five-and-dime stores) by the Royal Navy, was a small and slow type of aircraft carrier built using merchant ship hulls and typically half the length and one third the displacement of the larger fleet carriers. Although they were slower, less armed and armored, and carried fewer planes, they were less expensive and could be built in less time. This was their principal advantage, as escort carriers could be completed in greater numbers as a stop-gap when fleet carriers were scarce. However, the lack of protection made escort carriers particularly vulnerable and several were sunk with great loss of life.

For Arctic convoy escort duty, the escort carriers usually carried between fifteen and twenty aircraft, typically a mixture of Hawker Sea Hurricanes, Grumman F4F Wildcats (referred to as "Martlets" by the British), or biwing Fairey Swordfish, or Albacore torpedo/reconnaissance/dive bombers. The escort carriers were used for close support of the convoy while larger fleet carriers accompanied the covering force.

Attacks by surface warships needed to be countered by opposing warships with their greater firepower. Although this is another ideal situation, on several occasions, merchant ships fought gun duels with enemy warships. Rarely did the merchant ship survive these encounters.

Impact of Convoy Loses

The following summary from a 1943 U.S. Naval Air Training Manual sheds some light on the significance of the loss of just three ships. Although it mentions U-boats, the impact also applies to losses caused by aircraft and surface ships:

> If a submarine sinks two 6000-ton ships and one 3000-ton tanker here is a typical account of what we have totally lost: 42 tanks, 8 six-inch howitzers, 88 twenty-five-pound guns, 40 two-pound guns, 24 armored cars, 50 Bren [weapons] carriers, 5210 tons of ammunition, 600 rifles, 428 tons of tank supplies, 2000 tons of stores, and 1000 tanks of gasoline. In order to knock out the same amount of equipment by air bombing, the enemy would have to make three thousand successful bombing sorties.

INTELLIGENCE

Knowing what your enemy plans to do and where his forces are is a crucial part of warfare. There are many ways of gathering this information, but four types formed the intelligence backbone for the Arctic convoys: spies, radio direction finding, crypto analysis, and visual observation.

Probably the oldest way to get information is by using spies. During World War II, both the Allies and the Axis powers had agents who either passed along information when convoys were leaving port or when a U-boat was about to go out on patrol. Once ships began carrying radios, it became possible to locate them through radio direction finding. RDF enables users to locate a target by taking a bearing on the direction the signal is coming from. If multiple receivers can get a bearing on the enemy's radio, a fairly accurate fix can be determined. The more bearings and/or the closer to the source, the more accurate the location.

A refinement on RDF was High Frequency Direction Finding (HF/DF), nicknamed "Huff-Duff." This type of intelligence was of significant value for the escorts. Using Huff-Duff, an escort could obtain a bearing on a U-boat that was transmitting, even if the U-boat was over the horizon. Using this information, the escorting force could take evasive action and/or send an escort to attack the U-boat. Because its range wasn't limited to line-of-sight as was radar, Huff-Duff proved more valuable in deterring attacks.

Crypto analysis is the ability to decode the enemy's radio messages. The most famous of these in World War II was Enigma, used by the Germans, which the British were able to break. British code-breaking operations were located mainly at Bletchley Park.

Decrypted German naval signals were referred to as "Z" intelligence or "Special Intelligence" and classified as "Ultra" for security purposes. Knowledge of the existence of the fact that decryption was being achieved was restricted to a very few senior officers and the staff actually engaged in the interception and processing of signals. Until May 1941, it was impossible to break any German Trident naval code. From May 1941 until January 1942, most signals could be read; then there was a blank until the end of 1942 so far as Atlantic submarine traffic was concerned. Thereafter, most German naval signal traffic could be read with increasing ease until the end of the war.

After intercepting an Allied signal regarding ship movements, *Beobachtungsdienst* (B-Dienst or BdU), the German naval code-breaking organization, would form a line of submarines across the probable line of advance of a convoy so that one boat would make contact and report, then issue the necessary orders. In order to use knowledge of an opponent's intentions, it is essential that:

1 The information is received in time to study it and act thereon.
2 The means with which to act are available.

3   There is sufficient time in which to act effectively, i.e., deploy assets,
    reroute convoys, etc.

Before the U-boats could attack, a convoy had to be located and
its position, course, and speed signaled to a command station. BdU
would then decide the action to take, bearing in mind the location of
other U-boats, and signal accordingly to effect a concentration of several
U-boats around the convoy to make a concerted attack.

If the Allies intercepted and deciphered a German order to form a
U-boat patrol line, then the Admiralty could divert the convoy around
the line to pass undetected. However, the speed of advance of a convoy
was about 8 knots, somewhat less than 10 miles per hour (mph), so
that the patrol line of the warning that had been received must have
been sufficiently far ahead of the convoy for effective alteration of
course to be made to carry the convoy clear of the line. Even in the best
circumstances, the interception of the signal, its decoding, transmission
to Admiralty, and plotting of the positions likely would have taken
several hours.

But code breaking went both ways, and the British by no means had
a corner on the market. BdU was successful in reading the Royal Navy's
secure communications for most of the war. The Finnish Intelligence
Service was successful not only in compromising Soviet secure
communications, but it also was able to compromise the classified
transmissions of other, non-Axis nations as well.

Lastly, visual intelligence consisted of reconnaissance flights and
stationing submarines along the enemy's projected track or at key access
points to his bases. As it pertains to the Arctic convoys, this method
was extremely successful for the German forces. Luftwaffe long-range
BV-138 flying boats and FW-200 Condors routinely spotted the convoys
and maintained contact throughout most of the passage. U-boats also
were effective, but convoys could avoid them by changing course or
holding a U-boat down with depth charges until the convoy was out
of range.

The Allies had less success with visual intelligence for several
reasons. Among these were the range reconnaissance aircraft had to
fly to their search areas, weather over the search areas, multiple exit
points from fjords for the Kriegsmarine, and limited Allied resources
for conducting the reconnaissance. The exception was the Norwegian
Resistance, which radioed information about German ship movements.
This was done at the risk of capture, torture, imprisonment, and death.

GEOPOLITICAL OVERVIEW
Northern Europe, Britain, and the United States

August 1939–August 1941
Setting the Stage

By mid-summer 1939, the threat of another cataclysmic war hung over Europe like the Sword of Damocles.

Germany had invaded Czechoslovakia on March 15, 1939. In response to Germany's aggression, Britain and France pledged their support to guarantee the independence of Poland, Belgium, Romania, Greece, and Turkey. During the first week of April, Poland and Britain agreed to formalize the guarantee as a military alliance, pending negotiations.

Ten weeks after invading Czechoslovakia, Germany and Italy signed the Pact of Friendship and Alliance, which secured Germany's southern flank from attack. This still left the possibility of war on two fronts: France and Britain in the west and the Soviet Union in the east.

Fueled by the opposing political ideologies of Communism and National Socialism, as well as being led by two of the world's most ruthless leaders, western governments believed there was no chance that Germany and the Soviet Union would ever form an alliance. This belief was rudely shattered when, on August 24, the two countries announced the signing of a nonaggression pact. Publicly the agreement stated that the two countries would not attack each other. The pact was intended to last for ten years.

A secret protocol was included in the pact: in exchange for the Soviets agreeing not to join the possible future war, Germany would give the Baltic States (Estonia, Latvia, and Lithuania) to the USSR. Poland was to be divided between Germany and the USSR. The new territories gave the Soviet Union the land buffer it wanted as surety from an invasion by the West. It also freed Hitler of the threat from the east.

On August 25, two days after the German–Soviet nonaggression pact was signed, Britain and Poland signed a Mutual Assistance Pact. These pacts were the death knells for continued peace in Europe.

War Begins

Germany invaded Poland shortly after midnight on September 1, 1939. Reaction from the rest of Europe was swift at least as far possible. France, Britain, New Zealand, and Australia declared war on Germany on September 3. This day also heralded the beginning of the sea war.

Without warning, *U-30* (Kapitänleutnant Fritz-Julius Lemp) torpedoed British passenger liner *Athenia* south of Rockall Bank in the Irish Sea. The liner was carrying 1,103 passengers; 118 men, women, and children were killed, including 28 Americans.

Lemp torpedoed *Athenia* in the belief that she was an armed merchant cruiser despite having been given strict orders that all merchant vessels were to be treated in accordance with Naval Prize Law (i.e., giving a warning before attacking). The attack gave the British the erroneous impression that Germany had commenced unrestricted submarine warfare.

Following Lemp's sinking of *Athenia*, the Royal Navy was heavily engaged in antisubmarine warfare against the U-boats, with losses on both sides. One early decision was to institute the convoy system starting on September 16.

Poland's fate was sealed when Soviet troops invaded Poland on September 17. Ten days later, Poland surrendered. The subsequent partitioning of that country was complete within a mere forty-eight hours.

At this point, the strongly isolationist United States was doing all it could do to stay out of the conflict. President Franklin D. Roosevelt issued a Neutrality Proclamation on September 5, as required by the Neutrality Act of 1937, which, among other provisions, forbade the shipment of arms and munitions to belligerents. This meant American arms could not be shipped to the Allies as was done in World War I. The President also ordered the U.S. Navy to establish a Neutrality Patrol. The purpose was to track any belligerent air, surface, or underwater naval forces approaching within a three hundred-mile zone off the U.S. Atlantic coast or the West Indies.

Norway and Denmark: April 9–June 10, 1940

As the war progressed, Britain and France became increasingly concerned about securing Norway and Denmark against German aggression and blockading shipments of Swedish iron ore, which were vital to Germany's economy. Much of the ore was transported by ship through Narvik and the Norwegian Leads.

Control of Norway by Germany would give the Kriegsmarine unhindered access to the North Atlantic, Baltic Sea, and the Arctic Ocean, as well as the approaches to the Soviet Union from the far north.

Winston Churchill, at the time the First Lord of the Admiralty, proposed a preemptive strike at Norway before Germany could do the same. However, the British government refused to take action on this proposal. All Churchill could achieve by April 8 was the mining of Norwegian coastal waters to deter German transports. It was a flagrant violation of Norwegian neutrality, but Churchill justified it by noting it would hurt Germany far greater than it would Norway. The move was too little too late.

In the early morning of April 9, Germany invaded Denmark and Norway (Operation *Weserübung*), ostensibly as preventive maneuvers against a planned Franco–British occupation of Norway. After the invasions started, German envoys informed the Danish and Norwegian governments that the *Wehrmacht* had come to protect the countries' neutrality against Franco–British aggression.

The invasion of Denmark lasted less than six hours before the Danes surrendered, making it the shortest military campaign conducted by the Germans during the war.

Norway was a more costly and prolonged battle, although the German attack was a stunning operational success. Kriegsmarine operations were conducted against strong British Royal Navy opposition. This opposition proved more costly to the Germans than to the British.

Britain and France moved quickly to reinforce the Norwegians. However, there was no coherent tactical or strategic plan for using these reinforcements, and they were defeated piecemeal by the better-coordinated Wehrmacht. The retreating Allied forces were evacuated on June 9. Norway capitulated to Germany the next day.

Western Europe: May–June 1940

As the Allies poured men and material into the Norwegian cauldron throughout the spring, Germany invaded the Netherlands, Belgium, and Luxembourg on May 10, and four days later struck France directly.

By May 26, the combined French and British forces were destroyed as effective offensive fighting units. Evacuation of the remaining troops began at Dunkirk and other French ports in Operation *Dynamo*, which lasted until June 4. The French sued for an armistice on June 17, which ended active combat in Europe.

Although fighting on land ended, the war at sea intensified. Kriegsmarine warship, armed commerce raider, and U-boat operations extended from the North Sea to the South Atlantic and into the Pacific. The number of Allied merchant ships sunk mounted monthly with no relief in sight.

Harking back to May 10, two other events occurred which would have a significant impact on the war. First, British Prime Minister

Neville Chamberlain resigned and was replaced by Winston Churchill. Second, British forces occupied Iceland without warning.

Iceland: May 1940

Winston Churchill wrote that, "It has been said 'Whoever possesses Iceland holds a pistol firmly pointed at England, America, and Canada.'"

At the time, the "pointed pistol" threatened the northern convoy route between Britain and the western hemisphere, upon which the island kingdom was dependent for delivery of most of the materials required to sustain its war effort, as well as much of what was needed for its very subsistence. Iceland was perched on the flank of these shipping lanes, which were under heavy attack by U-boats and Kriegsmarine surface warships. German air and naval bases on the island would almost certainly render the northern route unusable and put pressure on the longer and more vulnerable southern Atlantic route.

After the preemptive German invasion of Denmark and Norway, the British government grew concerned that Iceland would be next. Diplomatic attempts to persuade the Icelandic government to join the Allies and become a cobelligerent against the Axis forces failed. After diplomatic efforts failed, Winston Churchill, First Lord of the Admiralty, initiated planning for the occupation of Iceland. Code named Operation *Fork*, the invasion force consisting of 815 officers and men plus a small intelligence detachment was commanded by Colonel Robert Sturges. Departing Greenock, Scotland, on May 8 aboard two cruisers (HMS *Berwick* and HMS *Glasgow*) and two destroyers, the expedition entered Reykjavik Bay two days later.

Meeting no resistance, the troops moved quickly to disable communication networks, secure strategic locations, and arrest German citizens. Requisitioning local means of transportation, the troops moved to Hvalfjödur, south to Kaldaðarnes and Akranes, and east to Sandskeiði, thus securing landing areas against the possibility of a German counterattack. In the following days, air defense equipment was deployed in Reykjavik, and a detachment of troops was sent to Akureyri.

The Icelandic government issued a protest, charging that the neutrality of Iceland had been "flagrantly violated" and "its independence infringed" and noting that compensation would be expected for all damage done. In an effort to placate Iceland, the British promised not only compensation, but also noninterference in Icelandic affairs, favorable business agreements, and the withdrawal of all forces at the end of the war. Resigned to the situation, the Icelandic authorities provided the invasion force with *de facto* cooperation, though formally maintaining a policy of neutrality.

On May 17, 4,000 troops of the British Army arrived in Iceland to relieve the Marines. The British Army garrison was reinforced by Canadian Army units in early June.

Construction of naval facilities at Hvalfjödur began soon after the occupation, and these gradually grew into a large and important military complex. RAF presence likewise grew. Eventually there were five Sunderland flying boats and six Lockheed Hudson bombers for antisubmarine patrol and about a dozen Fairey-Battle seaplanes. However, after German reconnaissance planes overflew the island with impunity and strafed military camps at least once, Hurricane fighters were consequently dispatched in June 1941 to deal with the threat.

The United States: August 1939–July 1941

The United States was strongly isolationist when the war broke out and remained so through mid-1941. The Navy-enforced Neutrality Zone off the east coast was the outward sign of this. With Germany's increasing military success, President Roosevelt realized that neither a policy of isolation nor the vast Atlantic Ocean would safeguard the United States. However, under the neutrality legislation passed at the end of World War I, his options to assist Britain, and, initially, France, were severely limited.

A significant change in policy occurred on November 4 when the Neutrality Act of 1939 became law. It repealed the arms embargo and substituted a policy of "cash and carry," prohibited U.S. vessels and citizens from entering combat zones, and established the National Munitions Control Board, comprised of the secretaries of State, Treasury, War, Navy, and Commerce. The act was blatantly pro-Allies since German merchant ships couldn't successfully penetrate the British blockade and neutral ships carrying war materials to Germany were subject to seizure by British warships for carrying contraband.

Throughout 1940, the United States, under Roosevelt's leadership, continued to expand its role in the war. On May 3, Greenland, a crown colony of Denmark, sought U.S. protection so that Danish sovereignty could be maintained during the German occupation of Denmark.

It was on September 4 that Secretary of State Cordell Hull and British Ambassador Lord Lothian, Philip Henry Kerr, concluded an agreement to trade destroyers for bases; the United States provided fifty overage (built under World War I Emergency Program) destroyers in return for ninety-nine-year leases on bases in the Bahamas, Antigua, St. Lucia, Trinidad, Jamaica, and British Guiana. The British provided bases at Newfoundland and Bermuda as outright gifts.

Britain was running out of money to pay for food, weapons, and other materials. President Roosevelt's solution was unique, and he proposed it in a radio address on December 17, 1940:

> *It is possible—I will put it that way—for the United States to take over British orders and, because they are essentially the same kind of munitions that we use ourselves, turn them into American orders. We have enough money to do it. And there-upon, as to such portion of them as the military events of the future determine to be right and proper for us to allow to go to the other side, either lease or sell the materials, subject to mortgage, to the people on the other side. That would be on the general theory that it may still prove true that the best defense of Great Britain is the best defense of the United States, and therefore that these materials would be more useful to the defense of the United States if they were used in Great Britain than if they were kept in storage here.*
>
> *Now, what I am trying to do is to eliminate the dollar sign. That is something brand new in the thoughts of practically everybody in this room, I think—get rid of the silly, foolish old dollar sign. Well, let me give you an illustration: Suppose my neighbor's home catches fire, and I have a length of garden hose 400 or 500 feet away. If he can take my garden hose and connect it up with his hydrant, I may help him to put out his fire. Now, what do I do? I don't say to him before that operation, "Neighbor, my garden hose cost me $15; you have to pay me $15 for it." What is the transaction that goes on? I don't want $15 —I want my garden hose back after the fire is over. All right. If it goes through the fire all right, intact, without any damage to it, he gives it back to me and thanks me very much for the use of it. But suppose it gets smashed up—holes in it—during the fire; we don't have to have too much formality about it, but I say to him, "I was glad to lend you that hose; I see I can't use it any more, it's all smashed up." He says, "How many feet of it were there?" I tell him, "There were 150 feet of it." He says, "All right, I will replace it." Now, if I get a nice garden hose back, I am in pretty good shape.*
>
> *In other words, if you lend certain munitions and get the munitions back at the end of the war, if they are intact—haven't been hurt—you are all right; if they have been damaged or have deteriorated or have been*

lost completely, it seems to me you come out pretty well if you have them replaced by the fellow to whom you have lent them.

The "Lend-Lease" concept was brilliant but flawed: most of the material was either consumable or likely to be destroyed in combat. Congress passed the Lend-Lease Act (Public Law 77-11) on March 11, 1941. It permitted Roosevelt to sell, transfer title to, exchange, lease, lend, or otherwise dispose of any defense article.

Capping the events of 1940 was President Roosevelt's December 29 radio address during which he called for America to become a great "Arsenal of Democracy."

Lend-Lease and establishing the United States as an "Arsenal of Democracy" ended the charade of America's neutrality.

By early spring 1941, the British position in the Mediterranean had become untenable. Weakened by the withdrawal of some 50,000 troops to Greece and surprised by greatly reinforced German and Italian forces, Britain's Army of the Nile was driven back, with serious losses, across the African deserts to the Egyptian border. They seriously needed the roughly 20,000 British troops tied down in Iceland. Meanwhile, the Battle of the Atlantic had taken a critical turn when, in March, U-boats moved westward from their hunting grounds off England and the Irish Sea into the unprotected gap between Canadian and British escort areas due to the lack of long-range escorts at this point in the war. Shipping losses mounted steeply. Although the Royal Navy immediately established a patrol and escort staging base in Iceland, a dangerous gap in air coverage in the ocean defenses remained.

The Icelandic government took a pessimistic view of England's chances of survival, and had, as early as mid-July 1940, approached the U.S. Department of State concerning the possibility of Iceland's coming under the aegis of the Monroe Doctrine, which viewed efforts by European countries to colonize land or interfere with states in the Americas, Europe, or Africa as acts of aggression requiring U.S. intervention. If a garrison was required, it was thought that American troops, being those of a neutral power, would not draw German attacks.

American concern in the protection of the North Atlantic sea lanes and in the defense of Iceland as well, had been acknowledged in the recently concluded Anglo-American staff conversations. On June 4, President Roosevelt ordered the Army to prepare a plan for the immediate relief of British troops in Iceland. The question of where the troops were going to come from arose immediately. Although the

U.S. Army had reached strength of nearly 1.5 million men, the great bulk of its soldiers were raw recruits gathered in by selective service and recently called up National Guardsmen. By law, these men could not be sent beyond the Western Hemisphere unless they volunteered.

The only legal alternative was to send the Marines, who were all volunteers and, unlike the draftee-encumbered Army, could be ordered overseas. Moreover, the 1st Marine Brigade (Provisional), under Brigadier General John Marston, was already at sea prepared for expeditionary duty. On June 5, Roosevelt directed the chief of Naval Operations, Admiral Harold R. Stark, to have a Marine brigade ready to sail in fifteen days' time.

On July 7, President Roosevelt announced to Congress that an executive agreement had been made with Iceland for U.S. troops to occupy that country and that the Navy had been ordered to take all steps necessary to maintain communications between the United States and Iceland. Task Force 19 landed 1st Marine Brigade (Provisional) at Reykjavik.

Early that morning, as TF 19 approached Reykjavik, the sea was glassy calm; the sun was well up and bright, as it never set in July in northern lands. As the convoy approached the coast of Iceland, the pilots of the U.S. Army Air Force 33d Pursuit Squadron flew their P-40 Warhawk fighter planes off the deck of the aircraft carrier *Wasp* in what was, for Army Air Corps pilots, a most unusual performance. The same day, VP-73, another squadron of six PBYs as well as VP-74, a squadron of long-range five PBM Mariners arrived at Skerjafjördur (Camp SNAFU) from Argentia. The primary mission of the Navy aircraft was to patrol the Denmark Strait between Iceland and Greenland and fly Neutrality patrols over the transatlantic convoys up to 500 miles away.

On August 12, 1941, a secret conference concluded between President Roosevelt and Prime Minister Churchill on board the heavy cruiser *Augusta* (CA-31) in Argentia, Newfoundland. It was in Argentia that Roosevelt privately reassured Churchill that when the United States entered the war, it would accord the defeat of Germany first priority.

Out of this conference came a joint statement of principles called the Atlantic Charter. It endorsed the rights of all people to choose their own leaders, regain lands lost to them through force, trade freely with one another, have access to raw materials on equal terms, improve the lot of backward countries, disarm aggressors, and create freedom from want, freedom from fear, and "such a peace should enable all men to traverse the high seas and oceans without hindrance." This last phrase was directed at Hitler's U-boat campaign and served as justification for the United States to take part in the battle. Roosevelt also pledged that U.S. warships would escort British merchant ships between the United States and Iceland.

Following the conference, a directive from U.S. General Headquarters established the joint Army and Navy tasks and specifically interpreted the approach of Axis forces within 50 miles of Iceland to be "conclusive evidence of hostile intent" which would "justify" attack by the defending U.S. forces. President Roosevelt expressed his views as follows: "... I think it should be made clear that the joint Task ... *requires* attack on Axis planes approaching or flying over Iceland for reconnaissance purposes." Simply stated, it was a "shoot on sight" order six days before the *Greer* incident took place on September 4.

On that day, the USS *Greer* (DD-145), while tracking *U-652* 175 miles southwest of Iceland, was attacked but not damaged. Soon thereafter, *Greer* counterattacked with depth charges. Although no damage was done to either ship, the shots blew away the last vestiges of U.S. neutrality in the North Atlantic.

As of September 1, the U.S. Navy assumed the responsibility for trans-Atlantic convoys from a point off Argentia, Newfoundland to longitude meridian off Iceland on September 1. Admiral Ernest J. King, commander in chief, Atlantic Fleet, also designated a task group as a Denmark Strait patrol to operate in waters between Iceland and Greenland.

President Roosevelt's approval to search for and destroy German warships carried consequences that were not long in coming. USS *Kearny* was one of five destroyers escorting convoy ON-24 westbound from the United Kingdom to North America when the group was diverted to help a Canadian and British force defend the fully laden, fifty-two ship eastbound convoy SC-48. Two ships had been torpedoed on October 14, and a thirteen-boat wolf pack surrounded the convoy.

On the night of October 16/17, in the midst of the battle around that convoy, *U-568* laced a torpedo into *Kearny*'s starboard side, killing eleven men and injuring twenty-two. Surviving crewmembers stopped the flooding and regained power, and *Kearny* limped to Iceland. The Navy repair ship, USS *Vulcan*, provided timely and effective assistance to the destroyer.

The next encounter took place only two weeks later, when the Navy oil tanker, USS *Salinas*, was torpedoed south of Iceland on October 30 by *U-106*. While the crew worked to repair the damage, the U-boat surfaced and fired three more torpedoes. They missed. *Salinas* returned fire, forcing the attacker to dive. Escorting destroyers attacked with depth charges and reported sinking the U-boat. They hadn't.

USS *Reuben James* and four other U.S. destroyers were escorting the eastbound convoy HX-156 also on October 30. At 0539 hours on October 31, *Reuben James* was hunting down a U-boat contact when *U-552* fired a torpedo into the destroyer's magazines. The explosion broke *Reuben James* in two. As she sank, her depth charges exploded amongst the survivors; there had not been time to disarm them before the ship went down. Of the 159-man crew, 115 were killed.

Thus, the United States engaged in combat operations and sustained casualties more than a month before officially entering the war against Germany on December 11.

The Soviet Union: June–July 1941

On June 22, Germany invaded the Soviet Union. Code named Operation *Barbarossa*, it consisted of more than 4.5 million troops along a 1,800-mile front stretching from the Baltic Sea in the north to the Black Sea in the south. By the end of the first week, the Germans had achieved their major campaign objectives and continued toward Leningrad and Moscow.

Stalin made an effort to rally his demoralized nation on July 3. Calling on them as "brothers and sisters," something he had never done before and would never do again, he exhorted them to fight a "great patriotic war" against the treacherous fascist invader. Stalin asked them to fight, to take everything away before the advance of the invader, and to destroy anything that couldn't be removed, leaving nothing but "scorched earth."

Most western military experts believed that the Soviets would be defeated within a month. Despite this prediction, Britain and the United States immediately offered assistance. Notwithstanding the willingness to help, there were formidable physical and logistical problems of getting aid to Russia.

Among logistical problems were moving supplies to embarkation ports, assigning ships to carry the supplies, and detailing the warships for escort duty. The opening and protection of a new convoy route which, unlike the transatlantic ones, was exposed for a great part of its length to enemy-held territory on its flank was added to the Royal Navy's tasks. Already stretched almost to the limit by worldwide responsibilities, this additional requirement drained resources from other critical areas. The merchant marine fleet also was stretched almost to the breaking point. The German forces of U-boats, surface raiders, and Focke-Wulf Condors were sinking ships faster than new ones could be built or damaged ones repaired.

The Soviets held on through the summer, disproving military experts. The first convoy sailed for Arkhangelsk on August 21.

CHAPTER 2

SKIRMISHING
August 1941–March 1942

HMS *Adventure*, a fast, mine-laying cruiser, was the first ship to arrive in Russia on August 1, 1941, with a consignment of war materials including mines and depth charges, bound for Arkhangelsk. Combat cooperation between the Soviet Northern Fleet and the British Royal Navy began on July 31 when the Soviet destroyer *Sokrushitelnyy* rendezvoused with *Adventure* near Gorodetski Lighthouse and escorted her to Arkhangelsk along the intricate fairways of the White Sea and Dvina River. To Admiral Arseni Golovko, head of the Soviet Northern Fleet, the British mines were worthless. However, worthless or not, four Russian destroyers laid the mines on the seabed off the Fisherman's Peninsula in two mine barrages.

Outside the Kola Inlet on August 8, *V. Kuibyshev*, a ship of the same division, met the British submarine *Tigris*, the first that came to reinforce the North Fleet Submarine Brigade, located in the Polyarnoe Naval Base north of Murmansk. Later, destroyer *Uritzkiy* escorted a second British submarine, *Trident*, to her new home at the naval base.

Although the Kriegsmarine were not concerned about British operations at this point, they had already sown mine fields along the White Sea coast. The first victim was the cargo passenger ship *Pomorie* (Captain S. V. Varakin) on August 22. She was carrying thirty-two crewmembers and thirty passengers. Only two crew survived, a grim toll and a foretaste of what was to come for all who sailed these waters.

On August 21, "Dervish" was the first Allied convoy to sail from Hvalfjödur to Arkhangelsk. The convoy consisted of the merchant ships *Lancastrian Prince*, *New Westminster City*, *Esneh*, *Trehata*, and *Llanstephan Castle* and the Dutch freighter *Alchiba*. The convoy delivered 10,000 tons of rubber, 3,800 depth charges and magnetic mines, 15 Hurricane fighters, 1,500 tons of army boots, and a great deal of other essential equipment, as well as 534 pilots and ground crew from Britain who were carried on the convoy ships and escort vessels for service in Russia.

Escort of Convoy consisted of the destroyers HMS *Electra*, *Active*, and *Impulsive*; the antisubmarine warfare Shakespearian-class trawlers *Hamlet*, *Macbeth*, and *Ophelia*; and the Halcyon-class minesweepers *Halcyon*, *Salamander*, and *Harrier*. The minesweepers and their crews would remain in Arkhangelsk supporting the convoys.

Distant cover was provided by the heavy cruiser HMS *Shropshire* and the destroyers *Matabele*, *Punjabi*, and *Somali*.

At the same time, the old aircraft carrier HMS *Argus* carried twenty-four Hawker Hurricane fighters of the Royal Air Force's 151 Aviation Wing consisting of the 134th and 81st squadrons. Nearing the Murman coast, RAF 81 Squadron aircraft were flown off and landed at Vaenga airfield, 25 miles north of Murmansk. Taking off from a carrier deck is a skill usually acquired through much practice and done with aircraft specifically designed for carrier operations. But the RAF pilots had no training in carrier flight operations, and Hurricanes are land-based aircraft. This was a one-time shot. Fortunately, all fifteen aircraft got off without significant damage.

The Hurricanes reinforced the Soviet Air Force, which had lost approximately 3,000 aircraft during the initial stages of the German invasion. One of their most pressing needs was for fighters to assist in the defense of Murmansk, which the Germans were determined to capture.

A Luftwaffe base was located less than 50 miles away at Petsamo, making the Kola Inlet too dangerous for the ship containing the crated aircraft to dock in Murmansk. So it continued on to Arkhangelsk, where the aircraft were assembled with Russian assistance, and rejoined the rest of the wing at Vaenga on September 12.

The convoy arrived in the White Sea without loss, primarily because the Luftwaffe had only a few aerial reconnaissance forces in the region at the time. The Soviet Northern Fleet destroyers *Groznyy*, *Oritskyy*, and *Kujbyshey* met the convoy west of Cape Kanin Nos in the White Sea on August 30, and on the following day sailed down the Dvina River, arriving safely in Arkhangelsk. This first run was a quiet one for the escorts and merchantmen.

Though this initial run over the icy seas went smoothly, the welcome on shore was almost as cool as the weather. Ken Allen, a seaman on board the British freighter S.S. *New Westminster City* was not impressed with the reception from the Russians in Arkhangelsk:

I was Ordinary Seaman and later Sailor on the SS New Westminster City, *having joined the ship on 10th July 1940 and several voyages later re-joined her in Ellesmere Port on the 29th July 1941 for an unknown destination although large crates which contained "Kittyhawks" and "Tomahawks", [fighter] planes from the U.S.A. were clearly stenciled "Goods for Russian" and "Murmansk or Arkhangelsk". We sailed from Scapa Flow on the 21 August 1941, six Merchant ships and a large naval escort including the old aircraft carrier H.M.S.* Argus *with twenty-four Hurricanes of No. 151 R.A.F. Wing onboard.*

It was dark for most of the time and we saw no action during the whole round voyage, German intelligence seemed to have fallen down for once. One of the merchant ships was the Union Castle Liner Llanstephan Castle *with Commandos on board. The convoy laid off Spitzbergen early one morning for two or three hours and I understand the Commandos landed to blow up communication installations etc. but the event appears to have had little publicity.*

Despite us taking war supplies to Russia, at that time in the war there was very little cooperation from the Russians. We were to dock in Arkhangelsk but arriving off the quay there were no boatmen to take our ropes. Our Master wanted to lay alongside the quay and land crewmembers to take our ropes but armed guards stopped them because we did not have shore passes. Eventually officials came down and a few passes were issued but when the gangway was down the passes were collected and we were not allowed ashore for several days.

Little labour was available and we crew drove our steam winches and helped with the discharge of cargo. When we loaded a full cargo of sawn timber it was stacked by Russian women, we still drove the winches.

The first contact RAF officers had with the Russians in Arkhangelsk was very different, however, and left a deep impression on them. One of them later wrote about it:

> *I saw a couple of old Russian lumber-men and a party of a dozen Russian girls sawing up and loading timber into lorries as they arrived at the dockside. After they had loaded up all the timber that was in sight, they moved off to the next railway-shed, and from the coming and going of lorries it was obvious that the sawing and loading up was still going forward. The party was under the command of a girl about twenty, a qualified engineer. They worked away for three hours like absolute fury, the engineer-girl working the hardest of the lot. No one was looking on or supervising—but the speed of the work was prodigious. Once a lorry was loaded up with sawn timber, the girls would sit down for a breather and start smoking and singing. And then, when another lorry would come up, they'd start in all over again.*
>
> *The whole thing was, on their part, a marvelous exhibition of enthusiasm, energy and concentration. When they had finished loading every piece of timber in sight, they got to and swept down the whole quay-side (including all the rubbish chucked off the transport), a task which took an hour, and then buzzed off home. One had at last seen Russians at work, unwatched. Or rather—certain Russians at work unwatched. If there is anybody in Russia among the "higher-ups" making mistakes and blunders—and by what the Russian army is doing there is no evidence that any higher-ups are making mistakes and blunders—there is evidently a terrific mine of enthusiasm and energy backing the war effort among the "lower-downs."*

RAF 81 Squadron pilots and aircraft were welcomed with open arms by their Soviet counterparts. The British pilots were hesitant at first about letting the Soviets fly without extensive training, but the Soviets weren't ready to wait, as related by Soviet Air Force Officer Vasily Minakov:

> *In the first meeting of allies, the commander of a squadron, Captain B. F. Safonov with the pilots has come on landing the Hurricanes. They were met by the commander of English squadron A. T. Miller. Safonov has asked Miller to show the aircraft. Miller answered that the Hurricane [was] difficult to handle and only skilled pilots could tame it. But Safonov repeated the request. Miller gave in. After Safonov was seated in the cockpit, Miller stood with the translator on a wing and explained [the] appointment of devices, action with the basic panels and sequence of inclusion of toggle-switches for motor start.*

Safonov listened attentively. When Miller [had] finished explanations, Safonov addressed to the translator: "Tell, to the major that I ask it to check up, whether I have correctly understood all". Miller lifted his hands and has told to the translator: "Tell to Mr. Safonov I'm impressed."

Two minutes later, Safonov was airborne and handled the Hurricane with consummate skill.

During the following month, the Royal Air Force provided air cover to Soviet troops trying to hold off German forces from Murmansk and the Murmansk railway. In particular, they provided fighter escorts to Soviet bomber aircraft operating along the front. The RAF pilots carried out their final operational flight on October 8. At that point, they started handing their aircraft and equipment (including the pilots' flying helmets) over to the Soviet Air Force, a task they completed by October 22. The personnel of 151 Wing returned by sea on British ships, and they started arriving back in Britain on December 7, 1941. During thirty-six days of direct participation in combat, they flew 365 combat sorties, destroying or damaging twelve German planes at a cost of two RAF pilots killed.

On September 29, PQ-1, consisting of 11 merchant ships loaded with raw materials, 20 tanks, and 193 crated Hurricane fighter planes, sailed from Hvalfjödur for Arkhangelsk. Making the trip as part of the escorting force were the minesweepers *Britomart*, *Swan*, *Gossamer*, and *Hussar*, which were sent to reinforce three other minesweepers that had arrived as part of Dervish.

The first returning convoy, QP-1, comprised of the returning Dervish ships, four Russian merchant ships, and the fleet oiler *Black Ranger*, left Arkhangelsk and arrived at Scapa Flow on October 9. Both convoys arrived safely, having enjoyed good weather and no encounters with the Germans.

Arctic convoy duty differed from that of the North Atlantic or runs to the Mediterranean. John Squires, a seaman on board the destroyer HMS *Impulsive*, described the differences:

There was no real threat from the enemy at this stage of the war, which was fortunate really, as it was summer in the north and we had twenty-four hours of daylight, apart from the odd patch of fog in the Barents Sea.

It was an unusual experience to go on watch at midnight until 4am and to have the sun still shining, plus the clock had to go which played havoc with the watch keeping duties, and the meal times, still, it did not interfere with the Up Spirits or Nelson's Blood ration [the daily issue of grog to all hands].

Squires also recalled both the routine and the unexpected beauty he experienced:

These were the times during long days and nights, on convoy runs, when the ships companies' talents came to light such as model making, embroidery, sketching, rug making, you mention it.

To avoid the enemy we had to sail into the Greenland Sea between Bear Island and Spitzbergen and those Arctic waters are notorious for fog and it can be very scary in dense fog surrounded by many ships, straining one's eyes in case another ship got too close. But on a moonlight night the north can be quite pleasant. I remember one night, it was very misty and moonlight, and round the ship's bow was a white crescent, just like a miniature rainbow but pure white.

Also there was the beautiful spectacle (sometimes) of the northern lights, Aurora-Borealis. They are huge ribbons of fabulous colours, dancing and flickering against the black of the night, and as we approached our destination, we sailed through the sea of pack ice. Some of the ice flow had the odd seal or two on them who, I thought, looked at us reproachfully for disturbing their peace.

Minesweepers played an integral part in the Arctic convoy story. In September, the First Minesweeping Flotilla, comprised of *Bramble*, *Gossamer*, *Hussar*, *Leda*, *Seagull*, *Speedy*, and *Windermere*, was allocated to Arctic convoy duties with north Russia as its base. The flotilla joined the escort force for PQ-2 in Liverpool and sailed to Arkhangelsk without losses. John Douglas-Hiley on board *Bramble* remembered his arrival in Russia:

While waiting to enter the Dvina River for passage to Arkhangelsk itself, we were met by a small Russian icebreaker tug. Although it was only late September, we were all "rugged up" with thick clothing—two pairs of socks and a pair of oiled wool sea-boot stockings under leather sea-boots. The Russian Engineer Officer of the tug, a young woman, came on deck to look at us. She wore a short sleeved shirt, trousers and ordinary shoes and stood there for some time without a goose-pimple showing. We were amazed and impressed.

Our minesweepers followed the tug up to Brevennik Island, just opposite Arkhangelsk itself. On the island, there was a small dockyard at one end and what appeared to be a detention centre at the other. This was guarded by sentries, many of them women soldiers. We learned early on that when they called on you to halt, it meant just that. They were quite ready to shoot if in doubt. We were issued with Red Stars to wear in our caps to help identification.

Even when not escorting merchant ships, the British minesweepers were constantly employed, and their crews got a taste of the bitter Russian arctic weather. One of the first independent operations for them was to investigate "unknown objects" dropped from enemy aircraft in the strait at the entrance of the Kara Sea. One crewmember of this operation described it:

As we moved east from the mouth of the White Sea, the sea [became] frozen, which looked to one like a thick mixture of water and cellulose. When we reached the strait we observed that the shore was completely covered with ice, but in the middle of the gulf we could see separate ice floes. We made several tacks without results with the electromagnetic and acoustic sweeps and were coming to think that it was a false alarm when a very powerful explosion rang out ahead, throwing into the air a tangled mass of broken ice. Those on deck threw themselves into shelter from the ice rubble, crashing down on the ship.

This was a terrific introduction to minesweeping in the Arctic. But there was more to come shortly, as Douglas-Hiley related:

The minesweepers' task was to provide close cover, because the Germans concentrated their principal attacks at this point (the entrance to Kola Inlet). They knew that every convoy had to converge on this point, thus providing the maximum target.

During our early days at Polyarnyy, two of our ships were attacked by two large German destroyers, and one of them was hit by a 5.9-inch shell, but the Germans broke off the action for reasons no one could explain. The after 4-inch gun mounting was on the superstructure immediately above the wardroom where the Gunnery Officer was sleeping. When the alarm sounded, he dressed and put on his steel helmet. Just at that moment, the shell hit the gun mounting killing one man and severely wounding another. A splinter penetrated the deck and the Gunnery Officer's battle-

bowler [helmet]. It raced around the inside of his tin-hat till it fell down on his bald-head leaving him struggling like mad to get the helmet off. The severely wounded man was sent to a Russian hospital where a kidney wound was successfully operated on, but without anesthetic. They were short of medical supplies.

Douglas-Hiley got an unexpected insight to his Soviet allies one day, an insight that summed up why the Soviets were fighting so hard:

I learned to speak some Russian and was able to exchange our cigarettes for their awful papirossi, those smoke sticks with a cardboard tube at one end and tobacco at the other. The brand was called Nasha Marka [Our Brand]. Talking alone with one of them, I asked what he really thought of Communism. "You must be joking, Ivan," he said. "Don't you know that Communism is only for export?"
"What are you fighting for then, Sergei?"
"Two things—Rodina (the Motherland) and the hope that, maybe, my grandchildren will have a better life," he replied.

Initially the convoys were planned on a forty-day cycle. Prime Minister Winston Churchill insisted that the cycle be shortened to ten days, with Arkhangelsk handling the bulk of the deliveries. The protection of the convoys heading to north Russia was a responsibility of the Royal Navy Home Fleet based in Scapa Flow and commanded by Admiral Sir John C. Tovey.

The route, which was open to U-boat attack throughout its entire length, was limited to the west and north by ice and to the east and south by an enemy-occupied coast, well provided with anchorages whence surface forces could operate at will, and airfields from which aircraft could dominate 1,400 miles of its furthest east, and therefore most vulnerable, waters. The whole route, including the terminal ports at each end, lay within the range of enemy air reconnaissance and at two points was crossed by German routine meteorological flights. British shore-based air support was confined to what could be given from Iceland and Sullom Voe in the Shetland Islands.

The most critical logistical problem was refueling the escorts while at sea. Other problems included lack of facilities of any kind for both naval and merchant personnel at journey's end, which posed a serious threat to morale.

In Iceland, the U.S. Navy escort force primarily consisted of three 327-foot Secretary Class Coast Guard cutters (USS *Bibb* [WPG-31], USS *Duane* [WPG-33], and USS *Ingham* [WPG-35]) and four older Navy destroyers (USS *Babbitt* [DD-128], USS *Badger* [DD-126], USS *Leary* [DD-158], and USS *Scheck* [DD-159]). These ships ran shuttle service, escorting empty merchant ships to the Mid Ocean Meeting Point, where the British escort force was relieved by either an American or Canadian escort force, picking up fully loaded vessels from an eastbound convoy and returning to Iceland. If all went well, the round trip took about seven days. They also were called to reinforce besieged convoys fighting their way through the mid-Atlantic (known as "Torpedo Junction"), conduct search and rescue missions, assist in resupplying outlying garrisons, and conduct weather patrols. Despite their extensive operations, none of the escorts sank a U-boat during the war.

From Loch Ewe, additional ships for the Arctic convoys were sailed in a series of convoys designated "UR" (United Kingdom–Reykjavik) and "RU" (Reykjavik–United Kingdom). Although not routinely harassed by U-boats or the Luftwaffe, the ships were battered by lethal storms while their masters grew gray trying to navigate through impenetrable fog.

The Army Air Force wasn't idle in Iceland, either. The 342nd Composite Group was tasked with preventing Luftwaffe reconnaissance and bombing attacks. Army pilots flying P-38 Lightnings proved effective, shooting down a Focke-Wulf FW-200 Condor in August 1942. Although not tallying a significant number of kills, the pilots did prevent the Germans from obtaining accurate information on shipping.

Navy Patrol Squadron VP-73, VP-74, VP-84 flying Catalina PBYs and PBMs, and VB-128 flying Ventura PV-1s endured seemingly endless flights over thousands of square miles of barren ocean, often under appalling weather conditions. Winter in Iceland was the worst enemy of the patrol squadrons. The British withdrew their PBY squadron, feeling that the weather was too extreme for operation of the slow patrol aircraft. On January 15, 1942, gales reaching 133 mph struck the area, sinking three of VP-73's Catalinas and two of VP-74's PBMs.

The first victory over U-boats was long in coming. It wasn't until August 20, 1942, while on convoy escort in Skerja Fjord, near Reykjavik, that Lieutenant (JG) Robert B. Hopgood and his crew attacked and sank *U-464*, Korvettenkapitän Otto Harms commanding. Hopgood and his crew pressed home the attack even though the crew of the U-boat elected to remain on the surface and fight it out with the lightly armed Catalina. HMS *Castleton* rescued fifty-three survivors. Returning to base, Hopgood sent the following message: "Sank Sub Open Club" (Hopgood was awarded the Navy Cross for his heroic action).

Despite the hardships and boredom, these intrepid airmen sank five U-boats between August 1942 and October 1943.

For the men, Iceland was a bleak and often inhospitable place to live and work. Army and Marine garrison troops had little to do day to day, and there wasn't much in the way of entertainment.

As difficult as it was for the troops and flight crews, the escort sailors had it worse. The frequent shuttle runs strained the ships to the breaking point. Particularly hard hit were the destroyers, which literally began falling apart. Even the tough 327s weren't immune. Lieutenant (JG) Joe Matte on *Ingham* reported that, during a two-week period, the boot on the underwater sound gear was stove in by heavy weather, rendering that vital equipment almost useless; the ship was battered by various misadventures in coming alongside tankers in gale force winds; No. 1 boat was slightly damaged; No. 2 boat was stove in; the port gun sponson (aft) was partially broken; and the starboard gun sponson was completely smashed by a wave, broke adrift, and fell into the sea.

Hvalfjödur proved as dangerous as the open ocean. On January 15, 1942, a storm with wind velocity of more than 80 knots and gusts of more than 100 knots struck; heavy cruiser *Wichita* (CA-45) was damaged in collisions with U.S. freighter *West Nohno* and British trawler HMS *Ebor Wyke* and grounded near Hrafneyri lighthouse. Storm conditions lasted until January 19 and caused heavy damage among patrol planes based there and tended by seaplane tender *Albemarle* (AV-5).

The strain continued throughout the year. There was no peace on earth on Christmas 1942 for *Duane, Ingham,* or *Campbell.* At noon, a 100-knot gale struck from the mountains. *Duane* had both anchors down, but the wind blew so hard they dragged across the bottom. The harbor was in chaos as ships tried to save themselves, at times fouling each other's anchor chains, a move that hamstrung their chances of survival. *Ingham* and *Campbell* fought for their lives as winds pushed them toward the rocks, powerful engines and low slung hulls straining to hold clear, the crews on deck working the anchor windlasses, braced against the blow.

In-port time, usually anchored in the harbor in Hvalfjödur, was spent refueling, rearming, repairing equipment, chipping and painting, and standing anchor and radio watches. The rare shore liberty for the escorts' officers was in Reykjavik, which offered little in the way of night life, or for enlisted men, at the base canteen, which was limited to a few hours and two cans of beer per man. Coast Guard crews held boat drills every morning, regardless of the weather. Pulling boats were launched, and the men rowed for an hour or more before breakfast. They rowed not for fun or simply to provide exercise, but to gain proficiency in handling the boats in all types of weather, good practice for those times when they would be called to rescue survivors from torpedoed ships in the open ocean. On board there was no privacy, and even the rare quiet times were haunted by the knowledge that the men soon would have to go out to sea again.

Somehow through all this, the air crews and escort sailors from the United States and at least one Royal Canadian Navy minesweeper, HMCS *Canso*, kept their sense of humor. No one remembers how or when it started, but by the spring of 1943, they began to refer to themselves as members of the "Brotherhood of the FBI." This, in that more refined period of time, was a nice way of saying "Forgotten Bastards of Iceland."

Convoys PQ-1, 2, 3, 4, and 5, totaling twenty-nine ships, as well as the returning convoys QP-1, 2, 3, and 4, all made runs during autumn and early winter of 1941 without losing any ships. But they did suffer casualties in men and equipment.

PQ-3 ran into severe storms and patrolling Luftwaffe Ju-87 Stuka dive bombers. On this run in November 1941, Godfrey P. Hudson kept a diary, which tells the story:

November 16th. Leaving today. Stormy outside. Getting a bad buffeting by head seas which sweep over the fo'c'sle head and roar along foredeck.

November 20th. Full gale. Two ships turned back—one hit a small berg and the other had engine trouble. One of the tanks in our 'tween deck broke loose and charged into the ships side flattening the angle irons. Bosun and crew got aboard the charging monster and shored it up with baulks of timber. (Ship was eventually awarded the OBE for this act of bravery.)

November 22nd. Crossed Arctic Circle. Course for 75 North. I believe. Stukas dive bombed the convoy. The flutes under the wings gave a banshee wail and every seventh shell was a tracer so when one of the gunners on the port wing Oerlikon was hit by a tracer it cauterized the wound and he survived the rough handling when the skipper ordered "that corpse off the bridge" I put him in the shelter of the wheelhouse which was reinforced with concrete slabs and took over the gun for a few exciting seconds. We were in the vicinity of Jan Mayen Island at the extremity of the Stuka's range so it was a short lived raid. They lost two planes and the crews were dead when picked up. Temperature 40 below.

The British seamen and the first of the American merchant seamen learned bitterly in the winter of 1941–42 about Arctic weather. The gales blew across the 900-mile-wide space between Greenland and Norway and swept northeastward. The wind struck the slowly laboring columns of a convoy with an unbroken fury. The crews lived in almost perpetual darkness for 115 days during the dark winter when the sun barely rose. It was so dark that a lookout stationed on a ship's bridge could not even see the bow of his own vessel.

The positions of the ships ahead, on each side and astern were unknown; all were under complete blackout regulation. Convoy machine-gunners had orders to fire directly at any light shown. But another ship might be detected by a veering wind gust that held a tang of stack smoke, or her engine sounds, the thud of her propeller, the waves hammering her hull.

Men strained to hear and to smell as well as to see. They explored the caverns of the wind in the lulls between gusts with extremely sensitized perception. Buffeting wind blurred their vision, and the unwilled tears froze on their cheeks. Their eyebrows and eyelashes were frozen. Their lashes would fall off later, painfully, in the heated quarters of the ship. Breath was agony if taken fully before the wind; a man turned aside, breathed, swung back, and examined the reaching dark again.

Ships often were saved from collision, severe injury, and loss of life by a lookout's recognition at the last instant. The other ship appeared as a shape darker than night, marked by the pale run of the wake alongside in the somber sea. Then the shout to the helmsman was given: "Hard over!" The slick brass of the whistle handle was grasped and pulled down, and signals exchanged. The ships swerved apart from each other, back into the vastness of the night and the wind.

Mates and helmsmen stood breathing rapidly after such near-collisions. They sweated inside their layers of clothing. Shivering overcame them. When they tried to drink coffee, their teeth clacked on the rims of the mugs.

Winter was brutal for the men on the convoys, and summer was little better, bringing its own dangers. Ice was within 80 miles of the North Cape during the summer months. The Atlantic Drift, the last of the Gulf Stream, flowing northeastward, separated in two forks, and both brought fog. One went along the Norwegian coast and then the Murman coast of the continent, and kept Murmansk ice-free. The other went much higher north, past Bear Island, in 74°29′ North latitude and 19°10′ East longitude. Summer convoys found protection in the fog, but also wandered far off course due to poor visibility, and suffered badly from collision. Fog, some convoy shipmasters said, was worse than the winter darkness.

A British ship's captain who had experienced both brutal winters and summers remembered the dangers wrought by the weather.

From February onwards it is lighting up quickly. At the end of January there are four hours' daylight, end of February eight hours' daylight, end of April 20 hours', and July and August virtually twenty-four hours' daylight, with sun all the time, which works along the horizon. From April to August there's no really bad weather; conditions are ideal for enemy attack.

Winter starts in September, and from October to the end of December there's a lot of fog and heavy snowstorms, but not much wind. From the end of December you may get gales of hurricane strength which can last five days, but between gales the weather may be flat. In the winds, a big short sea is built up—seldom more than fifteen feet, even in bad weather, for the seas are comparatively shallow—but in those big short seas the ship rolls like hell.

Storm damage was in some instances so severe that ships were forced to leave convoy. The crews of the merchant ships worked with almost frantic haste to make repairs at sea and keep their vessels within the protective screen of the escort.

They took a very great chance of being sunk if they returned alone to Iceland. U-boats ranged across the straggler ship's course back to the Icelandic ports. The temperature of the water was less than forty degrees in summer. A man could live in it for about ten minutes. Chances of survival were small in a lifeboat, and death from exposure was slow, painful, and terrible.

Even just working outside on a ship's main deck in the Arctic night with a gale blowing and the spray freezing as it fell was very nearly impossible. Escort vessels, with a good deal more ease of maneuver than a heavily loaded cargo ship, lost boats, davits, and men on many occasions.

Deck cargo that had shifted during battering storms was the usual problem for a merchant ship. Tanks, planes, trucks, and locomotives were stowed fore and aft on the main decks in the loading ports. These were thick-coated with ice. During a gale, some ships accumulated as much as 150 tons of ice that covered all of their deck gear. Windlasses and winches were stubborn and sluggish, even though they had been kept running for days.

A ship's deck gang first tried to remove the thick ice with chipping hammers, mauls, picks, and axes to clear the gear. Ice clogged the block sheaves. Ice formed in the manila core of the wire rope and swelled the diameter; the rope would not lead through the blocks. Pins were frozen in shackles, and were beaten free with a broad-headed maul in the darkness. Blows missed the pins and hit the hands of the men who held the shackles. There was no use complaining; voices and shouts went unheard in the wind no matter how loudly the curses were uttered.

Wire and chain were shackled in place and hauled across the dimly seen pieces of cargo. New lashings were secured. Men groped their way, working without light. Their sea boots were full of water. The towels wrapped within their weather-coat collars had long since been soaked. Their hands, stripped of icy and useless gloves, were numb, clumsy, and bloody. Seas smashed over the deck, and the men were knocked headlong.

Each of them had been secured singly by the chief mate when they started work. Individual lifelines, strong manila, were attached to a main hawser stretched fore and aft. When the sea struck, they were swept only the length of the lifeline—rather than overboard—then fetched up, the bowline knot yanking at their chests as their backs, legs, and arms banged against the deck plates, seawater soaking them in a smacking torrent that made them gasp out in fear. Drowning was an ever-present danger.

Some ships were so badly damaged or their cargo so shifted that they sailed with as much as a 30-degree list. Speed was reduced to 3 or 4 knots. Steering was dangerous and kept to a minimum. A sudden change of rudder direction might send a ship beam-end under, never to right herself.

When the ships reached Iceland and went to anchor in the safety of the deep bay at Hvalfjödur, the men felt a giddy intoxication of relief. Shore leave was not allowed. Permission was asked to take ships' boats away, and the men went around the bay visiting various vessels.

Americans getting ready for their first Arctic convoy, who boarded British ships with veteran crews, were told that their luck was just a bit more than ordinary. The British gave accounts of conditions in the White and Barents Seas, where it easily took a ship sixteen days to move just 70 miles.

Coming out of Arkhangelsk in February, the men on bridge lookout had icicles on their eyebrows, noses, and beards. Icicles as thick as a man's arm hung from the rigging. The chief engineer turned over the propeller every ten minutes to keep it free from ice. Even inside the ship, ice formed on the bulkheads, and the portholes were frozen shut.

The British seamen at Hvalfjödur showed the Americans their Arctic clothing. They had been issued hooded duffle coats lined with lamb's wool and padded around the skirt. There was an extra hood for each man, with only slits for eyes and mouth. Standard-issue underclothing was as thick as a sweater and made of soft, white wool. So were the two pairs of seaboot socks, which reached high on a man's thighs. There were long, broad scarves, wristlets, and mittens with a separate thumb and first finger. Sea boots were made of leather, and were lighter, more compact, and easier on the feet than the rubber boots the Americans wore.

Gunners, coxswains, and signalmen, whose duties involved prolonged exposure, were issued knee-length sheepskin jerkins. These they wore leather-side out, with a leather duty belt holding the waist tight. The garments were sleeveless to allow full freedom of action. Under their helmet liners, the gunners wore balaclava hoods, knitted so that the bottoms protected a man's chest and back.

Men and ships alike were susceptible to the icy sea. One Russian merchant ship in QP-3, *Kuzbass*, was the first to be caught by the Arctic winter's fury. The convoy sailed from Arkhangelsk on November 27. K. A. Egorov, a Soviet Northern Fleet officer on board *Kuzbass*, told what happened after the convoy reached the White Sea and set course for Iceland:

> *As soon as the icebreaker left the mouth of the Northern Dvina River in the White Sea we [were] met by intense cold and a raging gale which lasted two days.*
>
> *In the Barents Sea, the convoy met another violent storm. The heavy seas smashed the ship's rudder and bent it ninety degrees to starboard. Kuzbass fell behind the convoy. The captain gathered the ship's officers in an attempt to reach a solution. Some suggestions were made including making a wooden rudder (luckily it was a lot of wood) and [making] our own way to England. Fortunately, in the twilight the steamer Arcos, a straggler from the convoy, hove into view. Her captain agreed to tow us to safety.*
>
> *Now began a desperate struggle with the seas. In twenty below zero temperature and the ships casting about like wood chips, a bad dressed team (not even enough mittens) filed with the tugs Arcos in the Kuzbass and vice versa. Tow-lines rushed like a thread, when one ship billowing like an*

elk on the ridge, and the other plunged into the abyss at the foot of the waves. Finally, Arcos broke down and towing became impossible.

When the storm died down, we tried to tow again, but there was [a] big swell and it did not happen and soon we were trapped in the ice.

On 10 December at 0900 hours the ice breaker Litke, rescue ship Squall, and SKR-19 found us. At 1100, the captain of Litke reported that the southern passage [was] clogged with ice and planned to go north of the island of Kolga. December 13, began a strong contraction of ice and the ship's hull cracked. The captain explained the situation and gave orders to prepare to leave the ship. Avoiding panic, we prepared clothes and food, but the ship wasn't crushed.

At last, on December 18, Kuzbass, towed by Litke, headed east to safety. Only on December 26 at 1400, again in a raging storm, did we enter the harbor Iokanka.

Winter's onset necessitated drastic changes in the convoy routing. In the middle of January 1942, navigation had been stopped in the White Sea and Dvina River due to heavy ice despite the concentration of icebreakers in the White Sea. From the war's beginning, Arkhangelsk accepted 52 vessels that delivered 699 planes, 466 tanks, and other cargo, accounting for 95 percent of all deliveries to Russia.

But the move to Murmansk did little to solve the convoys' problems. The condition of its port was even more pitiable than Arkhangelsk's. Not only was almost all valuable equipment evacuated when the war began, but there was no housing for the dock workers in Murmansk. Among these were 1,500 people who had been evacuated to the Kola Peninsula from territory threatened by the German invasion, another 2,000 mobilized in the Ryazan region east of Moscow, and 500 (mostly women) were sent from Arkhangelsk.

The work went on through the polar night in blackout conditions. The weather alternated between hard frosts and blizzards whipped by gale force winds. Regardless of the harsh conditions, 2,500 people worked every day to unload the transports, averaging one transport every ten to eighteen days.

In both Arkhangelsk and Murmansk, the civilians were on the verge of starvation. Evgraf Evlogievichu, a student at the Arkhangelsk School of Ship's Boys, remembered that bitter time:

All winter 1941–1942 Arkhangelsk was very hungry. Cut bread ration to 200 grams. Ate not only the skin and birch bark, spruce, even coats: removed the pile, cut the peel into strips and cooked. On the streets there were no cats, no dogs, no pigeons. At school for breakfast we [ate] bread and butter.

Up to this point, there had been no concerted effort by the Germans to disrupt the convoys, except for occasional attacks by the Luftwaffe. However, the military supplies being delivered were helping to stiffen the defenses in the Kola Peninsula and around Leningrad. This was noted by the German high command and great action against the convoys began in early winter.

PQ-4 was attacked by a small group of Ju-88 bombers in an area to the south of Jan Mayen Island. Single planes continued to attack the convoy until it reached the White Sea. However, the attacks were not driven home. At this stage of the war, Luftwaffe pilots, as a rule, approached at a height of 12,000 feet, winged over into a dive, and dumped their bombs out of anti-aircraft fire range.

PQ-6 was the first to have a run in with Kriegsmarine destroyers. Minesweepers HMS *Hazard* and HMS *Speedy* were scheduled to meet the convoy as it approached the Kola Inlet. But, at 1845 hours on December 17, 30 miles north of Cape Gorodetski, they encountered the German destroyers Z-23, Z-24, Z-25, and Z-27, which mistook them for Russian destroyers and attacked. The action resulted only in four hits on *Speedy*, which was damaged and forced to return to Murmansk.

The minesweepers cut their trawls and opened fire on the enemy, but the forces were obviously unequal. *Speedy* received four direct hits and lost two men killed, with damage to the after gun, damage to the propeller, and a smashed top-mast, which forced her to leave the action under cover of a smoke screen and return to base escorted by the Soviet ship *Leda*. Although her sister ship was out of action, *Hazard* continued on to meet the convoy. An attempt by the British cruiser *Kenya* and the Soviet destroyers *Groznyy* and *Sokrushitelnyy* to cut out the German warships failed and the Germans retreated unscathed.

Surprisingly, between the end of December 1941 and March 1942, out of a total of 158 merchant ships in convoy, only one merchant ship and one British destroyer were sunk; one other merchant ship was damaged by the Germans.

On January 2, *U-134* sank the British freighter *Waziristan* from PQ-7A. *Waziristan* had been stranded on the ice edge and was attacked by Luftwaffe aircraft before being torpedoed and sunk by *U-134*. None of her forty-seven man crew survived.

PQ-8 was hit next, and once again the minesweepers were part of the fight along with Northern Fleet units.

Reinforcing the escort of PQ-8 on January 17, 1942, the destroyers *Sokrushitelnyy* and *Gremyashchiy* were sent, together with six motor launches, six motor torpedo boats, and the minesweepers *Hazard*, *Sharpshooter*, and *Hebe*. That evening, about 20 miles from the Kola Inlet, the commodore's ship *Harmatris* was attacked and torpedoed by *U-454*. The torpedoes blew a hole in her stern and started a fire, which was quickly extinguished.

In a repeated torpedo attack, *U-454* fired her stern tubes at the British tanker *British Pride*. The torpedoes were heard running by the escorts on that side of the convoy and may have been aimed at the cruiser *Trinidad*. These found their target in the magazines of *Matabele*, sending a sheet of flame 700 feet high into the night sky—the destroyer had disintegrated, hurling her crew into the icy seas. Several of the destroyer's already-primed depth charges set to explode at various depths blew up beneath those who had not been killed. The survivors still on board had no option but to jump from the blazing portion of the hull still afloat into the icy sea, which also was in flames. *Matabele* sank in two minutes. Most of the crew abandoned ship safely, but when the minesweeper *Harrier* arrived on scene a few minutes later, she found the area covered with corpses gently bobbing in the swell. It was a grim reminder that survival time in Arctic waters is measured in seconds. Of *Matabele*'s complement of 238, only two survived.

Hazard and *Sharpshooter*, along with the patrol ship *Smerch* and four motor launches, escorted the damaged *Harmatris* while she was being towed by two tugs from the Kola Inlet.

During the tow, two German aircraft attempted to attack the convoy, but the motor launches opened a deadly anti-aircraft barrage, driving off the marauders. On January 25, the convoy with the damaged transport *Harmatris* reached the Kola Inlet.

Throughout fall and early winter, German forces stationed in Norway were still minimal, and the commitment to provide convoy escorts didn't strain British Home Fleet resources, a situation soon to change.

On the German side, Hitler was shaken by the British Commando raids on the Lofoten Islands in March, which played on his fear that Great Britain might invade Norway. In November 1941, Hitler decided to send the battleship *Tirpitz* to Trondheim rather than into the Atlantic. Hitler, "convinced that Norway is the 'zone of destiny' in this war," ordered a heavy reinforcement of land and air forces and demanded that "every available vessel be employed in Norway."

This was a major shift in German policy, and it was further reinforced by Hitler's decision that the cruisers *Scharnhorst* and *Gneisenau*, based at Brest, should join the *Tirpitz* in Norway. In an audacious operation in February 1942, the two battlecruisers with the heavy cruiser *Prinz Eugen* returned to German waters via the English Channel, causing considerable embarrassment to the Royal Navy and the RAF. Yet both *Scharnhorst* and *Gneisenau* received serious mine damage, while *Prinz Eugen* was torpedoed off Kristiansand and had to return to port. It was seven months before the *Scharnhorst* could rejoin the *Tirpitz* in Norway.

In addition, the heavy cruisers *Admiral Scheer*, *Lützow*, and *Hipper*, light cruiser *Köln*, two flotillas of destroyers, and fourteen U-boats were transferred to the north of Norway. To ensure that these ships were safe from attack, as well as to protect their communications, the Germans concentrated a significant number of minesweepers, patrol ships, and various support vessels in the area. They also intensified their coastal and air defenses.

Grossadmiral Erich Raeder, head of the Kriegsmarine, insisted that the heaviest concentration of ships in Norwegian waters would be ineffective unless the Luftwaffe strength was correspondingly increased. As a result, more airfields were constructed in Norway and Finland. Luftflotte 5 was reinforced with two specialized antishipping units, KG 26 and KG 30, which were transferred to the air bases at Bardufoss and Banak, as well as another squadron of FW-200 Condors bringing the total to five hundred aircraft.

The main concern of the British was that the German ships in Norway, particularly the *Tirpitz*, did not break out into the Atlantic to attack the convoys. Just after *Tirpitz* arrived in Norwegian waters, Winston Churchill described the destruction of *Tirpitz* as "the greatest event at sea at the present time. No other target is comparable to it." He asserted that the whole strategy of the war turned at this period on this ship, which was holding four times the number of British capital ships from other assignments to say nothing of the two new American battleships retained in the Atlantic.

By springtime 1942, the Arctic nights were shortening and daylight hours were growing long enough to allow German surface ships and aircraft a fair chance of attack since the ice barrier lies further south in March and April than at any other time of the year. The barrier forced convoys to pass south of Bear Island and within 250 miles of the Norwegian coast, approximately 100 miles farther south than in the summer months. In addition, a large increase in the scale of the convoys had been decided on, and the two scheduled to sail at the beginning of March—PQ-12 (sixteen ships) and QP-8 (fifteen ships)—were the largest to date. The escort force consisted of forty warships for PQ-12 and, initially, eight for QP-8.

For the British this meant that big ship cover would have to be provided for these and future convoys. It also meant an increased U-boat threat, which in turn demanded destroyers for screening the capital ships, whose radius of action, except in emergency, was thus limited by the endurance of the screen.

The British and Germans knew that the most obvious use for the *Tirpitz* was against the Arctic convoys, and she made her first sortie on March 6, 1942, against PQ-12, which had been spotted by a FW-200 Condor reconnaissance aircraft the previous day. In turn *Tirpitz* was spotted by the British submarine *Seawolf*, and Admiral Tovey, the British C-in-C Home Fleet, providing distant cover with three capital ships and the aircraft carrier HMS *Victorious*, turned toward PQ-12 and QP-8.

On March 8, bad weather prevented aerial reconnaissance. The two convoys, the British Home Fleet, and *Tirpitz* with *Friedrich Ihn*, *Paul Jacobi*, *Hermann Schoemann*, *Z-25*, *T-5*, and *T-12* as escorts, were all within 80 miles of each other. The two convoys passed each other at noon. Tovey, who unknowingly had approached to within some 75 miles of them, turned to the southwest, little knowing that at that moment his opponent was only 60 miles away to the southeast and steering toward him at high speed. At 1630 hours, when the *Tirpitz* had crossed to the north of the tracks of both convoys, having passed some 60 miles astern of PQ-12 and 50 miles ahead of QP-8, one of the German destroyers, the *Friedrich Ihn*, encountered *Izhora*, a Russian straggler from the homeward convoy QP-8, which she sank at about 1715 hours, but not before her victim had managed to get off a distress message, which was picked up by the battleship *King George V*.

Unfortunately, the position received was incomplete, but soon afterward radio bearings of a German ship which might possibly have been the *Tirpitz* were picked up by the flagship. So at 1750 hours, Tovey altered the course of his force to the east, the direction from which the bearing had come.

In the evening of March 8, Admiral Otto Ciliax, commander of the Kriegsmarine task force, decided to terminate the operation due to poor visibility, bad weather, lack of air reconnaissance, the vastness of the operational area, and complete ignorance of the enemy's position, all of which made success more than doubtful.

At 0640 hours the next day, several British scouting planes from *Victorious* located the German task force. Assuming that the carrier to which the enemy planes belonged would not have ventured so close to the Norwegian coast without the protection of other heavy fleet units, Ciliax ordered *Tirpitz* to proceed toward the Lofoten Islands at maximum speed.

At 0730, a dozen Albacore aircraft armed with torpedoes took off and headed for *Tirpitz*. An hour later, a questing Albacore located *Friedrich lhn* and *Tirpitz* proceeding south at high speed 80 miles east of the Home Fleet. A few minutes after the Albacore made contact, Chief Petty Officer Finselberger, at an after anti-aircraft position aboard *Tirpitz*, spotted the shadowing plane and all of the battleship's formidable array of anti-aircraft weaponry, sixteen twin 10.5-cm guns, and sixteen 3.7-cm twin flak cannon were made ready. Ciliax flew off an Arado seaplane in an attempt to gain a little local air cover and then turned for the coast with an alteration of course to east, which would, with *Tirpitz*'s superior speed, open out her distance from the Home Fleet. The observer in the trailing Albacore wrongly reported this alteration as being to the northeast, an error that, with the loss of surprise, now conspired to rob Admiral Tovey of any chance of victory.

At 0842, the torpedo-armed Albacores sighted their quarry to the southeast in the direction of the rising sun. The squadron commander ordered his aircraft to climb into cloud cover, hoping to get ahead of the *Tirpitz*, but as they overflew the battleship and the *Friedrich lhn*, a break in the clouds exposed them to flak. Nevertheless, the Albacores split into subflights, which attacked immediately.

The first subflight of Albacores released their torpedoes at long range on the *Tirpitz*'s port bow but at too fine an angle for them to hit the racing ship. With great skill and coolness, Captain Karl Topp on *Tirpitz* put his helm over to port and combed the approaching torpedo tracks. The second subflight attacked from the starboard quarter with the same lack of success. The third and fourth also approached on the starboard side, but were delayed due to the difficulties of maneuvering ahead of the speeding ship.

Topp applied counter helm, which reduced the angle of approach of their torpedoes, and *Tirpitz* succeeded in evading them all. The barrage of fire put up by the German ships, especially the *Tirpitz* herself, was terrific. Two of the Albacores were shot down and, though more were thought by the Germans to have been hit, so intense was their fire, these were the only losses. The British planes had themselves fired machine guns at the gray superstructure as they had roared past. It was a bitter disappointment. The attack, made from leeward and from astern, had robbed the Albacores of any tactical advantage to be gained from a high rate of speed of attack. As the biplanes headed back for the carrier, the unscathed *Tirpitz* was racing unopposed for Norway. *Tirpitz* and her escort made it back to Norway without loss, but also without finding the convoy they were sent out to destroy.

Izhora's sinking seems an incidental loss in this confrontation between giants. She was an old, slow, coal-burning freighter long past her prime captained by Vasily Belov with First Mate Nicholas Adayev. The thirty-one-person crew included three women: Anna Avdeeva was a former barmaid and the eldest at age fifty, Basov Agne had been a charwoman, and Raisa Mogutova was the youngest at just twenty years old. Among the men were nineteen-year-old Peter Panteleyev and two sixteen-year-old sailors: Yuri Shumkova and Lesha Makarycheva.

The battle began when the German destroyer *Friedrich Ihn* hove into view on that overcast afternoon. At 1645 hours on March 7, *Friedrich Ihn's* log noted: "At full speed have gone in this direction. The pipe [smoke stack] and two masts of the steamship, following a course on the West becomes soon visible."

Ihn ordered *Izhora* to stop, lower the flag, and not use the radio. The log continues: "17hrs. 20min. the Steamship informs the identification data: 'Timber carrying vessel *Izhora*, the port of registry Leningrad. Displacement of 2815 tons, I go with cargo'."

If the Germans seized the ship, the crew's fate was obvious: capture by a boarding team from one of the destroyers, and then a short trip to Norway, ending in a concentration camp. There wasn't a ghost of a chance that any would survive. Failure to comply with the order to stop would automatically mean a death sentence.

Knowing they would die one way or another, Vasily Belov increased speed and Nikolai Gusarov, the radio operator, immediately broke radio silence to report contact with the German squadron and its exact location. This was heard by the Germans, and *Ihn* immediately opened fire and destroyed *Izhora's* Radio Room, killing Gusarov.

The other destroyers and *Tirpitz* then opened fire on the unarmed freighter. Incredibly, *Izhora* remained afloat despite being pummeled by one of the strongest fighting ships in the world (eight guns in caliber 380 mm, and numerous smaller guns), and three destroyers (five guns in caliber 127 mm or 150 mm).

It should have ended quickly, for each warship was capable of sinking *Izhora* within minutes. *Izhora* couldn't fight back, and there was no chance of help from the escorts, which were miles away. However, though brutally beaten up by shells, the gallant ship refused to sink. Most of the crew suffered painful deaths, scalded by steam, burnt by fire, killed by shrapnel under hailstones of shells, or frozen to death after succumbing to hypothermia in the cold water. Naturally, nobody wanted to die, including those two sixteen-year-old boys who had taken the place of their lost fathers and that twenty-year-old girl who, possibly, had not yet tasted her first kiss.

But *Izhora* paid the Germans back for her crew's deaths as the smoke from the burning ship rose high into the sky and was visible from afar possibly alerting the British escorts to the German presence. The German commander, watching the protracted fight between three destroyers and one small transport, grew angry. What should have been an easy operation was turning into a big problem. The Germans lost their secrecy and had remained in one place for too long. Consumption of shells on the sinking of the transport was comparable to the cost of transport itself and its cargo. Therefore, the admiral asked Topp to have the destroyers attack *Izhora* with torpedoes.

Ihn fired a torpedo at close range, but the torpedo suddenly turned around and almost hit the destroyer. After that *Schoemann* attacked, but missed at point-blank range.

Failing in a simple torpedo attack, *Ihn* dropped depth charges set at a minimum depth of detonation. They broke the bottom of the Soviet ship, and it finally disappeared under the water at 1758 hours after a battle lasting for more than an hour and a half.

The Germans picked up the only survivor from the water: Nicholas Adayev. Neither fire nor ice water, neither hailstones of bullets nor large-caliber shells could destroy Adayev. But a year in the Shtutgof concentration camp was too much for him to endure. He died in captivity, thereby affirming the choice made by *Izhora*'s crew not to surrender even against overwhelming odds.

Summing up *Izhora*'s bravery Anatoly Lifshits, assistant navigation officer on the Soviet destroyer *Rattling*, wrote about the event in somewhat broken English:

> I remember, how have met on March, 12th in water area Kola a gulf transports PQ-12. We already knew about tragedy which was played on March, 7th with Izhora. Also it is necessary to tell that thanking a heroic

act of a command of a steamship Izhora's *convoy has not been crushed, and has reached whole and safe ....*

The Feat of Izhora *which was lost, but not surrendered to the enemy, was not in vain. Its radio signal has been accepted by escort PQ-12 that has helped it to avoid a meeting with a battleship* Tirpitz *and has rescued an escort from defeat.*

It [PQ-12] delivered the largest party of strategic cargoes received by the USSR in one caravan: 200 planes, 160 tanks and 180 armoured cars, 24 guns, hundreds trucks, machine tools, thousand tons of the equipment, raw materials and the foodstuffs. Also that is important these cargoes basically were used in Stalingradsky [Stalingrad] fight that, undoubtedly, has approached Day of Victories.

By the life the Soviet seamen have prevented death of many and many seamen of allied escort PQ-12 and QP-8, and also destruction of the ships of these escorts. And, how many lives of our people the military technology on the fronts could save up, what loss planes, tanks, and shells have put to the enemy, torpedoes which carried the escort ships, it is impossible to tell.

Four merchant ships had straggled from PQ-12 during its passage: the *Bateau* early on, the *Kiev* on March 3, *El Occidente* on encountering the ice on March 6, and the *Sevaples* as they broke out of the ice on March 11. One of the escorting antisubmarine whalers, the *Stefa*, had lost contact on March 6. *Kiev* and *El Occidente* reached Iokanka unmolested on March 10, and *Sevaples* sighted and joined forces with the *Stefa*, which, on March 13, shot down an aircraft trying to bomb the merchant ship. Ironically, despite the presence of a German battle squadron and a wolf pack of four U-boats strung out across the route of PQ-12 between Jan Mayen and Bear Island, this was the only engagement directly connected with the passage of PQ-12. *Bateau* returned to Iceland and sailed with PQ-13.

PQ-12 suffered one loss, but to the sea, not to the Germans. HMS *Shera*, one of four former Norwegian whalers being transferred to the Soviet Navy, capsized and sank on March 9. The weather at the time was not usual, and, although some icing of the upper deck had occurred, it was not severe. It is believed that *Shera*'s stability was affected by the ice, made worse by a low level of oil fuel on board and the excessive amount of guns and equipment on her upper decks. Only three of her crew survived: Lieutenant Hansen RNR, Ordinary Seaman Harris, and Steward Phillips, to be rescued by her consort, *Svega*, which reached

Murmansk independently on March 11, unaware that PQ-12 had altered course far to the north.

On March 14, 1942, Hitler decided to make the Arctic convoys a strategic target of major importance linked directly to the campaign in Russia. The Anglo-American deliveries of war supplies were "sustaining Russian ability to hold out." He declared that, "it is necessary that maritime communications over the Arctic Ocean between the Anglo-Saxons and Russians, hitherto virtually unimpeded, should henceforth be impeded."

The skirmishing was over and the now battle began in earnest.

CHAPTER 3

ARCTIC SHOOTING GALLERY
March 1942

A s winter warmed into spring, the Allies were fighting defensive battles—and losing. U-boats rampaged along the U.S. east coast, sinking ships in broad daylight, leaving funeral pyres of smoke visible to people on the beach 10 miles away. North Atlantic convoys fought east and west through an unremitting gauntlet of deadly wolf packs. In North Africa, British forces pushing west ran into a reinforced Afrika Corps under Field Marshal Erwin Rommel, which stopped the advance and forced a retreat toward Egypt. The Mediterranean Sea was closed to Allied shipping from Alexandria in the east to Gibraltar in the west. Japan's forces controlled the entire southwest Pacific, ruthlessly rolling over anyone who opposed them. After a brutal Russian winter, German forces were still within striking distance of Moscow, fighting house to house in Stalingrad and shelling Leningrad on a daily basis.

Although not in massive quantities, the supplies arriving in Russia via the convoys were enough to help the Soviet Union hold out through the winter. After assessing the reasons for the unexpected Soviet ability to resist defeat, the Wehrmacht and Hitler realized that the Arctic Convoys were making a difference and were a serious threat to defeating the Soviets. Although the Germans had been blocked in their attempts to capture Murmansk, they were determined to sink every ship at the docks and bomb the port into oblivion.

With the coming of spring, planning went on for more and larger convoys, which would have to sail during increasing hours of daylight, making them easier to find. Sailing of eastbound PQ convoys was synchronized with westbound QP convoys so that their courses would cross one another in the vicinity of Bear Island, where the cruiser covering force could cover both convoys in the most dangerous area.

Convoys still had to fight the Arctic's brutal weather, coupled with an ice pack pushing south ever closer to Norway, decreasing the maneuvering room to avoid attack. This narrowing gap meant the convoys were within range of Luftwaffe bases in Norway during most of the voyage. Long-range FW-200 Condors and BV-138 flying boat reconnaissance aircraft easily located the convoys in good weather and were impossible for the slow-moving ships to elude. Also, these planes were heavily armed and seemingly impervious to attack by the lightly armed British fighters accompanying the ships on the new escort aircraft carriers.

Eight convoys—PQ-13, 14, 15, and 16 and QP-9, 10, 11, and 12— totaling 163 ships sailed between March 21 and May 21. Only one, QP-9, made it through without loss to either the weather or the Germans.

There were nineteen ships in PQ-13, which sailed from Reykjavik on March 21. British Vice Admiral A. T. B. Curteis covered the western route on battleship *King George V* with a second battleship, *Duke of York*, the battlecruiser *Renown*, the carrier *Victorious*, and the cruisers *Edinburgh* and *Kent*, screened by eleven fleet destroyers. The cruiser *Trinidad* provided close cover together with two destroyers, *Fury* and *Eclipse*, which joined off Iceland. Destroyer *Lamerton* and the trawlers *Blackfly* and *Paynter* accompanied PQ-13 from Reykjavik, together with ex-Norwegian whalers *Sulla*, *Sumba*, and *Silja*, which were being transferred to the Soviet Navy in an attempt to beef up the local minesweeping force.

QP-9, also with nineteen ships, sailed from Murmansk on March 22. The convoy was covered west of Bear Island by the cruiser *Nigeria* and an ocean escort of the minesweepers *Sharpshooter* and *Britomart* and the destroyer *Offa*. Additional local support was given by five minesweepers led by *Harrier*, two Russian destroyers, *Gremyashchiy* and *Sokrushitelnyy*, and the British destroyer *Oribi*. These accompanied QP-9 two days into its homeward passage, until the early hours of March 23 when they turned back to Murmansk. Little more was achieved by the cruiser *Kenya*, intended to be performing the equivalent role of *Trinidad*, which left Kola on March 22 but failed to locate the convoy. She did, however, succeed in carrying home 10 tons of bullion.

On March 23, QP-9 ran into a severe southwesterly gale with heavy snowstorms, but the convoy managed to stay together. As the weather abated the next evening, lookouts aboard the minesweeper *Sharpshooter* spotted *U-655* 300 yards away. Lieutenant Commander David Lampen, *Sharpshooter*'s captain, immediately altered course to intercept, but his quarry submerged. *Sharpshooter* laid down a series of depth charges, which blew the U-boat to the surface, where she was rammed and sunk by *Sharpshooter* before she had time to dive again. None of the U-boat's forty-seven-man crew survived. *Sharpshooter*'s bow was damaged, but she stayed with the convoy.

During the course of its voyage, QP-9 endured additional attacks by U-boats and aircraft, all of which were beaten off by the escorts and intense fire from the merchant ships. The convoy reached Reykjavik on April 3 without loss.

PQ-13 was less fortunate, however. The convoy sailed from Iceland on March 21 and had four days of clear sailing before running into a savage storm.

"The Barents Sea became a fury of tumultuous water," said Ronald Adds, a stoker on board HMS *Fury*:

The waves reared up in enormous mountains of water sixty to eighty feet high. Then, there was the cold. Freezing spray formed into ice as soon as it hit superstructures, decks, and guard rails.

Imagine a destroyer climbing such waves at a slow speed and, leaving the quiet of the trough, meeting the full force of the tempest on the wave top. Then, there was the cold. At times there was so much ice—up to 3 inches thick—there was danger of capsizing.

To take over the watch in the engine-room of a destroyer dressed in a duffel coat, woolen socks and sea boots was an experience I had never had before. Beneath the duffel coat I wore full uniform, but with a roll-collar pullover instead of collar and tie. Beneath that were hand-knitted woolen long johns and a long sleeved vest. When I was issued with this kit in Scapa Flow,

I never imagined having to wear it. I had always worn cotton gloves on watch, but now I was wearing fur-lined mittens—and very happy to do so.

Every now and then flurries of snow would filter down through the air vents, whilst the three foot diameter copper pipes supplying cooling sea-water to the condensers under the turbines were inches thick in ice. The thermometer reading of the seawater showed 28 degrees Fahrenheit—way below the freezing temperature of fresh water. Due to this, the normal use of circulating pumps was considered unnecessary. I've never been so cold in my life.

We were all scared. There isn't a man who served on these convoys who would not admit to being scared. But I cannot recall any panic amongst Fury's ship's company, although some of them were at sea for the first time. Such was life in those days. Cigarettes were our main consolation, which, thank goodness, were duty-free. There was also the consoling effect of the daily ration of rum, all too often not drunk on the spot but illegally bottled for the provision of "Dutch Courage" at times of stress.

At times so much ice built up on decks, masts, guns, and superstructures that the ships were in danger of capsizing. This was the fate of *Sulla*, one of the whalers. Harold G. Neill, a crewman on *Sumba*, shared vivid memories of the storm and *Sulla*'s fate:

We all left on March twenty-second and as soon as we left the shelter of the fiord the weather was atrocious, gales with blizzards, it was impossible to see, the snow was so thick. We joined up with PQ-13 and lost them because of worsening conditions. I was personally involved in chopping ice as far as I could reach. I was on the engine room casing lashed to an iron stanchion, as fast as I cleared the ice it was back again.

This icing of the ship had to be experienced to believe it. I went into the C.O.'s cabin and there was a good inch thick of solid ice covering the whole of the bulkhead where he slept or was supposed to, I don't think any of us did much sleeping that trip.

The boxes which had been made to take the sweep on both Port and Starboard of the superstructure had been smashed to matchwood, iron stanchion had been bent and twisted, everything on the deck seemed to have disappeared such was the force of the sea and ice.

The Sulla was on a parallel course to us not too far away. One minute I looked over and she was there, the next time I looked she had gone, I assumed at the time that she had turned turtle and gone down with the weight of ice, there was no sound of an explosion just nothing, no debris visible or any sign of her; she had vanished.

Sulla sank on March 25, taking her entire crew of twenty-one men with her. The storm lasted three days and scattered the convoy across 150 miles. Because of the storm, Vice Admiral Curteis's ships ran short of fuel and returned to base, leaving only the close escort to cover the convoy.

On March 27, the senior officer of the escort force in HMS *Harrier* began trying to reassemble the convoy, but no ships were in sight. The Commodore's ship, the tanker *River Afton*, unable to steer within five points of the wind (roughly 55 degrees), had drifted toward the Lofoten Islands in northern Norway. The most easterly ship was the *Empire Ranger*, all alone and only about 80 miles north of the North Cape; 40 miles astern of her was a group of six merchant ships with an armed whaler in company; 35 miles further west was the SS *Harpalion* escorted by the destroyer *Fury*; while a further 65 miles astern was another group of six ships escorted by the destroyer *Eclipse*, the whaler *Sumba*, and the trawler *Paynter*. The cruisers *Trinidad* and *Nigeria* were searching for stragglers in an area 100 miles to the southwest of Bear Island.

March 28 dawned clear and sunny with occasional snow flurries, but the convoy was still dispersed, having been unable to reassemble since the storm that sank the *Sulla*. At 0700 hours that day, Kapitänleutnant Heinrich Brodda of *U-209* made the first contact after sighting the Polish steam merchant *Tobruk* escorted by the armed trawler HMS *Blackfly*. The encounter was inconclusive, as the U-boat missed the trawler with a stern torpedo and the depth charges dropped on her caused no damage. Soon thereafter the ships dropped out of sight in a snow squall.

Just after 1000 hours, *Trinidad* was spotted by a BV-138 flying boat. Two hours later, the Luftwaffe launched attacks by Ju-88 bombers, and for the rest of the day, gunners on the scattered ships tried to fight them off.

First blood was drawn by the bombers, sinking *Empire Ranger*, romping ahead of the convoy, and the *Raceland*, a straggler from the easternmost group of six ships. *Raceland* was attacked by two aircraft, two bombs hitting about 20 yards from the ship on the starboard side near No. 3 hatch. There were no direct hits, but the concussion of the bombs ripped a hole in the starboard side of the forward hull, breaking deck fittings and steam pipes and stopping the engines. The engine room flooded, and the ship took a 45-degree list to port.

Herman Torgersen, who was in the food storage room sorting potatoes on *Raceland* when the attacks began, said to the Canadian next to him: "Now it's getting serious." The aircraft came right above them, but disappeared again; a few shots were exchanged. The aircraft next came from behind. The alarm sounded again, and the men grabbed their lifebelts. Torgersen donned his tall sheepskin-lined boots—but not his socks, which he bitterly came to regret.

The *Raceland* was poorly equipped for taking defensive measures. German aircraft dropped two bombs from about 100 feet up; they exploded under the ship, destroying the plating in the engine room on the port side. The ship immediately started to list to starboard at a sharp angle.

Torgersen was assigned to the starboard lifeboat, which was difficult to launch because of the heavy coating of ice on the boat falls. Torgersen recalled that all forty-five crewmen got safely in the boats: the first mate had one boat with fifteen on board, the second mate one boat with eighteen men, and the captain and the boatswain a small boat with six men each. None of the boats had a motor. *Raceland* wasn't sinking, so the captain gave orders to wait, which they did—for twelve hours. During those long hours, Torgersen and Danish First Engineer Svend Svenningsen (who later died) went back on board to retrieve food, blankets, canned fruits, preserved milk, clothes, and anything else they might need. Years later, Torgersen could still remember how he had to break a lock in the food storage room in pitch dark: He put the lock in his pocket, and it's the one remaining souvenir he has of *Raceland*.

At 2230 hours, *Raceland* finally sank. A tall column of flames rushed toward the skies in the tremendous explosion that followed. In the middle of the fire, survivors could see the profile of a raft from the *Raceland* being flung to the skies. Now the lifeboats tried to set a course for Murmansk, about 600 miles away. All four were tied together. The second mate, who had a working compass, led the group.

That night, a terrible hurricane blew up, bringing with it indescribable cold. The boats became separated in the storm, and the men never saw each other again. The two smaller boats probably went down immediately.

Brutal weather lasted for the eleven days they were on the sea. Bitter cold and vicious storms constantly nagged the men. All the food was lost during the first day of the storm, and soon the real tragedy began. The first engineer, whom Torgersen remembered as a nice Danish fellow, suddenly stood up, snatched the precious compass, and flung it in the water. He then fell to his knees, wrapped his arms around his legs, and died. Torgersen struggled for hours to free the dead man's arms from his legs, but they were frozen stuck. The second mate gave the order to throw the body overboard, but no one wanted to do it. But the boat was overcrowded, and finally he was given to the sea.

After that, someone died every day, usually preceded by a period of varying degrees of insanity. One fellow from Bergen, Norway's second-largest city, suffered in pain from extraordinarily cold feet. He suddenly pulled off his tall, fur-lined boots, threw them into the sea, stuck his feet into the ice-cold water, and said, "This is lovely. Now I can get warm." His boat mates could see death creep over him from his feet to his heart. He was dead within five minutes. Another man threw himself overboard; they managed to get him on board again, but it was too late. Another mate wildly flung an ax, cutting the ropes while yelling and singing before falling silent and dying.

The second mate, Johansen, was the last of the eighteen men on the lifeboat to die. The young man from Bodø, a small town in north-central Norway, had proved himself a first class seaman. But he, too, lost his composure, sailing the lifeboat round and round in circles for days, which his boat mates all realized even though they were not navigators themselves. Eventually, he, too, was seized by a violent death cramp. Only five of the original eighteen men in the lifeboat were left alive when they reached the Norwegian coast and were taken prisoner by the Germans.

Air attacks continued as the opponents played a deadly game of hide-and-seek through snow squalls and low-hanging clouds. The freighter *Ballot* suffered bomb damage, and, although not in any danger of sinking, sixteen men demanded to leave the ship. The men in the lifeboat were picked up by *Silja* and later transferred to *Induna*. Both ships became stuck in ice the next day. Despite being short-handed, *Ballot*'s remaining crew stayed to repair the ship and brought her safely to Murmansk on March 30.

Based on the sighting report from the BV-138, the destroyers *Z-24*, *Z-25*, and *Z-26*, under the command of Captain Gottfried Pönitz, sortied from their Norwegian base at far northeastern Kirkenes to intercept the convoy. Adding to the forces arrayed against PQ-13 were *U-209*, *U-376*, *U-378*, and *U-655*, which were ordered by Rear Admiral Hubert Schmundt, Flag Officer Northern Waters (*Gruppe Nord*), to form a patrol line off the North Cape.

The destroyers spread in a line 3 miles apart, swept west along PQ-13's estimated track. At 2245 hours, *Z-24* came across *Empire Ranger*'s lifeboats and rescued the sixty-one survivors. Then, just after midnight on March 29, *Z-26* encountered *Bateau* and sank the freighter with torpedoes and gunfire, killing thirty-seven men. At the time of the sinking, the weather was bitterly cold with a blizzard blowing.

Robert Taylor, one of the two Maritime Royal Artillery gunners, survived. The other, Bombardier Richard Hector Waddy, only lived for about ten minutes in the frigid water.

"I was just about to go on watch when we were hit by two torpedoes amidships," wrote Taylor years later.

> I grabbed a kapok coat and tried to help some of the crew, but they seemed to want to go down with the ship. An air pocket in my heavy coat kept me afloat as I swam away. After about an hour, a German destroyer came up and they threw me a wire hawser and I grabbed it with both hands and my teeth. Soon they had me aboard.

The trapped air pocket in his upper body area apparently prevented the intense cold from reaching his heart—at least that was the explanation given to him by the German naval doctor aboard the ship that rescued him. Taylor was one of only six *Bateau* survivors.

By the morning of March 29, the convoy was in two groups about 80 miles apart from one another; the whereabouts of four ships were unknown. The westerly group of eight ships was being escorted by HMS *Eclipse* and the trawler *Paynter*. At 0645, they were reinforced by HMS *Oribi* and the Soviet destroyers *Gremyashchiy* and *Sokrushitelnyy*. *Trinidad*, accompanied by *Fury*, was steaming east at 0843 hours to collect the easterly group of four ships and bring them back to the other group. The weather started to deteriorate, the visibility shortening as heavy snow squalls driven by a bitter wind swept down, when *Trinidad*'s radar picked up a contact bearing 079 degrees at a range of 6.5 miles. Suddenly ahead at only 1.5 miles were the three destroyers, each carrying guns equal to the fire power of the British cruiser and much larger than British destroyers and at top speed.

Trinidad's commanding officer, Captain L. S. Sanders, gave the order to open fire with main guns, anti-aircraft weapons, and machine guns, sending a curtain of fire crashing into *Z-26*, the lead destroyer, immediately setting it on fire. Shells could be seen exploding amidships with flame and smoke. The German ship began to return fire, and two shells smashed into *Trinidad*'s port side. The German destroyer then broke off the engagement and headed northwest into a snow cloud. Sanders recalled the action:

As I knew the rough positions of my own force, these could only be the Germans, so when three shapes appeared out of the murk only a mile or so distant, I was able to open fire immediately without waiting to signal the challenge. They were Germany's latest Z class destroyers. It was an exhilarating moment to hoist, in earnest, the signal "Enemy in sight" and to wireless to the Naval world a real enemy report.

The enemy returned our fire. Several shells fell close and two exploded in my day cabin aft, killing the one man of the damage control party there who thought it foolish to lie down. My immediate reaction, and of those others on the bridge, was to duck! Quite pointless and soon stopped.

When I judged the time right, I turned a complete circle away from the enemy to avoid the torpedoes they had undoubtedly fired—two passed close by our side—and also because I did not want to get too close, which might encourage the enemy to split up and press home an attack simultaneously from different directions. This would have spelled disaster. We could only engage effectively one ship at a time, so at least one destroyer could have got in to point blank range and put a salvo of torpedoes into me. Thank God this move did not appear to occur to them. They were intent on running away.

They disappeared into the murk during our turn, but our radar kept contact as I hoped it would. I wondered what to do next. I remembered Nelson's order—"No Captain can do very wrong if he lay his ship alongside that of the enemy." So I gave chase and in time sighted the rear destroyer. She had possibly had her speed reduced by our earlier shelling. We passed a few wretched German sailors in the water, but this was not the time to pick them up. Our salvoes continued to fall around her but with only an occasional outburst of flame indicating a hit.

In an attempt to finish off Z-26, *Trinidad* fired a torpedo, which in the intense cold ran erratically, and, reversing course, returned and hit the cruiser. It struck underneath the bridge, leaving a gaping hole 60 feet by 20 feet, which flooded the forward boiler room and killed thirty-one men, forcing the ship to break off the combat.

Meanwhile, *Eclipse* located the badly damaged Z-26 and began to chase her, scoring at least six hits until the enemy stopped. *Eclipse* was attacked by the two other German destroyers but escaped by taking cover in a snow squall, though not before she had been hit aft by two shells and holed above the waterline in the forward part of the ship by two others.

Attracted by the gunfire, *Oribi* and *Sokrushitelnyy* joined the action. *Sokrushitelnyy* fired six salvos at a German destroyer, claiming one hit until losing contact in a snow squall. *U-376* (Kapitänleutnant Friedrich-Karl Marks) had observed the gunfire but only once sighted a destroyer, which proved to be German.

After the battle, the U-boat sighted the German destroyers picking up survivors from the sinking *Z-26* and was ordered to participate in the rescue operation. The sinking vessel took 240 crewmembers into the deep with her; most of the men died in the freezing cold water. Although *Z-24* and *Z-25* rescued ninety-six men, only eight were still alive when *U-376* came to the rescue. Three of the men died of exposure during the next few hours and were buried at sea.

Escorted by *Fury*, *Trinidad* made her way toward Murmansk and safety. *Eclipse*, short of fuel and with nine seriously wounded men in need of urgent medical attention, also set course for Murmansk, which she reached the next morning.

After the warship fight and despite the casualties, the battle wasn't over yet. Sixteen merchant ships were still scattered across hundreds of square miles, each a target for the Luftwaffe above and the U-boats below. With *Trinidad*, *Fury*, and *Eclipse* out of the fight, few escorts remained, and those that did weren't always near the missing ships.

One of the missing ships was the freighter *El Estero*. Hoping to avoid detection, her master headed into the ice field at the first warning that the convoy had been discovered. He was only partially successful. Greg A. Novak, a crewman on board *El Estero*, told the tale:

> Following our emergence from the storm the following relatively clement weather permitted a determined German attack upon the elements of our scattered convoy. We emerged from a stormy cloud-cover, heavily snow- and ice-clad, in nature's camouflage, dimming our presence near the iceberg-floes to be seen, closely north of us.
>
> At high altitudes, beyond the range of our AA Guns, bombers alone were to be seen. 50-foot geysers of sea-water shot upward where the dropping bombs hit the sea, generally of comfortable distances from our ship.
>
> The first mate, a seaman (names lost in memory) and I cast a heavy drum of smoke-screen material over the stem and into the sea as the ship headed into the ice-floes to minimize the Luftwaffe, warship long-range shell, and submarine activity.
>
> Once safely ensconced amidst the icebergs, difficult to get at, almost invisible to any other combatant within possible range, axe-wielding seamen

beat off the ice, coating shrouds, deck, etc. to prevent cargo-shifting or to prevent a top-heavy ship from capsizing. The ship carefully was slowly threading its way among the icebergs.

We emerged from the ice-floes into a clear day only to enter a floating mine-field. A spined floating-mine was to be seen nearly in collision with our motionless ship on our Port side amidships. Our black-bearded Captain J. Beatovich, in a sonorous baritone voice barked out an order to me from the bridge to me amidships. I being the lone unfortunate within earshot, directing me, calmly, to fend off the mine from the ship's port side with a piece of timber, two by four inches and eight feet long, retrieved from a midship hatch.

No legendary figure of the Spanish Main, nor any cut-throat apparition ever depicted in Robert L. Stevenson's Treasure Island, or Boy's Own or Chums Annuals, avidly read, wide-eyed, some sixty years ago in my boyhood, ever could have inspired greater respect than this man, in his only recollectible [sic] verbal exchange with me, whose bellow, moreover, could carry from a coast-wise tramp in transit to a distant shore, no matter the intensity of a prevailing gale. His bark could shatter glass.

In any event, not daring to offend this stalwart controller of our collective destinies, I managed carefully to avoid the trigger spines of the floating mine and fend off the deadly six foot diameter sphere from contacting the ship's hull. However, there can be no doubt that my personal motivation was less than altruistically sparing a ship and crew from harm, but rather one of mere self-preservation, yet it seemed to me that, from that day forward, the crew showed me a little deference, forgiving me future faux-pas, as if they owed me something.

A few turns, slowly, of the starboard screw saw the ship's stern separate further from the ball, slowly drifting away in our wash astern of us. But the very motion of the ship exposed, off our port-bow, among the drift-floes a second floating mine, which fact I called out to the bridge and it was summarily acknowledged, after a moment's pause, by the captain, who had probably seen it earlier in any event. Nevertheless, it was easily avoided.

Within an hour we came within earshot of a heavily-armed minesweeping Russian trawler and a nearby destroyer [Gremyashchiy and Sokrushitelnyy]. The destroyer was shortly to leave us, but the trawler escorted the lone straggler into the Kola Inlet on, I believe, March 28, 1942, taking but a few hours.

While the *El Estero* fought for survival under German attack, the whaler *Sumba* was running out of fuel in her attempt to maneuver through ice fields. She needed help. Harold G. Neill, an officers' steward, recalled what was going on with *Sumba*:

> We were on our own and running out of fuel and wondering if we broke radio silence it would give our position away to the enemy. Our luck held and our signal was answered by the Fury who gave us a time when to expect them. Our spirits were uplifted when she turned up and began putting a fuel pipe over to replenish our tanks, they also sent over fresh bread etc. which was a godsend.
>
> All too quickly we were refueled and the Fury was on her way, without her assistance I wouldn't be sitting writing this today, we were all eternally grateful to her officers and crew. We felt happier having Paynter with us for company but it wasn't long before we heard the sound of planes that proceeded to attack. Their firing lacked precision and I thought at the time we were not worth the cost of a bomb, we made a very small target in a large expanse of water.
>
> At the start of the attack we manned our gun forward of the wheelhouse but as we tried to fire it the barrel blew off—it was full of ice. The explosion shattered the glass in the wheelhouse. We had twin Lewis guns set in armoured shields and they had also been made useless by the weight of ice.

Induna with *Silja* in tow tried to clear the ice field. It wasn't until the afternoon of March 29 that they finally freed themselves and set course for Murmansk. That night, the tow parted in heavy seas and they were unable to find the trawler in snow squalls. *Induna* proceeded on her way alone, only to be torpedoed and sunk by *U-376* the next morning, March 30.

Forty-one survivors abandoned ship in two lifeboats, but by the time they were picked up by a Russian minesweeper on April 2, only thirty were still alive; two later died of exposure in a hospital in Murmansk. The weather had been horrible with temperatures around 20 degrees below zero Fahrenheit and freezing winds. The survivors had been sprayed by ice-cold water, and most of them, including David, a fourteen year-old cabin boy, lost limbs. The master, twenty crewmembers, six gunners, and eleven men from *Ballot* were lost. Nineteen crewmembers and four gunners from *Induna* made it. Only five of the sixteen men who had abandoned *Ballot* survived.

Induna's Engineering Officer William P. "Bill" Shorts remembered what happened after their ship sank:

I was preparing to go on watch when the torpedo struck and I went immediately to my boat station. The lifeboat that I should have been in had already been launched. The weather was so bad, that the boat had to be cut adrift. I ran around to the other lifeboat, only to discover that it had, too, been launched with a full complement. I realized then that, if I were going to get off the sinking ship, I would have to jump into the Sea, which is mighty cold in the Arctic in March, plus the fact that I could not swim.

Eventually, the overcrowded lifeboat, which was damaged during the launching, picked me up, and it was leaking badly. With so many onboard, we were packed in like sardines in a tin can. There was no room to move, but there was hope of being picked up, as an SOS had been sent and perhaps a naval vessel would be sent to look for us. Hope for the first day was high, but, as the night fell, we realized that it would be a bitter cold night with sleet, snow and forty foot waves to contend with. Little did I realize at that moment, what an awful experience that was to follow. Could one's courage and endurance stand the ordeal?

There has always been the impression that a "tot" of rum will keep out the cold. There was wine and whiskey aboard the lifeboat and some indulged and drank too much. Those who did went to sleep and no matter how they were shook, they did not stir, as by now, they had hypothermia and when they went to sleep, they never awaken. Sadly, the first night, six died and all we could do was slide them overboard and commit their bodies to the deep.

This went on for four days. A "donkeyman", who had been badly burned in the engine room after a flashover, was lying in the bottom of the lifeboat and there was nothing we could do for his wounds. He eventually died; frozen to the bottom of the lifeboat and it was impossible to remove him. The water keg was frozen solid, so we were licking ice. Water had gotten into the wireless transmitter so we could not send another SOS. All the rations that were to sustain us were frozen solid, too.

At the end of the fourth day, out of thirty-four men to start with, only seventeen were alive. One man went mad. The sea spray was freezing on the gunwale and he started to lick the ice. His tongue became swollen; he then became deranged, and died from suffocation. We had given up hope of rescue and from time to time, we sighted land through the snow and whiteout, but it seemed so far away.

On the fifth day of their ill-fated voyage, when only four or five men remained alive, fate played an almost unbelievable last cruel trick. A swirling mist descended on them, fanned by a bitter breeze. As the fog thickened, it blanketed visibility and muffled just about every noise. Only the ceaseless lapping of water against the boat could be heard. Then suddenly they heard a whistle. The sound faded then rose again, louder and more constant. Hearts raced with excitement. Surely it was someone from a rescue boat trying to locate them.

With what little strength was left, they tried to shout. Despite their efforts, there was no answer. Still the whistle persisted. First it seemed to be ahead and then astern. The sound was eerie, almost supernatural. In their low state of mind, the mystery deepened every minute and became almost frightening. Desperate and frustrated, their eyes tried to pierce the fog bank but saw nothing.

Minutes later, their hopes came tumbling when the riddle was solved. On the thwart, gently rolling with the movement of the sea lay an empty bottle. As the wind swept through the boat, it played on the open end of the bottle, trilling the whistling sound. Hope turned to despair, optimism to despondency. It was the worst moment of their ordeal.

At dawn on April 1, aircraft of the Northern Fleet sighted boats with people 15 miles to the west of Tsyp-Navolok headland off the Murman coast and directed the minesweepers *T-882* and *KT-406* to the boats. *T-882* was on scene first and took on board twenty-eight survivors.

Bill Shorts finished the story:

A Russian minesweeper eventually picked us up. By now we were so weak; we had to be hauled aboard by ropes around our waist. I actually tried to walk, to get circulation going in my legs but it was impossible as my legs would not support me. When the Induna *was torpedoed, we were 175 miles from Murmansk, Russia. When we were picked up, we were told later that we were a scant 25 miles from Murmansk. So, in four days, we had drifted 150 miles.*

Four merchant ships and a warship in the convoy were sunk, and two warships and numerous merchant ships were damaged—all in just two days. The Germans lost a destroyer and several aircraft. But, for both sides, PQ-13's ordeal was not over yet. The fifth and last merchant ship lost was *Effingham* on March 30. A torpedo from *U-456* (Kapitänleutnant Max-Martin Teichert) struck amidships on the port side, and the crew of eight officers, twenty-six men, and nine armed guards immediately abandoned ship with two lifeboats in rough seas as the ship began to settle by the stern. Two men fell overboard and drowned. After about two hours, the survivors watched the *Effingham* explode after *U-435* (Korvettenkapitän Siegfried Strelow) torpedoed the ship again.

On March 31, the master, the chief mate, and fifteen men in one of the lifeboats were picked up by HMS *Harrier*, which was on patrol off Kola Inlet, looking for stragglers from the convoy. The *Harrier* landed them in Polyarnoe the next day, but not before six men in the lifeboat had died of exposure. Sixty-five hours after the attack, eleven men and three armed guards in the second boat were picked up by a Soviet patrol vessel, but four men in that boat also had died of exposure. All of the survivors were taken to Murmansk. John Guthrie, a member of the U.S. Naval Armed Guard detachment, wrote about the events:

> *When the ship was hit they were only able to launch two lifeboats to the best of my recollection, I do remember the first two who froze to death and they were the warmest dressed two in our boat. After they died we took their heavy clothes and dumped them overboard. I don't recall how long we were in the boat but it was quite a few hours.*
>
> *I was quite excited when the H.M.S.* Harrier *came over the horizon. When they picked us up the 3rd mate believe who had been on the tiller the whole time hand had frozen to it so one of the crewman from the* Harrier *had to cut it off (tiller not his hand). After we were taken aboard they gave us some warm dry clothes and a couple of drinks of rum. Several of the crew didn't want theirs so I drank them so they wouldn't be wasted. I guess I must have passed out because they told me later we were again attacked by German torpedo boats going in.*

Although the Germans had drawn first blood, they were to suffer the last loss by killing one of their own, *U-585* (Korvettenkapitän Ernst-Bernward Lohse). On March 30, the U-boat hit a German mine that had drifted from the Bantos-A minefield in the Barents Sea north of Murmansk. All forty-four crewmen died with their boat.

After escorting the wounded *Trinidad* safely to Murmansk, *Fury* immediately left again to patrol off Kola Inlet, where she was joined by *Speedwell*. Their tasks were antisubmarine patrol and to search for any remaining ships from PQ-13. They spotted the drifting *Silja*, which was towed by *Harrier* to the Polyarnoe Naval Base. *Fury's* Ronald Adds recalled the event:

> *What was left of Convoy PQ-13 arrived in Murmansk at about noon on 30th March, which was, incidentally, my second wedding anniversary. Five*

merchant ships had been lost, the cruiser Trinidad *severely damaged and requiring considerable repair, and the destroyer* Eclipse *badly damaged by enemy gunfire. The survivors of this living hell now looked forward to a little respite in the calmer waters of a friendly harbour. We totally forgot that the German Air Force was only fifty miles away in Norway.*

Nineteen ships had started with PQ-13. Five were sunk. This was a loss of more than 20 percent, but the losses were deemed acceptable by the British Admiralty.

Because Murmansk suffered daily bombing raids, there was little rest for the convoy crews. In any event, the Russian city offered little in the way of recreation. Also, the wounded needed care, ships needed to be offloaded, repairs had to be made, and the convoy's dead still on board their crippled ships had to be laid to rest.

Of the ships to be repaired, *Trinidad* was the most seriously damaged, and she went into dry dock at Rosta, north of Murmansk on the Kola Inlet. Incessant bombing had put the electric power out of action, so the ship had to be pulled into dock manually by the weary and exhausted crew, following a recent harrowing experience of nearly being sunk by one of their own torpedoes.

Once in the dock, massive tree trunks had to be cut to size to shore the ship in place. As the water pumped out, the full extent of the damage could be seen: a gaping hole, three decks laid bare, and many bulkheads completely disintegrated. Steel plates were needed to repair the ruptured hull, but requests to the Russians for these plates were in vain. There were plates somewhere in the dockyard, but they were buried under tons of snow, making them impossible to find. An urgent signal was sent to the Admiralty for suitable plates to be sent in the next convoy, which was due to arrive in mid-April.

The crew, although safe, were stranded in Russia at Rosta with nothing around them except snow and ice, forced to gaze every day at their damaged, dry-docked ship, which they wouldn't be able to repair for weeks, a ship in which so many lives had been lost through enemy action and the malfunctioning of their own torpedo due to extremely cold weather. About all they could do was to undertake the grim task of removing the shipmates who had perished. "The next job was to collect and bury our dead," recalled Captain Sanders:

We had some sixty casualties, of whom thirty-two were dead or missing. The latter were scattered, many dismembered, in the compartments that had been flooded or damaged. This duty I gave to the splendid Royal Marines. It was a most unpleasant task that sickened everybody. I endeavoured to help them to face it by accompanying them and explaining that they must regard the remains as merely cast-off matter and that the souls had moved on to another plane.

We embarked the simple coffins, made by the Carpenters, in a minesweeper and buried them at sea at the mouth of the Kola Inlet, with the customary Naval Burial Service taken by our Chaplain. I wrote a personal letter to each of the next of kin.

In an attack on April 3, Luftwaffe bombers sank *Empire Starlight*, *New Westminster City*, and the Polish-manned freighter *Tobruk* and damaged the Soviet Survey ship *Ost* while the vessels were at docks in Murmansk. This raid is well remembered by crewmen who were there: Ted Starkey and Morris Mills on board *New Westminster City* and Greg Novak on *El Estero*.

The first account is from Greg Novak:

In Murmansk Harbor proper we tied up to a dock alongside a narrow-gauge railway spur connection that terminating in Leningrad and a grainery with an Army Field Hospital in its rear.

Despite numerous Air Attacks from nearby German-/Finnish-held Airfields, with low-flying planes generally coming from the west, flying low over the hills ringing Murmansk our ship, El Estero *came through completely unscathed. It's Anglicized name could well have been translated into "The (Lucky) Star." Shrapnel often fell like a light hail from the fiercely defensive Russian AA batteries ringing Murmansk harbor. We had endured everything from a 200-plane raid to nuisance raids of solitary dive-bombing Stukas, whose ominous wail was, to me, akin to the eerie night-cry of a lonely loon on some desolate Minnesotan lake.*

On one occasion, a stray bomb in a near-direct hit on a gun-turret aboard Empire Starlight *tied directly ahead of us and blown two brothers out of the turret. Miraculously, one survived intact but momentarily went mad, swinging a fire-axe at anyone near him until he was subdued.*

Ted Starkey and Morris Mills and *New Westminister City* weren't so lucky, as Starkey recalled:

We managed to get into Murmansk harbour and were all dismayed to see so many bits of ships, sticking up at odd angles. Several of our ships at that time were, like us, loaded with gunpowder in two of the holds. The Russians soon discharged the aircraft in crates from the 'tween decks, but before we could get the gunpowder off the big air raids started.

After about twenty minutes we were hit by three (I think) bombs, which all went through the decks before exploding. I was thrown violently onto the twin Oerlikons on the port bridge wing, where I had been assisting. The bombs set the ship ablaze, but luckily, did not set off the gunpowder.

As I lay on the bridge deck my left arm, especially my elbow, was a mess—but it didn't hurt to breathe! So, when asked, I said I was alright as we had several serious casualties which were taken off with difficulty, as the gangway was gone, and put into waiting ambulances. Not surprisingly, I seemed to have been forgotten—"sleeping" on the bridge deck. When I finally came to I was alone on the blazing ship—others were standing off about 600 yards away, waiting for the ship to explode as the flames neared the gunpowder.

There was no way I could get off so I returned to the gun, but as I swung it over to look through the cartwheel sight I saw not aircraft but Russian women, firing similar guns, on the roofs of the huge warehouses. The gun was in worse shape than I was—so no heroics for me!

I tried to slide down a mooring rope, but I was pitched off and in my dazed condition missed the quay as I fell into the icy water—which "sobered" me up. I was wearing a duffel coat, so my head was well above water. I watched the rivet heads in the ship's side and could tell that she wasn't sinking any further. I could hear noises inside the ship, which I thought must be the metal caps flying off the gunpowder cylinders.

Then a miracle happened! There was a lot of hissing steam, as the ship's fires became extinguished and the next thing I knew was a plain wide strop dangling in front of me. I wrapped the strop twice round my right hand, two little tugs and up I went. I must have weighed half a ton with all my sodden Arctic clothing, but everything held and I was soon shivering like hell on the quayside—courtesy of the Second Mate and four Russian firemen.

After some weeks I was discharged from hospital, left arm plastered from fingers to shoulder, and into the Hotel Arctica.

Morris Mills fared worse in the attack:

My recollections of the bombing are still vivid in my mind. That day we had been discharging cargo using the ship's derricks which were steam driven. The winches were driven by Russian Stevedores—mostly women—who were very inexperienced and tended to open the valves quickly, not taking the strain and resulting in many broken wires and strops. In one such incident a wire parted causing the load to slew round breaking the ship's Carpenter's leg.

After we had got the Carpenter ashore to hospital we continued with the backbreaking work of repairing and reeving cargo wires until we were knocked off at 1700 hours. After a meal I went ashore for approximately two hours and came back around 2000 hours and turned into my bunk and fell asleep.

I have no recollection of there being an Air Raid warning. I am convinced a single plane flew in undetected and bombed our ship prior to the main attack. The first bomb went straight through the bridge and exploded in No. 2 hold killing a large number of Russian dock workers. The explosion was immediately below my cabin and in a fraction of a second there was a vivid blue flash, a column of flame roared through the cabin and a bulkhead disintegrated revealing the occupant of the next cabin, and then darkness.

The detonation of a five hundred pound bomb within feet of one's self beggars description. A column of flame blasted through the accommodation, followed by a colossal roaring sound as the cabin disintegrated. The opposite bulkhead ripped apart like tissue paper revealing, for a split second, the horrified face of the Radio Officer. I was hurled into a corner and showered with burning debris.

The conflagration of flames, the hideous sounds of metal being torn apart, mixed with the cries and screams of the wounded, drove me to a mad desperation. Frantically I tore myself free of burning wreckage and hurled myself through a jagged hole where once the door had been. Out on the open deck, I ran blindly for several yards before collapsing in an alleyway. All around me the bridge was a blazing inferno and I could feel my skin scorching. I was quite rational and knew I had to get somewhere safer, so pulled myself upright only to fall down. "This is bloody stupid!" I thought. "What's wrong with me?"

Then I saw my left foot had been smashed to a bloody pulp and was only connected to my leg by strips of sinew, the white bone protruding at the bottom. Then the waves of agony raged through me in torrents. I may have screamed in my torment. If so, it was a silent scream, for I heard nothing. I was terrified the foot was going to drop off and sat cradling the bloody object in my hands, the hot blood pumping out through my fingers.

Put simply, I was a bloody mess and it was in this state that Captain Harris found me.

He realized that if I was to survive I must be got ashore as soon as possible however, this was no simple task because the explosions had blown the ship several feet off the quay and brought down the gangway. It was decided to tie a heaving line around my body, lower me over the side and swing me like a pendulum until I gained sufficient momentum for those shore side to catch me.

By this time the ship's side was glowing red hot and the ammunition exploding through the hull. Several times I was brought clashing against the ship's side until I was eventually caught and laid out on the wooden quay together with other wounded to await ambulances.

Whilst in this exposed position the ferocity of the raid grew with a large number of planes attacking ships. The Russians and naval ships were putting up tremendous ack ack fire but I saw the ship astern of us—Empire Starlight—receive several hits, and the New Westminster City was again hit. At this point I noticed our Arab engine room ratings who had been running around in a blind panic jumping off the ship onto the quayside and, even above the hellish din of guns and bombs, I heard their limbs breaking as they landed near to me.

At this point a plane came in low strafing the whole length of [the] quay and we were quickly dragged into a nearby warehouse. I remember some Russian women dock workers doing their best for us, trying to staunch the flow of blood, talking soothingly, stroking my hands and face, before a ramshackle ambulance arrived and conveyed me to hospital.

I must have lapsed into unconsciousness because my next memory is of coming to in a bare room with people grouped round me lying on a table and a Russian saying in broken English: "You very bad, must have blood, I give blood, you sleep."

They then put a mask over ray face for the gas, this was quite terrifying as I thought they were suffocating me and fought like mad to get the mask off before going under.

I was subsequently told that the Russian who had given blood was a Merchant Marine Officer who just happened to be in the hospital. Apparently he gave his blood direct, intravenously. Whether we were the same blood group—or not—I shall never know, but he certainly saved my life. Unfortunately, I never met him to thank him.

For some wounded survivors of lost ships, the agony suffered in open boats didn't end when they reached Murmansk. Bill Shorts, who survived *Induna*'s loss, tells a grim tale of his experience:

Murmansk had been heavily bombed and there were craters everywhere. All that was left standing were schools which were commandeered as military hospitals. Hospital, the conditions were unbelievable. The school had huge windows and the German bombers came over from Petsamo [Finland] every hour on the hour. Our hospital [was] also heavily bombed. One bomb exploded fifteen yards from the hospital, but the nurses did not pay attention to it.

We had no idea how hard it was for the Russians, until we saw the work of doctors and nurses. It seemed to us that they are working 24 hours a day.

In the hospital, I was covered with grease and bandaged from head to foot in an attempt to warm me up. A tube was put into my stomach. The tube had a filter on the end and tepid water was poured into my stomach to clear the ice that had formed inside my stomach. They managed to get the ice cleared out.

When the bandages were removed, it was found that gangrene had set in, in both of my legs. I was then taken to a makeshift operating theatre; a school classroom where there were six operations going on at the one time. Placed on an ordinary table, a white sheet was set to cover the front view I had and a voice told me, in broken English, "We're going to cut your legs off."

I was given no general anesthetic, no preparation, as medical supplies were non-existent. All I remember after that was excruciating pain in my legs prior to passing out. When I recovered consciousness, I was told that I had been delirious for three days.

When I became more aware of my surroundings, I discovered that both my legs had been chopped off, one below the knee and one above the knee and there were great incisions to the stumps in order to drain the gangrene away. It just flowed on the bed. No one was allowed near me for the real risk of infection. My legs had been literally chopped off just like chopping a roast of beef off. The bone was sticking out; the nerve endings exposed so when anyone [came] too close to me, the nerves reacted. It seemed very crude, but I would not be alive if the deceased parts had not been cut away, thus saving my life. Five months passed, my wounds were never stitched and bone still stuck out; nerves exposed.

Five of us had frostbite. Among them, two of them each had a leg amputated. Assistant Steward Jim Campbell, who was only 15 years old, lost a leg [and] all fingers of one hand. Food was not nourishing, for five months we had rice—stewed, fried, boiled and any other conceivable way. Some of the meat was supposed to be Yak meat.

My weight, I guess was about six stones [84 pounds], which was normally 12 stones. My leg bones were sticking out and I had close cropped *hair. Toilet facilities just did not exist and with no legs, my bowel, etc. were evacuated directly on the bed. I do not remember the sheets beings changed.*

There were very few nurses with too many patients. A very upsetting situation but we were all so weak that we couldn't do anything else. But, there was some humour. Dr. Opoprmenko sang "It's A Long Way to Tipperary" and "Pack up Your Troubles" he'd learned during the First World War. Natasha Mamonova, a translator, and Madame Wright of Leningrad [organized] competitions, where winners were rewarded with cigarettes. Then she discovered that some of us [could] sing and play musical instruments, and began holding concerts to support us.

Sailors, ships, and dock workers weren't the only ones who suffered from the air raids. Civilians also daily faced the risk of death, something Greg Novak witnessed firsthand:

In a log-topped earthen underground air raid shelter on one occasion I was denied refuge simply because it was overcrowded with peasants and their livestock. I then sought shelter from a low-flying, strafing Messerschmitt by diving into a ground-level coal bunker and buried myself below the remaining coal.

Subsequently I learned that some 300 peasants had perished in the overcrowded air raid shelter I had been denied entry. It took a direct hit and the majority of those inside had died from the concussion alone.

The ships and their crews at least could look forward to leaving with the next westbound convoy, even though it meant once more running the gauntlet of deadly weather and increasing German attacks. There was no escape for the civilians; all they could do was to pray for an early Allied–Soviet victory.

Because of massive German air raids on Murmansk, which cost men, ships, and equipment, British Naval Mission and officers of the Soviet Northern Fleet discussed the feasibility of having convoys once again go to Arkhangelsk.

In answer to this, according to Colonel V. V. Shehedrolosev and Captain of the First Rank Igor. V. Kozyr, the staff of the Northern Fleet, informed the British mission that before ships could use White Sea ports, the shipping fairways had to be swept for mines when the ice was breaking up. This would not occur until late April.

Northern Fleet staff officers repeatedly approached the senior British naval officer in January and February to request help in clearing the fairways. However, this help was slow in coming. Thus, the mine sweeping was only recommenced in June 1942, according to Shehedrolosev and Kozyr.

The representative of the British Mission declared that in the prevailing circumstances, they were forced to decline sending convoys to the USSR until the opening of navigation in the White Sea. The liaison officer attached to the staff of the Northern Fleet noted reasonably that the beginning of navigation in the White Sea coincided with the period of "white nights" (at the end of April, there are twenty hours of daylight, and from July through August it's light twenty-four hours a day), the most unfavorable period for the passage of convoys.

Despite the opinion of both Soviet Northern Fleet and British Admiralty officers, Churchill and Stalin insisted the convoys continue. On April 8, PQ-14, made up of twenty-four ships, left Reykjavik and headed east to Murmansk; westbound QP-10, comprised of sixteen ships, left from Murmansk on April 10. Both convoys were heavily escorted to contend with the growing German forces of aircraft, U-boats, and surface ships. And, there was still the Arctic Ocean to contend with.

CHAPTER 4

FATEFUL VOYAGES
April–June 1942

The heavy attacks on Convoy PQ-13 left no doubt in the mind of Admiral Sir John Tovey, commander-in-chief, British Home Fleet, that the enemy was

determined to do everything in his power to stop this traffic. The U-boat and air forces in Northern Norway had been heavily reinforced, the three remaining destroyers were disposed offensively at Kirkenes and the heavy forces at Trondheim remained a constant, if reluctant, threat.

As a result of known threats, all convoys were heavily escorted to contend with the growing German forces of aircraft, U-boats, and surface ships. However, there was no protection against or escape from the Arctic Ocean.

On April 8, PQ-14 made up of twenty-four ships, left Reykjavik headed east to Murmansk, and westbound QP-10, comprised of sixteen ships, left from Murmansk on April 10.

PQ-14 had as initial local escort the minesweepers *Hebe* and *Speedy* with the antisubmarine trawlers *Chiltern* and *Northern Wave*, and the *Hunt Wilton*. The convoy made for the rendezvous 120 miles south-southwest of Jan Mayen, where HMS *Edinburgh* (which was carrying a large deck load of steel plates needed to repair *Trinidad*); the destroyers *Bulldog, Beagle, Beverley, Forester, Foresight*, and *Amazon*; the British corvettes *Campanula, Oxlip, Saxifrage*, and *Snowflake*; and the trawlers *Lord Austin* and *Lord Middleton* were to have joined them on April 11.

Heavy cover was provided by the *King George V*, wearing the flag of Commander-in-Chief Admiral Tovey, *Duke of York, Victorious, Kent*, and eight destroyers, while the *Norfolk* cruised in an area about 130 miles to the southwest of Bear Island, in a position where she could support either PQ-14 or QP-10 during part of their voyages.

However, PQ-14 ran into thick drifting ice during the night of April 10/11 and became scattered. Sixteen ships, damaged by the storm, turned back for Iceland. Only the cargo ships *Empire Howard, Briarwood, Trehata, Dan-y-Bryn, Yaka*, and *West Cheswald* and the tankers *Athel Templar* and *Hopemount* carried on.

The four trawlers, *Chiltern, Northern Wave, Lord Austin*, and *Lord Middleton*, were new additions to the escort forces. They were among the more than six hundred coal-burning fishing trawlers, drifters, and whalers requisitioned by the Royal Navy that had been converted for wartime use by converting their fishing holds into messdecks, installing communications and ASDIC equipment, and mounting guns, some dating from World War I or earlier, on the main decks. They were manned by fishermen, tugboat men, and bargemen, with officers drawn from fishing fleet skippers and mates. Communications ratings often came from a multitude of civilian jobs, many of whom had never been to sea. Added to this eclectic group were men from the Royal Navy and Royal Navy Reserve to provide some naval discipline. Although this was a rugged group, the Arctic proved a challenge.

Lord Austin should have gone through to Murmansk with *Lord Middleton*, but didn't make it. Through frequent snowstorms she steamed with the convoy steadily north around the snowbound Icelandic coast, fog and icy winds making it difficult for her crew to keep their eyes open, and frozen snow having to be scraped regularly from the bridge windows. Iceland behind her she forged on, but on the third morning she found herself in company with six large merchantmen. The rest of the convoy had vanished. Not knowing where the convoy was, *Lord Austin* took them back, out of stormy seas to the naval base of Akureyri on the north coast of Iceland.

In addition to *Lord Austin* and her six charges, another ten merchant ships that had been battered by the storm returned safely to Iceland.

On April 15, the convoy's remaining eight ships and their escorts were spotted by a BV-138 flying boat, which was relieved by an FW-200 Condor. Later that day, the first air attack by Ju-88 bombers arrived, and attacks continued throughout the rest of the day. Aircraft circled the convoy, making occasional attacks, which were beaten off. One plane that crossed the convoy was believed badly damaged by anti-aircraft fire from all the ships. After that, the rest of the day was quiet.

But things were different the next day when at least two U-boats reached the beleaguered convoy and escorts, adding deadly torpedo firepower to the bombs of their Luftwaffe brethren.

The chief officer on *Hopemount* recalled what happened:

Continuous high-level and dive-bombing attacks were made by Ju-88s and were combined with intense submarine attacks in a series of co-ordinated waves. It was a process of attrition as they tried to pick us off. Sometimes the bombers attacked so low that the escorts used to fire into the water hoping the shells exploding on the water would send up shock-waves and water to disrupt the attacks.

U-boat torpedoes were another matter for the men on the merchant ships as they plodded doggedly along the appointed tracks of the carefully formulated zigzag pattern, closed up in two short columns. The water was so gin-clear you could see the two red and white bands on the torpedoes. They passed right across the bow ... I can see them now.

An anonymous ship's master added his memories of the U-boat attacks on PQ-14:

I had 63 men on deck at the time—all the crew and gunners. Only two engineers and three stokers were down below.

Each man has a whistle and he blows it when he sees a torpedo. The torpedo is actually travelling 50 yards ahead of its wash, so if the wash hits the ship you know the torpedo is safely past. A man who doesn't know that may lose his nerve.

I put the helm hard a-port and squeezed her through between the torpedoes. This ship will do a full circle in four minutes; if on the swing, she'll turn with the swing enough to dodge in about 30 seconds; if against the swing, one and a half minutes.

The German method, he said, appeared to be to fire what is called a "Browning shot" (possibly derived from the old term of browning a covey of partridges, i.e., aiming at none in particular) from ahead and the flanks of the convoy, each submarine firing two or more torpedoes. Having done this, the U-boats withdraw out of range and lay in wait, so far as possible, for the convoy to reach them once more. On this occasion, the U-boat battle went on for four days.

Another master, asked to picture the action said:

> One would hear six short blasts on a siren. That meant torpedoes. Two blasts would be a warning from a ship that she was going to swing, perhaps out of control. The Commodore would give a long blast to draw our attention. During an air attack you might well see eight separate fights going on between ships and aircraft.

In his opinion, the air is colder than the sea, and so he advised his men, if they found themselves in the water, not to climb out on to a raft but to lash themselves to the raft with the fathom of line tied to the lifejacket and remain in the sea until picked up by a ship.

U-403, beating the sharpest lookouts and most adroit maneuvering, fired a salvo of five torpedoes into the convoy from starboard side. Two torpedoes hit the commodore's ship *Empire Howard* at 1245 hours, while *Dan-Y-Bryn* and *Briarwood* avoided the other three torpedoes by quick helm action.

The first torpedo struck Commodore E. Rees's ship *Empire Howard* in the boiler room, killing all on watch below. A few seconds later, another hit the after holds, where her cargo of ammunition exploded, instantly cutting the ship in two. Observers watched as her tween deck cargo of army trucks fell from her port side into the sea. She sank in forty seconds.

The American freighter *West Cheswald* was astern of her in the column. The explosion was so violent that the men of the engine-room watch thought their vessel was mortally injured. *West Cheswald* yawed and reeled from the concussion. Pumps shook on their base plates and almost stalled. Paint flaked from the bulkheads. The frightful clangor of the blast rang back and forth through the engine room and fire room, and men opened their mouths wide to relieve the eardrum pain.

Men on deck gazed at a pillar of fire several hundred feet high and nearly as broad. It rose from the sea where the British ship had been. Fragments of wood, steel, and bits of human bodies dropped from the pillar and rained into the roiling seas.

Of *Empire Howard*'s total complement of fifty-four, about forty men jumped overboard just at the moment that the counter-attacking trawler *Northern Wave* dropped depth charges in the vicinity. Many of those in the water died horribly of broken bones and ruptured organs as a result. The remainder were dragged semiconscious aboard the second trawler, the *Lord Middleton*.

Lord Middleton was steaming close to the *Empire Howard* when the torpedoes struck. Engineman Douglas Finney on *Lord Middleton* recalled what happened:

> *As I looked across I heard three explosions, saw her* [Empire Howard] *shudder, and in three minutes she had gone, taking the Commodore and many others down with her. We managed to pick up fourteen survivors. Among these was a young lad no more than fourteen years old and in a state of shock. He had probably lied about his age to make the voyage. He recovered, but four others died.*
>
> *The night before entering Murmansk we stopped ship in a howling gale to hold a burial service and put them overboard. During the service we heard enemy aircraft overhead, but luckily the storm screened us.*

Of the eighteen rescued, only nine lived, including Captain John MacDonald Downie, who afterward ascribed their survival in the freezing sea to the oil from the ship's ruptured bunker tanks, which covered them. Twenty-nine of *Empire Howard*'s crew were lost. Commodore Rees was last seen smoking a cheroot and hanging on to wreckage, but neither he nor any of his staff of convoy signalmen survived.

Captain W. H. Lawrence, vice-commodore and Master of the *Briarwood*, took over as commodore. Activity on Friday, April 17, 1942, began at 0430 hours with the arrival of the *Sokrushitelnyy* and *Gremyashchiy*, which, having escorted QP-10, transferred to PQ-14. Shortly before 0500, the first Ju-88s were overhead, and *Briarwood* shot down one of them. The air raid was unsuccessful and soon broken off due to low visibility. Finally, on April 19, the seven remaining ships of PQ-14 reached Murmansk.

German reconnaissance planes located QP-10 just as the convoy cleared the Kola Inlet on April 10. Providing protection for the vulnerable merchant ships were five destroyers; Commander John E. H. McBeath, in *Oribi* was the senior ship; also sailing were *Punjabi*,

Marne, Fury, and *Eclipse;* the minesweeper *Speedwell;* and two trawlers, *Blackfly* and *Paynter.* The cruiser HMS *Liverpool* provided close-cover anti-aircraft support.

Ju-88s attacked at first light the next day. Concentrated fire from the merchant ships shot down two aircraft and damaged several others. Among the convoy escort ships was the Soviet destroyer *Gremyashchiy* with Captain 3 Rank A. I. Gurin in command and Lieutenant B. Gavrilov as senior artillery officer, whose gunners shot down one of the Ju-88s.

During the attack, the merchant ship *Stone Street* was damaged, and *Empire Cowper* was sunk. *Stone Street* returned to Murmansk under her own power. *Empire Cowper* had straggled and was away from the anti-aircraft support of other ships in the convoy, making her a prime target for the bombers. One Ju-88 made it through *Cowper's* barrage and dropped three bombs—one was a near miss, but the other two struck home and the ship began sinking. T. H. Effington, one of the surviving engineering officers, recalled what happened on board when the bombs hit.

> *I watched the dive bombers coming in on the starboard side and saw bombs leave the aircraft. One fell into the sea on the starboard side, another on the port side, but the one that did the damage fell directly down the coal bunkers and exploded in the bowels of the ship about ten feet in front of the boilers. One fireman died later because of lumps of coal buried in his face.*
>
> *After dropping its bombs, aircraft dived to about mast height and the pilot waved as he went past, but never regained height and crashed into the sea.*

Effington reached his lifeboat station and started down the ladder to reach the boat. "At the bottom of the ladder I had to wait," he said.

> *There was still some way on the ship and with the rough seas the boat was being dragged along [as] well as going up and down about fifteen feet from the bottom of the ladder.*
>
> *At this point a plane coming from the starboard side tried to machine gun the lifeboat below me. Fortunately, the boat was on its way down and the bullets struck the side of the ship between my feet and the boat.*
>
> *After drifting away from the ship, the Second Mate was in the bows praying to the Lord while a little Galley Boy, about sixteen years old, said "Let's all sing." I think he'd seen too many films.*

The hero of the hour was Lieutenant R. Mossiter, commander of the trawler Paynter, *who placed just the trawler's bow against* Cowper's *hull of the sinking ship just below the foredeck so the men still on board could jump to safety.*

Nineteen men died with *Empire Cowper*.

The minesweeper *Speedwell* added to her score one aircraft shot down and another damaged on April 11. Two days later, she attacked a German submarine 60 miles to the south of Bear Island, but without success.

The British minesweepers of the local escort also took an active part in repulsing flights of aircraft, but when *Stone Street* was damaged, they were ordered to escort her to Kola Inlet.

The convoy was engulfed in a snowstorm before the German planes could attack again. For once the crews welcomed the bad weather and nearby ice flows, which hid them from prowling aircraft and U-boats. Such luck couldn't last. Less than forty-eight hours later, on April 13, clearing weather brought clear skies, good visibility, and U-boats.

U-435, commanded by Korvettenkapitän Siegfried Strelow, was first to arrive, at around 1300 hours. After missing an attack on HMS *Punjabi*, Strelow succeeded in slipping through the escort screen and torpedoing the Russian ship *Kiev*. The torpedo hit aft between Nos. 5 and 6 holds, blasting an enormous underwater hole and damaging the propeller shaft. *Kiev* plunged down sharply by the stern and sank within six minutes. *Kiev*'s captain, L. K. Silin remembered the attack:

> *At the moment of explosion I went from a cabin on the bridge and gave the order to abandon ship. The crew together with First Lieutenant launched the lifeboats and released two liferafts over the side. Boats number 3 and 4 have left filled with people. Having seen [the] hopelessness of* Kiev's *position I headed for Boat number 1, but after it was launched, the sinking ship carried [it] away aft and it capsized, throwing people into the sea. We swam to some nearby rafts and managed to pull ourselves on to them. The trawler HMS* Blackfly *approached about a half hour later and by that time our clothes began to become covered by ice. The trawler removed people from boats 3 and 4, then picked us off the rafts.*

Seventy-one people were on board *Kiev* when she was torpedoed: forty-nine crewmembers, eight passengers including two children, and fourteen military personnel. Nine of the seventy-one were killed, but the children survived.

After sinking *Kiev*, Strelow returned thirty minutes later and, again avoiding the escorts, hit the Panamanian freighter *El Occidente*. The attack killed twenty of *El Occidente*'s crew; there were twenty-one survivors.

Dense fog followed by a westerly gale later that day forced the enemy to withdraw once again, saving QP-10 from further attack. The ever-persistent FW-200 Condors regained contact at dawn the next day, April 14.

At 0600 hours, twenty Ju-88s arrived, diving out of the sun. Heavy fire from the convoy discouraged the planes from coming too close, and the bombers pulled off to regroup. Returning twenty minutes later, they again ran into a wall of ack-ack, which cost them four aircraft while the convoy escaped mostly unscathed. The freighter *Harpalion*'s rudder was blown off, making the ship impossible to steer. She could not continue in this condition, and the escorts were forced to sink her after taking off the crew.

The Russian freighter *Sevzaples* and her captain, I. S. Karasev, were in the thick of the attack. He recalled the attack and his crew's selfless devotion to their ship:

> At five o'clock forty minutes, the convoy has undergone to an attack of four-motor bombers of type of Focke-Wolf and two-engine torpedo bombers Junkers-88 which went several waves of ten to twelve planes. On bombing they came in groups of three to four planes at once from different directions, at low height, to fifty meters.
>
> One plane has been lined (hit) by escort fire. The bomber has entered into a dive, has dumped bombs, but did not pull out and ran directly into water together with crew. The convoy has undergone to an attack from air the following wave, but without losses.
>
> Intensity of shooting by Sevzaples was such that barrels of 20-mm of guns of Oerlikon heated up so that they had to be cooled with water. Cooks, barmaids, and orderlies from the dining rooms recharged the ammunition for the guns and carried it to the combat positions. Hands and fingers were bloody with broken blisters, but there were no complaints from anyone.
>
> With a dawn it was possible to expect an attack of submarines. Pets of the wolf pack loved this maneuver when the sun shines on the horizon, accurately tracing a silhouette of steamships. It facilitated shooting, worked on unexpectedness, and suddenness attacks. Vigilance of watches,

continuous supervision overseas, attentiveness to trifles, endurance, and
patience were the unique weapons against it.

QP-10 arrived in Reykjavik on April 21, having lost four ships—
25 percent of the convoy—in exchange for shooting down six German
planes and damaging a seventh. For the Allies, this was a high price
to pay. Replacing planes and aircrews is cheap compared to ships, the
cargo they carry, and the large crews needed to man them.

On the Soviet side, the increasing German activity against the convoys
and increasing attacks on Murmansk stretched the Northern Fleet's
Air Force to the breaking point. So in March 1942, the Red Army Air
Force 95th Fighter Aviation Regiment, consisting of two squadrons of
Petlyakov Pe-3 twin-engine aircraft, reinforced the Northern Fleet Air
Force. The 95th's missions included convoy escorts, attacks on German
troops and airfields, and reconnaissance missions in support of the Fleet.
The 95th Fighter Aviation Regiment had experienced hard fights in the
German attack on Moscow and carried a rich tradition of excellence in
combat. Two examples of the regiment's actions illustrate that tradition.

On April 23, the First Squadron of 95th Regiment, led by Captain S.
S. Kiryanova, bombed the German airfield at Luostari in Finland. The
raid was so unexpected that German anti-aircraft fire opened up only
after the Soviets had released their bombs and were making strafing
runs. One fighter, a Messerschmitt Me-109, took off in the midst of the
attack. It was shot down by a Pe-3. Seventeen German aircraft were
destroyed that day.

Three days later, Number Two Squadron of the 95th Regiment
consisting of eight Pe-3s, headed by Major A. Sachkov, bombed the
airfield at Heybukten, where the Luftwaffe sometimes concentrated
hundreds of bombers, especially during periods when Allied convoys
were on the Barents Sea. According to the testimony of a captured
Luftwaffe pilot, X. Gunteya, six planes were destroyed, at least twenty
aircraft were partially destroyed, two hangars and several barracks
were burned, and fifteen soldiers and officers were killed. As the Soviets
headed home, they were jumped by twenty-three Me-109 fighters,
which shot down five Pe-3s. Only three of the eight Soviet aircraft made
it back to base. It was a costly raid for the regiment, with the loss of five
planes and ten men killed, but it guaranteed there were fewer German
planes to go after convoys PQ-15 and QP-11.

PQ-15, the largest convoy yet, consisting of twenty-five ships and two ice breakers, sailed on April 25. QP-11, with thirteen ships, set out two days later. The Germans were waiting for both convoys with the Kriegsmarine heavy ships *Tirpitz*, *Hipper*, *Scheer*, and *Lützow*, destroyers, and twenty U-boats. The U-boats, organized into the Northern Waters Flotilla, were painted white, with polar bear insignia on the conning towers. The crews were tough, seasoned veterans from North Atlantic duty, where they enjoyed unparalleled success against thinly escorted convoys.

Luftwaffe squadrons had been reinforced with Heinkel He-111s and Ju-88s modified to carry torpedoes slung under their wings. Two distinguished Luftwaffe officers were responsible for the structure and organization of air operations in North Norway: Major Blordon, operating the Junkers 88 Squadron KG30, and Colonel Ernst Roth, the flight commander at Bardufoss conducting operations of the air torpedo group, flying Heinkel He-111s. The strength of the Luftwaffe in north Norway now totaled 103 Ju-88 long-range bombers, 42 He-111 torpedo bombers, 15 He-115 torpedo bombers, 30 Ju-87 Stuka dive bombers, and 74 long-range reconnaissance BV-138 and FW-200 Condors.

For the first time, U.S. Navy warships would be part of the escorting force. Task Force 39, commanded by Rear Admiral John W. Wilcox, Jr., in the battleship USS *Washington*, had departed Casco Bay, Maine, on March 25. In addition to the *Washington*, the task force was comprised of heavy cruisers *Wichita* and *Tuscaloosa*, aircraft carrier *Wasp*, and Destroyer Squadron 8, commanded by Captain D. P. Moon in *Wainright*. The task force ran into exceedingly thick and foul weather, so rough that *Wasp*'s flight deck, 57 feet above the waterline, shipped green water. In the midst of this, Admiral Wilcox was swept overboard and lost, and a plane launched by *Wasp* to search for him crashed and was lost. Rear Admiral R. C. Giffen in *Wichita* then assumed command. This was the first heavy unit of the Atlantic Fleet to reach British waters since the declaration of war four months earlier.

On April 28, this group, without the carrier *Wasp*, combined in one covering force with several British vessels: the aircraft carrier *Victorious*, light cruiser *Kenya*, five British destroyers, and battleship HMS *King George V* flying the flag of Admiral Sir Tovey. They departed Scapa in order to cover the North Russia convoys.

Commander J. Crombie in the minesweeper HMS *Bramble* led the close escort, which consisted of two other minesweepers and four trawlers, joined later by four destroyers. The convoy's defenses were beefed up with the inclusion of the CAM ship *Empire Morn* and the anti-aircraft cruiser HMS *Ulster Queen*, which was stationed in the body of the convoy to augment the anti-aircraft barrage of the merchant ships.

HMS *Ulster Queen* (Acting Captain C. K. Adam) was a former Irish Sea mail and passenger packet capable of 18 knots that had been requisitioned and commissioned under the Royal Navy white ensign as a fighting ship. She was fitted with six high-angle 4-inch guns, four twin 2-pounder anti-aircraft guns, and ten 20-mm Oerlikons.

The convoy also was covered by a patrol of four submarines, *Unison* (P43, British), *Minerve* (Free French), *Uredd* (Norwegian "Fearless"), and *Jastrzab* (P551, Polish "Hawk"), off Norway, guarding against a sortie by German warships.

PQ-15 enjoyed a quiet passage until just before midnight on April 30, when an FW-200 Condor spotted it about 250 miles to the southwestward of Bear Island. Luckily, poor visibility and frequent snow squalls gave considerable cover. It wasn't until 2200 hours on May 1 that six He-111s, each carrying two torpedoes, made the first German air torpedo attack of the Arctic war.

The planes appeared as little dots at first, low on the horizon. They swept in from the south, their shape and size becoming more clearly defined as they approached. Barely 20 feet above the water, they came in line ahead then swept in a wide circle around the convoy.

On the flank of the convoy and closest to the attackers was the corvette *Snowflake*. With her single 4-inch gun and two machine guns firing at maximum speed and efficiency, she raced toward the line of aircraft. The near shell blasts and accuracy of machine gun fire was so disconcerting that the planes were unable to concentrate on their target and, in an instant of confusion, loosed their torpedoes, which sped on ineffectually to run harmlessly among the ice floes. During the next thirty minutes, the bombers made repeated attempts to break through but without success, losing one of their number to the intense anti-aircraft fire from the convoy. With their torpedoes expended and thwarted in their endeavors, the Heinkels returned to base.

Also on May 1, the Distant Covering Force suffered two losses when *King George V* and the destroyer *Punjabi* collided in fog. A signal had been sent to *Punjabi* to watch out for a floating mine, and to avoid this, she had turned to starboard, and cut across the bows of *King George V*, unable to avoid collision. *Punjabi* was cut in half by the larger ship. As the two sections began to sink, and with the crew jumping into the water, more explosions sounded as the primed depth charges rolled off the stern into the water amongst the crew.

The two sections, sinking fast, were surrounded with blood, oil, debris, and bodies of the crew floating in the wash of the gray silhouette disappearing into the fog. Although realizing something awful had happened, no one was aware of the reason or result and assumed the battleship had been hit by a torpedo or mine.

Signalman Eric Whyte was in the communications mess waiting to go on watch on the flagdeck of the *King George V*:

Suddenly I felt the ship make a violent turn and seemed to heave out of the water. Soon after a loud explosion could be heard along with ship's side. "Hands to Mine" stations was piped. My station was amidships near the catapult, visibility was poor. Although there was plenty of activity on the signal deck we seemed to be proceeding as normal. A destroyer on port screen signaled intention to haul out of position to aid the now known crippled destroyer Punjabi *astern of us. We then learned our bows had cut her in half and as a result of the collision her primed depth charges had rolled off the stern and exploded near us and in the area of the doomed* Punjabi.*

I was given to understand this tragic accident happened because the destroyer was out of position at the end of a maneuver and perhaps did not carry out the correct procedure. The sad fact remains that loss of life had been suffered and one of our own destroyers had been sunk and we felt for those lost and the thoughts of the Captain of this tragic accident.

Seaman Gerry Ricketts aboard *Punjabi* luckily survived the tragic sinking of his ship:

The sea was calm with frequent snow showers and dense fog patches, so the opening and closing of distance between the big ships and escorts was frequent and often frightening. As the fog closed in the escorts with fog buoys streamed formed port and starboard screens.

Punjabi *was second in the starboard column following the leader. As she turned towards the big ships to close the distance the fog buoy of the leader was lost. Within minutes* Punjabi *now blind crossed the line of advance of the 35,000 ton flagship* King George V, *who struck our port side aft of the engine room slicing through us like a knife through butter.*

The tremendous crash was heard, all power and lighting failed as the ship lurched violently to starboard with everything crashing around us. As the ship was slowly returning only temporarily to even keel we scrambled to the ladder and on to the upper deck when it was obvious that half had disappeared. We stood on deck the angle getting steeper every minute.

On the port side our stern could be seen vertical, some yards away and appeared to rise up out of the water as the depth charges exploded throwing up water and wreckage.

Looking aft, the battleship USS Washington *loomed out of the fog and altered course to starboard. Looking forward the huge hulk of the carrier* Victorious *swept across our bows. It became very obvious this was the time to leave so [I] went over to the starboard side. The ship's whaler was some distance and the water was rising fast up to my knees. Steadying myself on the boat davits I stood on the top guard rail when within seconds the water rose suddenly floating me off and away. I joined a messmate and shared his wooden staging where we could. I saw HMS* Martin *and HMS* Marne *coming towards us to pick us up as thankful survivors.*

Whilst in the water, oil, wreckage and other less fortunate bodies of our shipmates. Wichita *and* Tuscaloosa *passed close by before we were rescued by HMS* Martin.

For many of my shipmates the cold and oil fuel was too much and fifty-two of the crew of Punjabi *died that day.*

Stoker 1st Class George Stacey was aboard *Marne*, one of the rescue ships taking aboard survivors. He was on duty in the boiler room when the engine room rang for more steam:

We thought contact had been made with a U-boat. Then the buzz went round the ship, that one of the escorts had been sunk. We raced to the scene of disaster and then bridge rang down to stop engines. I came off watch and was standing on the upper deck. I have never seen such fog. Everything was deadly still, quiet and eerie.

As we drifted along silently, the sea became calm, all round was thick, black, oil fuel and trying to swim for their lives were the poor devils from the Punjabi. *Others that were past swimming just floated by looking terrible, just black oil covering their lifeless bodies amongst the wreckage.*

Again the silence was broken by further explosions from the depth charges rolling off the sinking stern of the doomed ship causing further havoc, injuries and death to the crew, before finally disappearing below the surface.

Norman Newton, a signalman on board HMS *Martin*, recalled the incident as well:

Upon entering any of the very dense fogs which prevail in the Arctic Ocean, the destroyers would form up in line ahead and drop astern of the capital ships. To assist station keeping, each destroyer towed a drogue astern. It was a nerve racking experience for those on the bridge, watching and following the spout of water created by the drogue, for very often the towing ship could not be seen.

It was during this hazardous manoeuvre that the destroyer ahead of Punjabi *must have made a slight turn; unfortunately the* Punjabi*, following the drogue, turned too much and sailed straight under the KGV's bows and was hit just aft of the bridge.* Martin*, which was following next in line and following* Punjabi*, also turned in towards the battleship, almost ramming her amidships. Fortunately our Captain (Commander C.R.P. Thompson, DSO., RN.) was able to do an emergency turn, which was followed by a nightmare journey travelling in the opposite direction through the oncoming capital ships.*

We saw these massive, ghostly shapes gliding past to port and starboard, accompanied by the noise of sirens signalling and foghorns wailing. After what felt like an eternity the fleet passed and, in the silence which followed, we turned to help Punjabi*. She was lying in two halves and the surrounding sea was covered in black oil fuel.*

We lowered every available boat and proceeded to pick up the poor souls struggling in the black mess. The stern soon sank, but the depth charges were all primed and, as soon as they reached the critical depth, they detonated causing a shock wave which stunned the men in the water, most of whom sank from sight. We managed to rescue quite a few survivors, including the Captain, from the forward section before it sank.

Our lads had great difficulty trying to haul survivors onboard, because it was almost impossible to hold them due to the fuel oil. Unfortunately several survivors died, due to inhaling fuel, and were buried at sea.

Punjabi's captain was on *Martin*'s bridge when an Aldis lamp signal came from Admiral Tovey on board *King George V*, apologizing for the loss of his ship. Gus Brilton recalled that:

When asked if he wished to reply, Punjabi*'s captain said "Yes, mate. It's a f—ing fine way to lose your shipmates". I wonder if* Martin*'s Yeoman of Signals, Harry Plaice, remembers making that reply and if it is recorded in the enquiry report that must have been made after the collision.*

Of *Punjabi*'s crew, 169 were rescued from the forward section and another forty were picked up from the sea by other escorts. Forty-nine crewmen lost their lives in the accident.

Punjabi sank directly in the path of the *Washington*, which had to sail between the halves of the sinking destroyer. *Washington* suffered slight damage from the detonation of the depth charges. *King George V* sustained serious damage to her bow and was forced to return to port for repairs.

Ill luck continued to dog the escorts on May 2 when the minesweeper *Seagull* (Lieutenant-Commander Pollock) and the Norwegian destroyer *St Albans* (Commander S. V. Storeheil) launched a depth-charge assault on an ASDIC contact which breached and revealed itself to be not a U-boat, but the Polish submarine *Jastrzab* commanded by Lieutenant Commander Bolesław Romanowski.

After a week of bad weather and only one U-boat contact, *Jastrzab*'s hydrophone operator detected warships approaching at about 1945 hours on May 2. Romanowski was able to see them through the periscope despite the fact it was snowing. After studying them for a few moments and consulting the ship recognition book, he announced they were friendly, but altered course and ordered the release of recognition flares to avoid being attacked. The flares broke from the casing and surfaced to release smoke signals.

These were not seen on either the *St Albans* or the *Seagull*, and there followed a chaotic few moments as the destroyer and minesweeper made a determined depth-charge attack, the consequences of which were serious. The main circuits were blown, and the submarine again lost trim. Seams burst and water soon was pouring into the pressure hull, contaminating the batteries and releasing chlorine. Romanowski blew his tanks and surfaced between the two attacking ships.

To surface ship crews, any and all submarines are enemies. As the *Jastrzab* broke the surface, she appeared to be heading toward the Norwegian destroyer, thus her identifying pendant numbers, P551, were invisible. However, her torpedo tubes also were laid upon the Norwegian ship, and a shot from a secondary 2.7-inch gun was fired at her as Romanowski, seconded by his British liaison officer and signalmen and the duty watch, scrambled up on to the conning tower, whereupon fire also was opened by machine guns from the bridges of both ships. Five people, including the two British ratings, were killed outright; six others, including Romanowski and his liaison officer, were wounded before it was realized aboard *Seagull* that an unfortunate error had occurred. This also had been realized aboard *St Albans* and both ships ceased fire and launched boats.

Commander Romanowski wrote in *Ice and Fire* about the attack from his perspective:

I saw ex-American destroyer [St. Albans] *at angle of 120° running to my left and ship I did not recognize* [Seagull] *at 2000 meters distance. Snow falls. Due to a huge wave we lost depth control and broached. When we regained periscope depth, the destroyer attacked us. He was too close and I shot a yellow smoke identification signals then a series of depth charges exploded fairly close.*

I shot another identification smoke flare—again, a series of five bombs, awfully close, and yet again just five more. All the bombs on the port side astern. I ran away as I could. The effect of explosions on the ship terrible: everything is broken off; the lights went out, stopped the motors, chlorine gas leaked from the batteries, short circuits, etc. I had to surface.

When I jumped on the bridge, the ship slowly twisted to the left [due to bombs]. I noticed the 200-meter trawler from us and destroyer at 800 meters. Both shot with machine guns. The English signaler, severely wounded, still tried to send the identification signals with the Aldis lamp, but killed on the spot. I got four bullets in the legs, I fell and could not afford, sat on the platform, holding the Polish flag over his head.

Seeing that the destroyer intends sink me, I ordered the crew go out of the boat. The destroyer passed astern of us then stood alongside the port side at a distance of fifty meters and opened fire. The trawler gave one burst from his pom-poms and stopped firing. Destroyer subsequently stopped the firing and from the bridge someone asked: "Are you German?"

In a strong voice I replied: "We are Polish submarine Hawk. *Cannot you see P 551, you bloody fool?"*

Romanowski, though hit by five bullets, brought his confidential codebooks off with him. *Jastrzab* was sunk by Seagull's 4-inch gun since there was no hope of saving her. Five crewmen, including the British liaison officer were killed and six injured, including Romanowski. The survivors were later transferred to the cruiser *London*.

PQ-15's luck finally ran out for good at 0127 hours on May 3, when six Heinkel He-111 torpedo planes attacked at wave-top height from the convoy's starboard side in the half light of the Arctic summer night. A wall of fire swept up toward the planes, blowing two of them out of the sky and damaging a third, which crashed.

Captain Julius Christoph Klepper, a veteran seaman of Finnish birth, was in command aboard *Expositor*. He handled her with immense care. Her cargo was 10,000 cases of TNT and 10,000 rounds of 75-mm and 37-mm ammunition.

There were only five men in her armed guard detachment, and at Tail o' the Bank in the River Clyde, extra guns had been mounted. Volunteer gunners from the ship's crew took over the two 20-mm Oerlikon pieces, the double-mount Hotchkiss machine guns, and a 50-caliber Browning machine gun. The merchant seamen were delighted with the Oerlikons, which delivered a shell about the size of an old-fashioned telephone shank. A few well-directed Oerlikon bursts could tear the leading edge off a Heinkel's wing and deflect her fast from her torpedo release point.

The volunteers remembered distinctly the famous warning given them in February 1942 by Hitler. The broadcast had been heard at sea and in all the sailor bars along America's East, West, and Gulf coasts. Hitler shouted hoarse-voiced into the microphone that American merchant seamen were fools. He warned that they should leave the ships and stay ashore. He promised those who sailed small chance of survival.

Now, having fired at the silver-painted Heinkels with the broad, black Iron Cross emblems on the wings and fuselages, the merchant gunners shouted, "F— you, Adolf! You and your sister!" They were not fully certain whether Hitler had a sister, but that was unimportant. They were shaken by rage and fear.

Three of the He-111s eluded the barrage, their torpedoes striking *Botavon*, *Jutland*, and *Cape Corso*, which was the first ship in the outboard starboard column. She carried an all-ammunition cargo. When the Heinkel torpedo found her, she was destroyed within seconds.

Leading Seaman Raymond Smith was aboard the trawler *Cape Palliser* when *Cape Corso* was hit. He recalled the incident:

> *Horrified, we saw one of the merchant ships go straight up and disappear in a purple flash. All that was left of her afterwards was a mass of floating debris of deck cargo, all else had gone to the bottom.*
>
> *Our four-inch was practically useless as the low-flying planes were on us before we knew it, and it was impossible to bring the gun to bear. As I was strongly built my action-station was on the stripped Lewis gun, a contraption which could be fired from the shoulder, like a rifle, instead of from the usual tripod. Only someone with a bit of weight could fire the monstrosity — if you didn't hold on tight you spun round with it.*
>
> *I was on the starboard side of the bridge near the wheel-house when a low-level bomber swept over us from the port beam. Its rear-gunner was "hosepipe firing" [strafing] and I could see him as clear as day working the gun in a figure of eight — and not too bad with his gunnery, either. I was told*

later that his shot fell just short of the starboard waterline—I don't think I'd time to look. I managed to get off somewhere near a pan-full, gradually spinning round and trying to keep the Lewis somewhere near the target; it was a hell of a thing to use. Our point-fives also got close to the target, but the two twin-Hotchkiss, one each side of the bridge, proved useless.

The survivors we picked up were mostly lascars, but among them was one Nigerian, whom they seemed to resent and wouldn't have in their presence, until after much trouble we told them they were all in the same boat—and lucky to be in it, too!

The escorts picked up 137 survivors from *Botavon* and *Jutland*. Seventy-three crewmen were killed in the attack, including twenty from *Botavon* and all fifty on board *Cape Corso*.

From about noon, May 2, to the afternoon of May 4, the convoy was shadowed by U-boats. The escorts made several attacks on what were believed to be U-boat contacts, but no U-boat was damaged or sunk.

A bombing attack took place at 2230 hours on May 3. Only *Cape Palliser* was slightly damaged by a near miss, and one Ju-88 was shot down during what was the last air attack PQ-15 had to face. The Soviet Air force helped divert the attack when a flight of Pe-3s, led by the commander of the 95th Regiment, Major A. Zhatkovym, found the convoy and jumped the low-flying Ju-88s. He recalled the incident:

The attack by our fighters in a remote area of the sea was a complete surprise to the enemy. The first volley [of] rockets created confusion in their ranks and they jettisoned their bombs then banked away from the convoy.

Our fighters circled over the convoy and several times enemy planes appeared on the horizon appeared, but dared to approach the ships.

Visibility deteriorated the evening of May 4, and a southeast gale sprang up, bringing with it heavy snow, which provided excellent cover for the remainder of the passage. Also on May 4, the destroyers *Sokrushitelnyy* and *Gremyashchiy* put to sea at 0100 hours to meet convoy PQ-15.

On May 5, Soviet Northern Fleet patrol ships *Rubin* and *Brilliant* and the British minesweepers *Harrier*, *Niger*, and *Gossamer* sailed from Polyarnoe to reinforce the convoy escort. At 2300 hours, the destroyers arrived at the convoy in the midst of the storm. The destroyer *Gremyashchiy* detected a U-boat with ASDIC and attacked her firing nineteen depth charges. The U-boat turned away and went deep.

The convoy arrived at Kola Inlet at 2100 hours on May 5.

Commander J. Crombie, commanding officer of the corvette HMS *Bramble* and escort commander, summed up the convoy's voyage to Murmansk in his report to the British Admiralty:

> *The feeling of being shadowed day and night with such efficiency is uncomfortable and considering the efficiency of the shadowing I am surprised that more air attacks did not take place. It is possible that although the weather was fine at sea (except for the last day) the weather at the aerodromes may have been different. It is surprising also that there is only evidence that one submarine attack took place—that on the night of the torpedo aircraft attack.*
>
> *I should like to record the excellent conduct of the convoy, the majority of which were American ships unused to convoy work. Their steadiness when the torpedo attack took place and leading ships, including the Commodore and Rear Commodore's ships were sunk, their speed of opening fire and their excellent station keeping made the task of the escorts very much easier. It was largely due to the good conduct and discipline of the convoy that twenty two ships out of twenty five arrived at Murmansk undamaged.*

Before leaving Murmansk, *Edinburgh* took on two large and unusual cargos. The first consisted of wounded merchant mariners from ships that had been bombed, torpedoed, or strafed in convoy or while in Murmansk as well as nearly two hundred passengers, including British Army and RAF personnel who had been training the Russians in the use of British tanks and aircraft, Poles released from Russian prisoner-of-war camps, and Czechs who had escaped from their country when Germany invaded in 1939.

As more casualties arrived aboard the cruiser, the vast hangar took on the appearance of a hospital ward and the small sickbay looked like an emergency operating theater. Day and night, Surgeon-Commander W. F. Lascelles, RNVR, Surgeon-Lieutenant D. C. Lillie, MB, ChB, RNVR, Surgeon-Lieutenant L. Cama, RNVR, and Surgeon-Lieutenant (D.) J. K. Donald, RNVR, worked ceaselessly, operating on the wounded seamen. In many cases, they found that wounds had become septic and amputations of feet and legs were necessary to save life. That section of the ship and those involved became caught up in a war apart. Surgically, it was a question of saving as much as possible of a man.

Among the casualties was Morris Mills who, after enduring having both legs amputated without anesthesia, was finally headed home to England:

Came the great day, the 27th April, and we were carried out into ambulances—in reality, battered old Army trucks with a canvas top and open back—they managed about six patients to a truck. We had not gone far before a ferocious air raid occurred. The vehicles came to a shuddering halt leaving us totally defenceless in the middle of the street. From the back of the truck we had a panoramic view of the raid. The air was full of bursting shells and shrapnel scythed through the air with a vicious whistling sound. From our grandstand view we saw buildings disintegrate in clouds of smoke and flames.

It was a miracle we survived that storm of shells and bombs, I can only liken it to being out in torrential rain and not getting wet. We had not gone much further when the next wave of bombers came in, again the ambulances screeched to a stop. In a mad haste we were rushed into a large building and laid in every conceivable space, corridors, hallways and tops of tables. To this day I have no idea what type of building it was—hotel, office block or barracks. I suspect the latter because it was crammed with soldiers destined for the Murman Battle Front, then only twenty miles away.

As we lay terrified, a Russian soldier came over and squatting down beside us, producing a balalaika (a stringed instrument), began singing haunting Russian songs, soon his comrades joined in. Before long, the mood changed as they broke out into rousing martial, marching songs, which they sang with such gusto they almost drowned out the dreadful din of battle. When it was time to leave my Russian placed the balalaika in my hands and said a few words, which I roughly translated as, "Good luck—this is a souvenir." I thanked him.

We arrived at the dockside and boarded a Fleet Minesweeper, I think it was HMS Gossamer, *and taken down river to Vaenga, where the cruiser HMS* Edinburgh *lay alongside the quay. I was in a bad way and cannot remember too much about it, but I had an impression of this magnificent 10,000-ton cruiser towering above me as I was carried on board. Here was the very pinnacle of British Naval power.*

There were some thirty to forty badly injured patients from Murmansk hospital. The ship's hanger had been turned into a temporary hospital, and most survivors were accommodated there. The most severe cases were taken into the ship's hospital, a small area with six cots, and as I found myself there it is reasonable to presume I was in a bad way. My verminous clothing was taken off and after being washed I was put into a clean cot.

Shortly afterwards, the ship's surgeon came down and said he wanted to have a look at my stump. He must have read the fear in my face for he said, "It's alright, lad, I'm going to give you a shot to kill the pain."

This was another world to what I had so recently left, everywhere efficiency, cleanliness, order, good food and medicine. Above all, the wonderful, cheerful, esprit de corps of the Royal Navy.

The second cargo arrived two days before *Edinburgh* sailed and was a rarity in the many tasks the Royal Navy was called upon to perform. Supply Petty Officer Arthur Start described in his own words what happened:

I had been asleep for about an hour when I was awakened by the bugler sounding off, "Both watches of the duty hands fall in, in the starboard waist". My messmate sat up with a start, looked at his watch and said— "What the 'ells going on—it's quarter to bloody midnight".

When we arrived on deck we could hardly believe our eyes. The scene was like something from a film. Secured along the starboard side were two barges and at vantage points aboard were about a score of Russian soldiers armed with "Tommy" guns held at the ready. On our own ship, stationed at regular intervals from the deck and up ladders to the flight deck were also our own Royal Marines keeping guard.

As we watched, a tarpaulin covering the barge's cargo was drawn back to reveal scores of ammunition boxes. The natural assumption at first was that these contained small arms ammunition—but why should there be such security for a routine job of work? And then in a matter of minutes the truth was out. The boxes contained not ammunition but gold—gold bullion. Over five tons of it to be stored in the cruiser and shipped to the United Kingdom.

The boxes, rope handled, were extremely heavy, each needing two men to lift them. In the dull grey daylight of the Arctic midnight we carried those boxes all the way up to the flight deck and there lowered them by ropes through a shaft trunking to the bomb room three decks below. All the time we were unloading the gold there seemed to be an aura of evil present. An uncomfortable feeling of impending disaster.

We all felt it—most expressed it. Superstition is a strong characteristic with sailors throughout the world. The ominous feeling persisted and when part way through the operation, sleet started falling and the heavy red stenciling on the boxes ran freely to drip a trail of scarlet along the snow-covered decks, apprehension redoubled.

One seaman expressed the thoughts of all of us when passing an officer he said, "It's going to be a bad trip, sir, this is Russian gold dripping with blood!"

More than 5 tons of pure gold was stacked in *Edinburgh*'s bomb room, a specially armored compartment deep in the bowels of the ship used for high-risk cargo, especially high-explosive ammunition. The value of the gold taken aboard *Edinburgh* was estimated then to be about £5 million and part of a deal between the Russian Government and the U.S. Treasury, a down-payment on thousands of tons of war equipment for the Soviet Army fighting the bitter war against the German invaders.

Convoy QP-11, consisting of thirteen ships, left Kola Inlet on April 28. Captain W. H. Lawrence, Master of SS *Briarwood*, was commodore. The close escort consisted of six destroyers, the *Bulldog* (Commander Richmond, senior officer) *Beverley*, *Beagle*, *Amazon*, *Foresight*, and *Forester*; four corvettes *Oxlip*, *Campanula*, *Snowflake*, and *Saxifrage*; and the trawler *Lord Middleton*. Close cover was provided by the cruiser HMS *Edinburgh* (Captain H. W. Faulkner), with Rear Admiral Sir Stuart Bonham-Carter commanding 18th Cruiser Squadron, on board.

Minesweepers *Gossamer*, *Harrier*, *Hussar*, and *Niger* accompanied the convoy until the evening of April 29, and the Russian destroyers *Sokrushitelnyy* and *Gremyashchiy* reinforced the escort through the Barents Sea.

Morris Mills recalled leaving Russia:

> *Lying in my cot, warm, fed, and partially sedated, I felt the ship dip her head into the seas, and felt a wonderful sense of suffocating joy surge through my body, such as almost made me fight for breath. I was going home on one of the most powerful warships in the British Navy. In my mind's eye I could see that dark, evil, shore receding into the distance.*
>
> *The following morning, Rear-Admiral Sir Stuart Bonham-Carter paid us a visit in the sickbay. A burly figure in a heavy naval coat without any insignia of rank—apart from his gold braided cap. The Admiral was full of bonhomie and confidence as he spoke with each of us. Before leaving he made a short speech. "Well, lads, you know we are escorting Convoy QP11 back to England. I don't think our German friends are going to let us pass without a fight, so you must prepare yourselves for action, but never fear, you are in the hands of the Royal Navy and we'll get you back safely." Stirring words.*

A German Ju-88 reconnaissance spotted the convoy on April 29, but there weren't any attacks that day. Everyone in the convoy knew attacks by German destroyers were inevitable and it was *Edinburgh*'s task to defeat them. Reports of U-boats kept the escorts alert and, instead of trailing the convoy at only 6 knots, *Edinburgh* was ordered to move 20 miles northwest and zigzag to avoid U-boat attacks. No destroyer escort was sent along to screen the cruiser from U-boat attacks.

The following afternoon, April 30, *U-456*, commanded by Kapitänleutnant Teichert, found *Edinburgh* steaming at a sedate 20 knots on a regular zigzag course, totally unescorted. Teichert's problem was that he only had two torpedoes left and could not afford to miss. He didn't.

The first torpedo, amidships, ploughed through to the region of the forward boiler room and below the stoker's messdeck, destroying compartments through to the port side, killing all personnel in the blast area and flooding other compartments in a deluge of oil and water.

The second struck aft, ripping off the stern, blowing the whole quarterdeck upward like a sheet of paper and wrapping itself around the guns of "Y" turret with the barrels protruding through the steel decking. With it went the rudder and two of the four propeller shafts. So great was the explosion that it blasted the bottom plates of the ship downward to form a distorted fin or rudder. With a noise of rending metal and the dreadful thunder of tons of seawater flooding through under enormous pressure, the cruiser shuddered to a stop, listing heavily to starboard. The proud warship, once the envy of cruiser squadrons, had in five seconds become a grotesque coffin of steel and smashed bodies, with two enormous gaping wounds lapped by the cold gray sea.

Within the cruiser, normal routine was being followed to the letter. The pipe had just sounded, "Fall out from action stations" and "Nonduty hands to tea." Most of the crew had been at "Stand by action stations" for the past forty-eight hours. This was the earliest opportunity for some to relax in the comparative comfort of their own messdecks. For the first time since the ship had left Murmansk, the pipe, heard throughout the ship including by those at their sea-going stations, seemed to dispense an atmosphere of relaxation. There was a natural buoyant air of optimism, a sense of security. It was in this unguarded moment that no one, not even the bridge lookouts, saw the torpedo wakes streaking toward the ship.

In compartments and gangways just above the explosion areas, men stumbled and staggered in the darkness, cannoning into one another as they made for the exits, cursing violently when they could not be found. The two torpedoes had destroyed all electrical power to the gun turrets. Only one of the forward turrets, "B" turret, could be operated at all.

Damage to the engine rooms and the stern was so extensive that only limited power could be applied to move the ship forward.

Below the cruiser's decks, conditions where the first torpedo had struck were chaotic. For the few who survived there it was a nightmare of living hell. Leading Stoker Leonard Bradley described the scene:

Just before the torpedo struck I happened to go into the stokers' messdeck which was fairly crowded at the time and was talking to a friend of mine, a young amateur boxer called Harrington. As we chatted, the torpedo exploded in the oil tank below us. The whole messdeck split in two and as the lights went out Harrington and I and at least another 50 men fell straight through into the storage tank which was partially filled.

The emergency lighting failed to come on and we were down there in complete darkness, floundering around in oil and water. In the blackness with men around screaming and shouting, I managed at last to get a footing and started to make my way towards where I thought the hatch might be.

As I moved, I heard Taff Harrington near me. I called out "Taff," and he grabbed me. The oil was now pouring in fast from burst pipes in adjoining tanks and rising up to our shoulders. Harrington tried to hold my hand but it slipped and he died in the oil. There was another boy called Harrison clinging to a stanchion. I tried to lift him above the level of the oil but he screamed blue murder for he had broken both collar bones and an ankle. All this time I was swallowing oil. Gradually the oil found its level and stopped rising. Everything went very quiet.

The hatch above us was sealed and we had no idea if the ship was afloat, partly submerged or at the bottom of the ocean. We must have been there nearly an hour when the miracle happened. The hatch was prized open and three stokers came down with ropes and pulled us to safety.

Above, on the fo'c'sle deck outside the galley, Engine Room Artificer Robert Sherriff was standing talking to the Chief Cook, "Dolly" Gray. The explosion split the deck open where they were standing and both fell through. Sherriff managed to cling to a projecting ledge and regain the deck but the Chief Cook was propelled on downward and was never seen again.

Supply Petty Officer Arthur Start, who, with his mate Petty Officer Bob Walkey, managed to save several trapped men, related his account:

I was in the Petty Officer's mess at the time the first torpedo hit. All the lights went out but fortunately I happened to have a torch in my pocket. Realising that the messdecks below might still contain trapped men, we lifted back the hatch cover of the vertical shaft down through which the gold had been lowered.

Sure enough within the compartment we could see men swimming around in oil and water. My mate ran to fetch ropes and ladders, but while he was away several of the men below managed to get into the shaft which was only two feet square. Within the trunking there were no ridges or ledges to provide a hold but in desperation those men somehow managed to come up through by working their knees and backs against the sides. Eventually the hatch was sealed. There were several men down there but they were dead anyway.

When the torpedoes hit, Morris Mills was in sickbay, propped up sipping tea while watching the ice-flecked seas racing past a porthole when the torpedoes hit. He, too, recalled the event:

Following the catastrophic explosions there was a split second's silence, the ship trembled like a wounded animal as the seas rushed into her gaping wounds, and then the all too familiar cries and screams of the wounded. Panic broke out in the sickbay as thick oily smoke reeking of cordite belched through the alleyways, filling our confined space. I felt sure I was about to die, but was terrified of dying like a rat caught in a metal box, sinking into the icy depths of the Arctic Ocean.

In a blind panic, I desperately struggled to pull myself over the cot side in order to fall to the deck and crawl out of this death trap. I had almost made it when a sailor rushed in and hoisted me onto his shoulder, "It's alight mate—I've got you."

With superhuman strength he battled his way over a tilting deck, through a milling crowd of seamen, up several iron ladders, and laid me on the open deck. He didn't wait to be thanked, even supposing I could have spoken any words through clattering teeth, but returned below to rescue others. A true, unsung hero.

Owing to the violent manner necessary to get me from below, my various wounds had all burst open, yet again I could feel the hot blood pumping from my stump. I might have bled to death, but for the fact I was laying on an open deck clad only in a hospital night-shirt, in a snowstorm, and minus 20 degrees F. the blood was literally freezing in my veins.

My body and mind were exhausted by the relentless punishment they had taken. The Arctic weather was rapidly freezing my thinly clad, tortured body, I felt no pain, even the spurting blood became bloody icicles. The vast ocean, the towering superstructure of the cruiser belching flames and smoke, the scream of escaping steam, the shouts and cries of crew about their various duties, all began to fade into a swirling, grey mist. I was dying and felt warm and contented.

The torpedoes' explosions were seen from the convoy, and the *Foresight* and *Forester* were detached to her assistance, followed shortly afterward by the Russian destroyers *Sokrushitelnyy* and *Gremyashchiy*. Escorted by them, she started the 250-mile return passage to Murmansk.

Although out of torpedoes, *U-456* continued to shadow and report the *Edinburgh*'s movements. Based on these reports, the Kriegsmarine Flag Officer, Northern Waters, ordered the destroyers *Hermann Schoemann*, *Z-24*, and *Z-25* put to sea and attack Convoy QP-11 with its depleted escort.

At 0540 hours on May 1, QP-11 was about 150 miles to the east-southeast of Bear Island when four Ju-88 torpedo planes attacked. John L. Haynes was part of the U.S. Naval Merchant Armed Guard detachment on board the cargo ship *Eldena*. As he remembered, it was his nineteenth birthday:

I wondered how we would celebrate the momentous occasion!! It didn't take long to find out. At 0445 six Junker Ju-88 torpedo planes attacked. Four of them came directly at us while two climbed into the clouds. Of the four on attack, two flew across our stern toward the ship aft of us, but turned off when both our ships opened fire. Both planes were observed to drop a torpedo but no tracks were seen. The other two bombers flew toward the ship ahead of us but veered off when we opened fire. Both, however, were seen to release their torpedoes. None of the torpedoes hit their intended targets. A plane flew around the convoy but was kept at a distance by gunfire from the escort ships. We had expended about 230 rounds of .50-caliber ammo.

At the same time, a U-boat was sighted and forced to dive by the *Amazon*. Frequent HF/DF bearings indicated that four U-boats were keeping pace with the convoy on different bearings, and at 0820 hours, course was altered to the southwest in an attempt to shake them off. Then ice was sighted in large quantities ahead, which extended some 20 miles to the south of the route, and course was again altered to the westward. The forenoon passed without incident. The weather was moderate, but frequent snow squalls caused the visibility to vary between ten and two miles.

At 1345 hours, the convoy was on course 275 degrees, skirting heavy drift ice to starboard, when the *Snowflake* reported three radar contacts bearing 185 degrees. At the same moment the *Beverley*, screening on the port bow, reported enemy in sight, bearing 210 degrees. The enemy proved to be the destroyers *Hermann Schoemann*, Z-24, and Z-25.

On receipt of the *Beverley*'s sighting report, Commander Richmond, who was on the starboard bow of the convoy, moved across to the threatened flank and ordered the destroyers to concentrate on him. At once, the convoy (with the corvettes) carried out an emergency turn of 40° to starboard, the destroyers making smoke to cover it.

At 1400, the *Bulldog* turned toward the enemy on a southwesterly course with the destroyers in line ahead, with *Beagle*, *Amazon*, and *Beverley* following. The Germans at this time were about 10,000 yards distant, heading toward the convoy. At 1407, both sides fired torpedoes; none hit the destroyers, but a track was seen to pass close astern of the *Bulldog*.

After three minutes (1410), the Germans turned away and the British destroyers returned toward the convoy, making smoke. Repeatedly the two destroyer forces, in line ahead and on parallel courses, blazed away at one another with both sides loosing torpedoes. Each time the enemy turned to double back on their last course, *Bulldog* and her consorts turned also, always keeping themselves between the enemy and the convoy.

The British ships were frequently bracketed with heavy shells as the enemy tried to establish the range, but with each salvo falling to port or starboard the British force maneuvered into a new line of advance. The German ships, mounting between them ten 5.9-inch and five 5-inch guns, were far more heavily armed than the four remaining British destroyers, which between them mustered only six 4.7-inch and three 4-inch guns.

Amazon, second in line, was caught in a salvo that straddled her in a sudden sheet of flame and black smoke. Still in line and maintaining top speed, she sped on. As the smoke cleared, her captain, Lieutenant Commander Lord Teynham, stunned and bruised from the explosion, looked down from the bridge on a scene of destruction. The forward gun had been torn from its mounting; its crew, dead or wounded, lay prone on the fo'c'sle deck. The 4.7-inch gun aft, the 4-inch amidships, and the anti-aircraft guns had been smashed with their crews killed or wounded. The wheelhouse was shattered, and the main and auxiliary steering positions rendered untenable.

Careening along at 30 knots, *Amazon* was now out of control. As *Bulldog* made a tight turn to double back on the previous course, *Amazon* could only speed onward. It was only by cleverly executed maneuvers of the engines that her captain was able to bring her back into line at the rear of the column. She was immobilized as a fighting unit but it would not do to let the enemy be aware of this. Despite the fearful damage the ship had sustained, Lord Teynham somehow managed to maintain *Amazon* in line, so that to the enemy she still appeared a potential threat.

The German torpedoes running loose among the ice floes rose to the surface in a trail of bubbles and headed toward the merchant ships. A straggler, the Russian freighter *Tsiolkovsky*, was dead in line and a torpedo plunged into the engine room, rocking her to a standstill. Slowly she settled down by the bows, her screws high out of water. With the pungent smell of oil from her ruptured tanks came cries for help as the crew tried to launch rafts and boats.

The port lifeboat, although overcrowded, was successfully floated off, but on the starboard side panic prevailed. Twenty-five of the crew had managed to climb into the boat with the davits swung out, poised over the water some 30 feet below ready for lowering. Unfortunately the stern fall had jammed in the reel, slightly tilting it.

Despite all efforts to release the obstruction, matters worsened with the weight of those in the boat. In the confusion that followed, one of the two men operating the lowering mechanism took an axe in a moment of panic and severed the fall. The boat swung down hanging by the bow, throwing every man into the sea. In increasing terror, the second fall was now cut and the heavy boat plummeted on to the men below, killing many of those swimming around. Within minutes, the ship plunged slowly to her grave, with a small crowd of men packed high in the stern waving and screaming for help.

Moments later, *Lord Middleton* reached the sinking ship. Those who had survived the explosion and the numbing shock of immersion in the frigid waters were hauled aboard more dead than alive. Saturated in the black oil, it was difficult to grasp the men and lift them over the side. After thirty minutes of search, only a pathetic collection of bodies remained, washing about among the oil and mass of wreckage, and *Lord Middleton* made off at speed to join the distant convoy after rescuing only five people, leaving twenty-seven dead behind them.

During the course of the next four hours, the Germans made five separate attempts to reach the convoy, each of which was foiled by the aggressive tactics of the escorting destroyers despite their great inferiority in firepower to the Germans.

After a final exchange of gunfire at 1742, the Germans once more turned away. The British held on toward them for a few minutes until the rear destroyer disappeared into the smoke to the southeast. The *Hermann Schoemann*, Z-24, and Z-25 had been ordered to attack the damaged *Edinburgh*, some 200 miles to the eastward, which is why they broke off their attacks.

Commander Richmond could not know this, and for the next three hours he kept his force cruising between the supposed direction of the enemy and the convoy. By 2155 hours on May 1, the convoy was in open water and the destroyers resumed their screening stations. The remainder of the passage was uneventful, and QP-11 arrived at Reykjavik at 0700, May 7.

Meanwhile, *Edinburgh*, unable to steer except with her engines, was making very slow progress eastward. On receiving information about the damage to the cruiser, Admiral A. G. Golovko, the Commander in Chief of the Soviet Northern Fleet, sent a message to the destroyers *Gremyashchiy* and *Sokrushitelnyy* that read: "If possible, render assistance to the British cruiser!" At the same time, the British minesweepers *Harrier*, *Niger*, and *Gossamer* were sent at 2150. At midnight on May 1, Soviet Tug No. 22 went out to the cruiser escorted by *Hussar*.

As the day wore on aboard *Edinburgh*, many acts of heroism and tragedy occurred in and around the explosion areas. Men trapped in small compartments were pulled to safety in the nick of time as oil threatened to engulf them. Men were caught in the blast of burst steam pipes in darkness until the flesh peeled from their bodies. Men were trapped alive in unreachable compartments, a voice tube the only link with the upper deck, as officers tried to reassure them they would soon be freed, knowing full well survival time was running out.

At 0630 hours on May 2, *Hermann Schoemann*, Z-24, and Z-25 came upon the *Edinburgh* making about three knots under her own steam and steering with the aid of the tug on her port bow and the minesweeper *Gossamer* secured astern. First to sight the enemy was the minesweeper *Hussar*, which boldly opened fire with her single 4-inch gun. *Edinburgh*, although almost unmanageable, fought back and hit *Schoemann* with her second salvo, resulting in heavy damage to the German ship.

By now the destroyers *Forester* and *Foresight* had joined in the battle, which became one of hide and seek in and out of the snow squalls and the smoke screen laid by the destroyers to cover the *Edinburgh*. At 0650 hours, just as she had fired three torpedoes at the enemy, *Forester* received three hits, which killed her captain, Lieutenant Commander G. P. Huddart, R.N., and brought the destroyer to a stop.

The *Z-24* had also fired torpedoes, which passed under the *Forester* and sped on toward *Edinburgh*. One of these, almost at the end of its run, struck the cruiser on the side opposite to that against which the U-boat's torpedo had exploded, almost cutting the ship in half. Nevertheless, she continued to engage the enemy, but it was now plain to both the admiral and his flag captain that there was no longer any hope of saving her.

A moment later, Commander Jocelyn S. Salter in the *Foresight*, who had interposed his ship between the enemy and the damaged *Forester*, drew on himself the concentrated fire of the enemy ships at a range of about 4,000 yards. He went on to full speed and sought to retire under the cover of smoke, but four hits, one of them in a boiler room, brought his ship to a halt.

Foresight's casualties included Lieutenant R. A. Fawdrey, seven ratings killed or died of wounds, and eleven ratings wounded. The *Forester* lost her commanding officer, plus twelve ratings killed and nine ratings wounded. In addition, one officer and two ratings belonging to the *Lancaster Castle*, who were embarked in the *Foresight*, were wounded, and her master, Captain Sloan, was killed.

After a time, the badly damaged *Forester* and *Foresight*, taking turns to screen each other while repairs were effected, managed to get under way again, but to everyone's surprise and relief, the two remaining German destroyers retreated after rescuing some two hundred of the *Hermann Schoemann*'s crew and then scuttling her. Later, fifty-six more survivors were picked up from rafts by *U-88*.

However, for *Edinburgh* the end was obviously near, and the Admiral ordered the minesweepers to take off her crew. The injured merchant seamen in sickbay were carried to the upper deck and transferred to the minesweepers.

Once the minesweeper *Harrier* was secured along the port side and *Gossamer* starboard, the loading of the wounded and passengers began—a formidable undertaking up and down a sloping deck between the two vessels. But there was no time to complain. With the ship almost in two and likely to break up at any moment, time was of the essence.

Most of the wounded were on stretchers and had to be lifted over the side of the listing ship and lowered by whatever means available. The deck of *Harrier* was at least 12 feet below that of *Edinburgh*'s, and the transfer was made more difficult by the lifting and falling swell. One by one the stretcher cases were lowered as carefully as possible, but almost inevitably there were accidents. A few became dislodged from their stretchers and crashed to the decks below. Others, almost naked from their sickbay beds fell over the side and became entangled in the scrambling nets, nearly freezing to death in the Arctic wind.

Years later, Morris Mills wrote about the incident:

My stretcher had been placed some distance from the disembarking point, and watching the press of men trying to get off, I began to wonder if I would make it in time?

At this stage a sailor settled down beside me and drawing a packet of cigarettes out lit two and gave me one. I thanked him through chattering teeth and inhaled deeply. We silently watched the desperate struggle to get the wounded onboard the Harrier, *while several hundred seamen patiently waited their turn.*

Then, quietly, as though to himself he said, "Christ, mate, it's going to take a bloody miracle to get that lot off before she goes down!" Taking a deep drag on his cigarette, "How you feeling, mate?"

"Bloody cold." I replied through chattering teeth. He nodded.

"Do you feel up to taking a chance?"

He pointed to a projection overhanging the Edinburgh's *side—it was either a piece of wreckage, or a torpedo tube—he had noticed that every time the* Harrier *rose on a swell it was level with her deck. "If I give you a bunk-up you could crawl across." The will to live flared through my body, and I nodded eagerly. Without hesitation, he picked me up and placed me on the projection. "Good luck, mate." I had no time to thank him as I started to inch my way across. The surface was rough and jagged and several times I struck my raw stump causing it to hemorrhage a fine spray of blood.*

There was no time to worry about that as I clung to the metal and looked down on the freezing sea. Willing hands grabbed me and I was rushed down to a small cabin and placed in a bunk. The ship's surgeon was called and he applied a tourniquet and gave me a shot of morphine before dashing off on another mission of mercy.

Once everyone on board had been taken off, the admiral ordered the *Foresight* to sink *Edinburgh* with a torpedo. A booming explosion rocked the vessel when it hit, sending a sheet of flame skyward that mushroomed into a pillar of black smoke. Slowly, *Edinburgh* rolled over on her side. The fore part broke away in a twisted mess of rending metal. The stern disappeared quickly, but the bow hovered for a moment before disappearing in a tumult of bubbling, gurgling water. Survivors were overwhelmed by the disgusting stench of oil fuel that coated the freezing water of the Barents Sea.

Edinburgh bore within her hull the bodies of fifty-seven men. Almost at the same moment, *Hermann Schoemann* was settling into her last resting place on the floor of the ocean with the bodies of those killed aboard her.

Aboard *Harrier*, the log recorded *Edinburgh* as sinking in position 71-51 degrees North, 35-10 degrees East. The time was 0900 hours May 2, 1942.

Minesweepers and destroyers moved away with one final look at the pool of oil and wreckage littering the surface over *Edinburgh*'s watery grave. The vessels geared up for their advance, moving forward again in the dark waters of the Arctic Ocean. They could linger no longer. It was time to make for the Kola Inlet.

As the battered British force moved toward safety, the crew of the Russian destroyer *Rubin*, which had joined them in the fight against the German force, found time to compose a wireless message. It was sent when the ships were off the coast and radio silence could be broken. It read:

SOVIETS SEAMEN HAS WITNESS OF HEROIC BATTLE
ENGLISH SEAMEN WITH PREDOMINANT POWERS
OF ENEMY. ENGLISH SEAMEN DID OBSERVE THEIR
SACRED DUTY BEFORE FATHERLAND. WE ARE
PROUD OF STAUNCHNESS AND COURSE ENGLISH
SEAMEN—OUR ALLIES.

When the badly battered force of warships returned to Murmansk, *Edinburgh*'s survivors had not had a hot meal for forty-eight hours, and the weather was bitterly cold. All the authorities were able to offer them was a bowl of thin, watery soup and a crust of hard rye bread. On this diet, supplemented by anything the visiting ships could spare, they would exist until repatriated. On arrival in camp, each man was issued one blanket and a piece of synthetic soap.

The Soviets had nothing better to offer. Food in the northern regions was short, and most of the population lived on a subsistence diet and were barely managing to survive themselves.

Merchant Navy survivors were taken up river to Murmansk, where a fleet of ambulances waited to take them back to the hospital they had so recently left. Morris Mills was one of those returning to the place he so desperately wanted to leave a few days earlier.

Quite a number of nurses who had waved us goodbye were there to greet us. Many cried and were quite desolate to find some of the original party had been lost. Those survivors who had thought themselves unlucky not to have been included in the Edinburgh party, anxiously questioned us as to what had happened.

We were too physically and mentally exhausted by our experience to go into detail, but what little we related caused great concern as they realised the insurmountable dangers of a return to the UK. Here and there, someone would ask after a shipmate only to learn he had not made it. An oppressive air of doom hung over the ward.

CHAPTER 5

WHITE NIGHTS
May 1942

After studying the reports from PQ-15, the British Admiralty recommended the Arctic convoys should be stopped, if not completely, at least until after the Arctic winter gave the protection of darkness to the ships. The First Sea Lord, Admiral Sir Dudley Pound, wrote to Admiral Ernest J. King, commander in chief of the U. S. Fleet, and informed him: "The whole thing is [a] most unsound operation with the dice loaded against us in every direction."

The problem facing British Prime Minister Winston Churchill and U.S. President Franklin D. Roosevelt was extremely serious. Shipments through the Arctic Circle to Murmansk and Arkhangelsk had reached only about half the amount that had been promised, and roughly 25 percent of every convoy was being sunk. For the USSR, the situation had become considerably worse since the beginning of the German spring offensive. The Caucasian oil fields were being deeply penetrated, and the Volga and the Don rivers were about to be reached by the invader. If supplies to the USSR were stopped, she very possibly would be unable to continue the fight against Germany, forcing her to sign a separate peace treaty.

Exacerbating the situation was the fact that the Allies were still losing the Battle of the Atlantic. U-boats ranged from the Arctic to the U.S. east coast to the Caribbean, South Atlantic, around South Africa, and into the Indian Ocean, sinking an average of thirty-three ships each week, and there was no end in sight. These losses far outstripped the combined British and U.S. shipbuilding capabilities.

Stalin learned early in May that ninety loaded ships were being kept at Tail o' the Bank and Loch Ewe in Scotland and at Hvalfjödur. They were bound for North Russia, but awaited convoy instructions. He sent a message to Churchill asking that "all possible measures be taken to ensure the arrival of the above-mentioned materials in the U.S.S.R. in the course of May as this is extremely important for our front."

Churchill understood the gravity of the Russian position and replied to Stalin: "Fight our way through to you with the maximum amount of war materials."

Churchill then addressed a meeting of the Chiefs of Staffs Committee:

Not only Premier Stalin but President Roosevelt will object very much to our desisting from running the convoys now. The Russians are in heavy action and will expect us to run the risk, and pay the price entailed by our contribution. The United States ships are queuing up. My own feeling, mingled with much anxiety, is that the convoy ought to sail on the 18th. The operation is justified if a half gets through. Failure on our part to make the attempt would weaken our influence with our major Allies. There are always uncertainties of weather and luck which may aid us. I share your misgivings, but I feel it is a matter of duty.

While these discussions were taking place, temporary repairs were completed to HMS *Trinidad*. The necessary repair plating was delivered by *Edinburgh* to the dry dock at Rosta. Russian women welders were brought in and, under the expert guidance of British construction engineers, the plates were jointed and fastened into positions with supporting girders of timber. But it was a temporary repair job, one that could not withstand an Arctic storm.

The *Trinidad*, escorted by the destroyers *Somali*, *Matchless*, *Foresight*, and *Forester*, left Murmansk in the evening of May 13. A force of four cruisers, *Nigeria*, *Kent*, *Norfolk*, and *Liverpool*, and four destroyers, *Inglefield*, *Escapade*, *Onslow*, and *Icarus*, under Rear Admiral Harold M. Burrough, was disposed west of Bear Island to cover her passage. In addition, a battle fleet, consisting of the *Duke of York* with Admiral Tovey on board as the senior flag officer, *Victorious*, *London*, USS *Washington*, *Tuscaloosa*, and eleven destroyers provided distant cover further to the south.

By May 12, about sixty *Edinburgh* survivors had arrived aboard the cruiser *Trinidad* as passengers, settling themselves in the canteen recreation space. This space had to be shared with an equal number of merchant seamen survivors of various nationalities from bombed and torpedoed ships of earlier convoys. Despite the cramped quarters, they were all happy enough to be returning home, particularly in a heavily armed cruiser which could well defend herself against attack. And those attacks would surely come in the sunlit nights that assisted the enemy but gave no cover to the British ships running the gauntlet between North Norway and the Ice Barrier. Just before midnight on May 13, *Trinidad* left the Kola Inlet in the gray aura of the Arctic night, with the sun low on the horizon peering through a thin veil of mist.

Throughout history, the sailing of a ship on the thirteenth of the month has been regarded by seamen as an omen of bad luck, and this was no exception. Many of the *Trinidad* and *Edinburgh* men openly expressed their apprehension. Two close friends of Jim Harper, a *Trinidad* seaman, confided in him that they did not expect to live much longer. They seemed aware of their fate, yet they behaved as though all was well. Strangely enough, the number thirteen had loomed significantly in recent months in respect of the Arctic convoys. The convoy in which *Trinidad* had torpedoed herself in March had been PQ-13. And QP-13, the convoy of thirteen ships *Edinburgh* had escorted out of the Kola Inlet on April 28, had resulted in her sinking. Now *Trinidad* was sailing on the dreaded date, the thirteenth.

At 0730 hours the next morning, *Trinidad* and her escorts were located 130 miles out by an FW-200 Condor. There were also several U-boat alarms, but no torpedo attacks or ice restricted the convoy's movement to the northward. By 1852 hours, two more BV-138 shadowing aircraft arrived. Their homing signals were intercepted by the British ships, but there was nothing they could do about it. Then at 2100 came the dreaded but expected news: In the radar compartment, bright against a black screen, the searching arm disclosed the approaching enemy with frightening clarity. Formation after formation of aircraft between the bearings 180 and 240 degrees were shown heading at speed in the direction of the cruiser. Reports to the bridge became almost continuous: "A wave of aircraft at 15 miles," "Another at 30 miles," "There are more coming in at 40 miles," "More at 60 miles." Then from the radar desk came a report that could not have been more complete in its bone-chilling finality: "The screen is full of aircraft, sir."

Air attacks developed shortly before 2200 that evening, when Ju-88s started dive bombing *Trinidad* and the destroyers. Frank Pearce was on *Trinidad*'s bridge that evening during the attacks:

Then came the first low whisper of the enemy. I was standing on the bridge beside Captain Saunders and Admiral Bonham-Carter heard the pulsating hum, growing louder with every passing second. There was no further need for radar reports for the first wave of bombers were already in sight. Small black dots against the ceiling of the Arctic world, they began a game of hide-and-seek, darting from the cover of one thin cloud to another. On the ship every eye peered anxiously into the scattered haze, while at the guns fingers closed more tightly around trigger keys. Darting out of the sky in concerted movement, the bombers peeled off and came screaming down at near vertical angles, their engines racing.

But even as they began their dives the cruiser's guns blasted a defensive curtain of fire. A deafening roar that set the senses reeling as the barrage from the combined power of the 4-inch anti-aircraft guns, 2 pounders, pom-poms and Oerlikons went into action. With it, barely audible in the thunder of battle, came the voice of the first lieutenant, Lieutenant Commander Jack Herrapath, air defence officer, over the loud speaker system directing gun crews on to targets from his observation position half-way up the mast. With startling clarity, the first of the bombs were falling.

Small and dark at first against the sky, they tumbled from the belly of the planes in a whining, wobbling descent of flight. Suddenly they were falling around the ship, missing by 40, 50 or 100 feet astern and abeam. Exploding on contact with the sea in ear-splitting eruptions, great waterspouts cascaded high above the ship's funnels, hanging momentarily before falling in an ice-cold deluge on the gunners in open cock-pits round the superstructure.

After about twenty-five bombing attacks, in which no hits were obtained though all ships experienced near misses, about ten torpedo bombers came in at 2237. Eight minutes later (2245), a lone Ju-88 roaring out of the thin cloud immediately overhead released its stick of four bombs from a height of about 400 feet. Pearce, along with personnel on the bridge, watched with bated breath as the wobbling, screaming bombs fell directly toward the superstructure. With them came both the roar of the Junker's engines pulling out from its dive barely above mast height and the thunder of the ship's guns blasting a stream of shells into the attacking aircraft. Reduced to a fireball, the German plane plunged into the sea away on the port beam.

"The impact of four 500 pound bombs exploding almost simultaneously was terrifying," continued Pearce.

The little world around the bridge superstructure disintegrated into a pocket earthquake, blinding the senses, sending the bridge deck leaping. Officers and ratings were hurled in all directions. The damage to the ship was catastrophic. Each of the bombs had been on target. One had fallen outboard, gliding along the side of the ship aft of the forward "B" turret, in line with the bridge. Here it exploded under the waterline, blowing off the temporarily welded plates and sending a wall of water into the magazine and cordite compartments below the turret. All were instantly flooded, drowning every rating battened down in the area. If the explosion had occurred above the waterline flame and not water would have reached the cordite, in which case the ship and every man aboard would have disappeared in one great ball of fire.

The ship listed 14 degrees to starboard, but was still able to steam at about 20 knots. The carnage in the area of the recreation space where the *Edinburgh* and merchant marine survivors had taken refuge defied description. The explosion tore away steel bulkheads like cardboard. Decking between the recreation space and the messdecks around and below were ripped apart; stanchions, handrails, and piping were twisted like wire into grotesque shapes. Few men in the area survived

Torpedoes then just arriving from the torpedo bombers were avoided, as were other torpedoes a quarter of an hour later. By 2350, the attacks began to ease off. Captain Saunders was at last able to lessen the fanning of the flames by reducing speed to 12 knots, but by now this was too late to do much good. At midnight, with the sun shining above the horizon, the fires burned out of control. Below were those who remained alive, dazed and wounded, trying to grope their way to safety past flames and through choking smoke. Below them, in compartments that had become sealed off by fire, men were trapped at their duty stations.

Bert Soper and his friend "Blackie" Cass, passing through the fire area on their way to the upper deck, were mesmerized by the sight of a fellow seaman trapped in a light steel bulkhead that had been wound tightly round him by the force of the explosion. As the flames roared nearer, he was screaming his way to death. Every fire main in the area was out of action, and nothing could be done to extricate him.

By midnight it was clear that the fire was out of control, and in light of the distance from the nearest port, the presence of U-boats, and the certainty of further air attacks, the decision was made to abandon ship. The wounded and passengers had already been taken off by *Forester*, and the remainder were then embarked in the other three destroyers.

Engineer Lieutenant John Boddy attempted a gallant rescue. Some of his stokers were trapped below, shouting for help. The tall, young, faired-haired officer stepped through a hatchway to the decks below with the remark, "Can't leave my men below—must try to get them out."

A raging inferno had engulfed that part of the ship. Boddy could find no ladder or rope to lower himself below decks. Intense heat foiled any rescue efforts, and both Boddy and the men he had tried to rescue perished. Married just a week or two before the ship left Devonport, Boddy had sacrificed his life to reach his men. He was posthumously awarded the Albert Medal, subsequently renamed the George Cross.

High up on the 4-inch gun-deck, commissioned gunner Dicky Bunt and gunner Charles Norsworthy were manning the guns to the last to cover the remaining survivors while they climbed aboard the destroyer. Bunt, running between the port and starboard sides of the gun deck, was the first to spot the oncoming plane. With a shout of "Nosser, there's one bastard coming in over there," he and Norsworthy jumped on to the port gun mounting and watched the aircraft through binoculars and telescopic sights.

The He-111, approaching fast, was only about 20 feet above the sea and a mile away when first spotted. All the electrical circuits used to train and elevate the gun had been destroyed, so the two men were reduced to controlling the mounting by hand. With both barrels loaded, they waited. With *Trinidad* listing to starboard, they found even more trouble when they tried to depress the sights sufficiently to pick up the target. Norsworthy applied his eye to the telescope and directed the gun as best he could.

Changing to look through the open cartwheel sight, Norsworthy lowered the guns a little to get a target sighting between the bottom of the plane and the sea. He fired both barrels. The shells burst about three feet under the plane's port wing, lifting it with such a jerk that it almost capsized. The men who watched let out a great cheer. The enemy's torpedo dropped off at a crazy angle while smoke and flame poured out of the fuselage. Turning sharply away, the *Heinkel* slowly disappeared into the sea. These were the last shells to be fired from *Trinidad*.

The four destroyers and the minesweeper *Gossamer* stood off for some minutes to watch the last moments of the cruiser. The canting deck and settling bows revealed the distressed condition of the stricken ship. To hasten her end, Admiral Bonham-Carter on *Somali* gave the unpleasant but necessary order to *Matchless* to sink *Trinidad* with torpedoes. The crew and survivors watched the tubes being trained on the burning ship.

From *Trinidad*'s main and after masts, the large battle ensigns flaunted their emblems as if in defiance of the enemy and the leaping flames below. From a signal halyard on the main mast, a short line of flags, scorched by the heat, fluttered in the wind, broadcasting her last message to the world: "I am sailing to the westward."

On the destroyers' decks, the survivors watched as *Trinidad* sank into the frigid seas. Within the sinking hull, a great number of their messmates were being committed to the deep. So many of *Edinburgh*'s men had embarked with hopes of returning home to be reunited with their loved ones, but now they were dead, entombed within the disappearing ship. As the water reached the bridge, the stern lifted itself clear of the water. There she seemed to hang suspended for a few seconds as if reluctant to die. Then with a rush she plunged forward to disappear in a cloud of smoke and steam. It was 0120 hours on May 15: Ascension Day.

Now four of the five ships, crammed with survivors, put as much distance as possible between them and the German airfields, increasingly aware of the German reconnaissance planes, which never left but shadowed them continuously. But the boiler damage inflicted in their gallant defense of the *Trinidad* still limited the speed of both *Foresight* and *Forester*.

The destroyers rendezvoused with Rear Admiral Burrough's force and steered for Iceland. They were shadowed by enemy aircraft until 2000 hours on May 16, when about twenty-five Ju-88s attacked with bombs. Walls of water thrown up by near misses would at times completely hide one or another of the cruisers, which were bearing the brunt of the bombing. The Germans developed attack after attack, but after five hours, as the distance from the enemy airfields increased, they became less frequent. Despite the ferocity of their assault, every ship survived the blitzing and came through unscathed.

This attack took place more than 350 miles from the nearest airfield, which meant that in the future convoys had to expect to be attacked from the air during five days of their passage.

Rear Admiral Bonham-Carter's experiences in the *Edinburgh* and *Trinidad* left no doubt in his mind as to the hazards and dangers to which the convoys to North Russia were exposed. In his report to the British Admiralty, he wrote:

> *I am still convinced that until the aerodromes in North Norway are neutralised and there are some hours of darkness that the continuation of these convoys should be stopped. If they must continue for political reasons, very serious and heavy losses must be expected. The force of the German attacks will increase, not diminish. We in the Navy are paid to do this sort of job, but it is beginning to ask too much of the men of the Merchant Navy. We may be able to avoid bombs and torpedoes with our speed, a six or eight knot ship has not this advantage.*

These views were endorsed by Admiral Tovey, who repeatedly expressed his anxiety and more than once suggested that the convoys should at least be reduced in size. But political necessity overrode military considerations. The companion convoy QP-12 comprised of seventeen ships left Murmansk on May 21. PQ-16, with thirty-five ships—larger than any convoy to date—sailed from Iceland the same day.

QP-12 enjoyed a relatively uneventful passage. The convoy included the CAM ship *Empire Morn* and was escorted by the destroyers *Inglefield* (Captain P. Todd, Senior Officer), *Escapade*, *Venomous*, *St. Albans*, *Boadicea*, *Badsworth*, the anti-aircraft ship *Ulster Queen*, and four trawlers (*Cape Palliser*, *Northern Pride*, *Northern Wave*, and *Vizalma*). Though the visibility was generally good, the convoy was not sighted till the morning of May 25.

That morning, an FW-200 Condor, a BV-138 flying boat, and two Ju-88s appeared. In favorable conditions, the *Empire Morn* launched her Hurricane. The pilot, Flying Officer John Kendal of the Royal Air Force Volunteer Reserve, immediately found he had lost touch with his fighter direction officer, Sublieutenant P. G. Mallett in the CAM ship; his radio transmitter was faulty, though his receiver was functioning. Moreover, he also had lost sight of his primary target, the BV-138, in the cloud.

Undaunted, Kendal swooped down on a Ju-88 and began a long and dogged chase that culminated in both aircraft flying the length of the convoy. Kendal rocked his Hurricane from one quarter of the

The Arctic convoys were the most dangerous of all, under threat of attack by submarine, surface raider, and aircraft. Here PQ-18, en route to the Soviet Union in September 1942, is seen fighting a heavy attack by the Luftwaffe. (*IWM A12022*)

Icebound conditions on the deck of a British cruiser during escort duty on the Northern convoy route to Russia in February 1943. A return to the ice age can easily be imagined by the crews of these vessels, but the convoy got through all the same. (*Topham/AP*)

KMS *Admiral Scheer*, a Deutschland-class heavy cruiser (also referred to as a "pocket battleship"). Commissioned on November 12, 1934, and sunk by RAF bombers on April 9, 1945, while docked in Kiel.

KMS *Tirpitz*, a Bismarck-class battleship. Commissioned February 25, 1941, and sunk by RAF bombers November 12, 1944.

HMS *Bramble*, a Halcyon-class minesweeper commissioned in 1939. She served in the North Sea and as a Polar Convoy escort. She was sunk on December 31, 1942, by the battleship KMS *Hipper* and the destroyer *Z-16 Friedrich Eckoldt*.

Blenheims were used as both medium-range bombers and night fighters. They carried a crew of three and were armed with four .303 machine guns.

Known as the "Stringbag" by its crews, the Fairey Swordfish was obsolete when the war started in 1939. Regardless of that fact, the aircraft achieved an impressive record in combat over the next four years. (*IWM MH23*)

Martlets had considerable combat service, flying from both shore bases and aircraft carriers. The F4F was very maneuverable by European standards, and heavily armed with six .50-caliber machine guns, they were a serious threat to enemy aircraft.

Hawker Hurricanes were the first fighter aircraft delivered to the Soviet Union under Lend-Lease. Soviet pilots found it inferior to both Soviet and German aircraft in performance and armament.

The He-111 could carry 2,000 kg of bombs in its bomb bay or up to 3,600 kg of bombs externally. With a range of 2,300 km and a ceiling of 6,500 m, it was an ideal bomber for antiship operations. (*Bundesarchiv*)

One of the most versatile aircraft in the Luftwaffe's inventory, the Ju-88 served as a dive bomber, attack bomber, heavy fighter, night fighter, and torpedo plane. (*Bundesarchiv*)

The Condor was originally developed as a long-range passenger airliner. Equipped for antiship operations, the standard armament was one 20-mm cannon in the forward gondola and four 13-mm machine guns in the dorsal and beam positions. Later models carried radar mounted in the nose.

Jastrząb was the former US Navy S-Class *S-25* launched in 1922 and transferred to the British Royal Navy in November 1941 under Lend-Lease.

SS *Dekabrist* of Odessa, commanded by Captain Stephen Polukarpovic Belyev, was bombed and sunk on November 5, 1942 while sailing independently from Iceland to Russia. Although 87 crew members survived the attack, only ten eventually survived after being marooned for eleven months on Hope Island.

The *Zharky* was one of fifty-one flush-deck destroyers originally transferred from the United States to Britain. Several of these were then transferred to the Royal Canadian, Free Polish, and Soviet navies.

Sailors place a depth charge into position in a depth charge rack for dropping from the stern of the destroyer HMS *Eskimo* just out of harbor (possibly Hvalfjörður) after a U-boat hunt in the Atlantic. (*IWM A7414*)

Escorts and merchant ships at Hvalfjörður before the sailing of Convoy PQ-17. Behind the destroyer *Icarus* (1.03) is the Russian tanker *Azerbaijan*. The sea voyage to the north Russian ports of Murmansk and Arkhangelsk was the shortest route for sending Allied supplies to Russia. But it was also the most dangerous owing to the large concentration of German forces in northern Norway. The convoy PQ-17 was decimated by U-boats and the Luftwaffe after a communication from the Admiralty on July 4, 1942, ordered the escort to scatter. (*IWM A8953*)

Above • The 7,457-ton CAM ship *Empire Lawrence*, which was sunk during the PQ-16 convoy battle. Note the disruptive camouflage on her foredeck and the Sea Hurricane I sitting on the bow catapult. (*via Andy Thomas*)

Left • The escort carrier HMS *Avenger* with her full complement of six Sea Hurricanes from 883 Naval Air Squadron embarked. Note the special "Arctic" camouflage applied to her flightdeck for the PQ-18 operation. *Avenger* was sunk by U-boat *U-155* during the early hours of November 15, 1942, while escorting convoy MKF 1(Y) off the Portuguese coast. A single torpedo hit the ship's bomb room and ignited the munitions stored there, causing numerous secondary explosions. With her back broken, the carrier sunk in under five minutes, taking 68 officers and 446 ratings with it. (*R. Mackay via Andy Thomas*)

Below • An ammunition ship exploding during a Russian convoy, as seen from the deck of an aircraft carrier. (*IWM A12274*)

Above • Gun crews of HMS *Duke of York* under the ship's 14-inch guns at Scapa Flow after the sinking of the German warship, the *Scharnhorst* on December 26, 1943. (*IWM A21168*)

Below • An unidentified U-boat under attack by an 86 Sqn Liberator at 68,38N 08,59E, Germany, on July 18, 1944, in the Arctic Circle off Norway. (*ww2images.com*)

enemy plane to the other in a tenacious and perfectly judged attack, firing two long bursts of gunfire before overshooting his quarry. Black smoke began to pour from the engine nacelles of the Junkers. Her aircrew jettisoned their bombs in order to maintain height as the engine failed. Finally, the plane crashed into the sea. By now the Hurricane was short of fuel and the other German aircraft showed no signs of pressing an attack.

Kendal prepared to ditch near *Boadicea*, but the destroyer was approaching a patch of low, rain-bearing clouds, and Mallett advised Kendal to select a rear escort. Though he received no acknowledgement, Mallett was gratified to see the Hurricane break out of the cloud and double back to circle over *Badsworth*, while Mallett signaled the change of plan to the senior officer. Kendal now flew a tight, left-hand circuit and waggled his wings to indicate he intended to bail out rather than ditch. Flying east, he turned and, heading for *Badsworth*, climbed to gain height and vanished in the cloud.

The hundreds of men now watching from every ship in the convoy heard sound of the victorious Hurricane's engine cutting out. Then the fighter dropped out of the overcast and fell into the sea. A second later the figure of Kendal tumbled out of the sky, his parachute unopened. Just 50 feet above the sea, the canopy fluttered into life, but it was far too late. Kendal hit the water with the parachute imperfectly extended. A few moments later, *Badsworth* signaled *Empire Morn* that the young man had been picked up with grave injuries. Ten minutes later, Kendal died. He was buried at sea.

Luftwaffe aircraft continued shadowing through the afternoon. No air attacks were launched, and there were no submarine attacks even though U-boats were known to be in the area. Thick weather aided the convoy in avoiding trouble, and QP-12 duly arrived at Reykjavik intact and undamaged early on May 29.

After leaving from Iceland the same day, PQ-16 initially was escorted by the minesweeper HMS *Hazard* (Senior Escort ship) and four trawlers (*St. Elstan, Lady Madeleine, Retriever*, and *Northern Spray*). *Retriever* considered her speed insufficient to keep up with the convoy and returned to Iceland on May 24.

Graeme Ogden, captain of the trawler *Lady Madeleine*, was making his first Arctic Convoy run. Although he had experience with escorting convoys, Ogden expressed some trepidation at the new assignment:

At the Ardrossan Naval Base we had gone in for a new type of camouflage. The colour scheme was white, with light-blue and green triangles. By far the largest proportion was white, so we really looked very like a yacht, but, as we shall see, this nearly proved our undoing.

We left home behind us; we knew we should not be returning for many months—if at all—for we were going on "The Northern Crusade". I only hoped that ours would not be as disastrous as its medieval predecessors, which had left disease, death and ruin in their train.

One the four Russian merchant ships in PQ-16 was *Stari Bolshevik*, whose veteran crew was headed home on their fourth convoy. A DEMS gun crew provided by the Royal Navy was on board to assist in the ship's defense. The crew itself came from bombed, smashed, and burned cities and territories occupied by the Germans. A number of them had lost their entire families.

Also among the crew were four women. Of these, one was the second engineer's wife, a young, rather fragile-looking girl. Two others were pretty blonde stewardesses. The fourth woman was *Stari Bolshevik*'s Third Mate, whose husband was a tank commander on the Stalingrad front. She had not heard from him in months since she'd been at sea.

Two days after sailing, the escorts were joined by the anti-aircraft ship *Alynbank*, the submarines *Trident* and *Seawolf*, and four corvettes: *Honeysuckle*, *Starwort*, *Hyderabad*, and the Free French-manned *Roselys*.

The *City of Joliet* was one of the American vessels in convoy PQ-16, and this was her maiden voyage. Her crew consisted of thirty-nine seamen plus twelve naval armed guards commanded by an ensign. None of these ratings or the merchant seamen had ever been in a real air attack. One of them, Davis Doyle, had been twice shipwrecked, both times as the result of a torpedo attack. The sinkings had been almost instantaneous: violent shocks that made the ships shudder, bits of iron and wood flying through the air, a column of steam as the boiler groaned like a huge wounded beast. Both sinkings had been similar down to the smallest details. Davis remembered that he had hardly had time to be scared.

Rear Admiral Burrough, flying his flag on the *Nigeria*, sailed from Seydisfjord on May 23, with the *Onslow*, *Oribi*, and *Marne* as his destroyer escort. The cruisers *Norfolk*, *Kent*, and *Liverpool* later joined the force from Hvalfjödur. Together these ships were designated Force "Q."

Shortly afterward, a destroyer escort, consisting of the *Ashanti* (Commander R. G. Onslow, S.O.), *Martin*, *Achates*, *Volunteer*, and the

Free Polish destroyer ORP *Garland*, was detached to join PQ-16, the remainder of the force standing to the north-eastward for a position where it could also cover QP-12 approaching from the east. ORP *Garland* was the first warship flying Poland's red and white flag to visit a Soviet port since the beginning of the war.

At 0600 hours on May 25, the first FW-200 Condor arrived over the convoy, but the day passed fairly quietly, and Force Q was detached in the afternoon and returned to Scapa Flow. Convoy QP-12 was sighted at 1400 hours, and also reported having sighted a U-boat. An hour later, *Martin* sighted a U-boat 7 miles on the starboard beam of PQ-16 and carried out an unsuccessful attack. Although safe from U-boats for the time being, the arrival of a BV-138 flying boat meant that dive bombers and torpedo planes were on their way.

The first attack by six Ju-88 dive bombers and seven He-111 torpedo planes began at 1910 hours. Two Ju-88s fell to the convoy's gunners while out of the seven torpedo-planes, Pilot Officer Hay in the CAM ship *Empire Lawrence*'s Hurricane shot down one in flames and sent another staggering away heavily damaged and unlikely to reach its base. Overeager gunners on American ships fired at Hay's Hurricane as it flew low over the convoy after the dogfight. Although wounded, Hay successfully bailed out of his aircraft and was picked up by *Volunteer*.

Not a bomb or torpedo found its mark, though a near miss had immobilized one ship, the *Carlton*, which had to be sent back to Iceland in tow of the trawler *Northern Spray*. The day closed with an ineffectual attack by twelve Ju-88s between 2315 and 2330 hours.

One of the most hard-pressed vessels was *City of Joliet*, the target of eight torpedo planes and eighteen dive bombers during four attacks on just the first day of the battle. The Ju-88s and He-111s came in on the starboard beam at about 150 knots in line abreast, about 75 feet apart. Breaking formation, the bombers dove at a 50-degree angle and released three to five impact bombs, averaging 300 pounds each, from a height of 1,000 feet. The torpedo planes attacked in two groups, coming in 30 to 50 feet above the water and releasing torpedoes simultaneously at about 3,000 yards on the starboard side of the convoy. *City of Joliet* escaped with a severe shaking-up from near misses that twisted and buckled the hull plates.

In the early morning twilight on May 26, the American merchantman *Syros* straggled behind the convoy. As she labored to return, Kapitänleutnant Heinz Bielfeld on *U-703* found her and fired two torpedoes at the laboring ship. Raymond P. Holubowicz, serving as cadet-midshipman aboard *Syros*, sighted it as the track described a dim white furrow across the slate-colored sea. The torpedo had taken an abrupt right turn and was heading squarely for *Syros*. Holubowicz reported later what happened:

> *Since I was the only one who had seen the torpedo up to this point and being the only cadet aboard, I shouted into the wheelhouse an order to put the wheel hard over. The third mate came running out to find what business I had giving the helmsman an order, and before he was able to say a word he saw the torpedo. He shouted an order to the helmsman. The captain, too, ran out to find why someone was giving the helmsman an order while he held the con. By the time the captain got out on the port wing, the torpedo struck. Just before the torpedo struck, I threw the General Alarm switch. But it was too late to do any good for the men on watch in the engine room, one of whom was my fellow cadet, John Brewster.*

Syros carried TNT and ammunition. The torpedo struck her amidships. She exploded and sank within eighty seconds, wrapped in a vast white sheet of flame. She broke in half; the pieces reared as they buckled, then broke and plunged. Debris, lifejackets, shards of hatch board, and potatoes from the adrift and smashed locker lay on the dark wave crests where she had gone.

The crew of the *City of Joliet* saw a column of blinding flame rise to 9,000 feet, followed by a deafening roar, a suffocating displacement of air, and a searing wind on the face. The pillar of fire grew larger, became a gigantic egg, and changed color. From a blinding white it turned carmine, scarlet, and yellow. Then nothing. Not even a wisp of smoke against the pale blue sky.

Hazard and *Lady Madeleine* were detailed to look for survivors. Ogden on *Lady Madeleine* remembered the scene:

> *I love ships of all kinds, and it hurts me to see them destroyed. They lie there in their death agony like some wounded animal. Some take longer than others to die—some sink gracefully and proudly and others break up in a frenzy of despair.*
>
> *When we got to her she was well down by the bows and her crew had abandoned ship. Hazard had arrived before us and was busy picking up survivors. We sent both sea-boats away and collected some more. She was an American ship, and I shall never forget one American seaman standing*

up alone on a small raft making the hitch-hiking sign to us. The Americans
were in very fine form and seemed to regard the whole thing as a joke. One
Negro went straight from the life-boat to the wardroom, polished up all the
glasses, borrowed a steward's white jacket and appeared on the bridge to ask
if I cared for a "high-ball."

The "hitchhiker" story was told by the *Hazard* crew:

He was called Boston Blackie. It seems that he didn't even get his feet wet
when Syros *sank. Blackie managed to step off the rail of the ship as she was*
sinking and onto a life-raft that was fortuitously floating by at that moment.
He was alone on the raft and was next seen using his thumb to hitch a ride
on an escort vessel that came alongside.

Incredibly, twenty-eight men from *Syros*'s crew of thirty-seven were
rescued by trawlers.

There was only one air attack on this day: an ineffective effort by
eight torpedo bombers and three Ju-88s at 1800. U-boats were sighted
at frequent intervals, but were chased away or attacked with depth
charges. The last encounter took place at 2300 hours, after which no
more U-boats were encountered during the remainder of the passage.

But the departure of the four strongly armed cruisers (*Nigeria, Kent,
Norfolk,* and *Liverpool*) meant a very serious reduction of firepower for the
convoy. *Alynbank* was practically out of ammunition for her 5.25 pieces.
Her decks were littered almost knee-high with empty shell cases. All
the destroyers except the recently commissioned *Martin* were equipped
with low-level guns. Their main batteries could not be elevated for
high-angle anti-aircraft fire. A number of the merchant ships shared the
same predicament as *Syros* before she was sunk; their ammunition was
completely gone.

The Germans failed to take immediate advantage of that fact, though,
and on May 26, delivered a lone, weak Luftwaffe attack, a combination
of high-altitude bombing by Junkers 88s and a few runs by Heinkel 111s
when torpedoes were released. *Martin* and *Alynbank*, supported by the
escort's automatic weapons fire, drove it off without loss to the convoy.

Fatigue became a very serious factor for the merchant crews. Many
of the men had no clear idea of their destination and had not been
informed in any way at the outset of the voyage about the dangers

they might encounter. Sleep had not been possible since the ships left Iceland. Clothing was not taken off, and most of the bunks were unoccupied. Instead, men sat briefly dozing in the mess rooms or the officers' saloons. They kept on their lifejackets, and some their rubber suits. Gunners who were off watch hung their steel helmets from their wrists by the chinstraps. The helmets were of the basin-shaped, World War I type, and the web linings served to hold cigarettes and identification papers.

Regular meals had been attempted for several days aboard a number of the ships. But it was impossible to keep the big galley ranges going while the vessels were under attack or while depth charges shook the frying pans spinning off onto the floor tiles. Sandwiches and coffee were the only rations.

Some men went mad. They sat babbling in the passageways, pitifully huddled, or screamed at each other when a near miss fell. One ran straight toward a descending bomb; another, bareheaded, stood for hours on deck, looking numbly aloft at the German planes. When he spoke, it was to ask why the Germans wanted to kill him.

The worst ordeal was for the men who served below in the engine rooms and fire rooms. They formed in little groups in the passageways a few minutes before they were to go on watch. It was useless for them to wear lifejackets, which were too bulky to move around in. They stood in their regular work clothes, dungarees, or khakis at the doorways, which led to the engine-room ladders.

They were pale with the terrible fear that gripped them. Sweat ran down their faces. Their eyes were deep-drawn, glaring. The fear was so great that some of them bent over, violently gripped with stomach pains from the stress. Many could not control the shaking of their hands. Men on deck duty who passed them looked aside from the group in a strange, irrational kind of shame.

Then one of the group moved. He stepped over the high, brass-bound sill and onto the grating at the head of the ladders. The others followed, closely crowding, eager now, wanting to return to the familiar warmth and noise, the white bulkheads, the shining steel, the gauges, the pumps, the massive turning of the main shaft, and the reddish orange throb of the furnace fires. They found reassurance below, although their fear could never be wholly checked.

The men on deck duty served emergency watches: four hours on, four hours off. The muster in some ships was reduced almost in half; too many men were no longer capable. Fatigue claimed them, and they sprawled, heads down on the mess-room tables, still wearing their mittens and helmets. There were others who were temporarily insane, or so shocked they moved as if in a trance.

For those who went in rotation from the guns to the wheel and then to lookout, time had begun to lose meaning. They walked the guns, around, around, once more around, gazing into the cloud-banked horizon from which the Heinkels veered low, black, fast. Their necks ached from staring at the planes in high-level flight. Cramps locked their arms and legs. They blinked the rheum from their eyes to regain full vision. Within the rubber suits, their bodies were clammy and had begun to stink.

Coffee mugs and bits of sandwiches were among the heaps of empties beside the guns. The men reeled, almost comatose, hanging to the gun grips to stay upright. When they were relieved by their watch partners or men of the next watch, they did not make the effort of speech. They nodded, and shuffled away along the catwalks over the deck cargo.

Bullet holes from German low-level strafing runs roughly barked the smooth khaki sides of the wooden cases that held trucks. The men noticed those and the scatter of shrapnel fragments without curiosity. When they came to the forward deckhouse and started to climb to the bridge, the effort was almost impossible.

Some men wept, not because of pain or fear, but from the weakness rent by exhaustion. They butted from side to side on the ladders, stumbled over the rungs, nearly tripped. Then, hauling themselves by the handrails, they went topside.

May 26 passed that way, and in the early hours of May 27, lookouts sighted pack ice close alongside. Some pieces were as high as the bridge wings. Men reported seeing polar bears that peered forth from caves in the ice. But the reports were disregarded.

On May 27, the air attacks reached a climax with attacks by Heinkels and Junkers lasting throughout most of the day. The German command was fully aware that the cruiser withdrawal meant a serious lessening of the convoy's defensive power. The weather was fair and the sea calm. The Luftwaffe pilots chose their targets at will. When their bomb or torpedo loads were expended, they returned to the six airfields they used in Norway and Finland, armed again, refueled, and flew back for another attack.

After an air attack that did no harm at 0320 hours, course was altered to the south-eastward for a couple of hours to avoid heavy pack ice. At 1115, there started a series of attacks by a large number of Ju-88s.

The dive-bombing attacks were pressed well home through the broken cloud cover at 3,000 feet, and the enemy was assisted by an intermittent filmy haze at about 1,500 feet, which made them very difficult to see.

Destruction reached across the length and width of the convoy. Immense hedges of explosive-surged water flung up between the ships. Dark and slick patches of oil from bombs and from ships whose hulls had been ruptured littered the seas. Dead men floated with their arms wide from the life jacket, heads lowered and faces beneath the surface. They were hurled waist-high from the sea with the impact of bombs, flopped back, and bobbed along the columns of ships. The wounded called out to the ships that passed, begging to be saved from the sea. But the ships could not stop. The order was to proceed at any cost.

At 1100 hours during the course of the attack, one of the bombers dropped a stick of bombs on *City of Joliet* from less than a thousand feet. The crew saw them falling obliquely and rather slowly. The pilot did not pull out as soon as he had dropped his load: he merely decreased his dive and continued toward the deck, machine-gunning as he came down. Green flames spurted from his wings. On the deck, one of the temporary wooden gangways built over the piled-up vehicles to allow the crew to circulate caught fire.

The bombs fell in the sea all around the ship. The Junkers streaked like a meteor over the deck at a hundred feet. Crewmen felt that they could almost have touched the huge black crosses bordered with white. They could see every detail of the aircraft, even the pilot sitting in his cockpit. The crew saw his broad shoulders, head, and goggles. It was strange to see an enemy airman at such close quarters. The Junkers did a thunderous zoom, still firing with its rear guns. Round, light-edged holes appeared on the new paint of the petrol trucks. The men put out the fire on the wooden gangway, which was blazing peacefully.

An hour later, another bomber dived on their ship. The pilot released his bomb, this time a large one, from less than five hundred feet. *City of Joliet*, whose helm was hard over to port at the beginning of the dive, was now swinging to starboard. The bomb fell in the sea 30 yards to port, making the ship shudder.

The first casualty occurred at 1310 hours, when the cargo ship *Alamar* was hit by two bombs and set on fire. She was abandoned at 1330, and Commander Onslow ordered the submarine *Trident* to finish her. The survivors were picked up by HMS *St. Elstan*, *Starwort*, and *Trident*. Charles J. Hayes, a U.S. Navy radioman on board *Alamar*, never forgot his Murmansk experiences:

I was a radioman third class at this time. However, there was nothing for me to do. The Alamar *already had a radio operator and there was just no sense to having both of us sitting in the radio shack monitoring the frequency for messages. (Transmissions were not allowed, as subs could zero in on the radio signals.) So, I became a volunteer loader on one of our .50 caliber machine guns. I teamed up with a young gunner's mate I'll call "Georgia" because that is where he hailed from. We had practiced in the quiet times before the planes came and we got to be a pretty good team.*

But on this particular day—May 27, 1942—they came in such numbers it was impossible to keep your eyes on them all. The Stuka dive bombers used the bright sun to their advantage. They came down from the sun and we usually couldn't see them, but fired at the sound they made in their dive. They made a piercing, screaming sound when they dived to drop their bombs and it could really unnerve you.

Our gun station was located amidships on the starboard side. There were ships on either side of us in the convoy and bombs were dropping between the ships. The noise was deafening between the planes, the bombs dropping and the antiaircraft guns firing from the ships.

While we were firing up at the Stuka coming in overhead, I bent down to get another load to keep feeding the gun. I looked back over my shoulder and saw a German Ju-88 bomber approaching us from starboard aft. I pounded on Georgia's shoulder and hollered at him. He swung the gun around to meet the plane, but it was too late.

We didn't hear the bombs coming down, but there was a tremendous explosion. The noise was unbelievable. The Alamar *leaned way over to starboard. The sea came up into the gun tub and both Georgia and I were picked up and carried over the side when the ship came back up and the wave of water went back down to the sea. I remember falling through what felt like a waterfall and then hitting solid water and going down like a rock below the surface.*

I came back up into the sunlight and there was Georgia a few feet away, hollering at the top of his voice. I looked back and saw the Alamar, *still afloat and listing to starboard. There was a lot of smoke coming from her deck and we could see the crew letting down the boats. Georgia was trying to let them know we were still around, but we were so far away I didn't think they could see or hear us.*

The next time I looked, Alamar *was gone. As far as we could see there was nothing but water. The ships and planes were all gone and just [us] two bobbing around in the ocean, we looked at each other and kind of nodded our heads. We were sure that this was as far as we would go.*

I don't know how long we were in the water. The cold Arctic water has the effect of putting you to sleep. I vaguely remember seeing a lifeboat and the face of Alamar's first mate as he pulled me into the boat.

When I came to, I was in a bunk on a British corvette. It was crowded with survivors. All of Alamar's crew, both merchant and Navy had survived. Georgia and I were the only ones who got wet.

Five minutes after *Alamar* was hit, the *Mormacsul* was sunk by a direct hit and three near misses; three of the ship's crew perished in the attack. *Starwort* and *St. Elstan* rescued the survivors (thirty-six merchant seamen and the nine-man Armed Guard) at 1330 hours.

Between 1405 and 1410 hours, five direct hits sank the *Empire Lawrence*, and another started a fire in the *Stari Bolshevik*, which was successfully fought by her crew for thirty-six hours; near misses damaged the *Empire Baffin* and *Garland*.

Garland seemed to be singled out for terrific attacks, but, for most of the day, neither bombs nor machine-gun fire hit her. Toward the close of that day, however, a Junkers 88, diving through a curtain of fire, dropped a stick of four bombs close alongside. *Garland* disappeared in a wall of water and of smoke.

The four bombs fell in a group abreast the bridge about 20 feet off. There was no underwater damage, but the *Garland* was riddled from stem to stern with splinter holes. It was thought that this unusual splinter damage was caused by the first bomb exploding upon striking the water and detonating the other three in the air. "A" and "B" guns, one Oerlikon, and No. 1 boiler room were put out of action. And, a fire was started in the fo'c'sle. *Garland* was not out of action, but she was badly damaged. Entire gun crews had been wiped out. Her decks were covered with dead and dying. Casualties amounted to twenty-five killed and forty-three wounded.

Yet *Garland* never ceased firing. Her gunnery officer, himself wounded, organized crews of artificers and cooks to keep the guns in action. At the stern sections, among the corpses of gunners, they continued to fire at the attackers. The paymaster, mortally wounded, handed over his store keys to a colleague before he died. One of the wounded, lying where he had been dragged to a precarious safety, wrote on the white paintwork above him, "Poland—how sweet it is to die for thee!"

The commanding officer of one of the British escort vessels said:

When I saw this happen, I said to my officers, "That's finished the Poles; what a tragedy; they fought so magnificently." But I didn't have time to finish what I was saying, as out from behind a wall of smoke and water emerged Garland, *still firing.*

Six Junkers sought the CAM ship *Empire Lawrence*, which they bombed and strafed. Bombs sent waves splashing over her decks, where the gunners fired as rapidly as they could load and serve. Great, frothy cascades tumbled down upon her wheelhouse and bridge. Cordite smoke from her guns drifted out to show that she still fought. A bomb hit her foredeck close alongside the catapult rig. The force of the explosion made the ship visible in almost her entire length for a second or so, and then she began to sink.

The crew of *City of Joliet* saw the ship bearing down on them like a hunted beast. The bombs from the first plane all fell in the sea. The second had no time to drop his. Hit by the ack-ack, he continued to plummet like a stone until he crashed with a terrible explosion on the bows of the cargo ship. An enormous column of seething black smoke billowed in the air. When it dispersed, they saw that the *Empire Lawrence* was listing badly by the bows.

Her stem post was only a few feet above the water. On deck a group of brand-new trucks were on fire, and the crew were running from this curtain of flame. The boats were lowered over the side, and the rafts were thrown overboard. The crew jumped into the water without waiting any longer. Unfortunately, in the rush several rafts had not been held alongside and floated away from the drifting ship. The men who had jumped into the icy sea had to swim a long way to reach them.

A number of her men got away in a lifeboat. They piled aboard her, released the davits falls, and paddled clear astern before she was caught by the suction of the sinking ship. Junkers pilots flew over the lifeboat, though, where the men lay two and three deep on top of each other. The Germans made strafing runs until all aboard the boat were killed.

Empire Lawrence passed quite close to *City of Joliet*, and they could see the unfortunate men swimming in the icy water. The lifeboats drew slowly away from the wreck. The exhausted swimmers seemed to find it terribly difficult to hoist themselves up on the rafts. Spent, they reached for their mates, who could see their white faces and even the fear in their eyes but could do nothing to help. Though screaming for help, their cries went unheard above the cacophony.

There was no question of stopping and picking them up. No merchant ship was allowed to do this, and the orders were categorical. They had to sail on, averting their eyes from these wretched men struggling in the water. Moreover, above the convoy other bombers had just broken formation and were selecting their targets.

Graeme Ogden in *Lady Madeleine*, assigned as one of the convoy's rescue trawlers, recalled the attack on *Empire Lawrence*:

> At 1420 the Empire Lawrence *was hit and pulled out of her place in the convoy. I could not see how badly damaged she was, so I took* Lady M *over to her to help take off her crew if necessary. When I was nearly alongside, I noticed that her port-side life-boats were hanging vertically down the side of the ship, so I yelled to her captain and asked if he wanted my boats in the water. He shouted back something which I shall never know, for at that moment Geoff (*Lady M's *Executive officer) and I heard the cruel whine of bombers, and, looking aft, saw three of them diving on us.*
>
> *I heard the swish of falling bombs, but couldn't move our ship. The next thing I remember is that Geoff and I were rolling about on our backs on the deck of the A/S bridge and the sky was full of strange shapes. We were covered with falling wreckage and enveloped in suffocating brown smoke. I thought we had been hit. When, minutes later, the smoke cleared away, there was no sign of the 12,000-ton* Empire Lawrence.
>
> *The first thing I did was to light my pipe—I wanted to know if I was still alive. An oily pool—fringed with wreckage and bodies—and the shattered remains of a life-boat were all that remained of the* Empire Lawrence. Lady M *was untouched, although we were lying with our engines stopped, the length of a cricket pitch away.*
>
> *We heard afterwards from* Hyderabad, *who was just astern of us, that when they saw* Lady M *emerge from the smoke cloud, her gay camouflage bright in the sunshine, they could hardly believe it.*
>
> *Onslow in* Ashanti *thought we were gone, for he signaled incredulously:* "Do you need assistance?"
>
> *I answered:* "Empire Lawrence *sunk, am picking up survivors."*
>
> *We had but a few yards to move to pick up the survivors. Some were terribly wounded, and our own lads jumped over the side to help get them inboard. Fortunately, trawlers have little freeboard, especially in the waist, and, the sea being like a millpond, I was able to manoeuvre* Lady M *alongside the badly wounded, who were unable to move, and get them aboard. Our sea-boats collected the others. Sixteen in all, including the radar officer, who was apparently unharmed.*

We agreed afterwards, when making out the report of the loss of the Empire Lawrence, *that of the six bombs aimed at her at least three must have been direct vertical hits and that they knocked the bottom out of her. She had sunk in a matter of seconds.*

Garland's casualties were twenty-five killed or subsequently died of wounds and forty-three wounded.

Meanwhile, *Stari Bolshevik* was hit by a bomb on her foredeck, starting a fire and forcing the crew to wage a double battle against the enemy planes and the conflagration. The gunners succeeded in bringing down one bomber and drove off the rest. The struggle to save the ship and its cargo continued, but the commander of the British escort instructed the crew of the *Stari Bolshevik* to abandon her and board one of the escorts. At the same time, he announced his intention of finishing off the damaged transport. In reply, the captain of the Soviet ship signaled, "We do not intend to inter our ship."

At 1415 hours, *Ashanti*, the escort leader, sent a signal to the corvette *Roselys*: "Go and help the *Stari Bolshevik*."

The *Roselys* drew in to within 10 yards of the burning ship and managed to convey hoses to the "old Bolshevik." While the two vessels sailed side by side, a new air attack developed. Luckily no aircraft dived in their direction.

Stari Bolshevik could not stay in column and dropped back astern, a vast black banner of flame-streaked smoke above her.

Lieutenant Ralph Wilson Gray Ransome-Wallis, RNVR, the doctor on board the destroyer HMS *Martin*, was sent to assist with *Stari Bolshevik*'s wounded. He later wrote about his most remarkable house call:

Stari Bolshevik *was starting to lag behind the convoy a bit, possibly having to reduce speed to keep the flames and smoke from sweeping back over the ship. A lull seemed to have arrived and* Martin *turned back towards the stricken Russian. We quickly loaded two Neil Robertson stretchers into the whaler which had been swung out and lowered in its davits until it was level with* Martin's *deck. As the boat's crew was scrambling into the whaler I realized that both my tin hat and an extra bag of dressings were still in the Sick Bay. I raced along the deck to the Sick Bay and grabbed them just as the alarm bell went for another air attack.*

I ran back towards the whaler but unfortunately just as I passed the 4-inch gun it fired over my head at some German aircraft coming in low on the beam. I did not realize it at the time, but it was probably the blast from this gun rather than bombs, which caused damage to my ears from which I did not fully recover until some years after the war had ended although it did not interfere with my service career.

I jumped into the boat as it was being lowered and in a trice we were on our own bobbing about in the Arctic Ocean with Martin wheeling away at speed, firing furiously at attacking aircraft.

Stari Bolshevik had stopped about 300 yards away still burning fiercely with black smoke pouring out of her forehold and we started to row towards her. However the Germans were making a dead set at the ship and to our dismay she started to get under way again.

The prospect of being left alone in a small boat in the Arctic and no doubt being machine-gunned by the Nazis, did not appeal and we started to row like blazes, the Sick Berth Attendant (SBA) and I double banking the oars. Several bombs fell between us and the Stari Bolshevik, one near enough to soak us and make the boat rock violently. What with gunfire, bombs and the screaming engines of the dive bombers the row was terrific, but the effect on our rowing was electrical and the whaler surged along.

A rope-ladder was hanging over the port side of the Russian ship and with a last despairing effort we got close enough for our bowman to grab it and hang on as the Stari Bolshevik gathered speed. I scrambled up to the bow of the boat and jumped for the ladder which by now had been made fast to the bow of our boat.

It was a horrible thing to climb as it was no longer vertical, as all good rope-ladders should be, but was being pulled out [at] an angle by towing our whaler. However I was spurred on to climb the high side of the Russian by seeing that our boat was being towed so fast that it was becoming unstable and was bumping alarmingly against the side of the ship. Eventually I arrived on deck to be met by three Russian women who were obviously and excusably very frightened but were making valiant efforts to be useful. They seemed to be acting as deck hands, but were probably cooks and stewards as well.

I tried to show the women the dangers that our boat was in but they failed to grasp this and led me to some bundles lying on the deck that I realized were badly wounded men. My SBA now appeared on deck with a line to which was attached the stretchers. Leaving him to haul these up with the help of the women, I ran towards the bridge and climbed a steel ladder but before I actually got on to the bridge I was met by an officer, possibly the Captain, who could not speak any English but quickly grasped my pantomime act demonstrating the necessity to slow down and after a minute or two speed was decreased.

Returning to the wounded, I found my SBA explaining to one of the women that it was not a good idea just to tie a rope round a badly wounded man and drop him into the boat. These women however were very helpful and one could not help admiring their astonishing courage in a situation in which no woman should be placed.

We lowered three men on stretchers and three other less severely wounded men were able to climb down the ladder with a rope attached to them.

I started then to look around me, noticing the ship had carried an anti-aircraft gun right up in her bow. The bomb which had done the damage had landed on this and had blown a hole deep into the ship into which most of the wrecked gun appeared to have fallen. Round the jagged edge of the hole were some bits of badly burnt bodies and a little further aft lay the twisted body of another seaman — very obviously dead.

I did not linger as there was nothing I could do, but I heard from some forgotten source later on, probably one of the wounded, that five men had been killed. We cast off our rope-ladder and the Stari Bolshevik, *belching smoke like a volcano, clapped on speed and drew away.*

I shall always remember her with admiration.

A near miss further opened *City of Joliet's* seams, and she could barely keep headway; her master was aware that she was fatally injured. The British ship *Empire Baffin* was in the same condition, held afloat by her pumps. A Heinkel torpedoed the British ship *Lowther Castle*, and she sank, losing only one man killed.

At 1945 hours, two bombs from a Junkers found the British merchantman *Empire Purcell*, which started a fire. The ship was abandoned; survivors were picked up by *Hyderabad* and *St. Elstan* under deliberate bombing attacks. Commander Onslow ordered *Trident* to sink any ships that were unable to proceed with the convoy. *Trident* went alongside *Empire Purcell*, some of her crew boarded the boat, an attempt was made to extinguish the fire, but it had gotten out of control. Much concern was felt for the safety of *Trident* and her crew because she carried several tons of TNT. Not long after the *Trident* parted, the *Empire Purcell* blew up. The blast, felt on the far side of the convoy, made men gasp. The scarlet pillar of her flame seared eyes and roiled the sea into a maelstrom.

At 1950 hours, the British Merchantman SS *Lowther Castle* was hit on the port side by a torpedo fired from an He-111, at 4,000 yards. The crew abandoned ship and she dropped astern. Commander Onslow ordered *Trident* to sink her, but observing that she was being subjected to repeated vicious dive-bombing attacks, Onslow then cancelled the order. It was obvious that the enemy would save *Trident* from wasting a torpedo.

On the other side of the convoy, Commodore N. H. Gale was knocked prone when his ship, *Ocean Voice*, was hit by a bomb that set her on fire and tore away twenty feet of her side plating abreast No. 1 hold within two feet of the water line and started a fire in her forward holds. The crew fought the fire for several hours until it was finally doused.

"I had little hopes of her survival," Commander Onslow later wrote, "but this gallant ship maintained her station, fought her fire, and with God's help arrived at her destination."

The day's last loss occurred later that evening. *City of Joliet* signaled that she was filling rapidly with water and sinking. *St. Elstan* took the crew off without injury or loss.

At 2130 hours, the enemy finally left PQ-16 in peace, except for the inevitable BV-138 shadower aircraft circling the horizon. Commander Onslow reported that the situation appeared far from rosy: in one day he lost five ships—20 percent of the convoy—and there were still three days to go before reaching Murmansk. Commander Onslow wrote in his daily report:

> *I felt far from optimistic. The question of ammunition began to worry me badly. I ordered all ships to exercise strict economy and restricted controlled fire in the* Ashanti *to one mounting at a time. We were all inspired however by the parade ground rigidity of the convoy's station keeping, including* Ocean Voice *and* Stari Bolshevik *who were both billowing smoke from their foreholds ...*

On the morning of May 28, the fog grew denser until visibility was reduced to a hundred yards. The ships lost sight of each other and began to sail whenever possible by the fog buoy towed by the vessel ahead. More often than not, they saw absolutely nothing. They had to sail a general course and maneuver to avoid the ice, listening for their neighbors' sirens, which were muffled by the fog.

PQ-16 sailed south through this ice on May 28 and 29 during hours of continual daylight. The ships had to maneuver the entire time. The escort vessels did their best to see that the slow procession was not broken up by ice flows or heavy fog.

On *Lady Madeleine*, Graeme Ogden was looking forward to finally getting to Murmansk:

At midnight the sun was still 5 degrees above the horizon, glowering at me like a sinister Polyphemus. To paraphrase Noel Coward's lyrics — "Mad dogs and Englishmen go out in the midnight sun." Well, there the wretched orb was, a beacon to incoming German torpedo-bombers and certainly devoid of any romance. I wondered how I was going to explain this to Sally [his fiancée]. I was beginning to hate the sight of the bloody thing: it was my enemy — Death in the Afternoon and Death in the Midnight Sun. I thought of it as an orange in a butcher's shop, surrounded by deep-blue tiles. We looked like being the meat on the slab if we weren't very lucky. To hell with the sun!

The Germans, however, had not forgotten that our most vulnerable position for a final attack would be as the convoy approached the Kola Inlet. The question was, would the Russian fighters turn up in time? We had one more day to go as we approached Kildin Island.

Early on Saturday, 30th May, we sighted a skein of high-flying single-engined planes, which we took to be the expected Russian fighters, but they turned out to be about forty Ju-87s from Petsamo, and a vicious dive-bombing attack developed. In the middle of this holocaust, as our gunners joined the A. A. barrage, I noticed a Heinkel-112 seaplane approaching us at sea-level. It just goes to show how wrong one can be, for I thought he was on fire, as there was a red glow under his wings. Seconds later, when his machine-gun bullets began to hit Lady M's *smoke-stack, I came to in a hurry.*

At A. A. action stations in Lady M, *I was alone on the upper bridge, except for my signalman. We had to grin and bear being shot together. I had a pair of skeleton Lewis guns, which I used as shot guns (not by Holland and Holland, but lightened to be fired from the shoulder, with pans loaded one tracer to three). I seized my No. 1 gun and opened up. The Heinkel's tracers were now coming close enough for me to have lit a cigarette from them. There was nothing I could do but to keep on firing and reach for No. 2 gun.*

I yelled to Bunts (the signalman) to lie down. It was like being in a cowboy film. I must say I was more than relieved when the plane swerved off at about 100 yards range, and crashed into the sea with a splash like a leaping salmon. I then had some bomb-dodging to do from the Ju-87s, but nothing came uncomfortably near us.

The convoy along with *Lady M*'s crew was shaken up, but escaped unscathed.

At 1150 hours on May 29, three Russian destroyers, the *Grozny* (S.O.), *Sokrushitelnyy*, and *Kuibyshev*, in their palely mottled camouflage designs, joined the escort—a very welcome addition to its anti-aircraft firepower. Later that evening, six minesweepers, under the command of Captain Crombie in *Bramble,* also joined the convoy. Under their escort, with the *Alynbank* and *Martin,* six of the merchant ships were detached to Arkhangelsk. At 2330, while the two sections of the convoy were still in sight of each other, the Murmansk section was attacked by a combination of eighteen Ju-87 Stukas and Ju-88 bombers and the Arkhangelsk section by fifteen Ju-88s. According to the official report, no damage was suffered by the ships. But the men who weathered the attack tell of different results.

Sixteen-year-old Newfoundlander George H. Evans, a stoker on the explosives-laden Dutch ship SS *Pieter de Hoogh,* witnessed the Soviet destroyers' response to the attack:

The Russian form of defence was direct counterattack. The destroyers sailed out onto the exact courses held by the dive bombers and then opened with every gun aboard, they followed the low-sweeping German Heinkels along the columns, and pursued them across open sea.

Russian gunners were deft in their use of the 37-millimeter Bofors cannon. They skipped shells from the surface of the sea; that of Kuibyshev *struck the Heinkels in the belly, she went away damaged. Two more German planes were shot down; no more of the convoy ships were lost.*

The Luftwaffe attack was intercepted by Soviet Northern Fleet aircraft. Admiral Arseni Golovko recounted their actions in the fight:

Our airmen are giving direct cover to the convoys en route. This is what we were doing in the last allied convoy in May, when we lost the commander of the air regiment, Lieutenant-Colonel Boris Pheoktistovich Safonov, by now a Double Hero of the Soviet Union and the first man in the U.S.S.R. to achieve this in the war. The order announcing this was received today, a fortnight after Safonov's death. He died on 30 May in defense of PQ-16. The details of his end are meager, although there were many witnesses of it.

The convoy was sixty miles from our shores when the Nazis hastened up to deliver a massive attack with bombs. Forty-five Junkers escorted by Messerschmitts took part in the raid. As soon as the alarm signal was transmitted by the escort ships, four of our fighters led by Safonov took off to intercept. The fourth machine (pilot Kukharenko) returned to base half-way out owing to engine trouble. The other three went on and gave battle. Three versus forty-five Junkers and an unassessed number of Messerschmitts!

None the less every attempt of the Nazi pilots to break through to the transports in PQ 16 was defeated by our fighters—Safonov, Pokrovsky and

Orlov, who excellently co-ordinated their actions with the barrage put up by the escorts. In full view of everybody Safonov shot down two bombers, and Pokrovsky and Orlov one each.

Soon afterwards Vaenga [Air Base] headquarters heard the words "Cover my tail" ... on the radio. These turned out to be Safonov's. Next the signalmen in the destroyer Kuibyshev, *escorting the convoy, saw Safonov rush in to attack a third Junkers, but at the same moment an enemy fighter dived out of the clouds and attacked him. After a short time headquarters picked up another message from Safonov: "Have damaged a third ... engine ..." The last word was a code word indicating the necessity of a forced landing.*

The rest, according to the ship's signalmen, happened as follows: Safonov's machine, losing height, glided toward the *Kuibyshev*, but fell into the sea about two miles short of the ship and sank immediately:

The air battle over the convoy had ended. Getting rid of their bombs anywhere and everywhere the Nazi planes made off in the direction of northern Norway, having failed to sink a single transport.

Two hours after the battle Kuibyshev *searched the sea for Safonov, but failed to find him. The cause of his death thus remains unknown. Possibly the engine failed owing to machine gun fire. One thing was certain— Safonov had died on his 224th operational flight and in his 34th air battle, after his 25th individual victory over the enemy.*

It is sad to have to admit this loss. It will remain forever linked in my memory with the code number of the last May convoy, PQ-16. The Northern Fleet lost an outstanding pilot and astonishingly talented officer. A courageous son of the Russian people, true to the Soviet Motherland and the Communist Party, Safonov was a model warrior of the air and commander-instructor.

Once more, Graeme Ogden on *Lady M* was in the thick of the fight:

The senior officer of the minesweeper flotilla, for some strange reason, took over command of P.Q.16 from Onslow and attempted to split up the merchant ships into a Murmansk section and an Archangel section. The result was complete confusion, and the Ju-87s pounced on the convoy.

We were ordered to join the Archangel section, then the order was reversed. Whilst steaming between the two sections, a low-flying German plane came at us on our beam; I turned towards him and yelled to McTavish, but that wily Scot didn't need any advice from me. He waited until the Hun was about

400 yds. away (during which time I must say his bullets were whizzing past my head) and then let go. That was the end of that. "Well done, Mac," I yelled.

"The cheeky so and so," he replied.

The Ruski destroyers really saved this situation, as, having plenty of ammo, they put up a terrific barrage over the convoy. Now, to add to the confusion, the tardy Russian fighters turned up. I saw several planes crash into the sea, but as the Russians didn't take any notice of their own barrage, or anybody else's, I couldn't tell if they were German or Russian.

Before we had rejoined our section we were dive-bombed and, by the grace of God, I turned the ship the right way. The bombs exploded in the exact place where we should have been if I hadn't altered course. Poor Lady M got lifted out of the water and her engine stopped with a shudder. I thought we were hit, and, telling Geoff to take over on the bridge, I ran aft and down into the engine-room. Here I found Whitehead and the second engineer armed with a spanner about as big as themselves.

The chief did not speak, but gave me a look which I understood. All was not well in the engineroom, even the stokers' soot-covered faces looked pale. The engine's main piston had stuck and the chief was about to try and turn it over, in the same way as you crank a car with a starting handle.

The engine-room was full of steam and I had a nasty feeling Lady M had taken on a pronounced list to port. As I stood there watching, there was a thunderous explosion outside and Lady M again took a mighty heave. The chief and the second dropped the giant spanner, and we all panted for breath. The steam escape was worse and clouded the daylight out of the engine-room. Through a wet fog I saw the chief again wrestle with the huge spanner and, with the others, try to heave the engine over its dead centre. As these men, their half-naked bodies covered with sweat, strained away, I knew that if they didn't succeed Lady M was a dead duck.

The second explosion I had felt while in the engine-room could only have meant more bombs aimed at Lady M. Now I couldn't move the ship, she was at the dive-bombers' mercy. We were very obvious in our gay camouflage and, don't forget, we had just shot down a German plane. After what seemed an eternity the piston once again began its downward movement.

"She'll go now," Whitehead said thickly.

"Well done, boys," I answered and tore back to the bridge.

From then onward, Soviet Hurricanes gave air cover to the convoy as the crews began seeing signs that they were at last approaching land: floating tree trunks and land birds. At 1100 hours, they sighted the coast with its dark, rocky, pine-covered hills.

It was 1600 hours on May 30 when the Murmansk section formed single file to enter Kola Inlet. They steamed past Toros Island and through the minefield, took aboard their pilots. Commander Onslow held *Ashanti* on standby as they passed. He signaled them: "Reduced in numbers, battered and tired, but still keeping Perfect station."

Admiral Tovey, the commander-in-chief, Home Fleet, was agreeably surprised that, in the face of such a scale of attack, four-fifths of the ships of this large convoy ultimately reached their destination. He wrote:

The success was beyond expectation. It was due to the gallantry, efficiency and tireless zeal of the officers and men of the escorts and to the remarkable courage and determination of those of the merchant ships. No praise can be too high for either.

On the German side, Admiral Dönitz's, Commander-in-Chief, U-boats, wrote in his War Diary about the operation:

My opinion as to the small chances of success for U-boats against convoys during the northern summer … has been confirmed by experience with PQ 16. Owing to the difficult conditions for attack (constant light, very variable weather and visibility, abnormally strong convoy escort, clever handling of the convoy, appearance of Russian aircraft forcing the U-boats to dive on sighting our own aircraft as well) the result, in spite of shadowing and a determined set-to by the boats, has been one steamer sunk and four probable hits. This must be accounted a failure when compared with the results of the anti-submarine activity for the boats operating … U-436, U-703 have depth charge damage, unfit to dive to greater depths. Three more boats have slight depth charge damage, the effects of which … will probably mean some considerable time in the dockyard.

Admiral Dönitz concluded, "The German Air Force would seem to be a better means of attacking convoys in the north in the summer" and suggested that these facts be taken into account rather more than they had been hitherto when U-boat operations in the north were planned.

The Luftwaffe greatly overestimated the effects of their attacks on PQ-16 and claimed to have destroyed the whole convoy. From the results of their reconnaissance flights, Luftwaffe officers were convinced that the convoy had dispersed as the result of the first attack in the evening of May 25. This was not the case.

The lesson the Germans drew from this attack was that the anti-aircraft defense could be dissipated and confused by high-level dive bombing closely integrated with the launching of torpedoes from a height of about three hundred feet. The method adopted for the torpedo attack, which was known as the "Golden Comb," was for the aircraft to approach in a wide line abreast and to drop their torpedoes simultaneously. It also was decided to attack at twilight with the ships silhouetted against the lighter sky. By June, forty-two torpedo aircraft had arrived in Northern Norway, and these tactics were assiduously practiced.

As a result, PQ-16 lost seven merchant ships: six to air attack and one to a U-boat. Seventy-four officers and 397 men were rescued from the seven ships. According to German sources, two U-boats were damaged during attacks by escorts and of the 101 Ju-88s and seven He-111s that attacked the convoy, three Ju-88s were lost with their two-man crews.

Even as both sides studied what happened to PQ-16 and QP-12, the next convoys, PQ-17 and QP-13, were being assembled.

CHAPTER 6

APOCALYPSE
June–July 1942

W hile the British and German commanders were planning their next moves, HMS *Gossamer* and her crew fought a desperate battle for survival far from the convoy routes. *Gossamer*'s flotilla had been in Murmansk almost a year, escorting convoys as they approached the Murman coast as well as ensuring shipping channels were kept free of mines.

Leading Signalman John Maddern was on board *Gossamer* on June 24 as east and west the ship rode at anchor in the Kola Inlet north of Mishukov Point. The weather was fine and warm and the sky was clear but the water was cold. The crew were in jerseys, trousers, and shoes in the pleasant weather, so different from the freezing cold of the winter months.

Then at 0900 hours came the warning by the shore-based anti-aircraft guns and warning flags from ships in the anchorage of approaching enemy aircraft. *Gossamer*'s gun crews were at their battle stations, and the crew waited for the impending attack. Eight minutes later, five Ju-88 bombers were seen flying from west to east through the slight haze. As they reached the sun, four turned toward the anchored merchant ships and began to dive. The fifth was lost sight of in the sun. Maddern was one of the first men on board to see the enemy, and he later wrote about the attack:

> *Five aircraft came out of the sun and at least one attacked with bombs. The gunners opened fire but no hits were recorded. Two bombs hit us, and one near miss, virtually blowing our stern off at the break of the upper deck and quarter deck. The wardroom just disappeared with our Engineer Officer and two Deck Officers and several crew. There was a great deal of carnage but no panic. Some men below decks managed to get clear, but others were trapped as the ship was sinking fast.*
>
> *After the first explosion, I said to the captain there seemed nothing for me to do on the bridge—could I help below? I had just got to the ladder when a louder explosion threw me across the wheelhouse. This was the bomb that finished her, as she took a heavy list to starboard. On the upper deck— aft—two seamen were supporting an AB—one of the gunners. We lowered our port whaler to get the wounded away. I looked at some of my mates sliding over the port side whilst on the starboard side the guard rail was the only part above water.*
>
> *I saw a messmate sliding on his backside portside until reaching the bilge-keel and jumping into the water. At the height of our survival he, being a mess-deck wag, was heard to say even at a time of crisis—"Those bloody barnacles ripped the arse out of my pants."*
>
> *Soon there was only a P.O. and myself on that part of deck and he said the order had been given "Abandon ship: every man for himself." Two stokers appeared from the boiler room escape hatch and went over the side. One I never saw again—one survived. So I decided to jump.*
>
> *The whole business of the sinking took only ten minutes or so. Some small Russian boats headed towards us. We hastily climbed aboard, but our ship was now turning over, and the boat was being pushed under by the mast, so we had to abandon that one and board another in the vicinity.*
>
> *This then was the sad end to yet another gallant ship and crew with one exception. One of the enemy aircraft, still not satisfied, returned to survey the kill—flying low over the scene, machine-gunning the survivors in the water. It has since been related to me that three of the survivors in the confusion were hit by machine-gun bullets and died whilst swimming for their lives.*

Gossamer turned over and sank at 0921 hours, eight minutes after being hit. Twenty-nine of her crew died in the attack. Three or four Russian powerboats and at least one rowing boat quickly reached the scene and pulled the survivors to safety. The loss seemed of little account to anyone—except the families of the men killed.

Even after the severe losses suffered by PQ-16, convoys PQ-17 and QP-13 initially were scheduled to depart on June 11 in order to keep with the three-week schedule as Churchill had promised Roosevelt. However, the British needed to mount a relief operation for the island of Malta in the Mediterranean. This operation required many of the British Home Fleet ships dedicated to supporting the Arctic convoys to serve as escort. Thus, the convoy sailing dates were moved forward to June 27.

This delay gave the Germans additional time to finalize their plans to ensure no ship made it through to Russia. Hitler had been informed on June 1 of the proposal to use Kriegsmarine surface ships against PQ-17; he was assured that the operation would take place only if it could be safely assumed that no superior enemy forces would be met with and that adequate air cover could be provided. Eventually he approved, but with the proviso that before the ships sailed, the Allied aircraft carriers' disposition must be ascertained so that they could be attacked by the Luftwaffe.

This proviso was tantamount to canceling the operation, as it would have delayed the sailing of the ships too long. Grand Admiral Erich Raeder therefore decided that the operation should be carried out in two phases. First, while waiting for the convoy to be located, the ships should transfer to sortie ports in the extreme north. Second, once in place, they should await Hitler's final sanction and orders to proceed.

On June 14, Admiral Otto Schniewind issued his orders for the operation, which was known as *Rösselsprung* (Knight's Move). The surface forces were organized in two groups: the Trondheim group, comprising the battleship *Tirpitz*, flying the flag of Admiral Schniewind, and the cruiser *Hipper*, together with six destroyers; and the Narvik group, comprising the pocket battleships *Lützow* and *Scheer*, with six destroyers.

On confirmation of PQ-17's approach, the Trondheim squadron was to move to Vestfjord and the Narvik squadron to Altenfjord. As soon as the convoy had reached the Barents Sea, the two German squadrons were to proceed to a rendezvous a hundred miles north of North Cape, and then attack the convoy west of Bear Island.

The Germans relied upon air reconnaissance and U-boats to provide early information about PQ-17's position. Of the ten operational U-boats available, three were sent to patrol the northeastern sector of Denmark Strait as early as June 5. By June 18, all had been disposed on the estimated convoy route.

As they prepared to assault PQ-17, the Luftwaffe applied lessons learned from PQ-16 a month earlier. The Luftwaffe had overestimated the effects of their attacks on PQ-16 and claimed to have destroyed the whole convoy. They were convinced that the convoy had dispersed as a result of the first attack in the evening of May 25. The lesson they drew from this attack was that the anti-aircraft defense could be dissipated and confused by high-level dive bombing coordinated with the launching of torpedoes from a height of about 300 feet. The method adopted for the torpedo attack, which was known as the "Golden Comb," was for the aircraft to approach in a wide line abreast and to drop their torpedoes simultaneously. It also was decided to attack at twilight with the ships silhouetted against the sky.

The British Admiralty was aware of the risks involved in sailing convoys in the face of growing German opposition. Ultra intercepts in June indicated that the Germans intended at last to bring out their main units to attack the next eastbound convoy to the east of Bear Island, and this threat formed the main preoccupation of the Admiralty. However, political considerations compelled them to continue with the sailings.

The Allies had suffered serious losses in the convoys, but they had been confined to what the British Admiralty considered acceptable limits. Nevertheless, those with personal experience viewed the prospect of continuing the traffic during the summer months with grave misgivings. It was difficult to see how the problem could be solved if the enemy chose to supplement his air and U-boat offensive by using his heavy ships for a surface attack in the Barents Sea. The strategic situation, wrote Admiral Tovey:

> ... *was wholly favourable to the enemy. His heavy ships would be operating close to their own coast, with the support of powerful shore-based air reconnaissance and striking forces, and protected, if he so desired, by a screen of U-boats in the channels between Spitzbergen and Norway. Our covering forces, on the other hand, if they entered these waters, would be without shore-based air support, one thousand miles from their base, with their destroyers too short of fuel to escort a damaged ship to harbour.*

Tovey proposed that the eastbound convoy, QP-13, upon reaching 10 degrees East longitude, should put back for twelve to eighteen hours, unless it was known that German ships were still in harbor or the weather prevented shadowing from the air. He hoped that this temporary course reversal would either tempt the German heavy ships to pursue, cause them to return to harbor, or compel them to cruise for an extended period among the eight British, one French, and two Russian submarines on patrol in areas off the North Cape, the Russians occupying the two inshore areas. These zones were to be moved east as the convoy passed north of them.

The Admiralty did not agree to this, though their instructions envisaged the possibility, under certain circumstances, of the convoy being temporarily turned back.

British Admiralty instructions also stipulated that the safety of the convoy against surface attack to the west of Bear Island must be met by British and American surface forces, and that to the east of that meridian, the convoy must be met by submarines. In addition, the cruiser covering force was not intended to go east of Bear Island, unless threatened by the presence of a German surface force which the cruisers could fight. In any case, they were not to go beyond 25 degrees East longitude.

This plan did not altogether meet Admiral Tovey's views, which from the first appearance of the German heavy ships in Norway had differed in several respects from those of the Admiralty as to the tactical dispositions best calculated to achieve the object. He was seriously disturbed to learn during the course of a telephone conversation with First Sea Lord Sir Dudley Pound under which certain circumstances the Admiralty contemplated ordering the convoy to scatter.

All the latest experience pointed to the vital necessity for ships to keep together for mutual support against the heavy air attack that was certain—weather permitting—to take place. Tovey strongly disapproved of an order to scatter, except as a last resort in the actual presence of attack by overwhelming surface forces.

PQ-17 sailed on June 27 with thirty-five merchant ships under Commodore J. C. K. Dowding on board the freighter *River Afton*, escorted by *Halcyon*, *Britomart*, *Salamander*, and four antisubmarine trawlers. One merchant ship grounded while leaving harbor, and another was damaged by drift ice in Denmark Strait and had to put back.

The Support Force under the orders of Rear Admiral L. H. K. Hamilton consisted of the British cruisers HMS *London* (flagship) and

Norfolk, the heavy American cruisers *Wichita* and *Tuscaloosa*, and three destroyers. The main task of this force was to intercept enemy aircraft and U-boats making their way toward the convoy.

The Covering Force, under the orders of Tovey on board the battleship HMS *Duke of York* (flagship), consisted of the American battleship *Washington* (in which Rear Admiral Robert Giffen flew his flag); the aircraft carrier HMS *Victorious*; the British cruisers HMS *Cumberland*, HMS *Nigeria*, and HMS *Manchester*; and a dozen destroyers and corvettes. This task force was to operate in the waters between Iceland and Spitzbergen, where it would shield PQ-17 from a possible thrust by German warships based at Altenfjord, Norway. It was also responsible for the safe return of a westbound convoy PQ-13. The close escort joined from Seydisfjord, Iceland, departed on June 30. It consisted of six destroyers: *Keppel* (Commander J. E. Broome, S.O.), *Leamington*, *Wilton*, *Ledbury*, *Fury*, and *Offa*; four corvettes: *Lotus*, *Poppy*, *Diayiella*, and the Free French *La Malouine*; and the submarines *P614* and *P615*, along with two anti-aircraft ships: *Palomares* and *Pozarica*. There were also three rescue ships: the *Zaafaran*, *Rathlin*, and *Zamalek*.

Westbound QP-13, also consisting of thirty-five ships, formed up off the Kola Inlet on June 27. This convoy was escorted by the minesweeper *Hussar*; corvettes *Honeysuckle*, *Hyderabad*, *Roselys*, and *Starwort*; the anti-aircraft ship *Alynbank*; destroyers *Achates*, *Volunteer*, and the Polish *Garland*; and trawlers *Lady Madeleine* and *St. Elstan*.

PQ-17's route skirted northern Iceland, took a north-by-east tack, went past the volcanic, glacier-covered Jan Mayen Island, continued northward toward Spitzbergen and Bear Island, and then swung southeast through the Barents Sea to skirt the Kola Peninsula and enter the White Sea.

The first few days passed quietly for the convoy, and all of the escorting forces proceeded on a northerly course through thick fog and heavy ice floes. The first sign of trouble came about 200 miles west of Bear Island on July 1 when a BV-138 reconnaissance plane sighted the convoy. The next day, six U-boats attacked but were driven off by the escorts.

Early on the morning of July 4, PQ-17 was about 60 miles north of Bear Island when twenty-six Heinkel He-111 torpedo bombers dove through the clouds and leveled off 50 feet above the water. The freighter *Christopher Newport* was hit by a torpedo from a Heinkel that dived in solo flight through a hole in the cloud cover. The crew immediately abandoned ship and was picked up by the rescue ship

Rathlin. One of the accompanying British submarines was detailed to finish the ship with a torpedo.

During the attack on *Christopher Newport*, one of her armed guard gunners rendered exceptionally gallant service. Seaman First Class Hugh Patrick Wright, USNR, manned a .30-caliber Browning machine gun in the starboard bridge wing of the ship and did his utmost to save her.

The torpedo released by the attacking Heinkel plane headed directly for *Newport*'s midships section. An order was passed to open fire on the German plane in an attempt to explode it before the ship was struck. Wright was squarely on target with his fire, but the small-caliber bullets bounced in futile ricochet from the torpedo. The merchant seamen who served as loaders for Wright's gun told him that the fire was wasted. They told him, too, that he should get out of the bridge wing before the torpedo hit.

But Wright kept on firing, bent down over the piece, cursing it for its lack of power. The merchant seamen ran for the port side of the ship. The torpedo struck the starboard side, almost directly below Wright's gun station.

Wright was still firing at the plane at the instant of explosion. He was flung off the flying bridge and down onto the main deck. That knocked him unconscious, and he also sprained an ankle. His shipmates hauled him into a lifeboat, and he was among the survivors brought aboard *Rathlin*.

At 1930 hours, there came a half-hearted attack by a few bombers whose nearest bombs fell through the cloud ahead of the convoy between the destroyers *Keppel* and USS *Wainwright*. It was meant to be a combined torpedo and bombing attack; half a dozen He-115 aircraft had been circling the horizon for some time, and a torpedo exploded harmlessly outside the convoy.

A more determined torpedo attack was made less than an hour later. The anti-aircraft ship *Palomares* detected twenty-five aircraft coming up from astern at 2020 hours. They attacked from the starboard quarter, flying fast and low. Their leader showed great determination, hitting the *Navarino* in the middle of the convoy with two torpedoes before he crashed in flames just ahead of the *Keppel*. The remaining pilots weren't as brave.

"Had they kept up with him, dividing and generally embarrassing the A.A. fire," wrote Commander Broome, "many ships would have been sunk."

As it was, the Heinkels did torpedo three other ships: the freighters *Navarino* and *William Hooper* and the Russian tanker *Azerbaijan*. The *Navarino* and *William Hooper* were so badly damaged they had to be sunk. At first *Azerbaijan*'s bow was engulfed by flames, and lifeboats were seen leaving the ship, but she didn't sink. Led by women crewmembers, the fire was put out and the lifeboats hoisted back aboard. Fortunately, *Azerbaijan* was loaded with linseed oil for paint making, rather than fuel. She regained her station and continued with the convoy.

Commander Broome remarked on the good shooting of the escort and the convoy; four aircraft were thought to have been brought down, including one by the *Offa* and one by the *Wainwright*. The three rescue ships proved their value by picking up survivors quickly and efficiently. All told, the convoy lost three ships and ten men to the attack.

The convoy was 240 miles west of Norway's North Cape and still had more than 1,000 miles—five days' run—to sail before reaching Arkhangelsk. From the convoy's standpoint, everything was going well despite the day's air attacks.

The Germans, however, were still awaiting approval from Hitler for sailing the heavy ships to the attack. But the naval staff, fearing it might be delayed too long, had sanctioned the *Tirpitz* force joining the pocket battleships at Altenfjord (this had been done on the night of July 3/4). Admiral Tovey's covering force had been sighted some 300 miles southwest of the convoy early on July 3, and since then nothing had been seen of it. In view of Hitler's stringent orders that the carriers were to be located and put out of action before launching the operation, Grand Admiral Raeder decided that nothing further could be done for the present. They remained at Altenfjord until the afternoon of July 5.

At the British Admiralty, the situation was being watched with increasing anxiety. It had been known since July 3 that the German heavy ships had left Trondheim, and since the afternoon of July 4 that the northern squadron had left Narvik, but none of the ships had been located. That evening, Pound called a staff meeting to consider the situation. There was consensus that an attack might develop any time after 0200 hours next morning, July 5. If the attack was pressed home in full strength while Rear Admiral Hamilton's cruisers were still present, it seemed it could result only in their destruction, in addition to that of the entire convoy.

Against such an attack, the more widely the merchant ships were dispersed, the better their chances of escape seemed. Once the alarm had been given, the enemy raiders would not wish to spend more time than necessary in the neighborhood, rounding up odd groups and ships. But an 8-knot convoy takes some appreciable time to scatter effectively, and the matter was further complicated by uncertainty as to the extent to which the ice would permit maneuvering to the northward, away from the probable direction of the attack. On the other hand, the convoy was still some 800 miles from its final destination. Air and U-boat attacks had already started and were certain to continue on a heavy scale. Once scattered, the isolated groups and units of the convoy would present comparatively easy targets. Heavy casualties had to be expected.

Shortly after 2100 on July 4, the decision was made to withdraw the cruisers and scatter the convoy immediately.

The Admiralty's decision was conveyed to Rear Admiral Hamilton in the following three signals:

> "Most immediate. Cruiser force withdraw to westward at high speed. (2111 B/4)"
>
> "Immediate. Owing to threat from surface ships, convoy is to disperse and proceed to Russian ports. (2123 B/4)"
>
> "Most immediate. My 2123/4 (message). Convoy is to scatter."

To Hamilton, these signals could only mean that the further information about the Kriegsmarine heavy ship movements the Admiralty had been hoping for at 1858 hours had indeed come in and was of such a nature as to render imperative the drastic measures now ordered. Actually, the emphasis on the use of high speed by the cruisers was due to reports of a massing of enemy submarines between 11 degrees and 20 degrees east, and the order to scatter was intended merely as a technical amendment of the term "disperse" (used in the previous signal).

The nuance in wording between "disperse" and "scatter" could not be known to the recipients, and the cumulative effect of the three signals—especially as the last had a more urgent priority marking than the middle one—implied that pressing danger was actually upon them. Ships in the convoy ordered to disperse would merely cease to keep formation, and each ship would proceed at her best speed to her destination. Because in the present instance all ships were bound for the same port, Arkhangelsk, they would obviously remain in fairly close company with each other for some hours. On the other hand, ships were ordered to scatter immediately; that is, they proceeded in accordance with a plan laid down on courses that would separate them from each other as quickly as possible.

Commander Broome expected at any moment to see the cruisers open fire and the enemy's masts appear on the horizon. In this belief, he decided to take the destroyers of the escort to reinforce the cruiser force and ordered the two submarines to stay near the convoy when it scattered and to try to attack the enemy, while the rest of the escorting ships were to proceed independently to Arkhangelsk.

The British Admiralty decision to withdraw the protective screen and scatter the convoy was based on false information: the German surface forces had not yet left their Norwegian bases, but simply moved to different anchorages. They did not leave them until the next day, July 5, when *Tirpitz*, *Scheer*, *Hipper*, seven destroyers, and three torpedo boats made a sortie off the North Cape. The Germans didn't find any Allied ships and returned to port without firing a shot.

Commander Broome relayed to Convoy Commodore Dowding the message to scatter. Dowding knew that such an order was used only in extraordinary emergencies. It had been issued only once before in the war, in November 1940 when *Scheer* attacked a British convoy in the North Atlantic. Thirty-seven merchant ships were guarded only by the British armed merchant cruiser *Jervis Bay*. After giving the order for the convoy to scatter, she was sunk by *Scheer*.

The *Jervis Bay* action was fought, though, in the middle of the Atlantic. Here, 240 miles east of the North Cape and within the confined waters of the Barents Sea, these merchant ships had a very slight chance of escape from the enemy. They were already at the edge of the pack ice and could go no further northward.

As the six escorting destroyers turned away, Broome signaled Dowding: "SORRY TO LEAVE YOU LIKE THIS. GOOD LUCK. LOOKS LIKE A BLOODY BUSINESS."

Within an hour, many of the ships had disappeared over the horizon, each sailing its own course to Arkhangelsk. Some ships stayed together in groups of three or four for mutual support.

Luftwaffe FW-200s and BV-138s combed the Barents Sea, searching for the convoy. What they found astonished them: merchant ships spread out all over the area without any escorts.

The planes' pilots sent radio messages that brought the Junkers 88s, the Heinkels, and the U-boats. The ships that had belonged to PQ-17 were sought singly and attacked until their ammunition was exhausted and they were defenseless. Then they were rapidly sunk unless in combat they had already received fatal damage.

Some ships' crews fought back after a bomb or a torpedo had hit. They believed it was better to keep on fighting than to freeze to death in the sea. Only three of the American merchant ships carried 3-inch cannon. The rest were armed with .50-caliber and .30-caliber machine guns. The ammunition used by the machine guns bounced off the armor plate of the German planes if not fired at almost point-blank range. Defense, the crews realized, did not mean much. But it was a relief for nervous tension and kept a man from going insane.

During that time, the Panamanian registry freighter *Troubadour* had engaged in some rather exceptional activity. She carried a U.S. Navy gun crew whose members shared action stations with the merchant seamen. *Troubadour* had been armed in the United States with a 4-inch cannon, four Browning .30-caliber machine guns, and a .30-caliber Lewis machine gun. But the supply of ammunition was inadequate.

Ensign Howard E. Carraway, USNR, the gunnery officer, emphasized the seriousness of this shortage to the master and chief officer. In his report made later in Arkhangelsk, the ensign wrote:

It was decided on 28 June to open the seals on one of the three M-3 U. S. Army tanks on the deck, part of the cargo, and to determine whether the 37 millimeter gun in it could be manned and used for the defense of the ship. This was thought advisable in view (1) of the small amount of mixed tracer and ball .30 ammunition in our lockers; and (2) of the short effective range of the .30 Lewis machine gun against aircraft. This done, the gun was found suitable for use. Ammunition (Armor Piercing with tracer) was broken out of the hold with the aid of the Chief Officer, the gun was test-fired and a two man crew trained and assigned General Quarters stations in the tank.

Next day a second tank was opened, the 37 mm. gun made ready and manned. One member of the Armed Guard and one of the ship's crew were used as crew for each of the tank guns.

The weather on July 5 was bright and sunny with some high, thin clouds. The sea was cobalt and retained the broad, white paths of the ships' wakes. Off on the starboard hand, to the northward, the ice wall lay lustrous and sheer. The Germans came quickly to the target and attacked in strength.

The British freighter, *Empire Byron*, was sunk by *U-703*. The combined attack of U-boats and Ju-88s destroyed four ships, which had bunched together farther north. These were *Earlston*, *Washington*, *Bolton Castle*, and *Paulus Potter*. Then the *Pan Kraft* was caught while she ran alone and sunk by aircraft. Commodore Dowding's ship, *River Afton*, was another victim of *U-703*. The fleet oiler *Aldersdale* was damaged and abandoned (she was finished off by a U-boat two days later). *Carlton* was destroyed, as were *Fairfield City* and *Daniel Morgan*.

Fairfield City was a sturdy American freighter with a good rate of speed. She used evasive tactics while her gunners fired furiously at the Heinkels. But her machine guns caused little if any damage. Three Junkers 88s stayed high out of range, and each dropped a stick of bombs. At 1645 hours, two to three bombs struck the ship on the port side at the edge of No. 2 hatch. The blast wrecked the wheelhouse, the Captain's house, and part of the Saloon house. All the ladders to the bridge were blown away, all the hatch boards were blown off No. 2 hatch, and the geyser of water from the explosion filled the lifeboats half full of water. The ship was stopped by the engineer on watch and reversed to get the headway off the ship. The ship sank by the head at 1740 hours with her American ensign still flying.

The thirty-four survivors abandoned ship in Nos. 1, 2, and 3 lifeboats. They were unable to lower No. 4. Two crewmembers jumped overboard and swam to a raft. They were taken aboard one of the lifeboats. Another man was picked up from the water. The master ordered the men in the boats to look for other survivors, but none were found. At 1850 hours, No. 2 and No. 3 boats were taken in tow by No. 1 lifeboat, which was the motorboat, and they headed for the island of Novaya Zemlya about 250 miles away.

Daniel Morgan, an American ship that mounted a 3-inch cannon, was not so easily destroyed. Her master maneuvered her away from nine sticks of bombs. The gunners drove off dive-bomber attacks, and shell bursts ripped the wings of two attacking Junkers. But then the breech action of the cannon jammed and could not be cleared. Two more attacks were made against her.

The German bombers pounded the *Morgan* from end to end. Though there were no direct hits, the enormous impact of the near misses in the water right around her sprung her plates wide at the waterline and below. Her pumps could not handle the rapid flow into her holds and engine room. She was abandoned, and her crew was picked up the next day by the Soviet tanker *Donbass*.

Washington's forty-six-man crew abandoned ship in two lifeboats. Despite the speed of her sinking, the wireless operators had had time to send out an SOS. But the men in the boats were convinced that the only effect of these messages was to let the Germans know the positive result of the attack.

The survivors in the lifeboats strove to avoid uninterrupted icepack. Then the ice seemed to be breaking up. Channels opened, and to the east beyond the fields of ice, the survivors could see expanses of sea dotted with ice blocks. In an easterly direction lay Novaya Zemlya, an archipelago 500 miles long situated between the Barents Sea and the Kara Sea and split in two by the Matochkin Strait. The lifeboats contained blankets, chocolates, pemmican (a mixture of fat and protein), powdered milk, sugar, biscuits, dried fruit, and watertight kegs of fresh water. The crew reckoned the archipelago to be a little less than 300 miles away, about five days' rowing. They were wrong.

The American freighter *Olopana* had heard their SOS and had gone off its course to pick up the shipwrecked men. Two crews from ships sunk at the same time as the *Washington* were rowing toward it.

The two lifeboats containing the *Washington*'s crew did not move. The sailors began to row toward *Olopana* and then stopped. The shipwrecked men from the *Washington* did not wish to be picked up. They thought that it would have been madness to reembark now in a ship, which, they figured, would suffer the same fate. In their lifeboats, they were comparatively secure. No planes would bother to drop bombs on them, and no U-boats would torpedo them. But to board another cargo vessel was to expose themselves for certain to bombs and torpedoes. It was far better to reach the shores of Novaya Zemlya.

Once they were there, the men thought, they could wait a few days until the Germans considered that their attacks on the PQ-17 were over. Then they would make their way close inshore to the south. It would be very odd if they did not meet some Russian boat, which, they figured, would pick up the shipwrecked men and take them to Arkhangelsk. The dangerous amount of open water to cross would then be shorter. The sailors of the *Washington* were fully aware that something unforeseen could happen in their plan, but anything appeared preferable to going aboard the *Olopana*. They discussed the matter while the ship was approaching, and all were in agreement.

The survivors of the other two ships climbed aboard *Olopana*, but the *Washington*'s crew refused to go aboard the *Olopana* and began to row eastward without waiting for *Olopana* to disappear to the east.

Meanwhile, after *River Afton* was bombed and sunk, Commodore Dowding managed to get aboard a raft with an able-bodied sailor and a messboy from her crew. They sat side by side on the flimsy plank-and-oil-drum craft, huddled close against the spray and the wind. Commodore Dowding was an Arctic veteran. He spoke to the others from time to time so that they would not lapse into the first phase of the drowsiness that led to immobility and then death from freezing.

There was no way to steer the raft. She drifted downwind, and across the men's backs spray became a crust of ice. Ice also formed on the planks of the raft. The freeboard was less than a foot. Within a few hours, as the ice load increased, the raft would sink.

Thrust by the wind, the raft slowly went past a lifeboat from a sunken British ship. A number of survivors were aboard her, and she was in a bad way. The boat was wooden. German machine-gun bullets had perforated the strakes, tearing jagged holes in the hull. She was taking on water, and most of the men she carried were soaked to the skin, cruelly chilled, and unable to use their hands in the simple motions of bailing.

But aboard the boat was a sailor who was determined to live and to keep his shipmates alive. He stuffed the bullet holes with pieces torn from his and other men's clothing. Cursing, prodding, shoving, he got men to bail, and small amounts of water were cast out of the boat. She began to show more broadside and became almost ready to be rowed. There was, though, one survivor who did not respond to any kind of incentive.

He sat stoop-shouldered on a thwart, a sodden and pitiful figure in the grayish haze, the boat herself spectral-seeming on the leaden sea. Dowding could barely distinguish the man, but he clearly heard the rasping, exasperated voice of the sailor who exhorted the boat survivors.

The sailor addressed the stoop-shouldered man. "Alfie," he asked, "why are you so bloody wet?"

Hours later, the Royal Navy corvette *Lotus* emerged from the haze and discovered Dowding's pitiful raft. Dowding and his two shipmates were taken off without having suffered serious injury. *Lotus*, at some risk, cruised slowly south and west, looking for other survivors. But the lifeboat Dowding had seen was never found.

Late in the day of July 5, the Germans found a group of four British vessels, and the rescue ship *Zaafaran* was sunk by aircraft. But HMS *Salamander*, a minesweeper, and the freighter *Ocean Freedom* saved themselves and escaped. *Salamander*'s crew took out of the sea the complement from *Ocean Freedom* and some of the people from *Zaafaran*. The men had not been in the sea too long and were saved before exposure became fatal.

But the day's destruction wasn't over yet. Aircraft destroyed the American freighter *Peter Kerr*. Torpedoes fired in unison by several U-boats sank another American freighter, the *Honomu*. Men were lost aboard each of these ships, and flotsam littered the sea where the survivors struggled. Lakes of oil stretched far and wide, glistening black and trapping bodies. The air smelled of cordite, scorched paint and steel, with, as a base, the bitter stench of the oil.

Ensign Carraway reported on *Troubadour*'s participation in the events after the July 4 order for the convoy to disperse had been obeyed:

> *We immediately swung out of column to port, took a Northwesterly course and headed for the East coast of Spitzbergen. At about 2200 a British armed trawler hailed us and directed us to follow her. Later we were joined by the SS* Ironclad *and the SS* Silver Sword. *On the morning of 5 July, we reached the southern edge of the ice fields and turned East, closely following the ice.*
>
> *During the afternoon the radio operator received several distress messages from other ships of the scattered convoy being attacked by planes of various types and submarines. Some of the ships attacked and abandoned gave positions as near as twenty miles from our D. R. [dead reckoned] position.*
>
> *The commanding officer of the trawler, the H.M.T. Ayrshire, signaled us to put as much white paint as was available on our starboard sides (to help camouflage the ships) and prepare to enter the ice. The Armed Guard was turned to and aided in this task. Within five hours the painting was completed and we were well into the ice.*

Before the ships were camouflaged, Lieutenant L. J. A. Gradwell, RNVR, in command of *Ayrshire*, had boarded each of the merchant vessels. He explained the need for banking ships' fires. A single wisp of smoke from a stack might betray their position here. He advised that the ships that carried tanks on deck follow the example set by *Troubadour*: open up the M-3s and use their 37-mm pieces to repel attack. Gradwell wrote in his report:

> *After going about twenty miles into the ice all ships stopped, turned their starboard sides to the sea and waited until late in the afternoon of 6 July, when they headed out of the ice, took an Easterly course along the edge of the ice fields, with the West coast of the island of Novaya Zemlya as the destination.*

The ships waited in the ice for three days. On July 9, Gradwell held a conference with all of the masters and commanding officers in the group while the ships were at anchor in an unidentified inlet on the coast of Novaya Zemlya. They agreed to proceed south to Matochkin Strait, where a radio station was thought to be located. Here a party would be sent ashore to attempt to get a message through to the British Naval Control in Arkhangelsk.

Ensign Carraway continued in his report:

The C.O. of the Ayrshire *requested that I prepare all available arms with adequate ammunition and select six men to accompany the landing party, prepared in case the station should not be in friendly hands.*

On 10 July at 1100 the Matochkin Strait was reached and a signal from the station assured us that it was friendly. The landing party went ashore, obtained the desired information and returned without incident. Early on the morning of 11 July we moved about two miles into the straits, where the SS Benjamin Harrison *was at anchor. On 12 July all ships moved about ten miles further East into the straits for protection against air detection and attack.*

Earlier in the day a Russian tanker, a Russian armed trawler and an armed Russian icebreaker had joined the other ships.

Three British escort vessels — corvettes — arrived in the straits on 20 July. A convoy was formed and at about 1400 we cleared the straits bound for the White Sea.

On July 6, *Olopana*, after answering the *Washington*'s SOS and picking up survivors, was torpedoed and sunk by *U-225*. All but six of her crew and the load of survivors she had picked up were able to escape into lifeboats or onto rafts as the ship sank.

HMS *Pozarica* and her sister anti-aircraft ship *Palomares* were kept busy guarding the small convoys as they made their way across the White Sea to Arkhangelsk, picking up men who for days had been stranded in lifeboats and on rafts. While off Kolguyev Island, 60 miles from the Russian mainland, the convoy the Royal Navy ships escorted came under very heavy German air attack when, at 2000 hours on July 9, forty high-level bombers emerged from the clouds.

The Germans bombed with precision. The American freighter *Hoosier* and the Panamanian *El Capitan* evaded direct hits. Near misses were so numerous, though, that both vessels were abandoned in sinking conditions. The American Liberty ship *Samuel Chase* veered between the bomb geysers, helm hard right, then hard left in evasive maneuvers, and avoided destruction. But many of her steam pipes were ruptured. When the ship bucked with the violence of a near miss right off the bridge wing, the compass was flung from the binnacle in the wheelhouse. The sailor at the wheel steered without one until a box compass was brought from a lifeboat and installed in the binnacle case.

The rescue ship *Zamalek* was almost as badly battered as the American vessel. Near misses shook her until waves clashed across her deck. Soot from her stack erupted in big, black flakes. The stubby 1,200-ton steamer carried survivors in all her quarters and on deck. Those who stood clung to each other or else were knocked from their feet. Her engines could not maintain the strain at full speed. Her master slowed her, and she fell astern with the bomb blasts very close.

Despite their losses, the Allies fought back. Gunners aboard *Pozarica* and *Palomares* were able to take four of the German planes out of the sky. The 5.9-inch shells went aloft with great accuracy whenever a bomber came within range. Showers of aluminum from torn wing tips stippled the sea, and then the smashed planes whirled down and disappeared, howling, in immense gouts of spray.

The enemy broke off the action at 0230 the next morning and flew southwest. Two Soviet Catalina flying boats arrived over the convoy half an hour later and protectively circled it. The ships slowed until *Zamalek* could get back on station. Commodore Dowding, who had assumed duties of command aboard *Ocean Freedom*, ordered a course steered for Arkhangelsk.

Three corvettes, *Poppy*, *Lotus*, and *La Malouine*, were on the coast to pick up survivors from the beaches and collect the merchant ships. Twelve men from *Olopana* were found in a poorly sheltered beach camp. Space to accommodate the 240 survivors picked up by *Empire Tide* was made aboard the naval vessels. They proceeded to Matochkin Strait, where Commodore Dowding picked up five more ships (*Silver Sword*, *Ironclad*, *Troubadour*, *Benjamin Harrison*, and *Azerbaijan*) as well as two other vessels, the Soviet ice-breaker *Murman* and a trawler.

The weather was bad. With a storm brewing, Commodore Dowding passed orders to get underway. Fog helped conceal the ships off Novaya Zemlya. Dowding brought the convoy through the White Sea and into Arkhangelsk on July 24, and the ships were berthed. It had been three weeks since PQ-17 had dispersed.

Meanwhile, as many as fifty boats with survivors were trying to reach Novaya Zemlya. The island was a prolongation of the Ural mountain chain, and extended to 77 degrees North latitude. Matochkin Strait was a transversal fjord, more than 60 miles in length and most of that a half-mile wide. The hills that rose 3,000 feet were shouldered by glaciers, and between them and the sea, in summer, were green fields.

A short and harsh grass spread across the fields. Willow trees and dwarf birches dotted the landscape. Further inland, pale in the distance, stood snow-capped mountains.

Sea birds in great, noisy crowds littered the shore-side cliffs. A few lemmings, wild reindeer, foxes, wolves, and bears existed on the plains of the southern part of the island. The local waters held cod, herring, and salmon. Seals crawled up over the pebbles among the masses of driftwood on the beaches. Whales cruised close offshore.

After being sunk on July 5, *Fairfield City*'s survivors hoisted sails on the boats and made landfall on Novaya Zemlya, 5 miles south of Matochkin Strait, on July 9. The men took the sails and boat covers ashore and made tents from them.

It was the birds that saved the survivors' lives. The men saw them first, dark, small specks high in the saffron-yellow sky above the land haze. Then they landed, and fumbling with weakness, the survivors killed enough to make a broth, providing each man with a meal, meager as it was. Time was not taken to catch fish; hunger was too insistent, and the birds were all around. Hunting of game for meat was not even considered.

A number of the survivors lacked sensation in their feet and lower legs. They hobbled ashore from the boats, helped along the strand by their shipmates. The prospect for them was gangrene and amputation. They sat rather still on the beach, seldom talking.

On July 10, the survivors were discovered by some Soviet Boy Scouts, who took a note to a nearby Soviet-manned radar station which sent word of the men to Northern Fleet headquarters Two days later, HMS *Ayrshire* picked them up and took them to Matochkin Strait. There they were placed on various ships. Eleven were put on the SS *Troubadour*, ten on the SS *Silver Sword*, and seven on the SS *Ironclad*; three remained on the *Ayrshire*.

Washington's crew reached Novaya Zemlya after spending six and a half days rowing through the icy seas in their lifeboats. By the time they landed, they were ravenous. They had finished the last of the boats' provisions the night before.

Hunger possessed the entire company of survivors. Geese cackled on the beach, but were too careless near the men. Eight goslings were captured, their necks quickly wrung. The armed guard officer from the ship, a young ensign, wore a .45-caliber issue Colt in a holster. He went hunting alone and shot a seagull. That sent the other gulls, hundreds of them, away in screaming flight. But the ensign's prize added materially to a soup cooked over a driftwood fire.

Alerted to the disastrous battle around PQ-17, the Soviet Ice Patrol vessel *Murmanez* was sent to search for survivors. Ice patrol vessels were charged with responsibility for both combat and transport operations in the Barents and Kara seas. The *Murmanez* crew included a five-man research and operations group. Among the crew was Valentin Valentinovich Dremlyug, the ship's twenty-four-year-old engineering officer. Later he wrote about what happened:

> As she was heading out of the White Sea, Murmanez *received a radiogram from the tanker* Donbass *informing us about the destruction of the ships of convoy PQ-17 by German submarines and torpedo-bombers. As it turned out,* Murmanez *proved to be the Russian vessel able to give the first and most important help to the survivors of PQ-17.*
>
> *As the* Donbass *departed, the* Murmanez *continued on her assigned mission. On 13 July, while off Gusinaya Island (south of the Novaya Zemlya Islands), we noticed a number of people on shore who were trying to get our attention with smoke and flag signals. Capt. Kotzov ordered a small boat put over. As the boat approached the shore, its crew—well armed with carbines—was prepared for anything. The two machine guns on the* Murmanez *also were aimed at the people on shore.*
>
> *Our hails to them in Russian brought no response, but when we tried English we were told that they were the surviving crewmembers of the SS* Olopana *(one of the PQ-17 ships), which had been torpedoed and sunk by a U-boat about 15 miles from Novaya Zemlya. After almost two weeks adrift in a lifeboat, the survivors—12 in all—had finally come ashore at Gusinaya Island.*
>
> *On 16 July we transferred the* Olopana *survivors to the settlement at Belushya Bay. An interesting footnote to the* Olopana *rescue is the gift to me, mentioned earlier, by the boatswain of the* Olopana. *As he was taken aboard the* Murmanez, *the boatswain still had with him the small tin cup with which each lifeboat was equipped for measuring out the daily rations of fresh water. He had carried it with him throughout his ordeal. He gave it to me as a token of gratitude. The cup, however, has been a treasured part of my household ever since.*
>
> *By 17 July we had seven lifeboats in tow, on which were about 100 American and British survivors from various ships. We towed the boats to the Gulf of Molier, where we transferred all of the survivors to the British transport* Empire Tide.
>
> *Between 13 and 17 July we were able to take aboard more than 100 seamen—survivors of the* Alcoa Ranger, Washington, Hartlebury,

and Paulus Potter—*in addition to the 12 crewmen from the* Olopana. *Our poor vessel was filled to overflowing.*

Later, we came upon the American transport Winston Salem, *which had been deliberately grounded in order to prevent her from sinking from the damage already inflicted by the U-boats. To prevent the* Winston Salem *from breaking up and going under, we took soundings to determine the depth of water in her vicinity, and prepared to tow her off at the next high tide.*

To tow the Winston Salem *we "married" our bow and stern anchors to her anchors to give us the leverage we needed to be able to tow her off at the next tide. We were assisted in this task by a Russian trawler and together were able not only to get her underway again but also, some time later, to witness the delivery of her full load of precious tanks and ammunition to the port of Arkhangelsk.*

Thirty-six ships left Hvalfjödur. Two had turned back to Iceland, air attack had destroyed thirteen (in addition to the *Zaafaran*) at a cost of six aircraft, and U-boats sank ten vessels without loss to themselves. The convoy started out carrying 156,492 tons of cargo. The ships that were lost took with them all but 57,176 tons of that—a loss of nearly two thirds of the precious cargo. The material sunk included enough to equip an army: 430 tanks, 210 planes, and 3,350 jeeps and trucks. The human cost was 153 dead men.

Winston Churchill said of PQ-17 in his history of World War II: "Unfortunately the destroyers of the convoy escort also withdrew (with the cruisers)."

Commander Broome, who had led the destroyer *Keppel*, wrote to the editor of the *Daily Telegraph* on October 30, 1950:

This [Churchill's] statement may reasonably create the impression that the destroyer force was free to remain with the convoy or withdraw.

It was from no misfortune that the destroyers under my command withdrew. It resulted from a direct order from the Admiralty to scatter the convoy. This order could only have been justified by the proximity of the enemy, and it demanded therefore that I should concentrate my destroyer force with the nearby cruisers.

The responsibility for the tragic events which followed must rest with those who, in contradiction to naval practice, elected to direct an Arctic convoy from London, instead of passing information and leaving the decisions to the commander on the spot.

QP-13, consisting of thirty-five ships (twelve from Arkhangelsk, twenty-three from Murmansk) under Commodore N. H. Gale in *Empire Selwyn*, left Murmansk on June 27. The convoy was heavily escorted by the minesweeper *Niger* (Commander A. J. Cubison, senior officer of escorts); *Hussar*; the corvettes *Honeysuckle*, *Hyderabad*, *Starwort*, and *Roselys*; anti-aircraft ship *Alynbank*; destroyers *Achates* and *Volunteer*; and trawlers *Lady Madeleine* and *St. Elstan*. Two days passed without alarm, but the ships were sighted by an FW-200, and everyone feared that Ju-88s, He-111s, and U-boats wouldn't be far behind. No attack came—partly because of heavy fog, but mainly because the Germans were concentrating on PQ-17.

Captain R. Kelsoe was the master of the big Panamanian registry freighter *Exterminator*. He was a tall Yugoslav with a shock of brown hair. A pair of Colt .45 automatic pistols were thrust inside the waistband of his trousers. A pair of ferocious German shepherd dogs followed him wherever he moved and stayed at his side in battle.

A. Andresen, a Norwegian national, was Captain Kelsoe's chief officer. Andresen was the best gunner aboard *Exterminator*. He was in command of the volunteer crew that worked the British 4-inch cannon mounted on the foredeck.

The chief officer went personally armed, a precaution taken by most of the other members of the crew. Everyone on board *Exterminator* was of several nationalities, and from countries under German occupation. Capture could mean instant execution by a German firing squad.

Captain Kelsoe and Andresen kept a terse logbook account of the PQ-13 voyage from Murmansk to Reykjavik, Iceland. The entry for June 29 read: "Day begins heavily overcast. At 10:15 a.m. altered course to 355°. At 2:45 p.m. altered to 297°. Day ends overcast with visibility good, speed 9 knots."

The entry for the next day marked the arrival of the first German patrol plane, the dreaded Focke-Wulf Condor, whose radio reports would bring the Junkers 88 bombers, the Heinkel torpedo planes, and the U-boats. It forecast very probable extinction. Captain Kelsoe's logbook read: "Tuesday, June 30th. Day begins overcast, visibility fair. Russian destroyers left the convoy. At 4:40 p.m. first air raid alert. At 5:30 p.m. all clear. At 10:20 p.m. altered course to 225°. At 11:00 p.m. altered course to 270°. Day ends cloudy and fine with speed 8.4 knots."

His entry for July 1 was: "Dense fog, heavily overcast. At 7:30 a.m. altered course to 254°. At 5:15 p.m. altered course to 263°. At 11:00 p.m. altered course to 228°."

Commodore Gale, within the fog cover, steered a series of evasive courses. He held on to the hope that he might lose the German reconnaissance planes that were sure to search the area as soon as the weather cleared. But they came the next day. Captain Kelsoe recorded the fact in *Exterminator*'s log: "Thursday, July 2nd. Overcast, visibility good. At 9:00 a.m. two Blohm & Voss (BV-138) sea planes were circling the convoy. At 11:00 p.m. the planes left. At 11:25 p.m. altered course to 241°. Speed 8.5 knots. Day ends with scattered fog banks."

During the hours while the enemy aircraft were in sight, the escort made repeated attempts to shoot them down. The destroyers gave full throttle and whipped forward in a white, high-bow splatter, cannon firing as rapidly as they could be served. *Alynbank* joined with her heavier pieces.

The range was too great, and the German planes kept close to the haze-rimmed horizon in elusive flight patterns. There was nothing more to be done. The ships kept thumping and grinding on through the fog banks around them. The escort moved slowly once more in its usual screen formation. But aboard the escort vessels, men stood close alongside the depth charge racks and the gun mounts. They knew that U-boat attack might come at any minute.

The long minutes of waiting stretched into the next day. Captain Kelsoe wrote at the end of it: "Friday, July 3rd. Weather overcast with very thick fog and some ice. At 3:30 p.m. altered course to 196°. At 7:00 p.m. altered course to 210°. Ships passing through drift ice. Weather overcast with thick fog. Speed 8.3 knots."

Then, on July 4, during the hours of late afternoon, the men of the PQ-13 convoy fully understood what had saved them. Since July 1, they had heard intermittent rumbling from the southwestward. The loaded, eastbound convoy, PQ-17, was being attacked. The far-away noise was interrupted by long periods of silence. Fog lay thickly on the sea here; perhaps it spread, too, along the PQ-17 course track, protecting the ships.

Arriving off the northeast corner of Iceland on July 4, the convoy was ordered to split up. Sixteen ships, including that of the commodore, with part of the escort being routed to Loch Ewe and the remainder with the rest of the escort, went along the north coast of Iceland to Reykjavik. Captain J. Hiss of the *American Robin* was nominated as acting commodore of this section.

The weather during the previous two days had been cloudy, and it had not been possible to take sights during that time. As a result, the position of the convoy was uncertain. The radar carried by some of the ships of the escort was at that time not very reliable, and as the Iceland section approached the land, the weather deteriorated. It was blowing a gale from the northeast, raining, with the visibility down to about a mile. At 2000 hours, Commander Cubison decided to go ahead and try to make it to Iceland

Cubison realized that the ships must pass between the rugged coast of Iceland—now wholly unseen under a blanket of fog and rain—and a minefield, which extended for several miles to the westward out into the Denmark Strait. He decided to steer close enough to take a bearing of some sort. Weather conditions had made it impossible to take celestial sights for the past two days. Radar was unreliable. Visibility was down to one mile.

At 2200 hours on July 4, Cubison saw what he believed to be the North Cape. It was, however, an iceberg. He took a bearing on it and gave a radical course change of forty-eight degrees to due west. The convoy was ordered at the same time to form two columns so that it might sail safely between the outer minefield and the land.

A new minefield, closer to the coast, had been set since the PQ-13 formation had gone to North Russia. There were no charts available that gave the exact location of the field. The lack of charts would prove disastrous for the *Niger*.

Niger had been on duty in Russia for eight months, and her crew would be given leave as soon as she reached Britain after delivery of the convoy. A number of her men were discussing that when at 2240 she struck a mine. Before the ship went under him and he drowned, Commander Cubison was able to send a blinker message. *Niger*'s signal yeoman, swiftly pressing the trigger of the Aldis lamp, told Captain Hiss: "Suggest alter course to 222."

This was the course that had been previously steered, and Captain Hiss as acting commodore in *American Robin* was at once aware of it. He swung his own ship instantly and relayed the message to the rest of the convoy. But he lacked a chart that gave the minefield position, and suddenly *American Robin* was struck and seriously damaged by an explosion.

Due to faulty navigation, the convoy had sailed directly into the field. Within a brief space of time, four ships of the convoy had struck mines and foundered, and two more were seriously damaged.

Pale flames illuminated the scene as *Niger* sank, taking her commanding officer, eight other officers, and 140 crewmen with her.

The freighter *Hybert* hit a mine and sank, as did *Heffron* and *Massmar*. *Exterminator* and *John Randolph* were damaged. One of those lost was the Russian ship *Rodina*, which was carrying the wives and families of Soviet diplomats stationed in London.

Maria Amosovna Naumova Vyushina, who had four years of experience on steamships, was the baker on *Rodina*. Among the passengers were a young Russian woman and her young daughter, who shared Maria's cabin during the trip. The woman was going to meet her husband, who worked at the Soviet embassy in Reykjavik. Originally they were to have sailed on *Stari Bolshevik*, but at the last minute got passage on *Rodina*, which was departing sooner. Years later, in somewhat broken English, Vyushina recalled the voyage and its terrible end:

> The night we were to arrive in Iceland there was an explosion. I jumped up, flung the door open and found the corridor filled with water. The mother rushed out of a cabin with the girl on hands, without lifejackets.
>
> We ran to the boat deck where the boatswain supervised loading people into the life boats. The strong gale howled in tackles. As we got into the boat someone removed his own lifejacket and put on the girl. A strong wave picked up the boat and threw it against the sinking steamship. The boat turned over and plunged us into the icy water. It felt like I was burning and it was hard to breathe.
>
> Nearby appeared wide thick wooden hatch and I grabbed it, my hands where like iron crampons. Abruptly waves carried away me all further from a steamship. When a wave lifted me on an abrupt crest I saw Rodina strongly tilted as she sank.
>
> A man passenger floated not far away. He tried to come nearer to me and to grasp for same hatch, but couldn't reach it. In a wave there was a large timber which has knocked him on the head. On the water appeared a dark circle of blood began to creep away quickly, the man did not surface after being hit.
>
> My hands and body and I wanted to be let go of the hatch—I cannot unclench my fingers. Nearby the daughter of the passenger floated. The lifejacket's belt was weak and gradually slipped off the girl and I cannot help her. I looked back once again, but the girl already had drowned and was floating face down in the sea.
>
> It is better for me to sink, I thought, trying to be let go, but hatch and hands were as if one. Small ice floes, cross ties, bags with the wool, any wooden subjects around floated.

A big foreign boat passed near the sinking, I didn't think they saw me and again began to try to be let go of the hatch. I was exhausted and started to faint. Suddenly on hatch was a line with a big knot on the end. It was with the last bit of my strength I seized it with my teeth.

I regained consciousness as someone kneaded my body. It was the doctor. He saw I had regained my senses, and has started talking in language I didn't understand. I asked: "Where am I? How many of us survived?"

He didn't understand, but guessed and showed me ten fingers then four and three — 17 persons escaped.

The doctor somewhere left. I lay there covered with a bed-sheet and reflected: "This is probably a fascist submarine and in an hour German officer which will torture and then shoot me."

Then door was quietly opened and I grew cold, but it was Katya Vushueva from Rodina. *She among the survivors was the mother of the little girl. Katya and I cried over the loss of our ship and comrades.*

SS *Massmar* carried a crew of thirty-eight merchant crew, sixteen Naval Armed Guard, and thirty-six survivors of the torpedoed SS *Alamar*, which had been sunk in PQ-13. Among these were the U.S. Naval Armed Guard detachment of the *Alamar*, all of whom survived the sinking and were assigned to *Massmar* for the return voyage to the States, via Iceland.

Charles J. Hayes, radioman second class, was one of *Alamar's* Armed Guard detachment. Later he wrote about that terrible night:

The night of July 5, 1942 was very cold with dark clouds, strong winds and heavy seas. My assignment as lookout was on a hatch cover just forward of the bridge. I felt certain that with the size of the waves, no sub could possibly fire a torpedo with any chance of success, although we took nothing for granted and still kept a sharp watch.

When I was relieved of my watch, I went to my bunk which was just off the main deck. Of course, at this time and in these waters, we had learned never to be without our lifejacket — eating, sleeping or whatever.

I had just laid down when there was a horrendous explosion that shook the ship. The noise was louder even than that on the Alamar *when the bombs hit. I hit the deck and started for the hatch when another powerful explosion sounded. When I reached the main deck, it was already only three or four feet above the water.*

I looked down midships and saw a crew member trying to get a lifeboat free. The water was coming up so quickly the boat was already floating in the water before they had time to unhook the davits.

When I next looked over the side just in front of me, the deck was only a few inches above the surface. There was someone standing next to me—I don't remember who it was—and we both just stepped over the side into the water.

The sea was running high and those of us in the water would ride up to the top of a wave and then ride down into the trough, something like riding a small roller coaster. When you rose to the top of a wave you could see many people floating in the water and when you dropped down, you could see nothing but huge waves overhead. An overturned lifeboat floated by but I was unable to get to it.

Later, a lifeboat sailed by with a Navy Armed Guard sailor standing up in it! He had a big smile on his face as he sailed by. Some people called out to him from the water, but he didn't respond. He seemed to be in some state of shock and didn't seem aware of his situation.

All of a sudden, an overturned lifeboat came over the top of a wave, directly at me. There was a merchant seaman clinging to it and I noticed a line wrapped around the upturned bottom. The merchant sailor tried to reach me, but he was exhausted and wasn't able to pull me out of the water. I was able to grab the line that was wrapped around the boat and with some help from him I was finally able to climb onto the boat. We both were able to secure our arms under the taut line and this kept us from falling off. Then, as happened when the Alamar went down, I fell asleep from the cold.

Seventeen of *Massmar's* crewmembers, including the captain, plus twenty-three crewmembers from *Alamar*, including her captain too, were lost. Nine of the combined Naval Armed Guard detachments also perished.

At enormous risk to herself, the French corvette *Roselys*, under the command of Lieutenant de Vaisseau A. Bergeret, spent a hair-raising six and a half hours smelling her way around and into the minefield to pick up 134 survivors who otherwise certainly would have perished—a heroic action.

The trawlers *Lady Madeleine* and *St. Elstan*, with complete disregard for their own safety, also steamed about in the minefield for six and a half hours rescuing survivors, which included some from the cruiser *Edinburgh*. Between them they picked up 211 survivors, some of whom later died of exposure.

Graeme Ogden in *Lady Madeleine* wrote about his view of the disaster:

At 2040 I saw Niger *come steaming out of the gloom and take up a position about half a mile off our port bow. She made a visual signal to pass on to the Commodore to steer 270 degrees. While the signalman was busy calling up*

*the nearest ship, there was a heavy muffled explosion and, on looking round,
I saw* Niger *had taken on a heavy list and was clearly in serious trouble.
I made a hurried entry in the log:*

HMS Niger *torpedoed 2040.*

Estimated position 66°3o'N 23°io/W.

I then took Lady M *at full speed to* Niger, *broadcasting as I went
that* Niger *was sinking. It was now a wild noisy evening but as* Lady
M *plunged towards* Niger *I heard to starboard a quick series of heavy
explosions. Through my glasses I could see merchant ships stopped and
apparently sinking.*

By the time we got to Niger, *her bows were pointing skyward like
a toy boat. The part of her bottom which was above water was unharmed.
I thought at the time an acoustic torpedo must have blown her stern off.
Some of her crew were clinging to the nearly perpendicular foredeck and
others covered in black oil were hanging on to a Carley float some little
way away. Within a minute, with a final hiss of escaping steam, she slid
backwards into the hungry sea and disappeared before our astonished eyes.*

*The heavy sea running made it necessary to get to windward, thus
making a lee and drifting on to the raft.* Lady M's *stern just missed the raft,
but a heaving line was grabbed by the men hanging on to it and now began the
struggle to get these men aboard. In those days we did not carry scrambling
nets to help survivors climb inboard, and the task of rescuing those oil-covered
sailors from the raft as it rose and fell in the heavy seas was heart-breaking.*

I actually had my arm round Niger's *oil-covered Australian first
lieutenant when a wave swept him away never to be seen again. Apart from
saving his life, if we had got this man aboard we might have solved the
mystery of* Niger's *fate. As it was, the men we did get were engine-room
ratings and very bemused as to what had hit their ship. As far as I know, all
of her officers perished including Commander Cubison, her captain.*

*During this time the gunners on the merchant ships had opened
fire indiscriminately, under the impression their ships had been attacked
by U-boats on the surface or a German raider. Shells were whining in all
directions and raising waterspouts as they pitched into the sea.*

*The convoy was now in a state of utter confusion. Nobody knew what
was happening. Merchant ships were firing at one another, or anything they
could see in the water, which was dotted with lifeboats from the sinking
ships.* Haiard *and* Hussar *had disappeared into the fog with the leading
ships and remained silent.*

Graham Butcher, in St. Elstan, *thought we had been attacked by
U-boats on the surface using gun-fire and torpedoes. So did I, as apart from*

having seen torpedoes I had seen a merchant ship which was stopped, hit fore and aft by shells. Conversation was difficult with Roselys, *the French corvette. I believe Lieutenant Bergeret, her captain, thought we had run into a minefield, but I couldn't see how this could be possible.*

Firstly, because while on the same course the van of the convoy had steamed over the same ground unharmed, and, secondly, from the state of the sea, we were clearly within a few miles of the land. A quick look at the chart showed me that on my reckoning we were roughly on the reverse track PQ-16 had taken going north-east. Unless somebody had sown a new minefield while we had been away in Russia, the only one I knew of, and which was shown on our minefield chart, was miles away to the north-east in the Denmark Strait.

We began to pick up boat-loads of survivors from the American merchant ships. Unfortunately, they were mostly inexperienced seamen and terrified by the huge seas. They rowed for the sake of rowing, not looking where they were going or watching the treacherous waves. Some of them even pulled to my weather side and broke themselves to pieces against the ship.

I never expected to survive that night and the next morning. We spent hours and hours picking up and searching for survivors. Had we been in a minefield, we should have assuredly been blown up. If U-boats were about we were a sitting target, and if a raider was present we were helpless — our only chance was the fog.

Only HMS *Hussar* knew exactly where she was and where the minefield was; she led the remaining eleven ships out of danger and led the convoy to safety, arriving at Reykjavik on July 7. *Roselys* made port with U.S. Navy Catalina flying boats overhead that discouraged submarine attack. The remaining ships had arrived without further incident, and were already at anchor in Reykjavik harbor.

Although badly damaged by a mine, Captain Kelsoe believed that *Exterminator* was able to make port. He rejoined the convoy and entered in his logbook:

Monday, July 6th. First friendly plane appeared. Weather moderating and we are proceeding at 8 knots. The vessel was straining in No. 3 hold and was going down by the head. We requested a ship with pumps to be sent to our assistance. At 5:40 p.m. tug Empire Bascobel *was alongside and tried to pump out No. 2 hold. This proved unsuccessful and she cast off. Pilot on board at 11:35 p.m. At 11:45 p.m. tug* Empire Larch *made fast alongside, and we proceeded into inner harbor anchorage at Reykjavik.*

His entry for the next day read: "Tuesday, July 7th. At 12:45 p.m. ship anchored off Reykjavik. Salvage people came aboard and commenced work, taking on board pumps, etc."

Two members of *Exterminator*'s crew were convinced that celebration should not be delayed. The worst hazards of the voyage had been surmounted. A bottle they found in the engine room did not contain grain alcohol, though. It was a poisonous compound used in the cleaning of boiler tubes. The men died in intense agony after ingesting the poison.

After being rescued, Charles J. Hayes didn't wake up until arriving in Reykjavik.

I have no idea of the time that passed between the lifeboat and the hospital. I was told that we had been rescued by a Free French corvette. There were other survivors in the hospital, some in bed and some walking around.

I looked around for my Armed Guard shipmates from the Alamar. *There was just one other with me. He was the one who rode alone, standing in the lifeboat. He had no memory of that, although many others told of seeing him go by them while they were in the water.*

My partner, the gunner's mate, "Georgia" was gone, as were other mates, whose names and faces I still remember, but have not mentioned here.

Although it has been a lifetime since the Massmar *went down, I still remember those young men of the Navy Armed Guard—seventeen, eighteen, nineteen years old—who fought against an overwhelming enemy and survived only to lose their lives in an Allied minefield.*

However, in the poor conditions of storm and fog, we can understand the mistakes the Niger *made and sympathize with their loved ones over their loss. And we can never repay the courage of the French ship* Roselys, *who so bravely saved so many lives at great risk to their own.*

PQ-13's losses were four ships sunk, two badly damaged, and *Niger* gone from the escort.

Following PQ-17 and QP-13, the British Admiralty suspended convoys until September 1942. The growing demands on the Royal Navy in the Mediterranean and North Atlantic made it impossible it provide adequate protection for the Arctic convoys. Other measures would have to be put into place to keep some supplies moving to the USSR until September.

CHAPTER 7

TASK FORCES
July–September 1942

A s the last survivors of PQ-17 limped into Murmansk, the British Admiralty was assessing the impact of the damage. News of the horrendous losses was first published in the United States, and the orders given by the British Admiralty were criticized by journalists and politicians in both the United States and the United Kingdom. Despite the public outcry, the Admiralty remained undaunted in its program to continue the convoys.

However, it was decided not to send more convoys across the Arctic Ocean until the days shortened. The uninterrupted daylight gave too great an advantage to the Luftwaffe, and no adequate anti-aircraft protection could be provided to defeat its attacks. Therefore the convoys were suspended until September.

This decision was reported to the Soviet High Command, which protested energetically. The USSR was hard pressed by the German offensive, and her troops had more need than ever of war materiel and munitions. In order not to leave the Soviets without at least some war-fighting materials, the Admiralty announced that it would send a special task force of transports consisting of warships. There was also the necessity of replenishing minesweepers, escort ships, and aircraft in Soviet ports with stores and ammunition that had been lost in PQ-17.

The question of providing better air reconnaissance and the possibility of bombing German surface ships also was raised. Air Marshal Sir Philip Joubert de la Ferté, commander-in-chief Coastal Command, pointed out that had torpedo aircraft been stationed in northern Russia, the Admiralty might not have considered it necessary to scatter convoy PQ-17. He obtained an agreement with the Soviet command to make arrangements for the temporary transfer of a balanced force of search and strike aircraft to Russian airfields during the period of the next convoy operation.

This force was comprised of four photographic reconnaissance Spitfires, No. 210 Squadron Catalina long-range seaplanes reconnaissance squadron, and Hampden torpedo-bomber squadrons No. 144 from the RAF and Royal Australian Air Force (RAAF) No. 455, all under the command of Group Captain F. L. Hopps, RAF.

The British destroyers *Marne*, *Martin*, *Middleton*, and *Blankney* were the first ships dispatched, sailing directly to Arkhangelsk, loaded with ammunition and new gun barrels, particularly for the anti-aircraft ships *Palomares* and *Pozarica*. They arrived on July 24.

A second task force, consisting of the U.S. cruiser *Tuscaloosa*, U.S. destroyers *Rodman* and *Emmons*, and HMS *Onslaught*, sailed from Glasgow on August 13. *Tuscaloosa* carried 300 tons of ammunition, explosives, radar parts, medical supplies, dehydrated foods, and thirty-six torpedoes. Each destroyer carried 20 tons of aircraft parts and 19 tons of mixed cargo. Seven British naval officers, three RAF officers, and 160 other passengers sailed with the three ships.

A German reconnaissance plane sighted the group on the evening of August 20 and apparently reported its position. The convoy's course was changed, and poor visibility helped concealment. *Tuscaloosa* broke radio silence to report the sighting to Commander in Chief Home Fleet, hoping that this would be interpreted by the enemy as routine patrol procedure.

And, as Captain Norman C. Gillette, commanding officer of *Tuscaloosa*, remarked, "God sent a fog," which concealed the ships for the rest of this anxious voyage. Two British and one Soviet destroyer met the group outside Kola Inlet and escorted them into Vaenga Bay on August 23. Their arrival had been timed to allow for unloading and fueling during a time of day when the Luftwaffe typically was grounded.

Arrangements had been made by local Soviet authorities and British liaison officers for discharging cargo, and all hands turned to with a will to get their lethal load on the beach. This was accomplished by 0700 hours the next day, August 24. *Tuscaloosa*, *Rodman*, and *Emmons*, plus the British destroyers *Marne*, *Martin*, and *Onslaught*, sailed that morning at 0749 with 240 PQ-17 survivors on board *Tuscaloosa* and an additional 300 men, including four Russian diplomats, in the five destroyers. Among the survivors on *Marne* were men from *Edinburgh* and *Gossamer*.

The Kriegsmarine command credited its successful operation against PQ-17 to the "exemplary cooperation between aircraft and U-boats," the results being in every way commensurate with those expected from the surface warships. It was decided in the future not to employ surface ships in attacks on the loaded PQ convoys, but rather to use them for attacking the returning QP convoys in the Barents Sea, which they could do with a minimum of risk. In addition to destroying the major Allied convoys, the Kriegsmarine command hoped to disrupt Soviet shipping in the Arctic that summer.

During August, two operations were set in motion to accomplish this. Operation *Unternehmen* (*Wunderland* [Land of Miracles]) was the most ambitious, employing the battlecruiser *Admiral Scheer* along with *U-209* and *U-601*. *Wunderland* was considered a preliminary stage for establishing control over the western Arctic. The second, Operation *Zar*, consisted of extensive mine-laying to be carried out by *Ulm*.

Preliminary moves of Operation *Wunderland* began three weeks before *Scheer* left Narvik. The moves were conducted by *U-601* and *U-209*, with primary attention focused on Belushya Guba, an administrative center located in southwest Novaya Zemlya, a move designed to distract the Soviets from *Admiral Scheer*'s raid in the Kara Sea.

The first action occurred on July 27, when *U-601*, under Kapitänleutnant Peter-Ottmar Grau, attacked the town of Malye Karmakuly near Belushya Bay and shelled two anchored seaplanes and three living and two storage huts.

I. P. Mazuruk piloted one of the Soviet seaplanes. He and his crew had spent a long day searching for survivors of PQ-17. They'd spent twenty-four hours flying, but failed to find anything. Utterly exhausted, they planned to rest and refuel overnight before setting out again. There wasn't enough room for everyone to sleep ashore, so the aircraft commander, Kozlov, and mechanic, Serov Kosuhin, stayed overnight in the plane while Mazuruk, the navigator Zhukov, and copilot and radio operator Syrokvasha Cholyshev made themselves comfortable in one of the huts. Later, Mazuruk recalled that evening in an interview:

> We'd started to settle in when Zhukov said: "Maybe everyone's found already and we'll find nobody" as he pulled off his boots.
>
> "Anyway, we will seek, as long as possible," I replied. "Tomorrow we'll go once more over the coast. Maybe someone landed ashore."

While the men bantered back and forth, Grau readied U-601's gun crew for the attack. For half an hour, Grau carefully observed the structures on the shore and the seaplane through the U-boat's periscope. Moving to within 2,000 yards of the shore, Grau took another look to ensure there were no threats to the U-boat. Seeing none, he surfaced and prepared to attack.

Mazuruk had just fallen asleep when a shell hit the window under which he was sleeping, splashing the airman with small fragments of glass. The embossed frame flew over his head and hit the opposite wall of the house. Stunned, Mazuruk jumped up and looked out the broken window. Mazuruk continued his story:

> The first thing I saw was a flaming torch, an aircraft and a submarine, sitting on the mirror surface of the bay. At the submarine's bow, gunners were busy reloading and an officer on the bridge in a fur jacket showing his gunners where to fire.
>
> Kozlov jumped from the burning plane and furiously swam to shore.
>
> Not paying more attention to the aircraft, the submarine officer waved his hand toward the shore, and immediately following a projectile hit the roof of a family hut. The roof of the hut, as if projected from below by an unknown force, jumped up and collapsed on the walls of the building. Immediately it caught fire from the barrack's oven. From the ruins half-dressed men jumped out and, bending down, and fled into the interior of the island under cover of the rocky spurs.
>
> I and my comrades ran out of the hut, and as soon as we got clear, it was smashed into splinters by a projectile.
>
> After firing more shots the gunners one by one dropped in the conning-tower hatch and the boat slowly sank into the water.
>
> Shivering from the cold and the shock of the shelling, people were returning to the village. Several people were injured, the plane burned with mechanic Serov trapped inside. The Ice Station was half destroyed.

Grau was satisfied and thought that the work was well started. Without expending a single torpedo, he destroyed most of the Soviet polar station and burned a seaplane.

On the night of August 1, Grau received orders to move north toward Cape Desire and be prepared to raid the Kara Sea. This order was the beginning of Operation *Wunderland*. But before heading north, Grau decided to inspect the area one more time. Through the periscope, he saw the white, rocky, snow-capped mountains of Novaya Zemlya, beaches, rugged coves, and numerous bays. All previous attempts to get there had been thwarted by Soviet patrols, a minefield, and an antisubmarine net.

Grau turned the periscope without regret from the shoreline toward the sea and sighted an unescorted Soviet ship approaching the island. At 0023 hours, Grau fired a single torpedo, which hit and the vessel started to sink.

His target was *Krestyanin* (Master A. G. Nikolaev). Loaded with coal, she was approaching Belushya Guba Bay (Beluga Whale Island) when the torpedo hit. She sunk in three minutes; five sailors and two passengers died in the attack. The survivors abandoned ship in two lifeboats and were questioned by the Germans, who gave them the direction to the shore.

F. Stepanov, First Lieutenant of *Krestyanin* (Farmer), wrote about the sinking in his memoirs:

Krestyanin was without escort. The short distance from Naryan-Mar to Belushya gave rise to the illusion that the area was safe since there hadn't been any attacks against our ships.

My first thought after the explosion was of our ship's carpenter Gennady Lebedev and his wife Tase. The torpedo struck their cabin.

The Boatswain's Mate Lebedev, rushed to a lifeboat and with the help of three sailors, quickly lowered it overboard. I was in the second boat that got away before the ship sank.

Sadly Engineering Officer Pavel Barabkin didn't have time to get out of the engine room. Sending up a young fireman, Lenya Baukova, Barabkin apparently tried to run pumps to bail out the engine room, but there wasn't enough time, and he went down with the ship.

The two boats filled with survivors remained near where our ship went down, searching for other survivors, but in vain. Tase was not among them. Neither was the Orderly Nikitichna Mezdrikovoy Olga, an elderly woman of fifty-three years nor was twenty-year old Ghali Kambuznitsy Bestuzhev.

Suddenly the surface began to seethe and the submarine conning tower with the number of U-601 soon appeared.

When the water subsided on the bridge officer appeared in a fur jacket. For several minutes he looked at the people in the boat, and then in pretty clear Russian said:

"What is the name of the ship? What cargo?"

"Farmer. Arkhangelsk. Went in ballast," I yelled, although I was aware that the Germans could see perfectly that the ship was loaded.

The German still for a moment looked at the sailors and, choosing his words carefully, said: "Sorry. It's a pity we spent torpedoes."

Then, not paying more attention to the remaining people in the stormy sea, the U-boat captain descended into the bowels of the boat, closed the hatch, and submerged.

The wind grew stronger and, worst of all it was blowing from the shore, taking the crippled boat out to sea. Sailors piled on top of the oars, but rowing only warmed the people and the boats drifted westward. Yet the sailors did not give up. Stronger men replaced the feeble. The storm didn't grow stronger; nor did it subside, although the wind direction changed a bit.

On the second day, the fireman Lenya Baucom died, although there were older and weaker survivors than him. For some reason he lost his strength. Perhaps he had a cold after having jumped out of the boiler room to chill stuffy air. Who knows why, since we didn't have a doctor among us.

For over two days we fought wind and waves, fighting to stay near the shore. Finally the day came when we were able to reach Novaya Zemlya. The boats, grinding their bottoms along the rocky shingle, got close enough for the people to jump overboard and make onto the beach. However, final salvation was far away.

We landed on the desert shore and for many miles around there was no shelter. For no particular reason we decided to move along the coast to the south.

Walking was a little easier than rowing. The road was blocked by piles of rocks, sometimes descending to the water's edge, narrow winding bays, far from crashing into the shore. We were forced to deviate from the straight path. Sharp rocks tore our shoes, and bruised our bodies.

The Novaya Zemlya bird rookeries were far apart, and the food from them now was not enough—there were no eggs in the nests, and we couldn't catch the larger chicks with our bare hands.

The starving, ragged, hard frozen survivors marched to the south. They were brave in a battle; they did not give up now. Courage and perseverance won.

*I went ahead, and climbing up to the next rock, saw in the distance,
at the foot of the mountains two fishermen huts. Above one of them rose
smoke. Happily smiling, I whispered "We live" then sat down on cold stone,
waiting for my friends.*

After sinking *Krestyanin*, U-601 continued its patrol and on August 8
entered Kara Sea to gather information about Soviet shipping as well
as ice and weather conditions. She took up a key position off the north
point of Novaya Zemlya island.

After unsuccessful hunting in Kara Gate and Ugorski Shar Straits,
U-209 (Kapitänleutnant Heinrich Brodda) at last got her chance to
leave a mark on the Arctic Naval War. This mark was destined to be
exceptionally gruesome. On August 16, an NKVD (Soviet Secret Police)
representative in Chabarovo, a small port on the south shore of Ugorsky
Shar Strait, authorized the departure of two ocean tugs, *Komsomolets* and
Nord, which were to tow barge *P 4*, lighter *Sh-500*, and the tug *Komiles*,
which had a malfunctioning engine, to Naryan-Mar.

The *Sh-500* carried construction materials, but the *P 4* had
328 construction crewmen and workers of the Pechora port,
Narjan-Mar, some of whom were probably political prisoners from
Norilskstroi Gulag concentration camps. According to long-standing
practice, the NKVD considered itself a separate and independent
power inside the state. As such, the Soviet Secret Police never bothered
to inform White Sea Naval Command about their departure, and as a
result, the convoy left harbor unescorted, even though minesweepers
T-54 and *T-62* were available in Chabarovo.

As noted in *All World Wars: Operation Wunderland*, at 0700 hours the
next day, two miles from the north shore of Matveev Island, near
the western entrance to Ugorski Shar Strait, Brodda spotted *Komsomolets*
with *P 4* in tow, behind her was *Nord* with *Komiles* and *Sh-500*.

Brodda ordered U-209 to surface and shell P 4. The shells ignited
fires that engulfed the barge, sparking chaos. Inmates were released
from the hold by the guards, and everyone began jumping overboard
to escape the flames. While U-209 shelled P 4, *Komsomolets* cast off the
towline and attempted to leave the area while her radioman, Kozhevina,
reported the attack to Chabarovo.

Brodda saw *Komsomolets*'s attempted escape and ordered his gun
crew to fire on the tug. After several direct hits, this tug, too, caught fire
and began to sink. Brodda was certain that *Komsomolets* was doomed
and returned to finish off *P 4*.

At 0720, after two failed attempts to torpedo the burning *P 4*, *U-209* turned to pursue *Nord*. In the meantime, *Nord* was able to bring *Komiles* and *Sh-500* closer to the shore of Matveyev Island, where she cast off the towline and left in the direction of Ugorski Shar. At 0800 hours, *U-209* shelled *Komiles*, whose crew abandoned ship and were able to reach the safety of the shore.

Ten minutes later came *Sh-500*'s turn. At 0810 hours, Brodda shelled *Sh-500*. After several hits, the cargo lighter slowly went down.

P 4 was still burning when *U-209* moved in to finish the job. Almost out of ammunition, Brodda launched a torpedo which smashed into the barge's exposed side, sinking it quickly. Brodda noticed that one ship escaped. Concerned that it had sent out an alarm, he headed north to the shores on the Novaya Zemlya.

As soon as the men stationed at Chabarovo learned about the massacre on Matveyev Island, minesweepers were dispatched to pick up survivors. At 1140 hours, *T-54* and *T-62* met *Nord*, which turned back and joined the rescue force. Four hours later, the ships picked up *Komiles*'s survivors and also found *Komsomolets*, which eventually reached the island with only five of the original nineteen crewmembers on board still alive. From the total amount of 328 men on board *P 4*, only twenty-three were rescued. Not one of the construction workers, inmates, or guards from *P 4* survived the ordeal, and 305 people remain forever at the bottom of the Pechora Sea.

On August 19, *U-209* attempted to enter Belushya Guba, but was spotted by the motorboat *Poliarny* and two Soviet minesweepers, *T-39* and *T-58*. A firefight promptly erupted. Neither side sustained any damage, but with so much opposition in the area, *U-209* headed for quieter waters.

As U-boats wreaked havoc in the Kara Sea, Luftwaffe reconnaissance planes detected two convoys on August 15. Consisting of more than fifty ships in total, the convoys had left Arkhangelsk a week before and turned to the east to Belushya Guba, heading toward the Vilkitsky Strait. Both convoys were accompanied by almost all the icebreakers the Soviet Chief Administrator of the Northern Sea Route had at his disposal.

Admiral Scheer, commanded by Wilhelm Meendsen-Bohlken, set out from Narvik to the Barents Sea on August 16. Because so much depended on the accurate decoding of Soviet radio traffic, *Admiral Scheer*'s crew was joined by a Kriegsmarine *Funkaufklärung* (radio intelligence) team, most of whom spoke fluent Russian.

Weather conditions remained a major concern, and German planners were careful to take this into consideration. In addition to submarines and a network of stations stretching from Spitzbergen to Novaya Zemlya and even to the mouth of Lena River, five BV-138s were to patrol along the most important shipping routes.

An ice conditions report, transmitted by *U-601* to Kriegsmarine headquarters in Narvik on August 15, looked promising. The Germans decided to proceed with Operation *Wunderland*. At 1500 hours on August 16, *Admiral Scheer*, accompanied by destroyers *Z-16 Friedrich Eckoldt*, *Z-15 Erich Steinbrinck*, and *Z-4 Richard Beitzen*, left anchorage in Ofotfjord, Norway. Reaching Bear Island, approximately 400 nautical miles northwest of Murmansk and on the main Arctic convoy route in complete radio silence, Meendsen-Bohlken parted with his escort and proceeded eastward at full speed.

Foggy, cloudy weather and poor visibility favored *Scheer*'s run across the Barents Sea. On the evening of August 18, *Scheer* entered the Kara Sea and lowered her Arado seaplane on the water for a reconnaissance flight. After nine days of searching fruitlessly for Soviet convoys, *Scheer*'s lookouts sighted an enemy ship at 1100 hours on August 25. It turned out to be the old Soviet icebreaker *Alexander Sibiryakov*

An Arctic workhorse, *Alexander Sibiryakov* was one of the most well-known ships to sail along the Northern Sea Route. After the start of the war, *Sibiryakov* was armed with two 76-mm naval guns, two 45-mm guns, and two 20-mm anti-aircraft Oerlikons, and her crew was joined by thirty-two gunners. During the first year of the war, *Sibiryakov* was employed mostly in the White Sea carrying troops, artillery shells, and food rations and evacuating the wounded.

On August 23, *Sibiryakov*'s captain Anatoly Kacharava was ordered to deliver supplies for the weather stations on Severnaya Zemlia near the Taymyr Peninsula across the Vilkitsky Strait between the Kara and Laptev Seas. The crew and construction materials also were to be delivered for the new planned station on Cape Molotov. *Sibiryakov* was loaded with 350 tons of supplies for the weather station and a large cargo boat known locally as a *kungas* used for delivering supplies to shore. In addition, three hundred barrels of gasoline fuel were stored on deck. *Sibiryakov* had a crew of 47 sailors, 32 gunners, and 23 civilians (mostly personnel for the weather stations), along with two officers of the White Sea Naval Command in charge, for 104 in total.

By midday on August 25, *Sibiryakov*, on course to Cape Olovianny on Severnaya Zemlia, approached three islands, Belukha, Centralny, and Dolgy, which already had become visible on the horizon in the clear and cold Arctic air. At 1317 hours, as the crew was going to have lunch, Senior Signalman Alexeyev reported that he observed smoke from an unknown ship. Kacharava ordered his radioman Sharshavin to request identification.

Three messages were sent, but *Scheer* didn't reply. "Large capital ship," reported Alexeyev. "Yes, battleship or cruiser," replied Kacharava, observing the ship with his binoculars. "Here goes the bridge, massive gun turrets … Emergency message to Dikson in clear: 'Battleship near Belukha Island, country of origin is unknown.'" Kacharava was puzzled: there was no reason to sail in friendly waters without a flag.

On board *Admiral Scheer*, Meendsen-Bohlken faced a difficult dilemma. He could open fire immediately and quickly sink the old icebreaker, but with *Arado* grounded due to a lack of fuel, he also desperately needed information from the Soviets about ice conditions and the convoys' movements.

Scheer turned in the direction of the icebreaker, hoisted an American flag, and identified herself as *Tuscaloosa*. But the trick didn't work. Due to a German signal mistake, *Sibiryakov* signalmen read the name of the ship not as *Tuscaloosa*, but as the Japanese-sounding *Siyasima*.

Even if Alexeyev had got the name right, Kacharava knew that the American cruiser *Tuscaloosa* occasionally visited the Barents Sea and that, in fact, it entered Kola Bight in the evening hours of August 23 and left Murmansk on the following day. It was physically impossible for the American cruiser to be near Belushya Island on August 25, 1,300 miles from Murmansk.

Kacharava realized the approaching ship could only be German and ordered course to be set for Belushya Island. He then ordered a general alarm. Guns were quickly prepared for action as the firefighting crew connected water hoses and ship medics deployed a makeshift hospital to treat wounded.

At 1338 hours, Kacharava ordered his radioman to send a message in clear to Northern Sea Route Command in Port Dikson that an unknown battlecruiser had hoisted an American flag and was approaching fast. Dikson replied immediately that there were no American or Japanese ships in the area and that the ship in question could only be an enemy's raider, confirming Kacharava's suspicions. *Sibiryakov* was instructed to act according to standing battle orders.

The radio team on board *Scheer* was carefully monitoring radio messages from *Sibiryakov* and understood at once that their disguise hadn't worked. They demanded the Soviet ship stop radio transmission immediately. Receiving no reply, *Scheer* hoisted the Kriegsmarine battle flag and ordered *Sibiryakov* to stop her engine.

Sibiryakov was in a desperate situation. Belushya Island was still 10 miles away, and it would take the icebreaker more than an hour to reach it. At the same time, the distance between the ships was too large for *Sibiryakov*'s 76-mm guns to be effective.

Kacharava and his crew decided to fight. He sent a message to Port Dikson: "Enemy ship is closing on us, we will fight," followed shortly by one more message: "Shooting has started," and a last message, several minutes later: "... continue to fight ..."

The last two messages were not received by Dikson because *Scheer*'s powerful radio transmitter jammed all frequencies.

"Open fire," Kacharava ordered his gunnery officer Nikiforenko. *Sibiryakov*'s guns fired, but the distance was too great and the shots fell short of the German battlecruiser.

Nikiforenko saw through his rangefinder that the cruiser's dreaded 280-mm guns began to move. Kacharava ordered: "Smoke screen, helm to port, set course for Belushya Island, full ahead!"

The first German salvo slightly overshot the target, the close explosions shaking the ship. The phone line between the bridge and the guns was broken. Splinters cut down the fore-top-mast and destroyed the radio antenna.

At 1353 hours, *Scheer*'s next salvo landed right on target: a 305-kilogram shell struck the gun platform on the stern. The explosion was enormous. Kacharava saw pieces of boxes, trunks, boats, and spent shell cartridges flying high through the air. The stern gun was destroyed, its crew killed in the blast.

A third salvo straddled the icebreaker, this time hitting the bow. Hot splinters pierced gasoline barrels and many exploded, quickly spreading fire. Kacharava was heavily wounded and fell unconscious, his arm heavily damaged and bleeding.

The fourth salvo sealed *Sibiryakov*'s fate. Shells tore through the deck and exploded below, damaging the boiler and ripping gaping holes in the hulk. *Sibiryakov*'s engine went silent. At 1405, second in command Lieutenant Elimelach ordered everyone to abandon ship and launched the only undamaged lifeboat. But not everyone heard or followed this order. Some were left on board or were unwilling or unable to leave the ship, wounded or cut off by the wall of fire from the burning barrels of fuel.

An enormous column of smoke completely obscured the ship. Closing in on her victim, *Scheer* waited more than twenty minutes for the flames to begin to subside. *Sibiryakov* was visibly low in the water, but was refusing to sink. Miraculously, her last gun continued firing. Meendsen-Bohlken decided to deliver a *coup de grâce* and at 1428 ordered a final salvo from point-blank range, which at last silenced *Sibiryakov*. The valiant ship finally sank at 1500 hours.

Before the battle began, Kacharava ordered his chief engineer, Bochurko, to scuttle the ship in order to prevent the Germans from searching and seizing the icebreaker. Receiving word that Kacharava had died (a false rumor) and that a German launch was approaching, Bochurko decided to act and descended into the bowels of the ship, never to be seen again.

Meanwhile, still hoping to get information they needed, the Germans decided to capture survivors and lowered the launch, which quickly approached *Sibiryakov*'s lifeboat as it carried Soviet survivors. Stoker Matveyev, who was in the boat, threw an axe at a German officer and was shot on the spot.

German sources reported that some sailors refused to be rescued, instead jumping overboard. They were left behind in the ice-cold water, doomed for death. Several Germans jumped into the captured lifeboat and beat up survivors with gun butts, forcing them to board the German launch. Of the compliment of 104, the Germans picked up twenty-two survivors, including the wounded and unconscious Kacharava, radioman Sharshavin, and Zolotov, the head of the planned weather station on Severnaya Zemlia.

Meendsen-Bohlken was disappointed. *Sibiryakov* made *Scheer*'s presence in the Arctic known. The ensuing skirmish had warned the Soviets in the most deadly manner about the presence of the Germans, and the convoys certainly would react to the danger. Captured crewmembers could tell their captors only the name and destination of the ship. Because *Sibiryakov* was not part of any convoy, the Germans were unable to obtain any new information about other ships.

Meanwhile, the wounded Kacharava remained unconscious. The Germans assumed he was a regular crewmember; his true identity was only revealed much later. Also, as it turned out, Zolotov, the unlucky head of the polar station, was a geologist, not a meteorologist, and he knew little about the general conditions of the weather or the ice in the area. Nor was he aware of the current forecast, information that would be of the most value to the Germans.

At 1545 hours, August 25, the Germans intercepted a radio signal from the Soviets' Western Sector Command Headquarters of the Northern Sea Route Main Directorate, warning that an enemy auxiliary cruiser was operating in the Kara Sea. Soon *Scheer*'s lookouts spotted a Soviet boat, apparently looking for *Sibiryakov*, which at that time didn't notice the Germans. But with increasing Soviet naval activity, it was time for *Scheer* to leave the area.

Even after being discovered, Meendsen-Bohlken still stubbornly hoped to meet Soviet convoys near Cape Zhelaniya. But he received orders to turn northwest, into the empty Kara Sea. During the night, *Scheer*'s lookouts saw only the occasional ice field, and by the morning hours of August 26, Meendsen-Bohlken decided that because the element of surprise had been lost, he would be unable to intercept any Soviet ships in the open sea.

A more promising idea was to attack a port. There Meendsen-Bohlken not only could find merchant ships at anchor, but he also could capture senior commanders, enemy headquarters with documentation about convoy movements, detailed maps of the area, weather forecasts, naval codes, and other troves of information.

Meendsen-Bohlken could choose between two ports, both of which were among the most important centers of the Northern Sea Route in the Kara Sea: Amderma and Dikson Island. The Germans erroneously believed that Amderma was the key center for unloading Allied convoys because of the constant Luftwaffe bombing sorties against Murmansk. Meendsen-Bohlken knew, though, that if that were true, Amderma, located on the southwest coast, most likely would be well protected by shore batteries. In addition, the port was situated uncomfortably close to Soviet naval and air bases.

The remote Port Dikson looked like a much more promising target. Careful analysis of Soviet radio traffic during *Sibiryakov*'s ordeal indicated that Dikson functioned as a hub in the Arctic support network, transmitting orders to other ports and ships, and, because of the amount and type of radio communications it was most likely Western Sector Command Headquarters. If Port Dikson could be damaged or destroyed by heavy bombardment and searched by a landing party for intelligence information, the main aim of the Operation *Wunderland*— suppressing navigation along the Northern Sea route—could still be attained.

Unknown to the Germans was that in July 1941, the head of the Soviet shipping company Glavnoe Upravlenie Severnogo Morskogo Puti (GUSMP), Ivan Papanin, contacted Admiral Nikolai G. Kuznetsov and asked to reinforce Dikson defenses with "some guns." Papanin, an NKVD associate, had developed personal connections with Stalin and military brass and was able to submit his requests directly to Soviet leaders. Thus, Port Dikson's defenses were enforced with two batteries: #226 Naval with two 130-mm guns, and #246 anti-aircraft with two 45-mm guns. Later, another heavy battery, #569 equipped with two heavy 152-mm siege guns forged in 1910.

Dikson's senior officers met on board the *Dezhnev* during the evening hours of August 26 to discuss the port's defense. They decided to form two groups of local militia under the leadership of the Dikson polar station chiefs, Sidorin and Statov. Women and children were to be transported to a small hunters' settlement on River Lembrovka. GUSMP secret documents were to be stored there as well and prepared for burning on short notice.

Meanwhile, Lieutenant Kornyakov, commander of the battery #569 at Port Dikson, acting on his own initiative, ordered the 152-mm shells for his guns unloaded from the barge and selected volunteers for the gun crews from local longshoremen. Key commanding figures of the defense, Commissar Babintsev from the White Sea Naval Group and Senior Lieutenant Gidulianov, captain of SKR-*19*, decided to strengthen port defenses. Just before midnight, these two men left port on a motorboat to check the shoreline of Cape Kretchatik on Dikson Island to determine the best place to install 130-mm batteries. Their boat was accompanied by the port tug *Molokov* towing a barge carrying both the 130-mm guns and ammunition.

Dezhnev had the same light armament as *Sibiryakov* of four 76-mm guns, four 45-mm guns, and four 20-mm Oerlikons aircraft guns, none of which was remotely effective enough to fight a battlecruiser. Naval forces were not markedly enhanced when, later that evening, Port Dikson defenses were joined by the merchant ship *Revolutionary*, under the command of Captain Panfilov, of North Sea Route command. *Revolutionary* was armed with one 76-mm gun, one 45-mm gun, and two anti-aircraft Oerlikons, and she was carrying a cargo of timber. To make matters even worse, the third and the last vessel in Port Dikson was the unarmed cargo ship *Kara*, loaded with several hundred tons of ammonal, a powerful explosive used for mining and creating canals of clear water in the ice fields.

At 0105 hours on August 27, militia lookouts near the former position of gun battery #226 in the northwestern corner of Port Dikson caught a glimpse of the dark silhouette of *Admiral Scheer* moving to the south along the western shore of the island. The lookouts immediately contacted Dikson. An alarm was sounded, and the Port Dikson radio station began transmitting in clear the frightening news of the impending attack.

After the enemy's approach was reported, two lookouts picked up the only available rifle with a single 5-cartridge clip. They ran along the shore, keeping *Scheer* in sight and prepared to open fire on a possible German landing party. Indeed, if Meendsen-Bohlken had known that Dikson Island, GUSMP headquarters, and its radio station were not protected by any naval guns from the west, his landing party could easily have captured the island. Instead he chose to attack Dikson Island, Port Dikson on the mainland, and ships in the inner harbor simultaneously.

Dezhnev, standing near Conus Island coal terminal in the middle of the inner harbor, under command of Gidulianov's second in command, Lieutenant Krotov, began to move away from the terminal. But there wasn't enough time to take up a safer position under the protection of the shore. In twenty-five minutes, *Scheer* passed Skuratov navigation station at the entrance to the south harbor, 4.5 miles from the port.

Meendsen-Bohlken decided to take Dikson Island with a well-armed, 180-man landing party, supported by 280-mm and 150-mm naval guns. In order to minimize the landing party boats' exposure to the Soviet fire, *Scheer* had to launch landing operations as close to the GUSMP center as possible and needed to suppress any Soviet artillery. He foresaw no serious opposition, at most anticipating some disorganized and inaccurate fire from one or two merchant ships, several light guns of shore defenses, and counterattacks from the Port Dikson garrison, which, according to their estimates, consisted of the half-company (fifty to sixty soldiers) of NKVD border guards troops armed with rifles and, perhaps, a few machine guns.

In fact, the garrison also had two 37-mm antitank guns, one 76-mm anti-aircraft gun, and a 75-mm field howitzer. Border guards and approximately three hundred local militia armed with rifles, carbines, and hunting guns patrolled the port. But light artillery and hunting guns would not be enough to survive for long under the 280-mm guns firing at point-blank range.

Since Port Dikson already started hectic radio transmissions, the Germans knew they had lost the element of surprise and the shock effect of the heavy naval bombardment.

Meanwhile *Dezhnev* at last left the coal terminal, and Krotov changed speed from slow to full ahead, turning his ship toward the enemy. He decided to attack *Scheer*'s portside. If *Dezhnev* was damaged, he figured, the ship could be sunk between Pirozhok Island and the Vega shallows, blocking the entrance to the inner harbor. As *Dezhnev* passed the pier, her crewmen saw artillery crews and volunteer longshoremen trying to manually maneuver the heavy, unwieldy artillery pieces into firing position on the dock.

As *Scheer* closed to within 4 miles, Krotov, who wanted to buy as much time as possible, ordered his signalmen to send a message to *Scheer* asking her to identify herself. This time the Germans didn't try the "Tuscaloosa routine" again. As soon as *Scheer*'s fire control got visuals on the ships in the port, the German battlecruiser opened fire.

Dezhnev's bow guns fired back and then Krotov turned slightly to port to open *Scheer* for the guns on the stern. Gunners targeted not the impenetrable steel hulk, but her bridge, fo'c'sle, and rangefinders. It was their only chance to inflict at least some damage. They claimed later that they observed several bright flashes from hits on the battlecruiser's superstructure, but German sources don't mention any.

Soon *Dezhnev* was buffeted by two salvos. She then was hit by a third, between the third and fourth cargo holds. At first the Germans used armor-piercing shells, which passed almost harmlessly through *Dezhnev*'s hull, but the German gunners soon understood their mistake and switched to the high-explosive shells. Heavy shells damaged *Dezhnev*'s rangefinder, both 76-mm guns, and a heavy machine gun. Splinters ripped open a number of underwater holes; the biggest, found later in the hulk, was two square feet. Splinters also produced some leaks in the coal storage compartment, which were inaccessible for quick repairs. Six members of the crew were killed instantly from the blasts. One more died later the same day, and twenty sailors were wounded.

Dezhnev put up a smoke screen and started to move slowly to the entrance of Samoletnaya Bay, which provided better protection from the murderous fire of the heavy naval guns. At 0146 hours, *Dezhnev* discontinued the battle. She already had taken on tons of water, and her captain, Gidulianov, was determined to prevent capsizing. But he soon faced another problem. Eight minutes later, the ship ran aground and became a stationary target with almost all her armament out of action. The damage control party later reported that it would take at least three hours to cover all holes and pump the water out.

With *Dezhnev* out of the picture, *Scheer* concentrated her fire on *Revolutionary*, which was barely visible through the smoke screen. In just five minutes, *Revolutionary* took three hits which started fires on the deck and wooden bridge, damaged several compartments inside the ship, and destroyed the steam line and anchor winch, preventing the ship from weighing the anchor and making her an easy target.

Luckily for the defenders, *Scheer* had yet to observe the third ship, *Kara*, heavily laden with explosives and invisible behind the protection of the rocky shore and *Dezhnev's* smoke screen. Even one well-placed shell would spark a huge explosion and completely obliterate the port and defense forces. That hadn't happened yet, but *Kara's* discovery was only a matter of time.

In mere minutes, the Soviets had found themselves on the verge of complete annihilation. All their naval forces were out of action, and it seemed nothing stood between the German landing party and the command center of the Northern Sea Route.

In this crucial moment of Operation *Wunderland*, Kornyakov's 152-mm guns opened fire. No hits were registered, but high columns of sea water rose in the air close to *Scheer*.

According to *All World Wars*, Kornyakov had positioned his guns not on the pier itself, where they would be visible against the water, but near where the pier connected to the shore, making the guns much less visible. Because of this position, with its dark, rocky background, along with the murky haze of the late summer Arctic night, fog, and *Dezhnev's* smoke screen, no one on board *Scheer* knew how many guns the Soviets had or where they were located.

Nor did Meendsen-Bohlken know that he was dealing with vintage siege guns of pre-World War I design or that they were standing in the open without any camouflage, firing blindly through the smoke and fog without any rangefinders or any observation posts. He didn't know that the guns were serviced by poorly trained crews and untrained, though enthusiastic, volunteers under the command of an inexperienced lieutenant from backwater Arctic shore defenses.

But Meendsen-Bohlken had been well aware of the fate of the heavy cruiser *Blucher*, which was sunk by the antiquated Norwegian gun battery in Oslo-Fjord on April 9, 1940. He also knew about the disastrous end of the battleship *Bismarck*, which, in May 1941, received a hit in the fuel tank and later another hit in the steering compartment, enough for the British to close in for the kill. He thought that if *Scheer* attempted to move closer, sooner or later she could be hit and that any damage, even minor, in the middle of the inhospitable Arctic might prove fatal.

The main problem for Kornyakov, in the meantime, was not *Scheer*'s return fire, but how to handle the enormous recoil at unprepared artillery positions. The guns' spades were sliding on a slippery surface, and, weighing in at almost 8 metric tons, the artillery pieces were being thrown by recoil so far back that crews had to use a small port truck on the pier to return the guns into position. Later, the men used logs to block the spades and the rate of firing increased.

At 0146 hours, after battery #569 fired forty shells, Meendsen-Bohlken decided to disengage. After laying a smoke screen, *Scheer* disappeared behind Cape Anvil four minutes later. But Meendsen-Bohlken was still certain that even now, when the enemy's heavy artillery remained unsuppressed and the landing part of the operation had to be aborted, his trump card—accurate fire—could still overcome the Soviet defenses, or at least inflict irreparable damage on the port.

Moving north along the shoreline of Dikson Island, from 0214 to 0219 hours, *Scheer* shelled the Great Bear Island weather station. Kornyakov's battery again opened fire, aiming at the sounds of *Scheer*'s guns and the reddish glare of distant salvos, but didn't hit anything.

Scheer stopped firing to assess inflicted damage to the port infrastructure. Meendsen-Bohlken apparently was satisfied with the report: the oil depot and coal storage on Conus Island were burning fiercely, several radio masts were cut by splinters or toppled over, and the radio center and its power station were ablaze, as were several buildings in the settlement.

During the bombardment, Meendsen-Bohlken received reports that 20 percent of the ammunition on board the *Scheer* had been expended. Fire from the Soviet 152-mm battery continued, and he at last decided to lay a smoke screen once again and disengage rather than risk wasting precious ammunition. *Scheer* turned sharply starboard and disappeared in the vastness of Kara Sea. The battle for Port Dikson was over.

The Germans considered the battle a success. Two ships were heavily hit, one of which ran aground; port installations were destroyed; oil storage was burning; and the radio center and weather station on the Great Bear Island had been shelled into oblivion. It looked like the hub of the Northern Sea Route was put out of action for a long time. In addition to optimistic observation reports, the Germans soon intercepted a Soviet message that the Soviet ship *Valerian Kuibyshev* was lost. Meendsen-Bohlken assumed that she was on the Port Dikson anchorage as well, though in reality *Kuibyshev* was sunk on August 24 by *U-601* to the northwest of Dikson. The ship's crew perished and it was two weeks before the wreck was found.

In fact, the permanent damage inflicted by the bombardment was negligible. The port was not taken, and no vital information about the Northern Sea Route was captured. Steel radio masts were promptly fixed and erected, the power station remained intact since shells hit only barrels with spent oil stored nearby, and the fires on Conus Island were soon extinguished. Port Dikson resumed regular transmissions in just two days, even before *Scheer* reached Narvik.

Revolutionary was repaired in three days, *Dezhnev* in six. Miraculously, except for seven sailors aboard *Dezhnev*, nobody else was killed by *Scheer*'s shells. The icebreakers *Litke* and *Taimyr* were sent to Port Dudinka on the Enisei River and in three days returned with enough fuel to supply Port Dikson for the next Arctic convoy.

Scheer's retreat was uneventful. At 2000 hours on August 28, the battlecruiser met with her escort destroyers near Bear Island. Two days later *Scheer* entered anchorage at Tielzund in Schemenfjord. Soon after returning to her base, British reconnaissance planes discovered *Scheer* at anchor. The British Admiralty informed the Soviets that because all German capital ships were found at their Norway bases, the Kara and Barents seas were at last free from German surface raiders.

While the battle for Port Dikson was raging, the Kriegsmarine minelayer *Ulm* left Narvik at 0400 hours on August 24. Mine-laying was to have started on the night of August 27. But before reaching her destination, *Ulm* ran afoul of the British destroyers *Marne*, *Martin*, and *Onslaught* on their way back from Arkhangelsk. In addition to their normal crews, the three destroyers were carrying *Edinburgh* and *Gossamer* survivors.

The morning after leaving Arkhangelsk in company with USS *Tuscaloosa* on August 24, as a consequence of an Ultra intercept, the Admiralty ordered Joe Selby, commanding officer of *Onslaught*, to leave the escort of *Tuscaloosa* and take *Marne* and *Martin* with him.

Selby had been given a position to steer southeast of Bear Island, then a second position due south to North Cape. Naval intelligence informed him that he likely would encounter light surface warships that were suspected to be in the area.

At 2155 hours, British lookouts reported a well-camouflaged enemy merchant ship in the area. A minute later, the three destroyers increased speed to 25 knots, while the enemy turned to port until she was steering directly away. Six minutes later, *Onslaught* opened fire at a range of 9,000 yards, followed immediately by *Marne*.

According to a November 1942 British report, upon first sighting the group of destroyers, Kapitänleutnant der Reserve Ernst Biet, *Ulm*'s commanding officer, at once realized the hopelessness of his position and gave the order to haul down the German flag and hoist the U.S. flag, hoping to deceive the approaching enemy ships. Many in *Ulm* thought the destroyers were Russian, which made them even more anxious owing to the Russians' reputation for taking no prisoners.

Ulm altered course to the westward and then back to southwest and started zigzagging. Her executive officer, Leutnant zur See der Reserve Heinrich Birckenstadt, was on the signal deck. He pointed out to the captain that the U.S. flag was still flying. Biet replied, "Yes, yes, I know" and appeared very agitated. He ordered it to be hauled down and the German flag to be hoisted instead. He then ordered the 10.5-cm gun to open fire.

Ulm was no match for the three British destroyers. While *Marne* and *Martin* straddled *Ulm* with their 4.7-inch armament and the minelayer replied with her only two guns capable of returning fire, *Ulm* scored two hits on *Marne*, knocking out "Y" gun and killing an ordnance artificer. In addition, three men among the *Edinburgh* and *Gossamer* survivors were killed and another five were wounded.

By 2216 hours, the range had closed to 2,500 yards, and the British opened their anti-aircraft guns onto *Ulm*'s bridge to destroy any radio or fire control gear. According to Biet, this burst of fire was responsible for most of the casualties among his ship's company, nearly all of whom had mustered by the bridge preparing to abandon ship.

Marne's salvoes began to fall close to *Onslaught*, so the latter increased speed to 30 knots past the enemy to clear the line of fire. When clear of the smoke, *Marne* was ordered to cease fire and *Onslaught* turned to fire another torpedo. The enemy was swinging slowly to port at the time and eventually stopped, heading approximately 030 degrees.

After firing two torpedoes that missed, *Onslaught* fired her third torpedo at 2231 hours, hitting *Ulm* abreast the foremast and causing a huge explosion and detonating onboard ammunition. An officer who survived the blast reported that it hit *Ulm*'s magazine. The ship broke up completely, sinking in just two and a half minutes at 2235.

Marne closed the sight and rescued fifty-four survivors, but some thirty to forty survivors were left swimming in the water, the British ships considering it imprudent to remain any longer in the vicinity due to the presence of enemy aircraft. Of *Ulm*'s complement of 186 souls, 132 died. Those left behind in the water were among the dead.

After the ground support crews transported to Russia on board USS *Tuscaloosa* were in place, Royal Australian Air Force (RAAF) 455 Squadron and RAF 144 Squadron readied their thirty-two Hampden bombers for the long flight from England. The flight was about thirty minutes beyond the normal endurance of a Hampden. There was some apprehension among the aircrews; it was a long flight toward an unknown destination over inhospitable country and enemy territory, with little hope of a safe forced landing.

On Wednesday, September 2, the aircrews packed small kits of personal belongings into cardboard containers to be carried in the empty bomb bays. It was a beautiful day, and the airmen were in high spirits for an easy flight to the departure point at Sumburgh in the Shetland Islands (the closest airfield to Norway). First into the air was 144 Squadron. They wheeled around and beat-up their home base of Leuchars airfield, some aircraft actually hopping over parked aircraft as they flew around showing off. Wing Commander Grant Lindeman, 455 Squadron's commander, came onto the radio and sternly announced "455 will take off like gentlemen." The ensuing flight was routine as they crossed over the North Sea, which sparkled as they headed north.

The group commander toyed with the idea of sending the aircraft off on the night they arrived to get ahead of bad weather. Fortunately the idea fell through on account of the refueling necessary to make the long trip to Soviet bases. The squadrons were told too late that they would be expected to operate within a day or two of their arrival at the Soviet airbase. Naturally, the squadron commanders objected to this short notice, pointing out that they might easily be held up by bad weather. The arrangements were fixed to a rigid timetable that did not take the weather into account.

Weather was the greatest concern, and it was not looking good. The Group Command was worried that if the squadrons could not fly and be in place at the Soviet airbases in time, questions would be asked in high places. On September 3, Group Command got overexcited and tried to dispatch the squadrons despite a shocking weather report, believing the next day might be even worse. Wing Commanders James McLaughlin and Lindeman refused to take their squadrons into certain disaster, unwilling to lose half their aircraft and men simply to save

Group's face; it would be no use if only a handful of survivors made it to Russia. Their only chance against capital ships was to attack in large formations; anything less would be an ineffectual sacrifice.

So the squadrons waited for the weather to clear. A reasonably clear forecast came in the afternoon of September 4. The decision to go was made. The thirty-two aircraft dispersed around the crowded taxiways of Sumburgh and had their fuel topped off. At the final briefing for pilots and navigators, they were warned of a "nomad," or breakaway barrage balloon, drifting across their track and were warned to steer clear of Rovanimi fighter airfield in Finland.

The support party and reserve crews stood watching as the small airfield resounded to the throb of so many engines starting. Engines were run up to full power against brakes before the aircraft began to slide down the downhill runway. There was no room for error: the airfield runway ended with a 200-foot drop to the sea.

On the ground, Squadron Leader Jimmy Catanach, RAAF, couldn't restrain himself to wait his turn; he taxied into the first gap in the line and was away. Catanach was full of unbridled energy. He didn't drink or smoke and talked at an incredible speed. He couldn't stand still, hopping about all the time. For all that, he was an excellent flight commander and one of the most liked men in the squadron.

Once airborne the aircraft turned north, heading for Burra Firth at the top of the Shetlands. From there they were to set a course to cross the Norwegian coast at 66 degrees North (the Arctic Circle is 66.6 degrees North). The last light faded from the sky as they flew up the Shetlands, and the islands below looked grim and black.

Occasionally they saw a glimmer of light from the window of a cottage below. Lindeman mused about the scene and their situation:

How cosy the occupants must be by their fire in the lamplight, whilst we airmen roar through the night high above with a long stormy passage ahead. In an hour or two they'd yawn and go off to bed and we'll be miles away over the North Sea, bucketing about in rain and cloud, not knowing what evil ones might be lurking in the murk.

These thoughts made him so miserable that he gave up and brooded over the engine gauges instead. Everything was normal. "George," the automatic pilot, was behaving. After take-off, the autopilot often seemed to want to fly at a fixed altitude, and Lindeman had worried he would have to fly manually all the way.

They departed from Muckle Flugga lighthouse, far north in the British Isles, flying over the sea under some unpleasant low cloud. A positive sign was the sight of flickering flame floats, which had been dropped by leading aircraft to calculate drift. They felt less lonely up there in the great empty blackness as they followed the friendly trail—each of those fairy lights bobbing on the water was being watched by someone else who had passed a few minutes earlier. Navigator Les Oliver observed, "Gosh look at 'em all. It's like Bondi Esplanade [in Sydney] on a Sunday night."

The cloud base thickened as they went north, and to stay below it they were forced down to 500 feet, a mucky altitude where great white-capped waves lashed underneath. One aircraft actually bent the tips of one propeller after clipping a wave-top.

Lindeman decided to try to climb above the thick cloud and heavy rain. At 7,000 feet, he broke into clear sky with stars overhead. After some time, he and his fellow flyers noticed the cloud below breaking up, and they soon were able to see the sea and make out the horizon.

Ahead of them was a faint glimmer on the horizon. As they approached, it grew bigger and looked like an orange flame flickering on the sea. Lindeman estimated it to be at about the point where they would turn east to the Norwegian coast. He called up his navigator, Les Oliver. "Yes," replied Oliver. "I've been watching it for some time. Looks like an aircraft burning on the water, doesn't it?" That agreed with Lindeman's assessment, and he instructed his crew to look out for German night fighters in their path. Colin Bastian, the upper gunner, searched the sky ceaselessly.

Lindeman was puzzled: the flame was growing larger, but they didn't appear to be getting any closer. At last the penny dropped. It was the horn of the moon rising out of the sea, partially masked by some low black cloud, which gave it an odd shape and a flickering effect.

Turning toward the Norwegian coast, they could see the thick cloud ahead, which rose to 6,000 feet. To clear the Swedish mountains, they needed 8,000 feet, so they began a steady climb to get above the cloud.

Breaks in the cloud as they crossed the coast and the rising moon made flying easier. Ahead were the great black mountains; below fjords and lakes. But they could not see enough detail to fix their position. Oliver advised everyone that they were on track. Lindeman hoped he was right. Flying under radio silence so as not to give their position away to the Germans, they could not use radio navigation to fix their position. They had kept to their compass course faithfully but had no idea what navigational errors had been introduced by wind drift, compass variation over Sweden, or even the angle of dip caused by using unsuitable compasses in high latitudes.

The weather forecast was for fine weather at dawn over Finland and Russia. The plan, if their track was approximately correct, was that they should be able to spot the Gulf of Kandalaksha on the western end of the White Sea. This and a single railway line were the only landmarks in the surrounding wasteland. Crossing Sweden, the cumulus clouds gave way to a great flat expanse of low-level cloud blotting out the ground. They droned on at 7,000 feet.

Aircraftman Murray Cryer was an engine fitter in August 1942 when he found his name on the noticeboard as nominated to fly overseas on aircraft "A" (for "Apple"). It was replaced by "K" (for "King") just before they left. Cryer noted during the flight that the autopilot required constant course adjustment to maintain track, and over Sweden the crew were surprised to fly over towns with lights on. The rest of Europe was blacked-out each night.

As UB-K (King) ("UB" was the squadron designator for 455 Squadron) climbed to 10,000 feet over the Swedish mountains, Colonel C. Storry and his crew, including Snowy Lovell, Bluey Collins, Sargent R. Sheedy, and Murray Cryer, found the cold unbearable, even with the hot-air pipe jammed up the trouser leg of the heavy Arctic Tropex kit they wore. The ventral gunner at the end of the pipe was the worst off. Over Finland, gun flashes split the darkness as forty anti-aircraft guns opened up. Storry dived to 3,000 feet as a cannon shell passed through the tail and two more hit the wings.

On board UB-H P 5304, after crossing the Norwegian coast, the aircraft was tracked by a German fighter from Bodø across the Swedish border before being shot down. The entire crew was killed in the subsequent crash, though it was many years before facts became known.

As dawn broke over Finland and Russia, the airmen's worst fears were realized—they didn't know where they were and their fuel was running low. Below was a cold, barren wasteland, sparsely wooded with light trees and dotted with myriad lakes. The land was without a significant landmark. A forced landing looked possible for a pilot mindful of his fuel position, but for how many days would they have to walk to find help? Who would help them: Russians or Germans?

Jack Davenport piloting UB-B had only one thought as he looked down: Finding a tree, lining up, and having a pee. After eight hours flying in the cold, he was busting. The crew was jumpy. Now it was dawn, and the scene they saw below was different from any they'd seen in Scotland, England, France, or Germany. Harry Harrison, the upper gunner, sent a chill through the crew when he shouted "Fighters!"

"It's okay! They're Hurricanes!" Davenport fired the recognition flare colors of day.

"They're attacking!" screamed Harrison. The Hurricanes wheeled around, guns blazing. The fighter-like qualities of the Hampden were handy as Davenport avoided first one attack and then a second. Between jinxing, Davenport lowered the wheels and waggled his wings. Harrison waved both arms to the Russians.

The Hurricanes then came alongside and forced the Hampden down. Only late in his approach did Davenport realize he was landing on an airfield. Earth-covered shelters for the Hurricanes camouflaged it so well he wasn't able to make out the field. Later, Squadron Leader Dennis Foster of 144 Squadron also was escorted into what he later learned was Monchegorsk aerodrome.

UB-R, flown by Robert Holmes, was also well north of the track and weren't sure of their position. Earlier he and his crew had been fired on by light, accurate flak while over Finland. Navigator Frank Dick was lost because their compasses were so affected by the iron in the mountains and the angle of dip (i.e., where the compass needle points downward to the North Pole) in the high latitudes.

With "R" for Robert flying at about 8,000 feet in the brightening sky over Finland, Dick spotted light flak coming up. To relieve the boredom, he called up the supernumerary, Bob Raebel, who had probably not seen flak from the receiving end. "Bob," he said, "if you look out to port you'll see some light flak coming up."

Silence.

"Bob? Bob, you there?"

"Yeah."

"Did you want to see the flak out to port?"

"No," came the sullen reply. "I don't want to see any bloody flak!"

At last the crew sighted the coast bordering the Barents Sea. Below was an airfield. They set down cautiously. There appeared to be Hampdens in the dispersal area. As they circled, a green light winked, inviting them to land.

The Hampden was often visually confused with the German Dornier Do-17 bomber. On the final approach, Frank Dick in the nose suddenly called to his pilot Robert Holmes: "Bob, those planes have got crosses on them!"

Holmes pushed the throttles open and got the undercart up. As they went over the end of the airfield, anti-aircraft mortar bombs called "Flying Onions" whistled past them trailing cables.

Now they knew they were at Petsamo in Finland. Following the coast, they located the Kola Inlet. Again they were met by a barrage of anti-aircraft fire, this time from the Soviet Naval Base at Polyarnoe. Turning south, they flew past Vaenga and picked up the Murmansk–Kandalaksha railway, which would lead them to the Soviet Afrikander air base.

To Dick, Afrikander appeared busy with Hampdens dispersed around the field. Fuel was getting critical, and there was a light mist at ground level. Holmes made a normal approach down to 20 feet when suddenly the mist thickened and the ground disappeared. Below, airmen ducked as wheels came through the mist and Holmes went around again. The mist held off on the second approach, and they were able to land.

In PL-K, Sergeant John Bray, also lost in the Petsamo area, was shot down by a Messerschmitt. Bray parachuted clear, but his crew was killed in the ensuing crash.

"Jeep" Patrick in UB-L came a little later into Afrikander. After several attempts at landing in the mist, his fuel position also was critical. He flew toward Kandalaksha, searching for an emergency landing ground. All he could find was an area where the silver birch trees had been cut down, leaving tall thin stumps. Jeep elected to make a wheels-up landing. Turning to approach, both motors stopped. He was gliding. With the supernumerary aboard, it was cramped as the crew braced themselves against the wing spars. In the cockpit the navigator, Leo Clohessy, braced himself for the crash.

The Hampden hit and slithered on her belly, tree stumps tearing at her until she came to rest. Miraculously, she was largely intact and on an even keel, and no one was hurt. Ronny Bryans, the supernumerary, rushed back to collect the cardboard container holding his kit. These containers were strewn along the crash path when the bomb bay had been torn open.

As Bryans reached for the container, a bullet smacked into the ground at his feet. He dropped to his knees, thinking of the revolver stashed in the container. Looking around, he could see no one. For the second time that morning, an Australian acknowledged the Russian mastery of camouflage.

Heeding the warning shot, Bryans ambled nervously back to the others at the aircraft, forgetting the revolver. As they waited, knowing that they had an unseen guard, Bryans removed the clock from "L" for London's instrument panel as a souvenir.

Further north Sergeant W. Hood, piloting a 144 Squadron machine AE356, broke through cloud over the Kola Inlet. Suddenly the crew found themselves in the middle of a fighter dogfight. It was unclear whether Soviet or German bullets brought them down. Hood brought the aircraft down to a forced landing in a lake.

Everyone except the lower gunner, Sergeant W. Tabor, was more or less unhurt and tried to get out of the aircraft. They came under Soviet rifle fire from the shore. The Soviets knew it wasn't one of their aircraft. Meanwhile, a desperate struggle developed to get Tabor from his compartment in the sinking aircraft. But they failed, and Tabor was trapped. Later, he was buried at Vaenga.

In UB-K, Murray Cryer, the engine fitter, sat nervously on the D spar behind the pilot.

"Fighters! Coming in from port!" yelled Sheedy, the upper gunner.

Cryer grabbed a spare Vickers machine gun from its rack and attempted to push it out through the beam-gun port. He had to fight the slipstream to get the gun mounted, and then he found the port wingtip occupied most of his field of fire. The moment passed as the gunner called, "Hurricanes! They must be Russian Hurricanes!"

Jimmy Catanach's aircraft UB-C had crossed the mountains, but compass error had pulled him well north of the track. Catanach crossed the coast over the Barents Sea near Kirkennes on the Finnish–Norwegian border when he was forced down by flak from the German armed trawler, *Ubootjager 1105*.

With his fuel tanks punctured and leaking, Catanach knew he could neither return nor go on, so he elected to make a wheels-down landing on a beach. Fate stepped in as the aircraft stopped exactly where a German patrol was waiting. The crew was captured before they had time to destroy their aircraft. Catanach himself, Australia's youngest squadron leader at the time, was shot by the Germans two years later in reprisal for his part in the "Great Escape" (a mass escape attempt of Allied prisoners in 1944; fifty men were summarily shot as a warning to others). The Germans found papers on the aircraft referring to the radio organization for PQ-18 and QP-14, which when put together with a deciphered signal to the Soviet 95th Naval Flight Regiment, gave them a good picture of the convoys' routes and timetables.

Mystery surrounded Sargent Sandy Smart and his crew in UB-H. Some airmen were positive that he was seen over Afrikander, while others stated that fighters over Finland were seen chasing him. Another firmly held theory was that he had been brought down by Swedish flak;

this is unlikely given the desolate area they crashed in. It was learned later that the entire crew was killed when their aircraft crashed at Aravst Uttar, Sweden.

144 Squadron was less fortunate, losing six aircraft, the most spectacular of which was PL-J serial AE436, piloted by Pilot Officer I. Evans. With one motor overheating, the pilot could not maintain altitude as he crossed the Swedish mountains. He flew into rising ground on a scree-covered slope of Tsatsa Mountain, about 15 miles north of their track. The aircraft broke up badly, wrapping around on itself, nose against tail, but staying right-side up. Only the pilot and supernumerary survived. Relatively unscathed, they walked for three days before happening on the village of Kvikkvok, 20 miles southeast of the crash site.

It quickly became apparent that very few Russians had been told the Hampdens were expected. Even the Soviet pilots covering the narrow air corridor assigned to the flight seemed largely unaware. The whole area north of Kandalaksha was a war zone, and isolated crews were thought to be Germans by the simple soldiers and peasants—and they were treated accordingly.

Davenport, after landing at Mongiegorsk, found his aircraft surrounded by peasants with pitchforks. "Harry," he called to the upper gunner, "the natives don't look friendly, better stay by your guns." Still harboring a strong desire to empty his bladder before negotiating, Davenport climbed down. Relief was almost his when suddenly the embarrassed young Australian noticed there were many women among the peasants. "Angliyskiy," he called pointing to himself. "Churchill, Stalin, RAF."

His words were met with blank stares. The English gunner called down insubordinately, "Tell 'em the truth you mug. You're a bloody Australian."

At last the Russian-speaking Commissar, Kapitan Nikolaev, arrived. Recognizing they probably weren't German, he had Davenport and his crew escorted to an underground bunker. What the British believed to be glasses of water were offered around in an amusing ceremony, and the young fliers followed the Commissar's example, knocking them back in one gulp. They had never drunk vodka before. Breathless and reeling from the fiery spirit, they fought to speak.

Milling around near the wreck of their aircraft UB-L, Jeep Patrick and his crew fidgeted, knowing they were being observed and guarded by an unseen sniper just 15 miles inside the Eastern Front.

Eventually a troop of soldiers arrived and, thinking the Australians were the hated Nazis, treated them quite roughly. One story has it that Jeep Patrick was bayoneted in the backside, though Ron Bryans had no memory of the incident.

Things got better when they were taken to an underground interview room. An English-speaking commissar was able to understand their wondrous tale and verify it through Afrikander. Later they were reunited with the squadron at Afrikander.

The next day, a Russian SB3 bomber escorted the Hampdens, three at a time, to Vaenga. As Cryer's aircraft made a port turn onto its final approach to land, the port motor quit, probably due to a mix-up changing fuel tanks. The loss of an inboard motor was normally fatal turning at low altitude and low speed. The inner wing of the turn would stall; the faster outer wing still giving lift would flip the aircraft over into an incipient spin. Typically, the aircraft would crash into the ground before the pilot could recover control. On this occasion, however, Cryer managed to keep control and land normally. Even the Russians came forward to congratulate him on saving the aircraft.

Overall the losses were a disaster, losing nine of thirty-two aircraft, precisely the loss rate anticipated for an attack on a major warship. 455 Squadron lost three aircraft; 144 Squadron was less fortunate, losing six aircraft.

Challenges continued throughout the month of September for the Allies working in and around the Arctic Circle. On September 26, 1942, sailors of the Soviet timber ship *Sacco*, passing near Belushya Island, saw a strange bearded man on the beach wearing rags, desperately waving a large white flag and obviously trying to attract their attention. *Sacco* stopped the engine, but was unable to launch a rescue boat because of high waves.

The ship's radioman reported the sighting to Port Dikson and got everybody at GUSMP HQ highly agitated. The stranded man could only be a sailor from the icebreaker *Sibiryakov*, sunk by *Admiral Scheer* in August. Fortunately, a Soviet seaplane piloted by Kaminski was in the air at the time, not far from Belushya and Dikson, and was ordered to pick up the survivor or to at least drop some food and a note for the man, asking him to hold on until he could be rescued.

Due to stormy conditions, the seaplane wasn't able to land, so the pilot dropped a bag with cacao powder, condensed milk, bread, medications, and warm winter clothes, along with a note promising rescue as soon as the storm subsided. Three days later, Cherevichny, one of the most experienced polar pilots, approached the shore to rescue the man. Excited, the man couldn't wait, jumped into the icy water, and started swimming to the seaplane. After being rescued, he was treated for malnutrition in the hospital. Later, he told his incredible story.

Nikolai Vavilov had been a stoker aboard *Sibiryakov*. He had been on board the burning icebreaker with two other men, sailor Safronov and gunner Dunayev, but couldn't escape in time, cut off by the flames and almost suffocated by smoke. When *Sibiryakov* went down, sailors were sucked under by the huge water maelstrom. Safronov and Dunayev drowned, but Vavilov managed to clasp a piece of wood and surface, alone in the middle of the Arctic. He was about to give up when he saw an empty lifeboat floating on the icy sea, survivors from which had only recently been transferred to the *Scheer*. Vavilov managed to reach the boat and pull himself out of the water. In the boat he found the corpse of fellow stoker Matveyev, who died of a gunshot wound.

When *Scheer* disappeared on the horizon, Vavilov decided to set out for Belushya Island, still 5 miles away but likely his only chance for survival. On his way to the island, he found and rescued a blind dog, heavily burned, and collected some floating debris, including a bag with wheat middling (fine particles of wheat bran and fine particles of wheat shorts, wheat germ, wheat flour, and offal from the "tail of the mill"). He also located an emergency supplies box under the bench and secured an invaluable emergency kit with three cans of food, two axes, a loaded handgun, a compass, a sleeping bag, some clothes, matches, a bucket, a flask with water, and a couple of signal flares.

When Vavilov reached Belushya, he unloaded all his treasures on the shore and started his polar odyssey, which would last thirty-four days. Belushya was completely deserted. Vavilov found only the ruins of an old lighthouse. His situation soon became desperate after his boat was crushed by waves during a stormy night and his food and matches were depleted. Vavilov was preparing to give up and die when he saw *Sacco*'s silhouette on the horizon.

Officials visited Vavilov in the Port Dikson hospital, but all he really knew was that the ship went down and that he was the only survivor.

Hopes of the relatives of *Sibiryakov*'s crew, who thought that, after Vavilov's miraculous rescue, other survivors would be found, quickly vanished.

While these battles were being waged, planning went ahead for PQ-18 and QP-14. Both German and British commanders alike believed they had the situation under control and would come out of the next confrontation victorious. No one asked the men at the sharp end of the spear what they thought about the situation.

CHAPTER 8

AN AUTUMN IN HELL
September–December 1942

B y the end of August, the British Admiralty was ready to sail
convoys PQ-18 and QP-14. Because German reconnaissance
aircraft were patrolling over Iceland, where most of the previous
convoys had sailed from, it was decided to sail PQ-18 from Loch Ewe
on the northwest coast of Scotland.

On September 2, the forty-four ships in PQ-18 under Rear Admiral E.
K. Boddam-Whetham serving as a commodore set out for Arkhangelsk.
In company were the two tankers *Gray Ranger* and *Black Ranger* for
refueling the escorts and the rescue ship *Copeland*. As soon as the long
line of ships cleared the Outer Hebrides, they encountered the full force
of an Atlantic gale, which delayed their progress. They were thirty-six
hours late at the rendezvous with the ocean escort.

The ocean escort comprised the two anti-aircraft ships (*Ulster Queen* and
Alynbank), three destroyers, four corvettes, and four trawlers, all of which
joined the merchant ships on September 7. The escort was augmented on
September 9 when Rear Admiral Robert L. Burnett in command of the
fighting destroyer escort, flying his flag in the anti-aircraft cruiser *Scylla*
(commanded by Captain Ian Macintyre), joined the convoy.

For the first time the escort aircraft carrier *Avenger* sailed with the convoy, carrying twelve Sea Hurricane fighters and three Swordfish antisubmarine aircraft. However, the Hurricanes were of the oldest type, and as Admiral Tovey remarked to Churchill, it was ironic that transports crammed with the latest type of Hurricanes for Russia had to be protected by their outworn predecessors.

Additional cover was provided for Convoy QP-14 by a cruiser force under Vice Admiral Stuart Bonham-Carter, consisting of his flagship *Norfolk*, *Suffolk*, and *London* with two destroyers, which operated to the westward of Spitsbergen between September 17–20, in support of *Cumberland*, *Sheffield*, and *Eclipse*, which were landing reinforcements and stores for the Norwegian post at Barentsburg.

Four submarines were stationed close off the coast of Norway to intercept enemy ships going north from Narvik. These were soon joined by three more submarines, forming a shifting patrol line to cover the passage of the convoys east of Bear Island.

In addition to the *Avenger*'s aircraft, improved antisubmarine protection, and reconnaissance by Coastal Command aircraft from Iceland and Russia, the convoys had the support of the two squadrons of torpedo-carrying Hampden bombers based in Russia against possible attack by surface ships in the Barents Sea.

The number of warships assigned to cover PQ-18 and QP-14 totaled seventy-six, a massive accumulation of firepower, but the Germans were ready for them. As mentioned in Chapter 7, Jimmy Catanach's Hampden of RAAF 455 Squadron crashed in Norway, and the Germans found papers referring to the radio organization for PQ-18 and QP-14. This information, when combined with an intercepted signal from the Soviet 95th Naval Flight Regiment, gave the Germans a good picture of the convoys' routes and timetables. The Luftwaffe, whose torpedo bomber strength had increased to ninety-two, was ready and anxious to try to repeat its success against PQ-17. Also, between eight and ten U-boats formed a scouting line across the convoys' projected paths.

German reconnaissance aircraft located PQ-18 late on September 8, but the Germans soon lost sight of it. Thanks to low-lying cloud and occasional fog banks, reconnaissance planes did not find it again until 1320 hours on September 12. However, U-boats had managed to gain and maintain contact during this period, although they were kept at a respectful distance by the *Avenger*'s antisubmarine aircraft, which made several attacks on them and assisted the escort ships in their attacks. It was estimated that there were now no fewer than eight U-boats around the convoy, and the destroyers had a busy time fending them off. In one of these attacks, the destroyer *Faulknor* sank *U-88* at 2100 hours on September 12.

The following day at 0855, *U-408* and *U-589* avenged the loss of their comrade by sinking the freighter *Stalingrad* and tanker *Oliver Ellsworth*, in the outside starboard column. *U-408* fired three torpedoes, one of which hit *Stalingrad* on the starboard side at the coal bunker. She sank in less than four minutes. The starboard lifeboats were destroyed by the explosion, leaving only the portside boats for crewmembers and passengers to use. Adding to the loss, one of the portside boats capsized when reaching the water. Sixteen crewmembers and five passengers were lost. Master A. Sakharov was the last to leave the *Stalingrad*. He spent forty minutes in the freezing water before being rescued.

One of the torpedoes hit *Oliver Ellsworth* (Master Otto Ernest Buford), igniting her cargo of oil. Her crew immediately abandoned ship. But the vessel still had headway, which caused both starboard boats to swamp. One of the portside boats struck a raft and sank. Due to the quick reaction of the British rescue ship *Copeland* and HMS *St. Kenan*, forty-three crewmembers and eighteen gunners were picked up; one armed guard drowned.

The U-boats had scored; now it was the Luftwaffe's turn. The first attack came at 1500 hours when half a dozen Ju-88s dropped their bombs through gaps in the clouds from a height of about 4,000 feet, with no loss to either the convoy or themselves. This was only a taste of what was to come.

Half an hour later, thirty Ju-88s and fifty-five He-111 torpedo bombers carried out a mass attack, the latter employing the Golden Comb technique, approaching in line abreast, 100 to 150 yards apart at a height of about 35 feet above the sea in perfect formation. Each aircraft carried two torpedoes, and all were dropped simultaneously, threatening the convoy with 170 torpedoes.

The pilots launched their torpedoes only at the precise moment when they had just enough space to pull out before crashing into the ships' masts. Riddled by anti-aircraft fire, some of them caught fire and crashed into the sea, but none failed to press home the attack. Ships fired on the planes, the trajectories of their shells crossing the fire of the targeted ships and forming a net of fire over the sea.

Above the deafening din of the ack-ack could be heard the explosions of ships hit by torpedoes. In every ship, the crew was certain that it was quite impossible that their vessel could come unscathed through this inferno.

For Boddam-Whetham, convoy commodore, the contingency plan for massed torpedo attack was a simple 45-degree alteration of course, either to port or starboard using the appropriate international sound signal backed up by a single flag hoist. Its efficacy relied upon good lookouts, prompt response, and coordinated repetition of the signal down the columns. The commodore made his port-turn signal, but the ninth and tenth columns failed to respond due to the sheer size of PQ-18. The outer starboard ships failed to execute the turn and caught the worst of the attack.

One plane flew so close to *Wacosta* that the torpedo failed to hit the water and instead dropped through her No. 2 hatch, exploding inside her hull. The ship had been slowing down, her engines disabled by the terrible explosion of the ship immediately ahead. Leading the ninth column, the *Empire Stevenson* was suddenly enveloped in a tower of flame and smoke, which, when it cleared, left only an oily slick on the water. This was the dreadful penalty of carrying explosives. Although no one from the *Empire Stevenson* survived, all the crew of the *Wacosta* were rescued.

Similarly loaded with tanks and war materials, the *Macbeth*, second ship in the tenth column, succumbed to two torpedoes, while the *Oregonian* ahead of her capsized rapidly after three torpedoes stove in her whole starboard side. Only twenty-seven of her fifty-five-man crew were rescued by the *St. Kenan*, many of them in a fearful condition having swallowed oil and been immersed in the freezing sea.

Macbeth's crew was rescued by *Offa*, whose commanding officer, Lieutenant Commander R. A. Ewing, ran her alongside the Panamanian freighter, so close that several of the destroyer's guardrails and stanchions were crushed. Torpedoes also hit the Russian ship *Sukhona*, as well as *Afrikander*, a Panamanian ship chartered to the U.S. Maritime Commission. Both were abandoned as they sank, their crews efficiently picked up by the close escort ships. Although the rescues were a bit of good news, the day was going poorly for the convoy. With the exception of the *Mary Luckenbach*, the outer two columns of PQ-18 had been annihilated.

The loss of the two outer columns was by no means the end of it all. More losses would come. Leading an inner port column, *Empire Beaumont* was set on fire after a torpedo struck in the only hold not containing explosives. The ship was successfully abandoned. Less fortunate, however, were the crew of the *John Penn*. The three men on duty in her engine room were killed when two torpedoes exploded in their midst.

Amid the confusion, *Copeland*, the trawlers, and the motor minesweepers picked up the merchant sailors from their rafts, lifeboats, and the freezing sea. *Daneman*, one of the four trawlers, was steaming at the rear of the convoy. Seaman Gunner G. R. Lunn, one of the survivors from *Empire Stevenson*, wrote later:

> *One of these four seamen couldn't swim and we put it down to his threshing madly about in the sea which kept him afloat and warm enough to survive. Another older man was about to be rescued when the planes attacked again and we had to get under way and leave him to drown. I can still see him, cold in the water, trying to reach one of our sailor's hands to get a grip so that he could be pulled aboard to safety, but we were being attacked by a torpedo-bomber and the skipper rang full-ahead.*
>
> *We had to leave him and watch his bald head and red football jersey, vanish behind us; as we were the last ship in the convoy he would never be picked up.*

St. Kenan rescued sixty-four survivors during and after the mass torpedo-bomber attack. These included survivors from the American SS *Oregonian*. Ten of her survivors were snatched from the sea, all in horrible condition after swallowing oil and water and being plunged into the icy seas.

Among *Sukhona*'s survivors were a man and his wife who had suffered several broken ribs. Their two children were not among the survivors.

Eight ships had been lost in less than fifteen minutes. Luftwaffe losses amounted to only five aircraft.

The following day, September 14, began with another loss for the convoy. Returning to station from an ASDIC contact, HMS *Impulsive* obtained a second echo and had begun a run in to depth-charge it, but before she could, *U-457* (Korvettenkapitän Karl Brandenburg) torpedoed the tanker *Athel Templar*. *Impulsive* then lost contact as *U-457* dove under the convoy amid the noise of the propeller races and escaped.

Although she was hit in the engine room, the tanker's volatile cargo did not explode. But fire soon made it impossible for her crew to do anything more than abandon ship. The master, forty-two crewmembers, and eighteen gunners were picked up by *Copeland* and *Offa*, one of whose crewmen, James Green, jumped into the icy sea in an abortive attempt to rescue a drowning boy. Green was recovered and revived with difficulty after his exertions. Another sixteen *Athel Templar* crewmembers later died from their injuries.

HMS *Onslow*, following a sighting by one of *Avenger*'s Swordfish, bagged *U-589*, which was stalking the convoy. At 1235 hours, the Luftwaffe again joined the battle with about twenty torpedo aircraft targeting *Avenger* and *Scylla*. The attack cost the Germans another eleven planes, but the losses didn't deter them from further attacks.

As the initial wave of torpedo bombers in this attack disappeared over the horizon, a dozen Ju-88s appeared overhead and started dive-bombing. Several ships, including the *Avenger*, made narrow escapes while the Germans lost another aircraft. Almost immediately, twenty-five torpedo aircraft came in from ahead, dividing as before into two groups, one of which made a dead set for the *Avenger*. *Avenger* had ten fighters in the air, and these, together with the ship's guns, shot down nine more enemy aircraft, but one ship, *Mary Luckenbach* in the starboard wing column, was torpedoed. She blew up with such force that *Nathaniel Greene* right behind her in the column was covered with debris and several of her deck cargo crates burst. Sublieutenant Robert Hughes witnessed the explosion from his gun director on *Scylla*.

> *Tracers began to fly upward from all over the ship as a plane skimmed the masts. Oerlikon gunners lay backward, strapped to their guns, the muzzles pointing skyward and slewing as the gunners scrabbled the deck for purchase to move sideways. The plane kept on steadily though shells kept hitting her, and headed for the* Mary Luckenbach *on our starboard side. She headed on pursued by a few shells, and other targets presented themselves. Suddenly there was a dull roar from starboard, and Freeman shouted and pointed. "Look !"*
>
> *The* Mary Luckenbach *had gone. In her place a stupendous column of smoke was rocketing to heaven, and as we looked an immense glow lit the column, and great cerise, orange-and-yellow fragments arched outwards towards us.*
>
> *"Oh, Good God Almighty," prayed someone.*
>
> *I shuddered in fear. "Oh, God," I prayed. "Oh, God, why have you sent us here? What have we done, what have we done?"*
>
> *"Duck!" came my voice from somewhere deep down, and five heads bent as in prayer, and perhaps we did pray.*
>
> *Still we waited and the seconds flitted past, but there was no crash of metal on top of us. We raised our heads. Fluttering down into the director came large pieces of ash.*
>
> *Mead caught a piece on his hand and smeared it into his palm. "Just like burnt paper," he said quietly and wonderingly.*

The great smoke column was still thousands of feet high and mushrooming out where it met the clouds. At its base flames still flickered, and the following ship was altering course to avoid them. The Mary Luckenbach *had gone, and forty men had died. This was their memorial and the smear on Mead's palm.*

The death toll from *Mary Luckenbach* was forty crewmen and twenty-four armed guards. Incredibly, one man did survive. He was walking along the deck carrying a cup of coffee for the captain when the ship exploded. Next thing he knew, he was in the water a half mile away. Unfortunately, Hughes wasn't able to record his name, just his story.

During this action, three Hurricanes were shot down by the convoy's guns, but the pilots were saved. The final attack of the day began at 1430 hours when about twenty aircraft approached from astern and bombed intermittently through gaps in the cloud for about an hour. Despite the difficult conditions that provided only fleeting glimpses of the attackers, another aircraft was shot down.

The next morning, two large Russian destroyers, *Gremyashchiy* and *Sokrushitelnyy*, and two smaller ones, *Uritski* and *Kuibyshev*, joined the convoy escort screen. When rounding Cape Kanin at 0820 hours on September 18, twelve He-111 torpedo aircraft delivered an attack from the starboard quarter of the convoy dropping their torpedoes at between 3,000 and 4,000 yards range. Although in the commodore's opinion the ships had a good opportunity to avoid them, one ship, *Kentucky*, was hit. Fortunately no one was killed.

A similar attack an hour later was synchronized with a bombing attack by Ju-88s. *Kentucky* was hit again and sunk. All her crew got away safely. The Hurricane aircraft in the CAM ship *Empire Morn* shot down three aircraft and damaged another. The pilot then flew on and successfully landed at a Russian airfield with only four gallons of fuel left in his tank.

At last, on the evening of September 19, the convoy reached the Dvina River leading to Arkhangelsk. PQ-18 lost fourteen ships, more than a third of the total convoy, during the voyage.

Meanwhile, westbound QP-14 with twenty ships sailed from Arkhangelsk for Loch Ewe on September 13. With the convoy of fifteen ships were the rescue ships *Zamalek* and *Rathlin*. The commodore was J. C. K. Dowding, on board the *Ocean Voice*, which also was his ship in PQ-16. The close escort of the two anti-aircraft ships *Palomares* and *Pozarica*, two destroyers, four corvettes, three minesweepers, and three trawlers was under the command of Captain J. F. Crombie, R.N.

After the air battle around PQ-18 on the afternoon of September 16, Admiral Robert L. Burnett began transferring forces from PQ-18 to QP-14. He did this gradually in three groups so as to make it less obvious to the enemy. In addition to *Scylla* and her destroyer escort force, he took the aircraft carrier *Avenger*, the anti-aircraft ship *Alynbank*, the tankers *Gray Ranger* and *Black Ranger*, and the submarines *P 615* and *P 614*.

The weather during the convoy's passage through the Barents Sea was thick with patches of fog and intermittent snow squalls, which favored the defenders and hampered the work of the enemy shadowing aircraft. It was bitterly cold, too, and severe icing conditions impeded the work of the *Avenger*'s antisubmarine aircraft in maintaining constant air patrols around the convoy. Catalina aircraft working from the Kola Inlet assisted in the patrols.

As for the Kriegsmarine, instructions had been given to eight U-boats to patrol along a line 200 miles to the east of the passage between Bear Island and the South Cape of Spitzbergen, but by the time this line was established, the convoy was well to the west of it. When this was discovered from a report of a shadowing aircraft that caught sight of the convoy at 1100 hours on September 18, the U-boats took up the chase at full speed. Escorts sighted three of them astern and northeast of the convoy that afternoon.

The thick weather seemed to offer an excellent opportunity to throw the U-boats and Luftwaffe off the scent, and Burnett decided that when the convoy passed the South Cape of Spitzbergen on the morning of September 19, he would alter its course to take it up the west coast of Spitzbergen, which would increase its distance from the enemy airfields in north Norway.

The deception worked for twelve hours before the U-boats again found the convoy. Their first victim was the minesweeper *Leda*, stationed astern of the convoy. She was torpedoed and sunk by *U-435* (Korvettenkapitän Siegfried Strelow) at 0520 hours on September 20, resulting in the loss of forty-six lives, including two merchant seamen survivors. Six others were among the eighty-six of the ship's company who were rescued.

It was estimated that five submarines were in contact with the convoy. Counterattacks by destroyers and aircraft continued throughout the day, but without success. Then at 1720 hours, *U-255* (Kapitänleutnant

Reinhart Reche) laced two torpedoes into the American freighter *Silver Sword* (Master Clyde Wellington Colbeth). The first struck in the bow, and the explosion destroyed the forward part of the bridge. The second hit the stern, blowing off the stern post, the propeller, and the rudder and causing the after magazine to explode. The seven officers, twenty-nine crewmen, twelve armed guards, and sixteen passengers abandoned ship in two lifeboats and one raft. Of the sixty-four survivors, fifty-five were picked up by the British rescue ship *Rathlin* and nine by the *Zamalek*, but one oiler later died aboard of wounds. The sixteen passengers aboard *Silver Sword* also had survived ships lost in PQ-17: fifteen from *Honomu* and one survivor from *Peter Kerr*, which had been sunk by German aircraft on July 5.

Silver Sword was one of the ships of Convoy PQ-17 that Lieutenant L. J. A. Gradwell of the trawler *Ayrshire* had preserved from destruction. It was tragic that a ship that had survived such great dangers should have been stricken when she was two thirds of the way back on the return trip.

In the afternoon of September 20, Admiral Burnett decided to detach the carrier *Avenger* and his flagship, the cruiser *Scylla*, to return to base independently because the convoy was now beyond the range of heavy air attack. He had requested aircraft from Coastal Command to take over the antisubmarine air patrols and so relieve the *Avenger*'s pilots, who were exhausted after ten days of continuous operations under extremely severe conditions. Burnett also considered that the U-boat threat was so great that it was inadvisable to retain these two valuable ships close by any longer.

After transferring his flag to the destroyer *Milne* (Captain I. M. R. Campbell, R.N.), the two ships parted company, but hardly had they disappeared over the horizon before U-703 (Kapitänleutnant Heinz Bielfeld) fired a spread of three torpedoes at the destroyer *Somali*, commanded by Lieutenant Commander C. D. Maud, R.N., at 1955 hours. One torpedo struck home. The explosion blew the torpedo tubes over the side and cut all of the port side main stringers so that the ship was held together only by the upper deck and starboard side as far as the keel. The port engine fell through the bottom of the ship, and the engine and gear rooms filled with water. The leaking bulkheads on either side were promptly shored up and seemed to be holding, but there was no light or power except from an unreliable auxiliary diesel generator that powered the bilge pumps.

The British rescue ship *Zamalek* was alongside within minutes after the hit, but she was sent back to the convoy. The trawler HMS *Lord Middleton* took off most of the 190-man crew and transferred them to other ships. Only a skeleton crew of eighty men were left aboard *Somali*, and all of them were forbidden to go below except for any critical work. HMS *Ashanti* then took her crippled sister ship in tow, cruising at a slow 7 knots in a flat and calm sea, to crawl to Akureyri, Iceland.

Three more destroyers and *Lord Middleton* were detailed to escort her. This left the convoy with twelve destroyers and the close escort of nine ships. The presence of twenty-one escorts didn't trouble the U-boat captains and their veteran crews, which *U-435*, commanded by Korvettenkapitän Siegfried Strelow, proved in dramatic fashion.

At 0630 hours on September 22, *U-435* penetrated the screen and torpedoed three ships within five minutes of each other. They were the tanker *Gray Ranger* (Master Howard Douglas Gausden, DSO), the *Bellingham* (Master Soren Mortensen), both of which were survivors from PQ-17, and the Commodore's ship *Ocean Voice* (Master Harold James Kay). Once again Commodore Dowding found himself waiting to be picked up out of an icy sea. *Gray Ranger* suffered the loss of six of her crew of thirty-three. Surprisingly, no one on board either *Bellingham* or *Ocean Voice* was lost.

This was the last attack, as soon afterward the U-boats were ordered to withdraw. But now another hazard beset the convoy in the shape of a northerly gale, which swept down upon the ships riding high in ballast and tossed them about, making steering and station-keeping a torment. Thankfully the storm didn't claim any ships, so the battered sixteen made it safely into Loch Ewe on September 26.

Meanwhile, *Somali* was slowly making her way south under tow. All but two officers, one of whom was the commanding officer, Lieutenant Commander Maud, and eighty ratings had been taken off the *Somali*. By that time, everything possible had been done to make her seaworthy, but as the wind increased and the rising sea caused the water-logged ship to labor more and more, the towing hawser sprang taut out of the sea one moment, only to fall back slack the next. It soon became obvious that disaster was in the offing.

The captains of the two ships conferred over a telephone line that had been run between them. It was a battle against lengthening odds. Maud ordered all hands on deck as a precaution. It was well that he did so, for the end came with dramatic suddenness. Early on the morning of September 24, with the wind howling through the darkness and the angry hiss of the waves rolling up from astern, there was heard the ugly, frightening sound of rending metal as the ship broke in half. This was followed by the shattering thud of bursting bulkheads as the two sections drifted apart, slowly turned over, and sank. Only thirty-five of the eighty men on board were plucked out of the icy water, including Maud, who was unconscious when rescued.

Captain Richard Onslow (later Admiral Sir Richard Onslow), commanding HMS *Ashanti*, wrote about rescuing *Somali*'s survivors:

> We had come up on the weather side, beam to sea, drifting fast down over the position where she had sunk. The rescue nets were over the side and some of our better swimmers ready with lines round their bodies. I signalled to the other two ships to get to windward of me. In that weather it was hopeless to try to hold the ship head to sea. The only possible manoeuvre was to stay beam on and, by backing and filling, pick up as many as we could to leeward.
>
> It was heartbreaking work. The ship was rolling drunkenly and we were drifting so fast that inevitably a few of those in the water were trapped under our bilge keel before we could grab them. And a few swept past our bow or stern, when to have moved the ship would have meant losing those we nearly had.
>
> We could only pray that the ships to windward would see them in the blinding snow and spindrift. I was proud of our men that night. Many of them showed great courage and endurance, particularly those who went over the side, at the risk of themselves being caught under the bilge keel. But their courage was of little avail. Of those they brought on board none was still breathing, and only one responded to artificial respiration. He was the captain, Lieutenant Commander Colin Mead.
>
> When we could see no more men to leeward we worked round to windward again. Between us we covered the area until all hope was gone. The three of us could count the living on one hand, and it took some time to find out from the Lord Middleton how many she had.
>
> We had lost sight of her in the storm and could get no answer on the wireless, so we spent a very anxious time while we spread on a line of search to find her. When she got her radio working again we learnt that she had rescued over thirty (men). Thank God for the Lord Middleton was our thought. But we had lost some forty gallant officers and men. I am haunted still by the thought that perhaps I should have foreseen and avoided it.

In the two convoys, sixteen merchant ships had been lost (a loss rate of 29 percent), together with the large destroyer *Somali*, minesweeper *Leda*, fleet tanker *Gray Ranger*, and four fighter aircraft (three of whose pilots were rescued).

The commander in chief, Admiral John C. Tovey, did not consider the losses excessive in view of the scale of air and submarine attacks to which they had been subjected. The Germans lost thirty-three torpedo planes, six Ju-88 dive bombers, and two long-range reconnaissance aircraft—a total of forty-one; three U-boats had been lost and five damaged, and another had been sunk by a Catalina aircraft off Iceland while lying in wait for QP-14. Approximately 250 aircraft torpedoes had been fired in order to sink ten ships. No one tallied the human losses to death or injury or to the incredible amount of stress each person suffered.

Convoy PQ-19 was cancelled because Operation *Torch*, the invasion of North Africa, required the support of a large number of British Home Fleet units. In order to keep supplies following to the Soviets, the British Admiralty started a series of independent single-ship sailings, both east- and westbound, codenamed Operation *FB*.

It is not clear whether the British or Americans originated the idea for Operation *FB*. What is known is that it initially was to entail twelve merchant ships, then in Iceland, sailing at twelve-hour intervals (roughly equivalent to 200 miles distance between sailings) from October 29 to November 2, 1942, with British and American ships alternating departures. At the last moment, the Russian ship SS *Dekabrist* was added, bringing the total to thirteen ships.

No escorts were provided for the individual ships, but the trawlers *Cape Palliser*, *Northern Pride*, *Northern Spray*, and *St. Elstan* were spaced along the route from Iceland, while *Cape Argona*, *Cape Mariato*, and *St. Kenan* were sailed from Murmansk to cover the eastern end of the passage. In addition, two submarines, HM submarine *Tuna* and the Dutch *O-15*, were ordered to provide protection for ships sailing between October 23 and November 9.

The first ships, *Richard H. Alvey* and *Empire Galliard*, sailed on October 29 without being spotted by the Germans. These were followed by *Dekabrist* (Russian) and *John Walker* and *Empire Gilbert* (British) on October 30; *John H. B. Latrobe* (U.S.) and *Chulmleigh* (British) on October 31; *Hugh Williamson* (U.S.) and *Empire Sky* (British) on November 1; *William Clark* (U.S.) and *Empire Scott* (British) on November 2; and, finally, the last two British ships, *Daldorch* on November 3 and *Briarwood* on November 4.

Of the thirteen ships, three (*John H. B. Latrobe*, *Briarwood*, and *Daldorch*) returned to Iceland, five completed their voyages (*Empire Galliard*, *Hugh Williamson*, *Richard H. Alvey*, *Empire Scott*, and *John Walker*), and five were sunk (*Chulmleigh*, *Dekabrist*, *Empire Gilbert*, *Empire Sky*, and *William Clark*). For the crews of *Chulmleigh* and *Dekabrist*, their tales of survival are epics of suffering and endurance. For the five crews whose luck ran out, their stories also endure.

At 0118 hours on November 2, 1942, *Empire Gilbert* (Master William Williams) was hit on the port side by two torpedoes from *U-586* (Kapitänleutnant Dietrich von der Esch). She sank within two minutes, southwest of Jan Mayen. The U-boat had chased the ship for about two hours but missed with a first spread of two torpedoes at 0017 hours, only to hit a minute later. Within thirty minutes, the Germans arrived at the sinking position and rescued two men who were sitting on a beam, floating in the icy water. Von der Esch tried to question six survivors on a raft but received no answer, so he took gunner Douglas Meadows as prisoner aboard. The Germans took good care of their prisoners and landed them at Skjomen Fjord, Norway, on November 5. However, the master, forty-six crewmembers, and seventeen gunners aboard *Empire Gilbert* were lost.

The crew of *Empire Gilbert* was typical of a British merchantman in time of war. The merchant navy part of her crew tended to come from one area of the United Kingdom, though not exclusively. In this case it was from Tyneside in northeast England. The large complement of Defensively Equipped Merchant Ship (DEMS) gunners came from all over the country. There was a strong element of experienced men in all departments, together with many who were only in their first few years of seafaring.

Twenty-one-year-old Eric Aisthorpe was a quiet, conscientious lad. During his youth, he learned to play the harmonica and the accordion very well. He was looking forward to seeing more of the world when he joined *Empire Gilbert* early in September 1942. But apart from a short visit to Iceland, he would see no more of the world before he lost his life.

Two other young men, John Stewart and Alex Souter, grew up only a few doors from each other in Lossiemouth, a small town in Scotland. Inseparable friends, they shared good times as well as bad. The bond between the two was as strong as ever when they both signed on *Empire Gilbert* in early September 1942.

Bombardier Arthur Hopkins of the Maritime Royal Artillery had already completed five wartime voyages in merchant ships: two to Canada, one to the United States, one to Freetown, and then to the Middle East on a troopship, sailing around the Cape of Good Hope. After joining *Empire Gilbert*, Hopkins said the voyage from England to Iceland was uneventful.

Empire Gilbert sailed as ship number five from Hvalfjödur on October 30 and remained undetected for about two days until a German aircraft found them on November 1. The plane did not attack, instead flying around, well out of anti-aircraft range, making signals to base. Bombardier Hopkins was on watch when, at 2200 hours, he spotted a U-boat running parallel to them on the port side. He raised the alarm, and the ship was brought to action stations immediately. Soon afterward, though, a torpedo hit *Empire Gilbert* on the port side, sinking her. There was no time for lifeboats to be lowered. Only three men survived.

Bombardier Hopkins and those around him were forced to jump into the icy sea. In the frigid November waters of the Arctic Ocean, it would have taken only minutes for most of them to succumb. Though Hopkins recalled hearing men shouting in the darkness around him while he was still in the water, as Harry Hutson described in *Arctic Interlude*, Hopkins remembered little else about the event until being rescued by a U-boat. There, he found two of his shipmates also on board.

Ralph Urwin also signed on *Empire Gilbert* in early September 1942. Just seventeen years old, he signed on as deck boy, as did three other seventeen-year-olds: Thomas Stobbs, George Carey, and Ronald Birch.

After *Empire Gilbert* sank, like Hopkins, Urwin remembered little until he awoke on board the submarine and found himself being rubbed down by the German crew to try to bring warmth and circulation back to his numb limbs.

The third survivor was also a DEMS gunner: twenty-year-old Army gunner Douglas Meadows of Gloucester.

In mid-December 1942, Urwin's mother received a letter from the ship's managers, Turner Brightman & Co., telling her that the *Empire Gilbert* was overdue and must be presumed lost with all hands. It was not until March 1943 that Mrs. Urwin received a letter through the Red Cross from her son, saying that he was well but a prisoner of war.

The day after *Empire Gilbert* was sunk, *William Clark* (Master Walter Edmund Elian) left the safety of Hvalfjödur, sandwiched between *Empire Sky* and *Empire Scott*. The passage from Hvalfjödur to the North Cape of Iceland was uneventful. No warships were seen, though one or two white lights were observed in the distance from time to time, most likely from small Icelandic fishing vessels. Soon after leaving

North Cape on November 2, a British Catalina aircraft buzzed them and then flew off. Hutson notes that, if it was an RAF aircraft, then it likely was from 330 (Norwegian) Squadron, RAF, based at Akureyri, or one of the long-range Catalinas of No. 210 Squadron, based at Sullum Voe in the Shetlands. The American VP-94 Squadron of the U.S. Navy was based at Reykjavik and also flew Catalinas.

By the morning of the November 4, *William Clark*, an American Liberty ship, was in the vicinity of Jan Mayen. At 1333 hours on November 4, she was hit on the port side amidships by one of three torpedoes from *U-354* (Kapitänleutnant Karl-Heinz Herbschleb) off Jan Mayen Island. The torpedo struck in the engine room, disabling the engine, flooding the room, and killing the five men on watch below.

No one aboard *William Clark* had seen anything suspicious before the attack. No one saw any signs of the submarine or the first torpedo. Seven lookouts had been on duty at the time: one in the crow's nest, two in the bows, two on the flying bridge, and two on the after gun platform.

The surviving sixty-six crewmen, officers, and naval armed guards of *William Clark* abandoned ship in three lifeboats after the hit. The U-boat missed the ship with a torpedo at 1400 hours, but hit her ten minutes later with a *coup de grâce* on the starboard side amidships. She broke in two forward of the midship house and sank in a few minutes.

The three boats got together, and the motor lifeboat (No. 1), under the charge of Elian attempted to tow the other two, but because of the danger of swamping, he ordered the lines cast off. Elian told the other two boats he was going to try to sail to Iceland so that he could send help to them. This boat with the master and twenty-two other men was never seen again, presumed to have been swamped with all hands lost.

First Mate William F. Goldsmith was in charge of No. 2 boat. On the strength of the briefing before sailing from Hvalfjödur and the fact that a distress message had been sent, he decided to stay in the vicinity, for the time being at least. The remaining two boats drifted apart. After three days and two nights of suffering through brutal, unrelenting Arctic weather, rescuers finally arrived.

The telegraphists of *St. Elstan*, which also had sailed with PQ-16, had received the distress call from *William Clark* and knew she was astern of their own position. The vessel was turned round and steamed at full speed toward the given position. She searched for several days before Able Seaman Anstey, a Newfoundlander who was on look-out aft, sighted the flare sent up by Goldsmith's lifeboat astern of the trawler. After some confusion over the bearing, the trawler steamed off at full speed on the correct course to find the boat. Approaching quietly and smoothly, *St. Elstan* was almost alongside the lifeboat before most of the occupants realized it.

The long and cold days and nights of searching for the survivors of the *William Clark* were made up for by the sheer joy displayed by those rescued. The lifeboat had drifted roughly 20 miles from the given position during the day of November 7. Quickly taking the twenty-six men on board, *St. Elstan* was under orders to continue her patrol until all of the independently sailing merchant ships were clear of her area. Thus, it was not until November 17 that she landed the survivors at Reykjavik.

HMS *Cape Palliser* picked up No. 3 lifeboat and its fifteen survivors and two dead crewmembers—the second mate and a utility man—on November 12. All the survivors in this boat were near death when rescued, and a Navy gunner among them died shortly after being rescued. Two of the survivors lost their legs due to exposure. All of the survivors were landed at Akureyri, Iceland.

Eighteen-year-old Anthony Spinazzola had joined the SS *William Clark* in August 1942, in New York, after having already served as an Armed Guard gunner on board SS *James Gunn* and SS *Valley Forge.* He recalled the events in the Arctic:

> *My boat station was with the Chief Mate's crew while my duty station was aft on the 4.5-inch gun, 12 to 4 watch. November 4th was a calm morning and we were about to sit down to chow when the torpedo hit directly amidships, right into the engine room, just below the crew's mess hall on the port side. We all rushed out to the port side passageway but the outer door was jammed shut. We went over to the starboard side passageway and had to pass the engine room hatchway by this route. I remember looking down as we passed but I could see nothing but steam, fire and smoke. I did not think anyone down there could have survived that explosion.*
>
> *I made my way to my boat station, stopping to pick up some extra warm clothing on the way. The Chief Mate's boat had been destroyed by the explosion and the other port lifeboat was hanging by one of its falls. We crossed to the starboard side but both these boats were already full so we went back to the port side.*
>
> *The Chief Mate organized us into getting this boat into the water. The greatest danger was from the water being continuously washed in and out of the hole in the ship's side made by the torpedo. We managed to get the boat launched and to heave on the line fastened to its stern. This kept us*

clear of the yawning hole. We had to row with all our might when we cast off, but we made it clear of the ship. All three boats came together and the Master said he was going to use his motor to try and reach Iceland to get help for us all.

The Second Mate hoisted his sail and also left. Mr. Goldsmith, however, decided to wait near the scene to see if rescue came. We did not see the submarine at all. The weather got worse and I do not know how we managed to stay afloat. Morale slumped rapidly as the weather deteriorated. We had seen a Catalina while we were in the boat but there was still no sign of rescue. I remember being suddenly engulfed by a bright ray of light which frequently disappeared below the wave tops. We did not know then if it was a rescue ship or a submarine. Fortunately it turned out to be HMS St. Elstan and the Captain was warning us to keep clear of the propeller.

Soon we were all on board the rescue ship and all her crew did everything they could to make us comfortable. Some of us had frozen feet and hands. I cannot remember how long we were on board, but we searched for other survivors, unsuccessfully. When we reached Reykjavik we said our farewells to the rescue ship crew and were taken by ambulance to the Quonset hut hospital. I was there for a month before being taken back to the States on board the USS Polaris. I was sent to Brooklyn Naval Hospital for two months until my frozen feet got better and then I returned to sea until the war ended.

I spent all my remaining sea-time in warmer climates!

The final death toll for the *William Clark* was thirty-one men: four officers, fourteen crewmen, and thirteen armed guards.

While *Empire Gilbert* and *William Clark* were unsuccessfully fending off attack, *Empire Sky* was dealing with troubles of her own. At 2224 hours on November 6, *Empire Sky* (Master Thomas Morley) was torpedoed and sunk by *U-625* (Kapitänleutnant Hans Benker) south of Spitzbergen, Norway. The master and forty-one crewmembers were lost, as were eighteen DEMS gunners (ten from the 4th Regiment Maritime Artillery and eight from the Royal Navy).

Only a year old at the time of this sailing, *Empire Sky*, a British cargo steamer, likely was the first victim of *U-625* (Kapitänleutnant Hans Benker) when she was listed as missing as of November 14, 1942. British records show her as sunk off Murmansk, cause unknown, with no survivors from her crew of sixty. Most historians agree that the missing ship almost certainly was *Empire Sky*, as no other missing vessel was unaccounted for in this northern area at the time.

Empire Sky had loaded at Hull, England, during August and September 1942, and two teenage boys from nearby Grimsby joined her there. Victor James Jennings, sixteen years old, signed on as mess room boy. The second youngest of ten children, Jennings was a quiet boy, who, after leaving school, had begun work at a local cycle shop until he had joined the merchant navy in 1941. After working on *Empire Sky* for about two weeks, he was given permission to sign off and did so. He told his family that he had seen rats on board and that he considered *Empire Sky* an unlucky ship. This action saved Jennings's young life—for a time. But his luck would not hold. He signed on the SS *Almenara*, a much smaller ship than *Empire Sky*. He sailed in this vessel on his seventeenth birthday, bound for the Mediterranean. The vessel was mined off Taranto on September 20, 1943, and Jennings died in the tragedy.

George Rhodes was the other teenager who had signed on *Empire Sky* at Hull. He had signed on as cabin boy. Like Jennings, Rhodes, too, came from a large family His father, Bill, was a ship's carpenter. This left his mother, Ethel May, to bring up the family on her own while his father was at sea. Rhodes's first job upon leaving school was on a farm, but his heart was not in it. There was salt water in his blood, and so in 1940 he joined the merchant navy as a cabin boy. He had already been shipwrecked off Australia and had two years sea time under his belt when he signed on *Empire Sky*. He decided to stay with the ship when Jennings signed off. This decision was to cost him his life.

Sergeant Edward Edgar Stoackley joined *Empire Sky* at this time, too. He was the senior Army gunner on board. He enlisted in the Royal Artillery before the outbreak of war, and early in 1941 volunteered for duty as an anti-aircraft gunner on merchant ships.

During the last week of October 1942, *Empire Sky* was in Hvalfjödur. Three men, including two firefighters, were discharged there. Fireman James Carr, thirty-nine years old, signed on as one of the replacements for this fateful voyage. The other two firemen also joined *Empire Sky* at Hvalfjödur shortly before she sailed on her fateful journey: Robert Hall and John Murray.

The only records regarding the loss of *Empire Sky* are from the log of *U-625*. The entry for November 6 shows that after attacking the stranded SS *Chulmleigh*, the U-boat set off to return to her designated patrol area. An hour later, she dived to reload her torpedo tubes and while submerged the sound operator detected propeller noises on a bearing of 150 degrees true at 1830 hours. The U-boat surfaced ten minutes later and set off at high speed on this bearing, looking for the contact.

Fifty minutes later, the lookouts on the U-boat could see a dark shadow off the port bow. It was a large merchant ship, steering an easterly course at about 9 knots. The U-boat rapidly gained on the ship and overtook her to get into a suitable attack position. By 2000 hours, *U-625* was beginning her run in. At 2014, she fired two torpedoes. Both missed.

U-625 increased speed to get ahead of the merchantman, and once again Benker maneuvered his submarine in a favorable position to attack. He waited half an hour as the sky grew bright with shimmering waves of light from the Aurora Borealis. Benker intended his next attack to be from close range in order not to give *Empire Sky* any time to avoid action, should she spot his torpedoes running toward her. Meanwhile, the forward torpedo tubes had been reloaded, and Benker ordered Tubes 1 and 2 to stand by. At 2224 hours, he then ordered them to be fired. One hit the bow. The other struck just aft of the midship's superstructure. Benker wrote in the logbook:

> *The ship is listing to starboard then to port. The bows sink deeper. Transmits a radio message, name of ship not recognized. Boats are lowered. Astern is an aircraft on a catapult were fitted with a fighter on a catapult which straddled the foc'sle head, not the stern. [None of the ships taking part in this operation were CAM ships.] On deck aircraft are lashed and there are large boxes. On the bow and stern there are guns. Ship has six holds. Estimate 6,500 tons. Ship now stopped.*
>
> *Fire torpedo from tube five (stern tube), hit after thirty-five seconds. Ship explodes in a great detonation, night is brightened to daylight, a fire column rises in the sky, wreckage splashes around in the water, which seems to boil. Many splinters hit our boat. Only a short time later, smoke marks the scene of the disaster. The lifeboats have also disappeared. Return to patrol area.*

Late in 1942, George Rhodes's mother was informed that her son was missing. The terrible uncertainty of his fate remained a burden for her until February 1946, when she received a letter from the ship's managers. The letter said that a postwar examination of German records indicated that *Empire Sky* had been sunk by a U-boat and that none of the crew survived.

On October 31, *Chulmleigh* left Hvalfjödur for North Russia, carrying a cargo of government stores. The weather was overcast, and heavy snowstorms made it difficult to fix positions. A snowstorm was raging, and visibility was very poor. Master Daniel M. Williams had made good progress, when at 2300 on November 5, his ship struck a reef. The *Chulmleigh*, stuck firmly amidships on the reef, with her stern almost out of the water. She was so much down by the bows that the foredeck was almost awash and the captain was afraid the swell then running would break her back. A wireless message was issued, and after an hour and a half the men were ordered to the boats.

The captain remained on board with Chief Officer E. J. Fenn and Second Engineer Richard A. Middlemiss. The numbing cold so affected the men in the boats that they seemed incapable of action. The master at length got *Chulmleigh*'s engines started, but the ship only settled more down by the head. Finally she hogged amidships. The engines were stopped for fear that the ship would break in two. A further wireless message was sent, and by 0400 hours, *Chulmleigh* had been abandoned. The boats seemed to be in a horseshoe-shaped lagoon, with heavy seas running and breakers all around; the boats were kept alongside the ship, as otherwise they would have been crushed on the reef.

At the first sign of daylight on November 5, the fifty-eight men in three boats moved off toward an opening in the lagoon. Almost at once, five Ju-88s flew over the ship at masthead height and scored two direct hits with their bombs. A column of black smoke rose high into the air, but the *Chulmleigh* did not catch fire. Williams decided to make for the nearest settlement, which he calculated to be about 150 miles away.

At 1558 hours on November 6, *U-625* torpedoed the stranded *Chulmleigh* and completed the destruction of the vessel with gunfire. Later, the wreck was again bombed by a Ju-88.

The following account, based on the report by Williams and Third Officer David F. Clark, conveys a graphic illustration of the appalling hardships suffered by the survivors.

The men of the *Chulmleigh*, struggling to remain connected in three lifeboats, could not easily keep together. One of the boats was in dangerous condition and was soon abandoned, its crew divided between the two remaining seaworthy boats. They proceeded along the Spitzbergen coast, which was visible during the few hours of twilight that relieved the otherwise perpetual darkness. A gale blew up on November 8, but on November 9, the two boats turned toward the shore and regained contact with each other. Captain Williams's boat had a serviceable motor, and it was agreed that he should go on ahead to the settlement to fetch help. It was very cold, and a lot of water was shipped; the wind froze the sails, and the crew's clothing became rigid with frost and ice.

The night of November 9/10 was so severe that the steward became delirious and died. On the afternoon of November 10, some huts at the entrance to a fjord were sighted, but as Williams and his crew were making toward them, the motor froze up and could not be restarted. Without the motor helping them, the wind and current made it impossible to make landfall, and the boats drifted out to sea, losing sight of land.

At about 0200 the next day, after several hours among the reefs, they were suddenly washed up on the beach, where a heavy sea broke over the party and the master regained consciousness at the shock. By good fortune, they found several wooden huts within 20 yards; two of the crew had died in the boat and another died on the beach, but the survivors managed to reach the huts, although the youngest among the crew had to be carried.

They at once fell fast asleep. In the morning, the twenty-three men who remained from the original ship's company of fifty-eight moved into one of the larger huts. This proved to be quite habitable; it had a small coal stove, and there was enough wood and coal to make a good fire. Although no trees were in sight, there was plenty of driftwood and a great many old boxes they could burn. "After we had slept that first night," Clark recalled, "we all felt a little better."

> We collected what was left of the lifeboat's rations and at once made ourselves hot drinks, coffee and Horlicks, melting the snow for water. This revived us considerably and we became terribly hungry. We also found some tins of corned beef and biscuits in one of the huts, so we managed very well.
>
> As long as we had food for tomorrow our morale remained good. Captain Williams encouraged us to take about two hours' exercise each day, but after a time most of us suffered so much from frostbitten feet that it was impossible. Feet and hands became gangrenous and I became very ill.

After a few days on land, Captain Williams recovered enough to take charge. Most of the men had swollen hands and feet and could do very little, but the four Army gunners were hardly affected. One man in particular, only 4 feet 11 inches tall, was phenomenally tough; the captain said of the gunners that they "looked after us all, nursing the men who were ill, going out to collect firewood, and generally running things."

Clark and Lance-Sergeant R. A. Peyer made two attempts during their first few days on land to reach the settlement, but the intervening country was barren and strewn with rocks. Deep ravines and great stretches of snow and ice were further hindrances to the explorers, who had to turn back and arrived back at the huts completely exhausted.

During the first week, thirteen more men died from frostbite, gangrene, and exposure. "They seemed to give up hope," said Williams, "and then died; but I believed right to the end that we would come through."

Expeditions of any kind were never easy. The men had only a few hours of twilight during which to work, and visibility often was reduced to 10 yards. Another sortie, in a northeasterly direction up the fjord, revealed a small hut in which there was a sack of flour and some tins of corned beef and cocoa. This was brought back, and the flour, mixed with water and cooked in the form of small cakes, kept the party alive for another three or four weeks. There were dozens of boxes of matches in their hut, and with the petrol from the lifeboat's tank they managed to keep two Primus stoves working. They had hot drinks three times a day; and when the coffee and cocoa ran out, they made do with hot water. They also found some tins of whale-blubber preserved in oil; this sustained them for another five or six days, and they also drank the boiled oil.

A second attempt to reach the settlement was unsuccessful, and toward the end of December, the situation was becoming desperate. According to the master's statement:

> By now the Third Officer and an Able Seaman were suffering badly from gangrene, as were several of the others; their feet and hands were discharging and the smell was awful. Another man died on Christmas Eve. I therefore decided to make a final attempt to get help, or die in the effort.

When they were halfway to the settlement, Williams's two companions broke down. They could not go on. So they turned back, and upon reaching the hut, all three collapsed. On January 2, 1943, one of the gunners went out to collect firewood; almost at once he came rushing back in a state of complete terror. Captain Williams could get nothing out of him, and the nine men still alive could think only that they were about to be set upon by polar bears. Luckily, it was nothing more fearsome than two hunters who were on a trapping expedition wearing white furs. They took word of the survivors' plight to the settlement, and a rescue party was sent with sleighs.

"We were all in a pretty bad condition," said Captain Williams, "as we had ceased to have the energy to exercise ourselves. Our clothes were soaked with pus from gangrenous limbs and gave off a horrible stench."

After two months in bed, Williams and the remaining survivors were allowed to get up. They spent most of their time learning to ski. This pastime provides an ironical footnote to the long story of endurance, as Williams noted: "There had been a pair of skis in the hut, and if only we had known how to use them we could probably have got help much sooner."

At 2000 on January 4, the survivors reached the settlement, where they stayed until June 10, 1943. The survivors eventually boarded the cruisers HMS *Bermuda* (Captain T. H. Back, RN) and HMS *Cumberland* (Captain A. H. Maxwell-Hyslop, RN) and landed at Thurso, Scotland, on June 15, 1943. The master, three crewmembers, and nine gunners survived. However, thirty crewmembers and nine six gunners were lost, many to gangrenous infections brought on by frostbite. Their ordeal lasted 217 days.

SS *Dekabrist* of Odessa, under the command of Captain Stephen Polukarpovic Belyev, had already survived two convoys: PQ-6 in late 1941 and QP-5 in early 1942. Now, in autumn 1942, she loaded her cargo in the United States and sailed in convoy to Iceland, originally intended to be part of convoy PQ-19.

Dekabrist was located on November 4 by Junkers Ju-88s from Norway. She was attacked several times with bombs and torpedoes and then strafed with machine guns. *Dekabrist*'s gunners drove off all of the attacks, leaving the ship undamaged.

The ship was attacked again just after midnight, this time by three aircraft, soon followed by five more. The final aircraft made its attack when one well-aimed torpedo struck the vessel in the bows. The Russian crew struggled all day to keep the water at bay, expecting more attacks to come, but no other aircraft found them.

By 2000 hours, it was obvious to Captain Belyev that the water was gaining on them at an ever-increasing rate. The vessel was going to sink. Belyev ordered the crew to abandon ship once she was well down by the head and the foredeck was awash. A final distress message was transmitted soon after midnight on November 5, giving their position as 7530N 2710E.

All four of *Dekabrist*'s lifeboats were launched safely, well stocked with food and other supplies. Once the boats were safely in the water, the captain ordered the crew to stand off the vessel but to remain in the vicinity in the hope that rescue would come to them from one of the two submarines. *Dekabrist* was east of Spitzbergen when she was attacked, and the trawlers were much further to the south and west.

None of the submarines arrived in time to save the *Dekabrist*. Soon after dawn, another flight of German aircraft found her and sent her to the bottom of the Arctic Ocean. While the crew watched the vessel sink, a thick blanket of fog developed, and the four lifeboats soon lost sight of each other. A few hours later, the fog lifted and the survivors in the captain's boat saw land and a hut on Hope Island to the east of Spitzbergen.

People were running along the beach, waving frantically. One of the other lifeboats came into view, too, and they closed on each other. Under the command of Third Mate Treticyn, this boat confirmed the sight of human habitation. Treticyn's boat managed to land safely through the surf, but Captain Belyev's boat could not make it through the breakers. The crew was not strong enough to prevent her broaching and so the captain stood off the beach, his men totally exhausted. Belyev and his crew never again caught sight of Treticyn or of any survivor from his boat.

After failing to land with Treticyn, Belyev's boat drifted further north with the wind for another four days before the weather changed and they began to drift south again. The crew was in a very bad way, unable to assist themselves. On November 14, nine days after they abandoned the *Dekabrist*, they spotted land (Hope Island, southeast of Spitzbergen). A few hours later, they found themselves washed up onto the beach. All nineteen survivors reached the shore before the next wave smashed the boat.

The men had no idea where they were. They were weak from hunger and dehydration. The conditions in the lifeboat had been very bad indeed. There was only four ounces of water per person a day early on after the sinking, but this soon had to be cut in half and finally there was only enough water to wet their tongues. Food was more plentiful, but without water, the men found it difficult to eat because of swollen tongues and cracked lips.

The ship's doctor, Nadejda Matvevna Natilich, had brought the ship's cat with her into the lifeboat, and more than once it was suggested that the pet should be killed and used as food. Natilich, however, strongly resisted this, and the cat was reprieved after long and heated discussions.

Four lifeboats had left *Dekabrist*. The crew numbered around eighty, about twenty people per boat. The reports of Belyev and Natilich quote a total figure of nineteen survivors in this boat. By the time they reached the beach, the survivors from Belyev's boat could barely walk. Miraculously, no one drowned when the boat was smashed by the pounding surf.

Once ashore, the survivors set to work. The sails were recovered from the lifeboat, and the fittest among them erected a makeshift tent. Two small parties were organized from the fittest men to search for better shelter, one going south, the other, led by Belyev, heading north.

Belyev's group located a seal hunters' hut. The rotting hut was in poor condition, large holes dotting the walls. The floor was covered in ice. But with an ancient stove and some bunks, it was better than their makeshift tent. Not long after reaching the hut, the weather deteriorated to hurricane-force winds and blizzard conditions. Before long, snow several feet thick covered the hut.

The survivors made a rough chimney from wet wooden boards and this worked well—until the boards dried out and caught fire. As soon as the weather moderated sufficiently, they dug themselves out and everyone went back to find the tent, three men, the doctor, and the cat. They eventually located the tent, but all the men had died from exposure. They were left where they had died.

It was at first thought that the doctor was dead, too; as there was no reaction from her, but the cat was still alive and kept close to its mistress. Able seaman Vasiley Nichalovich Borodin investigated further and realized that Natilich, although close to death, was still alive—barely. Every effort was made to revive her. About three days later, she was taken to the northern hut. Not long after, Soviet Navy seaman Kamenskji became gravely ill and died, most likely from pneumonia. He was soon followed in death by seaman Nicholas F. Ivanov.

The survivors soon established a routine, the fittest making daily forages for firewood, others melting snow and boiling water for treating victims who suffered from gangrene. Scouting the shoreline for goods that had been washed up proved fruitful as they frequently found a keg of butter, a sack of flour, and other valuable items of food, all of which helped to sustain them throughout the long winter and spring months. The hut itself also contained meager supplies of flour and butter, as well as an ancient shotgun (though only a few cartridges).

One evening after settling in for the night, an enormous polar bear pounded open the flimsy door of the hut. Belyev kept his head and picked up the loaded shotgun, not knowing for sure whether it would fire correctly or explode in his face. He pointed it in the general direction of the bear and pulled the trigger. There was a tremendous explosion, and the bear fell mortally wounded. The crew made the most of its quarry. Its body was skinned for the fur, the meat used for food, and the less savory parts for baiting fox traps.

On Saturday, 1 May 1943, almost six months after the Russian survivors had first set foot on Hope Island, a Heinkel He-115 seaplane from Banak in Northern Norway, flown by Luftwaffe pilot R. Schutze, had been ordered to overfly the island just in case the Allies had put ashore a weather station during the winter. The aircrew was amazed to see the figure of a man against the snowy white background. The German pilot cautiously flew lower on his second run. He could see the castaway beckoning him to land. Instead, the pilot climbed and then sent a signal to its base reporting the incident. The reply ordered the aircraft not to attempt to land but to return to base immediately and make a full report.

German intelligence officers concluded that there could be only two possible explanations for human presence on Hope Island: Either the man was indeed a member of an Allied weather party and the beckoning had been a deliberate ploy, or he was a shipwrecked mariner who had somehow managed to reach the island. The Germans knew that they had sunk ships in the vicinity during the past few months, but they found it difficult to believe that any man could have survived without assistance.

This, however, gives rise to even more questions. If the hut had been occupied, presumably by shipwrecked mariners, then which ship were they from? What happened to them? Had they tried to reach safety in their lifeboat?

Other aircraft were sent to the island, and one reported finding a wooden hut, most likely constructed before the war by seal hunters. The aircraft also reported seeing not one but three castaways, one of whom was almost certainly a woman. None of the survivors had made any attempt to hide from the aircraft—quite the reverse: They all seemed happy to have been discovered, and all waved excitedly. When the aircraft returned and the crew was debriefed, the German authorities decided that they had no other choice than to order a U-boat to make a landing on the island to discover exactly what was going on.

On July 24, 1943, *U-703* (Oberleutnant zur See Joachim Brunner) was ordered to make a thorough search of Hope Island, take off the survivors if indeed they were shipwrecked mariners, and destroy the hut if it was, or had been, used as a weather station.

U-703 reached Hope Island the next day. The U-boat circumnavigated the island at a discreet distance while several members of the crew scanned the barren snow-covered rock with powerful binoculars. They found no signs of human habitation. Brunner decided to take a closer look. On the second run, a keen-eyed lookout spotted a wooden hut. A shore party was made ready while other members of the crew inflated a rubber dinghy, checked the 88-mm deck gun, and made it ready for immediate action. Light machine guns were mounted on the conning tower and small arms, grenades, and ammunition for the shore party were checked. A small, well-armed group were put into the dinghy and paddled to the shore.

The group approached the hut with caution, not knowing exactly what to expect. After bursting through the door, they discovered the hut was empty, although there were signs that it had been recently occupied. They soon found a second hut, and once again the shore party of four men under the command of Leutnant zur See Heinz Schlott went ashore.

Once the shore party was in position surrounding the tiny refuge, they signaled the submarine and a warning shot from the 88-mm deck gun on the U-boat was fired. This brought forth a solitary figure, hands crossed behind his head in sign of surrender. The shore party advanced and eventually found that no one else was inside the hut to pose a threat.

Inside the shelter they found an old revolver, ammunition, a few meager rations, old newspapers, and animal skins. They discovered the foul-smelling castaway was Russian. Although he could not speak any German, he could speak a few words of English. The Germans soon discovered it was Belyev.

Captain Belyev told his rescuers that he would be more than pleased to guide them to the survivors who were living in other huts. He was taken back to *U-703*, where he showed Brunner where the other huts were situated. The first hut was found easily. It was empty when investigated, though it, too, showed definite signs of having been occupied quite recently. The shore party was again recovered, and *U-703* set off for the next position.

By that afternoon, the third hut was sighted, and a few short bursts of light machine gun fire were used to attract attention before deciding whether to put men ashore. The gunfire immediately brought three people from the hut. Two seemed quite fit, but the third was obviously seriously ill or injured. Captain Belyev used the megaphone to instruct the people to come out to the U-boat in the small boat that could be seen on the shoreline.

The two fit survivors placed the sick man in the boat and then rowed out to *U-703*. Brunner and his crew were surprised to find that one of the fit survivors was a woman.

While the Russians were on board *U-703* being questioned and given food, clothing, and facilities to wash, a small landing party went ashore to examine the survivors' hut and its contents. When they returned they reported that the hut was indeed only a refuge. There was no sign of weather or radio equipment.

Brunner decided that because he still had to lay another weather buoy and because accommodation on the U-boat was limited, he would take only the Russian captain with him. The others would be left behind. Brunner ordered his crew to assemble a survival kit from the U-boat's stores while he explained to Belyev what he proposed to do.

When Captain Belyev translated this to his compatriots, their disappointment was obvious, but they accepted the fact that they had no choice. They were sent ashore with the survival kit, which contained medical supplies, vitamin tablets, food, clothes, diesel oil, matches, cigarettes, and tools. The U-boat crew gathered firewood from the shore and brought it to the hut.

U-703 set off again for Narvik, arriving on August 3 without further incident. Belyev was almost in tears as he shook hands with every member of the submarine's crew before being taken away under a Navy guard.

On her next patrol, *U-703* received a signal ordering her to return to Hope Island. Aircraft had reported seeing at least two people still alive, nine months after they had first reached the island. The message indicated that the middle hut seemed to be their base. Brunner was ordered to bring everyone off the island.

When *U-703* arrived, the shore party found only two survivors in the hut, the woman and, amazingly, the man who previously had been so ill. The third survivor also was still alive, living in a separate hut further away along the shore. After bringing the doctor and the man aboard the U-boat, *U-703* then made her way to the more remote second hut. The lone Russian, Lobanov, came out of the hut, crawling on his hands and knees to meet the landing party.

Lobanov was placed in the rubber dinghy by the four Germans, and they set off to paddle back to the submarine. They soon ran into difficulties in the choppy water and found they could make no headway against the surf. Brunner brought the submarine closer and managed to float a line to the exhausted dinghy crew. They retrieved the line and made it secure, and *U-703* went slowly astern, pulling the dinghy and its occupants through the turbulence and alongside.

The rescue had come too late for Lobanov. He died a few hours later and was buried at sea with a formal ceremony. The two remaining Russians,

Borodin and Natilich, were put ashore at Harstad, Norway, on October 9, 1943, almost eleven months after first being marooned. Seventy-seven of their comrades had died as a result of the sinking of the *Dekabrist*, lost to the enemy and to the even deadlier Arctic.

As the eastbound ships fought their way through storms, ice, and the patrolling Germans, eight Soviet ships sailed westward between October 29 and November 25. Eighteen additional Soviet ships ran the gauntlet, the last one sailing on January 24, 1943. All but three of these arrived safely.

The first lost was the hard fighting *Donbass* (M. I. Pavlova, Master), which had survived PQ-17 in summer 1942 and rescued fifty-two survivors from the *Daniel Morgan*. On November 7, *Donbass* ran into a Kriegsmarine battle group consisting of the heavy cruiser *Admiral Hipper* and the 5th Destroyer Flotilla (*Z-27, Z-30, Friedrich Eckoldt,* and *Richard Beitzen*). After an unequal battle against *Z-27*, she was sunk, and forty-nine of her crew were killed. Pavlova and fifteen crewmembers were taken prisoner. The other two losses were cargo ships *Krasny Partizan* (Captain A. F. Belov) and *Ufa* (Captain L. I. Patrikeev), both sunk by *U-255* in late January 1943.

Krasnoe Znamya left the Kola Inlet on January 26. She sent a message later that day that German aircraft were attacking, but then contact was lost. According to U-boat records, at 1100 hours on January 26, *U-255* sank an iced-up steamer with two torpedoes west of the Bear Island. The ship had just escaped from the chasing *U-625* (Kapitänleutnant Hans Benker) when it was torpedoed by *U-255*. *U-255* surfaced after the attack and tried to question the survivors who had taken refuge in a lifeboat, but they only spoke Russian, which the Germans could not understand and the U-boat left without taking any prisoners. No distress message was heard by shore stations or any ships, and the survivors were never found. *Krasnoe Znamya*'s captain Belov and fifty crewmen were lost.

Ufa had set out from the Kola Inlet a day earlier, on January 25. At 0547 hours on January 29, *U-255* fired a torpedo at a steamer, identified as a Myronich-class freighter, which was located south of Bear Island in the Barents Sea and observed it sinking by the bow twenty-five minutes after being hit. Two torpedoes had missed at 0231 and 0233 hours, possibly passing underneath the vessel. When the U-boat surfaced after five hours, they still found survivors at the sinking position and tried to question them, but they only spoke Russian. Once again, there is no record of a distress message being sent and, like *Krasnoe Znamya*, *Ufa*'s captain and thirty-eight of her crew were never found.

The loss rate of eight out of thirty-nine unescorted ships that ultimately sailed as part of Operation *FB* was significantly better than that of the heavily guarded convoys. But all loss is relative. We'll never know what hell most of the survivors went through before dying or how their families suffered not knowing, often for years, what had happened to their loved ones. Regardless of the personal tragedies, Operation *FB* with its 20 percent casualty rate, was considered by the British Admiralty, militarily and logistically, a success.

The last PQ/QP convoy series was QP-15, which sailed from Arkhangelsk on November 17 consisting of twenty-eight ships with Captain W. C. Meek as commodore. Protection was provided by the anti-aircraft ship *Ulster Queen*, five minesweepers, four corvettes, and the Soviet destroyers *Baku* and *Sokrushitelnyy*.

A gale sprung up on November 20, and by the time QP-15 reached the vicinity of Bear Island, it was badly scattered. Ted Balaam, a British telegraphist on board one of the escort ships, wrote graphically about what happened when the gale hit QP-15:

> *A story regarding QP15, a convoy in which our Russian allies lost ships in tragic circumstances.* London (Flag), *with* Suffolk, A.A. *ship* Ulster Queen, *5 minesweepers, 4 corvettes, one trawler, destroyers* Onslaught *and* Orwell, *Russian destroyers* Baku *and* Sokrushitelnyy, *left Arkhangelsk with 28 ships formed into a convoy. More destroyers, two flotillas, had been promised as an enemy cypher had been decyphered by the Admiralty under the "Ultra" system informing Admiral Hamilton that German surface craft, including* Hipper *and attendant destroyers, had express orders to proceed and destroy QP15 and escorts.*
>
> *However, after leaving port we ran into what developed into a hurricane, and within no time at all convoy lines were broken. The close escort screen was fighting to stay afloat. When* Suffolk *could be seen, her four screws became visible before plunging into the depths again.* London, *since the 1939 refit, rolled even at anchor and was going over to 45°, then 50°.*
>
> *The height of the swell was measured and the seas running were eighty feet. A little later the anemometer screamed and took off, the graph in the plot came off the paper and ceased, the last reading was 110 mph.*

The wind and sea increased, as did the icing up, suddenly we went over to 70°, everyone wedged themselves into something as we listened above the wind to hear the crashing of crockery, and many unidentified items moving. To our relief we came upright again and slewed to Port to receive a huge wave which did not break until it reached "B" Turret and all but drowned us. As we surfaced we were horrified to see Baku *listing badly and her entire bridge went over the side.*

We tried with the largest signal lamp to tell her to go home and tried to find Sokrushitelnyy *to tell her the same. On the crest of an eighty-foot wave we saw her in a 'Vee' shape and tragically watched as she broke in half amidships and foundered, with all aboard we feared.*

The only consolation was that the weather kept the aircraft grounded and Hipper *in harbour, not that they could have done much in the prevailing conditions and with the convoy completely scattered and fighting damage.*

At 1430 hours on November 20, *Sokrushitelnyy* was hit by a large wave, tearing off her stern and sinking her within ten minutes, killing six men. Other destroyers managed to take off 191 men, but thirty of them were lost during the rescue effort. At 1530, the other destroyers in the convoy began to leave due to a lack of fuel, leaving a crew of thirteen to man *Sokrushitelnyy*. She was not seen again.

The storm kept the Luftwaffe at bay, but it didn't deter the U-boats. Two of them struck the badly scattered convoy on November 23. *U-625* (Oberleutnant zur See Hans Benker) was the first, sinking the British freighter *Goolistan* (Master William Thomson) at 0145. Second was the Soviet motor merchant *Kuznets Lesov* (Master V. A. Tsibulkin), when *U-601* (Kapitänleutnant Peter-Ottmar Grau) fired a spread of four torpedoes, one of which hit home. *Kuznets Lesov* sank in four minutes. Neither ship's crews, totaling eighty-two men, survived.

The battered remnants of QP-15 began arriving at Loch Ewe on November 30. The last limped in four days later. With its arrival, the PQ/QP convoys passed into history.

CHAPTER 9

GERMAN GÖTTERDÄMMERUNG
December 1942–May 1945

B etween December 1942 and March 1943, the Axis Powers' (Germany, Italy, and Japan) tide of success reached its high-water mark and began turning in the Allies' favor. In North Africa, the British Eighth Army had pushed the German Afrika Corps a thousand miles westward. At the western end of North Africa, Anglo-American forces, firmly in control of Morocco and Algeria, were slugging eastward through Tunisia. The Allies encircled and then defeated their foes on May 16.

In Russia, Soviet Red Army troops fought bloody house-to-house battles for control of Stalingrad and, during its winter offensive, surrounded and captured 300,000 German Army troops that had threatened the city. On the other side of the world, U.S. soldiers and Marines slowly eliminated Japanese forces on Guadalcanal, the first step in driving the marauders out of the Pacific. Guadalcanal was secured on February 9, 1943, six months after the Marines landed on August 7, 1942.

In the Atlantic, U-boats still reigned supreme through the bitter winter months, wreaking havoc among almost every convoy they encountered. They were finally fought to a standstill and their dominance broken at the end of March, following three months of cataclysmic convoy battles.

As these battles raged, the British Admiralty resumed regular convoys, sailing in mid-December to the Soviet Union. There were several changes in these new convoys. The most important was replacing the PQ and QP with the randomly chosen designations "JW" for eastbound convoys and "RA" for the westbound ones. This was done in a futile attempt to confuse German Intelligence. Another significant change was that the eastbound convoys would sail from Loch Ewe instead of Reykjavik. What hadn't changed, though, was the heavy force of escorts accompanying the convoys.

The first of the dual eastbound convoys to sail from Loch Ewe was JW-51A with sixteen ships on December 15, 1942, escorted by seven fleet destroyers and four smaller vessels. It was a quiet passage, and all the ships arrived safely off the Kola Inlet just five days later, on December 20.

The second, JW-51B consisting of fourteen ships, left on December 20, escorted by six fleet destroyers (*Onslow*, with Captain R. St. V. Sherbrooke, senior officer of the Escort Force, *Obedient*, *Orwell*, *Obdurate*, *Oribi*, and *Achates*), the corvettes *Rhododendron* and *Hyderabad*, the minesweeper *Bramble*, and the trawlers *Vizalma* and *Northern Gem*. Distant cover was provided by the battleship *Anson*, flying the flag of Vice Admiral Sir Bruce Fraser, with the 8-inch-gun cruiser *Cumberland* and three destroyers, which sailed a few days later from Akureyri on the north coast of Iceland, on December 26.

For the first six days, the convoy's passage was uneventful. Then, on December 26, when the convoy was half way between Jan Mayen and Bear Island, a great gale overtook it. The five ships of the port wing column and the trawler *Vizalma* lost touch with the convoy. The next afternoon, the minesweeper *Bramble* (Commander H. T. Rust) was detached to look for the missing merchantmen. Three of the merchantmen rejoined the convoy the next day. The fourth, *Chester Valley*, and *Vizalma* found each other and proceeded independently to Murmansk. The fifth lost ship, *Ballot*, reached the Kola Inlet two days after the rest of the convoy, only to be wrecked afterward.

By the morning of December 31, the storm had abated, the wind had dropped to a mild breeze, the sea was slight with no swell, and the sky was overcast with occasional snow squalls. But the masts, rigging, and upper works of all the ships were coated with ice.

Unknown to Captain Sherbrooke was that on the previous day, U-354 had sighted and reported the convoy, which she described as comprising six to ten ships steaming eastward at 12 knots and weakly escorted. After receiving this report, Admiral Erich Raeder immediately issued orders for a force consisting of *Lützow, Hipper* (flagship for Vice Admiral Oskar Kummetz), and six destroyers to sail as soon as possible to attack the convoy. Operational command was to be exercised by the Flag Officer Northern Waters, Admiral Klüber, at Narvik. Tactical command was vested in Vice Admiral Kummetz.

Kummetz's instructions included the destruction of the convoy and avoidance of action with superior forces. No time was to be wasted rescuing enemy crews, and enemy ships were to be prevented from rescuing their comrades. The capture of a few merchant ship captains for interrogation—or even the capture of a single ship—was desirable. He was informed of where the convoy would be on the night of December 30/31 and that it was steering east at between 7 and 12 knots.

While the Germans were searching for the convoy, they found the corvette *Bramble*, returning from a search for stragglers. *Hipper* opened fire and badly damaged the little corvette. Later, the destroyer *Eckholdt* finished her off. Eight officers and 113 ratings were lost. The loss went unnoticed by the British until after the battle.

Sydney Parkins, a signalman on board HMS *Jamaica*, wrote about what was to be called the Battle of the Barents Sea:

This is roughly what happened on New Year's Eve 1942. A German Naval Force sailed from Altenfjord and split into two sections, the heavy cruiser Hipper *and three destroyers in one, and the battle cruiser* Lützow *and three destroyers in the other. They would attack Convoy JW51B from different directions. To locate the convoy in quite poor visibility, each section was deployed some distance apart to widen the search area. The* Hipper *was the first to find the convoy.*

Captain Sherbrooke on Onslow *was in command of the convoy escort. When* Hipper *was sighted,* Achates *made smoke to obscure the convoy, which enabled* Obedient, Orwell, *and* Onslow *to feign a torpedo attack by emerging from the smoke screen, advance toward the* Hipper, *and retreat into the smoke again, after which they attacked from a different direction. This was repeated several times without firing torpedoes, thus maintaining the threat.*

The Onslow *received a direct hit and sustained heavy casualties, including Captain Sherbrooke, who received a severe facial injury.* Onslow *retired from the action, leaving* Obedient *in command. Although* Achates *was also in a crippled state, she continued to make smoke. This small destroyer force out-maneuvered* Hipper *for a considerable time, thus preventing it from attacking the convoy and allowing the* Sheffield *and* Jamaica *to arrive on the scene.*

The cruisers under the command of Admiral Burnett closed the convoy at more than 30 knots and achieved complete surprise. They opened up with their six-inch guns and almost immediately scored direct hits. The Hipper *retired after sustaining damage and casualties, a six-inch shell entering her boiler room and another setting her hanger on fire. The German destroyer* Eckholdt *appeared on the scene and, mistaking the British cruisers for German ships, steered straight toward them. She was literally blown out of the water.*

The Lützow *then made a challenge with the aim apparently of protecting the* Hipper, *abandoning the operation, and making for base.* Sheffield *and* Jamaica *then broke off the engagement in order to cover the convoy, whose escort had been badly depleted. The trawler* Northern Gem *picked up the survivors of the* Achates, *which eventually sank. The fate of the minesweeper* Bramble *remained unknown, but it was assumed she was sunk by a German destroyer when searching for convoy stragglers.*

Captain Sherbrooke of the badly damaged Onslow *survived and was awarded the Victoria Cross, but spent the rest of his life with only one eye. The following signal was made by C. in C. H.F. (Commander in Chief Home Fleet—Admiral Tovey):—"To CS 10, 'Sheffield,' 'Jamaica,' Capt. D 'Onslow' (R), Escorts of Russian Convoy. Your defence of the convoy was most gallant. The boldness of your action was entirely responsible for the safe conduct of the ships under your escort, a feat of which you may all be proud."*

JW-51B completed its voyage without further trouble from either the sea or the Germans.

Succeeding eastbound convoys JW-52 and JW-53 totaling forty-two ships completed their voyages without loss, as did westbound convoy RA-51 with its fourteen ships. All three convoys endured Luftwaffe attacks and, although the ships got away cleanly, the attackers weren't so lucky.

The German air attacks always followed the same pattern. First, reconnaissance planes sighted the convoy, followed shortly by the arrival of bombers and torpedo planes. But the pilots had a tougher time in winter than they did during summer's long sunlit days. Shorter days allowed for no waste of time and no errors in navigation. Often flying toward their targets in storms and snow squalls, the crews were lucky to even catch sight of the ships. Wind buffeted them on their approach flight, which could knock them off target during the attack's crucial final seconds. A dozen aircraft took off on January 24 to attack convoy JW-52, but only three reached the convoy. In the midst of a squall and facing an almost solid wall of anti-aircraft fire, they pressed home their attack. All three were shot down.

The small, eleven-ship convoy RA-52 sailed from Kola Inlet on January 29, 1943. Despite the usual bad weather, it was smooth sailing until *U-255* (Kapitänleutnant Reinhart Reche) struck on February 3. In broad daylight, Reche fired two torpedoes at the freighter *Greylock*, one of which hit aft, sealing the ship's doom. The ten officers, twenty-six crewmembers, twenty-five armed guards, and nine passengers, including three survivors from *Ballot*, all abandoned ship safely in four lifeboats. Most were picked up quickly by HMS *Lady Madeleine* and HMS *Northern Wave*, while four crewmembers were picked up by HMS *Harrier.*

So far, the season's JW and RA convoys avoided the large losses experienced by their PQ and QP predecessors. But RA-53 wasn't so lucky. Sailing from the Kola Inlet on March 1, the convoy's thirty merchant ships were guarded by thirty-one escorts, including three cruisers and eleven destroyers. The relative peace and quiet lasted four days. At 0924 hours on March 5, Reche's *U-255* slipped through the escort screen and fired a three-torpedo spread, scoring a fatal blow on the *Executive* and damaging the *Richard Bland*. *Executive*'s sixty-man crew hastily abandoned ship without orders and were soon rescued, but not before nine men had died. Fortunately for *Richard Bland*, the torpedo passed through the ship without exploding, leaving 8-foot-wide holes on either side of the ship.

A dozen He-111 dive bombers arrived at 1430 hours, but none of them could penetrate the ack-ack barrage. Undeterred, the Luftwaffe tried several more times during the few remaining daylight hours, though with the same lack of success.

Having beaten off one enemy, RA-53 met another challenge for which there was no defense: an Arctic winter storm. The Liberty ship *J. L. M. Curry* was smashed by the heavy seas on March 7. The crews of the other ships saw to their horror a colossal wave lift her up and break her in two. Her crew was rescued, but the convoy was scattered. Twenty-two vessels arrived together at Loch Ewe and then four more in succession. Two others never made it to safety.

Having survived one torpedo from *U-255*, *Richard Bland* succumbed to another one fired by the same U-boat on March 10. Thirty-two of her crew were lost; the remaining thirty-five rescued.

The *Puerto Rican*, an American merchant ship, straggling far behind, was torpedoed and sunk on March 9 by *U-586* (Kapitänleutnant Dietrich von der Esch). Severe weather and ice had rendered three of the ship's four lifeboats frozen and useless. When the fourth one hit the water, its stern boatfall tackle could not be released due to the ice, and it capsized. Eight men swam to a cork life raft, and six later transferred to a larger raft.

From a crew of sixty-two, only eight managed to reach the raft. All except one of them were swept away by the waves or perished in the cold. The sole survivor, August Wallenhaupt, twenty-six years old, was picked up on March 12 by a British destroyer, half crazed and nearly dead. The military doctors at Reykjavik could not understand how he had survived. Both his legs had to be amputated at the knee, as were all the fingers on his right hand and all but the index finger and thumb on his left hand.

Wallenhaupt's story began on a stormy winter night in the Arctic Ocean, just 400 miles off the north coast of Iceland. The *Puerto Rican* was in convoy when she left a Russian port, but for two days the freighter had been alone, cut off from the convoy and the rest of the world by radio silence. The temperature was 30 degrees below zero and the water was 21 degrees above zero—just 11 degrees below freezing. The entire ship was caked with ice.

Wallenhaupt was asleep in his quarters when *U-586*'s torpedo struck at 2200 hours, instantly awakening him. Right away, he knew what had happened: He'd been torpedoed before. Wallenhaupt took time to dress warmly. He slipped on his rubber lifesaving suit, put on his life jacket over the suit, and donned a knee-length woolen seaman's coat with a hood to protect his head.

He went out to his position at No. 4 boat and found other members of the crew trying to free the lifeboats from the ice. They rammed the boats with their shoulders, but "it was like ramming your shoulder against the Empire State Building and expecting it to fall." The boat finally worked loose and was lowered into the water. Wallenhaupt feared that the lifeboat would capsize because of the heavy ice on the falls, which would make it impossible to release the lines.

But he didn't have time to lose: the *Puerto Rican* was sinking fast. He threw himself out of the boat and tried to get clear of the sinking ship. Just four feet from the side of the freighter, he remained afloat with little effort because she generated little suction as she went down.

Wallenhaupt spied a small doughnut raft just a short distance away. It was impossible to swim to it, but the heavy seas brought the raft to him and he climbed aboard. Within ten minutes, he'd pulled seven men aboard the tiny raft.

At some point during his ordeal, Wallenhaupt noticed that he'd lost his heavy fur-lined gloves. His hands were getting numb. In fact, all the men's hands were beginning to freeze, and they tried to warm them by holding them over the automatic flare light on the raft. Just then, a large wooden raft floated by. Wallenhaupt grabbed it and secured the two rafts together. The party, now numbering eight men, split up, five of them crawling over to the wooden raft. Two seamen, however, were sitting motionless in the doughnut raft. They could not be revived.

Wallenhaupt moved to join the men on the other raft but found that he no longer had control over his legs. The other men helped him crawl aboard, and they all huddled together in the center of the raft. Thirty-foot seas pitched the raft unmercifully. Soon the heavy seas, breaking wildly over the tiny craft, encapsulated them in a sheet of ice. A huge wave washed one of the men overboard. One man went mad. All of them prayed.

Their prayers did little good. By daybreak the next morning, one of the survivors had vanished into the icy seas. Wallenhaupt watched helplessly as a third seaman also went over the side.

The other man on the raft was lying on his stomach, his head bare and iced over. Wallenhaupt couldn't budge him: He had become frozen stuck to the bottom of the raft.

Wallenhaupt had been on the raft thirty-six hours without food or drink. He tried to quench his thirst by lapping up some snow with his tongue. He lay on the pitching raft beside his frozen shipmate, drifting in and out of consciousness as the seas washed over him. Shortly before daybreak on the third day, he heard voices. He opened his eyes and looked around in the darkness but saw nothing. The mysterious voices were unrelenting, he prayed aloud to drown out the sound.

Near dark, the voices became stronger. "Hello, there! Hello, there!"

Wallenhaupt said his prayers more loudly. Suddenly he felt a violent bump against the side of the raft: it was a destroyer. The men on the deck of the warship broke into cheers when they saw him move.

He was carried into the ship's sickbay and given a hot cup of Bovril (a salty meat extract), a few sips of water, and a shot of morphine. His hands and feet were wrapped in ice-cold towels. Although safe, he was in pain, his hands swollen to three times their normal size and white with frost.

Wallenhaupt was taken ashore at an Iceland port and transferred to a U.S. transport. In the transport's sickbay, they wrapped his legs in cotton and hoisted them on pulleys. Morphine was injected at four-hour intervals. That, along with frequent injections of blood plasma and intravenous feeding, was just about the only thing that kept him alive.

He was taken to a hospital (which caught fire while Wallenhaupt was there). Just two days later, he contracted pneumonia and pleurisy. But that wasn't the worst of his troubles: his legs and fingers, ruined by frostbite, were amputated.

RA-53 was the last convoy to sail that spring because the longer days brought increased Luftwaffe activity. The British Admiralty suspended sailing convoys until November 1943 for other operational reasons as well, including the invasions of Sicily in July (Operation *Husky*) and at Salerno, also in Italy, in September (Operation *Avalanche*). In addition, with the German defeat in North Africa, the Allies regained control of the Mediterranean Sea. This meant that supplies for the Soviets could be sent through the Suez Canal and to ports on the Persian Gulf, a longer, but significantly safer route. With the opening of the Mediterranean, the Germans permanently transferred several Luftwaffe torpedo and dive-bomber squadrons from Norway to southern France to counter this new threat. Coincidently, many of the British Home Fleet escorts provided coverage and faced their old Luftwaffe opponents from up north.

Although Allied merchant ships and the Royal Navy were out of the battle for seven months, the German and Soviet naval forces fought relentlessly from the north coast of Norway eastward into the Kara Sea and half way to Siberia. The most significant encounter was Operation *Wunderland II*.

Between August 1 and October 3, the Kriegsmarine ran Operation *Wunderland II* against the Siberian sea route. The first action actually took place on July 27, when *U-255* (Oberleutnant zur See Erich Harms) sank the Soviet survey ship *Akademik Shokalski*. The U-boat was on its way to establish a weather station near Sporyy Navolok on the northeast coast of Novaya Zemlya. While the station was being constructed, the U-boat refueled a BV-138 flying boat on August 4. This aircraft spent the following week reconnoitering the area as far as the Vilkitsky Strait in preparation for operations against Soviet convoys by the Viking wolf pack U-boat group, comprising *U-302*, *U-354*, and *U-711*, and by the cruiser *Lützow* standing ready in Altenfjord.

No convoys were sighted. When the flying boat was no longer available, a second operation from September 4 to September 6 with *U-255* and *U-601* produced no results. Three weeks later, on August 21, *U-354* sighted a convoy off Port Dikson and followed it eastward, but wasn't able to reach attack position. *U-255* and *U-601* were followed by *U-354* and *U-302* during the last week of August in the western Siberian Sea. They damaged the steamer *Petrovski* (3,771 tons) and sank the *Dikson*.

From August 13 to September 25, 1943, U-boats of the Dachs wolf pack carried out mining operations in the Kara Sea: *U-625* east of the Yugor Strait; *U-639* off the Ob Estuary; *U-960* east of the Matochkin Strait, where *U-711* was hunting in vain; *U-636* off Dikson; *U-629* off Amderma; *U-601*, which had been out patrolling; and U-*960* off Dikson. On September 18 and 24, *U-711* shelled the wireless Russian telegraph stations at Pravdy and Blagopoluchiya.

At the end of September *U-703, U-601*, and *U-960* relieved the boats of the Viking group. On September 30, they located the Soviet four-ship convoy VA-18 coming from the east escorted by the minelayer *Murman* and the minesweeper trawlers *T-31, T-63*, and *T-42. U-960* sank the freighter *Arkhangelsk* near the Sergeya Kirova Islands but missed the *Mossovet*. The next day, *U-703* sank the *Sergei Kirov. U-601* missed the *Murman* and was in turn shelled by her. *U-960* sank the escort *T-42* but missed *A. Andreev*. After these attacks, the U-boats returned to their Norwegian bases, declaring the operation a success.

The German U-boats had dealt a heavy blow to navigation in the western Arctic. So much so that Soviet authorities decided to leave fifteen transport vessels wintering in Port Dikson.

On November 15, 1943, the fall's first convoy, JW-54A, set out from Loch Ewe with eighteen ships, followed by JW-54B's fourteen ships seven days later. These two and the first half of December's convoys, JW-55A, all made it safely to Russia, as did the one returning convoy, RA-51, despite attacks by U-boats and aircraft.

The commander in chief of the Kriegsmarine, Gross Admiral Karl Dönitz, who had replaced Admiral Raeder on January 30, 1943, came under increasing pressure to sanction a sortie by his remaining heavy surface ships. An opportunity presented itself at Christmastime, as it became apparent that outbound convoy JW-55B and homeward-bound convoy RA-55A would pass relatively close to one another as they rounded the North Cape of Norway, only a short passage from the Kriegsmarine base at Langefjord. On December 25, the battleship *Scharnhorst* (Captain Fritz Hintze) with the destroyers Z-29, Z-30, Z-33, Z-34, and *Z-38* left Norway's Altenfjord under the overall command of Konteradmiral Erich Bey.

British intelligence intercepted and decoded messages about the German plan. To counter the Kriegsmarine threat, the British assigned Force 2 composed of the battleship *Duke of York*, light cruiser *Jamaica*, and four destroyers—the Norwegian *Stord*, and the British *Scorpion*, *Saumarez*, and *Savage*—under the command of Admiral Sir Bruce Fraser to escort convoy JW-55B. Force 1 commanded by Vice Admiral Robert Burnett in his flagship HMS *Belfast* with the cruisers *Norfolk* and *Sheffield* would cover westbound RA-55A.

At 0755 hours on December 26, Bey ordered the 4th Destroyers Flotilla to search for the convoy, placing each destroyer five miles from each other while *Scharnhorst* went on a southwest course, later turning to the west-northwest. Partly as a consequence of this and of poorly transmitted and executed orders, *Scharnhorst* and the destroyers lost contact with each other.

Forty minutes later, *Norfolk*'s radar picked up *Scharnhorst* at a distance of 16 miles. *Belfast* also picked up the contact, and along with *Sheffield*, they headed for the lone German ship. For Admiral Burnett and his senior officers, this was the opportunity they had been waiting for, and they accepted it calmly. When the cruisers closed to within 6 miles, they launched the opening salvos of what was to become the Battle of North Cape.

Belfast's crew described the battle in their diaries, journals, and interviews. *Belfast* Captain Frederick Parham was among those who recalled the battle:

> On the evening of Christmas Day 1943 we had a warning from the Admiralty that it was believed that the Scharnhorst was probably putting to sea and we were ordered to push on ahead ... and to cover another convoy which was on its way out from England and was about halfway to Murmansk. I remember very well having a long discussion with my Admiral ... in the Charthouse about what we should do ... that I think finished at about midnight.

The news about the approaching *Scharnhorst* was met with mixed emotions. On the lower deck, the information that the German battleship was at sea was greeted with a mixture of apprehension and disbelief. Bob Shrimpton, known as "Ping" by virtue of his role as *Belfast*'s ASDIC operator, thought that it was all "a load of rubbish." In the engine room, however, Lieutenant Charles Simpson, *Belfast*'s torpedo officer, remembered more of a sense of calm and reserve:

Nobody showed any apprehension ... after all this was the job for which we'd trained, in some cases for twenty years. This was it. You now relied upon the skill of the gunners to sink the enemy before he sunk you. This was where interdepartmental co-operation was seen at its most intense. We got the gunners to the position they desired as fast as we could.

Since the Christmas Day announcement that *Scharnhorst* had put to sea, *Belfast's* crew was at their defense (combat action) stations. Larry Fursland was part of the engine room staff and recalled how the day passed: silent, tense, everybody waiting. Finally, on the day after Christmas, St. Stephen's Day, the storm broke. Fursland recalled that:

Then came Boxing Day, St. Stephen's Day, I remember as only yesterday, twenty to nine in the morning that's 0845 Navy time, "Action Stations," bugle. The Padre (chaplain) gave a short service of prayer and we all had to go to our action stations ... well my place was down the port diesel, and that's where I went down and that's where I stayed for twelve hours ... Chief ERA came down and started up the diesels and left me. I was clamped up each side, watertight doors, and just a hatch to go down.

While Burnett's 10th Cruiser Squadron screened the vulnerable merchant ships, Admiral Fraser, in the battleship HMS *Duke of York*, with the cruiser HMS *Jamaica* and four destroyers, set sail to deploy to the south, between *Scharnhorst* and her base in Norway. The trap was set. If Fraser's *Duke of York* could bring *Scharnhorst* to action, she would enjoy an overwhelming superiority in firepower, with her 14-inch guns out-ranging and out-punching *Scharnhorst's* smaller 11-inch guns.

At 0730 on the morning of Boxing Day (December 26), the British superiority in numbers further increased when Bey's destroyers were detached to search for the convoy. They failed to make contact and, being notoriously bad sea boats (in part due to their oversized 5.9-inch gun turrets), they were ordered home as the weather worsened.

By this stage, JW-55B was 50 miles south of Bear Island, as the Germans headed north to intercept. Meanwhile, Admiral Fraser was 200 miles away to the southwest, and Admiral Burnett's cruisers were approaching the convoy from the east.

First contact took place just before 0900 hours on December 26 when *Belfast* detected *Scharnhorst* by radar, heading south only 30 miles east of the convoy. HMS *Norfolk* engaged and hit the German battlecruiser, followed by *Belfast* and *Sheffield*. Crucially during this action, *Norfolk* disabled

Scharnhorst's main fire control radar, leaving her almost blind. She turned north and away, still trying to circle Burnett's force and reach the convoy.

Belfast had never fired a full broadside before, and some of the effects were unanticipated. Alone down at his action station on the port diesel generator, Fursland was faced with a problem: the vibration from the first broadside knocked out the two circulating pumps that cooled it. Without the generator, two triple 6-inch turrets—half *Belfast*'s armament—would be out of action.

Acting quickly, Fursland diverted a fire main along the passageway above his position and down through the hatch. Without any tools, he connected it to the generator with his bare hands, bypassing the disabled pumps, and circulated salt water from the main through the generator for twelve hours. He was completely alone.

The first broadside had caused another problem on the bridge, where the armored door of the plot room had been blown off by the shockwave from the *Belfast*'s own after turrets. For Seaman George Burridge, the destruction had a silver lining: "for the rest of the battle we [were] literally able to see what was going on first hand!"

Admiral Burnett was faced with possibly the most significant decision of his career, as Captain Parham later recalled:

> *The* Scharnhorst *turned north and made away at high speed, and this is where my Admiral, Burnett, had to make his really big decision, and I am absolutely convinced it was the right one. Which was that he was not to follow the* Scharnhorst *... because we couldn't possibly have kept up. The weather was so bad that she would have probably outstripped us and would merely have got round us and probably back on to the convoy. And so my Admiral's decision was to fall back on the convoy and wait and see, I remember him saying to me "I'll bet she'll come again."*

Burnett was absolutely correct. *Scharnhorst* returned to the convoy, only to find the 10th Cruiser Squadron once more in her path. Contact was regained at noon, and all three cruisers opened fire. During a twenty-minute firefight, *Scharnhorst* was hit again, and *Norfolk* was badly damaged by the battleship's 11-inch shells.

The German ship fled south, away from the convoy in an attempt to return to Norway. This time, Burnett shadowed by radar. With *Norfolk* disabled and *Sheffield* suffering from engine problems, *Belfast* was at one point pursuing her formidable adversary alone. Burridge was rather less than impressed by this development:

I recall Admiral Burnett coming on and saying that we were at the moment alone and we were going to engage the Scharnhorst, *which frightened the life out of everybody! ... [The atmosphere] was as tense as it could be, because we knew we were in real danger then.*

Shrimpton was also painfully aware of just how dangerous this period was: "We had to do a cat and mouse game with it ... if she had turned towards us and opened fire with those massive gun turrets of hers she would have blown us out of the water."

Brian Butler, another gunner confined with twenty-six other men in one of the ship's 6-inch turrets, recalled how "During lulls in the action, you'd sit there with your eyes closed. There was no way you could sleep. It was cold in the turret, bitterly cold in the turret."

Admiral Fraser in *Duke of York* was to the south-southwest, ideally placed to cut off *Scharnhorst*'s retreat. Fraser made radar contact soon after 1600 hours at a range of 22 miles and closed in. At 1650 hours, *Belfast* illuminated *Scharnhorst* with star shell. Burnett's cruisers engaged from one side and *Duke of York* and *Jamaica* from the other.

Duke of York succeeded in hitting *Scharnhorst* with her first salvo and swiftly began to inflict severe damage. Shrimpton, his ASDIC unusable in the frantic high-speed maneuvering of a surface action, witnessed the death blows.

Once the Duke of York *got in there, with those tremendous guns, it was horrendous to watch ... they just smashed the thing to pieces ... it was just one blaze from one end to the other ... You could see these flashes in the darkness coming through and you could watch the fall of shot as it lit up ... we closed as close as possible so that we could open fire on it ... her guns kept firing, just before she went down.*

Scharnhorst's forward 11-inch turret Anton was put out of action early, jammed to starboard with guns in the elevated position. Turret Bruno, the remaining forward turret, soon followed when an outbreak of fire forced the crew to flood it to avoid a catastrophic explosion. At 1708 hours, a 14-inch shell hit *Scharnhorst*'s aircraft hangar aft of turret Caesar, starting another fire.

At 1725 hours, Admiral Bey signaled his high command, informing them that heavy surface forces had surrounded *Scharnhorst*. At this stage, the chance of escape was still good, as *Scharnhorst*'s superior speed still enabled her to gradually increase the range. Her greatest chance came at 1824 hours, when a lucky shot severed the connection for *Duke of York*'s main fire control radar, forcing her to cease fire. A young officer, Lieutenant Bates, recognizing the urgency of the situation, climbed the mast and reconnected the radar.

By this stage, unbeknownst to the British, *Scharnhorst* was already lost. A shell from *Duke of York*'s last salvo had penetrated No. 1 boiler room and severed a steam pipe. *Scharnhorst*'s only advantage slipped away from her as her speed dropped to 10 knots. Bey sent his last signal to his superiors: "We shall fight to the last shell." But the end was near. According to eyewitnesses, *Scharnhorst* was on fire from stem to stern.

As soon as Fraser recognized what had happened, he seized his chance and ordered his destroyers to close in to point-blank range and attack with torpedoes. Crewmembers reported seeing the destroyers approaching at high speed, a comforting sight.

HMS *Saumarez* paid the price for this daring attack. *Scharnhorst* was mortally wounded, but she still had teeth, and a German shell smashed into the flimsy director control tower of the destroyer, killing eleven men.

Seaman Eric Parry was aboard *Scorpion* when ordered to attack the *Scharnhorst* with torpedoes:

> *I could hear the orders from the captain to various officers so it became obvious we were close to the enemy. I thought at one time we were going right alongside as we seemed to be looking down the muzzles of* Scharnhorst's *armament.*
>
> *Our captain was calm with his orders — the S class destroyers being encouraged to attack on their own with torpedoes.* Savage *and* Saumarez *were on the battle cruiser's port quarter,* Scorpion *and* Stord *on the starboard. We closed at a range of 2,000 yards:* Scharnhorst *could have blown us out of the water. I could hear the torpedo officer calling off the fish as they fired, swinging away we fired all eight and heard them running towards* Scharnhorst, *two hits were reported. Gunner (T) reported to bridge "all torpedoes fired."*
>
> *The captain replied: "Good, let's get the hell out of here."*
>
> *As we turned away we could hear muffled explosions. The S force attack over,* Virago, Jamaica *and* Belfast *followed by* Musketeer *and* Matchless *went in. By now* Scharnhorst *was a dead duck. About 1930 I saw this once magnificent battlecruiser go down by the bows with her screws still turning as she rolled over and sank.*

Four torpedoes found their targets, leaving *Scharnhorst* dead in the water and a sitting target as *Duke of York* and the cruisers opened fire again. At 1928 hours, *Duke of York* ceased fire for the last time, having expended nearly five hundred 14-inch shells. Further torpedo attacks followed, although by now *Scharnhorst*'s captain had given the order to abandon ship.

At 1945 hours, *Belfast* was ordered in to deliver the *coup de grâce* to *Scharnhorst* with Lieutenant Andy Palmer's torpedoes. Years later, he described the moment:

> *In that very last stage she was a very clear point of fire because she was on fire ... she was a mass of flames all the way along the ship ... we closed a bit [but] Bob wouldn't go closer than 6,000 yards, at the beginning of this last phase, Scharnhorst was firing an occasional gun and Bob wasn't going to take the cruisers in any closer than 6,000 yards ... we swung the ship and fired the starboard torpedoes and I said to Captain Parham, "Swing her back the other way and we'll fire the other salvo" but by the time we got the ship swinging somehow or other the Norfolk had crept up ... and I would have torpedoed her so I had to say "I'm sorry she's fouled the range" so we turned round and then when we turned round and when we turned back again the flames had gone out and she's sunk ... I was so certain that we'd got a hit that I had a swastika painted on to that particular tube.*

In fact, as *Belfast* turned, a tremendous explosion ripped through the German ship, probably originating from her forward magazines. She rapidly began to settle, and at 1948 hours, as Lieutenant Palmer fired, her radar blip vanished, followed by a series of muffled underwater explosions.

The initial reaction aboard *Belfast* was one of elation, but as the full enormity of loss of life became apparent, that elation was soon replaced by more somber feelings. All that could be seen were a pitifully small number of red lifejacket lights, each representing a man fighting for his life in the oil-covered water. Seaman Jack Wright was conscious that, when all was said and done, the Germans were just "sailors like ourselves."

Shrimpton remembered a moment of dead silence. "I think a lot of people were thinking there's a hell of a lot of men on there the same as us, youngsters, families, wives, kids, and they're in that water. I think that was a subduing effect."

Seaman Eric Parry recalled picking up survivors:

In company with Matchless *we were ordered to move in as close as possible and pick up survivors. Being stopped, the ASDIC crew were sweeping the area in case U-boats were about. We were now attempting to rescue the poor bloody crew of the* Scharnhorst, *what few were left, as few survived. The survivors were drenched in oil and half dead with cold, and swallowing fuel, some were injured.*

One of them, a very "arrogant Nazi," seemed to want to die rather than become a prisoner of war. Whilst hanging on to the scrambling net over the ship's side he refused all help from me and my mates, but we finally pulled him aboard where he still struggled and was very arrogant and defiant. He was dragged on deck but refused to sit. He fell down and started to cry. I went over to him, pulled him to his feet, at the same time receiving a blow to the chest. Stripping most of the oily clothing from the young seaman, he was only 19, known as "Hans," we discovered a shoulder wound which was bandaged with a handkerchief.

The next day the survivors were transferred to the Duke of York. *As the "arrogant Nazi" left he walked over to me, put his hand on my shoulder, stood for a moment and smiled, shook my hand vigorously and then got into the boat. Opening my hand I found an oily, soggy photograph. I never saw him again but was proud to have known him. A German sailor, some poor mother's son who, in a small way, was saved from the cold Arctic waters of the North Cape.*

Boy Seaman David Jones, aged seventeen, added his recollections of the battle:

It was only when the Scharnhorst *caught fire and was burning; you could see it on the horizon. At that time I was on P2 twin 4-inch gun ... and we had a port at the front of the gun shield, open, and I had my head out there looking and I could see it.*

We could see the tracers and things like that, we couldn't actually see the ships because it was pitch dark ... that time of year there was just a couple of hours of daylight at noon.

About thirty odd survivors out of about 2,000. I sometimes think of them, particularly about Christmas and say a little prayer for them. I'm not a religious person but I think of them sometimes.

Just thirty-six survivors were rescued before the British ships were ordered to vacate the area due to the danger of attack by U-boats. The death toll was 1,927 men, many left on board *Scharnhorst*, as well as several hundred who perished in the water.

As a consequence, the command to abandon rescue operations has become the source of some controversy in recent years, but the U-boat danger was very real. Rear Admiral Bey had received a signal at 1911 hours stating that all U-boats and aircraft in the area were being deployed to assist *Scharnhorst*. But in the frozen waters of the Arctic, it was highly unlikely that any of the *Scharnhorst* men would have survived more than a few minutes waiting for rescue.

British dead numbered eighteen from *Norfolk* and *Saumarez*. This was bad, but the completeness of the victory could not be denied. As the triumphant *Belfast* made her way to Murmansk, Captain Parham ordered "spice the main brace," and extra rum was distributed to all. In Murmansk, eighteen-year-old Oscar de Ville was faced with the reality of battle, as the victorious destroyers, cheered by all the ships in the harbor, tied up alongside and their casualties were brought across *Belfast*'s decks to the waiting ambulances on shore:

> We went back to Kola ... there was a small assembly of ships, some damaged, and I think the experience [I] had there that I remember the most was being detailed to be one of a hospital party to take some of the wounded to a hospital locally, which meant helping them across the decks of destroyers onto land ... and that was quite a harrowing thing at 18 to be doing. I thought they were very very brave guys—one felt very bad about leaving them in a hospital in a one-off village like Kola ... goodness knows how good it was.

Fraser's forces entered the Kola Inlet in triumph, although not without genuine regard for an enemy they believed had fought bravely in very unfavorable circumstances. In a moving ceremony aboard *Duke of York*, the German survivors were assembled and the flagship's officers somberly saluted them, after which Admiral Fraser paid tribute to the courage and determination of the enemy ship and her crew. Privately he later told his officers: "I hope that if any of you are ever called upon to lead a ship into action against an opponent many times superior you will command your ship as gallantly as *Scharnhorst* was commanded today."

The ship's company was aware of the importance of their achievement. With the destruction of *Scharnhorst*, any hopes the Germans had of mounting a serious surface threat to the Arctic convoys disappeared. Palmer summed up the victory later: "We'd been waiting for this opportunity for a couple of years and we knew that once the *Scharnhorst* was eliminated the real threat to arctic convoys would be removed ... we returned to Scapa and great jubilation."

Although the Kriegsmarine's large ships were no longer a threat, the U-boats were still a force to be reckoned with. New types of torpedoes were being added to their arsenal, making them even more deadly to merchant ships and escorts.

The first was the FAT (*Federapparat Torpedo*), which came into service in late 1942. Instead of running a straight course after being fired, a FAT followed a preprogrammed wandering course with regular 180-degree turns. Convoy JW-56A would be the first Arctic convoy to encounter U-boats with FATs.

The *Zaunkönig* (German for "Wren" and designated as "GNAT" by the Allies) was introduced in autumn 1943. Designed to be an escort-killer, it worked by locking onto the loudest propellor noise after a run of 400 meters from its launch. Its one drawback was that the loudest noise often proved to be the U-boat itself.

Another innovation was the snorkel, which, when raised to the surface, allowed a U-boat to recharge its batteries without surfacing. A low-lying camouflaged float attached to the snorkel was all that betrayed the U-boat's presence. It was almost invisible to the eye and no radar could detect it.

JW-56A, a twenty-ship convoy, sailed from Loch Ewe on January 12, 1944, heavily escorted by the cruisers HMS *Brunswick* and *Kent* in addition to destroyers *Hardy* (SOE), *Inconstant*, *Obdurate*, *Offa*, *Savage*, *Venus*, *Vigilant*, *Virago*, and the Norwegian *Stord*. Three days later, the convoy ran into heavy weather off the Faroe Islands, and many of the ships set off for Akureyri, Iceland, where they took shelter until January 21. After clearing Iceland and setting course once more for the Kola Inlet, the convoy's troubles were far from over. Waiting for the rich merchant ship targets was a line of ten U-boats.

Penelope Barker was the first victim, falling to *U-278* (Kapitänleutnant Joachim Franze) leaving sixteen dead and fifty-six survivors to be picked up by *Savage* on January 25. The British destroyer *Obdurate* (Lieutenant Commander C. E. L. Sclater, DSO and Bar, RN) was damaged by a GNAT from *U-360* (Kapitänleutnant Klaus-Helmuth Becker) and left the convoy. The next day *Andrew G. Curtin* was sunk by *U-716* (Oberleutnant Hans Dunkelberg) this time with three dead; sixty-eight survivors were picked up by *Inconstant*.

The final blow that day was struck by again by *U-360*, which damaged *Fort Bellingham*. The wounded ship fell behind the convoy and later that same day was sunk by *U-957* (Oberleutnant Gerd Schaar). Master James Ninian Maley, Convoy Commodore Commander I. W.

Whitehorn, RN, four naval staff members, twenty-two crewmembers, and seven gunners were picked up by HMS *Offa* (Lieutenant Commander R. F. Leonard, RN) and landed at Murmansk. Two crewmembers were taken prisoner by *U-957*. Eighteen crewmembers, sixteen gunners, and two naval staff members were lost. In less than a day, U-boats had destroyed 15 percent of the convoy, fifty-five men, and tons of valuable war supplies in addition to eliminating one of the escorts as an effective weapon.

U-278 struck again with a GNAT on January 30. The destroyer HMS *Hardy* was severely damaged and had to be sunk by HMS *Venus.*

HMS *Mahratta* as part of the escort for JW-57 was the next warship felled by a GNAT. JW-57, consisting of forty-two merchant ships, two tankers that doubled as oilers, and the rescue ship *Copeland*, all under the command of Commodore R. D. Binks aboard *Fort Romaine*, departed Loch Ewe on February 20, 1944. In addition, three Soviet-manned coastal minesweepers and three patrol craft were being delivered to the Soviet Northern Fleet.

The corvettes *Bluebell*, *Camellia*, *Lotus*, and *Rhododendron* provided close escort, along with a local escort of *Burdock* and *Dianella*, also corvettes. Also joining were two Western Approaches support groups, one under Commander Ismay J. Tyson in *Keppel* with *Beagle*, *Boadicea*, and *Walker*. The second support group, under Commander Louis B. A. Majendie, had two frigates, *Byron* and *Strule*, in addition to destroyers *Wanderer* and *Watchman*. Rounding out the escort force was the escort carrier HMS *Chaser*. Distant cover forces were commanded by Vice Admiral Irwin G. Glennie in the cruiser *Black Prince*. With him were the cruisers *Berwick* and *Jamaica* and the Polish light cruiser *Dragon*, as well as a destroyer screen including *Mahratta* (Lieutenant Commander Eric A. F. Drought, DSC, RN).

Lying in wait were eight U-boats of the Werewolf wolf pack.

On February 23, HMS *Chaser* flew off her F6F Wildcat aircraft to chase an FW-200 Condor shadowing the convoy. *Chaser*'s aircraft also flew patrols around the convoy and located several U-boats in the area. They were almost immediately detected by a Swordfish patrol, whereupon Commander Tyson's *Keppel* depth charged and sank *U-713* (Oberleutnant Henri Gosejacob) with its fifty-man crew.

Two days later, a long-range PBY Catalina from 210 Squadron RAF flew above the convoy and attacked the trailing *U-601* (Oberleutnant Otto Hansen), sinking the boat along with the fifty-one men on board. So far U-boats hadn't got close enough to attack thanks to the air patrols, but flight ops ended at dusk, leaving the ships vulnerable to the U-boat's night surface attack tactic.

On HMS *Wanderer*'s bridge, there was a certain amount of criticism from Lieutenant Commander Reginald F. Whinney about Vice Admiral Glennie's plan for night screening positions of the convoy. In the prevailing rough seas, the convoy was thought to be even more vulnerable than usual to a stern attack, but only *Mahratta* and one other destroyer had been assigned to cover this vulnerable sector. Whinney's misgivings were proved justified.

On the evening of February 25, Whinney received a message from one of the destroyers calling up the flagship on radio telephone: "Have been hit by a torpedo, aft, and am stopped." Soon after he heard another message: "Have been hit amidships by a second torpedo."

A GNAT from *U-990* had struck *Mahratta* at 2055 hours. The destroyer exploded and sank within minutes. HMS *Impulsive* (Lieutenant Commander P. Bekenn, RN) and *Wanderer* quickly arrived on the scene to pick up survivors. *Wanderer*'s antiquated guns illuminated the scene with star shell so they could search for survivors. Only sixteen men were recovered from the freezing waters; the commander, ten officers, and 209 ratings lost their lives.

Noel Simon was on board *Chaser* during the convoy and later wrote about what happened when the ships reached Murmansk:

> On arrival in Murmansk, the survivors were transferred to Chaser for the passage home. I talked to a group of Mahratta ratings—none of the officers had survived—who told me of the heroism of their doctor. Having managed to climb onto one of the few Carley floats to have come through the sinking, he set about hauling the others aboard. The float soon became overcrowded.
>
> Remarking almost casually, "There's not enough room for us all," the doctor slipped over the side into the sea and was never seen again.
>
> The straightforward manner in which the survivors recounted this event, and the admiration and affection with which they spoke of their doctor—whose name (oddly enough) none of them knew—made a deep impression upon me.
>
> Not until months later, and then quite by chance, did I discover that Mahratta's doctor was none other than Peter McRae, a contemporary of mine at school. As a boy he had been one of the most delightful and gifted of people. A good all-rounder, successful in all he undertook, yet completely unassuming. I remember him as an exceptionally fine rugger player—certainly the most outstanding fly-half in the school during my time there.

*Several years after the war, a proposal was made that his self-sacrifice should
be recognized by a suitable award but, sadly, the Admiralty did not concur.*

The succeeding convoys, RA-57, JW-58, RA-58, and RA-59 totaling 161
ships, only lost one merchant ship: *Empire Tourist* from RA-57. After
RA-59 arrived in Loch Ewe on May 6, 1944, the British Admiralty
again halted the convoys until mid-August. Although the large Allied
convoys had ceased, a constant flow of small Soviet convoys and single
ship sailings continued to work their way through the eastern Arctic.

Freed of the need to fight the large convoys, the Germans turned
their attention to disrupting this traffic. It was during this time that one
of the most tragic events of the Arctic sea war occurred, when *Marina
Raskova* (the former U.S. freighter *Ironclad*) under command of Captain
V. A. Demidov, was sunk on August 12, 1944.

On August 8, *Marina Raskova* put to sea with a load of general cargo
and 354 passengers, including 116 women and 24 children, as part of
convoy BD-5. She was accompanied by three escort trawlers, T-*114*,
T-*116*, and T-*118*, with escort commander Captain of 1st Rank A. W.
Shmelev. By order of Shmelev, the trawlers protected the transport with
a half circle, ahead and to the left and right of *Marina Raskova*.

Among the crew on *Marina Raskova* was twenty-year-old Claudia
Mihajlovna Nekrasov, who had just finished a course at the Arkhangelsk
Medical Institute. The diploma of doctor of general medicine was nestled
in a small suitcase among her simple belongings. Nekrasov lodged with
two girls aboard *Marina Raskova*: medical assistant Shuru Galstuhovu
and doctor Revekku (years later, Nekrasov no longer remembers her
surname). Both were young and cheerful. Revekku was twenty-four,
and Galstuhovu had only recently turned eighteen.

On the evening of August 12, 1944, Nekrasov conducted First Aid
lessons with crew. It was the first time she had led a class, and she was a
little worried. To make a good impression upon her listeners, she wore
her best dress and shoes. She recalled the events of the voyage in her
somewhat broken English:

> *Suddenly a blow shook the vessel. Doors swung open, boxes flew off tables,
> heaps of medicine vials scattered on the deck. I was flung away from a door,
> at falling painfully and was kicked by something.*
>
> *Limping, I headed out in a corridor only to find it filling with water.
> She ran out on deck and was drenched from above [by] the cold stream of
> sea water.*

Children and adults rushed about on deck, searching for rescue. Shouts were heard:

"Torpedo!"

"Boat!!"

"We're sinking, help!"

Panic became ripe. And in the sea new explosion thundered ...

On the bridge of T-118, Shmelev and the commander of a trawler, Captain Lieutenant Kuptsov, heard the explosion. Although sonar did not find any hint of U-boats nearby, messages received from Dikson asserted that they prowled somewhere nearby.

Shmelev ordered a course change to close in on White Island, 60 miles away, where he hoped shallow depths will not allow submarines to steal up to an escort.

Then at 2151 hours, the trawler's hull shuddered from the deaf explosion distributed behind the stern. Having turned back, Shmelev with Kuptsov had seen Marina Raskova's *right side foamy in the water and wreathed in smoke.*

With a rage Shmelev punched on gunwale.

"It seems it was a mine," he signaled the other ships.

"Typically for not contact mine," he thought.

"Ask Marina Raskova *how they're doing."*

Raskova replied: "I have a hole on the starboard side."

"Let's go to their aid," Shmelev ordered. "Have 116 and 114 there too."

As T-118 rushed off to the transport, she was torpedoed in the stern and a minute later began to plunge quickly into the sea.

This explosion also was heard on Marina Raskova.

Marina Raskova's *Captain Victor Alexandrovich Demidov and crew quickly put things in order on a deck, calmed the frightened people and stopped the beginnings of panic.*

"Women and children—forward!"

On Marina Raskova, *the first boats had been loaded with children and women. Only then did the other passengers begin to abandon ship.*

On a deck the senior assistant to Captain P. I. Menynutkin with group of sailors tried to get a patch under a hole. Unfortunately, all efforts of crew to rescue a vessel were vain. Having tilted to starboard, Marina Raskova *slowly plunged into the sea.*

Boats from T-116 and T-114 began rescuing passengers and seamen from Marina Raskova *and the sinking trawler T-118. T-114's boats picked up all the women and children from the steamship. In total on this small craft were over two hundred persons.*

After the explosion, the trawler T-118 with the torn-off stern held on the surface of 27 minutes, then its depth charges, which had rolled down from the racks, exploded and the flagship disappeared.

Without sparing any effort, seamen struggled to keep their ship afloat, but the outcome was inevitable.

Shmelev, who was onboard T-114 after the destruction of his ship, analyzed both explosions and not finding any suspicious underwater noises, concluded that the escort has got on a minefield and no submarine was nearby.

But it was.

Six thousand yards away from DB-5, *U-365's* commander, Oberleutnant Heinz Eckelmann, carefully raised his periscope, looking for the next victim. Meanwhile, the commander of T-*114*, Captain Lieutenant I. O. Panasjuk, started rescuing passengers of *Marina Raskova* and stopped his antisubmarine search. The weather began to worsen, but rescue operations went ahead at full speed. The evacuation of passengers, and then of the vessel's crew, went smoothly. During these dramatic and dangerous hours, the seamen of the steamship *Marina Raskova* showed the best human qualities: courage, selflessness, and readiness to offer themselves for the sake of the lives of others.

Nekrasov did not consider herself as the weak woman among the valiant men aboard *Marina Raskova*. When it came time for her to abandon ship, she did the same as the crewmembers, leaving the vessel with them. She also helped the other women into the lifeboats and handed them the children who were on board.

Claudia Mihajlovna Nekrasov continued her story:

Suddenly the trawler T-114 was rocked by a deafening explosion. A high water column and smoke shot up, ship fragments, and when the smoke has dissipated, only the bow part of the trawler was seen. In three minutes it turned over and disappeared.

Horror captured all who observed this picture. On the lost trawler were over two hundred persons rescued from Marina Raskova *and trawler T-118 and most terribly, 136 of them were women and small children.*

Shaken by the awful tragedy played before their eyes, passengers noticed at once that their little craft has ceased to move. T-116 had chopped off the towline and at full speed left the scene.

The commander of a trawler Captain Lieutenant V. A. Babanov, at last understood that the escort was exposed to attacks of the submarine or submarines and was afraid for life the 186 survivors he had on board and the life of his ship.

Shortly after T-116 disappeared behind the horizon, at two fifteen. A double explosion shook the sky and the sea: fascist pirates had finished Marina Raskova.

When the steamship disappeared from a surface from sea depths, the submarine slowly emerged. The boat passed by the overflowed boats, heading west after the surviving trawler.

In a stormy sea remained more than 150 persons. Except for the kugas [small boats] there were three whaleboats, several lifeboats, and a boat from the lost trawler T-114.

It is difficult to describe sufferings of these people. Semi-undressed, hungry, tormented by thirst, doused by ice splashes, and penetrated by a gale, they behaved differently in these hours and days of heart-rending experiences. The general misfortune is a litmus piece of paper that showed sincere qualities of everyone. Here was heroism and cowardice, selflessness and egoism, hope and despair, struggle and capitulation.

The high call of duty and courage was shown by such people as the senior technician-lieutenant M. P. Makarovsky, the captain purser. S. Rashev, the third assistant to the captain of a steamship Marina Raskova I. D. Vondruhov, chief petty officer N. I. Alekseev, engineer Malinin, captain Voevodkin, science officer Kuharev, nurse Galstuhova, and others.

For more than twenty days, searches by the people scattered across Kara Sea which have endured tragedy at White island proceeded. In them participated seven ships of the Belomorsky military flotilla, eight seaplanes, field men, and polar explorers on island White Island and peninsula Yamal.

When still hundred miles from White Island, we were found out by a seaplane piloted by Captain S. V. Sokola, and it happened that after almost in three weeks of drift only fourteen persons were still alive.

Samples of courage and heroism was shown by the pilots. Unprecedented, the feat was made by Lieutenant Colonel M. I. Kozlov. So overloaded with rescued people, the aircraft couldn't take off. The pilot, Matvej Ilyich, used it as a boat for twelve hours on a raging sea among the huge waves ready the entire fifty to the White Island.

Remember the names of those who risked their lives, tearing the survivors from the icy grip of death. These were military pilots Kozlov, Sokol, Fedukov, Khotulev, Evdokimov, Ruban, Belikov and their comrades. Looking for crews of warships involved, DO-203, BO-2W, MO-501, T-60, T-61, T-116, and T-117. Vice Admiral S. Kucherov, commander of the White Sea Flotilla, personally led the search and rescue effort.

The boat with *Marina Raskova*'s captain V. A. Demidovym, First Lieutenant P. I. Menyputkinym, the second assistant to captain A. A. Kazimirom, the fourth assistant N. A. Vaganov, A. N. Volochkovym, the assistant to the captain V. I. Vennikovym's military gunners, and four rank-and-file members of crew, whose names it was not possible to establish, completely disappeared in the cold open spaces of Kara Sea.

At the end of August at Rogozin's Cape on White Island, a boat with twenty bodies was found. It proved impossible to identify individuals or which ship the boat was from, so all were buried in a communal grave on this far polar island.

Claudia Mihajlovna Nekrasov's grief was enduring:

> For about a month I had still nightmares connected with memoirs on torpedoing. I could not see relatives of victims on Marina Raskova which, having learnt that I survived, came in hope of learning about destiny of the relatives. What could I tell them?

Of all the losses suffered at sea in the Arctic regions during World War II, this was the greatest single loss of life and, perhaps, the greatest tragedy. On board *Marina Raskova* and the two minesweepers were 618 people. Sailors and airmen rescued 256 people. The 362 dead included all of the children.

On August 15, 1944, JW-59 with thirty-three ships left Loch Ewe for the Kola Inlet. This was the beginning of the end for the Arctic Convoys.

Although on the defensive in the air, on land, and at sea, Wehrmacht forces continued fighting tenaciously. After the destruction of its surface units, Kriegsmarine U-boats continued to strike in the Atlantic and Arctic. For boats operating in the Atlantic, each mission meant almost certain death from Allied hunter-killer groups, which were often built around escort carriers or radar-equipped long-range aircraft that flew day and night in all weather. With the loss of their bases in France's Atlantic coast after the D-Day landings in June, the boats stationed there transferred to Norway, operating against the Arctic convoys with occasional forays west to the British coast.

A FEW FINAL WORDS

Sixteen convoys sailed between August 1944 and April 1945. U-boats claimed seven merchant ships and four Royal Navy escorts. Three of the escorts, HMS *Bluebell*, *Lapwing*, and *Goodall*, were lost in the final nine weeks of the war.

Although World War II in Europe ended on May 8, the last convoy, RA-67, sailed from the Kola Inlet for the River Clyde on May 31, 1945. The convoy had to contend with the ice barrier and leftover drifting mines, and it was deemed prudent to sail one more convoy. Then it was over, the convoy system was dismantled, and, except for the tragedy of PQ-17, the memories of the Arctic Convoys were overshadowed by other World War II events.

Between August 1941 and May 1945, seventy-seven Arctic convoys sailed the Arctic Ocean, not including Operation *FB*, which totaled roughly 1,400 merchant ships. Of these, 104 were sunk and 829 lives were lost. It cost the British Royal Navy eighteen warships with 1,944 of their crews. The German toll was five war ships, thirty-one U-boats, and an unknown number of aircraft and dead. The Soviets lost at least twenty-nine other merchant ships as part of the Arctic Convoys as well as an uncounted number of warships, aircraft, and casualties. Although these numbers pale in comparison to the losses sustained in the Battle of the Atlantic or to millions of men, women, and children killed during the Great Patriotic War and throughout the world, the losses still reverberate.

Regardless of the comparison, Arctic Convoys were proportionately the deadliest for ships and crews of any in the war. Yet the sacrifices brought on by these convoys have been largely ignored or forgotten in Europe and America, except for a few isolated locations in England and Scotland. The Russians remember and have raised monuments honoring all those who fought regardless of nationality. Even there, though, memories are fading as veterans of the war die. So it remains for us in later generations to remember their sacrifices.

So long as we live, they too shall live,

for they are now a part of us,

as we remember them.

—R. B. Gittelsohn

RESOURCES

The research material and stories used for this book came from a variety of sources. Many of the books and publications are out of print and their authors have passed on.

BOOKS (BY LANGUAGE)

English

Blond, Georges. *Ordeal Below Zero*. Mayflower-Dell: London, 1956.

Brookes, Ewart. *The Gates of Hell: The Terrible Story of the Arctic Convoys in the Second World War*. Arrow Books Ltd.: London, 1962.

Carse, Robert. *A Cold Corner of Hell: The Story of the Murmansk Convoys 1941–45*. Doubleday & Company, Inc.: Garden City, New Jersey, 1969.

Campbell, Ian and Macintyre, Donald. *The Kola Run: A Record of Arctic Convoys 1941–1945*. Futura Publications Limited: London, 1958.

Churchill, Winston S. *The Grand Alliance*. Houghton Mifflin Company: Boston, 1950.

Clifford, Kenneth J., Lieutenant Colonel USMCR, Ed. *The United States Marines in Iceland, 1941–1942*. Historical Division Headquarters, U. S. Marine Corps: Washington, D.C., 1970.

Donovan, James A., Colonel, U.S. Marine Corps (Ret). *Outpost in the North Atlantic: Marines in the Defense of Iceland*. "Marines in World War II Commemorative Series." Marine Corps Historical Center: Washington, D.C., 1991.

Evans, George H. *Through the Corridors of Hell*. Formac Publishing Company Limited: Antigonish, Nova Scotia, Canada, 1980.

Fairchild, Byron. *Command Decisions*. Center of Military History, Department of the Army: Washington, D.C., 2000.

Griffith, Hubert. *R.A.F. in Russia*. Hammond, Hammond and Company, Ltd.: London, 1942.

Hague, Arnold. *The Allied Convoy System 1939–1945: Its Organization Defense and Operation*. Naval Institute Press: Annapolis, Maryland, 2000.

Haynes, John L. *Frozen Fury: The Murmansk Run of Convoy PQ-13*. PublishAmerica: Baltimore, Maryland, 2010.

Hazell, Martin. *Poles Apart: Polish Naval Memories of World War II*. South West Maritime Society: Exeter, England, 2007.

Hughes, Robert. *Flagship to Murmansk*. Futura Publications Limited: London, 1956.

Hutson, Harry C. *Arctic Interlude: Independent to North Russia*. Merriman Press: Bennington, Vermont, 1997.

Llewellyn-Jones, Malcolm, Ed. *The Royal Navy and the Arctic Convoys: A Naval Staff History*. Routledge: Abingdon, England, 2007.

Lund, Paul and Ludlam, Harry. *Trawlers Go to War*. New English Library: London, 1972.

Mansergh, Audrey, Ed. *With the Red Fleet: The War Memories of the Late Arseni G. Golovko*. Putnam: London, 1965.

Moore, Arthur R. *A Careless Word ... A Needless Sinking*. American Merchant Marine Museum: Kings Point, New York, 1983.

Morison, Samuel Eliot. *History of United States Operations in World War II, Volume I: The Battle of the Atlantic, 1939–1943*. Little, Brown and Company: Boston, 1975.

Mills, Morris O. *Convoy PQ-13: Unlucky for Some*. Bernard Durnford Publishing: West Sussex, England, 2000.

Naval Historical Center. *The Official Chronology of the U.S. Navy in World War II*. Washington, D.C., 1993.

Ogden, Graeme. *My Sea Lady: The Story of HMS Lady Madeleine*. Hutchinson of London: London, 1963.

Pearce, Frank. *Last Call for HMS Edinburgh*. William Collins Sons & Co. Ltd.: London, 1982.

Raebel, Geoffrey W. *The Royal Australian Air Force in Russia—1942*. Australian Military History Publications: Loftus, New South Wales, Australia, 1997.

Reminick, Gerald. *No Surrender: True Stories of the U.S. Naval Armed Guard in World War II*. The Glencannon Press: Palo Alto, California, 2004.

Rohwer, J. and Hümmelchen, G. *Chronology of the War at Sea 1939–1945* (2 volumes). Arco Publishing Company, Inc.: New York, 1973.

Ruegg, Bob and Hague, Arnold. *Convoys to Russia: Allied Convoys and Naval Surface Operations in Arctic Waters 1941–1945*. World Ship Society: Kendal, England, 1992.

Rutter, Owen. *Red Ensign: A History of Convoy*. Robert Hale Limited: London, 1943.

Schofield, B. B. *The Russian Convoys: Heroes of the Murmansk Run— Allied Seaman Who Fought Stukas, Nazi Subs and Frozen Arctic Seas in WWII*. Ballantine Books: New York, 1967.

Tye, Chris E. *The Real Cold War*. Delco Creative Services Ltd.: Rochester, England, 1994.

U.S. Department of State. *Peace and War: United States Foreign Policy, 1931–1941*. (Publication 1983.) U.S. Government Printing Office: Washington, D.C., 1943.

Woodman, Richard. *Arctic Convoys 1941–1945*. Pen & Sword Maritime: Barnsley, England, 2004.

Polish

Borowski, Michael. *Memories*. Naval Museum: Gdynia, Poland, 2007.

Boruciński, Henryk. *W Lodach I Ogniu [In Fire and Ice]*. Krajawa Angencja Wydawnicza: Poland, 1975.

Russian

Alexandrov, J. E., Ed. *Polar Convoy: Memoirs of Participants Anniversary Collection for the 60th Anniversary of Great Victory from Dateastvo Island*. Island Publishing: St. Petersburg, Russia, 2005.

Blinov, Vladimir, Ed. *Trips of Fire: Murmansk Shipping Company in the Great Patriotic War*. Murmansk Shipping Company, Murmansk Book Press: Murmansk, Russia, 2005.

Bitsnob, B. M., Ed. *Murmansk Shipping Company in the Great Patriotic War*. Murmansk Publishers: Murmansk, Russia, 2005.

Dremliug, Valentine V. *War Years in the Arctic*. Federal State Institution "Seaport Authority." Big Port of St. Petersburg, Russia, 2010.

Grishanov, V. V. (Chairman). *Arctic Allied Escorts 1941–1945: Report on the First International Conference of the Brotherhood of Northern Escorts*. St. Petersburg, Russia, 2000.

Ilyin, V. N., Editor-in-chief. *Fleet in Victory: All-Russian Socially-Scientific Readings (on May, 19–20th, 2004)*. Administration of the Arkhangelsk Region, Department of Information and Public Relations: Arkhangelsk, Russia, 2004.

Lifshits, Anatoly L. *Sea and on Land*. St. Petersburg, Russia, 2005–07.

Platonov, A. V. *War in the Arctic Seas 1941–1945: Protection of Domestic Maritime Transportation*. NIKA: St. Petersburg, Russia, 2010.

Somkin, Alexander. *We Remember You*. Publishing House "Homeland Lomonosov": Arkhangelsk, Russia, 1995.

PUBLICATIONS

"1941–1945: The Arctic Lookout." *The Russian Convoy Club Official Magazine*. Bob Allan, Ed. Articles selected from issues including Nos. 5, 6, and 29–37.

"Army Air Forces in World War II." Edited by Wesley Frank Craven and James Lea Cate. Office of Air Force History: Washington, D.C., 1983.

"Dictionary of American Naval Aviation Squadrons, Volume 2: The History of VP, VPB, VP(H) and VP(AM) Squadrons." Department of The Navy, Naval Historical Center: Washington, D.C., 2000.

"Guarding the United States and Its Outposts." *Stetson Conn*, Rose C. Engelman, and Byron Fairchild. Center of Military History, United States Army: Fort Lesley J. McNair, Washington, D.C., 1964.

"It Will Remain in Memory Forever" (Russian). Gymnasium 9: Arkhangelsk, Russia, 2009.

"Northern Light Murmansk—Archangel." Official Publication of the
    North Russia Club. Articles selected from issues including Nos.
    15, 23, 47, and 50.
"The Pointer, USN Armed Guard WWII Veterans." Charles A. Lloyd, Ed.
    Articles selected from issues published between 1997 and 2011.
"Polar Convoys 1941–1945" (Russian). Galea Print: St. Petersburg,
    Russia, 1999.

UNPUBLISHED WORKS

Hewitt, Nick. *"Guns in the Night:" HMS Belfast and the Battle of North Cape,
    26 December 1943.*
Matte, Joseph, U.S. Coast Guard. Personal log from the USS *Ingham* (CG).

WEB SITES

"All World Wars:" http://allworldwars.com/Operation-Wunder-
    land-1942.html
"Feldgrau:" http://www.feldgrau.com/code.html
"Soviet Merchant Ship Losses:" http://www.shipsnostalgia.com/guides/
    Soviet_Merchant_Marine_Losses_in_WW2
"U-Boat.net:" http://www.uboat.net
"U.S. Navy Patrol Squadrons:" http://www.vpnavy.com/vpnavy_library_
    donated.html
"War Sailors:" http://www.warsailors.com/convoys/arctic.html

ABOUT THE AUTHOR

Mike Walling grew up in East Brunswick, New Jersey, the oldest of five boys. His parents, Don and Jean Walling, both served in World War II, Don as a meteorologist assigned to the U.S. Air Army Air Force 9th Air Force tactical fighter squadrons in Europe, Jean as a Navy WAVE officer in Boston and Vero Beach, Florida.

After graduating from Montclair State College with a B.A. in Biology, Mike served in the U.S. Coast Guard for six years as a commissioned officer and a senior petty officer. Most of his sea-going experience was in the North Atlantic and included two trips to the Arctic. His assignments included buoy tending, search and rescue missions, drug and fisheries law enforcement, and oceanographic operations. As part of the Boarding Party and Prize Crew on two cutters, he participated in the seizures of a Panamanian drug-runner and a Cuban fishing boat.

Mike's first book, *Bloodstained Sea: The U.S. Coast Guard in the Battle of the Atlantic 1941–1945*, was published by International Marine, a division of McGraw-Hill, and received critical acclaim by reviewers and veterans. The Naval Order of the United States honored him with its 2005 Samuel Eliot Morison Award for Naval Literature. *Bloodstained Sea* is now available through Cutter Publishing (www.cutterpublishing.com).

In conjunction with Flat Hammock Press, he published a new edition of *Sinbad of the Coast Guard*, the adventurous, true story of the USCGC

Campbell's mascot, whose exploits during World War II became legend. Appropriately, Sinbad's story was told by a fellow member of the Coast Guard, Chief George F. Foley, Jr., while the fine pictures were drawn by the outstanding Coast Guard Reserve artist, George Gray.

His book *In the Event of a Water Landing* tells for the first time the full stories of the Bermuda Sky Queen and Sovereign of the Skies rescues, the only two completely successful open ocean ditchings in Commercial Aviation history. These two stories encompass many facets of ditchings: bad weather, engine failure, horrific sea conditions, and indomitable courage in the face of death. Between these two are tales of other ditchings, as well as the journey we humans have undertaken from the beginning of transoceanic flight to today.

Mike's first novel, *Choke Points* (Cutter Publishing, 2009), addresses the real threats to Maritime and Port Security. It's the first of a ten-book Fletcher Saga series spanning 250 years.

In different venue, Mike produced a new version of the old song "I'd Like to Find the Guy Who Named the Coast Guard," originally written and recorded by Paul Yacich and the Coast Guard Band in 1945. The music has been lost, but working with Alison Freemen, this wonderfully humorous tune has been given a new lease on life and updated with three verses reflecting today's Coast Guard global missions.

He has spent more than fifty years collecting stories from veterans from World War II, Korea, Vietnam, and Iraq, as well as those of pilots, merchant seaman, and civilian personnel with NATO and EUFOR in Sarajevo. His research has included visits to London; Sarajevo; Baska Voda, Croatia; Halifax, Nova Scotia; St. John's, Newfoundland; New Orleans; and St. Petersburg, Arkhangelsk, and Murmansk, Russia.

Mike and his wife, Mary, live in Hudson, Massachusetts. He can be reached through his web site: www.mikewalling.com.

INDEX